This item is to be returned or renewed before the latest date above. It may be borrowed for a further period if not in demand. **To renew your books:**

- **Phone the 24/7 Renewal Line 01926 499273 or**
- **Visit www.warwickshire.gov.uk/libraries**

3 0 DEC 2015

Discover • Imagine • Learn • *with libraries*

2 9 SEP 2015    **Warwickshire** County Council   Working for Warwickshire

0135421839

TIME GOES BY

Kathy Leigh never knew her mother, who died many years ago in a freak accident. Raised by her father, Albert, and her Aunty Win in 1950s' Blackpool. Albert Leigh loves his daughter, but has never fully recovered from the shock of losing his wife. He struggles to form and maintain relationships, hounded as he is by the devastating secret that haunts him. Time passes, and Kathy grows up, falls in love and marries her childhood sweetheart; what more could a girl wish for? But when her father dies, Kathy uncovers his shocking secret which threatens to blow their family apart.

TIME GOES BY

TIME GOES BY

by

Margaret Thornton

Magna Large Print Books
Long Preston, North Yorkshire,
BD23 4ND, England.

British Library Cataloguing in Publication Data.

Thornton, Margaret
    Time goes by.

    A catalogue record of this book is
    available from the British Library

    ISBN   978-0-7505-3614-1

First published in Great Britain in 2011 by Allison & Busby Ltd.

Published in Large Print 2012 by arrangement with
Allison & Busby Ltd.

Magna Large Print is an imprint of Library Magna Books Ltd.

Printed and bound in Great Britain by
T.J. (International) Ltd., Cornwall, PL28 8RW

This book is dedicated to 'sand grown 'uns'
everywhere; those of us who feel proud to have
been born in the amazing town of Blackpool.

And with love to my husband, John, and my
thanks for his ongoing support
and encouragement.

PART ONE

Chapter One

1950

'Please, Miss Roberts ... what shall I do? I haven't got a mummy, you see.'

Katherine Leigh raised her hand a little timidly as she spoke to her teacher. She felt her cheeks turning a little pink as sometimes happened when she had to explain that she didn't have a mother as had the other children in the class.

It had been all right at Christmas. When they had made cards to take home she had written her card 'To Daddy and Aunty Win'. But it was different now because they were making cards for Mother's Day. She felt sure, though, that Miss Roberts would help her to solve her little problem. She was a lovely teacher and Kathy liked her very much.

Sally Roberts smiled understandingly at the little girl. 'Well, Katherine, dear ... maybe you could make a card for your aunt instead. Aunty Win, isn't it? Or for your grandma, perhaps?'

Katherine Leigh nodded, a little uncertainly, then she smiled back at her teacher. 'Yes, for Aunty Win, I think. She'll like that. But then ... I can't write "Happy Mother's Day", can I?'

'Oh, I don't see why not,' said Miss Roberts, 'because that's what it will be on Sunday – Mothering Sunday, although everyone seems to call it

13

Mother's Day now. And you can write "To Aunty Win", inside the card, "With love from Katherine", or "Kathy", if you like.'

'All right, then,' said Katherine.

Poor little mite, thought Sally Roberts, as she went round the tables of her 'top class' infants, giving out the paper required for the making of the Mother's Day cards. She had grown very fond of little Katherine Leigh, who had been in her class since last September. How awful it must be for her not to have a mummy, like all the other boys and girls in the class. Sally knew that Katherine's mother had died when she was a baby, only two years of age, so the little girl had no recollection of her at all. She was well looked after, though, by her father, and his sister whom she called Aunty Win, and Sally felt that she was well loved too.

She was always smartly dressed in a gymslip with a hand-knitted jumper beneath it, or a regulation white blouse in summer. School uniform was not compulsory, although most parents made an effort to conform.

Even in 1950, five years after the war had ended, there were restrictions, and many things were still in short supply. But Mr Leigh and his sister clearly did their very best for the child. Her dark curly hair was always well groomed and shining, tied back from her face in two bunches with red ribbons. Her father and aunt always came along on open evenings and other school functions and were pleased to hear of her good progress. They were, however, quite middle-aged; not old, of course, by any means, but considerably

14

older than the parents of most of the other children, and Sally was sure that Katherine must notice the difference. She guessed that Mr Leigh would be in his late forties, and his sister maybe a few years older.

Katherine was not an outgoing child, but she seemed happy enough and got on well with the other children, especially with her best friend, Shirley, who sat next to her at the table.

There were nine tables in the large classroom, around each of which were four child-sized chairs. A class of thirty-six children – aged six to seven – was really more than enough for any teacher to cope with, but it was the norm in those post-war days, as it had been for many years before. There had been a 'baby boom', with more children than ever being born as a result of fathers returning home from the war, and so classes were expected to become even larger in the next few years. Unless, of course, many more schools were built by the Labour government, elected in 1945 and still holding on to power.

'Now, boys and girls, listen carefully,' said Miss Roberts. 'The first thing we are going to do is write at the top of the card...' She wrote on the blackboard, in clear printing, 'Happy Mother's Day'. 'Now, pick up your pencils and copy this. Best writing, mind, because it will be going home... No, Graham, don't turn the paper over, or the writing will be on the back, won't it?' There was always one, she reflected.

The children were then instructed to make up their own design of a bowl with flowers in it. In the centre of each table was a selection of gummed paper in bright colours: green, blue, red, yellow, orange, pink and purple; four pairs of scissors with rounded ends; and cardboard templates of bowl shapes, leaf shapes, and various types of flowers – daffodils, tulips and daisy shapes.

It was, in that year of 1950, the beginning of the heyday of 'free activity' in the classroom, when infants, for certain times in each day at least, were free to express themselves in all sorts of ways. Painting easels with jars of brightly coloured poster paints; tables with crayons and drawing paper, plasticine, jigsaws, and creative games; building bricks; a sand tray and a water trough; and a fully equipped Wendy house with a dressing-up box; these were to be found in most infant classrooms. And what chaos was left for the teacher, single-handedly, to clear away after each session! The children, of course, were supposed to do it themselves, but it was more often a case of 'if you want a job doing, do it yourself!'

Sometimes, though, handwork had to be partially directed, and that was the case when cards – for Christmas, Easter, or other festivities – were being made. The children's efforts would vary, helped in some instances by the intervention of the teacher, but parents would be delighted at the finished masterpieces, however messy they might turn out to be.

'Why haven't you got a mum, then?' asked Timothy Fielding, one of the boys who was sitting opposite Katherine.

'Because I haven't, that's why!' she retorted.

'Why? What's happened to her? Has she run away and left you?' he persisted.

16

'That's quite enough, Timothy,' said Miss Roberts who was passing near to their table. 'Leave Katherine alone, please.'

'Well, that's what my mum says when I don't behave myself,' retorted the irrepressible Timothy. 'She says she'll go away and leave me.'

'I don't suppose for one moment that she really means it,' replied Miss Roberts. 'Now, get on with what you're supposed to be doing, and stop pestering Katherine.' She reflected that some parents did not show a great deal of sense in some of the things they said to their children. Although it was doubtful that Timothy believed his mother either; no doubt it was an idle threat not meant to be taken seriously. Timothy Fielding could certainly be a pest; most likely he drove his mother to distraction sometimes, as he did with Sally if she didn't sit on him hard when he became too troublesome.

'As a matter of fact...' Shirley Morris was saying, with a toss of her flaxen plaits as Sally moved away, 'Kathy's mummy died when she was a baby. Didn't she, Kathy? Not that it's any of your business, Timothy Fielding.'

'Yes, she did,' said Kathy, in quite a matter-of-fact manner. 'But I've got a dad, and a very nice aunty who looks after me. Aunty Win; that's who I'm making the card for.'

She didn't feel particularly upset; it was certainly nothing to cry about. She had never known her mother; only sometimes, now and again, in the dim recesses of her memory, she seemed to recall a pretty lady with dark hair and a smiling face holding her in her arms. But she could not be sure whether it was a true recollection or something she was imagining. Only occasionally did she feel the lack of a mother in her life. Times such as now, when they were all making cards for Mummy, or when she was invited to tea at Shirley's house and she realised what a difference it must make to have a mother in the home.

'OK, then,' said Timothy with a shrug of his shoulders, seeming for a brief moment to be a little subdued. But he soon bounced back. 'My mum's all right, I suppose. I'm glad she's there, anyway; I wouldn't want her to be dead. But she isn't half bad-tempered sometimes, much worse than me dad. You should hear her shout!'

'I'm not surprised, with you to put up with!' laughed Stanley, the boy who was sitting next to him, giving him a dig in the ribs.

'Shurrup you!' countered Timothy, shoving him back. A scrap seemed likely to break out until Miss Roberts clapped her hands and demanded silence – or comparative silence, which was all she could hope to get from thirty-six infants – with a threat that those who couldn't behave would have to stay in at playtime.

Peace reigned as they all settled down to creating their cards. Katherine chose blue for the bowl. She painstakingly drew round the template, then cut out the shape, licked the back of the gummed paper and stuck it to the bottom of the card. Then she cut out some yellow daffodils, red tulips and white daisies, and green leaves, and arranged them as though they were growing out of the bowl. Then she coloured in the stalks and the centres of the daisies with wax crayons. Each child had a box of

18

these in their drawer beneath the table. Katherine's were still in quite a good condition as she was a methodical little girl and she always returned them carefully to the container after they had been used. Timothy's, though, were broken and several of the colours were missing.

'Kathy, give us a lend of your green,' he said. 'I've only got this titchy bit left.'

'That's your own fault, then,' Shirley told him. 'Why should she? I know I wouldn't.'

But Kathy uncomplainingly handed over her green crayon. She was amused to see Timothy stick his tongue out at Shirley.

'Well, I wasn't asking you, was I, clever clogs!' he jeered.

Kathy quite liked Timothy really. He could be a bit of a pest, but she knew there was 'no real badness' in him, as her Aunty Win might say. He brightened up the day sometimes and made her laugh, recounting the jokes that his dad had told him. His shock of fairish hair stood up on end like 'Just William's'; in fact, he resembled her favourite fictional character in quite a few ways.

'Ta, Kathy,' he said. 'I've gone and put too much spit on me bowl an' all, an' it won't stick.' He banged his fist on the table, but the red bowl refused to stay put. 'Oh crikey! What shall I do?'

'Cut another one out,' said Kathy. 'Miss Roberts won't mind. I don't suppose you're the only one who's made a mess of it. You have to lick it carefully, you see. Look, I'll stick it on for you when you've cut it out.'

'Gosh! Thanks, Kathy,' he said. 'I'll give you one of my sherbet lemons at playtime.'

19

Shirley tossed her plaits and looked disdainfully at Timothy. 'I don't know why you bother with him,' she said. ''Specially when he's been so rude to you.'

'He didn't mean to be,' said Kathy. 'He didn't know, you see ... about my mother.'

She was pleased with the completed card and so was Miss Roberts. Her teacher told her it was very artistic and that her aunt would like it very much. Kathy wrote on the inside, 'To Aunty Win with love from Kathy.' Then she put it away in her satchel to take home at the end of the afternoon.

Sure enough Timothy was there at playtime, true to his promise. He handed out a cone-shaped paper bag of sherbet lemons. 'Here y'are, Kathy,' he said.

'Ooh, thanks!' she said, popping a bright-yellow sweet into her mouth. 'They're my favourites, them and pear drops.'

'Ta very much for helping me with my card,' he said. 'It looks OK now but it's not as nice as yours. Me dad says I'm all fingers and thumbs when I try to help him, when he's putting up a shelf, like, an' all that.'

'Never mind; it's the thought that counts,' Kathy told him, something that Aunty Win often said. 'And your mum'll like it, won't she?'

''Spect so,' said Timothy. 'I'm gonna buy her a Mars bar an' all. She likes them best.' As an afterthought he held out the bag of sweets to Shirley who was standing at Kathy's side, looking a little disdainful. 'D'you want one, Shirley?' he said.

20

'No, ta,' said Shirley, although Kathy suspected that she would like one really. She thought it was very generous of Tim to offer her one. Shirley cast him a scornful look as she skipped away.

'Please yerself, then,' said Timothy to her retreating back. 'See if I care!... I've got a joke for you, Kathy,' he went on. 'It's a good one; me dad told it me.'

'Go on, then,' she encouraged him.

'What d'you get if you cross a kangaroo with a sheep?' he asked, his grey eyes full of merriment.

Kathy frowned a little, then shook her head. 'I don't know,' she replied. 'What do you get?'

'A woolly jumper!' he cried, falling about laughing. 'D'you get it? You get wool from a sheep, and a kangaroo–'

'A kangaroo jumps – yes I know,' she said. 'You don't need to explain. I get it...' Although she was not sure that she did, not entirely, not the bit about crossing the animals. 'It's very funny,' she told him. 'I'll tell it to my Aunty Win.' Perhaps her aunt would be able to explain it.

She glanced across the playground to where Shirley was talking to another friend, Maureen, and at the same time looking a little crossly at Kathy. 'I'd better go and see what's up with Shirley,' she said.

'She doesn't like you talking to me,' said Timothy, 'but I don't care what she thinks. Ta-ra, Kathy...' He dashed off to kick a football around with Stanley and some of his other mates.

Shirley was indignant. 'I've told you before, I don't know why you bother with him,' she said to her friend. 'You'd better watch out or else they'll all be shouting out, "Kathy Leigh loves Timothy Fielding!".'

'Don't be so stupid!' retorted Kathy, feeling herself go a little pink. 'He's all right, though, is Tim. Anyway, we're not going to fall out over a silly boy, are we? Here – you can have a lend of my skipping rope. I tell you what; Maureen and me can turn up, and you can be first in if you like, Shirley.'

'All right, then,' said Shirley, somewhat mollified. So whilst the other two girls turned the rope she jumped up and down. They all shouted in chorus, 'Jelly on a plate, jelly on a plate, wibble wobble, wibble wobble, jelly on a plate' ... taking it in turns to be 'in' until the whistle was blown for the end of playtime. By the end of the afternoon Kathy and Shirley were the best of friends again.

'My mum says you can come to tea on Monday, if you like,' Shirley told her friend. 'And me dad'll see you home afterwards.'

'Gosh, thanks!' said Kathy. 'I'll ask my Aunty Win as soon as I get home.'

Chapter Two

Home for Katherine was a boarding house in the area of Blackpool known as North Shore, not too far from the sea, quite close to the north railway station, and about five minutes' walk from the town centre.

The name of the house was Holmleigh. Her father and Aunty Win liked to describe it as a 'private hotel' rather than a boarding house. There was, in point of fact, very little difference between the two, excepting, perhaps, that the small hotels had names and the boarding houses didn't. Aunty Win had told her that 'Holmleigh' was really just a posh way of spelling the word 'homely'. That was what they hoped their hotel was, a home from home, and it also made quite a clever use of their surname.

Her father, Albert, and his sister, Winifred, ran the hotel between them. Kathy knew that it had been started in the beginning by her grandparents, way back in the early years of the century, which seemed to her to be ages ago. Grandma and Grandad Leigh – Alice and William – who were now well into their seventies, had retired a few years ago, at the end of the war in 1945, and now lived in a little bungalow in Bispham. That was when Albert and Winifred had taken over the responsibility of the boarding house and had given it a name.

Kathy knew that her father was a very good cook – he called himself a chef– and he did most of the cooking when there were visitors staying there. Aunty Win looked after everything else: all the office work and bookkeeping and the organisation of the domestic help. They employed waitresses and chambermaids when it was their busiest time, usually from the middle of May to the end of the 'Illuminations' season – commonly known as the 'Lights' – at the end of October. For the rest of the year they took occasional visitors, usually to oblige their 'regulars', and during the slack period they took the opportunity to catch up with any decorating or odd jobs that needed to be done.

When Kathy arrived home on that Friday afternoon in mid March her father was up a ladder papering the walls of one of the guest bedrooms, whilst her aunt was busy at a trestle table in the centre of the room putting paste onto the next length of paper.

'Hello, dear,' said her aunt when the little girl's head appeared round the door. 'Have you had a nice day at school?' That was what she always asked, and as usual Kathy replied that yes, she had. She had never minded going to school, but it had been especially nice since she had been in Miss Roberts' class.

'Goodness, is it that time already?' said her father. 'I think it's time for a cup of tea, Winnie. You go and put the kettle on, eh? Hello, Kathy love. Go and help your Aunty Win, there's a good girl.'

Her dad was always saying that, and Kathy actually quite enjoyed helping out in the boarding house. When she was a tiny girl, before she started school, she had loved going round with her Aunty Nellie – not a real aunt, just a friend of Aunty Win – who came in once a week to 'do' the bedrooms. There were fifteen bedrooms on three floors, including two attic bedrooms. Kathy used to accompany her aunt with her own little dustpan and brush, and a duster, to help with the dusting and polishing. Aunty Nellie sometimes let her put a tiny amount of polish onto the

24

surface of a dressing table, and then rub hard to make it all shiny and gleaming.

She helped Aunty Win, too, in the kitchen when she was making pies or fruit tarts. She had her own pastry cutters and rolling pin and could already make jam tarts that they were able to eat. She did not help very much, though, when her father was in charge of the kitchen; he was not quite as patient as her aunt. She realised, though, that at the moment she was only playing at helping. But Kathy also understood, with all the wisdom of her six – nearly seven – years, that this would eventually be her job of work. When the time came for her to leave school – a long time in the future – she knew that she would be expected to work in the family boarding house, or whatever they wanted to call it, just as Aunty Win and her father had taken over from her grandparents.

'I'm coming, Aunty Win,' she called. 'I'm just taking my coat off, and I've got something to put away in my drawer. It's a secret, you see.'

On the way home from school she had called in at the local newsagent's shop and bought a small box of Milk Tray for Aunty Win for Mother's Day. She had been saving up from her spending money each week until she had enough. She put the purple box and the card in her drawer underneath her knickers, vests and socks, then went down to the kitchen to join her aunt.

'So what have you been doing at school this afternoon?' Winifred asked her niece. 'You don't do much work on Friday afternoon, do you?'

In Winifred's opinion they didn't do much work at all in the infant classrooms of today. It all seemed to be painting or playing in the house, or messing about with sand and water, from what Katherine told her aunt. Not like it was in her day. She had been born in 1900 and when she started school at four years of age Queen Victoria had been dead for three years. Her photograph had hung in the school hall for many years, so Winifred's parents had told her – they had both attended the same school – and then it had been replaced by one of Edward VII, her corpulent son. Winifred remembered his rather kindly face regarding them as they sang their morning hymns and recited their daily prayers.

She recalled, too, the rows of wooden desks where the children sat in formal rows – 'Straight backs, boys and girls, no slouching'; the chalk and slates on which to write the letters of the alphabet; the map of the world on the classroom wall, with a goodly part of it coloured in red, showing the parts that belonged to the British Empire. She remembered a strict male teacher, too, with a long swishing cane; not that it was often used. The children of yesteryear knew they had to behave themselves; one look was usually enough.

Times had changed, she pondered, and not always for the best, although Kathy seemed to be getting on well since she went into that nice Miss Roberts' class. There didn't seem to be as much messing about, and she could now read very nicely from her book that told of the exploits of Janet and John.

'No...' replied Kathy, in answer to her aunt's query. 'Miss Roberts usually lets us do a jigsaw or read a book on Friday afternoon, while she does her register for the week. She has a lot of adding up to do, she says. But today we were making cards for–' She suddenly stopped and put her hand to her mouth. 'Oh dear! It was meant to be a surprise. Pretend I didn't say that, will you, Aunty Win?'

'Of course, dear,' smiled Winifred. 'I didn't actually catch what you said anyway.'

The child had given the game away already, though, talking about hiding something in her drawer. Mother's Day, Winifred had thought to herself. That was one of the times when she felt most sorry for the little girl, not that Kathy ever seemed too worried about occasions such as those.

Winifred poured the tea into three mugs and added milk and sugar. 'Now, Kathy,' she said. 'Do you think you could manage to carry this mug upstairs to your daddy? Be careful, mind, but I've not filled it too full. And there's a custard cream biscuit for him. Pop it into your gymslip pocket, then you've got both hands free. Off you go now.'

Winifred loved the little girl more than she could say. She had tried to make it up to her for not having a mother, and she hoped and prayed that she had succeeded. She felt that she had, to a certain extent, although she realised it could never be quite the same. She had wondered if her brother might marry again, but he had been so distressed at losing his beloved Barbara that he had never, since that time, taken any interest at all in the opposite sex. He was a taciturn sort of man who did not show his feelings. Winifred was sure

27

that he loved his little daughter very much, but he found it difficult to tell her so or even to show her much affection. Any cuddles and hugs, or comfort when she was upset, came from her aunt or grandparents. It was only natural that she should sometimes ask questions about her mother – all her schoolfriends had mothers – and she was always told that her mother had died when she was only a baby, but she must never forget that her mummy had loved her very much.

Albert never spoke of his wife. He had settled into a comfortable little rut. He worked his socks off in the hotel. He was a first-rate cook – or chef, as he liked to call himself – and there was nothing he would not tackle when there were any jobs to be done in the off season. His only means of recreation was to go to the pub two or three evenings a week – he was a member of the darts team – and he was also an ardent supporter of Blackpool's football team. He was there every Saturday during the winter months, in his orange and white scarf, taking his place on Spion Kop. But Winifred could not imagine him ever cheering and yelling encouragement – or even booing! – as many enthusiastic supporters did. She guessed he was as silent there as he was in other aspects of his life. Blackpool was a First Division club and boasted of their most famous player, Stanley Matthews. Albert looked forward to the day when they might – when they would, he was sure – win the FA cup. He filled in his football coupon regularly. Winifred was not sure how much he allowed himself to bet, but he had never, as yet, had a substantial win, only the odd pound or two. They had to be quiet every Saturday evening after the six o'clock news when the football results were read out and Albert checked his coupon.

Winifred was looking forward to the start of the holiday season in a few weeks' time. It would begin slowly, with visitors coming for the Easter weekend and the following week – they were already almost fully booked for that period – but then there would be a lull for several weeks until the Whitsuntide holiday. It was then that the season would start in earnest and would, hopefully, continue until almost the end of October.

Blackpool was beginning to make its name as the foremost resort in the north, maybe in the whole, of England. The town had gained more than it had lost during the Second World War. Many of its competitors on the south and east coasts had been forced to close down for the duration of the war because of the threat of invasion or bombing. Admittedly, the curtailing of the Illuminations in the September of 1939 had affected the income of the Blackpool boarding house keepers and hoteliers. However, following on from that, many of these people were able to make up for their losses by accommodating RAF personnel who were training in the town. Over three-quarters of a million RAF recruits passed through the town during the war. There were also the child evacuees at the start of the conflict, but they did not all stay for very long; in fact, by 1940 the majority of them had returned home.

Later in the war there were American GIs stationed at the nearby bases at Weeton and Warton, and the Blackpool entertainment industry enjoyed a prosperity they had not seen since the end of the First World War.

The war had not deterred holidaymakers from visiting the resort, in spite of the wartime propaganda posters asking 'Is Your Journey Really Necessary?' Many families obviously thought it was still essential to take a holiday, and Blackpool was a relatively safe place in which to stay. The Whitsuntide holidays had been abandoned in 1940 by government decree, but the annual wakes holidays of the textile towns in Lancashire and Yorkshire recommenced in July and from then on Blackpool had never looked back.

The advent of rationing, rather than being a hindrance, had been quite a boon for the hotel keepers, and more especially for the boarding house landladies. They took charge of the visitors' ration books, and this led to the change from the old system of lodging houses to that of full board. Winifred remembered only too well the old days, when visitors brought their own food, which was cooked for them by the boarding house staff. The visitors paid only for their lodgings and for services rendered, such as cooking, laundry, cleaning of shoes, and – in some lodging houses – the 'use of the cruet'.

The system of 'full board' which had begun during the war years was now the norm. It consisted of cooked breakfast, midday dinner, and a 'high tea'. In some residences, as at Holmleigh, supper was also served in the visitors' lounge from nine o'clock in the evening.

In the previous year, 1949, the return of the Illuminations had marked a turning point from post-war austerity. The years of darkness and depression were over, exemplified by the return of the 'Lights'. Blackpool had become the envy of many of its rivals. It was well and truly back in business, catering for a full cross section of the public, from the working classes to those who considered themselves to be the 'elite'.

The hotel had become – almost – Winifred's whole life, the focus of her existence and her ambition. She was proud of what they had achieved since the end of the war. They were coming to be known as one of the best of the small private hotels in Blackpool, with the same visitors returning year after year. She had never done any work outside of the boarding house. It had been taken for granted when she left school at the age of fourteen that she should work in the family business. That was in the year of 1914; the start of the Great War had coincided with the end of Winifred's schooling.

It had been the height of the holiday season in Blackpool, but the initial disruption – when visitors trying to return home found that the trains had been commandeered for the fighting forces – proved to be of short duration. By mid August it was 'business as usual' in the resort. The holiday industry carried on and thrived throughout the First World War as, twenty years later, it was to do the same in the second conflict. It was an emotive issue, as to whether seaside holidays and leisure times, such as professional sport, should continue when the country was at war. The lists in the daily newspapers of deaths in action were becoming longer and more disturbing. But the 'powers that be' in Blackpool felt that it was good for morale that people should be encouraged to take holidays, as before. It was decided, however, that to continue with the Illuminations would be going too far, and so, despite their initial success, plans to make the Illuminations an annual event had to be cancelled, due to the outbreak of war.

And so the accommodation industry benefited, not only through the holidaymakers, but with the arrival of Belgian refugees, and then by the billeting of British troops. During the winter of 1914 to 1915 there were ten thousand servicemen billeted in the town, along with two thousand refugees.

The Leighs' boarding house played its part in accommodating both the troops and the refugees. Winifred was fascinated and, at first, a little shy of these men who teased her good-humouredly. But as the war went on – with, regrettably, the loss of many of the soldiers they had known – she began to grow in confidence.

It was not until 1917, though, when she was seventeen years old, that she fell in love for the first – and what she believed was to be the last – time. Arthur Makepeace was a Blackpool boy; he was, in fact, almost the 'boy next door', living only a few doors away from the Leigh family. He was three years older than Winifred and had joined up, as soon as he was old enough, in 1915. After a few outings together, when he came home on leave, they had realised that there was a good deal more than friendship between them. They had vowed that, after the war was over, they

32

would get married. Despite their age neither of their families had raised any objections. Many young couples were 'plighting their troth' in those uncertain days.

Arthur was granted leave in the early summer of 1918, then he returned to the battlefields of France. It was universally believed that the war was in its last stages and the young couple were looking forward to the time when they would be together for always.

Then, in the August of that year came the news that Winifred, deep down, had always been dreading. Arthur had been killed in one of the last offensives on the Western Front. It was his parents, of course, who had received the dreaded telegram, and they wept along with the girl who was to have become one of their family.

It was said that time was a great healer, and gradually Winifred picked up the pieces of her life and carried on with her duties in the boarding house. Like thousands of women of her age she had never married, had never even fallen in love again. She had settled down to a life of compromise. But there were compensations to be found: in her local church where she was a keen worker, and in the dramatic society – also attached to the church – where it was discovered that she was, surprisingly, quite a talented actress. And, above all, in her love for her little motherless niece.

Winifred was now fifty years of age and, by and large, she felt that life had not treated her too badly. She had missed out on marriage, though, and children of her own. And she still wondered, despite her quiet contentment with her life, what it would be like to experience the fulfilment of a happy marriage.

Chapter Three

'That's lovely, dear, really beautiful,' said Winifred. She felt a tear come into her eye as Kathy proudly presented her, on Sunday morning, with the card she had made. 'I love the flowers, such pretty colours. And this is your best writing; I can see that you've tried very hard.'

'Miss Roberts said it had to be our very best, 'cause it was going home,' said Kathy. 'It says "Happy Mother's Day", and I know you're not really my mum, but I couldn't put "Happy Aunty's Day", could I? Because it isn't. And Miss Roberts said it would be alright... And I've got you these as well, Aunty Win.' She held out the small purple box she had been hiding behind her back.

'Chocolates as well! And Milk Tray – my very favourites!' exclaimed Winifred. She hugged the little girl and kissed her on the cheek. 'Well, aren't I lucky? That's very kind of you, Kathy.'

She didn't say, as she might have done, 'You shouldn't go spending your pocket money on me', because she knew that it must have given the child pleasure to do so. She, Winifred, had always encouraged her to be generous and thoughtful for others; and she knew that Albert,

34

despite his gruff manner, tried to teach her not to be selfish.

'I shall enjoy these tonight while I'm listening to the *Sunday Half Hour* on the wireless,' said Winifred.

'All the class made a card,' Kathy told her. 'But Timothy Fielding made a bit of a mess of his. He licked his bowl too much and it wouldn't stick on, so I helped him to make another one.'

Winifred smiled. That boy's name often cropped up in Katherine's conversations. She gathered that he could be rather a pest in the classroom, but she suspected that Kathy had a soft spot for him.

'He told me a joke,' Kathy went on, 'but I didn't really understand it, Aunty Win, not all of it, though I told him I'd got it.' She told her aunt the joke about the kangaroo and the sheep and the woolly jumper, frowning a little as she did so. 'But a kangaroo and a sheep, they couldn't have a baby one, could they? I didn't know what he meant about crossing them, but I laughed because Tim expected me to.'

Winifred laughed too. 'It's just a joke, love,' she said. 'Quite a funny one actually.' Oh dear! she thought, knowing that it would be her job, when the time came, to explain to her niece about the 'facts of life'. And already, it seemed, she was beginning to question things. 'No; a kangaroo and a sheep wouldn't be able to ... er ... mate, to get together,' she began. 'It would have to be two kangaroos, a male and a female, or two sheep, a ram and a ewe, to ... er ... to make a baby kangaroo or a baby sheep. Just like you need a father and a mother, a man and a lady, to ... er ... produce a baby,' she added tentatively.

But Kathy's mind was already off onto another tack. 'Baby sheep are called lambs,' she said. 'Everybody knows that. But Miss Roberts told us that baby kangaroos are called joeys. That's funny, isn't it? There's a boy in our class called Joey, and everybody laughed when she said it. Did you know that, Aunty Win, that they're called joeys?'

'Yes, I believe so,' replied Winifred, relieved that the subject had been changed. 'Come along now; let's have our breakfast. Bacon and egg this morning because it's Sunday. I'll keep your dad's warm for him and fry him an egg when he comes down. He likes a bit of a lie-in on a Sunday, when he can.'

Albert was usually up with the lark, summer and winter alike. During the summer months, of course, there were the visitors' breakfasts to prepare for eight-thirty. And in the winter, too, he reckoned nothing to lying in bed when there were jobs to be done. On Sunday mornings, however – but only when there were no visitors in – he liked to take his ease for half an hour or so. Winifred took up the *Sunday Express,* if the newspaper boy had delivered it in time, and a cup of tea so that he could enjoy a little lie-in. It was something that the brother and sister had never been allowed to do as children, or even later when they had reached adulthood, and Winifred still did not think of ever allowing herself this little luxury.

Albert came downstairs just as Winifred and Kathy were finishing their breakfasts. He was washed and dressed – neither had they been encouraged to lounge around in dressing gowns – but not yet shaved, as far as Winifred could tell. She jumped up from the table to make some fresh tea and fry an egg, whilst Albert helped himself to cornflakes.

'I had a lovely surprise this morning, Albert,' she said, after she had placed his cooked breakfast in front of him. 'Look what Kathy has given me.' She showed him the chocolates. And a lovely card too, see.'

'Very nice,' he replied. 'So what is this in aid of? I haven't gone and forgotten your birthday, have I?'

'Of course not; don't be silly,' said Winifred. 'You know very well it's not till next month.'

'No, Daddy; it's Mother's Day,' said Kathy. 'Look, it says so on the card. We made them at school, and because I haven't got a mum, Miss Roberts said I should make one for Aunty Win.'

Albert's face took on a morose look. He nodded soberly. 'Oh, well then…Yes, I see. But it's no more than you deserve, our Winnie.' Then, suddenly, he smiled at his little daughter and his face looked altogether different. His blue eyes, still as bright as they had been when he was a lad, glowed with a warmth that wasn't often to be seen there. Really, he was quite a good-looking fellow when he smiled, Winifred thought to herself. It was a pity he didn't do it more often.

'That was a very nice thought, Kathy love,' he said. 'Yes, your Aunty Win has been very good to you, and you must never forget it.'

'I won't, Daddy,' replied the little girl.

'Now, when you've finished, Kathy, you'd better go and get ready,' her aunt told her.

'Why? Are you two off somewhere, then?' asked Albert.

'To church,' Winifred told him, although he must have known very well where they were going. 'It's a special service today, with it being Mothering Sunday.'

'Oh, I see,' he replied, looking morose again.

'I'll wash up before we go,' Winifred told him, 'and I'll put the meat in the oven – I've got a shoulder of lamb for today – so you can see to it for me, if you will, please?'

'Don't I always?' he replied a little gruffly. 'I'll do the veg an' all, and knock up a pudding, no trouble. You go off and enjoy yourselves.'

There was a hint of sarcasm in his words, as Winifred knew very well. Albert didn't go to church anymore, so she knew it was no use asking him, not even for special occasions now. He had never entered a church since he had lost Barbara. He didn't understand, he said, how God could have been so cruel to him; in fact, he professed not to believe in him anymore.

Albert and Winifred had been brought up to go to Sunday school and church, as was the norm in those early days of the century. And the tradition was still continuing now, in the early 1950s, Winifred was pleased to see, though not to such a large extent. Winifred and Albert had both been confirmed at their local parish church, Albert and Barbara had been married there and Katherine christened. She, Winifred, still attended the morning service each Sunday, when there were no visitors in the hotel. During the holiday season, of course, it was more difficult and she was not able to attend regularly, but she felt sure that God would understand.

Kathy did not often go on a Sunday morning – she attended Sunday school, which was held for an hour in the afternoon – but today was a special occasion and she was accompanying her aunt there for the Mothering Sunday service. Winifred put on her best coat, made of fine tweed in a moss-green colour, with a fitted bodice and a shawl collar. It was mid-calf length, the style owing a lot to the 'New Look' brought in by Christian Dior a few years previously. She had bought it two years ago at Sally Mae's dress shop. With the matching neat little turban hat and her black patent leather court shoes – the heels a little higher than she normally wore – she felt quite pleased with her appearance. She liked to look nice, although she didn't overdo it; vanity was one of the seven deadly sins, wasn't it? But the weekly visit to church was one occasion on which she dressed up a little more than usual.

'You look nice, Aunty Win,' Kathy told her, and she felt pleased at the compliment.

'Thank you, dear,' she said. 'We must look our best to go to church, mustn't we?' There was no one else to dress up for, she pondered, a little wryly, so she might as well dress up for God; although she was sure he would not care one way or the other. Winifred had kept her slim figure and so the new fitted fashions suited her very well.

'And I like your little hat,' Kathy told her. It was

39

a new one, from the stall in Abingdon Street Market. 'The green matches your eyes, Aunty Win.'

What an observant child, she thought. 'Yes, I suppose it does,' she agreed, although she considered her eyes to be more hazel than green.

Just a little of her mid-brown hair showed below her close-fitting hat. She wore her hair in a short style which was easy to manage, as she had done for years. She had not, as yet, found any grey hairs, which she thought was quite surprising. Just the slightest dusting of face powder and a smear of coral-pink lipstick added the final touch to her Sunday appearance.

'And you look very smart too,' Winifred told her niece.

Kathy's coat was quite a new one, bought just before Christmas from the Co-op Emporium on Coronation Street. Both Winifred and her mother were keen supporters of the local 'Co-ops'. The 'divi' – the dividend awarded to each shopper on every purchase – came in very useful when it was collected each year, just before Christmas. The little girl had gone with her aunt to choose the coat. It was cherry red with a little black velvet collar, and complemented her dark hair and brown eyes. Her aunt had knitted her Fair Isle beret, fawn, with a pattern of red, green and black. A complicated knitting pattern, but Winifred had been determined to master it. Those woollen hats were quite the fashion amongst the younger girls and she liked Kathy to have whatever her school friends had. She had been delighted when she had received it on Christmas morning as an extra little present. Her black fur-backed gloves had been a Christmas present too, and her patent leather ankle-strap shoes that she wore with white knee socks.

'Now, are we ready? You've got a clean hanky in your coat pocket? Righty-ho then, let's go. We don't want to be late... Bye then, Albert,' said Winifred. 'We're going now.'

'Bye-bye, Daddy,' echoed Kathy.

Albert was ensconced in his favourite fireside chair in the family living room at the back of the hotel. He was puffing away at his pipe, engrossed in the sports pages, and he grunted from behind the newspaper. 'Hmm... See you later, then. Have a nice time...'

It was only five minutes' walk to the parish church, which had been built in the early years of Victoria's reign; greyish-yellow sandstone with a square tower and a clock which now stood at twenty minutes past ten. The organ was playing quietly as they entered and took their places in a pew a few rows from the front. Kathy's friend, Shirley, was in a pew on the opposite side of the aisle with her mother, but not her father, Kathy noticed. The two friends grinned and waved to one another.

At ten-thirty precisely the organist struck up with the opening bars of the first hymn, and the choir processed from the little room called the vestry to the back of the church, and then down the central aisle to the choir stalls. They were led by a man carrying a sort of pole – it was called a staff, said Aunty Win, and he was the churchwarden – and the vicar in his white gown and a black stole edged with green. In the choir were men, women, and boys and girls as well. The boys and girls were a few years older than Kathy. She recognised some of them from the junior school, especially Graham, Shirley's brother, who was ten years old and had joined the choir quite recently. He did not even glance in his sister's direction as they passed by, but kept his eyes glued to the hymn book. No doubt they had been warned not to wave or grin. Kathy reflected that he probably felt a bit of a fool with that ruffle round his neck.

The men and the boys all wore white gowns – called surplices – but it was just the boys who had the ruffled collars. The ladies and the girls wore blue sort of cloak things, and the grown-up ladies had squarish hats on their heads. Kathy liked singing and she hoped that she might be able to join the choir when she was old enough. *'Awake, my soul, and with the sun, Thy daily stage of duty run...'* sang the choir and the congregation. Kathy tried to join in as well as she could. She could read quite well now and she soon picked up the tune, although she didn't understand all the words. *'Shake off dull sloth and joyful rise, To pay thy morning sacrifice.'* What was dull sloth, she wondered? She must remember to ask Aunty Win afterwards.

It was quite a short service, really, although there seemed to be a lot of standing up and sitting down again. Prayers, with the choir singing the amens; a reading from the Bible about Jesus and the little children; another hymn; then some more

42

prayers... Kathy's thoughts began to wander a little. She was fascinated by the windows of coloured glass; stained glass, Aunty Win had told her. The morning sunlight was shining through the one nearest to her, making little pools of red, blue, green and yellow on the stone floor. The picture on the window was of Jesus standing up in a boat, talking to some of his disciples: Peter, James and John, she guessed – they were the fishermen. And behind him the Sea of Galilee was as blue as blue could be...

Aunty Win nudged her as they all stood up for the next hymn. It was 'Loving Shepherd of Thy Sheep', and Kathy was able to sing it all as they had learnt that one at school. Then the vicar gave a little talk about families and the love that was to be found there. But he didn't just talk about mothers; he mentioned fathers, sisters and brothers, and aunts and uncles as well. Kathy was glad about that, especially the bit about aunties.

Then the children were invited to go to the front of the church where ladies were handing out bunches of daffodils from big baskets. The children took them and gave them to all the ladies in the congregation, not just the mothers but the aunties and grandmas as well, and some ladies who might not even have been married. They all received a bunch of bright-yellow daffodils. *'Here, Lord, we offer thee all that is fairest, Flowers in their freshness from garden and field...'* they all sang, and the organist carried on playing until all the flowers had been presented.

'What a lovely idea,' said Aunty Win, and Kathy

thought she could see a tear in the corner of her eye, although she looked very happy.

Shirley dashed across at the end of the service. 'Hello, Kathy... Have you asked your aunty if you can come for tea tomorrow?'

'Yes, she has asked me,' said Aunty Win, 'and of course she can go... It's very kind of you,' she said to Mrs Morris, Shirley's mother. 'Thank you very much.'

'It's no trouble,' said Mrs Morris. 'We love having Kathy, and my husband will bring her home afterwards.'

They said goodbye and Kathy and her aunt walked home, leaving Mrs Morris and Shirley to wait for Graham.

'It's going to be a busy week, Kathy,' Aunty Win told her. 'You're out for tea tomorrow; it's Brownies on Tuesday; and on Wednesday the drama group is meeting to cast the new play.'

'Are you going to have a big part, Aunty Win?' asked Kathy. She had gone to see the last one with her daddy. Aunty Win had taken the part of the mother and had had a lot of words to remember. Kathy hadn't understood it all, but she knew that her aunt had done it very well.

'I'm not sure,' smiled her aunt. 'I'll just have to wait and see. There are a lot more ladies as well as me.'

'But they're not as good,' said Kathy, loyally.

Aunty Win laughed. 'And then on Thursday it's your open evening at school, isn't it, dear? Your dad and I will be going to see Miss Roberts and find out how you're getting on.'

'Yes, we've been doing all sorts of special things

to make a nice display on the walls,' said Kathy.
'Yes, I shall look forward to seeing that. All in
all, a very busy week ahead,' said Aunty Win.

Chapter Four

Kathy loved going to tea at Shirley's home. It was
a small house, nowhere near as big as the hotel
where she lived. It was only a few minutes' walk
from Holmleigh in a street of what Shirley told
her were called semi-detached houses; that
meant that their house was joined on to the one
next door.

There was a small garden at the front with a
tiny rectangle of grass and flowers growing round
it. The garden at the back was not much bigger,
but Kathy thought it must be lovely to have a
garden at all. At Holmleigh there was just a paved
area at the front and a form where the visitors
could sit. And at the back it was just a yard with
a coal shed, a wash house and an outside lavatory. But they did have three toilets inside the
house as well, which were necessary for the visitors.

There was a small bathroom upstairs at Shirley's, and three bedrooms. One of them was very
tiny and that was where Shirley's brother,
Graham, slept. Shirley said he grumbled because
she had a bigger bedroom, but that was because
she had to share with her little sister, Brenda,
who was three years old. And Mr and Mrs

45

Morris slept in the other one.

Kathy had slept in lots of different bedrooms at her home, depending on whether or not there were visitors staying there. During the winter she had quite a nice-sized bedroom on the first landing, but she liked it best in the summer when she sometimes slept in one of the attic bedrooms. The ceiling sloped right down to the floor at the front and you had to kneel down to look out of the window. It was a lovely view, though, right across everybody else's rooftops. She could see Blackpool Tower, and the tiniest glimpse of the sea, sparkling blue if the sun was shining or a dingy grey if it wasn't.

They had a bathroom now at Holmleigh, but it had only been built last year, onto the kitchen at the back of the house. It was just for the use of the family, but there were washbasins in all the visitors' bedrooms. Aunty Win had told her that those had only been put in a few years ago. Until then the visitors had used big bowls and jugs that her aunt had filled with hot water every morning. There was still a bowl and jug in the attic room that Kathy used in the summer, very pretty ones with pink roses all over. And there was a chamber pot to match as well that went under the bed. Aunty Win called it a 'gazunder'. It was just there for emergencies because there was no toilet up in the attic.

Kathy remembered that until last year, when the bathroom was put in, she used to have her weekly bath – on a Friday night – in a huge zinc bath in front of the fire. The rest of the time the bath had hung on a hook in the wash house.

Kathy supposed that her dad and her aunt had used it too, perhaps, on different nights. She still had her bath on a Friday night. The new bath was gleaming white and shiny, but the bathroom was sometimes cold, and she missed the comfort of the fire and the big fluffy bath towel warming on the fireguard.

Shirley's mum made the two girls a drink of orange juice when they arrived home from school on that Monday afternoon, then they played with Shirley's doll's house, which stood in a corner of the living room. They liked rearranging the furniture and putting the tiny dolls on chairs so that they could have a meal. Kathy had a doll's house too. It had been her big Christmas present a few months ago. But this one of Shirley's was a bit different, a more old-fashioned sort of house; Shirley's mum said it was an Edwardian house, whatever that was. It was actually a bit bigger than Kathy's, but not nearly as posh; in fact it was a little bit shabby but Kathy wouldn't dream of saying so. She guessed it might have belonged to Shirley's mum before it was given to Shirley.

'I've called the girl Janet and the boy John, like those children in the reading books,' said Shirley.

'That's nice,' said Kathy. She didn't tell Shirley that she had christened her doll's house children Tim, after her friend, and Tina, because it sounded good with Tim. Shirley would only laugh and tease her about Timothy Fielding and say he was her boyfriend.

'They've had their tea now. Let's put them to bed,' said Shirley, rather bossily. 'Look, they've got a bedroom each, 'cause there's a lot of bedrooms upstairs. Mummy says they used to have a lot of children in Edwardian times, and that's when this house was made.'

Shirley liked to show off sometimes about all the things she knew. She was, actually, one of the cleverest girls in the class and usually came top in the spelling tests, and mental arithmetic – that was when you had to work out sums in your head. Shirley was in the top reading group too, and she, Kathy, was in the second one. Shirley was a bit of a 'clever clogs' – that was what Tim called her – but she was still Kathy's best friend for all that. Kathy knew she was not quite as clever as Shirley, but it didn't worry her. She knew that she always tried her best, and Aunty Win said that that was the most important thing.

'Look, there's a baby in the cradle too,' said Shirley. 'Wrapped in swaddling clothes, like Jesus was. But I'm pretending it's a girl baby. I've called her Jemima, 'cause it goes with Janet and John.'

'Can I play?' shouted Brenda from across the room. She had been playing on the floor, building towers of wooden blocks, but that, suddenly, was getting boring. What the older girls were doing looked much more interesting. She knocked over the pile of bricks and trotted across the room. 'Can I put the baby to bed, Shirley?' she asked.

'No, you can't! She's already in her bed.' Shirley gave her a push, not a hard one, but one that showed she was annoyed with her little sister. 'Go away, Brenda. You're a nuisance! Mummy says you haven't to play with my house. You're only a baby and you'll mess it up.'

48

Brenda's face crumpled and she looked as though she was going to cry. 'Not a baby!' she protested. 'I only want to help.'

'Oh, go on, let her,' said Kathy. She felt sorry for the little girl. She was such a sweet little thing, with wispy blonde hair the same colour as Shirley's plaits, and big blue eyes that were filling up with tears. 'She can't mess it up if we're here, can she?' Kathy thought how nice it would be to have a little sister like Brenda. Probably she could be a pest at times, but Kathy knew she would love her very much if she were her sister. And she was sure that Shirley did love her, really.

'Oh, all right, then,' said Shirley. 'Stop crying, Brenda. Don't be such a baby! Here, you can hold Jemima.'

That pacified the little girl and they all played happily together, until the next interruption. That was when Graham came into the room followed rapidly by his mother.

'Graham, how many times have I told you to take off your football boots before you come in the house. Just look at the state of you! Now there's mud all over the carpet! Go and get them off at once, and put your football things in the washing basket. Honestly! Whatever am I going to do with you?'

'OK, Mum,' said Graham, quite casually. 'It's only dried mud; it'll brush off. Keep your hair on!'

'And don't be cheeky,' said Mrs Morris, although she was smiling and so was Graham.

'He's a pest,' observed Shirley when he had left the room. 'Mum's always telling him about his football boots and stuff... But it goes in one ear and out of the other,' she added, in an old-fashioned way. 'I bet you're glad you've not got a big brother, Kathy. He drives me potty!'

Kathy didn't answer that remark. She was thinking it would be rather nice to have an older brother, just as she had thought, earlier, that she would like to have a little sister, or even a big sister.

Graham came back into the room a few minutes later and flopped into a chair with his *Dandy* comic.

'D'you want to come and play with us, Graham?' invited Brenda. 'I 'spect Shirley'll let you.' But her remark was greeted with scorn.

'Huh! Girls' stuff!' he sneered. 'No thanks! Anyway, shouldn't you be helping Mum to set the table, Shirl?' It was her job, sometimes, to put the cloth on the table and set out the cups and saucers.

'Why should I?' Shirley retorted. 'Why should it always be me? Why can't you do it?'

'Because I'm a boy, that's why,' replied her brother. 'It's women's work, cooking an' cleaning an' washing up an' all that stuff. That's what Dad says. And it's girls that have to help.'

Kathy gathered that Graham didn't reckon much to girls. He hadn't even said hello to her, although he knew she was there. Aunty Win said he was a lovely boy and so nice-looking too. But she had only seen him on a Sunday, dressed in his choir clothes and looking angelic. She didn't know what he was like the rest of the time. Kathy realised, though, that he might be considered

50

handsome, like princes always were in fairy tales. He was dark-haired, not fair like his sisters, and he had brown eyes with a roguish gleam. Like his dad, Kathy realised later when Mr Morris came in from work.

She had seen Shirley's dad before, but at the other times when she had been there for tea, the children and Mrs Morris had had their tea first – a sandwich tea followed by home-made cakes – whilst Mr Morris had had a cooked meal prepared specially for him. Today, though, they all sat down together to a meal of sausages and chips with baked beans. Kathy thought it was delicious. They didn't often have sausages and baked beans at home. Her father, and her aunt as well, were used to cooking rather different meals for the visitors, such as roast meat and two veg, and sausages were usually cooked as 'toad-in-the-hole' which she didn't like very much. Baked beans, too, were frowned upon, except occasionally in an emergency, as Kathy's dad reckoned nothing to 'eating out of tins'. And there was HP sauce, as well. She noticed that Shirley and Graham and Mr Morris put on great dollops of it. Kathy loved it, but was not often allowed it, although it was always put on the visitors' tables for them to have with their bacon and eggs.

'Nice to have you with us, Kathy,' said Mr Morris, giving her a friendly wink which made her feel shy. She smiled back, feeling her cheeks turning pink. 'Special tea an' all because you're here,' he went on. 'Don't tell anyone, but we usually have bread and dripping.'

Kathy knew that was not true and she laughed

51

a little uncertainly. Her own dad didn't often crack jokes or talk very much at all at mealtimes, but Shirley's dad was full of fun. She wondered if he was always like that.

'Take no notice of him, Kathy love,' said Mrs Morris. 'He's a terrible tease. He knows very well he has a cooked meal every night, don't you, Frank? The children and I have ours at dinner time when they come home from school.'

'Yes, I know that, Mrs Morris,' said Kathy quietly. 'I know he's … er … only joking. I have my dinner at dinner time too. But this is lovely,' she added.

'Aye, take no notice of me, love,' said Mr Morris. 'My missus looks after me real well, don't you, Sadie love?'

'Kathy's dad does the cooking in their house,' chimed in Shirley. 'Doesn't he, Kathy?'

'Well … yes,' replied Kathy. 'A lot of the time he does. But that's only because–'

'Aye, it's because they've got a boarding house, isn't that right, Kathy?' said Mr Morris. 'It's Mr Leigh's job; that's why he does the cooking.'

'Yes … he's a chef,' said Kathy in a little voice.

'A chef … aye, real posh that, isn't it? Like I said, it's his job. You wouldn't catch me in the kitchen. Not on your life!' Mr Morris grinned at his wife. 'Anyroad, my missus enjoys cooking, don't you, Sadie love?'

'I don't suppose I've got much choice,' said Mrs Morris with a sigh. But she was smiling. 'I don't mind a bit of help, though, sometimes.'

'Well, you've got a daughter to help out, haven't you? And soon there'll be two of 'em,' said Mr

52

Morris beckoning towards little Brenda. 'I don't reckon you're so badly off, love.'

Mrs Morris didn't answer. 'Now then, who's for pudding?' she said, a few moments later, getting up to collect the dirty plates.

'Do you need to ask?' replied her husband. 'All of us!'

'Yes ... please,' added Kathy politely.

Pudding was big pear halves – out of a tin, Kathy guessed – with lots of evaporated milk. Once again, it was delicious and a lovely treat.

When they had finished their meal Mrs Morris cleared the table. Kathy noticed that Shirley was helping, and so she did her bit too, carrying her own pots into the kitchen; she was used to helping Aunty Win at home. She noticed that Mr Morris and Graham got up from the table and sat down in the easy chairs, Mr Morris with the evening paper and Graham with his *Dandy*. But then her own dad did that as well. He didn't mind cooking – in fact he enjoyed it – but he wasn't all that keen on washing up.

'Thank you...' Mrs Morris smiled at the two little girls. 'A little help is worth a lot of pity.'

'My aunty says that,' Kathy told her.

Mrs Morris laughed. 'Yes, I daresay it's a common saying amongst us womenfolk. Anyway, off you go, you two. I'll soon have this lot cleared away, and then perhaps we can have a game or two – Ludo or Snakes and Ladders – before Kathy goes home. Can you find them, Shirley? They're in the sideboard drawer.'

'Oh, here's the tiddlywinks as well,' said Shirley, rooting in the drawer. 'Goody! Let's have a go at

53

that, shall we, while we're waiting for Mummy to finish washing up.'

Mrs Morris had put a velvety cloth over the table when it had been cleared. There was one just like it at Kathy's home, except that theirs was brown and this one was red.

'We need a flat surface,' said Shirley, 'or the tiddlywinks won't jump. I know; we'll use the Ludo board... Are you going to have a game with us, Graham?'

'What, tiddlywinks?' scoffed her brother. 'No thanks; that's kid's stuff.' He turned back to the doings of Desperate Dan.

'Can I play?' begged Brenda, running in from the kitchen where she had been watching her mother. 'Let me, please let me!'

'All right, then,' agreed Shirley. 'See, kneel up on the chair, then you can reach.'

Kathy thought the little girl was so appealing, shouting out in delight every time one of her tiddlywinks jumped into the pot. There were shouts of 'Shut up!' though, from her brother, and even Mr Morris winced a little at her piercing voice.

'Now then, that's all shipshape again,' said Mrs Morris, coming in from the kitchen. 'We'll have a game or two, shall we, before Kathy goes home. Frank ... Graham ... are you going to join us?'

To Kathy's surprise they both agreed that they would.

'There'll be too many of us, though,' said Shirley. 'It makes five and we only need four for Ludo.'

'And then there's Brenda,' said Kathy.

'Oh, she's too little,' said Shirley. 'I tell you what; she can play with you, Kathy, seeing that you seem to have taken to her... Let her think she is helping,' she added in a grown-up voice.

'And I'll have a look at the paper while you play,' said Mrs Morris. 'Then we can swap over later.'

Kathy enjoyed the games very much. Mr Morris was such good fun. Her dad could hardly ever be persuaded to join in games, and it wasn't much good with just herself and Aunty Win, although her aunt had taught her to play draughts and how to do patience, which you could play on your own. It was usually very quiet in the evening at Kathy's home, with her dad listening to the wireless and her aunt knitting or reading. She was enjoying playing immensely now, but she decided that Graham was not a very good loser. He wanted to win at all the games – she guessed that was why he wanted to play, so that he could show off – and he was really cross when Shirley won the first game of Ludo. He won the second one, though, so he cheered up a bit.

Then Mrs Morris joined in instead of her husband, and they played Snakes and Ladders. Graham was very annoyed when his counter had to go down a really long snake. And in the end Kathy won that game.

'It's only a game of chance,' remarked Graham. 'You don't have to be clever to win at Snakes and Ladders, not like you do at Ludo.' Mrs Morris told him off for being impolite to their guest, but Kathy didn't mind. She didn't know what he meant, really. Besides, it had all been such good fun.

When it was time for Kathy to go home Mrs Morris said she would walk back with her. 'I feel that I need a breath of fresh air,' she explained.

'But it's Brenda's bedtime,' said her husband.

'It's all right, Frank,' she replied. 'She can stay up a bit and I'll see to her when I get back. I won't be long. You can perhaps read her a story?'

'OK, then,' said Mr Morris. He didn't seem to mind that.

'Thank you for having me,' Kathy said to him when she had got her coat on, just as her aunt had taught her to do when she went to someone's house.

'That's all right,' he laughed. 'You're a very polite little lady. We've enjoyed having you. Come again, any time.'

'Can I come with you to Kathy's?' asked Shirley.

'No, you stay here,' replied her mother. 'Maybe you could read a story to Brenda as well. She'll like that.'

Shirley nodded. 'I'll read her the one about the three billy goats gruff. It's her favourite.' Shirley was very proud of her prowess at reading and never lost an opportunity to show off a little.

'Ta-ra, Kathy,' she called. 'See you at school tomorrow.'

Dusk was falling as they set off along the street and round the corner to the hotel where Kathy lived. She held Mrs Morris's hand as they crossed the road. She liked Shirley's mum. She was young and pretty, with blonde hair like Shirley's, and she wore bright-pink lipstick. She was nice and friendly too, and never seemed to get bad-tempered, not like some of the mums that Kathy had seen sometimes on the way home from school, shouting at their children.

'I want to have a little chat with your aunty ... about something,' she told Kathy. 'And I didn't really want Shirley to be listening, not until it's sorted out. She's a bit nosey, is our Shirley; she likes to know what's going on.'

'Little pigs have big ears,' remarked Kathy. 'That's what my aunty says sometimes, when she wants to tell my dad something private. But I don't ever tell tales.'

Mrs Morris laughed. 'No, I'm sure you don't. It's not really a secret ... but I was wondering if your aunt might find me a job at the hotel when the season starts... You're the only person I've told yet,' she added confidingly. 'But keep it under your hat for the moment. That means—'

'It means I've not to tell Shirley.' Kathy nodded. 'Don't worry, Mrs Morris. It's our secret.'

Shirley's mum laughed. 'You're a little cough drop, aren't you?' That was a funny thing to say. Her aunty said it sometimes when Kathy said something that made her laugh. She guessed it was a nice thing to be.

'We'll go in the back way,' said Kathy when they arrived at Holmleigh. 'The back door's usually open until everyone's in. Come in, Mrs Morris,' she said politely. 'I'll tell my aunty you're here.'

The door opened straight into the kitchen, and that led into the living room. It was the family dining room and sitting room and everything-else room, separate from the rooms at the front which were occupied by the visitors.

'Mrs Morris has brought me home,' called Kathy. 'She wants to ask you something, Aunty Win.'

Aunty Win was knitting and her dad was reading the newspaper and smoking his pipe. He looked up and nodded. 'Hello there. Thanks for having our Kathy.' Then he returned to his paper.

'Come in, come in. Sit yourself down.' Aunty Win jumped up and moved a couple of magazines off an easy chair.

'Thank you... I hope I'm not disturbing you,' said Shirley's mum.

'No, not at all... Kathy, go and take your coat off, there's a good girl. And then you can read in your bedroom while I talk to Mrs Morris,' said Aunty Win.

'Oh, it's all right; it's nothing private,' said Mrs Morris. 'I've already mentioned it to Kathy, haven't I, dear?' She sat down and paused for a moment before she started to speak. 'Actually ... I was wondering if you could perhaps find me a job of some sort, Miss Leigh, when the season starts. I could turn my hand to almost anything I'm sure; chambermaid, waitress or ... whatever you think best.'

'I'm sure I could employ you,' said Winifred. 'We, I should say, as it's my brother's business as well as mine. But he leaves that side of things to me, don't you, Albert?'

'Eh? What?' Albert looked up from his paper.

'Mrs Morris would like to come and work here during the season,' said Winifred. 'We'd be pleased to have her, wouldn't we?'

58

'Yes, of course,' replied Albert. 'You sort it out, Winnie.'

'Oh ... do call me Sadie,' said Mrs Morris. 'Most people do, and I prefer it.'

'And I'm Winifred; Win or Winnie for short. But you know that, don't you?'

'Well, yes; Kathy talks a lot about her Aunty Win. In fact, that's how I always think of you, as Aunty Win.'

Winifred smiled. '"What's in a name?" as somebody once said. Christian names it is, then. As you get older some people think it's too familiar to call you by your first name, but I've never minded at all. So ... Sadie, let's see what we can sort out, shall we?'

Kathy sat at the table, quietly leafing through her *Twinkle* comic, but she was listening as well. She heard Mrs Morris explaining that she hadn't been out to work since before she was married, but that she needed a job to 'make ends meet'.

'My husband, Frank, is quite old-fashioned, you see. I had a good job before we were married. I was a shorthand typist, and I worked for a solicitor in the town. But when we got married Frank made me give it up and stay at home. He thinks it's a man's place to provide, and he does earn quite a good wage; he's a bus driver for the Blackpool Corporation. He says it's a woman's job to stay at home and look after the house. Then the children arrived – Graham and Shirley and Brenda – and so, of course, I've spent all my time looking after them and Frank.'

'And making a very good job of it,' said Winifred.

'Well, yes; I've done my best. But we could do with a bit more coming in, to be quite honest. Graham and Shirley are always needing new things, they grow so fast. And Brenda has to have a lot of "hand-me-downs" that Shirley has grown out of. I sometimes feel they're shabbily dressed compared with some of the other children – your Kathy, for instance.'

'Well, we've only got Kathy to look after,' replied Winifred. 'And we try to make an extra effort ... under the circumstances, you see,' she added in a quieter voice. She means it's because I haven't got a mum, thought Kathy. 'But I think your children are a credit to you, Sadie.'

'Thank you. Well, I always make sure they're clean and tidy, and I try to see that they don't go short of anything, but it's hard at times. And I'd like to be able to buy a new dress for myself now and again, without having to ask Frank every time.'

Kathy, listening to it all, recalled that Shirley didn't have so many different clothes as she had. And the gymslip her friend was wearing now was too short, but she had never really thought anything about it before.

'I haven't said anything to Frank,' Sadie continued. 'He would only say no, we can manage, and there's Brenda to consider, and all that. I thought if I sorted something out first and then told him later, it would be a question of "fait accompli".'

Kathy didn't understand all that, but she thought how nice it would be to have Shirley's mum working at the hotel. She couldn't leave

60

little Brenda at home, though. Wouldn't it be good if she could bring Brenda with her, then she, Kathy, could look after her? It would be nearly as good as having a little sister of her own.

'Mmm...' Aunty Win was nodding solemnly. 'Yes, I see the problem ... Sadie. You don't want to cause trouble with your husband, do you?'

'Oh, I'm sure it won't come to that,' replied Mrs Morris. 'But he's like all men; he likes to think he's the one in charge.' She glanced cautiously at Kathy's dad, but he didn't seem to be listening.

'You could bring your little girl with you,' said Aunty Win. 'You'd look after her, wouldn't you, Kathy?' She seemed to realise that Kathy had been listening all the time.

'Ooh, yes! I'd like that,' agreed Kathy.

'And Shirley could come as well, if you like,' Aunty Win went on. 'They could amuse themselves, I'm sure, whilst you were busy. And Shirley and Kathy are such good friends, aren't they?'

Kathy pondered that it would have been rather nice to look after Brenda on her own. Shirley was inclined to be bossy and to want to be in charge all the time; like her mum had said that Mr Morris liked to be. Still, it would be good to have somebody to play with during the school holiday. It was often a lonely time with her dad and aunt busy working all the day.

Kathy heard her aunt suggest that Mrs Morris – Sadie – could be a waitress for the midday meals, except for Sunday when she would be at home with her family, and then perhaps she could help with the washing-up. 'It's a mammoth task when we're fully booked,' said Aunty Win. 'At the height of the season we might have as many as thirty guests.'

But Mrs Morris just smiled. 'It's all in a day's work,' she said. 'I've never minded washing up.'

'What I could really do with, though, is some help with the bookkeeping,' said Winifred. Albert leaves all that side of things to me, and it's a bit of a headache sometimes. The books have to be kept in order for the taxman, and maths has never been my strong point. We've muddled through so far, more by good luck than good management, but the laws are getting stricter now. I don't suppose you could...?' She looked hopefully at Mrs Morris.

'I'd be delighted,' said Sadie. 'That's a job I could do at home, if it's all right with you. I studied bookkeeping at night school. I've got a typewriter too – I've had it since I was doing my studying – so I could do any letters you want typing.'

'Do you know, this is like an answer to a prayer!' exclaimed Winifred. 'Except that I'd never have thought of asking God for help with my office work!'

The two ladies settled down to a long chat over a cup of tea. Kathy's bedtime seemed to have been forgotten, so she kept quiet. So had little Brenda's and Shirley's, she thought. She hoped that Mrs Morris wouldn't be in trouble with her husband when she got home.

Chapter Five

Winifred had been a member of the dramatic society ever since it had started, back in 1920. She had felt the need of an interest outside of the home which, in her case, was also her place of work. In some ways it had been a lonely sort of life compared with some of her friends, girls of the same age who had jobs outside of the home; that was until they married, when it was expected that young women would stay at home, caring for their husbands and families. But the recent war had taken its toll, and many young women, bereaved, as Winifred had been, viewed the future as one of inevitable spinsterhood.

The boarding house had been very much a family affair, with her mother, Alice Leigh, at the helm. Alice was just one of a vast army of seaside landladies, veritable matriarchs, who were becoming quite a force to be reckoned with. Blackpool landladies, in particular, were often the butt of music hall jokes and comic postcards, and even more so were their husbands. It was said that these downtrodden little men spent most of their lives in the kitchen, peeling endless amounts of spuds, and tackling great mountains of washing-up. This was not strictly true in all cases. William Leigh, Alice's husband, for instance, had had a job outside of the home. He was a painter and decorator by trade, the job he had been apprenticed to on leaving school and in which he was employed when he met Alice.

Alice's parents had 'not been short of a bob or two', as Lancashire folk were often heard to say. Soon after the marriage of the young couple they had helped Alice and William to buy the North Shore boarding house, and it had proved to be an excellent investment. It had been intended at first that Alice should run the business on her own, with just a little paid help. Later on, however, it had seemed only sensible that William should put his weight behind it as well, taking decorating jobs for other people during the winter months, at the same time doing the painting and decorating that was continually needed at the boarding house.

Now, in 1950, William and Alice were thankfully and happily retired. Albert was more or less in the same position as his father had been. His skills as a painter and decorator had been taught to him by his father. The difference was that Albert had also learnt to cook – in fact he was considered to be an excellent cook – something his father would never have dreamt of doing, and unheard of in the days of the old Blackpool landladies. And the boarding house – now a private hotel – was doing so well that Albert did not need to do jobs for other people. The ongoing work at Holmleigh kept him quite busy enough.

Winifred had never given a great deal of thought as to whether or not she would be able to act, when she had first joined the dramatic group. She had seen it mainly as a way of meeting other young people, and as a means of helping her to recover from the ache in her heart, still there after more than a year, whenever she thought about Arthur. Maybe, at the back of her mind, there had been the thought that she might, sooner or later, meet another young man who could come to mean as much to her as Arthur had done. But the years had gone by and this had not happened. There was, inevitably, a dearth of younger men – as the girls often complained, they were either too young or too old – and the few that joined the dramatic society, in the first instance and then in later years, had somehow never ignited that vital spark of interest in Winifred.

She had, many years ago, struck up a friendship with a friend of her brother. But he, like Albert, was five years younger than herself, not that that would have been of any consequence had they been truly attracted to one another. But after a couple of outings to the cinema and the music hall she had told him that she didn't wish to go out with him again. He had not seemed bothered at all, and she had wondered then if he had only asked her out at the request of her brother who, she knew, sympathised with her predicament.

Then there had been an older man, a solicitor in the town, who had been left a widower in his early thirties. There again, though, Winifred had known that there was no way she would ever want to spend the rest of her life with him, although he had seemed rather keen that she should consider doing so.

Nowadays she did not fret about her lack of a husband. Neither did she envy her married friends. Sometimes, indeed, she felt that she, as a spinster, had the best of it. Some men were so dogmatic and domineering. She was contented – happy, even – in her own quiet way. The dramatic society that she had joined initially to ease her loneliness had proved to be a source of inspiration and motivation to her. To her amazement she had found that she could act and, to her surprise and delight, after a year or two she was playing the female lead in some of the plays they performed.

She was not, by nature, an outgoing sort of person, but she did not find it difficult to take on the guise and the personality of the character she was playing. Neither would she have considered herself to be beautiful; she was certainly not at all like Joan Crawford or Gloria Swanson, the film stars of the time, but she supposed she had a pleasing face and figure, which, with her warm brown hair and greenish eyes, could be used onstage to her best advantage.

Her days of playing the young heroine, alas, were well past. However, she still enjoyed acting the more mature parts, as mothers or unmarried aunts. She had played the mother in J.B. Priestley's *An Inspector Calls*, and one of the middle-aged wives, which called for a certain amount of comedy, in *When We Are Married*, another of Priestley's plays. That one had been their last production. He was one of their favourite playwrights, but this year they were planning to put on a play from the end of the last century.

One of Winifred's best-loved roles, as a young woman, had been that of Gwendolen Fairfax in *The Importance of Being Earnest*. They had performed that way back in 1925 and now the producer – a different one by this time – had decided it was time to bring back Oscar Wilde's most famous play.

Would she be able to cope with the part of Lady Bracknell, she wondered? It was widely expected that it would be given to Winifred, but it was not yet cut and dried. There was to be a preliminary reading of the play at the next meeting. That would be on Wednesday evening.

But before that it was Kathy's Brownie meeting on Tuesday. They met in the church hall at six o' clock. Girls were supposed to be seven years old before they joined the Brownies, but as Kathy would be seven in June she had been allowed to join a couple of months early. This was really a special favour because Brown Owl was a friend of her Aunty Win, and also because Shirley, who had turned seven in January, had pleaded with Brown Owl for her friend to be allowed to join.

This would be her fourth time at Brownies and to Kathy it was one of the special times in the week. She was proud of her brown tunic, the real leather belt and silver buckle, and the yellow tie with a lovely little tiepin shaped like an elf that was fastened to it. Some of the older girls – the eight- or nine-year-olds – had badges sewn on to their sleeves that they had been awarded for passing tests: homecraft, needlework, artwork, music, swimming and all sorts of other things. Kathy was already learning to tie knots – that was one of the first tests they worked for – and she knew it would be quite easy for her to get her homecraft badge as well. That involved doing simple jobs in the home, like making a cup of tea, setting the table and washing up. She was already used to doing jobs like that.

Shirley was already there when Aunty Win left her at the church hall. Kathy took off her coat and hung it up and went over to join her friend.

'I've got something to tell you,' said Shirley excitedly. 'My mum's going to come and work at your hotel. She's going to be a waitress – I 'spect your aunty will let her be the one in charge, 'cause she says the two she had last summer were just girls helping out in the school holiday – and my mum's going to do the books as well; y'know, sorting out the money an' bills an' all that.'

'Oh ... that's nice,' replied Kathy. She knew that if she told Shirley that she already knew – or at least had heard something about it – then Shirley would be mad at her and get all huffy like she did sometimes.

'And your aunty says that me and our Brenda can come as well and play with you while my mum's busy working. That'll be good, won't it?'

'Yes, that's very nice.' Kathy nodded. 'Actually ... Aunty Win did sort of say that you and Brenda might be coming ... but I didn't know it was all decided. Why didn't you tell me at school today?'

'Because my mum's only just told me, that's why!' said Shirley, a little impatiently. 'Actually, they had a row – my mum and dad – when she got back from your house last night. It was past Brenda's bedtime, and she'd already had two stories read to her and Mum wasn't there to see to her. So Dad told me to help her to get undressed and have a wash an' all that. And he didn't half shout at my mum for being such a long time. I could hear them from upstairs.'

'Oh dear!' said Kathy. 'I thought he was really nice, your dad. He's good fun, isn't he?' She didn't say that he was not like her own dad who could be grumpy some of the time, because that wouldn't be a very nice thing to say.

'Sometimes he is,' replied Shirley. 'But he can get mad as well. He likes to be the boss, y'see; that's why my brother thinks he can boss me around – he's just trying to be like our dad. Anyway, my mum came upstairs then to see to Brenda and she looked real upset. I thought she was going to cry, but she didn't. She said to me not to worry, 'cause Daddy would get over it, like he always does.'

'So are they all right now?' asked Kathy.

'I think so. They seemed all right when Daddy came home from work. Mummy gave him his tea, then she had to come straight out to bring me here. But she told me and Graham at teatime about coming to work at your hotel. She said that Daddy wasn't too pleased at the idea, but she would work on him. That's when she said me and Brenda could come with her. And I think your aunty said we could have our dinner with you as well.'

'What about Graham? asked Kathy.

Shirley laughed. 'That's just what he said. "What about me? Who's going to make my dinner?" And Mummy told him he was just like Daddy, always thinking about himself.'

'So what will he do?'

'Oh, he's out most of the time in the holidays

playing football. I 'spect he might go to Jimmy's; he's his best friend. My mum certainly won't neglect him,' Shirley added.

Kathy pondered that family life – real family life, with a mother and father and children – must sometimes have arguments and fallings-out as well as fun and happy times. All the same, it must be rather nice, she thought.

Then it was time for the meeting to begin. They all stood round the big toadstool in the centre of the room. They saluted with three fingers and promised to do their best, to do their duty to God and the King, and to help other people every day. Then they went off into their 'sixes'; there were five of these groups. They were called Elves, Fairies, Pixies, Sprites and Gnomes. Kathy was an elf, and so was Shirley. The leader of each six was called the 'sixer'. Kathy knew it would be a long time before she achieved that honour, but for the moment she was enjoying the fun and games and learning the different skills. She could already tie a reef knot and a slip knot, and they were learning to knit – pearl stitch as well as garter stitch. The finished article would, hopefully, make a cover for a doll's bed.

She told her aunt on the way home what Shirley had said about her mum and dad falling out.

'Oh dear!' said Aunty Win. 'I do hope it isn't going to cause trouble. Sadie – Mrs Morris – is only trying to help a little with the money side of things. I'm looking forward to having her. I'm sure she'll be popular with the visitors; she's such a friendly young lady. Never mind, I expect it'll

70

all come out in the wash, as your grandma likes to say.'

Kathy thought again what funny things grown-ups said sometimes.

The play reading was to take place in the same church hall the following evening. The hall was in use every afternoon and evening for groups such as Brownies and Guides, Cubs and Scouts, Mothers' Union and Young Wives, as well as for all the social events that took place in the parish. Winifred was neither a young wife nor a mother, and although both those groups had said she would be welcome to join them she had not done so. She did not want to feel like a fish out of water.

She was, however, a person of some importance now in the drama group. She was always there early in her capacity as registrar to collect the subs and to welcome everyone. She was also vice-chairman of the group and next year it would be her turn to be in the chair.

When the present chairman, Mavis Peacock, arrived she was accompanied by a man that Winifred had not seen before. A new member, she wondered, looking at him with interest – she was careful not to show too keen an interest – although he was what might be called a hand-some figure of a man.

'Oh, hello there, Winnie,' said Mavis. She was a woman of Winifred's own age and they had joined the group at more or less the same time. Mavis, though, had always been more interested in the production side of things rather than taking much part in the acting. She was wardrobe mistress and was in charge of the props, and with her brisk efficiency she was an invaluable member of the society.

'This is my brother,' she went on. 'I think I told you, didn't I, that he was coming to live in Blackpool? Well, it happened all of a sudden in the end, and here he is! Jeff, this is Winifred Leigh, a very good friend of mine ... and one of our leading ladies,' she added with a nod of approval at her friend. 'Winnie, this is Jeffrey Bancroft, usually known as Jeff.'

The two of them shook hands, murmuring the conventional 'How do you do?' Winifred found herself looking into – and almost mesmerised by – a pair of shrewd grey eyes that seemed to be regarding her with more than the ordinary interest afforded to a stranger that one had only just met. He was not tall, little more than average height, like herself, with hair that she guessed had once been fairish, but was now a greyish blonde, still thick and with the natural waves that many straight-haired women would envy. He smiled at her in a friendly, but by no means a familiar, manner.

'Have you come to join us?' she asked. 'Are we about to welcome a new member?'

'I hope so,' he replied. 'But I've just come along to watch tonight.'

'And to see if you like us?' Winifred enquired.

'Oh, I'm quite sure I shall do that,' he smiled. 'I was a member of a drama group several years ago, but I haven't done much acting just lately. I will be quite content for the moment to act as an

ASM if you need one.'

'We certainly do, don't we, Winnie?' replied his sister. 'Our stage manager, Wilfred, is very good, but he's past retiring age now and he's always glad of extra help. Anyway, come along, Jeff, and I'll introduce you to some of the members.'

Winifred decided she would look forward to chatting further with him when they had their cup of tea halfway through the evening; but for now she must get on with the job in hand, collecting the money and welcoming the members.

The play reading began with the casting of the two roguish young bachelors, Jack and Algernon. It was more or less a foregone conclusion that the parts would go to the two youngish men, Dave and Tony, who were both in their mid-thirties. Possibly a little too old for the roles, but there was a shortage of really young men.

There were several young women who were willing and well able to take the parts of the two girls, Gwendolen and Cecily. There was total agreement though, fortunately, when the role of Gwendolen was given to Thelma Bridges, who was Tawny Owl to the Brownie pack. At twenty-three she was a little older, but not all that much so, than the character was supposed to be. The part of Cecily was awarded to Thelma's friend, Isobel, which pleased the pair of them.

When the tea and biscuits were served Winifred, purposely, did not seek out her new acquaintance, but she was not at all displeased, or surprised, when he came to join her.

'Your turn next,' said Jeff Bancroft, pulling up a

73

chair and sitting next to her. 'My sister says you're auditioning for Lady Bracknell?'

'Yes, that's right.'

'Pardon me for saying so, but aren't you too young and ... er ... attractive for such a role?' She could see that he was not trying to flirt with her. He was obviously sincere in what he was saying, so she took his words at face value. She smiled.

'Thanks for the compliment! I can assure you I'm quite old enough, although we don't know Lady B's exact age, do we? Yes, I realise I'm not the usual stereotype, but I don't see that that matters. I feel I could put my own interpretation on the role. Does she need to be corpulent and hatchet-faced? I don't really think so. Anyway, she's a character part I've always fancied having a go at. My days of playing the young ingenue have long gone, I'm afraid.'

'Mine too, alas,' he replied. 'But never mind; age has certain compensations.'

Winifred nodded. 'Yes, I suppose so.' She smiled at him questioningly. 'Such as?'

'Well, now you ask me I'm not quite sure, but there must be some.' Jeffrey laughed. She recognised the Yorkshire accent as he spoke, not too pronounced, but typical of the folk from the rugged northern hills, gravelly and issuing from way back in the throat. She remembered Mavis saying that her brother lived in Bradford, the city where Mavis also had been born. 'No, I'm joking,' he went on. 'Of course there are compensations. For a start, we're wiser now, aren't we? Years of experience must have taught us something. We're not so ready to rush into things or make mistakes, or perhaps not quite so many.'

'It's said, isn't it, that the person who never made a mistake never made anything?' answered Winifred thoughtfully. 'I don't think I've ever made any really drastic mistakes ... but sometimes life takes over, doesn't it, and you haven't much control over what happens to you. You can't always please yourself; sometimes decisions are already made for you.' She realised she was becoming rather introspective. 'Sorry...' she smiled. 'I didn't mean to start soliloquising. But don't get the wrong impression. I'm not complaining about my lot. I lead a very contented life.'

'And a very full one, I believe,' answered Jeff. 'My sister has told me about your hotel, and about how you look after your little niece. You've no children of your own?

'No, I've never been married,' she replied. 'I was one of the very many girls who lost someone in the first war. It's a long time ago, though. Who can tell whether it would have been a good marriage ... or a mistake? We were very young, but it seemed right at the time. However, it just wasn't to be.' She was finding it very easy to talk to Jeff, but she realised she hardly knew the first thing about him. Mavis had mentioned, casually, that her brother was coming to live in Blackpool when he had managed to sell his house in Yorkshire. And now, here he was, and he did seem to be quite interested in talking to her.

'Yes, it was a dreadful conflict,' he replied. 'Well, both wars were, but I'm afraid I can't speak from any real experience. I was just too young to join up in the first lot, to my parents' great relief. My elder brother was wounded on the Somme. He lost an arm, but at least it meant that he didn't have to go back. And he's still going strong, I'm glad to say. Then I was called up with my age group in the second war, but I never got any further than the very north of England. I must confess I was relieved. I felt I was rather too old to be a "have-a-go hero", and life was too precious for me to want to throw it away. But at least I did wear the uniform for a while.'

'The same as my brother,' observed Winifred. 'He joined up – he was in the catering corps – but he didn't leave these shores.'

'And then he was widowed, I believe?'

'Yes...' answered Winifred. It seemed that Jeffrey Bancroft already knew quite a lot about her family circumstances. 'Albert lost his wife towards the end of the war, but we've both tried to do what we can for our little Katherine – Kathy, we call her.'

'Yes, I was widowed too,' said Jeff, 'three years ago. But my two children were already married with families of their own.' That answered a question that Winifred had been wanting to ask, but had not felt able to. Mavis had not mentioned whether her brother was coming to live here on his own, or whether he had a wife and family. And Winifred, at that time, had not really been curious enough to enquire.

She murmured the conventional, 'I'm so sorry ... about your wife, I mean.'

He gave a sad smile. 'Yes ... it's always distressing, but I have to confess that it was not an ideally happy marriage. We were young – too

76

young, as we both came to realise – but we stayed together for the sake of the children. It was a shock, of course, when I lost Beatrice. It was very sudden; an aneurism, and we weren't even aware that she had a weak heart. I grieved for a while, more than I expected to. But then I knew it was time to move on. Both my children have moved away. My son is in Canada, and my daughter's in the south of England, so I don't see them as much as I would like to...'

'So you decided to come and live in Blackpool?'

'Yes. Mavis is my only sister and we've always got on well together. I decided to move away from the grime of the mill towns – although it's not so bad as it used to be – and enjoy some of your famous fresh air and Blackpool breezes.'

'And are you enjoying it?'

'Yes ... but it doesn't half blow here! I was nearly blown off my feet on the lower prom the other day, to say nothing of getting soaked by an enormous wave crashing over the sea wall.'

Winifred laughed. 'Yes, we residents have learnt to beware of the tides. Do you live near the sea?'

'Yes, I have a little bungalow in an avenue near to Gynn Square.'

'And what about your job? You were able to find employment here?' Winifred realised then that she might be seeming rather nosey, but he was so easy to talk to. 'I'm sorry...' she said. 'I'm asking too many questions.'

'No, not at all,' he replied easily. 'Actually, it didn't make any difference to my work because I'm self-employed. I'm a freelance artist.'

'My goodness! That sounds very clever.'

Jeff smiled. 'Well, let's say it's one of my very few talents. I'll be able to help you with your scenery... I do illustrations for greetings cards and children's books, and for book covers. Anything, really, that I'm asked to do. I suppose you could call me a jobbing artist, but it keeps the wolf from the door.'

'I'm very impressed,' said Winifred. 'Oh ... I think they're ready to start again. It's been nice talking to you ... Jeff.'

'The pleasure is all mine ... Winifred,' he replied. 'And ... good luck! Or should I say "break a leg"?'

She laughed. 'It doesn't matter. I'm not superstitious.'

Her chat with Jeff Bancroft had enhanced her sense of well-being and had, somehow, imbued her with confidence.

The other lady auditioning for the part was older and plumper, looking altogether more like a typical Lady Bracknell. But there was little doubt when they had both been heard what the outcome would be. The part was awarded to Winifred and the other contender gave way graciously.

'Congratulations!' said Jeff, as they put on their coats ready to depart. 'I knew you'd do it.'

'Thank you,' said Winifred, humbly. 'I must admit ... I'm rather pleased.'

'Now, may I offer you a lift home?' he said. 'Or do you have your own transport?'

'No, I don't drive,' she replied. She knew it would be churlish to refuse; besides, she had no intention of doing so. 'Thank you,' she said. 'It's very kind of you.'

His car was parked outside, a Ford Popular, about two years old, she assumed, although her knowledge of cars was limited.

'So I'll see you next week,' he said when they pulled up outside Holmleigh. Like the perfect gentleman she had already assumed him to be, he jumped out and opened the passenger door. 'I'm very pleased to have met you, Winifred. Goodnight, my dear. See you soon...'

'Goodnight, Jeff,' she said. 'I'm pleased as well.'

She walked to the front door feeling a lightness of spirit that she had not known for ages.

Chapter Six

The spring open evening was one of the most important events in the school year. The children had been in their new classes for almost two terms, by which time the teachers knew them all very well and were able to discuss with the parents their varying strengths and weaknesses.

Each teacher did his, or her, very best to make their classroom as attractive as possible. Sally Roberts, at four o'clock on that Thursday afternoon towards the end of March, looked around her room with a quiet smile of satisfaction. The exercise books had all been marked up-to-date and were arranged in tidy piles on the children's tables, with a printed name card on the top that the parents could easily identify. Sally's own desk had been tidied, and a vase of daffodils and freesias added a spring-like and welcoming touch.

The display on the walls, though, was of the greatest importance. It consisted of the children's paintings and drawings, each one carefully framed and mounted; examples of stories the children had written, and their first attempts at poetry; and a large mural, taking up nearly the whole of one wall, depicting the story of *The Pied Piper* of *Hamelin.* Sally had read them Browning's poem and they had been fascinated by it. It was very sad, of course, the story of the children being lured away, and just one little crippled boy being left behind. But they had all seemed to take it in their stride, as they had done with Grimms' fairy tales. They certainly were grim, with their instances of wicked witches, cruel stepmothers and terrifying ogres.

Sally had learnt, though, that children liked to be scared at times. They seemed to understand that it was not real, and that they were safe, when the story came to an end, in their own comfortable little world. At least, that was true for the most part. She had reason to believe that one or two of the children in her class were somewhat neglected – and it was usually the case that the parents of this minority were the ones who did not turn up to open evenings or other school events. And there was little the teachers could do, unless the neglect bordered on cruelty or deprivation, when steps would need to be taken. However, this area of North Shore was, by and large, what was considered a good catchment area and there were few real problems.

The mural was the *pièce de résistance* of Sally

Roberts' classroom and she looked at it with a feeling of satisfaction. It was largely the children's own work, apart from the large figure of the Pied Piper that she had drawn and the children had coloured in red and yellow. There were rats of all shapes, sizes and colours: orange, brown, fawn, grey, black and white. The houses of Hamelin, likewise, varied in design, mostly with the black beams typical of that part of Germany, standing at crazy angles with steeply sloping roofs and crooked chimneys.

She gave a contented nod, then put on her coat that hung by the door and went out into the corridor, then out of the side door. Phil Grantley was in the car park. This was really a small area of the playground that had been sectioned off for the use of those teachers who had cars, although there were only four of them who felt able to afford one.

'Want a lift, Sally?' called Phil, and she was pleased to accept.

'Thanks, Phil,' she said, scrambling into the passenger seat of his small Morris car. 'Seeing that we have to be back at six, it doesn't give us much time.'

'All done and dusted then?' he asked as they drove off.

'Yes, all ready for the onslaught,' she replied. 'Most of the parents of my class have said they are coming, but it remains to be seen. Do you think this new system will work better?'

It had been decided by the headmaster, and agreed by the rest of the staff, that the parents should be given a five-minute slot, which was all that time would allow, in which to speak to their child's class teacher. It would, hopefully, do away with the queues and the melee that had sometimes occurred in the past.

'It ought to,' replied Phil. 'There was no end of a barney in my room last time, one chap saying that they'd been waiting half an hour and that another couple was barging in. There was very nearly a punch-up till I stepped in.'

'I shouldn't think they'd want to argue with you, Phil,' smiled Sally.

Phil Grantley was a six-footer and well built too. He did a little boxing in his spare time. He was the physical education teacher, as well as teaching one of the fourth-year junior classes, and was often to be seen in his tracksuit, as he was now, because he took most of the classes for games. No doubt he would be more suitably dressed that evening, in a suit and tie. Dress code was carefully observed amongst the staff, it being the view of the headmaster that teachers should set an example in tidiness and suitability of clothing.

'Do you fancy coming for a drink with us tonight, Sally, when we've finished here?' asked Phil. 'I'm hoping it will all be over by half past nine at the latest.'

'Thank you; that would be very nice,' she replied. 'Where are you thinking of going?'

'Oh … probably one of the hotels on the prom, the Carlton or the Claremont, maybe. The bars are not too busy out of season and they're not quite so rowdy as some of the town centre pubs. Us lads don't mind, but we must consider the ladies, mustn't we? Some of you prefer a bit

82

more class.'

Sally smiled. 'Why? Who'll be going?'

'Brian and Alan and me, and some of the younger lasses. I don't know about the older contingent or the married women. We can ask them, but they'll probably say no.'

'It's nice of you to include me,' said Sally.

The infant teachers were all women, as was the norm. Sally felt that she fell between two stools; they were either several years younger, or older, than herself. Sally was thirty-four and already felt as though she had been teaching for a lifetime; she had been at the same school for all of the time. Fortunately, though, she loved her job.

Several of Sally's colleagues on the infant staff were young women who were quite new to the profession, aged twenty-one to twenty-five. Some of them were already married and juggling the two jobs of looking after a home and husband, and full-time teaching. It was usual, though, to stay at home when the first child arrived. The other teachers were older, fiftyish and sixtyish, with two approaching retirement age.

Sally felt herself more drawn to the junior teachers, several of whom were of a similar age to herself. She found that the men on the staff – there were five of them, six including the headmaster – added a touch of levity and lightness to the atmosphere. Although all of them, it must be said, were very competent teachers, the men, on the whole, did not take themselves or their profession too seriously, or get as tensed up about it as some of the women did. She got on well with the women, some of them single, as she was, and some of them married with teenage families. She was often included in their outings, usually at Phil's invitation, and she appreciated it.

'We enjoy your company, Sally,' Phil replied, in answer to her remark. He glanced across at her and smiled, causing his craggy face to crease into laughter lines around his mouth and his warm brown eyes that always reminded her of those of her gran's spaniel.

She knew that several of the staff wondered whether the two of them were secretly going out together, but that was not the case. They were, at the moment, just good friends. Sally had discovered that beneath his brawn and his commanding appearance, Phil was really quite shy. He had joined the staff eighteen months ago, but had still not got round to asking her out on her own. Always supposing, of course, that he wanted to do so, and she was not even sure of that. Phil Grantley was something of an enigma. She knew, though, that he was roughly the same age as herself and, as far as she knew, quite unattached.

It was not far to Sally's home, and they did not converse very much on the journey, Phil being a careful driver.

'Cheerio then, Sally,' he said, as she jumped out of the car. 'See you later ... I shall look forward to our drink together,' he added, almost shyly. Then, 'Shall I pick you up tonight?' he asked, as though he had just thought of it. 'About a quarter to six, is that OK? It'll save you waiting around for a bus.'

'Thanks very much, Phil,' she replied. 'I'd be really glad of that. See you later, then. Quarter to

84

six will be fine.'

Well, that was a step in the right direction, she thought to herself, although she was not altogether sure, really, about the direction she wanted their friendship to take.

'Hello, dear; had a good day?' called her mother as she opened the front door. It was her usual greeting and Sally replied, as she usually did, 'Yes thanks, Mum... I haven't got much time,' she added. 'Shall I get ready before tea, or what?'

'Your tea's all ready for you, dear,' replied her mother. 'I remembered you have to be out again for six o'clock. I've made a nice shepherd's pie and it's keeping warm in the oven. Your dad and I will have ours later when he comes in from work. That's the beauty of shepherd's pie; it won't spoil.'

'Thanks, Mum,' said Sally. 'You're a treasure. I'll just wash my hands first, then I'll get ready afterwards.'

'Best bib and tucker tonight, eh?' Her mother beamed at her.

'Yes, that's right, Mum. We must try to impress the parents. Although they'll be looking at the children's work, not at the teachers' clothes.'

Sally knew that her mum, and her dad too, were very proud that she had been to college and had become a teacher. Her mother had told her many times that it was what she would have liked to do, but it had been impossible. She had been one of a large family of children; she had left school at thirteen and had gone to work in a store that sold clothing for both men and women. It was there that she had met her future husband,

Bill, and they had married when she was just twenty years of age. She had assured Sally that she had never regretted it, and Sally knew that that was true. She doubted that there could be many couples of her parents' age who were as happy or as satisfied with their lot.

But Millie Roberts had been determined that her children should have all the advantages of higher education that had been denied to her and Bill, should it be possible. Jack, though, their second child and only son, had had other ideas. He had joined the merchant navy as soon as he was old enough and, consequently, he was always away somewhere or other on the high seas. Fortunately he had come through the war unscathed, but it was a great regret to Millie and Bill that they saw him so infrequently.

And it was the same with their eldest child, Freda, who was five years older than Sally. She, too, had shown no aptitude for serious study. She had left school at fifteen and had worked as an office junior for a solicitor in the town. Her parents had been disappointed when, at the age of eighteen, she had told them she was pregnant and was going to marry Clive, the lad she had been going out with ever since she left school. They had supported her, though, rather than regarding it as a shameful event that brought disgrace to the family, as was the attitude of many parents of the time. Freda had made a good marriage; Millie and Bill now had three grandchildren, the eldest of whom, Jennifer, was now almost twenty. But, as it was with Jack, they seldom saw Freda and her family. They had moved several years ago to Birmingham where there was more scope for Clive in his work as a motor mechanic.

So it was that Millie Roberts had come to invest her hopes and dreams in her younger daughter. It had been a great joy to her when, after training for two years at a college in Manchester, Sally had been given a teaching post at a school in Blackpool, one that was practically on the doorstep.

Sally was still contented at home, but she knew that she stayed there now mainly for the sake of her mother. She did not mind her mum's cosseting because it was never too overbearing. Mum never asked too many questions about her private life and she had all the freedom she needed. It was very nice, she had to admit, to have her meals cooked for her and her washing done, although she did pay her way very generously and helped out with the household chores as well.

The sad fact, however, was that Sally should have been married by now with a family of her own. She had met Martin Crossley soon after she had started teaching. He had taught at a secondary school in the town, and they had met at a social gathering of the National Union of Teachers, the organisation she had joined on starting her career. He was the first serious boyfriend she had had. They were soon very much in love but were in no hurry to get married. Sally had felt she must teach for a few years at least as her parents had invested so much in her education; and Martin, too, wanted to save up so that they could have a good start with a home of their own.

But alas, the war intervened. Martin joined the RAF and within a year had become part of a bomber crew. He was the 'tail-end Johnny' which, he informed Sally, was the name for the rear gunner. He was involved, inevitably, in the Battle of Britain, and in the July of 1940 Sally heard the tragic news from Martin's parents that he had been killed in action.

She was overwhelmed by sadness, but it was fortunate that she had the long summer holiday from school in which to try to come to terms with her loss and to pull herself together. During the first couple of weeks, though, as well as the anguish of her loss she was also nearly out of her mind with worry. On his last leave, only a few days before he had been killed, she and Martin had made love together for the first – and the last – time. They had paid no heed as to what the consequences might be, which was most unlike the careful and considerate man she knew Martin to be. In the midst of her tears she prayed frantically that all would be well, although she knew it was rather too late for prayers to make any difference. Fortunately she knew, a fortnight later, that her fears had been groundless.

'Thank you, God, thank you...' she had murmured, over and over again. She remembered what had happened to her sister several years before. What a shock and a disappointment it would have been to her parents should it have happened again.

Gradually the pain of her loss eased and the grief became less intense. She had her teaching job to keep her busy. Eventually she found that it brought her contentment, even happiness and, for the most part, fulfilment. She loved the children she taught and she had made good friends amongst the staff. There had not been anyone else, though, who had caused her to feel the way she had felt about Martin.

Sally felt quite satisfied with her appearance as she regarded herself in the full-length mirror. She had decided to wear the dress she had bought just before Christmas and had worn for the family gatherings that had taken place around that time, but she had scarcely worn it since then. It seemed a suitable time now to give it another airing. The dress was a dusky pink colour, made of a fine woollen material, with three-quarter-length sleeves, a full mid-calf-length skirt and a nipped-in waist. She had kept her trim figure – some of her married friends had lost their waistlines after childbearing – and the black patent leather belt accentuated her slimness. With it she wore her black patent leather shoes and a matching handbag. She would take a light coat, although she would probably not need it. Phil was picking her up and would most likely run her home again after their visit to the promenade hotel.

'You look very nice, dear,' said her mother, when Sally appeared in the living room. 'That colour really suits you.'

'Do you think so?' queried Sally. 'I wondered if it was a bit wishy-washy – you know, with me being fair-skinned and my hair and everything.'

Her hair was a silvery blonde and had kept its colour without any artificial aids, and the one or two grey hairs she had found did not show. Her eyes were grey; a nondescript colour really, she thought, but tonight she had highlighted them with a slight touch of mascara and a pale-green eyeshadow. She usually chose pastel colours for her clothes, but she had wondered sometimes if a bright red or blue might make her look more striking.

'No, it's just perfect,' said her mother. 'And you've done your eyes as well.'

Sally laughed. 'Well, I don't often get a chance to dress up, do I? And we're going out for a drink after the meeting, a few of us.'

'You look a real bobby-dazzler,' said her father. He and her mother were sitting at the table, eating their shepherd's pie. Bill Roberts was manager now of one of the gents' outfitters in the town, having stayed in the same line of work ever since he had left school. 'You'll turn a few heads tonight, Sal,' he added.

'That's not really the idea, Dad,' she smiled. 'The parents are concerned with the children's progress, not with what their teacher looks like.'

'All the same...' said her dad, nodding approvingly.

'How are you getting to school?' asked her mother. 'Are you going on the bus?' That was her usual form of transport to and from the school, although she occasionally cycled there if the weather was good.

'No ... Phil's picking me up,' she answered. 'Didn't I say?'

'No, you didn't, actually.' Her mother smiled. 'So that's why you're looking so fetching, is it?

Eyeshadow an' all!'

'Give over, Mum!' said Sally. 'You know very well it isn't so. I've told you, Phil and I are–'

'Just good friends!' Her mother finished off the statement. 'Alright, love; I know it's none of my business. But Phil Grantley's a really nice young man; I've always thought so.'

A ring at the doorbell stopped any further comments. Phil was standing on the doorstep looking unusually smart in a grey suit with a dazzlingly white shirt and maroon tie.

'Wow! You look smart,' said Sally.

'Why? Don't I always?' He gave a quizzical grin.

'To be honest, no!' she laughed. 'But you scrub up very well, I must say.'

'And so do you...' Phil was looking at her admiringly. 'You look ... quite amazing, Sally.'

'Thank you, kind sir,' she joked, a little fazed by the intensity of his gaze. 'I can make an effort when it's necessary.'

'Come along, then.' He held her arm in a friendly way as they went down the path, then he helped her into the car. 'We'd best get moving or the parents will be there before us.'

Indeed, a few of the early birds were already there, waiting in the corridor outside the classroom doors.

'See you later,' said Phil with a cheery wink as he went further along the corridor to the junior part of the building.

The business of the evening began at once when Sally had hung up her coat and sat down at her imposing desk. There were two chairs at the opposite side where the parents could sit. This was one occasion when the children were not invited, so that the teachers could speak to their parents in confidence.

Sally tried to say something encouraging about every child, and never to be too critical or condemning. Some children were exceptionally bright, others average or only mediocre, and some, it must be admitted, were slow to learn, whether through lack of brainpower or through laziness or want of motivation. But they nearly all had some ability in one direction or another, some saving grace, however small it might be. It might be that they could paint or draw very well – some of the less able pupils were surprisingly good at art – or could run fast, or print neatly, or help the teacher with the classroom jobs (such as cleaning the blackboard), or were kind and friendly towards the other children. This was a quality in her pupils that Sally regarded as of great importance.

Shirley Morris's parents were some of the first to be seen. Shirley, in many ways, was a model pupil, at least as far as her schoolwork was concerned.

'Yes, our Shirley takes after my wife,' said Mr Morris with a proud glance at that lady. 'I was never all that good at book learning an' all that sort of thing. But Sadie got her School Certificate, didn't you, love?'

'Yes, Frank,' replied Mrs Morris, giving him a look that quite clearly was asking him to shut up!

'And I'm a bus driver,' he went on.

'Yes ... so Shirley said,' replied Sally. 'Actually, she wrote all about it in a little story.'

'Did she now?' He looked pleased at that. 'Yes, I've got a good job and I'm proud of what I do. Each to his own, that's what I say. I like to think Shirley takes after me in some ways, though. She's a confident little lass, wouldn't you say so, Miss Roberts?'

'Very much so,' agreed Sally. 'She's very self-assured...' Which was a polite way of saying that she was bossy and inclined to be cocky.

'She's bossy, isn't she?' said Mrs Morris, taking the words right out of Sally's mouth, although she would not have put it so bluntly. 'I've noticed her with her little friend, Kathy. She tries to rule the roost and she likes to get all her own way. Of course, that's another way in which she takes after her father.' She cast him a half-joking, half-reproving glance. 'I have told her about it, because I think it's a tendency we must try to discourage.'

'Bright little girls are inclined to be bossy at times,' said Sally, 'more so than boys.' She eyed Mr Morris warily, hoping that any ill feeling between them would not develop any further. It wouldn't be the first time she had had parents sniping at one another when they were supposed to be discussing their children. 'Don't worry about it, Mrs Morris. She'll probably grow out of it, and I don't let her get above herself. Kathy Leigh can hold her own, I assure you. Actually, the two of them are quite good for one another. Kathy's a sensible little girl, and she seems to be able to stop Shirley from getting too big for her boots ... if you see what I mean.'

Kathy's father and her aunt came about halfway through the evening. Sally had met them both on a couple of previous occasions, but this was the first time she had talked to them at any length.

'She tries hard at everything,' Sally told them when they had looked carefully at Kathy's exercise books: the sums, English, spelling and copy-writing books.

'A few spelling mistakes, though,' observed the woman that Kathy called Aunty Win. 'She's only got ten out of ten once, as far as I can see.'

'Well, I was never much good at spelling,' observed Mr Leigh with a grin. 'But I've got by, haven't I?' Sally reflected that she had heard similar remarks several times already that evening.

'How does she compare with the other children?' asked Miss Leigh. 'With her little friend, Shirley, for instance. Kathy tells me that she's a lot cleverer, in the top reading group and good at sums and everything. Kathy seems to set a lot of store by what Shirley does.'

'We try not to make comparisons, Miss Leigh,' replied Sally. 'There aren't any exams as such until they reach junior school age. Kathy works to the very best of her ability, and that is what is important. She's a trier, and she will do well because she'll have a go at anything, even if she finds it difficult.'

'What would you say she was best at?' asked Mr Leigh.

'Oh ... composition,' replied Sally. 'Story writing, we call it. As you've noticed, her spelling is not always one hundred per cent, but she expresses herself very clearly. I asked them to write a story about what they wanted to do when they were grown-up.'

'Yes, we've read that one,' replied Miss Leigh, smiling.

'Well, she starts off by saying that she would like to write books, like Enid Blyton...'

'Yes, she's just started reading some of them on her own,' said Kathy's aunt. '*Naughty Amelia Jane* and *Mister Meddle's Mischief,* and I've been reading the stories of the Faraway Tree with her, and I'm enjoying them very much myself,' she smiled.

Then, more prosaically, Kathy had gone on to write that until she became a story writer she would work in the hotel, like her dad and her aunty. 'She says she wants to be a good chef, like her daddy, and to look after the visitors and make them welcome, like her aunty does,' Sally told them. 'I was quite touched by that. She obviously admires you both very much. She's a grand little girl, and you must be very proud of her.'

'So we are,' replied Mr Leigh. 'Aren't we, Winnie?'

Kathy's aunt smiled and nodded. 'Yes, indeed we are.'

Sally had had time to appraise them both during their conversation. Mr Leigh she took to be in his mid forties; quite a good-looking fellow, she supposed, with fairish hair and blue eyes, unlike his daughter, who was dark-haired with brown eyes. Kathy must take after her mother who had died when she was a baby, she reflected. She had imagined Mr Leigh to be a taciturn sort of man when she had met him before, but he had seemed much more amenable this evening. He had a nice smile, that she guessed one saw only rarely. Sally was aware that he had smiled at her once or twice and his glance had lingered on her a time or two. Not in too obvious a way, though; just nice and friendly.

Miss Leigh too – Aunty Win – was a very likeable person, obviously dressed in her best clothes, a smart green coat with a matching hat. It was gratifying when parents took the trouble with their appearance for something as mundane as a school meeting. She had said goodbye to them with a feeling of satisfaction. They had thanked her sincerely for all that she was doing for Kathy. It was good to be appreciated; it was parents such as those who made the job even more worthwhile.

Chapter Seven

'Was it a successful evening, then, Sally?' asked Phil as they set off on the drive to the Carlton Hotel.

There were five of them in the car; Phil's mate, Brian, was on the back seat with Mavis and Eileen, two of the junior teachers. Sally had noticed that Phil had sorted out the seating arrangements, making sure that she had the seat next to him, at least that was how it had seemed to her.

'Yes, very successful,' she replied. 'All satisfied customers, as far as I could tell. How about you?

No punch-ups this time?'

'No, it all went very smoothly,' Phil replied. 'The odd query as to why our Jimmy isn't doing as well as Johnny, the boy who lives across the street. It's hard to tell them, isn't it, that Jimmy hasn't got as much upstairs as Johnny has; that he is, in fact, as thick as two short planks!'

Sally laughed. 'Yes, I know what you mean. I try to find something good to say about every child, but I must admit it's a struggle at times. And I suppose they get more competitive when they go into the juniors, especially in the top year, like you teach.'

'You can say that again,' chimed in Brian from the back seat. He, along with Phil, taught one of the fourth-year classes, the ones who had recently sat for the all-important exam. 'But it's the parents who are far worse than the kids. "Will our Mary pass the scholarship exam? Oh, we do want her to go to the grammar school, don't we, Fred?" It's hard to say that she hasn't a cat in hell's chance!'

'So what do you tell them?' asked Sally.

'Well, I just waffle on about us trying to get as many through as we can. But I try to explain that the secondary schools today are all geared up to what is best for the individual child. And that the secondary modern schools in this area have a very good reputation, and that they're more suited to those who are – what shall we say? – less academically gifted.'

'And do you think they believe you?'

'The more sensible ones do,' Brian replied. 'In some ways, you know, it's very damning to judge a child at the age of eleven. There are so many who turn out to be what we call late developers.'

'They get another chance, though, at thirteen, don't they?' enquired Sally.

'In theory, yes.' It was Phil who answered. 'But many don't take it. They get settled into their school and make new friends, and they possibly don't think it's worth the effort.'

'Do we have to talk shop?' asked Mavis, from the back seat. 'As far as I'm concerned I've done enough talking about it all for one day. I thought we were going out for a bit of relaxation, to get away from school, to say nothing of a boring husband!'

'Well, you married him!' countered Eileen. 'It's a bit late to say that now, isn't it?'

'What do they say? Marry in haste, repent at leisure?' remarked Mavis. 'Well, I certainly did that.'

'Didn't he mind you coming with us tonight?' asked Eileen.

'He doesn't know, does he? Not that he'd care. So long as he can listen to *Take It From Here* and he's got a good thriller to read, Raymond's not bothered what I get up to.'

Sally was listening with some amusement. The rest of the staff had heard it all before and had learnt to take Mavis's remarks with a pinch of salt. She was a buxom blonde, always ready for a laugh and a joke, a real tonic in the staffroom. She had been married to Raymond for five years, but they had no children. Sally guessed that, in spite of her banter, the couple were quite happily married. And that, contrary to her appearance –

she looked more like a barmaid than a teacher – and her seeming nonchalance, Mavis was a surprisingly good teacher. Certainly her class of eight- and nine-year-olds thought the world of her.

It was inevitable, despite Mavis's complaints, that they should talk 'shop'. For the most part it was almost the only thing that they all had in common. They sat in the bar lounge of the Carlton Hotel, the ten of them clustered around two small tables. Sally, who was sitting facing the window, watched the familiar cream and green tramcars, lit up now that darkness had fallen, rattling past on the tramlines on the other side of the wide promenade. And beyond that, the inky blackness of the sea.

They had decided to have a 'kitty', which was the fairest way of paying for the drinks. It would certainly not be right for the men to pay for them all. Brian and Alan were both married, but they joked that their wives had signed their permits for tonight. Sally sipped at her gin and lime and felt contented. Evenings such as this, when she could let her hair down and enjoy herself, had become all too rare. She had settled into rather a rut, although it was one of her own choosing, staying at home in the evenings with her parents, listening to the radio or reading the wide variety of books that she either bought or borrowed from the library. During the winter months she had been attending an evening class for French conversation. She knew the usual schoolgirl French, common to most grammar school pupils, and had decided it would be a good idea to learn to converse in the language. It was questionable, though, whether she would ever get to use the skill. At the moment she was contemplating a trip to Brittany during the long summer holiday, but would it be much fun on her own, she wondered? And would she be brave enough to go alone?

The shop talk had been exhausted and the little group around Sally's table – herself, Phil, Alan and two of the young women from the infant staff – were now discussing Blackpool's football team. They all, it seemed, were keen supporters. Sally went occasionally to the Bloomfield Road ground when her father – quite rarely – was able to get time off from the shop.

'Who are they playing on Saturday?' she asked. 'It's ages since I went to a match.'

'They're playing Preston North End. What you might call a local derby.' Phil leant closer to her. 'Would you like to come along with me?' he asked. He was not exactly whispering, but his voice was low enough for the others not to hear. She wondered, though, why he was being so careful that the remark should not be overheard. 'I shall be going on my own,' he told her. 'I usually go with a friend, but he's away this weekend.'

'Yes, I should love to go. Thanks, Phil,' she replied. 'I'd better dig out my scarf, then I'll look like a real supporter.'

At a quarter to eleven they were all ready to call it a day. Phil dropped Brian off, then Mavis and Eileen, leaving Sally till last. She knew he had gone quite a long way round. He stopped outside her home.

'I'll see you on Saturday, then, Sal,' he said. 'I'll

call for you... Is half past one OK, then we can get near the front? You'll be all right on the Kop, will you? That's where I usually go.'

'Of course,' she replied. 'That's where I stand when I go with my dad. But I'll see you tomorrow at school, won't I?'

'Yes...' he smiled. 'But it's just in case I don't have a chance to talk to you.'

She laughed to herself. 'Yes, I understand, Phil,' she said, still wondering why it needed to be such a big secret. 'Saturday, then. I'll look forward to it.'

'So will I,' he replied. He leant towards her and kissed her lightly on the cheek. 'Goodnight, Sally. It's been great this evening... After the meeting, I mean. I've really enjoyed it.'

'So have I, Phil... We must do it again sometime, perhaps just you and me,' she said, very daringly. She reached for the door handle, but he jumped up and went round to open it for her.

'See you, Sally...' he said, watching her as she went up the path. She turned to wave when she got to the front door; he was still standing by the car.

It's only a football match, she pondered, but at least it was a start. But she would quite like it if it should turn out to be a start to something more.

Winifred was pleased to see that her brother was a good deal more animated than usual after their visit to Kathy's school and their talk to Miss Roberts. She wondered, indeed, if it could be Kathy's teacher who had brought about this change in Albert. She had noticed that he had listened keenly to what the teacher had to say and had talked quite freely to her, unlike the way he often behaved with a young woman he scarcely knew.

'That was a very satisfactory evening,' he remarked, when they arrived home. Kathy was in bed. They had left her in the charge of their next-door neighbour, Mrs Walsh, who was very fond of the little girl and she had seen her into bed at her usual time.

'Will you stay and have a cup of tea with us, Mrs Walsh?' asked Winifred.

'No, thanks all the same,' replied the lady. 'I'll get back if you don't mind. I don't want to miss *Twenty Questions*. Your Kathy's been as good as gold; of course, she always is. What a little treasure she is. I expect you got a good report from her teacher, didn't you?'

'Yes, she's doing nicely, Mrs Walsh,' replied Winifred. 'Thanks very much for looking after her.'

'I'll make the tea just for you and me, then, Winnie,' said Albert, going into the kitchen. Another unusual happening; he normally ensconced himself in an armchair with his pipe and the newspaper whenever he came in from somewhere. She thought she could even hear him humming!

'I'm pleased with our Kathy, aren't you?' he said, when they were settled down with their tea and chocolate digestive biscuits. 'I know she's not exactly the brain of Britain, not quite as clever as some of the kids in the class, but what does it matter? She said herself in that little composition she wrote – well, her teacher called it a story, but they were always compositions when I was at school – she said she'd be working in the hotel when she grew up, so I'm glad she's looking forward to that.'

'Before she becomes a famous authoress!' answered Winifred, with a twinkle in her eye.

'Aye, well, that remains to be seen, doesn't it?' said Albert. 'But she does seem to have a flair for writing, doesn't she? And that painting on the wall that she'd done of the sands and Blackpool Tower, I thought that was really good.'

'She works hard, and that's the important thing,' said Winifred. 'And I don't think she's any trouble in class. Well we wouldn't expect her to be, would we? And she likes her teacher, which is always a good sign; and I rather think Miss Roberts is quite fond of Kathy too... Nice lass, that Miss Roberts, isn't she?' she asked, trying to sound quite nonchalant.

'Yes, a very sensible young woman,' replied Albert. 'Aye, she's got her head screwed on the right way, has that lass. She's a pretty young woman, an' all. I don't remember there being teachers like that when I was at school.' He chuckled. 'Most of 'em were right old battleaxes from what I recall.'

'Yes, they seem to be a different breed now, that's true,' agreed his sister. 'Of course, when we were children everyone over the age of twenty or so looked old to us, didn't they?'

'Yes, maybe you're right... How old do you think she might be, that Miss Roberts?' Albert asked casually.

'Oh, not all that young,' answered Winifred. 'Young compared with us, of course. Well, compared with me, I mean. I should imagine she's turned thirty, maybe a bit more. I wonder why she's not married? She's a very attractive young lady. Maybe she lost somebody in the war; she's about that age.'

'Yes, happen so,' said Albert. 'Not that it's anything to do with us.' He remained thoughtful, though, and Winifred could detect a gentleness in his eyes and a trace of a smile on his lips. She didn't dare to hint, though, even jokingly, that he might be smitten with Miss Roberts. If she did he would land on her like a ton of bricks. Besides, she was harbouring secret little thoughts of her own. She was looking forward to the next rehearsal at the drama group more than she had done for ages; and it was not just the challenge of getting to grips with a new play.

They both told Kathy the next morning that they were very pleased with her progress and that Miss Roberts had said she was doing well. 'She's a very nice young lady,' her father said. 'I reckon you've struck lucky getting into her class, Kathy.'

'Yes, we all like her,' said Kathy. 'She's called Sally. Timothy Fielding saw it on one of her books. It's a nice name, isn't it?'

'Yes, very nice,' agreed Albert, pleased that he could now put a name to the young lady who had impressed him so much. He had thought he was off women for good and all, but now he realised that it might not be so. What the dickens he could do about it, though, he had no idea.

There was almost a capacity crowd at Bloomfield Road on Saturday afternoon. Watching the weekly football match – either the first team or the reserves – was something that Albert liked to do on his own. He was an ardent supporter, but not by any means a shouter. He could feel the excitement inside himself, the suspense whenever the match was nearing an end and it looked as though 'the 'Pool' might lose or draw, and the release of tension when they finally managed to score. He heard the deafening roar of the crowd around him, the cheers, whistles and the raucous noise of the rattles, but Albert greeted each goal in silence; that was his way. Occasionally he had gone with mates of his from the darts team, but he could never bellow out his enthusiasm as they did, and he found that this, somehow, embarrassed him. He wore his orange and white scarf every week, as true supporters did, but not without a feeling of self-consciousness.

He felt the crowd surging around him now on Spion Kop, pressing against him from the back and sides as he leant against the crush barrier. There had been an accident there a while ago when a crush barrier gave way, but one tried not to think about that. It was turning out to be quite a good match, with Stanley Matthews on top form. Nothing electrifying, though, and the score was one-all at half-time.

The crowd relaxed and began to chat together after the whistle was blown, but it seemed to Albert that he was inconspicuous; nobody tried to engage him in conversation. He looked around him ... then he felt himself give a start of surprise as he noticed, a few yards to his right, the young woman who had been occupying his thoughts for the last few days. It was Miss Roberts – Sally, as he was allowing himself to think of her – looking most attractive with a little orange bobble hat perched on top of her silvery-blonde hair, and an orange and white scarf wound round her neck. She, too, must be a supporter, then. She was smiling up into the face of the young man who was standing next to her. Albert felt a stab of disappointment and almost anger. He might have known, though, that she would have a boyfriend; she was such a personable young lady. He looked again, more closely; she hadn't noticed him and he didn't think he wanted her to. The fellow looked familiar. Albert had only seen him once or twice before but he knew he was a teacher at the same school. Mr Grantley, he thought he was called, the chap who taught PE and games.

He watched them surreptitiously throughout the interval. It seemed to him that they were good mates, but possibly nothing more than that. They didn't appear to be at all 'lovey-dovey', and he told himself that it was only to be expected that two members of the same staff should attend a football match together.

Blackpool scored again in the second half, making it a win for the home team, the result they had hoped for. Albert hung back, but still kept an eye on the couple as they left the ground. They were not holding hands or linking arms or anything else to show that they were any more than good friends. He was thoughtful as he stood in the long bus queue on Central Drive and remained in a contemplative mood all the way back to North Shore.

'Was it a good match?' asked his sister.

'Yes, not so bad,' he replied. 'We won at any rate, so I suppose you can't ask for more. A bit slow off the mark, though, some of 'em.'

'Well, your tea's ready,' said Winifred. 'I've made a meat and potato pie. I thought you'd be a bit starved, standing outside all afternoon. Come on now, Kathy love. Let's get our meal while it's nice and hot.'

'You'll never guess who I saw at the match this afternoon,' said Albert as they tucked into their meal. He smiled confidingly at his daughter.

'Who, Daddy?' she asked.

'Your teacher, Miss Roberts. She had an orange scarf and hat on as well. I didn't know she supported Blackpool, did you?'

'No, I don't know much about her, really,' answered Kathy. 'Except that I like her. Well, we all like her. I know she's not married, because she's a Miss, isn't she, not a Mrs?'

'Was she on her own?' asked Winifred, watching her brother closely.

'No ... she was with that fellow that teaches games at Kathy's school. Mr Grantley... That's his name, isn't it, Kathy?'

'Yes, we don't see him much 'cause he's a junior teacher. I've seen Miss Roberts get into his car, though, sometimes,' said Kathy. 'Timothy Fielding says that perhaps he's her boyfriend.'

'That Timothy Fielding seems to know an awful lot,' smiled Winifred. 'I expect they're just friends, though, with them teaching at the same school.' She looked reassuringly at her brother as she made the remark.

'Yes … that's what I thought,' he replied.

It was later in the evening after Kathy had gone to bed that Winifred decided to broach the subject with her brother, about the thing she knew was on his mind; but she knew she had to be tactful.

'You've taken rather a liking to that teacher of Kathy's, haven't you, Albert?' she began. 'I can tell by the way you talk about her. Well, I can't say I blame you; she seems a lovely lass.'

He did not jump down her throat. She felt that he was pleased she had mentioned it. For his part, he was glad to confide in her, to get it off his chest and talk about this unusual and unsought feeling that had hit him like a bombshell.

'Yes … I must confess I'm rather smitten.' He gave a rueful smile. 'Ridiculous, isn't it? You know me, what I'm usually like with women. There's never been anyone since Barbara. I've never wanted anybody else.'

'But time goes by, Albert,' she told him. 'A lot of time has passed since you lost Barbara, and it's all "water under the bridge", as they say.'

'But what on earth have I got to appeal to a nice young woman like that? I'm in my mid-forties, set in my ways. A bit of a grump, I know, at times, and I'm not educated like she is. Anyway, how could I possibly ask her out? I don't even know her, do I, not really?'

'You're still quite a good-looking chap, Albert,' said his sister. 'Don't run yourself down. And it's about time you started looking positively at life, instead of being so negative. Maybe you don't know her very well, but everything has to start somewhere.' She was thinking of how she had met Jeff Bancroft, quite out of the blue. 'And you don't need to speak in a broad accent, you know. I think you put it on at times for effect.'

'Aye, I reckon I do,' he laughed. 'I daresay I could be as posh as the next man if I made the effort.'

'Well, think about it,' said Winifred. 'You never know. Something might turn up. There might well be an opportunity for you to do something about it.'

Sally had enjoyed Phil's company at the football match. They found, as they chatted easily together during the times when they were not watching the game, that they had quite a lot in common, more than she had realised. They liked the same sort of films. Sally was surprised that Phil liked musicals, and he was equally surprised that she enjoyed cowboy films. And they both read detective stories – Ngaio Marsh, Margery Allingham and Conan Doyle, as well as Agatha Christie – and some of the 'easier to digest' Victorian novelists. She was, therefore, somewhat taken aback and disappointed, too, when Phil brought the car to a halt outside her house and said, 'Cheerio then, Sally. It's been great, hasn't it? See you on Monday, then.'

'Yes ... great, Phil,' she agreed, trying to sound cheerful. 'Thanks for taking me.' At least he leant across and kissed her cheek, and then opened the door for her. But before she had reached her front door he had driven away with a carefree wave.

So what am I to make of that? she wondered as she took out her key and opened the door. She had expected, at least, that he might have asked her to go out with him that evening, for a drink or to the cinema, or to arrange to see her the following day. Phil Grantley was a mystery and no mistake. She dashed upstairs to her bedroom, unwilling at that moment to face her mother's cross-questioning.

Chapter Eight

Winifred couldn't help smiling to herself. It seemed that she and her brother, somewhat belatedly, were experiencing emotions and feelings that they had assumed were long past and gone. For her part, she had not told Albert about her meeting with Jeffrey Bancroft. Indeed, there was very little to say about it at the moment. He was just a very nice man whom she had enjoyed talking to and whom she believed had shown the same interest in her as she had in him. She tried to warn herself not to read too much into the situation. From the little she already knew of Jeffrey she had gathered he was a friendly man who would find it easy to get on with most people. But she knew she had not felt so attracted to anyone of the opposite sex since she had fallen in love with – and had then lost – Arthur all those years ago. She would be seeing Jeff again on Wednesday. She felt a lift of her spirits when she thought about it. And as she observed her brother she guessed that he would be glad of an opportunity to see again the young woman who had so appealed to him.

And then on Monday Kathy brought home a letter from school that seemed to provide an answer to his dilemma. There was to be a spring fayre on Friday afternoon, commencing at half past three, and this was a letter reminding parents of the event. They had had a similar letter a few weeks back but it had quite slipped Winifred's mind.

'You'll come, won't you, Aunty Win?' begged Kathy. 'And you as well, Daddy. There's going to be stalls selling all sorts of things.' There was a request in the letter for homemade cakes, handmade goods, books, 'bric-a-brac', items for a 'white elephant' stall; anything, in fact, that would be saleable, apart from old clothing (jumble sales were held from time to time as separate events).

'And there'll be games,' Kathy went on excitedly. 'Guessing the name of a doll, and how much a cake weighs, and a bran tub and a tombola – but I'm not sure what that is – and a raffle with lots of prizes. And cups of tea and drinks and things to eat, 'cause it's near teatime.'

'Good gracious! It sounds as though your teachers are going to be very busy,' observed Winifred.

'Some of the mums are going in to help as well,' said Kathy. 'Those that are on the committee of that thingy – you know, the PTFA. D'you think you could come and help, Aunty Win?'

'Oh, I don't know about that, love. I'm not on the committee, am I?' She imagined they would be all much younger than herself, like Sadie Morris. 'But I'll certainly come to the fayre. And I expect your daddy will come as well. You will, won't you, Albert?'

'I don't see any reason why not,' he replied in his usual non-committal way, but Winifred could see that he was not averse to the idea and was even smiling a little. 'There might not be many fathers there, though,' he added. 'Most of 'em'll be working, won't they?'

'The teachers are hoping they'll come later,' said Kathy, when they finish work. We're doing a concert, you see; well, just a little one, at half past five. The top class infants – that's us – we're going to sing some songs; well, those that can sing nicely have been chosen, and I'm one of them.'

'Good for you, Kathy,' said her dad.

'And some of the top class juniors are going to do some country dancing. It's going to be really good.'

'I'm sure it is. It all sounds very exciting,' said Winifred. 'We'll look forward to that, won't we Albert?'

'Yes ... I reckon we will,' he said reflectively.

Winifred had been reading through the script, trying to learn by heart as much as she was able, although they would not need to be word-perfect for a few weeks. It was always easier, though, when your movements were not hampered by a book in your hands and, fortunately, she had

112

been blessed with a good memory that had not let her down yet, despite her advancing years.

Jeff was not there when she arrived, nor had he put in an appearance when they started to rehearse. Snap out of it! she told herself, and concentrate on what you're doing or you're going to look a real fool. You've been given this leading role, so do justice to it.

He turned up about half an hour later and, noticing him from the corner of an eye, she felt a relaxing of her tension. She did not look at him but she was aware that he was watching her.

'Well done!' he said, coming to join her in the interval. 'You're getting to grips with Lady B already, aren't you?'

'I'm trying,' she said. 'It'll be easier when I don't have to rely on the script.'

'When is it being performed?' he asked.

'Oh, not till the end of July. We always give ourselves plenty of time, and make allowances for people going on holiday. We try to arrange our holidays for after the performance, though, if we can. Not that it affects me very much. I can never go away during the summer whilst the visitors are in. We have a break during August, then we meet up again in September... You've decided to stay with us, then, have you?' she asked tentatively.

'Oh yes,' he replied. 'I'd already decided after the first meeting.' He smiled at her, his grey eyes looking intently into hers. 'But, as I said, I shall just assist with the stage managing this time and give a hand with the scenery. I'll have a chat with Wilfred after the break and see what he'd like me to do. I don't mind being a "gofer", seeing that

I'm the new boy,' he laughed good-humouredly.

Jeff's sister, Mavis Peacock, stood up then to draw their attention to the notices. The main one was that there was to be a coach outing in a few weeks' time to the nearby town of Preston. A well-known amateur dramatic group from that town was also presenting *The Importance of Being Earnest* at one of the smaller theatres there. 'We don't want to pinch any of their ideas, of course,' said Mavis. 'And it's possible that their interpretation will be quite different from ours, but we thought it would make an enjoyable outing. If you're interested in going would you let me know as soon as possible, then I can book the theatre seats.'

'Will you be going?' Jeff asked Winifred.

'Oh yes, I fully intend to go,' she replied. The date chosen was the first Friday evening in May. 'Albert – my brother – sometimes has a darts match on a Friday, but I can always get my next-door neighbour to look after Kathy if necessary.'

'You won't have any visitors in?' asked Jeff.

'No, it's a slack time between Easter and Whitsun. And if we do have a few in we'll be able to sort something out, I'm sure. It's something I don't want to miss... What about you, Jeff?' she asked. 'Will you be going?'

'But of course,' he smiled. 'That's why I asked you. I'll put our names down straight away, shall I?'

'Yes please,' said Winifred, very pleased at the way things were progressing.

He was not watching the rehearsal when they started again, but he was there to run her home in his car at the end of the evening.

'Are you doing anything on Saturday?' he asked as he stopped the car outside Holmleigh.

'Not particularly,' she replied. 'Do you mean during the day or in the evening?' Could he possibly be asking her for a 'date', she wondered?

'I was wondering whether you would like to go to the cinema,' he said. 'I haven't checked what is on, but I'm sure we'll be able to find something that we'll both enjoy.' He laughed. 'I can't get over the number of cinemas that there are in Blackpool.'

'Yes, we're pretty fortunate in that respect,' agreed Winifred. There was the Odeon; the Princess; the Palace Picture Pavilion, as well as the Palace Variety Theatre in the same building; the Winter Gardens cinema; the Tivoli; the Regent; the ABC; and the Imperial, all near the centre of the town, as well as several more in the outlying suburbs. She enjoyed a visit to the cinema but it wasn't much fun going on her own, and Albert never seemed inclined to go with her. She occasionally took Kathy to a matinee on a Saturday afternoon if there was something suitable showing. The little girl loved the singing and dancing in the musicals of Metro-Goldwyn-Mayer and 20th Century Fox, featuring such stars as Betty Grable, Fred Astaire and Ginger Rogers, and of course, she loved the Walt Disney films.

'I'll look in the *Gazette* and see what's on, shall I?' said Jeff. 'That is, if you'd like to go?'

'Yes, I would, very much,' she replied.

'That's great, then.' He grinned at her. 'What sort of films do you like? Have you any preference?'

'Oh, my taste is pretty general,' she told him. 'But I'm not keen on cowboy films, or on gangsters. James Cagney is not one of my favourites,' she smiled.

'Nor mine,' he agreed. 'Laurence Olivier now, or James Mason; they're what I call real actors. But I must confess I'm not averse to something more light-hearted now and again. The 'Road' films, for instance. Bing Crosby and Bob Hope...'

'And Dorothy Lamour,' added Winifred. 'Yes, I like those too. I took Kathy to see *The Road to Morocco* and she loved it.'

'Will there be any problem regarding your niece?' Jeff asked her. 'Will your brother be able to look after her? He might be going out himself.'

'I very much doubt it,' said Winifred. 'He's usually in on a Saturday. His darts matches are during the week. Don't worry; we'll sort something out, I'm sure.'

'I'll phone you, then, shall I, when we've both looked at the paper?'

'Lovely,' she agreed, smiling at him and feeling like a twenty-year-old going on her first date. He put his hand over hers, then leant across and kissed her gently on the cheek, before getting out of the car and going round to open the door for her.

'Goodnight, Winifred, my dear,' he said. 'Sleep well...'

'You too,' she replied. 'And ... thanks, Jeff. I'll look forward to Saturday.'

'Me too.' He gave a broad smile and a cheery wave as he drove away.

Winifred decided not to tell her brother straight

116

away about her outing with Jeff. He could hardly object, though. She scarcely ever went out, except to church functions or to the drama group. It would be ironic, though, if he should happen to have a date of his own on the same night; two middle-aged people whose life had followed the same routine for so long, and who were now seeking just a little excitement. She forced herself to wake up to reality. She knew – and she knew that Albert would realise, too – that whatever might happen in their personal lives, Katherine had to come first.

Very little work was done on that Friday afternoon at the North Shore school; that is to say very little schoolwork. Lessons were largely abandoned as classes were 'doubled up', releasing half of the teachers to prepare the stalls and games for the spring fayre, helped by the ladies of the committee and their friends who would, later, be in charge of the refreshment room. Several of the older children, those in the fourth-year junior classes, were enlisted to help as well, and they considered themselves to be very important. The rest of the pupils had to contain their excitement all afternoon as they looked forward to what was one of the great social events of the year.

It had been planned to start at three-thirty, which was the finishing time for the infant classes; the juniors did not normally finish until four o'clock, but on this day they were all going home at the same time. It was hoped, though, that very few of them would be going home. It was assumed that mothers – and fathers – meeting their younger children from school would stay for the fayre, and that the older children would have persuaded their parents, grandparents and aunts and uncles to come along as well.

Sally Roberts felt very sad as she watched a few of her pupils, and some from the other classes, put on their coats and then walk dejectedly across the playground. There were only three such in her class, the very ones that she might have known would not be staying to join in the fun; they were the ones whose parents rarely supported the school events or even bothered to turn up on open evenings. Those parents were the ones, however, who would be there, with all guns blazing, should there be a complaint to be made about the teacher or the headmaster.

There was little time to brood, though, as the other children eagerly greeted their parents and guests, leading them proudly around the school. It was not a time for looking at the children's books or talking about their progress, but the teachers had pulled out all the stops to make the school look as attractive as possible. The corridors were decorated with large paintings and friezes made by the various classes. Sally's 'Pied Piper' was there, as well as springtime collages, a depiction of the 'Noah's Ark' story, paintings of Blackpool's attractions – the Tower, the big dipper at the Pleasure Beach, the bright yellow sands and the unusually blue sea, and the tramcars on the busy promenade – and drawings of Mummy and Daddy and 'my house' done by the youngest children, aged four and five.

Sally was in charge of the tombola game. Each

person, after paying their sixpence, drew out a raffle ticket and was awarded the corresponding prize. In a true tombola some of the tickets won nothing at all, but it had been agreed that this was too disappointing for the very young children; and so every ticket won a prize, although it might only be a few sweets or a tiny bar of chocolate. The initial outlay was worth it in the end as many were encouraged to have another go.

Kathy Leigh came into the tombola room about ten minutes into the proceedings, with her father and aunt.

'Now, Kathy, are you going to have a turn?' said Sally. 'There are some lovely prizes; you might not win one of the big ones, but you're sure to win something.'

'Yes, we'll all have a go,' said Mr Leigh, feeling in his pocket for some change. 'Here you are, Kathy. You go first.'

The little girl won a brightly coloured pencil and a rubber, with which she seemed highly pleased. Her aunt then won a bottle of Amami shampoo, and her father a bottle of ginger beer.

'It would go very nicely with that whisky,' he remarked, pointing to one of the star prizes.

'Have another go, then, Albert,' said his sister.

'OK. Nothing venture, nothing win,' he said, handing over another sixpence.

They were all astonished when he won the bottle of Black & White whisky.

'Well done!' exclaimed Sally, handing him the bottle. 'I'm very pleased it's going to such a good home! You're not teetotal, then, Mr Leigh?'

'No fear!' he chuckled. 'I'm wondering – Miss

Roberts – may we leave these bottles here and collect them later? It'll save us carrying them all round the school. We've a lot to see, haven't we, Kathy?' Kathy nodded, quite pink-checked with excitement.

'Certainly,' said Sally. 'I'll put them in the cupboard. Don't forget them, though.'

'There's no chance of that,' said Mr Leigh, smiling warmly at her.

A nice man, she mused as they went away. He had a lovely smile; but she reflected, as she had done before, that he probably did not smile all that often.

Kathy was enjoying herself immensely, showing her dad and aunty all the interesting pictures on the walls, and then leading them into the classrooms where the various stalls and games were going on. She chose the name of a doll from a long list of names.

'I think she might be called Sally,' she said, printing her own name carefully on the list. 'It's Miss Roberts' name,' she whispered to her aunt, 'but I don't think many of the others know that.'

It was a lovely baby doll with eyes that closed, dressed in a hand-knitted coat and bonnet. 'You might not win, you know,' her aunt told her. 'It's just luck, really, like the raffle and the tombola.'

'I'm not bothered,' Kathy replied. 'I've got my prize from the tombola and these books, and I'm having a lovely time. Are you enjoying it, Aunty Win?'

'Indeed I am,' Winifred replied. She was pleased to see how delighted Kathy was by everything. She was such a good little girl and so easily pleased.

120

Not like some badly behaved children who were to be seen in Woolworths on a Saturday afternoon, crying blue murder because they couldn't get their own way. Winifred noticed that her brother seemed to be getting into the spirit of things too, in his own quiet way.

In the next room, where there was a home-made cake stall, they met Shirley with her dad. Her mum, who was a member of the committee, was serving on the stall. Shirley had told Kathy that her dad would be able to come because he was on early shift that day and finished at dinner time. Introductions were made whilst Shirley and Kathy smiled at one another.

'I'm pleased to see that most of my fairy cakes have been sold,' said Winifred, 'and the fruit cake that I made.'

'Oh yes, they went very quickly,' said Sadie Morris. 'I didn't know they were yours. You could say they sold like hot cakes,' she laughed, 'whatever that means.'

'Can we go round on our own, me and Kathy?' asked Shirley, after a whispered consultation between the two of them.

'It's all right with me,' said Shirley's mum, 'but you're supposed to be showing your dad round, aren't you?'

'Oh, that's OK,' said Mr Morris, winking at Winifred. 'I think I'll just nip out for a quick smoke in the playground.'

'Behind the bike sheds, eh?' laughed Albert, seeming in a very good mood.

'I don't think there are any bike sheds,' Shirley remarked.

'It's just a joke, love,' said her dad. 'I won't be long, then we could perhaps all have a cup of tea in a little while, before this important concert starts.'

They all agreed that this was a good idea and Frank Morris hurried away, glad to make his escape, thought Winifred.

'Off you go, then, with Shirley,' she said, 'and we'll see you in the tea room in about twenty minutes. You've still got some money to spend, have you?'

'Yes, and I've got a watch on,' said Shirley importantly.

'Well, here's another shilling for each of you,' said Kathy's dad, reaching into his pocket for the two silver coins.

'Thank you, Daddy...'

'Gosh! Thank you, Mr Leigh...' The two girls beamed with surprise.

My goodness! thought Winifred. Her brother was feeling magnanimous today.

'Come on,' said Shirley. 'I want a go on the bran tub, don't you? And I've seen some hair slides that I like, and now I can afford them.'

Winifred bought some home-made flapjack. She made her own but it would be nice to try someone else's baking for a change.

'Would you like to buy a raffle ticket?' asked one of the older girls in another part of the room. She and her friend were in charge of a small table with books of coloured raffle tickets and a dish of money.

'What's on offer?' asked Albert genially.

'Well, the first prize is a meal for two in a posh

restaurant in Blackpool,' the girl replied. 'Then there's this box of fruit, and this big box of chocolates, and this tin of toffees.'

'Go on, then,' said Albert. 'I'll have two tickets, and two for my sister. Not that I ever win anything,' he said as they walked away.

'Don't tell fibs,' said Winifred. 'You won that whisky, didn't you? It might be your lucky day.'

'Oh yes, so I did,' he agreed. 'Remind me to pick it up later, Winnie.'

She didn't think he would need reminding. He had been in remarkable high spirits since his encounter with Sally Roberts.

There was a goodly crowd assembled in the school hall at half past five to watch the display of singing and dancing put on by some of the children. Winifred and Albert had met up again with Sophie and Frank Morris, and after they had all had a cup of tea and a buttered scone they had stayed together. Kathy and Shirley had gone off in great excitement as they were taking part in the musical entertainment.

Before the concert could start, though, it was time for the raffle to be drawn. The prizes were displayed on a table at the front of the hall, and the headmaster, Mr Williams, was asked to draw out the first lucky ticket. Everyone fumbled in their pockets and bags for the pink and green tickets, then waited eagerly to hear the result.

'Pink ticket, number 105,' called out the headmaster. 'First prize – a voucher for two for a meal at the Fishing Net; that's the newly opened seafood restaurant in Blackpool, for those who don't know. Now, who is the lucky winner?'

Winifred nudged her brother. 'Albert, it's yours!' He was sitting there quite unconcerned, like most of the men were, not bothering to check the tickets that his sister had taken out of her purse. 'Yours were the pink ones and I had the green. Didn't I tell you it might be your lucky day? Go on...' She gave him a push. 'Go and collect your prize.'

'Do I have to?' he mumbled. 'What do I want with a meal for two? I'd rather have that box of chocolates.'

'Go on with you!' she retorted. 'I don't think you've any choice. It's the first prize.' She waved her hand. 'It's here, Mr Williams. It's my brother's ticket. He's coming...'

'Congratulations, sir,' said the headmaster, handing him an envelope. 'Now, would you draw out the next ticket, please?'

Albert did so, and Mr Williams called out the next number. 'Green ticket, number 59, for the voucher to spend at Sweetens bookshop.'

'That might've been better,' Albert murmured to his sister as he returned to his seat. 'I could've given it to our Kathy to spend.'

'Don't look a gift horse in the mouth!' she chided him. 'You miserable so and so!'

'Well, we cook our own meals, don't we?' he persisted. 'Whoever heard of going out for a meal when you can have much better food at home? Especially at Holmleigh.'

'Shut up, Albert!' she told him. 'See, it's time for the entertainment to start now...'

Winifred was pleased to see that he did stop

muttering, and he watched with interest as the younger children filed in through the door and assembled themselves into three tidy lines, obviously well trained by their teacher – not Miss Roberts – who sat down at the piano.

About forty of the 'best singers', as Kathy had told her aunt, from the third-year infant classes, had been chosen to form a choir. They all looked very smart, the girls in their navy gymslips with the red and blue woven girdle, and the red and blue striped tie that they wore on special occasions. Most of the girls had red ribbons in their hair, Kathy's topping her dark curls and Shirley's tied at the end of her blonde plaits. The two friends were in the centre of the front row, smiling broadly, although Kathy had said they had been told quite firmly that they must not wave to their parents and friends in the audience.

There seemed to be more girls than boys in the choir. Kathy had told her aunt that the boys were inclined to 'grunt' rather than sing; but that her friend Timothy Fielding was one that had been chosen.

'He sits on the row just behind me,' she said. 'He's got a lot of fair hair that stands up like a hedgehog.'

A good description, thought Winifred, as she looked at the boy she had heard so much about. A shock of blonde hair and a rather cheeky face. He looked as though he might be a handful, but he was very clean and tidy, as were all the boys, dressed in their dazzling white shirts – she guessed they were not usually so clean – and red and blue striped ties.

The teacher played the introductory bars and the children started to sing, 'As I was going to Strawberry Fair...' They were surprisingly tuneful and melodious, and the parents and friends listened with obvious delight as the children went through their repertoire of folk songs and old English melodies, the same ones that they had sung at school many years before: 'Early One Morning', 'Dashing Away with the Smoothing Iron', 'The Miller of Dee', and the most poignant song of all, 'The Lark in the Clear Air'.

Winifred was pleased to see that Albert had got over his fit of pique by the time they had finished. He turned to her with a look of tenderness in his eyes. 'They were good, weren't they? I'm proud of our Kathy; she was loving it, wasn't she? By Jove, those songs take me back a bit.'

'Me too,' agreed Winifred.

There was another round of applause as the children and their teacher sat down at the front of the hall to watch the older children do their bit. These boys and girls were ten and eleven years old and they performed very ably the country dances they had been practising for several weeks: 'The Dashing White Sergeant', 'Strip the Willow' and 'Sir Roger de Coverley'.

'I think I'd have felt a bit daft if I were one of the boys,' Albert observed, 'but they didn't seem to mind, did they?'

'I don't suppose it's much different really from ballroom dancing,' said Winifred, 'and you're quite good at that, aren't you? Or ... you used to be,' she added. She remembered that he had hardly danced at all since the time he had used to dance with Barbara. Maybe she shouldn't have mentioned it.

'That's a thing of the past,' he replied, but he didn't look as morose as he usually did when reminded of the days gone by. 'I've been thinking, Winnie,' he said, as they went to find Kathy, who was waiting outside the hall. 'You can have that voucher for the meal. I daresay you can find somebody to go with you, can't you?'

For a moment she was tempted, but she had a better idea. 'No, Albert,' she said. 'You won it and you must use it.' She wondered if she dared suggest what was in her mind. 'Why don't you invite Kathy's teacher, Miss Roberts, to go with you?' she ventured.

'I wouldn't dare!' he replied. 'How could I do that?' But he looked as though he might well consider it.

'Of course you dare,' she replied. 'You can say it's a way of saying thank you for all she's done for Kathy.'

'But it's free, isn't it? It's not going to cost me anything. Not much of a thank you, is it?'

'You'd be buying drinks, wouldn't you? They wouldn't be free. Oh, go on, Albert,' she coaxed him. I think it would be a lovely idea. We have to see her now to collect your other prize. And what did I hear you say earlier today? Nothing venture, nothing win...'

Chapter Nine

The Fishing Net had opened up in the centre of Blackpool some six months previously and was becoming one of the most popular places to dine, or to 'eat out', as people often said. Eating out rather than dining at home was a pastime that was only just starting to be accepted as a popular thing to do. The older generation still regarded it as something strange and unnecessary. Why should anyone want to go out for a meal when you could eat just what you wanted at home and for much less cost?

Food was becoming a little more plentiful in the early Fifties, after the restrictive war years, although food rationing was still continuing. The restaurants, however, such as they were, didn't seem to have much of a problem in putting on a reasonable meal. Venues, though, were somewhat limited. There were hotel dining rooms where outsiders could book a meal, and some department stores had cafés for a quick snack. Lyons Corner Houses were popular in London, but there was nothing of that ilk in the provinces.

And so the Fishing Net was something of an innovation. As its name implied, it served mainly fish dishes. Crabs and lobster, usually served with salad; oysters and mussels for those who wished to be a bit more adventurous and were not too squeamish; and the more usual fish dishes – hake, haddock, halibut or plaice – served with chips or another potato alternative and an accompaniment of vegetables. One could also order gammon or steak, but the majority plumped for fish as the restaurant was best known for its good variety and excellent cooking of this commodity.

It was Sally's first visit to the Fishing Net, although she had often walked past it on her shopping trips to Blackpool and had thought how nice it would be to have a meal there. Which was why she had not hesitated for more than a few seconds – the delay in answering had been due to surprise rather than reluctance – when Mr Leigh had invited her to share in his raffle prize.

'Well ... yes, of course I will,' she had replied, feeling quite dumbfounded. 'Thank you for asking me, Mr Leigh. How very kind of you... Yes, I would love to go.'

The poor fellow had gone quite pink with embarrassment – she guessed he had been plucking up courage to ask her – and she tried to put him at his ease.

'It's ... it's just a little way of saying thank you ... er ... Miss Roberts – for all you have done for our Kathy,' he managed to say, with a little hesitation. 'She's very fond of you, I know. She never stops talking about you. It's Miss Roberts this, and Miss Roberts that, all the time.'

She smiled at him. 'Children are often like that about their teachers in the infant school. Sometimes we're a sort of mother figure, you see. They've had to leave Mummy at home and ... well ... I suppose we're the next best thing.' She had stopped then, aware of what she had just said. She could have kicked herself. Little Katherine, of course, didn't have a mother. But to apologise might only make things worse. She had noticed that Mr Leigh had looked a little disturbed; not angry, but the diffident smile had vanished from his face for a moment.

Then he replied, 'Kathy's mother died. She doesn't remember her, but she thinks the world of her Aunty Win. I don't know what I'd have done without Winnie.'

'Yes, I know she does,' Sally replied, a little confusedly. 'She thinks a lot of you as well, Mr Leigh. She often talks about you both... I was only speaking generally – about mothers. I didn't mean–'

'That's all right.' He smiled again, then he said, 'Shall we arrange a date, then, for this meal? It doesn't state any particular time.'

They had decided on the following Tuesday. This was an evening that appeared to be free for both of them. Mr Leigh mentioned that his darts match was on Thursday that week, and Sally's only regular engagement was night school on a Monday.

'I don't have a car,' he told her almost apologetically. 'I've never really seen the need for one so far, although it's something I've been considering.'

'Neither have I,' she answered. 'More to the point, neither has my father,' she added, as she could see that Mr Leigh was a little worried about his lack of his own transport. 'Dad works in town; he's the manager of a gents' outfitters, but he says it would be too much trouble to park.

Shall we go on the bus, then?'

'Certainly not,' he replied. 'I wouldn't dream of it. No, I shall get a taxi, and if you give me your address I shall come there and pick you up. What time shall we say?'

They decided on six-thirty, then they would be ready to dine at seven o'clock. He didn't think it would be necessary to make a reservation but decided to do so just to make sure.

As Sally watched him leave the classroom with his bottle of whisky – it certainly had been his lucky evening – to meet his daughter and sister who were waiting outside, she started to wonder what she had done. Was it ethical, she asked herself, to accept an invitation such as this from the father of one of her pupils? (She was reminded of the old joke about a woman teacher meeting a man on a crowded bus and exclaiming, 'Don't I know you from somewhere? Oh yes, of course; you're the father of one of my children!') She smiled at the thought, telling herself that it was, as Mr Leigh had said, just his way of saying thank you. But she had noticed a hint of regard in his eyes as he looked at her, not only tonight but at their previous meeting at the open evening. She was not averse to a bit of admiration from a member of the opposite sex. He was quite an attractive man, too, when he smiled, and she guessed he might be altogether different from the aloof and rather stern person that he seemed to be at a first acquaintance.

Should she tell the rest of the staff about it? she pondered. She decided to think about that over the weekend. She had been wondering whether another invitation from Phil Grantley might be forthcoming, to another football match or to something that might be considered more of a proper date. But since their visit to the match last Saturday he had said very little to her. Not that he had deliberately avoided her; he had just spoken to her in the same casual way that he spoke to the other members of the staff. Sally was hurt; she couldn't understand him at all. It really seemed as though there was something on his mind, but if he didn't want to confide in her – which he clearly didn't – then there was nothing she could do about it. She wondered if, unwittingly, she had accepted Mr Leigh's invitation as a way of getting back at him? That could only have some effect, though, if Phil knew about it.

When it came to the crunch she told no one about it except, of course, her parents. She didn't see the point in telling the rest of the staff. School would be breaking up on Wednesday for the Easter holiday and she wouldn't see any of them for the next two weeks. But she had to face something of a cross-examination from her mother.

'What do you know about this man?' she asked. 'I mean, what's his background, and should you really be doing this? Couldn't it be construed as unprofessional conduct, getting involved with one of the parents?'

'I'm not getting involved, Mum,' Sally had replied, rather testily. 'I'm old enough to look after myself and I know what I'm doing. He's a perfectly respectable man. He owns a hotel. He's the chef there, and his wife died several years ago. For heaven's sake, I'm only going out for a meal

132

with him!'

'All right, dear. I'm sorry,' her mother had replied. 'We just want what is best for you, and what is right for you, your dad and me, that's all.' Sally knew that although her parents were proud of her status as a teacher, they still thought, on the other hand, that she should be married by now with a couple of children.

However, her mother kissed her cheek and said, 'Have a lovely time, dear', when the taxi pulled up at the door. Mr Leigh didn't make any move to come to the house door, which Sally was glad about, nor did her mother remain on the threshold to have a 'nosey', but went inside and closed the door.

Mr Leigh got out and opened the taxi door for her, and she sat on the back seat next to him. He looked very smart in a navy suit with a faint stripe, a pale-blue shirt which, she noticed at once, matched the colour of his eyes, and a maroon tie with a quiet paisley design.

Sally had deliberated about what she should wear. She liked her dusky-pink dress and she knew it suited her; then she remembered she had worn it at the open evening and that Mr Leigh might remember it. If he was anything like her father, though, and like a lot of men, she suspected, he would not have noticed what she was wearing. How many times had she heard her dad say to her mother, 'Is that a new dress, dear? No? I don't remember seeing it before.' Anyway, what the heck did it matter? she told herself. It was just a casual dinner with someone who was little more than an acquaintance. She always liked to look her best, though, and in the end she had decided to wear her moss-green suit with the fashionable wing collar and the accordion-pleated, mid-calf-length skirt, with a pale-green silky blouse underneath in case she took off her jacket.

Mr Leigh smiled as though he was pleased to see her. 'Hello, Miss Roberts,' he began as the taxi drove off. 'I hope you're looking forward to this meal as much as I am.'

'I certainly am, Mr Leigh,' she replied. 'But I wonder if we might be a little less formal tonight? My name is Sally. I feel like a real old school ma'am when you keep calling me Miss Roberts.'

'Certainly,' he replied. 'I was waiting for you to suggest it, actually. I didn't like to, with you being Kathy's teacher an' everything. Anyway, I'm Albert.' He grimaced. 'Not surprising really, is it, that I was reluctant to tell you? I hate it, but that's what my parents called me and unfortunately I don't have another name, so I'm stuck with it.'

'A popular name at the time, I suppose,' she said, thinking to herself that she didn't like it much either. 'Queen Victoria's husband was Albert, wasn't he? I suppose that's why it became popular.'

'I'm not as old as all that!' he retorted, but fortunately he was laughing. She laughed too.

'No ... sorry... I wasn't suggesting that you are. But the next king – Edward VII – he was an Albert as well, wasn't he? Didn't they call him Bertie?' She guessed that Mr Leigh – Albert – would have been born during the reign of that monarch. She, Sally, was born in 1916, during the reign of George V, which made her feel very old when she thought about it; and she guessed that Albert Leigh must be quite a few years older than herself.

'You have a good knowledge of history,' he commented, 'but then you would have, with you being a teacher.'

'It's not terribly relevant to being an infant teacher, though,' she replied. 'But I've always been interested in history, especially modern history, if you know what I mean.'

'Yes, the First World War is being regarded as history now, isn't it?' he said. 'I wasn't old enough to be in that one, but I did my bit in the last one. Anyway – Sally – I'm pleased you agreed to come with me. I hope we'll have a very pleasant evening.'

'I'm sure we will,' she smiled.

The taxi dropped them right outside the Fishing Net and Sally waited whilst he settled up with the driver. There was a welcoming feel to the restaurant even from the outside. The paintwork was sea green and curtains that resembled fishing nets were draped across the windows.

There was a pleasant friendly ambience, too, when they entered the place. Albert gave his name, and a waitress in a smart green dress with a paler green apron and cap showed them to a corner table for two. The tablecloths were of green and white checked cotton, the silver cutlery was bright and gleaming and the table mats depicted seascapes of various resorts and fishing ports of the British Isles.

The same theme was continued on the walls. There were looped fishing nets, lobster pots, and sepia photographs of fishermen and trawlers;

stormy seas; herring girls – as the women who used to follow the fishing fleets around the coast of the British Isles were called – engaged on their task of gutting the herrings; and well-known fishing ports of Britain, with Fleetwood, a few miles up the coast, being featured more than once.

The menus were large, both in shape and in content, and the waitress handed one to each of them, at the same time lighting the candle in a green glass bowl in the centre of the table.

'Hmm...We're quite spoilt for choice,' observed Albert. 'Shall we have something to start with? I think the allowance they've given us will run to that... But it doesn't matter, of course,' he added hurriedly, as though realising that that might sound rather stingy. 'You choose whatever you want, Sally. We're here to have a good time.'

The list of starters was not quite as extensive as the main menu. Neither of them fancied hors d'oeuvres or soup. 'I'd rather like some shrimps,' said Sally.

'Yes, I'll go for that too,' agreed Albert. 'Morecambe Bay shrimps potted in butter; sounds good. Yes, let's push the boat out, if you'll pardon the pun.'

When the waitress returned in five minutes or so they had both agreed to order scampi with chips – plus vegetables – for the main course, a dish that was becoming very popular. From a separate wine list Albert ordered a bottle of Chardonnay.

'I'm not a connoisseur of wines,' he told her. 'Far from it, but I'm told that Chardonnay is considered to be rather superior to the ordinary Liebfraumilch.'

They all sounded quite glamorous to Sally. Wine drinking was becoming rather more fashionable now because many folk had discovered that pleasure on holidays abroad, but this was something that she had not yet experienced, apart from a short trip to France a couple of years ago with her parents.

'Do you serve drinks at your hotel?' she asked. 'Alcoholic ones, I mean.'

'No, we don't,' he answered. 'We don't have a licence. Very few of the smaller hotels have as yet. It's just the larger ones like the Norbreck and the Imperial, and lots of others, of course. Maybe one of these days...'

Conversation lagged a little while they were waiting for their meal. But just as Sally was searching in her mind for an opening remark the wine waiter arrived with the bottle of Chardonnay. He poured a little of the golden liquid into Albert's glass. He tasted it knowingly and when he nodded that it was acceptable the waiter poured out a glassful for each of them.

'Cheers,' said Albert, raising his glass. 'Here's to an enjoyable evening ... and the start of a friendship?' he added with a slight query in his voice and a quizzical look at her.

She nodded. 'Yes... Cheers, Albert,' she replied and they clinked their glasses. 'Mmm ... very nice,' she commented, after she had taken a good sip of the wine. 'Not too sweet, not too dry; very pleasant.'

'As I say, I'm not an expert,' Albert said, 'but it seems OK to me.' He grinned. 'Well then, Sally, are you going to tell me a little about yourself?

137

For instance, how long have you been teaching?'

She laughed. 'A good way of finding out how old I am, Albert?'

'No ... no, not at all.' He looked a little confused. 'That wasn't what I meant. Anyway, I don't know how old you were when you started teaching, do I?'

'It's no secret,' she replied. 'Why should it be? I've been teaching for fourteen years, all at the same school. I trained for two years at a college in Manchester and then I was lucky enough to find a post in my hometown, which pleased my parents, of course.'

'And you must have liked it there, at your school, or you wouldn't have stayed?'

'Yes, that's true. There has never been any incentive for me to move elsewhere. I was twenty when I started teaching, so that makes me thirty-four, doesn't it?' she added with a twinkle in her eye.

'All right, cards on the table,' he replied. 'I'm forty-five, and I see no reason to be secretive about it...' He hesitated for a moment. 'You're an attractive young woman, Sally. Have you no special boyfriend? Forgive me if you think I'm being personal, but you must have a lot of admirers?'

She laughed. 'If so, then I don't know where they are. No, I don't have a boyfriend.' She was soon to realise why he had asked.

'Actually ... I noticed you at the football match,' he told her. 'When they played Preston. You were with that young fellow from your school. And ... well ... I just wondered.'

'Oh yes, that's Phil Grantley,' she replied. 'I didn't see you there. You're a supporter of Blackpool, then?'

'Of course! You could say I'm one of their greatest fans,' he said with the most enthusiasm she had seen him show so far. 'I never miss a match if I can help it. What about you? Do you often go?'

'Occasionally, when I've someone to go with,' she said. 'I've been with my dad sometimes, when he's not working. And then Phil asked me to go with him, so I did. We're just mates,' she added. 'That's all. Just like I'm mates with most of the other fellows on the staff.' Any regrets that she had felt regarding Phil's lack of interest she was trying to push to one side.

'Actually ... I was engaged once,' she went on to say, just in case he should think there was something odd about her. 'To another teacher that I met soon after we both started working in Blackpool. But then ... well ... the war came along and unfortunately Martin was killed. He had joined up straight away and he was part of a bomber crew. They were shot down during the Battle of Britain.'

'How dreadful for you.' Albert looked most concerned. 'Yes ... that terrible war caused misery for thousands, in all sorts of ways. As I know from my own experience,' he added. He offered no further explanation and she did not ask. He looked almost angry for a moment, and she assumed that it might be something to do with losing his wife. Then he smiled rather sadly. 'But life has to go on. I expect you have learnt that, haven't you, Sally?'

'Indeed I have,' she replied. 'As I said, I enjoy my job; in fact it's become almost my whole life. Which, I suppose, is not entirely a good thing,' she added thoughtfully.

Their shrimps arrived – tiny pink morsels in butter in little brown earthenware pots, served with triangles of brown bread and butter. They both proclaimed them delicious, and just enough not to take the edge off the appetite.

The scampi dish, too, which soon followed, came up to expectations. The pink shellfish, which were really the tail ends of large lobsters, were moist and flavoursome, encased in crispy bread-crumbs. The chips, too, tasted like the very best home-made ones.

'I must confess I've never had this dish before,' Albert said. 'It's well worth the trying.'

'You don't serve scampi at your hotel, then?' asked Sally.

'No, we never have done. But it's something I may well consider putting on the menu. It would be a nice change for a high tea. I could learn quite a lot from this menu here. I'm pleasantly surprised at the quality of the food and the standard of the cuisine.'

'Yes, it really is excellent,' agreed Sally as she tasted the fresh garden peas and the green beans which complemented the fish.

'Do you know ... when I won the raffle prize I was not particularly pleased at first,' Albert told her. 'I thought it was a question of "coals to New-castle", if you see what I mean. I've never been in the habit of dining out. I was conceited enough to think that we put on a better meal at our own hotel, but I know now how mistaken I was. And then... well ... I thought of inviting you along, and I'm so glad that I did. And so pleased that you agreed to come with me.'

'I'm pleased too,' she replied, meeting his eyes for several seconds as he regarded her with obvious admiration. She lowered her gaze, a little discomfited. One 'date' – if you could call it that – was all right, but she was not sure that she would want to go out with him again.

'Now, do you think you could manage a pudding?' he asked, as the waitress arrived to take away their empty plates. They had done justice to the meal, only a few chips remaining on each of their plates.

'I'll leave you a few minutes to decide,' the waitress smiled as she handed out the menus again. 'But I can recommend the lemon meringue pie, one of our chef's specialities.'

'That's good enough for me, then,' said Albert. 'How about you, Sally?'

'Yes, I agree,' she replied. 'It's one of my favourites.'

'We'll both have that, then.' Albert handed the menus back. And then two coffees, please.'

'My mother makes lemon meringue,' said Sally. 'But she uses a packet mix; it's really good, though.'

'Yes, it's a very popular sweet at the moment,' said Albert. 'It always goes down well when we put it on. I must confess, though, that I use a ready-made mix as well. Shh...' He put a finger to his lips. 'Sometimes we have to consider the time factor and cut a few corners now and then.'

'I'm sure you have a good reputation, though,' said Sally. 'Have you had the hotel a long time?'

'For ever,' he said, smiling. 'At least it seems so.' He explained that the business had been started by his parents in the early 1900s, and it had been taken for granted that he and his sister should work there. When his parents had retired he and Winifred had taken over the boarding house and had tried to make it a little more 'high class'.

'We gave it a name,' he said. '"Holmleigh" – one of my sister's bright ideas – and we refer to it as a private hotel now.'

'And you are expecting that Katherine will work there as well, are you, when she leaves school?' asked Sally. He seemed to pick up on the note of slight censure in her tone.

'Yes, I hope so,' he replied, 'although it's a long time off; Kathy's only six, well, nearly seven. Who knows what might happen in the future? Why? Don't you think it's a good idea?'

'I believe in children being allowed to attain their full potential,' she replied. 'Katherine's a very bright little girl. She may well have other ideas when she grows up. I know she says that's what she wants to do at the moment, but she doesn't really know about much else yet, does she?'

'Well, we'll see,' he replied. 'We got the impression, Winnie and I, that Kathy was just an average sort of scholar. I know she tries hard – you said so – but she's not top of the class or anything like that, is she?'

'No, but children often develop later and surprise us all,' said Sally. 'Anyway, we can't really look so far ahead, can we?'

The lemon meringue pie arrived and they tucked into it with gusto. It was time for a change of direction in the conversation, thought Sally. She had noticed a certain edginess in Albert's remarks. A man who likes his own way? she pondered. But then her married friends told her that most of them did! She had noticed, too, that he never spoke of his wife and she assumed that this must be a 'no-go' area.

'Scrumptious!' he declared, spooning up the last morsel of his lemon meringue. 'That's one of our Kathy's words, and it sums it up very nicely.' His earlier tetchiness seemed to have vanished. He leant across the table, looking more intently at her.

'You were saying earlier, Sally,' he began, 'that teaching seems to have become your whole way of life. And I'm pretty much the same with the hotel; my life revolves around it. Not entirely a good thing, as you also remarked. It seems to me that I need a change, and so do you.' He paused for a moment before saying, 'Would you consider coming out with me again? We get along very nicely, don't we, and ... well ... I would like to see you again.'

She did not answer for a moment. She had assumed that this would be an isolated occasion, but maybe she should have guessed that he might have other ideas. It might be churlish to refuse. She didn't need to get too involved with him if she didn't wish to do so. And where could be the harm in accepting? Invitations were pretty thin on the ground at the moment. She liked him, perhaps more than she had thought she might, although his company had kindled no real spark of attraction or excitement in her.

'Yes, why not?' she answered, smiling at him in a friendly way. 'Thank you, Albert. Yes, I'll go out with you again, sometime.' She wanted to make it clear to him that it might not be a regular occurrence, and maybe not just yet either, if that was what he had in mind.

'That's good,' he replied. 'I thought you might say no.'

She could see that he would have been disappointed if she had refused. The relief he was feeling now that she had agreed showed in the more relaxed tone of his voice. She decided she would go along with her decision to see him again with as much enthusiasm as she could muster. It was no use being half-hearted; but at the same time she pondered that she hardly knew the man. It might well turn out that they had very little in common, or that they didn't like one another very much on a further acquaintance.

But he seemed determined to please her. 'What sort of things do you like to do?' he asked. 'The cinema, theatre, dancing ... or another meal? I don't think you're the sort of young lady who makes a habit of going to pubs, are you?'

She agreed that this was true. 'It's the way I've been brought up,' she told him. 'Like many girls – women, I suppose I should say! – of my age. It wasn't the thing for women to go into pubs on their own, was it, or even with men at one time? Not until the war; I suppose that has changed things to a certain extent. I do have a drink – occasionally – with some of the members of our staff. Yes ... I enjoy the theatre and cinema, when I go, which isn't very often. I used to enjoy dancing, but I haven't been for ages.' Hardly at all since Martin was killed, she mused. They had spent many happy times dancing at the Tower or the Winter Gardens ballroom. 'The only thing I do regularly – once a week – is my French conversation class.'

'And I have a darts match once a week,' he replied. 'Not always the same night, and occasionally it might be more than one night; but I'm sure it's a problem we can get round. I must admit I go to the pub ... oh, possibly two or three times a week, but it's mainly for the company. There's just my sister and myself at home, apart from Kathy, of course. We get on quite well, but sometimes I like a change of company and so does Winnie.'

'You'll be getting busy at the hotel very soon, won't you?' Sally enquired.

'Yes, it'll be Easter this weekend, of course, and the first of our visitors will be arriving. After that there's a lull until Whitsuntide, then it's all go until the end of the Lights. At least, we hope it will be. But the boss has to be allowed a night or two of freedom. Bosses, I should say; Winnie and I sort it out between us.' He smiled. 'I'm sure we'll be able to come to some arrangement.'

Sally smiled back, a little hesitantly. It seemed as though he was assuming he would still be seeing her during the summertime. Well, that remained to be seen.

'Actually, I had a bit of a surprise last weekend,' he went on. 'My sister, Winnie, she had a date, of all things! With a man, I mean.'

'And that was unusual, was it?' asked Sally.

'I'll say so! You could've knocked me down with a feather when she told me. Apparently she's met this chap at her drama group. He's only just joined, just come to live in Blackpool, and they seem to have taken quite a shine to one another.'

Sally laughed. 'And why not? Your sister is an attractive-looking woman.' She had been going to say, for her age, but decided not to.

'Well, yes ... happen she is. But there's never been anyone for Winnie – well, not that I know of – since Arthur was killed. He was her fiancé; at least, I think they were engaged, I'm not sure. I was only a young lad at the time. He was killed right at the end of the first war, not this last one.'

'Good gracious! That's a long time ago,' said Sally.

'Aye ... er ... yes, so it is. A lot of women were in the same boat, though. There was a great shortage of men and – like I say – she never seemed to be bothered once she had got over losing Arthur. Then, blow me down! She tells me she's met this Jeff fellow.'

'Have you met him?'

'Yes, just once. He came to call for her last Saturday and they went off to the pictures. He's quite a good-looking chap, I suppose, and he seems very nice. About Winnie's age, I should say, and he's a widower.'

'So you're thinking it will be more difficult if you both want to go out at the same time, is that it?' asked Sally.

'Aye ... yes, I reckon it might be. But I'm sure

there'll be a way round it. I'll have a chat to her... So, what do you think, Sally? You'll risk another outing with me, will you?'

'Yes, of course, Albert. Why not? I've already said so.'

'So shall we say the cinema, then? Not this Saturday – our guests will be settling in. Is the Saturday after all right with you?'

They agreed that they would both consult the *Evening Gazette* and see if they could find a film they would both enjoy; there were cinemas enough to choose from in Blackpool. Albert would ring Sally at her home; fortunately they were on the phone.

'Please don't think I'm in the habit of doing this, Sally,' Albert made a point of assuring her. 'Taking young women out, I mean.'

'I didn't think so.' She laughed. 'Anyway, it's really nothing to do with me, is it, however many lady friends you have had.'

'But I haven't,' he insisted. 'Not since Barbara...' He shook his head. 'I've never been interested.'

'Well then, I'm honoured,' she said quietly.

After they had finished their coffee Albert settled the bill and the waitress called a taxi for them. He shook her hand in quite a formal way when the car drew up at her door.

'Thank you for a lovely evening,' she said. 'I'm pleased you invited me.'

'And I'm pleased you came,' he answered. 'Good night, Sally. I'll be in touch with you.' He raised his hand in salute as the taxi drew away.

She was a little dazed with a surfeit of wine; between them they had emptied the bottle. She decided not to give too much thought to what the future might hold until she had had a night's sleep.

Chapter Ten

When Sally returned to school after the Easter holiday she was surprised to find Phil Grantley waiting for her outside her classroom door.

'Hello, Phil...' She greeted him cheerfully, as though there was nothing amiss between them. There wasn't, really, as far as she knew, apart from his recent aloofness, which had led her to think that it might be best if she tried to forget her awakening interest in him. 'Have you had a good holiday?' she enquired.

'No ... not really,' he replied. 'Actually, that's what I want to talk to you about, so I thought I'd have a word with you away from the rest of the staff.'

'Whatever's the matter, Phil?' she asked. He didn't look his normal cheerful self, but then, as she recalled, neither had he seemed so for the last week or so, before the school broke up for Easter. 'You're not ill, are you?' He did, in fact, look rather pale, with dark shadows under his eyes.

'No, I'm not ill,' he replied. 'I've not been sleeping too well; I've had a lot on my mind... Look, I can't tell you now. The bell will be going soon, and there isn't really much opportunity to chat at school, is there? There's always someone else around. I'll run you home from school tonight, and then I'll tell you all about everything ... if that's all right with you?'

'Yes, that's fine, Phil,' she replied, feeling very mystified. 'We'll try and get away on time, shall we?'

He nodded. 'Yes, and ... er ... Sally...' He was looking at her rather solemnly. 'I'm sorry if I've been a bit offhand with you lately. I realise now that I might have been. I didn't mean it, and I hope you still think of me as a friend?'

'Of course I do, Phil.'

He smiled then, but a little uncertainly. 'OK then; I'll see you later. Back to the grindstone now, eh?' he added, sounding more like his normal self.

Whatever could be the matter? Sally wondered, as she went into her classroom, ready to greet the return of thirty-six eager children. Most of them were keen to get back to school at their age. It was only as they grew older, usually not until they were of secondary school age, that they could be compared with Shakespeare's schoolboy, 'creeping like snail, unwillingly to school'.

The bell sounded a few minutes later and there was a charge of small bodies into the room.

'Hello, Miss Roberts...'

'Have you had a nice holiday, Miss Roberts...?'

'We've been away, Miss Roberts. We went to see my aunty in Wigan...'

'We went on the sands, but it was a bit cold...'

She was greeted on all sides by her enthusiastic pupils. 'Hello, everybody,' she said. 'Come along now and settle down. You can tell me all about your holiday later and what you've all been doing.'

She heard Timothy Fielding, as he passed by her desk, saying in an audible whisper to his friend, Stanley, 'I reckon she'll have us writing about it, don't you?'

She smiled to herself. Spot on, Timothy! she thought. That would be one of the first things on the timetable, to discuss their 'news' and then to write about a day they had enjoyed during their holiday.

Katherine Leigh smiled shyly as she went to her table. Sally wondered if she knew that her father had been out on two 'dates' with her teacher. She and Albert hadn't actually talked about whether he should tell Kathy. It wasn't as if they were courting, she thought to herself, or regarding it as a long-term friendship, although she had agreed to see him again on Saturday. She suspected that Kathy might already know about it. Her smile, to Sally, had seemed to be rather a secretive one. But she hoped that the little girl would keep it to herself and certainly not confide in her friend, Shirley Morris! She was a little busybody, if ever there was one. Sally didn't want it all round the playground that 'Miss Roberts is going out with Kathy Leigh's dad!' Well, she would just have to trust to Kathy's common sense, which she felt the child had in abundance.

Anyway, she had other things on her mind at that moment as well as her friendship with Albert Leigh. What on earth was the matter with Phil Grantley?

The infant classes finished at half past three, half an hour before the junior department. Sally tidied her desk, cleaned the blackboard and sharpened the pencils ready for the next day. Then she put on her coat and went out into the playground to wait for Phil.

She stood by his Morris Minor car and he arrived a couple of minutes later. 'Hi there, Sally; sorry to keep you waiting,' he greeted her.

'You haven't; I've only just arrived,' she told him, clambering into the small blue car.

He got in beside her and soon they were out of the gate and bowling along the road at a fair pace. He turned into a side road where there were no parking restrictions and stopped the car.

'Here we are, then, Sally,' he said. 'Time for us to have a little chat, I think. At least ... time for me to talk and you to listen, if you will?'

'Of course, Phil,' she answered. 'I've been rather concerned about you.'

He took a deep breath. 'Where can I begin...?' He smiled quizzically at her.

'Well, it's usually best to start at the beginning,' she said.

He nodded, then paused for a few seconds before he began to speak. 'I'm not sure whether you know – probably you don't – that I was engaged to be married before I came to Blackpool.'

'No, I didn't know that...'

'Well, it came to an end, quite amicably, but I decided I was ready for a change. So, as you know, I was fortunate to get the post that I applied for here in Blackpool.'

She nodded. She knew that he had come from

151

Yorkshire – a village near Bradford, she believed – and he now lived in a flat somewhere in the North Shore area. He would have been at the school for two years, come September.

'I stayed on good terms with my ex-fiancée, Pamela,' he continued. 'It would have been hard not to do so, really, as her parents and mine had always been close friends. Anyway, about a week before the end of term I had a phone call from my mother, in great distress. Pam had been badly injured in a car crash and she was in hospital.'

'Oh dear! What a shock for you,' said Sally. She recalled that that must have been round about the time that Phil had started to be friendly with her, Sally, and then had so abruptly seemed to go off the idea. 'And ... is she all right now?' she asked.

He shook his head slowly. 'I realised then that although I was no longer in love with her – I wonder if I ever was, really; we had grown up together, you see, we were sort of childhood sweethearts – I still had feelings for her. I went over to Bradford that weekend, but she was in a bad way. She was still unconscious; she had internal injuries and broken bones and possibly brain damage.' Sally remained silent, not knowing at all what she should say.

'And then – actually it was on Easter Sunday – my mother rang me to say that Pam had died...'

Sally gasped. 'Oh ... how dreadful!'

'Yes, it was ... dreadful. It was the funeral a few days ago. I only came back last night in time for school; I've been staying with my parents.' He shook his head in a bewildered manner. 'I still can't believe it, can't come to terms with it all. She was so lively and pretty, like you, Sally. Well, no – not just like you – but you know what I mean. She had everything to live for. Life is so very cruel...'

'Yes, it can be sometimes,' she agreed. 'Phil, I'm so terribly sorry. And I do understand. I knew there was something wrong, but I didn't like to ask too much.'

'And I didn't want to talk about it,' he replied. 'But I do know that life has to go on. It's a cliché, isn't it, that folk always trot out at times like this?'

Sally nodded. 'Yes, that's very true. I know that from my own experience. I lost my fiancé, during the Battle of Britain. I don't talk about it now; it's quite a long time ago, and lots of other girls lost boyfriends in the war. Another thing that people say is that time heals.' She smiled sorrowfully. 'Well ... yes ... it does, but it can take a while. If there's anything I can do, Phil, you know you can think of me as a friend.'

'I know that, Sally. That's why I'm talking to you, rather than to any of the others. Actually, I was wondering ... would you come out with me tonight? Just for a quiet drink somewhere. I feel that I need to get out. There's no point in sitting on my own, brooding. Like I said, Pam and I were no longer together, but I've been surprised how the fond feelings are still there, and about how upset I've been.'

'I'm sure I would feel exactly the same,' Sally replied. 'Yes, I'll go out with you, Phil. I shall look forward to it. Just what we need after the first day back.'

'Good...' He smiled at her. 'Let's get moving, then, now, shall we?'

They drove to her home, neither of them saying very much. 'What time, then? he asked as he stopped the car outside her house.

'Oh, half past seven? Is that OK?' she asked. 'It'll give us a chance to wash off the chalk dust.'

'Yes, that's fine.' He chuckled, seeming rather more cheerful. 'Cheerio then, Sally. See you in a little while.'

Poor Phil! She was quite stunned at his news. It certainly explained his strange mood. She felt no compunction about seeing him tonight. She had agreed to go out with Albert on Saturday. But both of them, Albert and Phil, they were just friends and nothing more ... weren't they?

Phil seemed to want to talk about Pamela, and Sally didn't mind listening. She knew that it was cathartic for him to do so. She remembered how, when Martin had been killed, she had felt the need to talk about him. It had seemed, somehow, to alleviate the grief she was feeling.

They sat near the window of the lounge bar of a seafront hotel, looking out across the promenade to the vast expanse of the Irish Sea. The days were lengthening now as it was well past the spring equinox. Dusk was falling and they watched the sun gradually disappear behind the grey-green sea. It was not such a spectacular sunset that evening – the sunsets in Blackpool were sometimes breathtaking in their beauty – but the mass of cloud, tinged faintly with pale orange and pink, was still a lovely sight.

'I'm glad I came to live in Blackpool,' Phil remarked. 'It took me a while to get used to the flatness of the Fylde. Where my parents live, where I was brought up, in a village called Baildon – it's a suburb of Bradford, really – it's surrounded by hills. Factory chimneys as well, of course, although not so many as there used to be, but there's a rugged charm to it despite the dark satanic mills. It's much cleaner and fresher here, but, as I say, I miss the hills and dales.'

'There are hills quite near here,' Sally told him. 'Not much more than half an hour's drive away. There's the Bleasdale Fells and the Trough of Bowland. And the Lake District, of course, further north. I went on a coach trip once, with my parents, to Ambleside on Lake Windermere; that was long before the war.'

'Much easier to explore, though, if you have a car,' said Phil. 'I had a few days in the Lake District last year, with Alan.' That was one of his colleagues from school. 'We did a spot of fell walking. I've never been to those nearer hills, though, the Bleasdales. Perhaps we could go sometime, could we, Sally, just you and me, I mean? Have you ever done any fell walking?'

'No, actually, I haven't,' she replied. 'It's something I've never really thought about. Fiona – you know, the girl who joined the infant staff not long ago – she was telling me that she'd joined a walking club in Blackpool. She seems to be enjoying it.' Sally didn't answer his question about going exploring with him. It would all depend on when, and on how things worked out for her.

'Was it something you and Pamela used to do?'

155

she asked.

'No, not really,' Phil replied. 'We used to go for short walks, but she wasn't really an outdoor sort of girl, even though she was brought up in the country; well, I suppose Baildon's sort of in the country. I think we both realised, in the end, that it wouldn't work out for us. We weren't very much alike – very few shared interests, you see.'

'Was she a teacher?' asked Sally.

'No, she worked in the local library...' He had told her earlier that he and Pamela had been in the same class at infant and then junior school, but had gone to different secondary schools. She had still been there, though, waiting, when he had done his two-year teacher training, and when he had returned from his war service. Sally already knew that he had been in the Eighth Army, in the Western Desert with Monty, something of which he was very proud, and he had returned relatively unscathed.

'When I came back from the war – I was one of the lucky ones, although it's something you never forget if you've been through it – I think I knew then that Pam wasn't the right girl for me. But she'd waited so faithfully for me all the time I was away. My mother told me how she used to go round to see them every week, how she looked forward to my letters, and that she never thought of going out dancing and having a good time as a lot of her friends were doing. So I thought how callous it would be to let her down, how devastated she'd be... And so we went on with it. We were actually saving up to buy a house; that was why we didn't get married there and then. And for me ... well ... it was an excuse, really. But, as I said in the end we both knew that it would not be right to carry on. She was really more like a sister to me, and that's how I feel now, that I've lost a dearly loved sister.'

'I'm sorry...' Sally said again. 'But it will get easier. 'You've got your job – I know how much you enjoy it – and lots of friends around you.'

'Yes...' Phil nodded. 'I've told Mr Williams, and Alan and Brian, about Pamela. If anyone mentions that I'm rather subdued, perhaps you could tell them why, Sally. But I will try and pull myself together. I feel I've made a start already, seeing you tonight...

'So, what about you and me, then?' he continued. 'We got off to a bad start, didn't we? I must explain to you about the day we went to the football match. I would have liked to take you out that evening, but it was my flatmate's birthday. He'd asked me, only the night before, if I'd go to the pub with him and a few more of his mates – strictly men only! – and I couldn't very well refuse.'

'No, of course not,' said Sally, thinking that the explanation had been a long time coming.

'So I thought I'd ask you out later on in the week, and then ... well ... there was all this awful business with Pamela, and I just couldn't think about anything else.'

'It's all right, Phil, I understand...'

'Anyway, I've enjoyed tonight, Sally. It was just what I needed. Thanks for coming and for being such a good listener. But I would like to see you again, and I promise I'll be in a more cheerful mood. What about Saturday evening?' Sally felt her heart sink; she had already had a feeling about what was coming next.

'I remember you telling me that you enjoy those big musicals,' Phil went on. 'Well, they're showing *State Fair* again at the Imperial on Saturday. A few years old now, I know, but it was one of my favourites at the time; Jeanne Crain and Dana Andrews, they were wonderful singers.'

'Yes, and Dick Haymes,' said Sally. 'It was one of my favourites too. But I'm sorry, Phil, I can't manage Saturday. I've already promised to go out with somebody.'

The smile on Phil's face vanished, to be replaced by a look of surprise, then disappointment, even a trace of annoyance. 'With ... a man, do you mean?' he asked.

It would have been easier, perhaps kinder, to lie, but she knew she couldn't do so. 'Yes, it is ... actually,' she replied.

'So ... who is it, then? Anybody I know?'

She was tempted to tell Phil that it was none of his business, but he was already in quite a vulnerable state of mind and she didn't want to hurt him any more. 'No, you don't know him,' she replied. Well, he didn't, not really, except perhaps by sight. 'I've been out with him a couple of times. Nothing serious,' she added. 'But it wouldn't be right...'

'No, I can see that,' he said. 'I've left it too late, haven't I? Just my luck! I might've known this would happen.'

'I'll see how things go,' said Sally, feeling rather uncomfortable. Maybe she shouldn't have agreed to come out with Phil this evening after all. 'As I said, it's not as though this is a serious friendship; I've not known him very long...'

'It's OK, Sally,' Phil said, a trifle abruptly. 'There's no need to explain; I understand the way things are. Now, drink up, and we'll get away before they throw us out. I don't want to get caught up in the confusion in the car park at closing time.'

Sally drank the last of her gin and lime, and Phil hurriedly finished his half pint. They spoke very little on the way home. She felt uneasy about the situation. What, at first, had seemed a pleasant sort of evening was ending under a cloud.

'Goodnight, Sally,' Phil said, as he pulled up outside her door. 'I'll see you tomorrow.' It was obvious that he didn't want to sit around chatting; there was nothing more to be said.

'Goodnight then, Phil,' she replied. 'And ... I'm sorry, really I am.'

'Forget it...' He shrugged. 'I'll get over it. Cheerio, then...' He drove off hastily, scarcely giving her time to close the car door.

Chapter Eleven

Sally had enjoyed her visit to the cinema with Albert, far more than she had anticipated. They had gone to see a rerun of one of the Ealing Studio comedies, *Kind Hearts and Coronets*, which was showing at the Dominion cinema in Bispham. It was a film that neither of them had seen the first time round and they both enjoyed it. Sally was surprised to hear Albert chuckling quite openly at times. At their first meeting she had come to the conclusion that he was something of a sobersides; but she was gradually changing her mind as she came to know him better.

It seemed there was more to Albert Leigh than met the eye. She had also gained the impression, at first, that he may have been a little self-conscious about his lack of formal education, compared with her own. She knew he had left school at fourteen, as had many lads of his age, and had gone to work straight away in his parents' boarding house. His prowess as a chef had been largely due to his own efforts. He had watched his mother, an excellent cook, at work, and he had learnt a lot from recipe books. His army service too, in the catering corps, had added to his experience. By and large, though, he seemed unwilling to speak much about his time in the army. Maybe he felt rather guilty that he had not taken part in any real fighting; but she guessed it was more to do with the fact that his wife had died round about that time.

In other directions, too, he was self-taught. She had imagined that, in his own home, he was very much a pipe and slippers and daily newspaper sort of man, when he was not hard at work in the kitchen, of course. But she learnt that the newspapers were not his only reading matter. His taste in literature was wide-ranging and by no means lightweight. He enjoyed the works of Somerset Maugham, A.J. Cronin and John Steinbeck. Sally mentioned that she had read, quite recently, the two books by Lloyd C. Douglas that had become very popular: *The Big Fisherman* and *The Robe*. Her comment had received a frosty reception.

'Religious, aren't they? I've got no time for 'owt–' he corrected himself hastily, 'for anything like that.'

'They're good stories, though, the sort that anybody might enjoy,' she told him, half apologetically.

'I've no time for any of that mumbo-jumbo,' he went on. 'I've never set foot inside a church since ... since my wife died. If that's God for you, then you can keep him.'

'Yes, I suppose I understand,' she replied. 'One is tempted to wonder, at times, what it's all about.'

She didn't tell him, as she might have done, that she had wondered why Martin had had to be killed ... but then thousands of young women must have felt exactly as she did. She had changed the subject quickly. She knew that Kathy went to Sunday school, and Sally had occasionally seen the little girl in church with her aunt. She, Sally, was not a regular attender; she went from time to time with her mother and would, if asked, call herself a Christian.

One thing that had surprised her was when Albert told her that he had, at one time, loved ballroom dancing. She supposed it was something that both he and his wife had enjoyed, and that he had not felt inclined to dance since he had lost her.

She had been somewhat taken aback, therefore,

161

when he had said, following their visit to the cinema, 'Would you like to go dancing on Saturday night, Sally?'

'Well ... yes, that would be very nice,' she replied. 'Where are you thinking of? The Tower, or the Winter Gardens?'

'I was thinking of the Palace, actually,' he said. 'It's a nice homely ballroom, from what I remember, and they have old-time dancing there as well as the modern sort. I used to dance a pretty nifty veleta.' He smiled; he had smiled more often that evening as they grew more used to one another.

They were sitting at the time in the lounge bar of one of the seafront hotels, to where they had walked after their visit to the cinema. Albert had, once again, ordered a taxi to take them to the cinema and would, no doubt, order one for their journey home.

Sally noticed that Albert was not slow in knocking back a pint. He was already into his second one while she was still sipping at her port and lemon. She guessed that he might be quite a heavy drinker when he was with the darts team at his local, and that he was used to speaking in the vernacular of the ordinary man. She noticed that he moderated his fairly broad Lancashire accent when he was with her and tried to act in a more gentlemanly manner. Not that it mattered greatly to Sally. Her father was pretty much the same sort of man: Lancashire born and bred and proud of it. Bill Roberts had learnt to talk 'posh', as he called it, as befitted his position as manager of a gents' outfitters, but could easily revert back to his more familiar accent and dialect.

Sally told Albert that she would be very pleased to go to the Palace. They decided they would go, first of all, to the first-house variety show, and then follow this with dancing in the ballroom. The Palace building, on Bank Hey Street, with its front entrance opening on to the promenade, was a multipurpose building. It housed a cinema, a theatre, known as the 'Palace of Varieties', and a ballroom, as well as various bars, seating areas, cloakrooms and kiosks. It was a very popular venue, especially on a Saturday evening. So that was the date that Sally had referred to, the one that had prevented her from accepting Phil's offer.

She was not altogether sure how she felt about that. Disappointed, she supposed, if she was honest with herself. She liked Phil very much; he was nearer her own age, of course, and was more her sort of a person really than was Albert. But a promise was a promise. She had accepted Albert's offer to go dancing and, in a way, she was quite looking forward to it. She hoped that Phil would not sink into a depressive state again. He had had a severe shock with the death of his former fiancée and seemed to be taking a while to recover.

But with regard to that, it soon seemed as though she was flattering herself. When she encountered him at school the following day he was cheerful and friendly and appeared not to bear any ill will that she had refused his offer to take her out. She did not refer to it again; and she could console herself that maybe it had done him good to talk to her, even though they could not take their friendship a step further.

'That fellow of yours must be loaded,' remarked Sally's father as she awaited Albert's arrival in a taxi, again, on Saturday evening. 'Taxis everywhere! I don't know...'

'He's not my fellow, Dad,' she replied. 'He's just a friend, and I don't think for one moment that he's all that wealthy. He has a hotel, as you know, and I think it does quite well, but there's a lot of competition in Blackpool. He's only ordered a taxi because, well, I suppose he thinks it might not be very gentlemanly to take me on the bus.'

Sometimes they had famous stars appearing at the Palace Variety theatre, singers such as Anne Shelton or Vera Lynn, or comedians like Arthur Askey or Jimmy Edwards. That night it was the Andrews Sisters who were topping the bill, along with the comedian Frank Randle, who was very popular with Blackpool audiences, and Wilson, Keppel and Betty, a trio dressed as Egyptians – two men wearing red fezzes and a somewhat scantily dressed lady in the centre – who performed a sand dance. They, too, always went down well with audiences. The rest of the acts consisted of a conjuror, a ventriloquist, another lesser known comedian and his stooge, and a soprano and baritone duo who sang love duets.

Sally had seen Frank Randle before and was not impressed with his portrayal of a drunk, guzzling from a whisky bottle. His catchphrase, 'I'll be glad when I've had enough of this!', had most of the audience in fits of laughter, but Sally could not do with drunkenness in any shape or form. It seemed to her that Albert was not very impressed either.

'He goes down a treat with the hoi polloi,' he whispered to her, 'but I can't say he's a favourite of mine. Sorry about this, Sally, but it's always the luck of the draw at the Varieties.'

Sally enjoyed the chirpy and cheerful Andrews Sisters, though, singing their bright and flirtatious little songs, 'Don't Sit Under the Apple Tree', 'It's Foolish but it's Fun' and 'An Apple for the Teacher', which caused Albert to nudge her elbow and grin. And she was impressed by the duettists, Mervyn and Maria, virtually unknown, but deserving, she thought, of a higher billing. It was obvious that the audience appreciated their performances of 'We'll Gather Lilacs' and 'I Can Give You the Starlight'. Ivor Novello's melodies always brought a lump to Sally's throat, so she was in a mellow, quite sentimental frame of mind when the show came to an end, and Albert took hold of her elbow to lead her upstairs to the ballroom.

The Palace building was remembered by many of the older Blackpool residents as the 'Alhambra'. It had opened with that name, and was also known as 'The People's Popular Palace of Pleasure', in the early part of the twentieth century; but following a financial crisis it had been bought by the Tower Company and renamed simply as the 'Palace'.

The ballroom was smaller than that of the Tower or the Winter Gardens, and had a more intimate and friendly ambience. It was, however, just as opulent as its rivals, the interior of the Palace having been fashioned in the style of the Italian Renaissance. Gilded pillars and curving balconies led the eye up to the frescoed ceiling, with its brilliant chandeliers. The seats were of red plush, and the highly polished parquet dance floor was a geometrical design of wooden blocks of mahogany, oak and walnut. At one end was a stage for the small orchestra that played for the dancing, alternating with the Wurlitzer organ.

Sally had opted to wear a summery dress that evening as the weather was warmer. As they had travelled to the theatre by taxi and would, presumably, be returning in one, there had been no need for her to wear a coat. Such an article of clothing could be rather a nuisance; it involved leaving it in a cloakroom whilst you were dancing, and then queueing up to retrieve it afterwards, and hoping that you could find the little pink cloakroom ticket. Her dress was one of her favourites, a Horrockses cotton with black and white polka dots on a pink background, with a full skirt and the waistline accentuated by a black shiny belt. With it she wore black patent leather shoes with heels that were suitable for dancing – not too high and not too low – and a small matching black bag, that she could sling over her arm and would not be too intrusive whilst she was dancing, completed her ensemble. Over the dress she was wearing a white lacy cardigan in fine wool that her mother had knitted for her.

The old-time dancing was in full swing when they entered the ballroom. They took to the floor for a military two-step followed by a veleta. She discovered that what Albert had told her was true; he was a very nifty dancer, light on his feet and his lead was easy to follow. By the time they had also danced the 'Gay Gordons' and a Saint Bernard's Waltz, Sally was glad to agree with his suggestion that they should adjourn to a nearby bar for a refreshing drink. She was pleased to see that he ordered a shandy for himself, just a small one, rather than his customary pint of bitter, and so she had the same.

'Well now, are you enjoying yourself?' he asked.

'Yes ... yes, I am, very much,' she replied, smiling at him.

'That's what I like to hear,' said Albert. 'I am too. It's ages since I danced, and I'm pleased to see I've not forgotten any of the steps.'

'I don't think you forget things you learnt in your youth,' said Sally. 'I can't remember when I first learnt to dance; at church hops, I suppose. But they seem ingrained into your memory, like poetry that you learnt at school.'

'Mmm ... yes ... "I wandered lonely as a cloud..."' quoted Albert. 'I left school when I was fourteen, but I can still recite that poem word for word. And we learnt "the quality of mercy is not strained". I remember struggling with that, though, I don't think I can go much further. Shakespeare, isn't it? Though I'm blessed if I can remember which play.'

'*The Merchant of Venice*,' said Sally. 'Yes, we learnt that as well. It's a favourite passage with English teachers.'

'I must bow to your superior knowledge,' said Albert, slowly bowing his head to her.

'I just stayed at school a few years longer, that's all,' said Sally, with a dismissive shrug, 'and I took English at a higher level to get into training college. Anyway, never mind all that... Thank you for suggesting that we came dancing, Albert. It was a jolly good idea.'

She was surprised, indeed, at how much she was enjoying the evening. Albert seemed much more relaxed and at ease with her, as she was beginning to be with him. And the close proximity to him whilst they were dancing hadn't worried her at all. He had, so far, made no move to kiss her good-night when they parted or even to hold her hand. She was wondering how she would feel about that. Most men were inclined to make a move in that direction sooner rather than later. She didn't think she would mind too much.

So when Albert said, 'We must do this again soon, seeing that we are both enjoying it,' she answered quite readily, 'Yes, I would like that.'

'We'll be getting busier at the hotel very soon,' he went on, 'but, as I've said before, the boss has to be allowed some time to himself, and so has my sister, of course, especially now she's got her gentleman friend.'

He explained that their busiest time of the day, as it was in most hotels and boarding houses, was at lunchtime, usually referred to in the north as midday dinner. It was then that they served the main meal of the day. High tea at five-thirty was a much simpler meal.

'So I can usually get away early evening,' Albert explained. 'We will be engaging girls to help with the washing-up, and we have a very competent

168

lady starting soon as a waitress and general help; at least my sister seems very taken with her. She gave us a hand at Easter time, and she's tackling the bookkeeping as well. You probably know her, come to think of it. Mrs Morris – Sadie, she's called – her little girl is in your class with our Kathy.'

'Yes, of course,' said Sally. She smiled. 'As a matter of fact, I already knew about it. There's not much that I don't hear about what goes on at home! Katherine hasn't said anything to me, though, about you and me...' Not that there was much to say yet, she reminded herself. It was early days and she didn't want Albert to think that she was too eager. 'About you winning the raffle prize, I mean,' she said, 'and us having the meal together.'

'I think she feels a bit – oh, I don't know – embarrassed, like, about me going out with her teacher,' said Albert. 'But she'll get used to it in time.' He paused for a moment, looking at her enquiringly. 'We'll still be able to get out and about, dancing or whatever, even during our busy time,' he continued. 'Now, shall we go back to the ballroom if you've finished your drink?'

He was taking a lot for granted, pondered Sally, assuming they would still be friendly come the summertime. This time he tentatively took hold of her hand as they moved back to the dance floor.

The band had now progressed to more modern melodies. The dancers were engaged in a waltz to the tune of 'Faraway Places', which had been a popular song the previous year. As Sally and

Albert joined the dancers the music changed to 'I Wonder Who's Kissing Her Now', and finally, 'You're Breaking My Heart'. They stood and clapped, as did all the other couples, as the band finished on a somewhat discordant crescendo.

When the band started again with 'Slow Boat to China', Sally recognised the rhythm of a slow foxtrot. 'I'm not really very good at this,' she said.

'Oh, come on, let's give it a try,' said Albert. 'Just follow me; it's only walking backwards, really, with one or two twirls.' She found, as she had with the waltz, that she could follow his lead quite easily. He was holding her closer too, and the sensation was not unpleasant. Then the music changed to 'As Time Goes By', a sentimental song from several years ago.

There was a woman vocalist singing about lovers kissing and saying 'I love you', of lovers remaining constant to one another as the years went by, but also of feelings of jealousy and discord. Sally noticed a change come over Albert. She felt his body stiffen and his accurate steps began to stumble. A surreptitious glance at his face, partly turned away from her, showed his mouth set in a grim unsmiling line. She guessed at once that this song must once have meant something to him. Maybe, to him and his wife, it had been 'their song'. She tried to laugh it off.

'I'm not doing very well,' she said. 'I feel as though I've got two left feet. Let's sit this one out, shall we?'

Albert nodded. He took her arm and led her from the floor. They sat in an alcove and he was silent for a few moments. Then, 'I'm sorry, Sally...'

he said. 'It was that song; it brought back memories.'

'I guessed so,' she answered. 'Songs can be so evocative. I've had that feeling myself... I understand.'

He nodded slowly. She wondered if he was about to descend into a black mood of despair. She didn't know him well enough to be aware of his possible highs or lows of temperament. Just as suddenly, though, he glanced across at her and reached for her hand.

'I'm sorry, Sally,' he said again. 'It's been a long time since I heard that song. But, as the words say ... time goes by. It doesn't do any good to live in the past. I've been learning that lately.' He smiled at her then, a half-rueful smile, but she could see, also, the light of a growing affection in his eyes.

'It's time for me to move on,' he said. 'And I'm so glad I've met you, Sally.'

Chapter Twelve

Kathy was feeling very excited. Miss Roberts was coming to the hotel on Saturday night to have a meal that her dad was cooking for them. A special meal, to be eaten when the visitors had all finished their own meal and had gone off to do whatever they wanted to do on a Saturday evening. They were full up with visitors that week, it being the middle of July. Kathy had heard her father and Aunty Win talking about how they were almost fully booked for the rest of the season, and she knew that that was good.

She was now sleeping in one of the attic bedrooms, her favourite room in all the hotel. There were two single beds in the room, which left space for not much else besides: a small wardrobe, an even smaller dressing table, and the washstand with the bowl and jug, not forgetting the pot that Aunty Win called the 'gazunder'.

Another exciting thing was that the grown-ups had agreed that Shirley could spend the night in the attic room with Kathy occasionally, as a special treat. Mrs Morris had been working at Holmleigh for quite a while now, as a waitress and general help, as well as helping with what Aunty Win called 'the books'. Her times had to be fitted around her husband's shifts. Mr Morris was a bus driver; he drove one of the cream and green Blackpool buses, and did not always work the same hours each day. Shirley had told Kathy that her mum and dad had had quite a few arguments about it.

'He doesn't really like Mum working at your hotel at all,' she said. 'But she's not taking much notice of him. She says she enjoys it, and she likes being able to earn some money of her own again. And so long as me and our Graham and our Brenda aren't being neglected, then she says she's going to carry on doing it. And it'll be great soon, won't it, when it's the summer holidays an' I can come with her?'

'Yes, and your Brenda as well,' Kathy had reminded her.

'Mmm ... yes. Well, we'll have to look after her,

I suppose,' Shirley frowned. 'She can be a bit of a pest, but she's all right, really. She'll have to do as she's told, though; I won't stand for any non-sense!'

All this would be happening in a few weeks' time, but first of all there was the meal to look forward to. It was going to be something of an occasion, or 'a bit of a do', as she had heard her dad say. Aunty Win's new friend was invited as well – Mr Bancroft, the man that her aunty had met at the drama group. He had been to their hotel a few times and Kathy liked him very much. He had said she could call him Jeff, but Aunty Win had decided that 'Uncle Jeff' would be better. Kathy liked that because she didn't have any real uncles. But the best thing was that Miss Roberts was having a proper meal there for the very first time, and she, Kathy, as a special treat, was being allowed to stay up and dine with them.

She knew that her dad and her teacher had been going out together for quite a while now; but Kathy also knew that they didn't really want it to be talked about. Her dad had put a finger to his lips and said 'shhh...' in a mysterious sort of way. So she hadn't even told Shirley about it; she would only go and blab it all over the playground. She supposed everybody would soon know, though, if they kept on going out together. Anyway, she wouldn't be in Miss Roberts' class much longer, so it wouldn't matter as much. In September she and Shirley and Timothy and all of them would be moving up into the juniors.

She kept wondering what it would be like if her dad were to marry Miss Roberts. Because that was what people did, didn't they, when they'd been going out together for a while? Then, she pondered, Miss Roberts would be her mum ... sort of. That was a very strange thought. She liked her teacher ever such a lot; she loved her, she supposed, nearly as much as she loved her daddy and Aunty Win, but it would be a very odd state of affairs.

And what about her Aunty Win and Mr Bancroft, Uncle Jeff? Would they be too old to get married, she wondered? She knew that her aunt was a few years older than her father, and he seemed a lot older than some of her friends' fathers. And where would they all live if such a thing were to happen? Uncle Jeff had a house of his own, and she knew that Miss Roberts lived with her mum and dad. And another very exciting thing was that her dad was talking about buying a car...

Winifred had been surprised at the change in her brother since he had started seeing Sally Roberts. He was happier in himself, much more amicable towards her and Kathy, friendly and unusually jolly with the hotel guests; all in all, much easier to get along with. He seemed to have shed several years. He was no longer a middle-aged man, which was the impression he had once given, but a young – well, youngish – man, enjoying life to the full.

It was his awakened interest in ballroom dancing that had been the main reason for his changed outlook on life, besides, of course, his friendship with Sally Roberts. Winifred remembered how he and Barbara had enjoyed their visits to the Tower and Winter Gardens, and sometimes to the Palace. He had not danced at all since he had lost Barbara, and Winifred had thought that that was something he would never want to do again. He had admitted to her, however – amazingly – that he had been wrong, that life had to go on, and, although he hadn't actually said as much, she guessed that he was hopeful that he had found someone with whom he might share his future life.

But how did Sally feel about it? Winifred wondered. Although she, Winifred, had encouraged him to ask the young lady out in the first place, she had feared afterwards that Sally might well bring the friendship to an end almost as soon as it had started. But this had not happened. Sally appeared to enjoy his company and especially to take pleasure in their visits to the Palace ballroom. They went there once a week – usually, though not always, on a Saturday, following a visit to the cinema or the variety show.

It was ironic, Winifred thought, after all the time that she and Albert had remained in their single status, that they should both, now, have found someone that they cared about. Her own friendship with Jeff Bancroft was progressing steadily. It was widely recognised now, by their friends at the drama group, that Jeff and Winifred were keeping company, or 'courting', to use the old-fashioned phrase.

They met on other occasions as well as the drama rehearsals, although their meetings had to be fitted around the workings of the hotel and now, of course, around the times that Albert wanted to spend with Sally. One thing that she and her brother had agreed was that Kathy had to be given priority. She must never be made to feel that the grown-ups were having to curtail their pleasures to attend to her needs. It was happening quite often now that she and Jeff would stay in on a Saturday night, enjoying a cosy evening listening to the wireless or gramophone records whilst Albert and Sally were out dancing. They would have supper together when they had attended to the visitors' requests. Then, at about eleven o'clock he would kiss her goodnight and depart for his own home.

His kisses had been chaste at first, now they were loving and were gradually becoming more amorous in nature. It felt strange – strange but pleasurable – to Winifred, who had not experienced the love of a man for so long. She wondered, and worried a little at times, how it would be if Jeff should become more ardent.

And how did Kathy feel about all that was going on around her? Winifred wondered. The little girl seemed contented enough, but who could tell what was really going on in that little mind of hers? Winifred noticed she had been a good deal more thoughtful recently. She had taken a liking to Jeff, which pleased Winifred, and he obviously enjoyed being with Kathy. She had been out with them once or twice at weekends. Jeff had driven the car northwards to Cleveleys, or south to St Annes; they had enjoyed a walk on the promenade and eaten ice creams, just like holiday-makers. Jeff had grandchildren of his own, rather younger than Katherine. His son in Canada and

176

his daughter who lived in Exeter each had two children, and it was a great regret to Jeff that he didn't see them more often. There was a baby grandson in Montreal whom he had not yet seen, and a two-year-old granddaughter he had only seen once. So Katherine, it seemed, was something of a compensation to him, and Winifred could foresee no complications should their relationship progress further. She did not, however, allow herself to think too much about what might happen. There was many a slip ... she told herself.

Albert had told Sally that the meal would be served at about seven o'clock. When she arrived at six-thirty Winifred greeted her with a glass of sherry, then Winifred and her gentleman friend, Jeff, and Sally chatted together at one end of the family living room whilst Albert was busy in the adjoining kitchen.

The family living quarters were rather limited, especially during the holiday season when the visitors took up nearly the whole of the house. The living room, however, was large, as it had to act as a dining room and sitting room as well. The table was already set at one end of the room, with a snowy-white cloth and gleaming silver cutlery. Albert popped out of the kitchen in his blue and white striped apron to say hello, and then disappeared again.

'He says that he's in complete charge of the meal this evening,' said Winifred, 'and it's my job to do the entertaining. We're very pleased to have you here, Sally. You've met my friend, Jeff Bancroft, haven't you?' They shook hands again, although Sally had met him before, briefly.

Sally was glad she hadn't dressed up too much. It was, after all, only a casual sort of family meal. She was wearing a shirtwaister dress in blue and white candy striped cotton, with a white square collar and white cuffs to the elbow-length sleeves. Winifred, also, was wearing a summery dress in green spotted rayon, and Jeff had taken off his jacket, revealing a blue short-sleeved shirt and a gaily striped tie.

'You look very nice, Miss Roberts,' said Kathy shyly.

'Thank you, Kathy,' said Sally. 'I don't wear this dress at school,' she added confidingly. 'It's one of my best ones.'

'Yes, you might get it all mucked up with paint, mightn't you?' said Kathy.

Sally laughed. 'Yes, that's true... You look very nice as well, dear.' The little girl's dress was bright red and she had matching ribbons that went well with her dark hair and eyes. Sally felt a bit awkward at being addressed as Miss Roberts, but she couldn't very well invite the child to call her Sally. It would be better to leave things as they were. Kathy seemed to have the sense to make the distinction between Sally as her teacher and as her father's lady friend – if that was what she was! – and to keep the identities separate.

The meal was Albert's cooking at its best, although he had not served anything too extra-ordinary. They started with prawn cocktails, and the main course was roast chicken. The large bird provided each person with white breast meat and dark meat from the plump legs. Sally was impressed by the roast potatoes that were crisped and browned to perfection. (Sally's mother was a good cook, but even she did not get them quite so tasty.) Brussels sprouts, diced carrots and garden peas, with sage and onion stuffing and rich gravy complemented the excellent meal. The sweet was a simple one, fresh strawberries with caster sugar and ice cream, mainly for Kathy's benefit.

'I'm so full up I think I might burst!' the little girl exclaimed at the end of the meal. She seemed to have forgotten her previous shyness.

'That's not terribly polite, Kathy,' laughed her aunt, 'but I think we all probably feel much the same way. Thank you, Albert, for such a lovely meal.'

He grinned. 'All in a day's work.'

'You must have been very busy today, though,' remarked Sally, 'with the visitors and everything else.'

'Oh, Saturday's not too bad really, as far as the cooking's concerned,' he answered. 'It's change-over day – you know, one lot of visitors leaving and the next lot arriving – so we don't provide a midday meal, and we try to make the high tea a simple one. We have two women who come in to change the bedding in the morning, and make everything shipshape... And as for the washing-up tonight, that's all taken care of. Kathy's going to do it for us!'

The little girl's mouth dropped open with surprise as she stared at Albert. 'I didn't know that, Daddy!'

He laughed. 'I'm only joking, love. That worried you for a minute, didn't it?' Sally wondered if, maybe, Albert didn't joke with his daughter very often. He wasn't really the most jocular of men.

'We'll see to all the washing-up in the morning,' he went on. 'Get up extra early, eh, Winnie?'

'I expect so,' she agreed. 'Now, Sally and Jeff, you go and sit down and my brother and I will clear away, then we'll have some coffee. And you, Kathy love, you'll have to go to bed soon, when your dinner has digested.'

Kathy asked Sally, still rather shyly, if she would read her a bedtime story. 'Aunty Win and me, we're reading *Milly-Molly-Mandy*,' she said. 'Well, I can read most of it myself, but it's nice to read it together.'

'I'd love to,' agreed Sally. So when Kathy was in her pyjamas and in bed they read the book together.

'Thank you...' said Kathy when they finished the story; she didn't call her Miss Roberts that time. 'I won't tell any of the others about this...' she added in a confidential whisper.

'That's all right, dear,' said Sally. 'I don't suppose it matters, but it can be our secret.'

She felt a tear come into her eye as she kissed the little girl's cheek. 'Goodnight, Kathy love. Sleep tight...' She was really getting very fond of the child.

After they had enjoyed a cup of coffee it was decided that the four of them should play a game of Monopoly. Sally couldn't remember afterwards whose suggestion it had been in the first place. She rather thought it was Albert's, which was ironic considering the way things turned out.

She was soon to see a different side to him, one

that she had not hitherto suspected. It soon became clear that Albert liked to win. If things were not going his way, then he could easily become frustrated and peevish. She had often seen children – more particularly boys – in the playground behaving in a similar manner. If they lost control of the football or failed to win a race some were liable to go off in a tizzy. It was excusable in children; it was all part of the growing-up process and they usually grew out of it. But in a man it was really rather reprehensible.

'I'm afraid my brother takes it all too seriously,' Winifred whispered to Sally, when Albert got a 'Go to Jail' card for the second time and had to miss another turn. 'He regards himself as quite an expert at Monopoly.'

'But it's a game of chance, surely?' said Sally. 'It all depends on the fall of the dice, doesn't it?'

'I suppose there's a certain skill involved in buying the property,' said Winifred, 'but I've always regarded it as fun. It's not real money, is it? But the way Albert behaves you'd think he was really going bankrupt!'

'What are you two whispering about?' he asked then, a trifle snappily, although he was trying to smile.

'Nothing,' replied Winifred. 'Come along, it's your turn now, brother dear.'

Things went from bad to worse for Albert. He was cock-a-hoop when he managed to buy houses, then hotels, on Park Lane, but was soon to lose all his wealth to Jeff who was gradually sweeping the board.

Albert was the first out of the game and almost

threw, rather than handed, his little red hotels and the remainder of his paper money to Jeff.

'Bad luck, Albert,' said Sally, trying to make a joke of it. 'Never mind, you've got a real hotel, haven't you? It's only a game, but you were unlucky.'

'Yes, so unlucky that he can now go and do the washing-up,' said his sister, who was obviously not too pleased at his behaviour.

'Huh! You must be joking!' he retorted. 'I'm going to read the newspaper.'

'All right, suit yourself,' said Winifred. 'Come on, Sally. Let's see if we can get some of Jeff's hotels off him. He's having too much of his own way.'

Jeff grinned good-humouredly. Sally couldn't imagine him ever behaving so childishly as Albert was doing, should the game have gone the other way. He seemed, altogether, a splendid sort of fellow, and just right for Winifred.

Albert seemed to think better of his conduct in a little while. He put down his newspaper and went towards the kitchen. 'I'll see to the washing-up,' he said, 'then we won't have to bother with it in the morning.' He sounded almost apologetic and managed a sheepish smile in Sally's direction.

'Good!' said his sister, quite curtly.

The outcome of the game was a foregone conclusion. Jeff won hands down, just as Albert emerged from the kitchen having completed his chore. It was just turned eleven-thirty. The game had taken more than two hours, which was not really long compared with some marathons;

182

Monopoly could sometimes continue on to the early hours, or even be postponed to the next day.

'I think it's time to call it a day now,' said Jeff. 'I'm thinking of you good people who have to be up to get the visitors' breakfasts.'

'Yes, that's true,' said Winifred, trying to hide a yawn. 'It's been a good evening, hasn't it? It's been lovely having you here, Sally. We must do this again sometime.'

'Yes...' said Sally, though not overenthusiastically. 'Thank you very much for the meal ... and everything. I've enjoyed it.'

'I'll run you home, Sally, if you like,' said Jeff. She lived not too far from his home near Gynn Square. 'Unless...?' He looked enquiringly at Albert.

'Yes ... thank you, Jeff,' replied Sally hastily. 'It's OK, Albert. I wouldn't expect you to walk back with me when I can go with Jeff. You need your beauty sleep!' she quipped. The truth was that she had seen enough of him for the time being.

'All right, then, if you're sure,' said Albert. He kissed her briefly on the cheek. 'Goodnight, Sally. See you soon...'

Jeff kissed Winifred, a little more lovingly, Sally noticed. They didn't say much on the journey home as Jeff was concentrating on the busy road; it was closing time at the pubs.

Sally was thoughtful. If Albert could behave in such a way over a game, then how might he react if things did not go his own way in real life? And there was another consideration. She had enjoyed the evening, but all of them, Albert, Wini-

183

fred and Jeff, were several years older than herself. She didn't want to grow old before her time. She realised it was mainly her own fault for carrying on seeing Albert for so long. It might be difficult now to make a break.

Chapter Thirteen

School had broken up and five glorious weeks of freedom lay ahead. Even though Sally loved her job she was not sorry to be having a break from both the children and the other teachers.

Her relations with Phil Grantley had remained cordial; but she had been surprised to learn, about a fortnight before the end of term, that Phil had found 'other fish to fry', to coin a phrase. It was her colleague, Joyce, who had told her that he was now seeing Fiona, the newest teacher to join the infant staff about a year ago. Sally remembered telling Phil that Fiona was a member of a local rambling club. Now it appeared that he, too, had joined the group and that the two of them, with the rest of the club, were going on a week's rambling holiday in the Lake District. It hadn't taken him long, Sally mused, to transfer his interest in her to someone else. She had to admit that she felt a little peeved, although she knew she had no reason to feel that way. It was her own admission that she was seeing someone else that had caused Phil to look elsewhere.

As for Sally, she was still seeing Albert, when he

was able to be absent from the hotel. She felt that he was getting keener and was regarding her now, quite openly, as his lady friend; whereas she, Sally, was not so sure that she wanted things between them to get too serious. Following his show of peevishness during the game of Monopoly he had tried to be more amenable and not to show himself up again, although he had, of course, not referred to the incident since.

He had now bought a motor car, a Ford Prefect about two years old, so they no longer needed to rely on taxis when they went out together.

'Will you be able to drive it?' Sally had asked. She knew he had never owned a car.

'Yes, of course,' he had replied. 'Actually, I already have a licence and I can soon brush up on my driving skills. I learnt to drive my father's car before I was twenty. You didn't need a licence in those days, but I got one as soon as it became compulsory – in 1935, I think it was.'

It turned out that Albert was a competent driver. Sally enjoyed, most of all, the times when Kathy went out with them. They had driven out into the countryside and picnicked by the banks of the River Wyre at St Michael's, or by the stream at Nicky Nook, a favourite beauty spot not far from Blackpool.

Kathy was more at ease with her now when they were not at school, and she no longer referred to her as Miss Roberts. She didn't actually call her anything on those occasions, but the feeling of affection and warmth between her and the child was growing. Sally wondered if Albert was now regarding her almost as a substitute mother for the little girl. Winifred had formerly assumed that role and was still doing so; but Sally speculated as to what would happen if Winifred should marry her friend, Jeff. This was seeming more and more likely from hints that Albert had dropped.

And Sally had seen for herself how proud Jeff had been of Winifred when they had attended the performance of *The Importance of Being Earnest*, just before the end of the school term. Kathy hadn't understood all the action of the play, but had enjoyed seeing her aunt in such a very different guise. The two young ladies in the cast, Gwendolen and Cecily, were presented with bouquets of flowers by the stage manager; but it was Jeff, in his capacity as ASM, who presented the bouquet to Winifred, Lady Bracknell. He kissed her lovingly, seemingly not caring about who was watching, and his regard and affection for her were clear to everyone as he stood beside her on the stage.

Drama meetings ceased during the month of August, but Jeff and Winifred were still very much together. Sally watched Albert becoming more and more concerned.

'I rely on Winnie so much in the hotel,' he told her. 'We're a good partnership, our Winnie and me. Of course, she's a perfect right to please herself whatever she does, and if she wants to set up house with Jeff Bancroft – if they get wed, of course – then I suppose there's nowt ... er... nothing I can do about it. I know it'd be a wrench to her, though, if she had to leave our little Kathy.'

Sally was relieved that she would be getting

away from Blackpool for a week during the school holidays. Following on from her night school class in French conversation, she was joining a group of the students who had decided to test their prowess in the language by spending some time in France; they had booked places on a coach tour to Normandy and Brittany. Joyce, Sally's colleague from school, was going as well. The two of them had become quite friendly recently. Joyce was a few years younger than Sally, but was the nearest one in age to her on the infant staff. She was married, but there were no children as yet, and she had said she would be pleased to accompany Sally, especially as her husband would be away on a fishing trip that week. They would be sharing a room during what looked like being quite a hectic few days of travelling from one resort to another.

'I shall miss you,' Albert told Sally. 'I can't remember the last time I had a holiday.' He sounded a little put out. 'Perhaps we could manage a few days away – just you and me, eh – when it's your next half-term holiday? The Lights will have finished then and all the visitors gone home. What do you reckon to that?'

'I don't really know, Albert,' said Sally rather evasively. 'I shall need to think about it.'

'Well, give it some thought while you're away... And don't forget to send us a postcard. Kathy's going to miss you as well, aren't you, love?'

Kathy nodded. 'Yes, I will,' she said. 'But I shall be busy. Shirley's here with her mum, you know, during the holidays, and we're looking after little Brenda, Shirley and me.'

'Oh yes, I remember,' smiled Sally. 'I'll send a postcard for you and Shirley, then, shall I?'

'Yes, that'll be nice,' agreed Kathy.

It was good fun having Shirley with her, and Brenda as well. They spent a good deal of the time in Kathy's room up in the attic, playing games or crayoning, or looking at books. They were allowed to play in the backyard if the weather was fine, skipping or playing with balls or whips and tops. They couldn't play out in the street, not with Brenda, because of the traffic.

The first two weeks were quite fine, then on the third week it started to rain. It was the week that Miss Roberts – or Sally, which was how Kathy now thought of her – was away. She hoped that the weather was nice and sunny in France.

'I'm bored!' said Shirley, when they had played Snakes and Ladders and tiddlywinks, and gone through their pile of comics. 'What can we do, Kathy? You think of something.'

'I don't know,' said Kathy. 'I'm helping Brenda to colour in this picture.'

'Oh, never mind her,' said Shirley. It was something she said quite often, leaving most of the looking after Brenda to Kathy, who really didn't mind at all.

Shirley stood up on the bed that Kathy slept on and started jumping up and down. 'It's dead springy, your mattress,' she said. 'Come on, Kathy; let's see who can jump the highest.'

'No! I'm not supposed to jump on it,' said Kathy. 'It's quite a new one, and Aunty Win says it'll damage the springs.'

''Course it won't!' retorted Shirley. 'Is the other

bed the same?' She took a flying leap from one bed to the other – there was a space of about two feet between them – then started to jump on the opposite bed. 'Yes, it's just as springy. Come on, Kathy. Don't be such a baby! I know... Let's pretend it's a river and we've got to jump from one bank to the other. Your Aunty Win'll never know. She's busy in the kitchen, isn't she?'

Kathy knew she shouldn't, but her friend was so bossy and she hated being called a baby. Somewhat reluctantly she climbed onto the bed and jumped across to the other one.

'I know...' said Shirley. 'You jump one way an' I'll jump the other way, then we'll cross in midstream. Mind you don't fall in or you'll get wet.' Actually, Kathy thought it was a pretty daft sort of game and she hoped her friend would soon get tired of it.

'Let me! Let me!' shouted Brenda. Before Kathy could stop her she had clambered onto the bed.

'No ... don't!' yelled Kathy, but it was too late. The child took a leap, as she had seen the bigger girls do, landing with a loud bump on the floor between the beds. 'Ow! Ow!' she cried. 'My leg, my leg, it hurts!'

The two friends looked at one another in horror then rushed to her side. She had landed with her leg bent underneath her. She yelled even more when Shirley tried to straighten her leg.

'Stop it! Stop it! You're hurting me. I want my mummy...' The child burst into tears.

'You'd better go and get your aunty, and my mum as well, I suppose,' said Shirley in a whisper.

189

'She's going to be dead mad with me... Don't cry, Brenda. It'll be all right.'

Kathy dashed down several flights of stairs and along the passage to the kitchen. Her father and aunt were both in there. 'Aunty Win,' she called. 'Can you come? Brenda's hurt her leg.'

'Yes, of course,' said her aunt. 'We'd better tell Sadie – Mrs Morris – as well; she's setting the tables. What was Brenda doing, anyway, to hurt her leg?'

'She was jumping,' said Kathy, a little sheepishly. 'She fell off the bed.'

'I see,' said her aunt, looking rather stern. 'Well, we'd better go and get Brenda's mummy, hadn't we?'

Mrs Morris was in the dining room setting the tables with the cutlery needed for the midday meal and tidying up the napkins.

'I'm afraid Brenda's had a little accident,' said Kathy's aunt. At the look of consternation on the woman's face she hurried on to say, 'It's all right; nothing too bad as far as I can make out. Kathy says she's hurt her leg.'

'Oh dear!' Sadie Morris put down the serviette she was folding and followed Kathy and her aunt out of the door and up the stairs. 'I don't know what my husband will say,' Kathy could hear her muttering. 'Well, actually, I do know. He was dead against me bringing her here; he expects me to be watching her every minute of the day.'

Brenda started crying again as soon as she saw her mother. 'Mummy, Mummy! My leg hurts. Make it better!'

She didn't cry out in pain this time as Mrs

Morris gently straightened out her leg and felt tentatively at the ankle. 'You're alright, darling,' she said. 'No bones broken as far as I can see. I think you've sprained your ankle.'

'I'll get some cold water and a bandage,' said Winifred, who had a little first-aid knowledge, as had Mrs Morris. The ankle was bathed and bandaged, and Brenda did not complain too much, although she couldn't put any weight on her foot. There was no word of recrimination at first, then Mrs Morris turned to question her shamefaced daughter.

'Whatever were you doing, Shirley, to let her fall? I told you to look after her.'

'We were jumping off the beds, that's all,' said Shirley, a trifle belligerently. 'It wasn't my fault. Kathy said we could.'

Kathy was shocked at her friend's betrayal, especially as it had been Shirley's idea. 'It wasn't my fault either!' she retorted. 'But I'm very sorry, Mrs Morris.'

'That's all right, dear,' the lady replied. 'It could have been worse.'

'I think you'd better let the doctor have a look at her, just to be on the safe side,' said Aunty Win. 'You can go now if you like.'

'No, thanks... I'll stay and finish my shift,' she replied. 'I'll call on my way home. Oh dear! Brenda won't be able to walk, will she?'

'Don't worry – Albert will run you to the doctor's,' said Winifred, 'and then take you home. It's the least we can do. Now, young lady, you'd better sit quietly in a big chair in the living room, seeing as you're a wounded soldier!'

Her mother carried her downstairs, with Kathy and Shirley, rather subdued, following behind. They all had their dinner after the visitors had been served, and when the washing-up was done, Albert took Brenda and her mother to the doctor's surgery.

'She was very worried about what her husband's going to say,' Albert told his sister later that day as they were preparing the salads for the teatime meal. 'From what I gather, things are not too rosy there. I wouldn't be surprised if we lose Sadie before very long. You'll have to be prepared for her giving notice, Winnie.'

'Yes, I can see the way things are,' agreed Winifred. 'Mr Morris'll have even more of an axe to grind now, won't he? I bet it was Shirley at the root of this, though Kathy won't say very much. She's a loyal little soul. She's very upset about it, so I haven't been too cross with her. But I saw the look on her face when Shirley tried to blame her. She's a bit of a minx, that Shirley... Mind you, I don't think Sadie's helping matters at home much either. I don't like saying this, but I've noticed she's got rather too friendly with Barry Proctor. He was here at Easter, if you remember, and I thought then that they were getting on very well together. And now he's here again. I was quite surprised, I must admit, when he booked up for another week.'

'Hmm... It doesn't take some fellows long to forget, does it?' remarked Albert. Barry Proctor, with his wife, had visited Holmleigh on a few occasions. Then two years ago Barry had written with the sad news that Joan had died following a

192

bad attack of flu, but that he would still be spending his summer holidays at Holmleigh. He enjoyed the seasonal variety shows in Blackpool, and the bracing winds and clean fresh sea air, a far cry from the rather grimy town of Burnley where he was an overseer in a mill.

'His wife's hardly cold in her grave,' Albert went on. 'I thought he was devoted to her, but it just goes to show... Mind you, I blame the women for doing the chasing. I'd have thought better of Sadie Morris, though...'

'We can't condemn her when we don't know all the facts,' said Winifred. 'Anyway, it isn't our place to act as judge and jury. I hope she's not acting foolishly, though, more for the sake of the children than anything.'

Albert didn't answer. His sister knew he wasn't in the best of humours that week with Sally being away in France.

Mrs Morris arrived the next morning without Brenda. 'My dad says Brenda can't come here anymore,' Shirley told Kathy. 'He was dead mad with my mum, far more mad than he was with me, and they had an awful row. He didn't want mummy to come either, but she said she had to, and he hadn't to try and stop her.'

'So where's Brenda, then?' asked Kathy.

'She's next door with Mrs Murray. She said she'll look after her, because she's got a little girl the same age, so they can play together. I don't think she'll do it every day, though, so I don't know what's going to happen.'

'What shall we play, then?' asked Kathy. 'We

mustn't do any more jumping!'

'I know, I know!' snapped Shirley. They started a big jigsaw of circus clowns, and when they tired of that they each read an Enid Blyton book. But Kathy knew they were not getting on as well as they used to do.

Things went from bad to worse. It was on Saturday morning, changeover day, that Sadie arrived in a very agitated state.

'I can't come anymore,' she told Winifred. 'I can't even work my notice. I'm really sorry to leave you in the lurch like this, but I can't carry on with the waitressing and helping in the hotel. I'll still do the books for you, just for the moment; I don't see how Frank can object to that, but I don't know for how long...'

She explained that her son, Graham, had fallen in the sea the previous day and had to be rescued by a holidaymaker. He had been brought home drenched and frightened, and her husband, understandably, had hit the roof. Graham had gone to the beach with his friend Jimmy, with whom he had been spending most of his time. They had been given strict instructions not to go near the sea, but boys would be boys. Graham had protested that they were only paddling, but a big wave had swept him off his feet.

'Oh, goodness me! That's bad news,' said Winifred, 'and for Graham as well, of course. Is he all right now?'

'He's fine,' said Sadie. 'But I've got to stay at home and see to them now. I daren't do anything else under the circumstances. I'm really sorry, Winifred...'

Winifred noticed, though, that she went to find Barry Proctor before he started on his journey home to Burnley.

Chapter Fourteen

Sally was enjoying herself in France. Whether or not her French conversation was improving was beside the point – they spoke so fast that it was hard to understand them, let alone converse with them! – but it was turning out to be a jolly good holiday. They travelled by coach, then by the Channel ferry. Their first stopping place was Dieppe. From there they visited the Normandy beaches, renowned, not all that long ago, for the D-Day landings, and the picturesque old town of Rouen where Joan of Arc was martyred. Then they moved on to Brittany to stay two nights in the fishing port of St Malo, and lastly in the medieval town of Dinan. They were enchanted by this quaint place with its stone ramparts and wood-fronted houses leaning crazily towards one another across the narrow streets.

They were enjoying the different sights and sounds and smells – a mixture of Gauloises cigarettes and fragrant coffee – of a foreign country. Although it was so near to England, it seemed so very far away. Possibly, above all, they were savouring the tastes of France. The country seemed to have recovered from the restrictions of wartime. They dined on pancakes – crêpes –

served as a savoury dish with scrambled egg, ham and cheese or meat, or as a dessert with fruit, ice cream or chocolate; the fish and seafood – monkfish, red mullet or John Dory – fish they had never encountered at home; or the speciality of Brittany, the *plateau de fruits de mer*, an assortment of exotic sea creatures served on a bed of seaweed. This last creation they only looked at in shop windows, but were not brave – or rich – enough to try. The sweets were their downfall, though; eclairs topped with coffee cream, chocolate gateaux, and featherlight sponges flavoured with Grand Marnier and served with almonds, fruit and cream.

Sally and Joyce had grown closer to one another that week, away from the strictures of the classroom. On their last evening they sat at a pavement café on the long street that led down to the quayside, enjoying the rich dark coffee they had grown accustomed to, and a bottle of Muscadet, the favourite drink of Bretons.

'It's been a good week,' said Sally. 'Thank you for coming with me, Joyce; I've enjoyed your company.'

'Likewise,' answered Joyce. 'There's not much time at school, is there, to socialise? I didn't realise until now that you and me ... well, that we could be such good friends. I mean, you're older than me and...'

'Don't rub it in!' laughed Sally. 'Yes, I do know what you mean, but age shouldn't really make a great deal of difference. Anyway, here's to us...' She raised her glass. And to our new-found friendship.' They clinked glasses and smiled at one another. 'I expect your husband will be glad to see you home again, though, won't he?'

'Yes, he will,' agreed Joyce. 'It'll be nice to see Roger again, I must admit. Although it doesn't do any harm to have some time apart now and again. It helps to stimulate the relationship. I expect Albert will be missing you too, won't he?'

Word had gradually got round the staffroom that Sally was seeing Mr Leigh, the father of one of the girls in her class, but, to her surprise, little had been said about it, in her hearing at least. Sally sighed.

'Yes, I daresay he'll be missing me... I'm not sure that I can really say the same myself, though.' She decided that she would like to confide in Joyce; she had not, so far, talked about Albert to anyone.

Her parents had met him and appeared to like him, but they had kept their own counsel, probably thinking that she was old enough and wise enough to know her own mind. But did she? That was the problem. She liked Albert; they got on well together for the most part. She knew he could be moody at times and liked things his own way, but she told herself that nobody was perfect. She guessed that since he had met her he had, in a sense, recaptured some of his youth; she was thinking in particular of the ballroom dancing. But she predicted that, should they embark on a more permanent relationship, he might revert to being set in his ways, to being as intransigent and unbending as she guessed he had been in the past. Winifred had remarked to her that there had been a big change in her brother since the two of them had been friendly. But, she reminded herself, he was eleven years older than she was...

'Why?' asked Joyce, in answer to Sally's remark. 'Don't you get on well with him? I met Mr Leigh when Kathy was in my class, and I can't help wondering... I mean, he seemed such a morose sort of chap. No, that's very unfair of me.' She shook her head. 'I don't really know him, do I? You don't need to tell me anything if you don't want to. It's none of my business, is it?'

'But I'd like to tell you,' said Sally. 'Yes, we're OK together; he's not really such a sobersides when you get to know him. I've got on with him much better than I expected to. I didn't mean it to carry on so long but ... well ... it has done. And now, you see, he's getting keener, wanting to see me more often and ... everything. And I don't really think that's what I want.'

'Then you'll have to tell him, won't you?' replied Joyce. 'Before he "pops the question", as they used to say.'

'Mmm... I suspect that might be in his mind, even though I've only known him for – what? – about five months. And I can't help thinking that he may well be wanting a mother figure for Kathy. Her aunt's always been like a mother to her, and she still is. Winifred's a wonderful person; I like her very much. But I think it's quite likely that she'll be getting married herself, so she may no longer be there to see to Kathy. I don't know, of course, but it's looking as though it might happen. I'm very fond of little Kathy; I always was, and she's grown closer to me since I've been seeing her dad.'

'Yes, she's a lovely little girl,' agreed Joyce. 'She was in my class, as you know, before she moved up, to you. I never felt she was any worse off, not having a mother; far happier, in fact, than she might have been in some of the homes I can think of. Is she still friendly with Shirley Morris?'

'Oh yes, they're bosom pals. Shirley's inclined to be bossy, as you probably know, but I think Kathy's learning to hold her own... Yes, I think you're right, Joyce. I shall have to tell Albert that there's not much point in us going on seeing one another. I don't mind being friendly with him, but I don't want it to go any further. I would like to get married one day, I suppose. Maybe have children of my own, if I don't leave it too late. 'That's another issue; I doubt that Albert would want any more children...' She was silent for a moment, deep in thought.

'I lost my fiancé, Martin, during the Battle of Britain,' she went on, 'and there's never really been anyone else since then that I could feel the same way about. I know that I don't love Albert, so it wouldn't be right, would it, for either of us?'

'No, it wouldn't, if you want my honest opinion,' said Joyce. 'I had heard that you lost someone during the war; I'm sorry about that... Weren't you getting friendly with Phil Grantley, not so long ago? I know some of the staff thought so – you know how they can gossip at times – and then he started seeing Fiona Wilson.'

'Yes, we were friendly; in fact, I thought at one time that it was really going somewhere. To be quite honest, I think I was on the way to falling in love with him, then it all seemed to go wrong. I suppose I went on seeing Albert on the rebound. The first time Phil asked me to go out on what you might call a proper date, I had already promised to go out with Albert, so that was that. Then, as you say, he started seeing Fiona...'

'Never mind, Sally,' said Joyce. 'There's more fish in the sea.'

'That's what I keep telling myself,' replied Sally. 'But why won't a prize catch swim my way?' She laughed. 'Thanks for listening to me. I know now what I have to do. I can't let it drag on any longer... I suppose we'd better be heading back, hadn't we? We've a long journey ahead of us tomorrow.'

It was hard to tell whether Albert had anticipated Sally's news that she didn't want to go on seeing him.

He had phoned her at home soon after she had arrived back and she had agreed to go out with him the following evening; but just for a quiet drink, she had said, not to the cinema or to go dancing. He had kissed her eagerly when she got into the car, but she could not respond to his ardour.

She told him almost as soon as they had ordered their drinks and sat down in the lounge bar of the Cliffs Hotel.

'I like you very much, Albert,' she told him, 'and I've enjoyed our times together, but it wouldn't be fair to go on seeing you.' She explained that, although she had grown fond of him, she didn't love him, and that rather than get more involved with him – which she felt was what he wanted – it would be better for them to part.

'But I think I love you, Sally,' he protested. She noticed that he had said only that he thought he loved her. 'And I've never loved anyone else, not since I lost Barbara. I really thought we might have something good.' He looked so disappointed and dejected that she felt sorry for him. 'But I suppose it was too much to hope for. I'm too old for you, Sally. That's the problem, isn't it? You want somebody more lively and go-ahead, not an old stick-in-the-mud like me.'

'But you're not like that,' she insisted. 'It's not the age difference, not really. I just feel that – in the end – it wouldn't work.'

'Fair enough,' he mumbled. 'I suppose I should have seen it coming. Kathy's going to be disappointed, I know that. She's got used to you coming round. She thinks the world of you, you know.'

'Yes, I suppose so, but I've told you how young children get attached to their infant teachers. I'm very fond of Kathy too. But I shall still see her at school, even though she won't be in my class.'

'Poor Kathy!' Albert shook his head. 'She's got another shock coming as well. She's about to lose her best friend, Shirley.'

'Why? Whatever has happened?' asked Sally. 'Shirley's not ill, is she?'

'On no, it's nothing like that. You know that Sadie Morris has been helping us at the hotel, and Shirley and her little sister were coming along to play with Kathy?' Sally nodded. 'Well, there was a bit of trouble; the little girl had an accident – nothing serious – but the father was furious. And then, to make matters worse, the next day the boy, Graham, fell in the sea.'

'Oh, goodness me! Is he all right?'

'Yes, he's fine. But Mr Morris hit the roof, understandably, I suppose. He had never wanted his wife to work for us in the first place. So the upshot of it is that he's forbidden Sadie to come anymore. Kathy knows about that, but what she doesn't know yet is that Mrs Morris is leaving her husband and taking the children to live with her parents in Southport.'

'Good gracious! That's a drastic step,' said Sally. 'Is it for good, or have they just had a tiff?'

'Rather more than a tiff. Sadie came round to tell Winnie about it this morning. She and her husband have had no end of a bust-up; apparently things have not been too good for a while. So she's off at the end of the week, to Southport. I think she's hoping to get a job there, and her mother will look after the children.'

'That's bad news,' said Sally. 'Poor Shirley ... and her brother and sister as well, of course. I hope they manage to sort things out and get back together.'

'Well, that remains to be seen,' said Albert. 'I'm afraid Sadie has got rather too friendly with one of our visitors – a man, I obviously don't need to add. So that won't have helped matters. She hasn't admitted as much, but Winnie's very astute and she got a fair idea of what's going on.'

'Good gracious!' said Sally again. 'I'm stunned, really I am. I would never have thought that about Mr and Mrs Morris.'

'It just goes to show,' said Albert grimly. 'You can never tell what's going on in a woman's mind.

"La donna è mobile"... Didn't you tell me that it meant "woman is fickle"?'

'Yes, that's right; so it does.' Albert was looking at her quizzically. 'You mustn't think... There's no one else involved, for me, I mean,' she tried to explain.

'I didn't think that, Sally,' he replied. He looked very sad for a moment and she felt sorry if she had hurt him so much. 'I didn't mean you. I was just speaking generally. Some women can be very fickle.' He gave a sad smile. 'I'm sorry ... about you and me. It was good while it lasted. I suppose that's all I can say. I'll take you back home when you're ready. There's not much point in staying on here, is there?'

He downed his half pint almost in one gulp. She was glad it wasn't a full pint as he had to drive home and she knew he would be preoccupied about recent happenings.

He kissed her on the cheek as they said goodbye outside her house. 'I'll see you around, no doubt, Sally,' he said. 'Take care of yourself ... and good luck.' He nodded unsmilingly as he got out of the car to open the door for her.

'Goodbye, Albert,' she said. 'You take care of yourself as well.' She hurried up the path without a backward glance.

It was Winifred who told Kathy, one night just after the little girl had got into bed, firstly, that her father was not seeing Sally Roberts anymore, and then that Shirley had gone with her mum and her brother and sister to live in Southport with her grandparents. Kathy, understandably, was puzzled about both issues.

'Why?' she asked, regarding her father and Sally. 'Have they had a row?'

'I don't think so, not exactly a row,' Winifred replied. 'They've decided that maybe they're not right for one another. Your daddy is a few years older than Sally – Miss Roberts – and people have to be very sure, if they're thinking of staying together, that they're always going to get on well with one another.'

'Did he want to marry Miss Roberts, then?' asked Kathy.

Winifred smiled. 'I think he might have done, but it wasn't to be.'

'I like Miss Roberts,' said Kathy. 'Well, I always liked her, but we've got more friendly – you know, as though she's not just a teacher – since she's been going out with Daddy.'

'Well, you'll still see her at school, won't you? And I'm sure she'll be just as friendly, even though it didn't work out for her and your daddy.'

'Are you going to marry Uncle Jeff?' Kathy asked, surprising Winifred by the suddenness of the question.

'I think that might be ... quite likely,' said Winifred cautiously. 'But a lady has to wait until she's asked, you know. So don't go saying that to Jeff, will you, or to anybody else?'

'No, I won't,' said Kathy. 'But would you like to marry him?'

'You're a nosey parker!' Winifred laughed. 'Jeff and I get on very well together. I like him very much and I think he likes me. But, as I said, you have to be very sure. Now, I don't think I want to say any more about that at the moment, young lady!'

'No, that's all right,' said Kathy. 'But why is Shirley's mum going to live somewhere else? Don't Mr and Mrs Morris love one another anymore? I thought he was nice, real good fun; he made me laugh.'

'You can't always tell what people are really like,' said her aunt. 'Sometimes they can be quite different with their own families.'

Kathy nodded. 'Yes, Shirley used to tell me about her mum and dad having rows. And I know he was real mad about Brenda getting hurt, and then Graham falling in the sea.'

'That's what caused the big fall-out,' said Winifred. 'Mr Morris wants to be sure that his children are being looked after properly, just like your daddy cares about you. And he thought Mrs Morris was neglecting them by coming to work here.'

'But she wasn't, was she?' Kathy frowned. 'I mean ... it was Shirley's fault – and mine as well – that Brenda got hurt. We'd been told to look after her. And Graham wasn't doing as he was told either, was he? He'd been told not to go near the sea.'

'Yes, it was all very unfortunate,' said Winifred. 'But you mustn't worry your head about it anymore, Kathy love. Maybe when Mrs Morris has had time to think about it she'll be sorry she's moved away. And perhaps Mr Morris will be sorry for all the things he said. It's what happens sometimes with married people. I know you'll miss Shirley, but you've got lots more friends at school, haven't you?'

'Oh yes, there's Maureen and Dorothy ... and Timothy. Actually, Aunty Win, Shirley was a bit bossy. I liked her, though.'

Winifred laughed. 'It'll all sort out, I'm sure.' She kissed her cheek. 'Now, you snuggle down and go to sleep. Goodnight, darling; God bless...'

Kathy settled down well in her new class. Her teacher was called Mrs Culshaw, whom the children soon decided was good fun but could be strict as well when the need arose. They still sat in tables of four, not at desks yet, like the older classes in the junior school. Kathy was pleased to be put on a table with Maureen who, after Shirley, was her next-best friend. It seemed as though Mrs Culshaw had been warned to separate Timothy Fielding and his sparring partner, Stanley Weston. To Kathy's disappointment, although she didn't admit it to anyone, Timothy was not on their table, but was seated at the other side of the room. Sitting opposite her and Maureen were Stanley, whom she knew and didn't mind too much, and a boy called Neville who was quiet, well behaved and clever.

She encountered Timothy, though, in the playground the first day. 'Hi, Kathy,' he greeted her. 'Would you like a pear drop?'

'Ooh yes, thank you.' She popped the pink and yellow sweet in her mouth.

'I've got another joke for you,' he said. 'What did the caterpillar say when he fell off the leaf?'

'I don't know,' she replied dutifully. 'What did he say?'

'Earwigo...!' He fell about laughing. 'D'you get it? Here – we – go. Eer – wig – o!'

'Yes, of course I get it,' she said a little impatiently. 'It's ... quite funny.'

'I can't hear you laughing,' he said. 'I 'spect you're upset about Shirley going, aren't you? My mum found out about it and she told me. I 'spect they'll be getting a divorce, Shirley's mum and dad.' Kathy wasn't sure what that meant but she didn't admit it.

'Oh ... I don't know,' she said. 'My aunty thinks they might come back when Shirley's mum's thought about it.'

'I don't think so,' said Timothy. 'My mum says if they get a divorce they'll be able to get married to somebody else.'

'Oh...' said Kathy, feeling even more confused. 'Look, I'll have to go, Tim. Maureen's waiting for me to turn the other end of the skipping rope. See you...'

'Aunty Win,' said Kathy that night as she was getting undressed ready to go to bed. 'What's a divorce?'

Winifred was startled. 'Why?' she enquired. 'Why do you want to know?'

'Because Timothy Fielding says that that's what Shirley's mum and dad are going to do, get a divorce. And I don't know what it means.'

'I think that your friend Timothy Fielding says a great deal too much,' Winifred replied.

'It was what his mum said...'

'Well, I'm sure she doesn't know,' said Winifred indignantly, 'and she shouldn't be spreading rumours like that.'

'But what does it mean?' Kathy persisted.

'Well, a divorce is what happens when a husband and wife decide that they don't want to live together any longer. So the judge grants them a divorce ... so that they're not married anymore.'

'And then they can get married to somebody else?'

'Well, yes... Is that something else that Timothy said?'

'Yes, he did...'

Winifred sighed. 'I don't think for one moment that Mr and Mrs Morris are going to get a divorce, or marry somebody else ... so you just forget about it, love. I've told you, sometimes grown-up people fall out, but very often they make it up again. You mustn't talk about Shirley's mum and dad. You won't, will you? And don't take any notice of what people are saying.'

'No, of course I won't.' Kathy shook her head. 'Aunty Win ... the Illuminations are on now. D'you think we could go and see them?'

'Yes, I'm sure we could,' said Winifred, glad about the change of subject. 'That will be something nice to look forward to, won't it?'

'That's a good idea,' said Albert, when Winifred told him about Kathy wanting to see the Illuminations. 'Why don't we all go? You and Jeff, and Kathy and me. We could go in my car. An evening during the week would be better than the weekend; it gets very busy on the promenade. Then perhaps we could go and have a fish and chip supper afterwards. That'll be a treat for Kathy, seeing that it's something we hardly ever do.'

'Aren't you forgetting something?' said Winifred. 'Somebody will need to stay here to see to the visitors' suppers. I don't see how we can all go, although I must admit I'd like to see the Lights as much as anyone.'

'Yes, that's a thought,' agreed Albert. 'We haven't got all that many folks in, though, next week. Perhaps Betty could come in for the evening, just for once; we'd pay her extra, of course.'

Sadie Morris's departure had meant that they had to employ another waitress-cum-general help. Betty Jarvis, a member of the church that Winifred attended, had been pleased to step into the breach. She had no children to worry about as they were both married, her husband had no objection to her working – in fact, he had welcomed the idea – and she seemed to be fitting in very well. It was the bookkeeping, though, that was the problem. Winifred had got used to having someone else to cope with it, and now, for the moment, she was once again doing it herself.

She was pleased that Albert was so enthusiastic about the visit to the Illuminations. He had been very downcast after the ending of his friendship with Sally, and she had feared that he would revert to being as miserable and uncommunicative as he had been when he lost Barbara.

'I shall never try again,' he had moaned. 'What's the use? I really thought Sally and I were getting on well. It just goes to show...' What it showed, Winifred was not quite sure. 'Anyroad, that's it for me as far as women are concerned.'

'Don't say that, Albert,' she had tried to console

him. 'You never know, do you? I didn't think I would ever meet anyone; it was really unexpected the way I met Jeff. Try not to be downhearted.'

'Well, at least I've got Kathy, haven't I?' he said. 'She's a bit upset an' all about Sally, and about Shirley, though she was a little madam, if you ask me! I'll have to try and make it up to her.'

And the visit to the Illuminations was one way of doing so. The Lights had recommenced the previous year after the years of darkness during and following the war. They were a great boost to Blackpool's economy, especially to the boarding house and hotel trade.

Betty agreed to come in to see to the suppers on the Monday evening at the start of the last week in September. Albert drove along the backstreets to the southern end of the promenade; the customary route for the traffic to take was from south to north. Kathy sat at the front with her dad, with Jeff and Winifred in the rear seats.

The Lights really were a fantastic spectacle, living up to the proud boast that they were 'the greatest show on earth'. All along the several miles of the promenade they sparkled like diamonds, rubies, emeralds and sapphires – a long, long necklace of jewels. Here and there were dazzling arrays of shooting stars, crescent moons and shining rainbows. There were juggling clowns and acrobats, colourful fishes and tropical sea creatures, and nursery rhyme characters, all dancing and darting about against the night sky. Now and again an illuminated tram passed by on the tram track on their left-hand side, transformed into a gondola, a paddle steamer or a rocket.

On the cliffs at North Shore were the tableaux, huge illuminated boards depicting jungle animals, fairy tales and circus scenes. One tableau, called 'The Rejuvenating Machine', showed a group of old men and women going into a strange-looking engine, and coming out at the other end as youthful boys and girls; such was the life-enhancing benefit to be found by taking a holiday in Blackpool.

Winifred was touched to see Kathy's delight at the new experience. She had 'oohed' and 'aahed' at first, then grew silent as her eyes took in one amazing vista after another.

'That was terrific!' she pronounced when they came to the end of the tableaux and turned off the promenade into the comparative darkness of Red Bank Road.

There was a fish and chip shop about halfway along that served meals to eat out or to eat on the premises. Albert parked the car on a side street and they went into the dining area at the rear of the shop. They sat at a table for four, covered with a red and white checked tablecloth, on top of which were large canisters of salt and pepper and a giant-sized vinegar bottle.

The fish and chips were delicious; the fish was white and flaky and covered in crispy batter, and the chips were hot and steaming and a perfect golden brown. At the side of each plate was a small carton of mushy peas. Even Albert declared that he couldn't have cooked it any better himself! They hadn't had a meal that night, after serving the visitors' high tea, and so between them they demolished the pile of bread and butter that accompanied the meal, and drank the huge teapot dry.

'Well, it's home time now, I suppose,' said Albert. 'It's been a grand evening, it has that!'

They got into the car and Albert set off driving, as carefully as he always did, back towards the sea. He would turn off soon and make their way home through the quiet back streets of the town.

Winifred could never say exactly what happened next. All she saw was a motorbike heading towards them, on the wrong side of the road as it tried to overtake a car.

'Look out, Albert!' she cried, but it was too late. 'There was a deafening crash as the motorbike plunged into the front of their car, and then a piercing cry as Kathy was thrown forward towards the windscreen.

Chapter Fifteen

'It wasn't your fault, Albert. How many times do I have to tell you? That thing was coming straight towards us. There was no way you could have avoided it.' Winifred had told Albert the same thing umpteen times, but he was still in need of reassurance. She knew how guilt-ridden he was feeling, and would continue to be so until he knew that Kathy was going to be all right. And how Winifred was praying that the little girl would open her eyes. She had been unconscious now for two days...

It had all happened so quickly, and even now it was still largely a blur of confusion in Winifred's mind. The almighty bang; the motorbike skidding away out of control and the rider lying motionless in the middle of the road; Kathy's cry of anguish, and then her silence; and Albert cursing as she had never heard him do before. In the back of the car she and Jeff clung to one another. They were, miraculously, unhurt, just suffering from the inevitable shock and a few minor bumps and bruises. A police car and an ambulance, then a second ambulance, arrived – she could not have said how long it had taken – called, no doubt, by a bystander. It seemed as though Albert might have a broken arm and a dislocated shoulder, and bumps and bruises, of course, but little else. It was Katherine who had borne the brunt of the collision, and Albert was still finding it hard to forgive himself for that.

They had all been taken off to hospital. Winifred and Jeff were treated for shock and then discharged, although they stayed behind for a while for news of Albert and Kathy. As they had guessed, Albert's arm was broken and he would need to stay in hospital overnight. Kathy, too, had a broken arm and the bang to her head had resulted in concussion.

They had waited anxiously for news. Then, at midnight, a doctor had informed them that the little girl was still unconscious, but not too seriously injured, as far as they could tell, apart from the broken arm, which had already been set. Winifred and Jeff went home as there was nothing else they could do.

They had phoned Betty Jarvis at the hotel, explaining that they would be delayed; they could not say for how long. She was shocked to hear of the accident, but assured them that she would wait there, no matter how long it might be before they returned. It was, in fact, one o'clock in the morning when the taxi dropped Winifred and Jeff off at Holmleigh. Jeff insisted on staying the night there, and Mrs Jarvis went home – only a few streets away – promising to be back in a few hours to help with the visitors' breakfasts. Fortunately there were only six guests booked in that week. Albert would be incapacitated with his broken arm; but Winifred, who was almost as good a cook as her brother, declared that she would be able to manage, with help from Betty and the part-time staff who came in for a few hours each day.

Their main concern, though, was for Kathy. Albert was discharged on the Tuesday morning, and he and Winifred went to the hospital whenever they were able to do so, after the visitors' requirements had been dealt with.

They sat at her bedside on Tuesday evening, then again on Wednesday afternoon, but there was no change in her condition. The doctor assured them, however, that there was no real cause for alarm; it was just a matter of time whilst her body recovered from the shock. Kathy looked very peaceful, but very small and helpless in the large bed, with her broken arm – fortunately her left one – encased in plaster.

'Poor little lass,' said Albert as they sat there on the Wednesday evening. 'I've not been much of a father to her, have I?'

'Albert, you must never say that!' Winifred remonstrated with him. 'You love her very much. She knows that, and she loves you too. We are all a victim of our own personality, and losing Barbara ... well, that had a great effect on you, didn't it? But I don't think Kathy has suffered from not having a mother.'

'And that is thanks to you, Winnie. You've been wonderful. You've loved her just as much as any mother could have done.' Albert was not often moved to utter such words of praise. She had felt, at times, that he took her largely for granted; but she could see the remorse in his eyes now, and the trace of a tear. 'But I'll be different,' he went on. 'If she comes round... I'll make it all up to her.'

'Albert, there's no "if" about it,' said Winifred. 'She will get better; the doctor has said so. Now, you must be positive about this; she's going to be all right.'

Albert nodded. He continued to look at the motionless figure in the bed. Suddenly, her hand moved, grasping at the sheet.

'There, what did I tell you?' said Winifred, in a hushed voice.

They hardly dared to breathe as they watched the little girl's head begin to move, slowly, from side to side. Then she opened her eyes. She blinked, then her eyes wandered around the room, as if to familiarise herself with her strange surroundings.

'Thank God...' whispered Winifred. 'Oh, Albert... I can scarcely believe it. I tried to believe, but ... Oh, thank you, thank you, God.' She buried her head in her hands, unable to stem the tears of relief.

'Yes, indeed ... thank God,' muttered Albert.

Kathy was looking at them now. 'Daddy ... Aunty Win...' she said, in such a tiny voice. 'Where am I?' She raised her head a fraction and tried to look around. 'I feel a bit funny,' she said. 'What's happened?'

'You had an accident, darling,' said Winifred. 'You hurt your arm and your head. You're in hospital.'

'Oh...' Kathy glanced down at her arm encased in plaster. 'My arm, yes... Is it broken?'

'It was,' said her aunt. 'But the doctors have mended it. And you're going to be fine. Now, just lie still and I'll go and fetch the nurse. She'll be so pleased that you've opened your eyes.'

'Have I been asleep, then,' asked Kathy, 'for a long time?'

'Yes ... for quite a little while.'

'Like Sleeping Beauty,' smiled Kathy.

'Well, not quite as long as that, love,' chuckled Albert. 'Not a hundred years. But quite long enough for your aunty and me to have to wait. See, your old dad's got a broken arm an' all. A couple of old crocks, aren't we?'

Kathy smiled at them, and there were tears in Albert's eyes as well as Winifred's as he and his sister looked at one another, almost too choked to speak.

'I'll go and get the nurse...' murmured Winifred.

Kathy, of course, needed to stay in hospital for a while longer. But they knew now that she was out

216

of danger. It was fortunate that she had suffered only from a broken arm and concussion. It could, indeed, have been much worse. Albert knew that they could all have been seriously injured or even killed. They were pleased to hear, also, that the motorcyclist was out of danger. His injuries were more severe, but he was recovering. What was more, he knew he had to take full responsibility for the accident; but that would all be sorted out in the not-too-distant future.

Winifred knew that she must ask Albert about the comment he had made when Kathy opened her eyes. 'You said "thank God",' she told him, but not in words of recrimination. He had sounded as though he really meant it. 'I thought ... well, you always refused to believe in him.'

Albert nodded. 'That's true; "thank God" ... that's what I said, and I meant it. I prayed, Winnie, when our Kathy was unconscious. I told myself that if God doesn't exist, then it would make no difference. But if he really was ... somewhere up there, listening to us, then maybe he might answer our prayers. I knew you would be praying as well, you see, and that he would most likely take more notice of you than he would of me.'

'Don't say that, Albert,' whispered Winifred. 'I believe that he listens to everyone. We don't always get the answer that we want, but this time ... we did.'

'Yes, thank God, we did,' echoed Albert.

'I'm glad you've changed your mind about God.' Winifred smiled at her brother. 'He can make such a difference to life.'

'Well, I shall certainly give him a try now,'

replied Albert. 'What have I to lose? I nearly lost the most precious thing in my life. But I shall be different now, Winnie, you'll see. I'm going to be a father that Kathy can be proud of...'

Chapter Sixteen

Kathy had no memory at all of what had happened. The last thing she remembered was sitting next to her dad as he drove along Red Bank Road ... and then she had woken up in hospital with a broken arm and a fuzzy head. Aunty Win told her that there had been an accident with a motorbike, and that she had been asleep for two whole days. They had all been very worried about her, but her dad and aunty assured her that she was going to be fine. Her broken arm would heal, and so would the few bumps and bruises caused by the accident. She would need to stay in hospital for a while and then stay at home until she was fit to go back to school.

She cried a little bit that night when her dad and aunty said goodbye. But the nurses and the doctor were very kind to her and after a day or two she started almost to enjoy being in hospital.

She had quite a few visitors – not all at once because the nurses were very strict about not having too many people round the bed – and that cheered her up a lot. Mrs Culshaw, her teacher, came to see her and brought her some flowers and chocolates and an Enid Blyton book, as well as letters and cards from all the children in the class. She had laughed at the one from Timothy Fielding. He had done a little drawing of himself with his sticky-up hair and a sad downturned mouth because Kathy was poorly. And Maureen, her best friend now that Shirley wasn't there, had sent a pretty card she had made herself with a pattern of flowers and butterflies.

And there was even more of a surprise the next day when Miss Roberts – Sally – came to see her. Kathy had been so disappointed when Sally had stopped seeing her dad. She, Kathy, had even been hoping that the two of them might get married and then Sally would come and live with them. And then, suddenly, it had all come to an end. She hadn't seen her favourite teacher nearly so much as she had hoped she would since moving into the juniors. But now, here she was!

Sally hugged her and kissed her cheek, and Kathy was almost too overcome to speak.

'All the teachers send their love,' said Sally. 'We were all sorry to hear about your accident, but you're looking quite bright-eyed and bushy-tailed, aren't you, dear?' Kathy had a broad smile on her face and her cheeks were pink with excitement. 'And here's a little present from me,' Sally went on. She opened her bag and took out a box of jelly babies and a book, quite a large green one. 'This is a book I enjoyed when I was a little girl,' she said. 'It's called *The Green Book of Fairy Tales*, and I'd like to give it to you now, Kathy.'

'Gosh, thank you!' said Kathy. 'I'll look forward to reading it. I'm feeling a lot better now. Daddy and Aunty Win, and sometimes Uncle Jeff, come to see me every day, and I might be going home next week. Daddy broke his arm as well. Did you know that ... Miss Roberts?'

'Yes, I called to see him and your aunty,' said Sally. 'He seems to be managing all right. He's more concerned about you, Kathy, about you getting well again... Your daddy loves you very much, you know.'

'Yes, I know,' replied Kathy. 'He's been ... sort of ... kinder, you know, while I've been in here. He used to be a bit grumpy sometimes. I was ever so sorry, Miss Roberts, when you and daddy stopped seeing one another.'

'Yes, I know, dear,' said Sally. 'But you mustn't worry about it anymore. Grown-ups know, you see, when something isn't going to work out. And we didn't think it would. But you and me, we'll always be friends, won't we?'

Kathy nodded. 'Yes, I hope so.'

'I'll let you into a little secret,' said Sally, leaning closer to her. 'You remember Mr Grantley? Phil – that's what he's called.' Kathy nodded again.

'Yes, I know Mr Grantley. He teaches one of the top classes and takes PE and Games.'

'Well, we've started going out together again, Phil and I. We were quite good friends, you see, and then your dad asked me to go out with him – to the restaurant, you remember, when he won that raffle prize? And so Phil and I drifted apart; it was all rather a mix-up, really. But we're friendly again now, and I'm very pleased about that.' Sally smiled and she looked really happy.

'Oh ... that's nice,' said Kathy, quite pleased

that Miss Roberts had confided in her, just as though she was a real grown-up friend. 'I like Mr Grantley. He looks as though he's good fun... Are you going to marry him, then?'

Sally laughed out loud. 'Oh, goodness me! It's early days to be thinking about that, Kathy love. Anyway, a lady has to wait until she's asked, you know.'

'Yes, that's what Aunty Win said when I asked her if she was going to marry Uncle Jeff,' replied Kathy. 'But I think they will get married, you know,' she added confidingly. 'They're quite old, really, but I don't suppose that matters, does it?'

Sally chuckled again. 'I don't suppose it matters at all. But what they are all concerned about at the moment is you getting well again.'

They chatted for a little while about what was going on in the hospital. Kathy said that the food was quite nice and that she liked all the nurses and the doctor who was in charge of her. And Sally told her about her new class of top infants.

She stayed for about half an hour, and Kathy breathed a sigh of contentment as she left. It had been really lovely to see her. With her good arm she opened the book. It was quite an old-fashioned one with lovely coloured pictures on shiny paper. Kathy knew she would enjoy reading the stories of fairy tale princesses, wizards, witches and dragons. And how nice it was to have a book that had belonged to Miss Roberts. 'Sally...' she whispered quietly to herself.

Sally was on top of the world at the moment. It had been a dreadful shock to hear, in the staffroom, about the accident that had put Kathy Leigh in hospital and caused injuries to Albert as well. It was Mrs Culshaw – Mavis – who, as Kathy's class teacher, had been given the news. At that time the little girl was still unconscious, and Sally had found it hard to concentrate on her work for the next day or two until the news came that she was recovering.

She was surprised, but pleased, to see Phil Grantley coming into her classroom after lessons had finished that day.

'It's good news about Kathy, isn't it?' he began, leaning casually against the teaching desk where Sally was sitting. 'I know how worried you must have been about her. You grew very fond of her, didn't you, whilst you and her father were friendly? I don't know her very well, but she seems a dear little girl.'

'Yes, so she is,' agreed Sally. 'I shall go and see her soon. I'll ask her Aunty Win first to make sure it's OK for me to go.' She hesitated, then she went on. 'It was never really serious between Albert Leigh and me, you know. At least... I think he wanted it to be, and that was when I decided to call it a day. It would never have worked out, although he's quite a nice chap when you get to know him. But not right for me.'

'Yes, I see...' replied Phil. 'That's the main reason I've come to see you, Sally, apart from saying that I'm pleased to hear about Kathy. You and me ... it all went wrong somewhere along the way, didn't it?'

Sally gave a rueful smile. 'Yes, so it did. Bad timing, you might say, and things happening that were out of our control.' They looked steadily at one another, and Sally knew that the stirrings of love that she had started to feel for him a few months ago were still there.

He reached out a hand to her across the desk. 'Could we try again, Sally?' he said. 'I really have missed you, and we've wasted such a lot of time.'

'What about Fiona?' she asked. 'You went on holiday together, didn't you?'

'With a crowd of others,' he replied. 'No, that has come to an end. Fiona and I had nothing much in common, really, only that we are both teachers, and are both quite keen on walking. But it's not enough. We know we're not right for one another. How do you feel, Sally? Would you come out with me ... tonight?'

'I'd love to, Phil,' she said simply as she squeezed his hand. She stood up, and he put his arms around her, kissing her gently on the lips.

'Come along,' he said. 'I'll run you home now, then I'll call for you tonight. Seven-thirty OK?'

'Very much OK,' she smiled.

He kissed her far more ardently as they said goodnight that evening, after a quiet drink at a seafront hotel. 'How about a meal and then the pictures on Saturday night?' he said. 'We'll paint the town red!'

They didn't exactly do that. They were both, deep down, quite reserved people, not given to extremes. But they both knew that they were at the start – though somewhat delayed – of something good.

Plans were afoot, too, at Holmleigh. Jeff Bancroft

223

had asked Winifred if she would marry him and she had quietly agreed that of course she would. They had both known that it was inevitable.

He had proposed to her on the evening that Kathy had regained consciousness. They sat together in the family living room, Albert having tactfully left them alone for a while, as if he knew what was about to happen.

'I know you're concerned about Kathy,' said Jeff, 'especially now, after the accident. And I know you won't want to move away from here and leave her.'

'That's true,' she replied. 'I'm not saying that Albert wouldn't look after her well, but he's always left a great deal of her bringing up to me, and I know she would miss me. I did think he might get married again, but I feel now that that isn't likely to happen.'

'Well, I'd like to suggest that I sell my bungalow and come to live here,' said Jeff. He smiled. 'That is, if you and Albert will have me?'

Winifred smiled. 'I think that's a splendid idea. I'd thought of it, I must admit, but I didn't like to suggest it myself. After all, it's your home that you're going to sell, isn't it? Besides, I had to wait until you popped the question!'

Jeff kissed her lovingly. 'My home is anywhere that you are, my dear,' he said. 'But I don't want to wait too long. There's no point in waiting, is there?'

They agreed on a quiet wedding just before Christmas. They hoped that, by that time, Jeff's house would be sold and they would then settle in their own private rooms at Holmleigh.

'Come on, let's go and tell Albert,' said Jeff.

Albert was quietly pleased to hear their news, although it was not his way to enthuse too much. 'I can't say I'm surprised,' he remarked. 'You two are made for one another. By Jove, this calls for a celebration. Your good news, and our Kathy getting better.' He took out a bottle of rich dark sherry from the kitchen cupboard and poured it into three glasses.

He raised his own glass. 'Here's to the pair of you. I wish you all the happiness you deserve. And to our dear little Kathy, God bless her...'

Winifred noticed that her brother's eyes were moist with tears.

They had been told that Kathy would need to stay in hospital for at least another week just to make sure that all was well. As Winifred was getting ready to go to church on the following Sunday morning she was feeling that she did, indeed, have a great deal to be thankful for that day. Jeff, who had also started attending the morning service, would be calling for her shortly. To her surprise Albert joined her, dressed in his best suit with a clean white shirt and a colourful tie.

'I'll come along with you, if you don't mind,' he said, just a trifle sheepishly. 'I reckon I've a lot to thank him up there for an' all, don't you?' He grinned as he gestured towards the ceiling.

'You have indeed,' said his sister. And I'm so pleased that you realise it, Albert.' There was a ring at the doorbell.

'There's Jeff,' she said. 'Come along; let's go.'

PART TWO

Chapter Seventeen

1961

Kathy stood by one of the large pillars that surrounded the Empress ballroom. She was trying
to look nonchalant as she watched the dancers
drifting by, as though she was not a wallflower or
at all eager that someone – anyone – should ask
her to dance.

She had come with her friend, Marcia, whom
she had met at night school. Her father approved
of Marcia; he thought she was a decent, well-
brought-up girl as, indeed, she was. But there was
another side to Marcia that Albert Leigh knew
nothing about. She could be very silly and giggly
when she had had a drop too much to drink; and
it didn't take much – only a couple of shandies –
to make Marcia lose her inhibitions, although, to
be honest, Kathy thought that she put it on a bit.
And, besides that, she was a dreadful flirt. Kathy
watched her now as she jigged past with the RAF
lad who had asked her to dance, laughing up into
his face and behaving in what both Kathy's father
and her aunt would consider to be a most in-
decorous manner.

Marcia was a blonde, a very attractive, vivacious, blue-eyed blonde, although she could
appear sweet and demure when she wanted to. It
seemed that the old adage that men preferred

blondes was true, because Marcia was always the first to be asked to dance.

But it didn't worry Kathy all that much. She knew that after the dance Marcia would come back to her. The RAF lad would most likely be only a bit of fun, easily forgotten, and the two girls would go home together at the end of the evening. Marcia, in fact, was engaged to a young man who was doing his national service in Germany. She was twenty years of age, two years older than Kathy, but she saw no reason, she said, to stay at home being miserable whilst Eric was overseas.

Kathy enjoyed her company and she liked to think that, maybe, she was a steadying influence on Marcia, there to prevent her going completely off the rails. It was only quite recently that Kathy's father had agreed to her going to the local dance halls. He drew the line at the Tower, which he considered for some reason to be 'common'; but he had set his seal of approval on the Winter Gardens – the Empress ballroom – or the Palace which, Kathy gathered, held certain memories for him. But he was not one to give too much of himself away. She seemed to remember that he used to go dancing at the Palace with Sally Roberts before that friendship had come to an abrupt end. That was round about the time of the accident. And it was following that occurrence that her father had started taking a good deal more interest in her, Kathy.

The dance was coming to an end, the couples applauding as the band stopped playing, as they always did. Marcia would be back with her soon. But before she saw her friend she heard a voice at the side of her.

'Kathy? It is you, isn't it? Kathy Leigh...' She turned to look at the young man in the khaki uniform of a soldier who was addressing her. A thickset young man, not very tall, with a shock of fair hair that stood up on end, a pair of bright blue eyes and a wide smiling mouth.

'Tim!' she cried. 'Timothy Fielding! Well, fancy that! I haven't seen you for ages. Where have you been?'

He laughed. 'Well, that's pretty bloomin' obvious, isn't it? I'm in the army!'

'National Service?' enquired Kathy.

'No, the regulars,' replied Tim. 'I joined the REME when I was seventeen and a half – as soon as they would take me! I signed on for three years.'

'REME?' queried Kathy.

'Royal Electrical and Mechanical Engineers,' said Tim. 'I would have just missed National Service, you see – it finished last year – and I didn't want to miss out on the experience. Call me daft, if you like!' he laughed. 'Actually, it was to give me a good grounding in my career, which I find it is doing. I'm training to be an electrician. I'm stationed up at Catterick Camp, and I've just got a spot of leave. It's great to see you again, Kathy. Come and have a drink with me, will you? Or ... are you with someone?'

Marcia was coming back, on the arm of the RAF lad.

'Yes, I am, actually,' she replied. 'I came with my friend, but I'm sure she won't mind. Marcia, this is Tim, an old friend of mine from schooldays.'

The two nodded at one another and mumbled, 'How do you do?'

'We're going to have a drink and catch up on old times,' said Kathy. 'Is that OK with you?'

'Sure it is,' replied Marcia. 'This is Simon; he's taking me for a drink as well, but we won't play gooseberry.' She winked at Kathy. 'I'll meet you later, then, shall I? In the usual place at eleven o'clock?' They usually met in the Floral Hall, at the top of the steps that led down to the cloak-room, when the dance was coming to an end.

Kathy nodded. 'Yes, see you later.' She drew her friend to one side. 'Watch what you're doing now,' she said in a whisper. 'Don't forget about Eric!'

'It's all right.' Marcia grinned. 'Simon's a good laugh, that's all. I've already told him I'm spoken for. So is he, actually. He's from Birmingham and he's got a fiancée there. Cheerio, then. Don't do anything I wouldn't do!'

Marcia's new friend was one of the myriad RAF men, mainly the last intake of National Service recruits, who were to be seen in the streets of Blackpool and in the local dance halls and cinemas. They were stationed at the nearby camps at Weeton and Warton.

Timothy led Kathy to a quiet corner of a bar near to the ballroom. 'Now, what are you drinking?' he asked. 'A pint of best bitter, or something more ladylike?'

She laughed. 'A shandy, please; just a small one, with ginger beer, not lemonade.'

'Okey doke...' He was back in a few minutes with a brimming pint glass for himself and a smaller one for her.

'Cheers,' he said, raising his glass. 'It really is the most wonderful thing, bumping into you. I must say, you're looking stunning! You always liked red, didn't you? I remember your red jumpers at school and the red ribbons in your hair.' He was smiling at her with the fondness of their remembered friendship.

'Yes, I run pretty true to form, don't I?' she replied, smiling back at him.

She knew that the dress suited her. It was a pinkish shade of red, like crushed strawberries – a simple sleeveless shift style in the new terylene material, with a knee-length skirt, a rounded neckline, and a neat black bow at the low waistline. Her Aunt Winifred often helped her to make her own clothes, but she had bought this one from her favourite dress shop, Sally Mae's.

'It's great to see you again, Tim,' she told him. 'It's been years, hasn't it? I'm surprised you recognised me.'

'You haven't changed at all,' he said, looking at her admiringly.

'No, neither have you,' she answered.

She had lost touch with him when they had both left junior school as they had gone to different secondary schools; most schools in Blackpool were single-sex ones anyway. Tim had attended a secondary modern school – he was a bright boy but one who did not apply himself as well as he might – whereas she, Kathy, had attended the only commercial school in the town.

She had almost – but never entirely – forgotten about him. She had seen him occasionally at church dances, which were the only dances her father would let her attend when she was in her early teens. Tim had never asked her to go out with him; it was doubtful, anyway, that she would have been allowed to go out with a boy before she was sixteen. And Tim, at that time, had been far more interested in knocking around with his mates, although he had always seemed pleased to see her and have a chat with her. Then, a few years ago, he had seemed to disappear off the scene completely. She asked him about that now.

'Do you still live in Blackpool – I mean, when you're not away doing your army service?' she asked. 'I don't think I've seen you for – what? – it must be three or four years.'

'Yes, my parents still live here, and my younger brother and sister,' he replied. 'You didn't see me because I was working away. When I left school I started an apprenticeship with a firm of electricians, and I was sent away on a lot of jobs out of town – Preston, Wigan, Blackburn, some as far away as Yorkshire – so I wasn't in Blackpool very much. Then I decided to join up.'

'How long have you been in the army?'

'Since a year last March.' It was now September. 'So I've another eighteen months to do. I'm on leave till Tuesday, so it's a nice long weekend. I came here with a mate tonight, though I have to confess I'm not much of a dancer. He lives in Blackpool, South Shore, though, so I didn't know him until we joined up at the same time. I daresay he's got himself fixed up for the evening.' He laughed. 'He can charm the birds off the trees, can Jerry. But the bird rarely stays around for more than one date.' He paused, looking at her fondly, and she thought how lovely it was to see him again. And he was just as garrulous as ever!

'What about you?' he went on. 'When I asked if you were on your own I wasn't referring to your friend. I meant ... is there a boyfriend on the scene?'

'No,' she smiled. 'Not at all.'

'Phew! That's a relief!' He gave an exaggerated sigh. 'Maybe we could meet again, then, before I go back on Tuesday?'

'Yes, I'd love to,' she replied without hesitation.

'Tell me what you've been doing, then, Kathy.' He leant forward eagerly.

'Well, I'm working at our hotel,' she began, 'as I've been doing ever since I left school. It was more or less taken for granted that I would, so I didn't have much choice in the matter, with it being a family business.'

'So what do you do exactly? Are you training to be a chef, like your dad?'

'Oh no. Dad and my aunt are in charge of that side of things. You remember Aunty Win? She's still living at the hotel. She married her gentleman friend, though, Jeff Bancroft, and they have their own rooms at Holmleigh. I'm in charge of the accounts and bookkeeping and all that side of things. You remember I went to the commercial school on Palatine Road? It was ideal for what I was going to do: shorthand and typing lessons, and accountancy. Then I took a further course at night school, so I'm quite well qualified.'

'And you're not hankering to do something else? I seem to recall that you wanted to be a writer – like Enid Blyton!'

She laughed. 'That was a childhood fantasy. Although I do write short stories, after a fashion, in my spare time. There's not always too much of that, though, especially in the summer. We're kept pretty busy at the hotel. Don't ask if I'm published, because I'm not! Perhaps one day, though; I live in hope!'

Timothy nodded. 'Yes, you were always top of the class at composition, weren't you?'

'I might have been,' she replied dismissively, 'at junior school at any rate. I missed quite a lot, though, after the accident I had.'

'Yes, I remember that,' he replied. 'We had just gone up into the juniors, and we were all real worried about you. You broke your arm, didn't you, and weren't you unconscious for a while?'

'Yes ... and when I woke up I remembered nothing about the accident. Then Mrs Culshaw came to see me and brought me some flowers and chocolates, and a new Enid Blyton book! And letters and cards from all the children in the class. I remember yours especially, Tim,' she smiled. 'Sally Roberts came as well; I was so thrilled when she came to see me.'

'Yes, we all liked her, didn't we? Mrs Grantley, of course, as she is now. Wasn't she friendly with your father at one time, before she married Phil Grantley?'

'Yes, my dad and Sally had been going out together for a little while, then it came to an end just before we had the accident. My dad was like a bear with a sore head when they finished, and I remember I was very disappointed as well. Of course, I'd just lost my best friend, Shirley, when she moved to Southport with her mother. You remember Shirley Morris, don't you?'

'Yes; what a bossy knickers she was! She and I never got on very well. You had some other friends, though, didn't you, after she left?'

'Yes, but it was quite traumatic for me at the time – Shirley going, and then my dad and Sally splitting up, then the accident on top of it all. That was why my aunt and Jeff stayed at Holmleigh. I'd always been very close to Aunty Win – she was like a mother to me – and they didn't want to upset me by moving away. So Jeff sold his bungalow and moved in with Aunty Win – after they were married, of course!'

'Of course!' smiled Timothy.

'Jeff's a freelance artist,' Kathy went on. 'He's always done very well, but they seem content to stay where they are, especially with my aunt still working at the hotel.'

'And what about your father? Did he never get married again?'

'Oh no... After my mother died – I don't remember her, of course – he was very bitter for ages. That's what my aunt has told me, and there was never anyone who could match up to her, in his eyes. I think Sally Roberts might have done, but I think it was Sally who finished their friendship, not my dad. I wish I'd known my mother...' she added wistfully. 'I used to feel ... not exactly envious, but I used to wish, sometimes, that I had the sort of family life that Shirley had – a nice friendly mum and dad, and a brother and sister. But then ... well, it all went wrong for Mr and Mrs Morris, didn't it?'

'Yes, Shirley never came back, did she?'

'No, her mum got married again to a man called Barry Proctor. Apparently she met him at our hotel, and she'd already got rather too friendly with him before she moved to Southport. My aunt said she felt terrible about it, with them getting friendly under her roof. I didn't know anything about it at the time, of course, and I've never seen Shirley again. I've seen her brother, though, Graham. He came back to Blackpool to live with his dad, and Mr Morris got married again as well.' She shrugged. 'So much for the family life I was so envious about!'

'It's not always like that, though, is it?' said Tim. 'My parents are still very happy together. And what about Sally Roberts – Sally Grantley – and Phil? Do you hear anything of them?'

'Oh yes, Sally and I are very friendly. Funny that, isn't it, with her being our teacher? She kept in touch with me after I had the accident, and then she asked me to be a bridesmaid at their wedding; that was the following summer.'

'Oh yes – I seem to remember that now,' said Tim. 'You were always quite a favourite of hers, though, weren't you?'

'I think it was because I didn't have a mum,' said Kathy. 'I was a bit worried about the brides-maid thing, in case some of the others said I was a "teacher's pet". But Sally said not to bother about it. I wasn't in her class anymore. Anyway, she'd become quite friendly with my Aunty Win and that was one of the reasons that she asked me. We still see her and Phil and their children, and my dad's come to terms with it all. Actually, my dad's quite a changed man now.'

'Mr and Mrs Grantley have a family, then?' enquired Tim.

'Yes, Lucy's eight and Daniel's six. I babysit for them sometimes. They're smashing little kids.'

'And ... what were you saying about your father? That he's changed quite a lot?'

'Yes, he really has. So I suppose, in a way, some good came out of the accident. From what my aunt says he was out of his mind with worry and guilt when I was injured. Then when I recovered, he saw it as an answer to prayer. He'd always said he didn't believe in God; he'd stopped going to church after my mother died. But now, well, he's never away from the place. He started going with my aunt and Jeff, then he became a sidesman, and now he's a churchwarden! He still plays darts, though, and has the occasional pint – and, of course, he still goes to football matches. But he's so much happier in himself.'

'So you and your dad are happier together as well?'

'Yes, we are,' she smiled. 'He was never very affectionate before, although I always knew, deep down, that he loved me. Now, though, he can't do enough for me. It has its downside, though. He always wants to know where I'm going and who I'm with. Especially if there's a lad involved!'

'And have there been ... some boyfriends?'

'Only a couple of lads from church. Nothing to write home about, as they say!'

'And what do you think your father will say about me?' Tim smiled at her, with his head on one side. 'Because I'm going to see you again,

Kathy. There's no doubt about that, is there?'

'No, none at all, Tim,' she replied. He reached out his hand across the table and she took hold of it. They smiled into one another's eyes, knowing already that this was what they both wanted so very much.

Chapter Eighteen

Kathy and Tim agreed to meet again the following day, which was Sunday. It was mid September and the hotel was fairly busy, although not completely full, with visitors who had come to see the Illuminations.

Kathy would be busy during part of the day as she helped out doing a spot of waitressing, but she agreed that she would see Tim in the afternoon after the midday meal was finished, and again in the evening.

She decided to put her cards on the table, so to speak, right at the start, so she asked Tim to come and call for her. Her dad would want to know where she was going and who she was with anyway, so it would be best to be up front about it. She had already confided in her aunt that she had met Timothy Fielding the previous night at the Winter Gardens, and that she was seeing him again that afternoon.

'How exciting!' said her aunt, looking quite delighted. 'You always liked him, didn't you?' she added roguishly. 'I remember when you were in Sally's class you were forever talking about him.'

'Was I?' said Kathy, laughing. 'Yes, I suppose I was, but it's a long time ago. He hasn't changed much, though. He still chatters as much as ever. I've asked him to come here, then he can meet my dad, and you of course, Aunty Win.'

'Yes, that would be best,' said Winifred. 'You know what your dad's like. He likes to keep an eye on you and what you're up to. It isn't that he doesn't trust you, but I suppose he still sees you as his little girl. I keep trying to tell him that you're grown up now.'

'He's not such a bad old fellow, though, as dads go,' said Kathy affectionately.

'Not so much of the old!' teased her aunt. 'I'm five years older than Albert, and I don't consider that I'm old, not by a long chalk!'

'No, of course you're not, Aunty,' laughed Kathy. 'Neither is Uncle Jeff. You two don't seem any older than on the day you got married.'

Winifred smiled. 'That's because we're so happy together,' she replied, her cheeks turning a little pink.

When Tim arrived at half past two Kathy took him into the living room where her father was taking his ease for a little while with his pipe and the Sunday paper.

'Dad,' she called. 'There's somebody here that I think you might remember. It's Timothy Fielding – we were at school together – and I met him again last night.'

Albert took off his reading glasses and looked at the young man, seeming a little puzzled. Then he

241

said, 'By Jove, yes! I do remember you. Our Kathy used to talk about you quite a lot. And I remember watching you at sports days and suchlike. You were a bit of a scallywag weren't you, when you were a youngster?'

'Dad, honestly!' said Kathy reprovingly.

Tim laughed. 'Yes, you're quite right, Mr Leigh. I think I gave the teachers a run for their money. But I never got into serious trouble. My mum and dad made sure of that.'

'So you're in the army now, lad,' said Albert. Tim was wearing his uniform, as many soldiers did when they were home on leave. 'Enjoying it, are you?'

'Yes, I am,' said Tim. 'I joined the regulars – the REME – to help in my career. I'm an apprentice electrician, you see. And my job's still here for me when I'm demobbed. I'm up at Catterick Camp, and I must admit I'm quite enjoying it, really.'

Albert nodded. 'Aye, that's where I was an' all, during the war, in the catering corps. So, I suppose you're off out now, you two?'

'Yes, I think we'll have a walk on the prom,' said Tim. 'Catch up on old times.'

'I'll be back to help with the teas, though, Dad,' said Kathy.

'Oh, that's all right,' said Albert. 'We're not full up this week. Winnie and I'll manage. Off you go and enjoy yourselves. Good to see you again, Timothy.'

'Thank you, Mr Leigh,' said Tim. 'It's good to see you as well.'

'Cheerio then, Dad,' said Kathy, thinking to herself that her father was in a remarkably good mood. And he seemed to have taken to Tim at once.

She took him to say hello to her aunt and Jeff and they were very nice to him as well.

'How lovely that you two have met up again,' said Winifred. 'I remember you very well, Tim. I used to hear such a lot about you. Kathy was forever talking about you and telling me jokes that you'd told her. Quite the class comedian, weren't you?'

'Aunty!' said Kathy, a mite embarrassed as she had been at her dad's remarks. But it was clear that Tim was already making a good impression.

Tim laughed. 'Yes, I liked to think I was,' he replied in answer to Winifred's remark. 'I must have been a real cheeky little brat. I've calmed down a lot ... er ... Mrs Bancroft. That's your name now, isn't it?'

'Yes, it has been for quite some time now, Tim,' said Winifred, as she and Jeff exchanged fond glances. 'It's getting on for eleven years now.'

'Good grief!' said Tim. 'How time flies, as my mum is always saying. Anyway, as I was telling you, I don't think I'm as cocky and such a damned nuisance as I used to be. And it's great meeting Kathy again.' Their happiness was clear to see as they smiled at one another.

'Off you go, then, and enjoy yourselves,' said Winifred, just as Kathy's father had already said. 'I hope we'll see you again, Tim.'

'Oh, I don't think there's much doubt about that,' replied Tim, putting an arm gently and caringly around Kathy's shoulders as they went out of the door.

'Well, that wasn't too bad, was it?' he remarked as they set off down the street, heading towards the promenade. He took hold of Kathy's hand. 'I think I've managed to convince them I'm OK and not the obnoxious little squirt I used to be.'

Kathy laughed. 'You were never that. As you said to my dad, you never got into any serious trouble, did you? I think you've made a really good first impression.'

They walked hand in hand along the promenade, northwards towards Bispham. There were several people, most likely visitors in the main – residents did not often take advantage of their resort's attractions – strolling along the prom, hand in hand, or arm in arm, and children bounding along ahead of their parents. It was a pleasant early autumn afternoon with the sun shining in a blue sky patterned with fluffy white clouds. There was a nip in the air, though, that gave a hint of the coming change in the season.

'Let's stop and have an ice cream,' said Tim, and they found a little café just off Gynn Square. They indulged themselves with vanilla and strawberry ices topped with chocolate flakes and nuts, covered with a gooey pink sauce.

'I really should be watching my weight,' said Kathy. 'I don't often spoil myself like this. I shall have to cut down on the cakes for a while to make up for this.'

'There's no need, is there?' smiled Tim. 'You look all right to me. In fact, you look pretty damned amazing...' He was regarding her with a look almost of wonder in his eyes. He recalled that she had been a pretty little girl, but now she was

244

a good deal more than just pretty. Her dark curly hair was almost shoulder length, framing a rounded fresh-complexioned face, out of which shone a pair of lovely luminous brown eyes. She was not dressed in her favourite red today, but the bright-yellow jacket with the stand-away collar suited her colouring just as well. She looked, he mused, like a ray of sunshine. Tim knew at that moment that he had fallen in love with Katherine Leigh, and how he hoped and prayed that she might feel the same way about him. He vowed that he must do nothing to mar this budding relationship.

Kathy lowered her eyes, a little fazed by Tim's adoring glance. She already knew, though, that she was so very glad that they had met again, and she felt sure that their friendship would blossom and go from strength to strength.

'No, I really do need to watch what I eat,' she said now, quite definitely. 'I wear size twelve in dresses now, and I mustn't get any bigger.'

'Well, I don't know what that means,' said Tim. 'But it sounds OK to me. Come on, then, if you're ready. We'll go and walk it off.'

North of Gynn Square there were large tableaux on the cliffs, stretching as far as Bispham, depicting fairy tales and colourful scenes of all kinds. In a few hours' time they would be lit up, forming one of the main attractions of Blackpool's famous Illuminations.

'No point in looking at them now,' said Tim. 'Shall we come and see them tonight? We could take a tram up to the end and then walk back. What d'you think, Kathy?'

'That would be great,' she replied. 'I haven't seen the Lights for ages. Funny, isn't it, that when you live here you never bother about them. I used to like them, though, when I was a little girl. That was when we had the accident, of course, after we'd been to see the Lights...'

'Well, you're going to be quite safe tonight,' said Tim, putting an arm around her and drawing her close. 'I shall take care of you, Kathy ... always.' She noticed his remark with a feeling of warmth and delight, but she did not comment on it.

Tim called for her again that evening at seven o'clock. 'So where are you off to now?' asked Winifred. She and Jeff were watching a variety show on the television, and Albert had gone to church. He went twice every Sunday now, apart from the times when the hotel was extra busy, to fulfil his duties as churchwarden.

'We're going to see the Lights, like a couple of day trippers,' laughed Kathy. 'It's ages since I saw them last.'

'That's nice,' said her aunt. 'I thought you might have been going to the pictures. It doesn't matter so much to me, but I know that your dad doesn't approve of the cinema on a Sunday. It's the way we were brought up, you know. And, of course, your dad's been much keener on Sunday observance since he started going to church regularly. But he won't object to you going to see the Lights.'

'We wouldn't want to do anything to upset him,' said Kathy. 'But in some ways he's much easier to get on with now, isn't he?'

'That's true.' Winifred nodded. 'Have a good time, then. We'll perhaps see you the next time you're home on leave, then, Tim?'

'Sure thing!' he replied with a broad smile. 'It's been good meeting you again.'

'And you, Tim,' added Jeff. 'Take care of yourself now.'

'What a grand couple they are,' said Tim, as they made their way once again to the promenade.

'Yes, Jeff's a great guy,' replied Kathy. 'He's made Aunty Win so happy. I don't think my dad imagined she would ever get married. And I'm sure my dad won't, not now. He's not taken much interest in women since that brief episode with Sally. He's happier in himself, though. He used to be such a grumpy old so-and-so at times.'

Tim laughed. 'Well, I seem to have got off on the right foot anyhow. I hope I can keep it that way.'

They boarded a tram near to North Pier. It took them along the prom to Bispham where the tableaux and the garlands of overhead lights came to an end. It was completely dark by now and the myriad multicoloured lights shone out brilliantly against the midnight-blue sky.

When they alighted from the tram they crossed the road to get a better view of the tableaux across the wide promenade. The scenes were a spectacular display of man's ingenuity and creativity, and it was often remarked that they got better each year. They had been shining in Blackpool since the early years of the century, apart from the duration of the two world wars.

Kathy recognised many familiar scenes – a

circus scene with jugglers, clowns and acrobats; jungle animals and creatures from under the sea; favourite characters from nursery rhymes and fairy tales – and overhead, strung across the promenade and decorating the lamp standards, there were Chinese lanterns, shooting stars and arching rainbows. It was a wonderland of colour and fantasy that brought out the child in everyone who was drawn into its spell. No more so than Kathy. She was filled with awe and delight, not only at the scene around her but at her closeness to Tim as they strolled along with his arm around her.

When they had walked a mile or so back towards the town centre they crossed the road and the tram track and made their way to the lower promenade. It was dark and quiet there away from the brilliant lights and the noise of the crowds and the clanging trams. There were a few other couples, who, like themselves, were seeking solitude. They had not kissed properly yet, apart from a peck on her cheek that Tim had given her as they walked along.

But it was all the better for the waiting. He drew her into a secluded corner in the shadow of the sea wall, and there they exchanged their first real kiss. It was tender and loving, filled with memories for both of them of their childhood friendship. There were still vestiges of the old Tim in his cheeky grin and his cheerful chatter that led him effortlessly from one thing to another. But he was grown-up now, and so was Kathy. Their next kiss was more passionate, holding promise of an awakening love of which they were both aware.

They drew apart after a few moments. He had not sought to do any more than kiss her. Nor did he tell her, yet, that he loved her. It was too soon; but the affection had been there long ago when they were children, and they both knew now that it would grow stronger. All he said, in a whisper, was, 'I'm so glad that I've met you again, Kathy.'

'So am I, Tim,' she whispered back.

'Come along; I'd best take you home,' he said. 'I must keep on the right side of your dad. Anyway, I'd better spend a bit of time with my parents.'

It was not yet ten o'clock but Kathy understood what he was saying. 'I'll see you again tomorrow, though, won't I?' he asked. 'D'you think your dad would let you off to come to tea at our house? I told my mum and dad how we met, and they'd love to see you again. Then we can go out tomorrow night.'

'I am allowed a little time to myself,' said Kathy. 'So I'm sure it will be OK with my dad and Aunty Win. I shall look forward to meeting your parents. I remember your mum, but not your dad.'

He kissed her again as they stood at the gate, then smiled and winked in the irrepressible way that she remembered, before walking off, with his soldier's gait, along the street.

He called for her the following day at five o'clock. The Fielding family lived only ten minutes' walk away, in a semi near to the school that Kathy and Tim had attended.

She was made most welcome and felt at home straight away. Tim's mother was quite young –

not yet fifty – and pretty, with a rounded face and a plumpish figure.

'Oh, I remember you very well, dear,' she said. 'You've hardly changed at all.'

'I must be rather bigger,' smiled Kathy. 'It's lovely to see you again, Mrs Fielding.'

Tim had a younger sister, Linda, who was fifteen, and a thirteen-year-old brother, Bobby. She remembered seeing him in his pram, but she didn't say so. Kathy could hardly remember Mr Fielding at all. She had known that he worked as an electrician for the local council, a job he was still doing. Tim had followed the same trade but for a different firm.

When he came home from work at six o'clock he, also, greeted her in a most friendly manner. Then they all sat down to a meal of steak-and-kidney pie and chips, followed by apple crumble with fresh cream. They finished off with a 'nice cup of tea', without which no northern meal was complete. Mrs Fielding had been hard at work in the kitchen for the latter part of the afternoon preparing the meal, as she did each day. She was, as she said herself, 'a full-time housewife and mum, and proud of it.' Like the majority of her generation she had not gone out to work after her marriage, nor had she ever wanted to.

'Times are changing, though, I realise that,' she remarked. 'I daresay you will want to go on working, Kathy, after you get married... Not just yet, though,' she added in the rather awkward silence that followed. Kathy felt herself blushing a little; was Tim's mother already thinking of her as a future daughter-in-law? But it seemed that she was just speaking in general terms. 'I mean, that's what today's young women seem to be doing, to help with the mortgage and everything, till the children come along.'

'Let 'em have a bit of freedom first, eh, Elsie?' joked her husband. 'Although there's nowt wrong with getting wed young if you're sure it's what you want.' Kathy wondered if he, too, was looking at her with an eye to the future.

She and Tim went out soon after the meal to catch the start of the film, *I'm All Right, Jack,* which was showing at a local cinema not far from both their homes. It was a rerun from a couple of years back that neither of them had seen the first time round. They laughed out loud with the rest of the audience at the antics of Ian Carmichael, as a graduate, trying to find his niche in industry; and the superb performance of Peter Sellers as the shop steward.

Tim bought her an ice cream in a little tub at the interval, and they held hands all the time, like a real 'courting couple', which she knew they almost were already.

They walked back to Kathy's home through the dark streets, both a little sad because it would soon be time to say goodbye, at least for the moment. They kissed several times as they stood by the gate, marvelling again at how wonderful it was that they had found one another again.

'You will write to me, won't you?' asked Tim.

'Of course I will, all the time,' she assured him. 'But you'll write as well, wont you?' She knew that a lot of young men were not great at correspondence.

'I'm not the world's best letter writer,' he confessed. 'My mother complains about it, but for you ... yes, I promise I'll write every week, at least. But I'll see you again very soon, I hope, in a few weeks' time if I can wangle it.'

After another tender kiss and a fond backward glance he was gone. But Kathy could not feel too sad at their parting. She knew that what they had found was 'for keeps'.

Their courtship followed the pattern of many of their peer group, where the young man was completing his national service. Tim still had a year and a half to do. He managed to get leave, though, every couple of months and they spent most of the time together. Their love for one another grew stronger and deeper. They had both uttered the 'three little words' that meant such a lot quite soon in their courtship, both of them knowing that 'I love you' meant for now and for ever.

It was not until the Christmas of 1962, though, that Tim asked Kathy to marry him, knowing that she would say yes. Holmleigh was open for four days over the Christmas period, so the two of them had not been able to spend as much time together as they could have wished; Kathy wanted to make sure that she pulled her weight at what was a very busy time. Tim had given her a ring that he had chosen himself, a sapphire surrounded by tiny diamonds which she loved.

They agreed, though, that it would be better to approach Kathy's father – to ask for his consent, in the old-fashioned way – when he was not quite so fraught with his hotel duties.

Kathy and Tim said goodbye at North Station the day after Boxing Day, hoping that it would not be very long before he was home again. Tim intended to wangle a forty-eight-hour pass at the end of January, then he would ask her father if he would agree to them being officially engaged.

Chapter Nineteen

Kathy and Tim had decided that she should broach the subject in advance. She guessed, although he didn't admit it, that Tim was a tiny bit nervous about approaching her father. She brought up the subject one morning over the breakfast table. Albert would not be running true to form, however, if he did not have something contrary to say.

'You want to get engaged?' He stared in astonishment at his daughter. 'But you've only known the lad five minutes!' Kathy could see, though, that there was a twinkle in her father's eye, and she knew he was not as surprised as he was pretending to be.

'Now, that's not true at all, Dad,' she replied, 'as you know very well. I was at school with Tim; we've known each other since we were five years old. I should think that's quite long enough for us to know what we want.'

'Aye, but you were only kids then, weren't you? What I mean is ... you've not been together all that much recently, with him being in the army. You've not had a chance to get to know him properly.'

Kathy smiled. 'Tim and I are very sure about what we want, Dad. Anyway, he's coming home on leave this weekend, and he's coming to see you. I know it might seem a bit old-fashioned, but he wants to do things properly, to ask your permission to marry me. I'm just paving the way, like, because I think he's a bit nervous.'

'It's not old-fashioned at all,' retorted Albert. 'You're only nineteen ... well, twenty in June, and he's not much older, is he? Anyroad, I'm pleased he's going to do things correctly. You'll not be wanting to get wed just yet, though, will you?'

'I'm not sure,' said Kathy evasively. She and Tim were planning to have a short engagement with a wedding later that summer. It was now January, 1963, and Tim was due to be demobbed in March. His job with Fothergill's electricians, an old-established local firm, was there for him to return to. They could see no point in waiting any longer as they were both sure of their feelings for one another, and had been so ever since they had met at the Winter Gardens, some sixteen months previously. They had both seen it as fate that they had met again, and felt sure that if they hadn't met at that time, then they would have done so at a later date.

'Well, he's a nice enough lad, I must say,' said Albert. 'Aye, you could have done far worse, Kathy. But I want you to be very sure, both of you. It's too late once you've tied the knot. We don't want any divorces in the family, like that

Sadie Morris. She was a flibbertigibbet if ever there was one! But she had us all fooled. I'd never have believed it.'

'But that's ages ago, Dad,' said Kathy. He did tend to harp on so about things that had happened in the past. 'Don't start on about divorce when we're not even married yet. Anyway, that's not going to happen, I can assure you, with Tim and me.'

'You can never be too sure,' said her father, shaking his head in a mournful way.

'Dad, for goodness' sake!' Kathy was starting to get cross with her father, but she could see the funny side of it as well. 'Don't be so bloomin' pessimistic!'

Albert smiled. 'No, you're right. I'm being silly, aren't I? But you know how I feel, Kathy love, don't you? I want the very best of everything for you. I want it all to be just right.'

'I know, Dad,' she replied. Indeed, she did know. He had been so caring and loving – overprotective at times – ever since she had had her accident and he had feared that he might lose her. She couldn't say, though, that he had ever been domineering or dictatorial with her; besides, her aunt and Jeff had always been there to stick up for her if he had ever been too intractable.

They were taking their ease at the breakfast table. There would be no more visitors until the week before Easter, unless some of their regulars asked to come and stay for a few days. They were always willing to oblige their clients, and that was why the hotel had a deservedly good reputation.

Kathy's aunt spoke up now. 'Well, I think this is

very good news, and I'm not surprised at all. You've only to look at our Kathy and Tim to see that they're made for one another.' Her eyes twinkled. And I've a feeling that Kathy thought so when she was only seven years old!'

Kathy laughed. 'Yes, I always had a soft spot for Tim.'

'I'm sure you'll be very happy together,' said Winifred. 'So let's not have any negative thoughts about it, eh, Albert? You should be looking forward to your only daughter getting married, and then some grandchildren coming along!'

'Well ... yes, so I am,' Albert admitted, looking affectionately at his daughter.

'I must love you and leave you now,' said Kathy, putting her pots together and getting up from the table. 'I'm sorry – I've left it a bit late to help with the washing-up, Aunty Win.'

'Don't worry, dear; I'll have it done in a jiffy,' said Winifred. 'Then I'm going to have a day of leisure before we make a start on the attic bedrooms tomorrow.'

Kathy had a part-time job during the winter months when the hotel was quiet. She did the accounts for a nearby newsagent's shop all the year round, but during the winter she served at the counter as well, to give the newsagent's wife a well-earned rest. Albert and Winifred still caught up with decorating and general maintenance of the hotel during the off-season, with help from Jeff in between his commissions for book illustrations and greetings cards.

The four of them were a contented little family group. Winifred and Jeff had found happiness that they had not anticipated so late in life. Kathy was looking forward to marrying the man whom folk were referring to as her childhood sweetheart. She hoped that they would be married sooner rather than later, if her father could be persuaded to give permission for her to marry before she officially came of age at twenty-one. And as for Albert, he seemed to have come to terms with his situation. He was no longer bitter about the death of his young wife, the event that had altered his view of life for so long. Nor did he resent his daughter's friendship with Sally and Phil and their young family. He could see that the young woman with whom he had – almost – fallen in love was happy with a man of her own age, one who was far more suited to her than he, Albert, would have been. The only women in his life now were his beloved daughter and his sister. And, along with his devotion to them, his commitment to his church and his rediscovered faith were a great solace to him.

Albert did not take much persuading to allow his daughter to marry before she was twenty-one. The wedding took place at the church that Albert now thought of as 'his' church, on a glorious sunny Saturday in mid August. What did it matter that it was the height of the holiday season? This was Kathy's day and she must have priority for once over the needs of the visitors. It was Tim's day as well, of course, although the bridegroom usually found himself overshadowed, and Tim was no exception to the rule.

Kathy had insisted, however, that she did not want a huge fuss, just a simple buffet meal after the wedding ceremony, with family members and friends. There were very few relatives on Kathy's side of the family, only her father and her aunt and Jeff; her grandparents had died a couple of years previously. But Tim's family made up for the sparsity; there were grandparents still living, as well as aunts, uncles and cousins.

Her wedding dress was a simple style: white silken satin with a boat-shaped neckline and an ankle-length bell-shaped skirt. Her short silk-tulle veil flowed from a neat pillbox hat decorated with seed pearls. Her bridesmaids were her friend, Marcia, Tim's sixteen-year-old sister, Linda, and Sally and Phil's ten-year-old daughter, Lucy. Their dresses, too, were simple, in keeping with the fashions of the day – sky-blue silken rayon in the now very popular shift style. Their matching pillbox hats complemented that of the bride, and they all, bride and bridesmaids, carried small posies of white and cream flowers: roses, sweet peas, lily of the valley and stephanotis.

The wedding breakfast – although it was at midday – was at Holmleigh, prepared in advance by Albert and Winifred and then laid out ready for their return from church by a team of hired helpers who would, later, see to the clearing away and washing-up. Kathy's father and her aunt wanted to be entirely free that day, and so guests who would normally have arrived on the Saturday had been asked to delay their arrival until the Sunday.

It was a joyful occasion, with the toast to the happy couple drunk in champagne.

'To Kathy and Tim...' The chorus of good

wishes echoed around the room, and tears welled up in Albert's eyes – a rare sight – as he gazed lovingly at the daughter who meant so much to him.

The couple departed for their honeymoon in Scarborough, a train journey from coast to coast as they, as yet, had no motor car. Tim had a driving licence, as he drove his firm's van, but they knew they would have to wait a little while before they could afford a vehicle of their own.

It was Kathy's first visit to the Yorkshire seaside resort, although Tim had been a couple of times with his parents when he was a child and he assured Kathy that she would love the place.

And so she did. In some ways it was like Blackpool – busy and bustling at this time of the year, and it also had its fair share of amusement arcades, ice cream and hot dog kiosks and 'Kiss me quick' hats. She had to admit, though, that Scarborough had a beauty of its own that Blackpool lacked.

They stayed at a small hotel near to the Spa Bridge. Kathy was captivated by the view from the bridge, across the wide expanse of the bay to the busy harbour. There the fishing boats were unloaded, and beyond was the huddle of fishermen's cottages on the steep slope of Castle Hill. And on the horizon the ruins of the old castle were silhouetted against the blue of the summer sky.

Kathy would have loved the place wherever it happened to be, because she was with Tim, who was now her beloved husband. She had felt a little apprehensive about the honeymoon and all that it entailed. Their love had not yet reached its fulfilment, partly because the opportunity had not arisen. They were both a teeny bit old-fashioned about such things. The time and the place had to be right; besides, they knew that their respective parents would not have approved of them anticipating the wedding date.

She soon realised that Tim was as concerned as she was about the matter. They were good friends and companions, though, as well as being very much in love, and they knew that all would be well. Very soon they discovered that they were as attuned physically as they were in every other way.

After a gloriously happy week it was time to go back and settle into their new little home. They knew that they were very fortunate. They were getting off to a very good start, far better than that of many young couples embarking on married life. They had saved up themselves for a deposit on a terraced house, and both sets of relatives – Tim's parents and Kathy's father, aunt and uncle – had contributed as well. The house was quite small, but it had a little garden at the front and also at the rear. It was only five minutes' walk away from Holmleigh, and not too far, either, from Tim's place of work.

Kathy intended to carry on working at the hotel, with Tim's wholehearted agreement. The majority of young wives went out to work now, as well as running the home, but Tim had promised to help his wife as much as he could. Kathy, remembering his efforts at school, reminded him that he was not much good at handiwork! Between them, though, they had made quite a good job of wallpapering their bedroom and the living room.

It was an ideally happy marriage with scarcely a wrong word to mar their contentment. As a young married couple Kathy and Tim were a part of what soon was to be called 'the Swinging Sixties'. As a popular song of the era said, the times were a-changing. The Fifties had started off with a period of austerity, when food was still rationed. But by the end of the decade Britain was again finding its way in the world and it was regarded by many as 'the best of times'.

The Sixties came in with an explosion of colour, sound and vitality. Kathy knew she must buy a miniskirt to be in the fashion. The new tights, too, instead of nylon stockings, were essential to wear with the short skirts. And a maxi-coat, almost floor length, and knee-high boots to compensate in winter for the cold around one's thighs. She had her hair cut shorter, and tried to make it less curly with backcombing and lacquer, whilst Tim grew his hair longer...

They listened to the Beatles, the Rolling Stones and Bob Dylan on records and on the radio and television. And they actually saw the Beatles live at a performance they gave at Blackpool's ABC Theatre.

They watched *Six-Five Special*, *Juke Box Jury*, *Steptoe and Son* and *Morecambe and Wise* on the television; and went to the cinema to see kitchen sink dramas such as *Alfie*, *A Taste of Honey* and *Saturday Night and Sunday Morning*.

They both wanted to start a family, though, to complete their happiness. They were delighted when their first child, Sarah, was born in 1965, followed in 1967 by Christopher; and so were the doting grandparents. Winifred was, in fact, a great-aunt, but as near as could be to a grandparent. She had always regarded Kathy as the daughter she had never had.

Kathy stopped working at the hotel when the children came along; that was to say, she no longer went in each day, as had been her custom, to help out wherever she could with the waitressing or general duties. She continued to help with the bookkeeping, although she could foresee a time in the not-too-distant future when her father and aunt might decide to retire.

The hotel and boarding house trade was gradually changing; it was necessary to keep up with modern trends to run a successful establishment. There were some regular visitors who still came year after year, but many had dropped away. Holidays abroad were now very tempting and, in many cases, just as affordable as staying in Britain. In this way, too, the Sixties was a time of change.

It was in the early spring of 1970 that Winifred told Kathy of their intentions.

'Your dad and I have decided it's time to sell up,' she said. 'Guests are wanting so much more these days. A bar, for instance, because they would like to be able to order drinks – alcoholic ones, I mean – with their meals. It's not that your dad and I are against that, but it would mean applying for a licence, and then paying extra bar staff. And there's another thing... A lot of the hotels now have gone over to what they call "en suite" facilities.' Kathy knew what that meant: a private bathroom or shower – or both – and a toilet attached to the bedroom.

Winifred shook her head. 'That would be no end of an upheaval for us, but if we stayed much longer we would have to do it. Times have certainly changed, Kathy. In the old days it was a jug and bowl in each room. Mind you, that was jolly hard work carrying water up the stairs every day...'

'And a "gazunder" underneath the bed,' laughed Kathy. 'I remember that up in the attic rooms.'

Winifred smiled. 'Yes, but it wasn't often that we had guests sleeping up there. We put in the required number of toilets, one on each landing, and a bathroom on each landing too, and washbasins in every room. It used to be quite acceptable – the norm, in fact – but folks seem to want a bath every day now instead of once a week.'

Kathy nodded. 'Yes, that's true...' So did she and Tim and the children, but she guessed her aunt still stuck to the tradition of bath night on a Friday. Winifred was always very clean and tidy, though, and still quite modern in her outlook in many ways.

'Anyway, we've decided to put Holmleigh up for sale,' Winifred went on. 'It would be best to let the new owners do any renovations they want in their own way.'

'And they'll be getting a place with a very good reputation,' said Kathy loyally.

'Yes, I must admit that's true,' said Winifred. 'And it's time for us to have a change and a rest. I'm seventy now, so is Jeff, and your dad is sixty-five. It'll be a big upheaval for us and no doubt it'll take some getting used to. Do you know, I have lived in this house all my life, and so has Albert, apart from his time in the army, of course, and you were born here, Kathy...' Her aunt looked pensive for a moment.

'So ... where will you retire to?' asked Kathy. 'You'll want to stay in Blackpool, I suppose?'

'Of course,' said Winifred. 'I'm a true "sand-grown 'un". I don't think I could live anywhere else now. Jeff and I rather fancy living in Bispham. We're going to look for a semi-detached house, not too far away from the sea. We'll have time to walk on the cliffs and ride on the trams! Things we never have time to do now. And your dad will be coming with us. We've talked it over with him and he agrees it's the best thing to do. We get along very well, the three of us. And if we get a large enough house he can have his own rooms. A sitting room as well as a bedroom, I mean; then he can be private when he wants to be.'

They did not have much difficulty in selling the property. A youngish couple from Blackburn, who seemed to be 'not without a bit of brass' as Albert put it, bought Holmleigh. They said they would carry on as usual with the visitors who were booked in for that summer, then start the alterations they required when the season came to an end. Albert, Winifred and Jeff found a house that suited them all on an avenue leading off the promenade, in the area known as Little Bispham.

In 1971 Kathy and Tim and their two children moved to a larger house, a semi-detached, not too far – but not too near – to that of their relatives. Tim was doing well at work and had been made a partner in the firm. On the strength of this they had bought their first motor car, a second-hand Morris that was roomy enough for a family of four. Sarah, aged six, was now at school, and Christopher would very soon be starting; he already went to a playgroup a few mornings a week.

Kathy now had more time to herself. She had continued with her story writing and was determined not to give up despite the inevitable rejections. Sally, whose friendship still meant a great deal to her, had insisted that she must keep on trying. It was a great day when, in the autumn of 1971, her first children's story was published by the magazine *People's Friend*. That was only the beginning. By the summer of 1972 her stories, both for adults and for children, were to be found in several of the women's magazines.

'I knew you would do it!' Sally told her delightedly. 'I knew when you were in my class that you had a talent for storytelling.' And Kathy knew that it was thanks to Sally and to teachers who came later for fostering her love of literature, without which she would not have been able to express herself so well.

And no one was more proud of Kathy than her father when her first serial story was published. 'That's my girl,' he said. 'I always knew you were a clever lass. My goodness! An authoress in the family. Just wait till I tell them all at the club and at church!'

Kathy was touched at her father's pride in her. She had seldom known him to be so excited about anything. The father and daughter were good friends now, something that at one time she could never have imagined. They all settled down to what seemed to be a period of stability, all of them well contented with the lives they were leading.

Chapter Twenty

It was in 1972 that Albert's health started to fail. He had two minor heart attacks and was warned to take things easy.

'I've done nowt else but take it easy ever since I retired,' he grumbled, showing a little of the tetchiness that at one time had been typical of him. 'I don't see how I can do much less than I'm doing now.'

Albert had not settled too well into retirement, although he had thought it was what he wanted. He still rose early every morning from force of habit. Then he bought a newspaper from the local shop, and after reading it he took a leisurely walk along the cliff top, if the weather was fine. He found then, for the rest of the day, that he had too much time on his hands. He still played darts, he watched Blackpool's football team – now, sadly, relegated – on a Saturday afternoon, and carried on with his church duties each Sunday.

His grandchildren were a source of delight to him. He had to admit, though, to a feeling of self-reproach as he realised that he was finding much more pleasure in their company than he had in that of his daughter at a similar age. He knew that this had been entirely his own fault, and he hoped that he had made it up to Kathy in later years. Indeed, he and his daughter were closer now than they had been at any time.

There was still a void in his life, though, after so many years in the cut and thrust of hotel life. Kathy discussed her fears about him with her aunt one afternoon when she called to see her. Winifred was on her own as Albert had gone to the bowling green. He didn't play himself but he liked to watch the team from his 'local'.

'Dad's not himself,' she said. 'At least, he's not the same person that we've all come to know and love. You remember we said how much he had improved? And I've been getting on with him much better than I did when I was a little girl.'

'Yes, it's since you had your accident, dear,' said Winifred. 'He realised then how much he loved you. He always did, you know, but he found it difficult to show it.'

'I was so pleased about the change in him,' Kathy went on. 'But now it seems to me as though he's going back to how he used to be. You know – those bouts of moodiness and silence. Sometimes I think he has something on his mind.'

Kathy thought then that her aunt gave her an odd look, as though there was something that she knew, but wasn't divulging it. 'Oh, I think he just gets a bit fed up sometimes,' Winifred replied. 'Retirement has not been quite what he expected. He's been so active all his life that he can't adjust to all this freedom. And those heart attacks he had scared him quite a lot.'

'He appears to have recovered from them, though,' said Kathy. 'He looks quite well in himself ... but I still have the feeling that there's something troubling him.'

'He's probably just concerned about his health,' replied Winifred, a trifle too quickly. 'We are inclined to be, you know, as we get older and we find we can't do everything that we used to do.'

'Well, I've really come to invite you all to come to tea on Sunday,' said Kathy. 'You and Jeff and my dad. That might cheer him up a bit. I know how much he likes to see the children...'

But the tea party did not take place. It was on the Thursday prior to the planned event that Albert had another heart attack. Winifred knew at once that this one was much more severe. It was now September, 1973, over a year since the two minor ones he had suffered. She called an ambulance and he was taken to hospital without any delay. Kathy and Tim were informed and they, too, rushed to the hospital. All the family spent an anxious evening awaiting news of him. Eventually they went home to rest, knowing there was nothing else they could do but leave him in the capable hands of the doctor and nurses.

He had recovered a little by the following day

when Winifred and Jeff went to see him again in his private room. He stretched out his hand towards Winifred and she took hold of it. He looked imploringly at her and he began to speak in an urgent manner.

'When's our Kathy coming?' he asked. 'I want to see her...' It was clearly an effort to speak. He was short of breath and his voice was husky and weak. 'There's summat ... summat I've got to say to her...'

'Kathy will be here very soon,' his sister told him. 'But ... leave it be, Albert. It's too late now.' She had a good idea what it was that Albert might want to tell his daughter. Kathy had been quite right when she had said that her father appeared to have something on his mind. She, Winifred, had noticed it as well. 'Just concentrate on getting better, there's a good lad,' she told him. 'Things are best left as they are.'

Albert shook his head regretfully. 'I'm done for, Winnie. I know that, and I know I've not been fair to the lass... I should've told her.'

'Leave it, Albert,' she said again. 'It would be for the best.' She stooped to kiss his pale cheek and he closed his eyes. It was obvious that he was exhausted and he said nothing more. He appeared to be sleeping, so they decided after a while that there was no point in them staying any longer.

'We're going now, Albert,' said Winifred, just in case he could hear her. 'We'll see you tomorrow, Jeff and me. Goodbye, dear. God bless...'

'He's not good at all, is he?' she whispered to Jeff as they made their way out of the hospital.

'No, I'm afraid not, my dear,' said Jeff, 'but he's in good hands. All we can do is trust, and say our prayers.'

'I'm worried about Kathy,' said Winifred. 'I'm bothered, Jeff, about what he might say.'

'I think he's too weak to say much at all,' replied Jeff. He kissed her cheek. 'Don't worry, darling. He probably wants to tell Kathy that he loves her, that's all.'

Kathy and Tim went to see her father later that afternoon. He was awake again but looked very frail and ill. He reached out a hand to his daughter. 'Kathy ... Kathy love, come here ... I want to tell you summat.'

She moved closer and took hold of his hand. 'What is it, Dad?'

'I've not been a good dad to you... I should have told you ... I know I should ... but I couldn't do it. But I always loved you, Kathy ... I loved you, so much...'

'I know that, Dad,' she replied. 'I always knew. You're worried that you didn't tell me so, aren't you? But I always knew that you loved me.' She leant over to kiss his papery cheek. At that moment his head lolled sideways and his hand dropped away from hers. She knew that he had gone.

'Tim, Tim ... call the nurse!' she cried. 'But I think it's too late. Oh dear! I think my dad has ... gone!'

Kathy was filled with a deep sadness at the death of her father. She could not have said, truthfully, that she was heartbroken. She reflected that she might well have been more grief-stricken if it had been her aunt who had died. She had always felt much closer to Winifred, who had been everything to her that a mother might have been. However, this was her father, and she knew he had done his best, according to his lights, especially of late. She recalled how, when she was a child, he had seemed remote at times and uninterested in her, but she knew he had been coping with his resentment and bitterness at the death of her mother. Following her accident, however, he had been much more approachable and caring, and this had awakened in her a strong affection for him. She had had a premonition, though, that he would not 'make old bones' as the saying went, so his death had not been too much of a shock to her.

He had died on a Friday, and the funeral was arranged for the middle of the following week; a service at the church followed by the burial at Layton Cemetery. Kathy went round to her aunt's home on the Saturday morning to help to sort out certain matters. Sarah and Christopher stayed at home with Tim, who worked a five-day week.

'We'll have to find your dad's will,' said Winifred. 'There should be a copy in his bureau, and the original one is with our solicitor. It's pretty straightforward, though.'

Kathy knew that the house belonged jointly to her father, Winifred and Jeff. It had been bought with the proceeds from the sale of the hotel plus a contribution from Jeff. The house would now belong to her aunt and uncle, and after their

271

deaths would be willed to Kathy. Also, the remainder of Albert's share of the profit from the hotel and any other monies he had accrued in his lifetime would now go to his daughter.

'I'll have a look in his bureau, shall I?' said Kathy. 'Although I must admit I shall feel rather guilty, as though I'm prying. He was always very secretive about the contents of that bureau, wasn't he? I know it's always kept locked, and once, when I was a little girl, I tried to open it and he was furious with me.'

'Well ... yes,' replied her aunt, evasively. 'There were certain things that your dad was secretive about. Never mind about it now, Kathy love. I'll see to it later. I'm not quite sure where the key is anyway.' Winifred looked flustered and ill at ease.

'It'll be on that jug on his chest of drawers where he keeps – sorry, kept – his odds and ends,' said Kathy. 'I know his spare door key is in there and his football season ticket.'

'Yes, perhaps so,' said Winifred. 'Go on, then, you're his daughter. I daresay you've more right than anyone to look at his private papers.' She looked doubtful, though, and more than a little anxious.

'I won't, if you really don't want me to,' said Kathy.

'No, you carry on, dear,' said her aunt. 'It'll happen be for the best.'

As Kathy had thought, the key to the bureau was in the pottery jug on her father's chest of drawers, along with other odds and ends: pencils and biros, books of stamps, a screwdriver, a penknife, and his season ticket for Bloomfield Road, the home of his beloved football team. He had only used it a few times that season, and Kathy pondered that it would be a shame for it to go to waste. Jeff didn't attend the matches regularly, and neither did Tim, who preferred to spend his free afternoons with the children and herself. Kathy decided, if her aunt approved, that she would give it to Phil Grantley, whom she knew was still an ardent supporter.

But there were other more important issues to be dealt with at that moment. The bureau, a solid-looking piece of furniture made from mahogany, was in her father's sitting room. It had a pull-down front that served as a writing desk. The key turned easily in the lock, and Kathy looked inside for the very first time. Everything seemed to be very neat and tidy.

The first thing that caught her eye was what appeared to be several photographs in stiff cardboard covers. She pulled them out, then looked in amazement at what she recognised at once was the wedding photograph of her father and the mother she had never known. She gasped as she gazed at the young woman in the photograph, knowing that she might almost be looking at a picture of herself. The bride had the same dark hair that fell in natural waves, framing a rounded face, the same mouth and nose, and she guessed that the eyes, like her own, would have been brown. Kathy realised then that she had never before seen a photograph of her mother, and what was more strange was the fact that she had never even asked if she might see one; for the life of her, now, she could not imagine why she had been so lacking in curiosity.

The young woman was wearing a dress that was obviously a wedding dress, but not a conventional long one with a veil. It was impossible to tell the colour from the black and white image; it could have been a white dress, or possibly pale pink or blue. It had padded shoulders and a sweetheart neckline, a yoke trimmed with lace, puffed sleeves and a knee-length skirt. The small hat was trimmed at the side with a posy of flowers, and she was carrying a small bouquet of what looked like roses in bud. The bridegroom – Kathy's father – was dressed in the uniform of a soldier; the three stripes on his arm denoted that he was a sergeant. 'What year had it been, she wondered? She was born in 1943, so it would be 1941 or 1942, she guessed. The war had been going on since 1939, and she knew it had been a period of quite severe austerity in Britain, hence the less-than-formal wedding dress.

Another photograph showed a wedding group. There were the bride and groom, a much younger Aunt Winifred, and another young man and woman whom she did not know – the bridesmaid and the best man, she supposed. She recognised her Grandma and Grandad Leigh who had died a few years ago, and there was another middle-aged couple whom she did not know. Her other grandparents? she pondered, the parents of her mother. Then why had she never met them or heard anything about them? Kathy realised now that a whole chapter from the past had been closed to her. When she thought again about her lack of curiosity, she recalled that she

274

had never been encouraged to ask questions about her mother. Her father had always been evasive or short-tempered on the few occasions she had dared to broach the subject, and even her aunt had been unwilling to say very much. She supposed that eventually she must have understood that it was a closed book, and so she had stopped worrying about it.

There were two more photographs. In one of them her father and the woman she had now gathered was her mother were seated, and the woman was holding a baby, a very young one, wrapped in a shawl. The baby's chubby face was crowned with a cap of dark curls, and the dark eyes seemed to be looking up at the mother, who was gazing at the child with a look of wonderment and love. Myself as a baby, thought Kathy, looking at the photo in bewilderment. The second one showed the same couple with the baby. In this one the woman was smiling straight into the camera, with the same look of joy and contentment in her eyes. Behind the couple, standing, were Aunt Winifred and, again, the couple whom Kathy had assumed were the bridesmaid and best man at the wedding, two people whom she had never met, at least not as far as she could remember. 'These, then, must have been her godparents, because these obviously were christening photographs. Curiouser and curiouser, thought Kathy, shaking her head in amazement.

She laid the photos to one side and took out a pile of foolscap envelopes from the next cubbyhole. She opened them one by one, no longer feeling that she was prying, but that she was gradually uncovering a mystery that had been hidden from her, but which she felt she had a right to know about.

The first envelope contained the marriage certificate of her mother and father. The marriage had taken place at the church the family still attended, on 27th June, 1942. She, Kathy, had been born in the June of the following year. So there was no question of it being what they called a 'shotgun wedding', she pondered. There was the name of her grandfather – Albert's father – with his occupation, given as hotel proprietor. And for the first time she knew the full name of her mother. She had heard her referred to as Barbara, but here was her name in full: Barbara Jane White. Instead of her father's name there was the name of a man referred to as her guardian, Benjamin White, presumably an uncle or a grandfather.

Opening the remaining envelopes she came across her own birth certificate; a baptism card, given as a memento to every child that was christened at the church – a custom they still followed; and the death certificate of her grandparents, Alice and William – Alice had died in 1960 and William the following year. She still hadn't come across the will that she was supposed to be looking for.

She opened the next envelope and drew out another certificate covered in the black spidery writing that seemed to be the typical handwriting on all of them. Then she gasped, first in astonishment, then in gradually dawning shock and horror, as her mind tried to make sense of what her eyes were seeing. For this was a certificate of divorce – the divorce of her parents, Albert Leigh and Barbara Jane Leigh, in the July of 1945. And there was the name of a co-respondent ... Nathaniel Castillo. Kathy knew little of such matters, but she thought that the co-respondent was the person named as having committed adultery with the respondent. But this was not what really mattered to her. The amazing – awful – truth that was now being revealed to her was that her mother had not died, as she had always been told. Her parents were divorced, something that Kathy had been brought up to believe was a shameful thing. Her mother, in fact, might still be alive!

Her hands were trembling as she drew out another sheet of paper that was in the envelope. It was a letter from her mother to her father. It was dated January 1945, a few months before the divorce. Kathy could hardly read what was written there because her eyes were blinded with tears. She gathered, however, that Barbara, her mother, was agreeing to leave baby Katherine with Albert and was promising never to contact any of the Leigh family again.

She snatched up the letter and the certificate and fled from her father's room, downstairs to the living room used by Winifred and Jeff. Her aunt was sitting motionless in an armchair. She looked up, her eyes full of apprehension, as her niece stormed into the room.

'Aunty Win...' she shouted. 'What can you tell me about all this?' She waved the offending papers at Winifred. 'You *were* going to tell me, weren't you? I should hope you were! Don't you think it's time I knew about it?'

'Oh ... Kathy love, I'm so sorry,' her aunt began.

'I guessed it would all come to light now, although I didn't really know if your dad had hung on to ... everything. I wasn't able to tell you. It was a promise I made, so long ago...' Her aunt's eyes, too, were moist with tears, but it made no difference to Kathy, her anger was so great.

'But my mother wasn't dead!' she cried. 'She might still be alive. Most probably she is...'

'That's something we don't know, dear,' said Winifred. 'But I'm sorry, so dreadfully sorry.'

'It's too late to be sorry now,' said Kathy, in a tone of voice she had never before used to her aunt. She couldn't remember ever having a real quarrel with Aunt Winifred, but this was unforgivable. 'You deceived me, Aunty Win,' she yelled. 'All these years, you've known about my mother and you never let on. I shall never forgive you.'

Scarcely knowing what she was saying or doing, Kathy grabbed her coat from the back of a chair where she had left it and fled out of the room, out of the front door. She leant against the garden wall, brushing the tears away from her eyes and trying to steady her breath. Her aunt had not followed her. She discovered she was still holding the papers and she shoved them into her handbag.

What should she do now? She had walked to her aunt's house, although she was able to drive the car – she had recently passed her driving test. Perhaps by the time she had walked home she would be feeling slightly more composed. She would start crying again, though, when she saw Tim, and the children would be upset.

She decided to go and see Sally. Her former teacher had been a good friend to her over the years. Despite the difference in their ages – Sally, and Phil too, now must be in their fifties – they had a lot in common and were able to talk about all manner of things. Sally and Phil also lived in Bispham, but it was a fair distance away. Kathy decided she would take a bus, but before that it might be as well to let Sally know that she was coming. She popped into the nearest phone box.

'Kathy, how nice to hear you,' said Sally. Kathy had rung her the previous day, of course, to tell her of Albert's death. 'Yes ... of course you can come round; I'll get some coffee ready... No, I'm on my own; well, Phil's out in the garden, taking out all the dead flowers ready for autumn, and the kids are out, as usual.' Lucy and Daniel were now in their teens and were usually pursuing their own interests. Are you all right, Kathy? You sound a little upset... Well, I suppose you're sure to be, about your father... That was a daft thing to say.'

'Actually, I am upset,' replied Kathy. 'Not just about Dad; it's something else. That's why I want to talk to you... Yes, see you in a little while...

'Come along in and tell me all about it.' Sally ushered Kathy into the comfortable living room.

Sally Grantley had not changed much over the years. She was still a most attractive woman. Her silvery-blonde hair had kept its colour; it was a shade that turned to grey very becomingly. It was always beautifully styled. Kathy guessed that her friend could afford some little luxuries. She was now the headteacher of a nearby infant school, not the one that Kathy had attended. And Phil had moved on too, to become the head of department for English at a comprehensive school, where he also taught games and PE.

'The coffee's all ready,' said Sally. 'Go in and make yourself at home.' Sally went to the kitchen and Kathy made herself comfortable in an armchair in the homely room. It was never over-tidy; evidences of Sally's and Phil's occupation were to be seen on the sideboard and in corners, mixed up with the usual teenage possessions: a pile of books waiting to be marked; football boots; an orange and white scarf; library books; and an assortment of long-playing records on top of the radiogram.

'Now, what's it all about?' asked Sally, handing Kathy a mug of hot coffee and a plate. 'You don't mind a mug, do you?' she said, offering her a biscuit, which Kathy refused.

'No ... thanks, and a mug is just fine. It's what we always use... I don't know where to begin, Sally, I really don't,' she started. She placed her mug on a mat on the small table next to her. 'Well, perhaps it might be better if I showed you these, then you'll understand... Not that I really understand any of it myself,' she added. She unzipped her bag and handed the papers to Sally.

Her friend perused them. 'Good gracious!' she muttered, after a few moments. 'I don't wonder you're upset. Have a drink of your coffee, love. It'll do you good. This has knocked you for six, hasn't it?'

Kathy sipped at her coffee, feeling the warmth

flow through her. She had felt cold all over, although it was quite a pleasant autumn day. 'It's unbelievable,' she said in a small voice. 'You know that I was always told she was dead. She might still be alive.'

'And your aunt never said anything, never even hinted?'

'Not a word. I'm afraid I've fallen out with her, the first time ever. I stormed out ... and came here. Tim doesn't know yet.'

'I'm glad you came,' said Sally. 'It's a shock to me as well.'

'When you were friendly with my dad ... you didn't have any idea then?' asked Kathy. 'You didn't suspect that his wife might not be dead?'

'No, never,' said Sally. 'I must admit I found it rather odd, though, that he would never talk about her. I mean ... a lot of men lose their wives, don't they? But they get over it in time. I remember, though, when we were dancing at the Palace, soon after I'd met Albert, he got quite upset when they were playing ... now, what was it? "As Time Goes By"; I think that was the song.' She began, softly, to sing the first line... 'Yes, that was it. I wondered if it might have been "their song"; you know what I mean. He said something about it bringing back memories.'

'I can't understand why I never asked any questions,' said Kathy. 'But I suppose, as a child, you accept what you are told. My mother was dead, or so I'd been led to believe, and they as good as told me not to ask any more about it. My aunt always assured me, though, that my mother had loved me very much.' She was thoughtful for a

281

moment. 'But she deserted me, didn't she? It looks as though there was someone else involved. This ... Nathaniel Castillo. 'What am I to make of that? He sounds like an Italian to me...'

'More likely to be American,' said Sally. 'The Americans entered the war in 1941.'

'Yes, of course,' said Kathy. 'Then she ... my mother ... she committed adultery. Maybe ... maybe she was a "bit of a flibbertigibbet", as my father used to say about some women! All the same, she was my mother.'

'We can't conjecture,' said Sally. 'We don't know all the facts. I'll say one thing, though, Kathy... Your father wouldn't have been the easiest person to live with, would he? If you'll forgive me for saying so.'

Kathy gave a wry laugh. 'You can say that again! Although, in all fairness, he did improve a lot as the years went by ... and I shall miss him,' she added wistfully.

'Of course you will,' Sally smiled at her. 'But now, I really think you should go and sort things out with your aunt. I know you're angry with her, and you have every reason to be. But Winifred's a remarkable person, you know, Kathy. And I'm sure she believed she was acting in your best interests.'

'Yes...' agreed Kathy, meekly. 'I'm sorry now. She's been like a mother to me. That's how I always thought of her, and I know she'll be feeling dreadfully upset.'

'She'll be able to explain everything to you,' said Sally. 'I daresay she's wanted to do so for a long time... Oh, here's Phil.' Her husband had just come in from the garden; he had not seen Kathy arrive.

'Hello there, Kathy,' he greeted her. 'I was sorry to hear about your father. Sally and I will be there, at the funeral. Is that what you've come to tell us about?'

'Partly...' began Kathy. 'But there was something else. Sally will tell you about it...'

'Yes, Kathy's had a shock,' said Sally. She told her husband, very briefly, about what had happened. 'And I think, Phil, that Kathy needs to go back now to sort things out with her aunt. You'll take her back in the car, won't you?'

'Of course,' said Phil. 'Right away. Oh dear, Kathy. I'm so sorry.' He shook his head, as bewildered as the rest of them. 'You never know, though. Good may come out of this.'

'I certainly hope so,' agreed Kathy. 'It feels like a dream at the moment, but whether it's a good one or a bad one, I'm not sure.'

Sally gave her a hug as she put her coat on. 'Chin up, love. And remember, we're always here if you need us.'

Winifred rushed to greet her when she came in through the back door, which was always left open during the day. 'Oh, Kathy love, I've been so worried. Where were you? I rang your number, but Tim said you weren't there. So now he's concerned as well.'

'Oh dear, I'm sorry, Aunty Win,' said Kathy. 'I was at Sally's.' She put her arms round her. 'I shouldn't have said all those awful things, but it was such a shock.' They clung together for several moments, each finding solace in the embrace.

'Of course it was a shock,' said Winifred. 'And I'm more sorry than I can say. Now, you give Tim a ring and tell him you're here. You can explain everything to him later. Then we'll sit down and I'll tell you everything that you ought to have known long ago...'

PART THREE

Chapter Twenty-One

1942

'Aunty Myrtle ... Albert asked me to marry him last night, and I've said that I will.' Myrtle White turned to smile at her niece. Barbara, too, was smiling and she looked quite pleased, but Myrtle could not have said in honesty that the girl looked ecstatic at the news she was telling.

Myrtle put her arms around her and kissed her cheek. 'Well, that's wonderful news, my dear. Albert's a grand young man; I've always thought so, and I'm sure he'll make you a very good husband.'

'Yes ... I think so too,' replied Barbara, sitting down at the breakfast table in the large kitchen. 'We don't want a long engagement. We're going to choose the ring this afternoon and we plan to get married in the summer; June, we think. Albert should be due for another spot of leave by then.'

Albert Leigh was home on leave at the moment. He was in the army catering corps, stationed up in the north of England, and there didn't seem to be any likelihood of him being sent overseas. He was now thirty-seven, considered rather too old for active service. Besides, all troops were at their various camps in Britain now, in this spring of 1942 – apart from those fighting in the desert areas in the Middle East – and had been ever since the debacle of Dunkirk.

Albert lived next door in the boarding house that was run by his mother and father and his sister, Winifred. He had worked there ever since he had left school, until he joined the army. They were a lovely family, on very good terms with Myrtle and Ben White who ran a similar boarding house next door.

Albert was a quiet man, but Myrtle was sure he was a good reliable one. She sometimes wondered why he had never married, but she had guessed he had been sweet on her niece, Barbara, ever since the girl was seventeen or so. But it was only quite recently that they had started going out together. Barbara was twenty-two, and her aunt thought that marriage to Albert would be a very good thing.

She glanced at her now, tucking into the plate of porridge that her aunt had placed in front of her. She enjoyed her food, did Barbara, and didn't seem to mind that she was a wee bit plumper than some girls of her age. She was a most attractive girl, with dark-brown hair that had a natural curl, warm brown eyes and a flawless pink and white complexion. Myrtle was not surprised that Albert had been attracted to her, and there had been one or two others who had been smitten. But since she had lost Mike, two years ago, Barbara had quietened down considerably. She had a lovely disposition too, very kind and thoughtful, and that was what was important, really, far more so than a beautiful appearance.

Myrtle was very proud of this young woman, her

niece by marriage; she loved her as though she were her own daughter. She and her husband, Benjamin, had had custody of her ever since Barbara's parents, Thomas and Lilian, had been killed in a car crash when the little girl was eighteen months old. Benjamin was Thomas's elder brother; there had been just the two of them, eight years apart. Ben and Myrtle had not been blessed with children, although they had been married for ten years and were extremely happy. And so they had brought Barbara up as lovingly as they would have done with any child of their own. They had decided, though, that she must know the truth when she was old enough. It would have been quite easy to pretend they were her real parents, but Barbara had been well aware that Ben and Myrtle White were her aunt and uncle, and therefore they shared the same surname.

'See you later then, Aunty,' said Barbara, finishing her toast and tea and getting up from the table. 'Must go or I'll miss the bus.' She gave her aunt a quick kiss. 'It's my half day, though, as you know. Albert's meeting me from work, then we're going to choose the ring.'

'How exciting!' said Myrtle. 'Perhaps we could all get together tonight – your uncle and me, and Albert's parents and Winifred, and you two, of course, and have a drink of sherry to celebrate.'

'Good idea,' said Barbara, smiling, as she departed.

She worked as a telephonist at the GPO in Blackpool, as she had done since leaving school, helping out in the boarding house as well when required. Benjamin White was a postman and had left much earlier that morning to start his duty at 5 a.m. An ungodly time of day but he was used to it. He finished work, however, at lunchtime and then he was free – after he had had a quick nap – to help his wife in the boarding house.

At the present time they had RAF recruits billeted with them. It had been so since early 1940, one batch of young men following another. The Leighs' house next door was also an RAF billet, as were the majority of boarding houses in this area of North Shore, Blackpool, and also in the centre and south of the town. It was the largest RAF training centre in Britain.

When the first lot of recruits had arrived at the Whites' boarding house in 1940, the young woman, Barbara, who was assumed by the men to be the daughter of the house, had attracted a goodly number of admiring looks and wolf whistles, as well as invitations to go out to the pictures or dancing.

But Barbara White was quite indifferent to the fact that Blackpool was now a veritable sea of air force blue. These young men were everywhere: drilling in the streets; practising manoeuvres on the sands; and in their spare time, walking in twos along the pavements; frequenting the cinemas, dance halls and shops. Barbara, aged twenty, was already engaged to her soldier sweetheart, Mike Thompson. He was stationed in the south of England and she did not see him very often. They corresponded regularly, though, and planned to marry quite soon, depending on the progress of the war and the availability of leave.

But Mike did not return from Dunkirk with the thousands of other retreating soldiers. He was shot by gunfire from an enemy aeroplane. Barbara was devastated at his death, and it was little consolation to her that she was only one of many girls to have lost a loved one in similar circumstances. She did accept invitations, later that year and in 1941, from some of the RAF lads, but there was still a deep sadness at the heart of her.

She had known for a long time that Albert Leigh from next door carried a torch for her. She liked him very much, but he was fifteen years older than herself, and at times seemed like a different generation. He was kind, though, so very kind, and well mannered towards her. His manner of speech betrayed his Lancashire origins, but she, Barbara, was a Lancashire lass too, and proud of it, and she didn't hold with snobbery or pretentiousness. Before he joined the army, Albert had spent a lot of his time, when he was not busy working in the hotel, with his mates at the local pub, where he played in the darts team, and she knew that he was an ardent supporter of Blackpool's football team. A man's man, one might say.

She had wondered, over the years, why he had never married. She could not be so vain as to think that he was waiting, hopefully, for her to smile encouragingly at him. He must have seen her in the company of lads when she was growing up, and then there had been Mike... Albert had told her how sorry he was on hearing of her fiancé's death.

But then, during the autumn of 1941, when he was home on leave, he had plucked up courage to

291

ask her to go out with him. He had told her then how much he had always admired her, had loved her from afar, and how it would make him so happy if she would go out with him when he was home on leave, and write to him whilst he was away.

And he was so kind and thoughtful, so gentle and loving in his conduct towards her, that she had agreed readily. She had discovered that he was not so serious as she had once thought. He was able to make her laugh – not frequently, but often enough – and pull her round from the bouts of sadness that still came over her from time to time. She noticed, too, that he was not a bad-looking fellow. He looked much younger when he smiled, and his blue eyes sparkled with merriment, in between his far more sober moods.

When he asked her to marry him she did not hesitate before agreeing that she would do so. He had kissed her passionately then, as they stood on the promenade looking out across the dark sea.

'You have made me the happiest man in the world,' he told her. 'I shall look after you, and love you always, my lovely Barbara. I shall never let you down.'

'I know that, Albert,' she replied meekly, quite overcome that someone should love her so devotedly. Mike had loved her, as she had loved him, but theirs had been a happy, carefree relationship, not so serious and ardent as this was showing signs of being. All the same, she felt that she was doing the right thing. Her aunt and uncle were good to her and she knew that they loved her dearly. She was contented living with them; after all, it had always been her home and she had never known any different. But she could not say that she was always entirely happy or completely satisfied with her lot. Aunty Myrtle was inclined to fuss and be overprotective of her at times. Barbara knew that it was because of her love for her niece, and that she was being true to the promise that she and Uncle Ben had made to look after her. She felt, though, that marriage to Albert would give her more independence. She would be more of a person in her own right, and to be married was, of course, something of a status symbol. It was all to the good that her aunt and uncle approved wholeheartedly of her engagement to Albert.

He met her out of work that day in February and they went to Beaverbrooks, the jewellers, in Blackpool, to choose a ring. Barbara, with Albert's approval, chose a sapphire with a diamond at either side, and it fitted her perfectly. He placed it on her finger there and then, in the shop. He kissed her, though not quite so ardently this time, in front of other people, and told her again that he was the happiest man in the world. The shop assistants looked on with smiles of approval, although they had probably seen it all before; but Barbara felt a mite embarrassed.

The wedding, after an engagement of only four months, was a somewhat quieter affair than it would have been in peacetime. Barbara did not choose to wear a traditional white dress, which would cost an extravagant amount of money and clothing coupons. She opted for a pale-blue dress that she might be able to wear again, and a small hat that would not look out of place at church on a Sunday morning. Her friend, Dorothy, whom she had known since she was at school, was her bridesmaid, and likewise Dennis, an old school friend of Albert's, acted as best man.

Just a few friends and family members met together at the Whites' boarding house after the church service. The buffet lunch, consisting of various sandwiches, meat pies, sausage rolls, fancy cakes, and trifles – topped, inevitably with synthetic cream, as fresh cream was by now an unobtainable luxury – had been prepared beforehand by Myrtle White and Alice and Winifred Leigh. Not a lavish spread, because of the rationing and because people believed it was their patriotic duty to be prudent. There was, however, tinned red salmon on the sandwiches, as well as a wedding cake that was quite rich with fruit. Both Mr and Mrs White and Mr and Mrs Leigh were not averse to a discreet amount of what was known as 'hoarding'. And so, between them, they had been able to provide tinned salmon, and tinned pears and peaches, as well as a fair amount of dried fruit, ground almonds for the almond paste, and icing sugar, to make a really acceptable wedding cake. It had been baked by Alice Leigh and iced by Myrtle White.

At many wartime weddings a large white cardboard structure, shaped like a cake and known as a 'whited sepulchre', was displayed, with a tiny fruit cake hidden inside. But that was not the case at this wedding reception. Although it was only of medium size, the cake for these newlyweds was the real thing, and was duly cut by the

294

bride and groom whilst their health was drunk in brown sherry.

The honeymoon was spent in the seaside resort of Southport, often regarded as a rival to its near neighbour, Blackpool. Southport could be seen clearly across the Ribble estuary as one stood on the promenade of nearby Lytham St Annes, but could only be reached by a roundabout route by road or rail.

'Is Your Journey Really Necessary?' the propaganda posters enquired of civilians, but Albert considered, as a serviceman, that he and his new wife were entitled to travel away on honeymoon, be it only for a long weekend.

Barbara knew that her new husband was blissfully happy. He was more cheerful and amusing to be with that weekend than she had ever known him to be. He told her time and time again how much he loved her.

'I'll never let you down, Barbara, my darling,' he told her once again. 'I'll always be there for you. I'll love you for ever.'

It was flattering, if a little discomfiting, to know that she evoked such feelings in Albert, especially as she knew he was not a sentimental sort of fellow. At least, that was the impression he gave to others. As for Barbara, she told him that she loved him too. It would have been churlish not to do so; besides, she was very fond of him already and she felt sure she would grow to love him in time.

Although Barbara had had a few boyfriends before she met Mike, she was still a virgin when she married Albert. She had been brought up to believe that it was right to save oneself for marriage. She had, therefore, been a little apprehensive about the wedding night, but she had found that there was no need to be. Albert proved to be a sensitive and considerate lover, and although the experience was not what she could call earth-shattering, she knew she need no longer worry about it. Anyway, she knew it was a part of married life, something her husband would expect of her. She did not know whether or not it was the first time for Albert. She guessed that it might not have been, but it was something she would never know.

Albert went back to his camp a couple of days after they returned to Blackpool. Barbara continued to live with her aunt and uncle. It seemed pointless to move next door to the Leighs' boarding house to the room that Albert slept in, seeing that her husband was not there. They hadn't really discussed the future very much, but the idea was that they would save up and buy a home of their own when the war was over.

Barbara continued with her job as a telephonist. She stayed at home most evenings, writing letters to Albert in answer to the long loving letters she received from him, or listening with her aunt and uncle to their favourite programmes on the wireless: *Monday Night at Eight*, *In Town Tonight* (broadcast on a Saturday), *Happidrome, Garrison Theatre,* and *ITMA*, with the irrepressible Tommy Handley, the comedy show above all others that managed to keep the people's spirits up in those depressing wartime days.

Occasionally she went to the cinema with a

friend from work. She enjoyed *Gone with the Wind*, and the light-hearted Hollywood musicals, starring such glamorous female stars as Betty Grable, Veronica Lake and Alice Faye, as well as the movies put on for propaganda purposes to boost the morale of a population becoming more and more war weary: *Mrs Miniver* and *In Which We Serve*. She could not be persuaded, however, to go out dancing. Albert, to her surprise, was a very good dancer and she looked forward to stepping out on the ballroom floor with him the next time he came home on leave.

That was in September, when he was granted a whole week's leave. They went dancing a few times that week, to the Tower, and to the Empress ballroom in the Winter Gardens. But their favourite venue was the smaller Palace ballroom, a more intimate place, but just as splendid in its own way as its larger counterparts. The superb ballroom floor was perfect for the thousands of dancing feet that trod it each evening.

They danced to an old-time medley; the veleta, the military two-step and the St Bernard's Waltz, as well as the quickstep, the modern waltz and the foxtrot. Albert confessed that he had been to lessons in ballroom dancing some years ago, and he was certainly a very accomplished dancer. Barbara had never been able to master the slow foxtrot, but under Albert's patient guidance she found she was now able to do so, following the expert lead that he gave.

Barbara sang softly beneath her breath to the music of 'As Time Goes By', a sentimental song that captured exactly the mood that they and

297

hundreds of other young couples were feeling that night; a tale of moonlight and kisses and sighs, and of love that would last for a lifetime.

'I'll always love you, my darling,' Albert whispered to her. 'No matter how the time goes by ... you will always be the only girl for me.'

Barbara felt, almost, as though she might be falling in love with her husband. One thing she was certain about was that their child was conceived later that same night.

Baby Katherine Louise was born on 30th June, 1943.

Chapter Twenty-Two

As 1943 dawned there was hope, at long last, that the tide was turning. It seemed that victory – hopefully in the not-too-distant future – was now a possibility; some, indeed, believed that it was assured. Civilians and servicemen alike were now starting to look towards the long-term future and to think about what sort of a world would emerge after the war-torn years.

A significant event had been when the Russian armies defeated the Germans. Hitler's greatest mistake had been, undoubtedly, his belief that Russia could be conquered along with the rest of the Western nations. He had not reckoned with the severity of a Russian winter, which proved to be the undoing of the German armies. The last of the German troops at Stalingrad surrendered on

2nd February, 1943.

The surrender of Italy followed a few months later. The North Africa campaign had ended in total victory for the Allied forces, and that army was now freed to take part in the planned invasion of Europe, which was being known as the 'Second Front'. The ongoing Battle of the Atlantic in May was another turning point. Forty German U-boats were destroyed and the trans-atlantic supply line was secure once again.

On 17th May came the news that nineteen Lancaster bombers had successfully breached the two largest dams in the manufacturing district of the Ruhr Valley, by means of what was known as the 'bouncing bomb'. The devastation and loss of life was tremendous, giving way to the thought in many thousands of minds that the majority of the casualties must have been innocent civilians. It had been reported in the newspapers that four thousand Germans had lost their lives in the flooding, and one hundred and twenty thousand had lost their homes.

The loss of life in Great Britain had been equally catastrophic in the blitz of the major cities – London, Liverpool, Manchester, Plymouth, Coventry – in the earlier years of the war, and still there was continuing loss of life amongst the soldiers, sailors and airmen who were fighting and believing in an ultimate victory. Indeed, it was reported that several of the bombers that had taken part in the breaching of the Ruhr dams had not returned.

At the time that baby Katherine was born on the last day of June, a mood of optimism was prevalent in the majority of households, none more so than in the homes of the Leigh and White families.

It was a straightforward, comparatively easy birth. Barbara stayed at home for the confinement, and the baby was born in the bedroom that had always been hers and in which she and Albert sometimes slept when he was home on leave.

All babies are beautiful, at least to their parents and close members of the family, but Barbara believed that her baby was, truly, the most beautiful baby she had ever seen. Her head was already covered with a mass of dark hair, clinging to her scalp in damp curly tendrils. Her cheeks were a rosy pink and her eyes, when she opened them, were a sort of inky grey. Barbara knew that babies couldn't focus properly, not so soon after the birth, but they seemed to be staring right into those of her mother, who already adored her. Tentatively, Barbara reached out a finger, placing it in the tiny palm of the baby, and the minute fingers, like a little pink starfish, closed around her own. She felt a deep thrill, unlike anything she had experienced before, and a feeling of wonder that she should be entrusted with the care of this tiny child.

'She looks just like you,' her aunt and uncle, and Albert's parents, told her.

'And I think she'll have your brown eyes when she's a few weeks older,' said Aunt Myrtle. 'Babies' eyes change, you know. They always look a sort of muddy grey at first.'

Albert was granted a forty-eight-hour compassionate leave, and he was delighted with his new daughter. 'I didn't believe I could ever be any happier than I was when you said you would marry me,' he told Barbara, 'but now I know that I am even happier. I'm the happiest man in the world. Thank you, my darling. She's ... just perfect.'

Between them they chose the names Katherine Louise, just because they liked them. But before long the little girl became known as Kathy.

She was a good baby, waking only once in the night for a feed, and by the end of September, when she was three months old, she was sleeping right through the night.

'You're lucky,' Albert's mother told her. 'I had endless trouble with both of mine. I forgot what a good night's sleep was like until they were more than twelve months old, especially with our Albert. He was on a bottle by that time, mind you, so I made sure that Bill took his turn...'

Albert, of course, could not take his turn at feeding the baby because he was not there, but Barbara was pleased that he did his share whenever he was home on leave. By the time baby Katherine was four months old she was being bottle-fed. In spite of Barbara's somewhat shapely figure – she could not be called plump, but she was certainly not skinny and had a bust that might be the envy of many girls – she found that her supply of milk soon dried up. She had no regrets about this and Kathy took to the bottle without any problems.

Albert came home on leave for the Christmas of 1943, but only on a forty-eight-hour pass. Barbara was sad to see him return to his camp, although, in a way, it was nice to have the baby all to herself again. He had, in fact, seemed at times to be more interested in the baby than he was in her, or had she been imagining it, she wondered? He was certainly taking his duties as a father very seriously. He watched her continually to make sure she was doing everything correctly – that the bath water was not too hot or too cold, the same with the bottle of milk, and that the nappies and little vests were well aired before the baby wore them.

'How do you think I manage when you're not here?' Barbara asked him jokingly.

'I'm sure you manage perfectly,' he replied, kissing the end of her nose. 'You're a wonderful mother, but I like to do my share. I'm hoping it won't be too long before I'm home for good, once we've got the better of old Hitler, then we can see about getting a little place of our own. Just you and me and little Kathy...'

Yes, it would be nice to have their own place, thought Barbara, although her aunt and uncle, and Albert's parents too, were very good to her. She had, of course, finished work well before the baby was born and there was no talk of her going back. Besides, mothers with young children were exempt from war work.

Despite having the baby to care for, time began to hang rather heavy for Barbara and she was even feeling a little depressed, an unusual state for her. She had enjoyed her job as a telephonist and the camaraderie of the other girls. Her aunt persuaded her to go to the pictures now and again with a girlfriend; Dorothy was the young woman who had been her bridesmaid. She was unmarried, although she had a fiancé serving in the merchant navy. She was now working at a munitions factory in Blackpool.

'Go out and enjoy yourself,' said Barbara's aunt, 'and don't worry about little Kathy. You know she'll be quite all right with me and your uncle Ben.'

And so Barbara and Dorothy started to go to the cinema once a week, very occasionally twice, and Barbara knew that her baby was in safe hands. She liked to get home by ten-thirty if possible, as her aunt and uncle did not keep late hours. She had her own door key, of course, but she did not want them to think she was taking advantage of their kindness. Her friend had been trying – though unsuccessfully at first – to persuade her to go dancing, to the Tower Ballroom, which was a favourite haunt of Dorothy's.

'No, I don't think so,' said Barbara. 'It wouldn't really be fair, would it? I mean, with Albert away. I don't think he would like the idea of me dancing with ... well, with other men.' She knew, in fact, that Albert would hate it.

'You have to wait to be asked!' joked Dorothy. 'You'd be surprised how many girls you see dancing together. Although I must admit there's no shortage of male partners, especially now the Yanks are here. I'll dance with you. I can do a pretty nifty quickstep, and Albert can't object to that, can he?'

'What does your Raymond think about you going dancing whilst he's away on the high seas?' asked Barbara.

'I don't know, because I don't tell him,' answered Dorothy, laughing. 'He wouldn't mind, though. He knows I don't intend to stay at home knitting. I write to him every week, but I don't see why I shouldn't go out and have a good time. Life can be pretty grim, and boring too, you must admit, in spite of them saying that victory's just round the corner. Please say you'll come with me, Barbara, just for once and see how you like it.'

And so Barbara agreed, although she was very unsure about it, to accompany her friend to the Tower Ballroom the following Saturday, the first Saturday in the February of 1944.

'Good for you,' said her aunt. 'Off you go and enjoy yourself. And don't worry about what Albert would say.' In Myrtle White's opinion, although she liked Albert very much, she had realised after spending more time in his company that he was something of a fusspot. He was clearly devoted to Barbara, and to the baby, but she had a feeling he might turn out to be rather critical and possessive, once the euphoria of marrying the girl of his dreams had worn off. 'There's an old saying, you know,' her aunt went on. 'What the eye doesn't see, the heart doesn't grieve at. And it isn't as if you're doing anything wrong. Lots of girls go dancing, even those whose husbands are away. I know how much you used to enjoy going dancing at the Palace.'

'That was with Albert,' replied Barbara. 'It was Albert, really, who taught me how to dance properly. I wasn't much good until he took me in hand.'

'Well, there you are, then,' said Myrtle. 'Go and trip the light fantastic and you'll feel better for it. And take your key. I know how you always try to get back early, but there's no need. It isn't as if you're still a fifteen-year-old, is it? You're a married woman now, and your uncle and I understand that.'

'I shouldn't be all that late, anyway,' agreed Barbara. 'I think the dance halls all close round about eleven o'clock. And I'll be walking home with Dorothy, so we'll be quite all right.'

'Well, don't forget to take your torch...'

'No, I won't forget,' smiled Barbara, 'and my gas mask. Although folks don't seem to be bothering quite so much now. The danger seems to be past ... thank God,' she added.

The blackout was still in force, though, but everyone had grown quite used to going out in the dark, armed with a torch, and finding their way by means of the white edgings on kerbs and road crossings.

'I'm ever so glad you decided to come with me,' said Dorothy, squeezing her friend's arm as they stood at the bus stop, waiting for the bus that would take them to the Central Station stop, near to the Tower. 'You'll enjoy it, I know you will. It's been ever such fun since the Yanks came to Blackpool.'

There were two American bases where the GIs were stationed, at the outlying villages of Weeton and Warton, a few miles distant from Blackpool.

'You hear a lot of tales about them,' Dorothy continued, 'but they're real nice guys, the ones I've met at any rate. And you should see them do the jitterbug! They're not supposed to do it on the ballroom floor, because it's a bit dangerous, all that prancing about and throwing the girls around. But they usually find a spot away from the ballroom where they don't get in the way of the more ... what shall I say? ... more prim and proper dancers.'

'And can you do it?' asked Barbara, smiling. 'This jitterbugging?'

'I've not tried yet,' said Dorothy. 'I've not been asked. But you never know, do you? Oh see, here's our bus. We're going to have a whale of a time, Barbara, I know we are.'

Chapter Twenty-Three

America had entered the war two years previously. It had been on 7th December, 1941, that the war had entered upon a new and significant phase. The Americans, led by President Roosevelt, had delayed entering the conflict, believing it to be a solely European war and, therefore, of no real concern to them. However, the Japanese attack on the US naval base at Pearl Harbor, Hawaii, forced them to change their outlook. The neutrality and isolationist policy of the American people was at an end, and when the USA eventually did enter the war they did so with determination.

The arrival of the American servicemen – known as GIs – had, so far, had little impact on Barbara or on her family and that of Albert's family next door. At the time of their marriage both the Whites' and the Leighs' boarding houses were still being used as billets for the RAF personnel, one group of men following upon another as their initial training came to an end.

Barbara had seen the GIs, of course, strolling around the streets of Blackpool. Their smart uniforms – a sort of brownish green and made of a fine cloth – contrasted greatly with the coarse material of the RAF and army uniforms of the British troops. Those had been designed for practicality and hard wear, not to enhance the figure! 'And not to attract the birds, either,' Barbara had overheard one of the RAF lads saying to his mate. The higher ranks in the British services wore uniforms of a finer material, but all ranks of American servicemen, both privates and officers, were dressed in the same impeccable manner.

Barbara had also heard the phrase 'overpaid, oversexed and over here' on the lips of some of the RAF lads who were billeted at the boarding house; it was a phrase that was being bandied about both by servicemen and civilians. In some instances it could be seen as a question of 'sour grapes'. It could not be denied that the American troops were overpaid, at least by British standards. They were paid five times as much as their British counterparts. The wages of an ordinary soldier in the US army was, in some cases, as high as those of a British officer.

As well as that, the GIs had access to what was known as the PX (Post Exchange), a sort of NAAFI, where all kinds of luxury goods were available, goods such as had not been seen in Britain for years. Chewing gum, sweets (which they called candies), oranges, butter, spirits, cigarettes, razor blades, and sweet-smelling soap – a contrast to the hard carbolic soap being used in the British households, and even that was rationed. Ice cream had been banned for the duration in the September of 1942, but it was available on the American bases.

Barbara's friend, Dorothy, had even managed to acquire a pair of the newly invented nylon stockings, which no British girl had ever seen before. She had been given them by her friend, Mavis, a girl who worked with her at the munitions factory. Mavis was keeping company – for the time being, at least – with a GI from Maryland whose name was Hank. It seemed that a goodly number of them were called Hank.

'Honestly, they're so fine you can't tell you're wearing them,' Dorothy had told Barbara. 'Except for the seam up the back, of course. They're just like gossamer, not that I'm really sure what gossamer is,' she laughed. 'I'll have to be real careful not to ladder them; they're so sheer, though, that a ladder might not even show. She's had chocolates from this Hank as well, my friend Mavis, and tinned peaches. And he got her dad a carton of Camel cigarettes. I didn't ask her what she had to do to get them, mind you, if you know what I mean.' Dorothy winked and sniggered.

'Dorothy, really!' exclaimed Barbara. 'You don't think, surely...?'

'Well, she's footloose and fancy free, is Mavis. She's not got a husband or fiancé, like you and me. And I must admit she's done the rounds; she's had a go with most of 'em. Our own RAF lads, Poles, Aussies, Free French, and now the Yanks. You've heard the expression about the Yanks?'

'You mean, overpaid ... and all that?'

'Yes, that's it. Of course, I don't really know about the "oversexed" bit. Mavis plays her cards very close to her chest. It may well be that she just likes to have a good time with no strings attached. She's a stunning-looking girl, I must admit; it's no wonder that the blokes all go for her. She might be there on Saturday night, at the Tower. If she is I'll introduce you to her. She told me that Hank is teaching her to jitterbug...'

It was not without a certain amount of trepidation that Barbara made her way to the Tower Ballroom on that Saturday night. The last time she had been dancing had been with Albert, and that had been long before baby Katherine was born. It had been the Palace Ballroom, rather than the Tower or the Winter Gardens, that Albert had favoured, and so Barbara had come to prefer that smaller and, she believed, much friendlier venue.

She had been to the Tower a few times, before Albert had come on the scene. She had danced there with her fiancé, Mike, who had been killed at Dunkirk. She had always felt that the Tower was somewhat brash and noisy, the place where the good-time girls hung out to 'click with a feller'. And there were plenty of those around at the moment, to be sure. But she told herself not to be stupid. She was a married woman now, mature and self-confident and well able to look after herself. She was going along solely to enjoy the music and gaiety, to have a change from the day-to-day routine and to forget the gloom and the deprivations that were a result of the ongoing war.

It was hard to believe that Britain had now been at war for more than four years. Admittedly there was no longer the despondency and fear for the future that there had been in the early years. Some believed that victory was assured and that it could even be brought about before the end of the year. All Barbara knew was that one had to go on hoping and praying...

The Tower Ballroom had been the dream, brought to life, of John Bickerstaffe – later Sir John – the first chairman of the Blackpool Tower Company. It had been his ambition to create a ballroom to equal, or preferably better, the Empress Ballroom in the Winter Gardens. To achieve this aim Mr Bickerstaffe had engaged the noted architect, Frank Matcham, to transform the room that was at first known as the Grand Pavilion. Frank Matcham was already well known and revered in the town, having designed Blackpool's Grand Theatre in 1894.

The ballroom was decorated in the French renaissance style and when it was completed in 1899 it was believed to be one of the three finest in the country; it had even been described as the finest in the whole of Europe. It was said that up to seven thousand people could be seated comfortably in the two tiers of balconies, supported by

310

massive gilded pillars. At one end of the room was a large ornate stage with a quotation inscribed above it in gold lettering. 'Bid me discourse, I will enchant thine ear' it read, a quotation from Shakespeare's *Venus and Adonis*. Large classical paintings adorned the ceilings and the surrounding walls, depicting idyllic scenes of nymphs, shepherds and shepherdesses, Grecian gods, and heroes taken from ancient legends; gilded motifs, too, bearing the names of famous composers, Bach, Beethoven, Mozart, Chopin...

Two large and elaborate chandeliers were flanked by a series of smaller ones, casting a radiance of electric light down onto the ballroom floor; this form of lighting was in its infancy at the end of the nineteenth century. The floor was a marvel in itself, comprising thousands of blocks of mahogany, oak, walnut and maple woods arranged in an intricate geometric design.

The Tower and the buildings underneath were now playing their part in the war effort, and not only by providing entertainment for the troops billeted in Blackpool and the holidaymakers – the many folk who were still visiting the town for a brief respite from the gloom and, in later years, the boredom of the war. The Tower top had been taken over by the RAF as an emergency radar station. A forty-foot section of the spire was replaced by a wooden structure bearing the receiving aerials, and a number of steel cantilevers were inserted into the iron girders of the Tower to carry the transmitting aerials.

The Tower top was also used as a lookout by the men of the National Fire Service and the

Home Guard, and the buildings below were used by the RAF and the Royal Artillery for training purposes. The ballroom and the circus became the venues for training sessions and lectures; and in the evenings they both reverted to their normal roles.

Barbara and Dorothy joined the queue of young women to deposit their coats in the cloakroom. When they had been handed the little pink cloakroom tickets they joined dozens of other girls at the mirrors in the washroom, titivating their hair, and applying a dusting of powder or a smear of lipstick before moving on to the ballroom. Barbara renewed her lipstick. It was a brighter red than the paler shades she usually favoured, but it had been the only colour that was available at the local chemist's shop; all types of make-up had been in short supply since the outbreak of war. Anyway, it matched her dress much better than a paler pink or coral shade would have done. She pressed her lips together, then, on second thoughts, wiped some of it off again; she hated to think that she might look tarty.

Her dress was a couple of years old, but it was one that she liked and thought suited her; new dresses were a luxury anyway, and considered an extravagance. She had toyed with the idea of wearing her wedding dress. She had chosen it believing, at the time, that it was one that she might wear again, but she had decided it was too pale and 'weddingy-looking' for a winter evening. The one she was wearing that night was of a silky rayon. It had a red background patterned with a bold design of black and white daisies; it was knee-length and had the fashionable padded shoulders.

'You look stunning in that dress,' Dorothy told her. 'It really suits you, with your dark hair and eyes and everything. You'll have the fellers queuing up asking you to dance.'

'Thank you ... but that's not really the idea,' replied Barbara; she was feeling, again, for a brief moment, that she shouldn't be there. 'You look very nice as well.'

Barbara and Dorothy were complete opposites as far as looks were concerned. Dorothy was blonde and petite. She had let her hair grow and it fell in a pageboy style almost to her shoulders; she had trained it to fall over one eye, in the style made popular by the film star, Veronica Lake. Her blue and white candy-striped dress with the puffed sleeves and sweetheart neckline enhanced her fair prettiness. She looked angelic, but she was a high-spirited lass, and Barbara looked to Dorothy to give her the confidence she needed to face the crowds in the ballroom.

It was, indeed, crowded, the girls two or three deep in some places at the edge of the ballroom floor. The dance floor itself was a rainbow of bright colours: red, blue, orange, green, pink, yellow, on the flowered, striped, and spotted dresses worn by the girls and some older women. They were a vivid contrast to the darker uniforms of the men: air force blue, khaki, the navy blue of the Royal Navy; and the brownish green of the Yanks' uniforms; there was scarcely a civilian man to be seen amongst the hundreds of couples circling round the dance floor. Many girls were dancing together, as Dorothy had said they would.

'Come on, let's give it a whirl,' Dorothy said to her friend, taking her hand and pulling her towards the ballroom floor. 'Can you lead, though? You're a few inches taller than me.'

'Yes, I think so,' said Barbara. 'It's a quickstep rhythm, so I should be able to manage that.' They stepped out to the music of 'Don't Sit Under the Apple Tree', the song that had been made famous by the Andrews Sisters.

The organist on the mighty Wurlitzer organ was the talented lady, Ena Baga. She had replaced Reginald Dixon, whose name had become synonymous with Blackpool, when he joined the RAF in 1940. His signature tune, 'Oh, I Do Like to be Beside the Seaside', had come to typify the jollity and the carefree mood of a holiday in Blackpool. Now, however, Ena Baga's signature tune, 'Smoke Gets in Your Eyes', was becoming almost as familiar to the dancers as that of her predecessor.

When the dance came to an end they moved off the ballroom floor. 'I don't know about you,' said Dorothy, 'but I don't fancy standing around with all these wallflowers.'

'No, neither do I,' agreed Barbara.

'Let's have a saunter around, then, and see if there's anybody we know, shall we? And in a little while we could go and have a coffee, or something stronger if you like.'

'No, coffee's OK for me, or tea,' said Barbara. 'Not just yet, though. We've not been here very long.'

She had been brought up with the belief that

nice girls didn't go into bars on their own, or even in the company of another girl. She had learnt, though, that Dorothy had no such inhibitions. She, Barbara, and her fiancé, Mike, had not frequented pubs and bars very much either. They had both been very young, only nineteen years old, when the war had started. Albert had enjoyed a drink, though, and probably still did, in the company of his fellow soldiers. Barbara had begun to feel more at ease in a bar when she was with Albert, but it was rather different now. She hoped that Dorothy would not consider her too much of a killjoy.

They made their way round the edge of the ballroom floor, pushing their way, as politely as they could, between the crowds of girls and servicemen. After a few moments Ena Baga struck up with the music of the 'American Patrol', a tune made popular by the Glenn Miller Orchestra and one which was being played more and more often in dance halls up and down the country.

As Dorothy had already told her friend, there was some jitterbugging going on in a space away from the ballroom floor where the music could still be heard, loud and clear. The couples on the dance floor were dancing a normal quickstep or, in some cases, a milder form of jitterbugging. Here, however, there were two couples who were really letting it rip.

'Hey, that's my friend, Mavis!' exclaimed Dorothy. 'You know, the one I was telling you about.'

'You mean the one who gave you the nylon stockings?'

'Yes, that's right. I'll introduce you to her when they've finished the dance. And I suppose that must be the famous Hank who's with her.'

Barbara's first impression of the girl, Mavis, was that she was the word 'glamorous' brought to life. 'Glamour' was a word much used with regard to the stars of the silver screen: Betty Grable, Vivien Leigh, Rita Hayworth, Ginger Rogers and countless others. This Mavis, to Barbara, was a Rita Hayworth sort of girl. Her bright-ginger hair, worn in a pageboy style, bounced around her shoulders as she danced. She was very pretty, and small, but curvaceous in the right places. Her tight-fitting emerald-green dress accentuated the swell of her bustline, and clung alluringly around her hips as she jigged and jumped about to the rhythm of the music, affording a frequent glimpse of shapely knees and thighs. Hank, if that was who it was, swung her around in an uninhibited way, pushing her away from him, then grabbing her and whirling her around in a frenzy. Barbara found herself gasping as the American lifted her off her feet then flung her over his shoulder, giving the onlookers a momentary glimpse of her stocking tops and frilly pink panties. The next minute she was back on the floor and upright again, seeming not a jot embarrassed.

The couple next to them were dancing in an equally reckless manner, and quite a crowd was gathering to watch the fun.

'D'you fancy a try?' said a voice at Barbara's side. She turned to see a pair of humorous grey eyes smiling down at her. A GI, of course; she could tell by his accent at first, and then by his uniform. She knew in that instant, though, that he was not aiming at a 'pickup'; he was just trying to be friendly.

'No, not me!' she laughed. 'Fun to watch, but ... no thanks! Not my scene at all.'

'Nor mine,' he smiled. 'But I wanted to see Hank doing his stuff. I've heard such a lot about it.'

'You know him, then?' she enquired.

'Yes, we're in the same unit, stationed at Warton. And the other chap, that's Marvin. Quite a lively pair, as you can imagine. And I'm Nat, by the way.' He held out his hand towards her. 'Nat Castillo. I'm pleased to make your acquaintance...' His eyes twinkled. 'Whoever you are?'

She didn't hesitate to shake his hand. He seemed such a nice fellow, or 'guy', which was what the Yanks said. 'Oh ... I'm Barbara,' she said. 'Barbara Leigh. I've come with my friend, Dorothy.' As she glanced around she could see that her friend, too, was talking to another of the GIs. 'I'm ... I'm pleased to meet you too.'

'You don't mind me talking to you, do you?' he continued. 'I know we Yanks have got a reputation for being brash and too familiar. Some of us are, or at least that's the impression we give, I guess. But me... I'm quite shy, really.' He grinned as he gave a little shrug. 'I'm just wanting to be friendly, that's all...'

And that was how it all started. In that instant Barbara's life was completely turned around, although she wasn't aware of it at first. She was aware, though, of the immediate attraction

317

between herself and the American soldier.

Looking back on how it had begun, a long time afterwards, she recalled a sermon she had once heard about temptation, and how one could either give in to it or turn away. She recalled the preacher's words... 'Maybe you can't help yourself at the first look, but you can avoid the next look, and all the subsequent ones...'

What, then, should she and Nat have done? Should she have refused to go for a drink with him, which was the next thing that happened? They had been in the company of others, though, and it would have been impolite to refuse. And after that, although it had begun so slowly and innocently, it was as if they both had known that it was inevitable; there had been no stopping the attraction they felt for one another.

She had known very soon that she and Nat were what was known as 'kindred spirits'. When she was in her early teens, Barbara's favourite book had been *Anne of Green Gables*. It was in that book that she had first come across the term. Anne Shirley, the heroine, with whom Barbara felt a great affinity, had gone on at length about how she and her friend, Diana, were kindred spirits. They thought and felt the same about everything, like the two halves of a complete whole; they were truly compatible.

Barbara was not sure that she had met anyone before, of either sex, to whom the term could apply. But now she had. She and Nat Castillo were, without doubt, 'kindred spirits'. And very soon they knew, come what may, that they belonged together.

Chapter Twenty-Four

When introductions had been made, the group of GIs and young women made their way to the nearest refreshment place, not far from the ballroom. It seemed perfectly natural for them all to gravitate there. The couples who had been jitterbugging were ready for some sustenance, as well as being too hot and dishevelled for comfort. Mavis and her friend Hilda, the other dancer, went off to the ladies' cloakroom to repair the damage done to their hair and apparel. They rejoined the party a few minutes later looking spruce and composed again.

'Over here, you guys,' shouted the fellow called Marvin, standing up and waving. 'We've already got yours in.' Barbara was to learn that everyone was referred to, in the American parlance, as a 'guy', whether they were male or female.

'Gee, thanks, Marvin,' replied Hilda. She had obviously picked up some of their vernacular already. 'Ginger beer shandy, for both of us? That's just hunky-dory!'

There were eight of them, and it seemed inevitable that they should pair off. Mavis and Hank, and Hilda and Marvin, already seemed to know one another rather well. Dorothy had struck up an acquaintance with Howard who was Nat's closest friend, or 'best buddy', as he called him. And so Barbara found herself with Nat.

Barbara had gone along with the rest of the girls and agreed that she would have a shandy, lemonade ones for herself and Dorothy. She and Nat were sitting side by side on a red velvet bench that ran along the side of the bar room, with Dorothy and Howard on stools opposite them. They were sharing a glass-topped table, and the other four were seated near to them.

Nat lifted his tankard – a pint of bitter – saying 'cheers', and so Barbara did the same with her smaller glass. They clinked them together, then smiled a little shyly and uncertainly at one another.

'So ... Barbara Leigh, are you enjoying yourself?' he asked.

'Yes, I am, very much,' she replied. 'I wasn't sure that I wanted to come here tonight, but Dorothy persuaded me. It's the first time I've been here for ... ooh, for ages.'

'The first time for me too,' agreed Nat. 'And I must admit I'm real impressed with your Tower Ballroom. I haven't seen anything like this back home.'

'Really?' said Barbara. 'I'm surprised. I thought everything in America was bigger than what we have over here.' She had been going to say 'bigger and better', but realised it might sound rather rude.

Nat laughed. 'Yeah ... I know that's how some of us Yanks like to talk. When we say bigger, we are sometimes implying that it's better as well, but it ain't always so. There are always guys who like to boast that everything's giant-sized in the good old US of A, but it all depends on where

320

you come from.'

'And ... where is that?' asked Barbara.

'Me? I come from a village called Stowe – well, a small town, really – in the state of Vermont. The loveliest little old place in the world to me, but we ain't got nothing like this.' He waved his arm around in the direction of the ballroom.

'Oh, I see,' replied Barbara politely. She sounded, and was aware that she probably looked, rather vague. She didn't think she had ever heard of Vermont, although she had heard of lots of places in the USA: New York, and Chicago, and Tennessee...

Nat smiled. 'Vermont is one of the New England states. You know ... the Pilgrim Fathers sailed from England in the *Mayflower* and landed in Plymouth?'

'Yes, I know a little about that,' replied Barbara. 'We learnt about it at school, but the facts are rather hazy to me; and so is my geography of the United States ... I'm sorry.'

'Nothing to apologise for,' said Nat. 'It can't be as bad as my scanty knowledge of your little country, and that goes for most of us Yanks... Anyhow, the settlers called the area New England, to remind them, I guess, of the old England they had left behind. That's why we have a lot of towns with the same names as yours. We have a Plymouth, of course, and a Portsmouth, Manchester, Boston, London, Norwich, Windsor... Dozens of them, I guess.'

'You must be missing your hometown,' said Barbara. 'Stowe, did you say? I should imagine it's nothing like Blackpool.'

He laughed. 'You can say that again! Nothing at all. Except that we depend a lot on tourists, as you do here. It sure is a lovely place where I live, surrounded by mountains, and in the winter we get hordes of skiers staying there; we have some of the best ski slopes in the whole of the USA. And in summer there's lots to do as well – rock climbing, fishing, canoeing, or just enjoying the scenery.'

Barbara smiled at him sympathetically. He surely must be homesick for that lovely place, although he was cheerful and bright, clearly determined to make the best of his exile in what must seem a very strange and different sort of land. 'And ... what do you do there, Nat?' she asked. 'Your job, I mean?'

'Like scores of others, my family run a hotel,' he replied. 'We're busy all year round with guests. I help out wherever I can, like the rest of the family, my parents and my aunt and uncle. I'm studying to be a chef, though, so that I can take over from my father, eventually ... God willing,' he added. 'And in the winter I'm a part-time ski instructor. We all learn to ski, from an early age.'

'That's quite a coincidence,' said Barbara, 'about the hotel, I mean, because that's where I was brought up as well, in a hotel. We call them boarding houses here, though, unless they're bigger and have more amenities, then they're called hotels. And ... my husband had a similar boarding house background. Actually, his family's boarding house is just next door to ours, and he helps with the cooking and everything else, like you do. At least he does when he's here. At the moment he's in the army, stationed up in the north of England...' She found her voice petering out as Nat looked at her thoughtfully.

'Yes, I noticed you were married,' he remarked. She was wearing her wedding ring, of course, which she never took off.

'We were married in 1942,' Barbara told him. 'We have a baby girl, Katherine. She's eight months old,' she said, trying to smile brightly.

'Gee, that's swell!' commented Nat. 'I can understand why you were hesitant about coming here tonight. You must miss her.'

'Well, yes, but I know she's being well looked after, by my aunt and uncle. They brought me up, you see, after my parents died when I was quite small. And I'm still living there, because it just makes sense to do so. When Albert – my husband – comes back, no doubt we'll move into a place of our own.' Why am I telling him all this? she asked herself. She had only just met him, but already it seemed as though they had known one another for ages.

'And ... what about you, Nat?' she asked; she knew she had to ask. 'Have you a wife, at home in the USA?'

'No, not me.' He smiled a little ruefully. 'I guess I never met the right girl ... not yet.' He paused, and they looked at one another steadily for a few moments, Barbara's brown eyes mesmerised by the intense regard in his silvery-grey ones. She knew then, as she often told herself later, that this was probably the point at which she should have said to herself, 'No! No more; turn away now before it's too late.' But, of course, she didn't turn away and neither did Nat.

He smiled then, and gave a little shrug. 'I guess I was always too busy working in the hotel, all the hours God sends... No, to be fair, that's not strictly true. I found time for leisure in between. I ski, as I told you, although that can be classed as work as well. I play baseball, though not very well; I canoe and I've done a little rock climbing. At least I did, until Adolf Hitler – and, of course, our own Franklin D. Roosevelt – thought otherwise, and now I've found myself over here.' He grinned. 'Yes, I know what they're saying about us – overpaid, oversexed, and over here!'

Barbara smiled at him. 'I believe you always have to speak as you find.' Then she added, rather daringly, 'You seem a nice normal sort of fellow to me.'

'Thank you kindly, ma'am!' He touched an imaginary forelock. 'You know, we were all given strict instructions as to how we must behave while we're over here in your country. In fact, we were all issued with a little booklet with a list of dos and don'ts. The worst thing we can say, apparently, is to tell a Britisher that, "We came over here and won the last one – and now we're here to see that you win this one."'

'It's true, though,' replied Barbara. 'We've stood alone for a long time, since 1940, when our allies were forced to surrender. None of us believed it would go on for so long.'

'Ye-eh, that's what it says in our little book, that the Brits are weary of it all. How the houses might look shabby because they haven't been painted for years; the factories are making planes now, not paint. And that British trains are cold because the power is being used for industry, not for heating. And how the rationing of food is affecting you all. That sure must be hitting you hard, being restricted to – what is it? – two ounces of butter a week, four ounces of bacon?'

'Something like that,' Barbara nodded. 'We manage. We've got used to it and I haven't heard of anybody starving. Actually, some people regard it as being fair shares for all.'

'You sure are a tough breed of people, and I take my hat off to all of you,' said Nat. 'That goes for most of us guys, I guess.'

Barbara didn't know how to answer that. She knew they all put up with the hardships and inconveniences because there was nothing else they could do. But they all did their share of grumbling from time to time, which was only human nature. It was probably true, however, that on the whole they had rallied round as a nation and supported one another, more than they had been inclined to do in peacetime.

'I notice you're a sergeant,' said Barbara, to bring a new topic to the conversation.

'Sure,' Nat replied, 'and so is my pal, Howard. We were both made up recently. And we're the genuine article, I can assure you. No badges of rank that we're not entitled to.'

'What do you mean?' asked Barbara.

'Oh, some of these corporals and sergeants that you might see around are real phoneys. They're privates in disguise. Artificial stripes that are taken off when they leave the dance hall, or if they're in danger of being seen by an NCO or an officer who knows them. Stripes put on to attract the girls, don't you know? Medals as well, sometimes; they're known as "Spam" medals.'

'Well, fancy that!' said Barbara. 'That's something I didn't know. Mind you, I've heard of some of our lads pretending to be something they're not. RAF lads telling stories of how many German planes they've shot down, when they're really ground crew... My husband's a sergeant as well,' she went on, feeling somehow that she ought to make some reference to him. 'Probably because of his age and maturity – he's fifteen years older than me – and he's in charge of the meals at the officers' mess. He's doing pretty much the same thing as he did at home.'

'So ... how long has he been in the army?'

'He joined up almost straight away, in 1939. He's never been sent abroad – he escaped Dunkirk – and there's not much likelihood of him having to go now. What about you, Nat?'

'Who can tell?' Nat shook his head. 'One never knows. We all know there are preparations going on for a second front later this year. That's why we're here. I sure would like to have a bash at old Hitler but, like your hubby, I'm in charge of catering. Coincidence, eh?'

Barbara nodded. 'Well, I'm sure it's as important a job as any other. I've been relieved that it's kept Albert away from the battle zone.'

'That's exactly what my parents say,' agreed Nat. 'But some think, of course, that we've got a cushy number. At least I'm seeing the world, aren't I? Or a part of it at any rate. I hope to see some more of your little old country before I'm through. Blackpool sure is a swell place.' He smiled and nodded appreciatively. 'I've walked along your prom a time or two, and been drenched when those mighty waves came crashing over the sea wall. Gee, what a sight! It puts me in mind of the coast of Maine. That's the furthest I'd ever been from home, apart from a week in New York.'

'I've never been very far from Blackpool either,' said Barbara. 'I spent a week in London with my aunt and uncle just before the war, and I've been up to the Lake District. But since the war started we've been encouraged to stay at home. Tell me, I know I may sound terribly ignorant but ... what does GI stand for?'

'General infantryman,' replied Nat. 'It's as simple as that.'

Barbara nodded. 'Well, I'm sure glad to know that,' she smiled. Another thing – I'm being real nosey, aren't I? Did you say your last name was ... Castillo?'

'Yes, that's correct. Nat – short for Nathaniel – Castillo.'

'It sounds Italian...'

'That's because, way back, my forefathers must have come from Italy. We're a cosmopolitan nation, you see. Folks from all over Europe came to settle in America: Italians, French, Spaniards, Germans, and the British, of course. We've got our fair share of Smiths, Browns and Robinsons, same as you have over here. But I suppose my great-great – I don't know how many greats – grandad must have been Italian. I can't speak the language, though. Eventually, you see, we all ended up speaking English.'

'Or your version of it,' smiled Barbara.

'Ye-eh, point taken.' Nat laughed. 'Some quite amusing differences, aren't there? I know that when we talk about a "bum" we mean someone who's lazy, but it has rather a different meaning to you, hasn't it? We have to be careful or we might be thought indelicate. Although, I asked where the restroom was, in one of your big stores, and the girl looked at me as though I was crazy. Apparently you have no qualms about calling it a toilet or a lavatory? Goodness knows why we Yanks have to be so discreet about it. On the whole, though, we're united by a common language, aren't we? And I've sure been glad of that. It would have been quite a problem to struggle with a new language as well as everything else.'

The band had now taken over from Ena Baga, and the music of 'Moonlight Serenade' was being played. Glenn Miller's captivating tunes had become very popular in Britain, especially since the arrival of the Americans. 'In the Mood', 'American Patrol', 'Pennsylvania, 6-5000', 'String of Pearls'; these tunes were heard on the wireless and in dance halls all over the country, but none was more popular than the haunting melody, 'Moonlight Serenade'.

Nat looked questioningly at Barbara. 'Would you care to dance?' he asked.

'Yes ... yes, I would ... thank you,' she replied.

They walked hand in hand to the ballroom floor. Barbara was aware of Dorothy's eyes on her, and she smiled at her friend. Dorothy winked; she, too, seemed to be getting along very well with Nat's friend, Howard.

It was a slow foxtrot rhythm, the most difficult

of all the dances to Barbara; but Albert had taught her well and she was able to follow Nat's lead quite easily. She wasn't thinking of Albert, however, at that moment. Nat was not tall, about half a head taller than Barbara, that was all. His hair was neither dark nor fair, just an in-between shade, cut short as regulations required, but it was quite abundant and had a natural wave. His silver-grey eyes were the first thing she had noticed about him; she had known at once that he was a kind and thoughtful sort of person.

He placed his hand in the small of her back and drew her a little closer, and she glanced up at him. His wide mouth curved in a tender smile, and she could not avoid the sudden indrawn breath that she took as their eyes met. The look they exchanged was one of perfect understanding. Barbara knew that was the moment when she started to fall in love with Nat Castillo.

Chapter Twenty-Five

Barbara and Nat were still dancing together as the last waltz was played, the evocative melody 'Who's Taking You Home Tonight?' They danced with their heads close together, scarcely moving, just taking small steps and swaying gently in time to the rhythm. Dorothy and Howard were near to them as the band ended the tune on a poignant diminuendo. The dancers all applauded, a tribute to the band and to Ena Baga, then the four of them together walked off the ballroom floor.

It was Howard who made the suggestion. 'May we have the pleasure of escorting you two ladies home tonight?'

'I don't see why not,' answered Dorothy cheerily. 'What do you say, Barbara? Shall we let them?'

'Yes … that would be very nice,' said Barbara with a shy glance at Nat. He did not speak, just nodded his head and winked.

'We'll see you at the top of the stairs, then, near the front entrance,' said Dorothy. 'Come on, Barbara; let's go and get our coats.'

'Nice fellow, that Howard,' Dorothy went on, as they stood in the queue for their coats. 'Good company; great to talk to and have a laugh with. I put him in the picture straight away, though. I told him about Raymond; I thought it was best to tell him. But it appears that he's married; he's got a wife and a kiddy – a two-year-old boy – back in the USA. His home's in Texas. What about you? You seemed to be getting on quite well with Nat. Did you tell him about Albert?'

'Of course I did!' replied Barbara, rather edgily. 'And about Katherine as well. He knew I was married, though, because of my wedding ring.'

'So that's all right, then,' said Dorothy. 'It's best to be above board, then we all know where we stand. Is Nat married too?'

'No, actually he isn't,' replied Barbara, as nonchalantly as she was able.

'Well, it doesn't matter, so long as he knows that you're spoken for. I don't see any harm in them walking back with us tonight. It's obvious that they're both very polite, well-brought-up

330

young men. They probably think it's the right thing to do.'

They left the Tower building at the promenade entrance, turning right towards Talbot Square. Dorothy and Howard were leading the way, with Barbara and Nat close behind as they walked up Talbot Road, then turned left along Dickson Road. At Nat's invitation Barbara linked her arm through his.

'It's good of you to see us home,' she told him. 'The blackout can be rather scary sometimes.' It was a dark night with only a dim crescent moon. 'Although we've all got used to it by now. What about you? How will you get back to your camp?'

'No problem,' answered Nat. 'There's transport laid on for us from the centre of Blackpool, in about half an hour.'

'Known as the passion wagons,' called out Howard, who had overheard the conversation. 'At least, that's what some of the guys call them. Those who've been up to no good.'

'Ye-eh...' Nat laughed. 'We've heard tales of some of your RAF lads taking revenge on the GIs and misdirecting them when they've missed their transport back to Warton. Some have found themselves on a tramcar bound for Bispham when they should've been going the other way, to Squires Gate.'

'Oh dear!' said Barbara. 'Well, it's not very far now to where we live.'

Dorothy lived slightly nearer to the centre of the town than did Barbara, so she was the first one to leave the foursome.

'What do you say that we do this again?' suggested Howard, as they stood together at Dorothy's front gate. 'Same time, same place, next Saturday? Is that OK with you girls?'

Dorothy looked at Barbara. 'What do you think? Is that all right with you? I've enjoyed it tonight.'

'Yes, so have I,' agreed Barbara in a quiet voice. 'Yes, that would be very nice.' She smiled shyly at Nat. 'Thank you, both of you, for seeing us home.'

It was Howard who answered. 'It was a real pleasure, ma'am.'

'Cheerio, then,' said Dorothy, walking up her path. 'See you next week. I'll be in touch with you, Barbara.'

Nat and Howard walked one on each side of Barbara, along the street and round the next corner to her aunt's boarding house. She was relieved that the house was in darkness. Her aunt and uncle had no doubt retired for the night, and probably all the RAF recruits, too, who were still stationed there. They were allowed a key if they knew they were going to be late back. The dark street was silent and the three of them found themselves whispering their goodnights.

'Thank you again,' said Barbara. 'See you next Saturday, then.' They had agreed to meet inside, near to the cloakroom, at seven-thirty.

'Goodnight, Barbara,' said Nat. She noticed the note of tenderness in his voice.

'So long, Barbara,' said Howard. 'It's been swell meeting the two of you. See you soon.'

Barbara and Nat exchanged a telling glance as Howard turned to walk away; then Nat followed him.

What have I done? What on earth was I thinking about? Barbara was to ask herself these same questions time and again over the next few days. She even tried to persuade herself that she must have imagined the intensity of feeling she had experienced on meeting Nat, and had only imagined, too, that it was the same for him. At one point she decided that she would not go on Saturday. This thing, whatever it was, must be nipped in the bud before it was too late. And yet she knew, deep down, that she would be there.

'I'm glad you're getting out and about a bit,' her Aunt Myrtle said to her, when she asked if she and her uncle would look after Katherine again on Saturday. 'Don't look so worried about it, dear. Kathy will be perfectly all right with us; she was as good as gold. And you're not doing anything wrong, going to a dance hall. Did you meet anybody else you knew?'

'Yes, we met some friends of Dorothy's,' said Barbara. 'They were dancing the jitterbug with some Yanks, and then a few of us got talking. It was rather good fun.' She didn't say, however, that they had agreed to meet up again.

Dorothy was unaware of the turmoil going on in her friend's mind, and Barbara intended to keep it that way.

They met again the following Saturday as they had arranged. Barbara felt dreadful lying to her aunt and uncle. Although it was not really a lie; it was what might be called a half-truth, a lie of omission. She was letting them think that she was just meeting Dorothy as she had done the previous week. The guilt she experienced made her feel that she was doing wrong, but she was to find that as the weeks, then the months, went by, her sense of guilt lessened. By that time she and Nat had fallen so deeply in love that all other considerations were of minor importance.

Excepting for the matter of her dear little daughter, Katherine. She loved her baby girl so very much. She was at the interesting stage now, sitting up and smiling at everyone; she was such a happy little girl. At ten months old she was even trying to talk. She repeated the sounds of 'ma-ma' and Barbara convinced herself, as all mothers did, that she was trying to talk to her mummy.

The sounds of 'da-da' did not, as yet, feature in her infant utterances. Albert was able to get a forty-eight-hour pass only occasionally, not long enough for his little daughter to form any lasting memory of him. He was clearly delighted with her; he made a tremendous fuss of her every time he came home, and the little girl would smile winningly at him as she did at most people. It was then that Barbara's guilt would surface, as she wondered what would be the outcome of this problem. She entered into lovemaking with Albert as she knew she must. She did not think he noticed any reluctance on her part. She was still fond of him and he was always gentle and considerate towards her at such times.

For the first few months the love that was gradually developing between herself and Nat did not reach its fulfilment. They both knew that the consummation was inevitable, but Nat was, deep down, an honourable man. Barbara knew that he was trying to show her that he loved her in every way, and not just in the physical sense; and she knew that she loved him in the same way. They were truly soulmates.

The relationship had begun quite slowly. She greeted Nat in a casual manner the second Saturday evening, the same way that Dorothy greeted Howard. They made their way to the ballroom first of all, where Ena Baga was already well into her stride, playing Deep in the Heart of Texas.'

'Gee whizz! She's playing my song!' exclaimed Howard. He sounded pensive for a moment, although he was still smiling. 'Come on, Dorothy, we must dance this one.' He took her arm and led her towards the dance floor.

'That's his state, Texas,' remarked Nat. 'I guess it means as much to him as Vermont means to me. He sure talks a lot about it.'

'But you've never been there?' asked Barbara.

'Gosh, no! It's about as far away as you can imagine from where I live, thousands of miles. And as different as you can imagine as well. Vermont's one of the smallest states in the USA, right up near the Canadian border, and Texas is one of the largest, way down in the deep south, bordering on Mexico. We get snow, and they get tropical sunshine and hurricanes. We get along great, though, Howard and me. We enlisted at the same time and we've stuck together ever since... Care to dance, Barbara?'

They moved easily together to the quickstep rhythm. Barbara had a feeling of rightness and familiarity with Nat's arms around her, although

335

he was not holding her too closely. He sang softly along to the tune of 'Deep in the Heart of Texas', about the bright stars and the prairie sky and the perfume of the sage in bloom, and she joined in as well. The song had become very familiar since the Yanks had come to Britain. The organist moved on easily from that melody to the rhythm of the 'American Patrol'. This was the signal for some of the more enthusiastic couples to start their jitterbugging.

Barbara and Nat danced carefully around them, avoiding a collision. The more energetic couples would, no doubt, be asked to move off before long, or would of their own accord continue their gymnastics away from the ballroom floor. When the sequence of dances ended the four of them met up again in the spot where they had all congregated the previous week.

'What do you say we have a little refreshment?' suggested Howard. 'I was thinking of tea and cakes actually, at the moment, rather than beer. That's one of your English specialities, isn't it?'

'That's true,' replied Dorothy. 'Usually in the afternoon, though; it's called "afternoon tea".'

'I thought you Americans preferred coffee,' remarked Barbara.

'Sorry to say it, but your coffee is undrinkable,' said Howard, laughing. 'Isn't that so, Nat?'

''Fraid so,' said Nat with a rueful grin. 'But I guess it's not your fault; another inconvenience caused by old Adolf, eh?'

'I don't think we were ever really coffee drinkers,' said Barbara. 'We used to drink Nescafé, but we can't get that now. We have to make do

336

with that Camp coffee that comes in a bottle. I must admit, it's pretty awful.'

'Well then, we'll have a nice cup of tea,' smiled Nat. 'That's what you Brits say, isn't it? A nice cup of tea. And I must say it's a mighty fine beverage, the way you make it.'

'Let's go to that posh place upstairs,' said Dorothy. 'There's a lot more to our Tower than just the ballroom, you know.'

She led the way to a refreshment room on the next floor up, where ferns and greenery, even a palm tree, added to the pleasant ambience of the place, a contrast to the rowdier downstairs bars and tea rooms. They sat at a table for four where a waitress served them with tea in a silver pot and a selection of cakes on a cake stand. The cream in the eclairs was 'mock' and, most probably, so was the filling in the 'almond' tarts, but they all agreed that they were as good as any you could get at the present time. 'It's rather more select up here, isn't it?' remarked Nat, 'away from the noise and the crowds.'

'I've told you, there's far more to the Tower than you see at a first glance,' said Dorothy. 'When we've finished our tea we could go and look at the animals.'

'Animals?' queried Nat.

'Oh, didn't you know? There's a zoo just over there. Or a menagerie, some people still call it. It's been there since the Tower opened, that's about seventy years ago, though no doubt the animals have changed.'

'Not much of a zoo by your standards, I don't suppose,' said Barbara, as the four of them, a

337

little while later, sat on the raised seating in the centre of the room watching, from a distance, the animals in their cages.

'A quaint idea, though,' said Nat. 'I guess the children like to come and see the monkeys.'

A few braver folk, including children with their parents, were pushing nuts through the bars of the cages, encouraging the monkeys to perform their tricks. But Barbara and Dorothy preferred to keep their distance, away from the lion and the rather fierce-looking bear.

'Is that the lion that the poem was written about?' asked Nat. 'Wallace, the one that had the "'orse's 'ead 'andle" poked in his ear?'

Barbara laughed. 'I'm not sure if it's the same one that swallowed Albert.' She felt a momentary spasm of guilt as she said the name that was also the name of her husband. 'I didn't think you Americans would know about that.'

'Oh yes, we've heard all about *Albert and the Lion* and Stanley Holloway since we came to Blackpool,' said Howard. 'Did he write the poem?'

'No, it was a man called Marriott Edgar,' said Dorothy. 'He's the man who writes the monologues for Stanley Holloway. I know because I recite it sometimes at church concerts, don't I, Barbara?'

'Yes, you do indeed,' answered her friend. 'And it always goes down well with the audience. Are you going to recite it for us now?'

'No, I'd rather not,' laughed Dorothy. 'Some other time, maybe. I say, it pongs in here, doesn't it? Shall we move on?'

'Yes, it is a bit niffy,' agreed Howard. 'And I

can't say I really approve of animals in cages, although they look contented enough.'

'There's an aquarium as well on the ground floor,' said Barbara, as they left the menagerie. 'And an aviary with exotic birds up near the top of the Tower. And in peacetime you could go up to the top of the Tower. Not now, though, of course; there's a radar station up there and a lookout post.'

The other two were a few steps in front as they all headed towards the ballroom again. They sat on one of the red plush seats in an alcove from where they could see the ballroom floor. If they vacated their seats, though, to dance or to seek refreshment, they were almost sure to lose them. The place was always crowded on a Saturday evening and that night was no exception.

'Have you been up to the top of the Tower?' asked Nat.

'Yes, once, when I was a little girl,' replied Barbara. 'I was with my aunt and uncle. I must admit it was a bit scary until I got used to it. Then I stopped being frightened and just enjoyed the wonderful views. You can see right across to Southport and the Welsh hills on a clear day, which it was at the time.' She smiled. 'We learnt at school that Blackpool Tower is five hundred and eighteen feet high. Not as tall as your Empire State Building, though!'

Nat's eyes twinkled with amusement as they met hers. 'No, I guess not. The Empire State is twice as high. Sorry about that, Barbara! Three hundred and eighty-one metres, so we're told; I guess that must be well over one thousand feet.'

'And have you been to the top?'

'Yes, so I have, on my one and only visit to New York. We went as a family when I was in my teens. We did all the sights: the Statue of Liberty, Central Park, Fifth Avenue, Broadway... It's a mighty fine city.'

'I'm sure it must be. I've only been to London once, ages ago,' Barbara said wistfully.

'I'm sure you will, one of these days,' said Nat, smiling understandingly at her.

'When the war is over...' mused Barbara. 'That's what we all keep saying, don't we?'

'Yes. All we can do is take a day at a time,' said Nat. 'None of us knows what's in the future. But we can try to make the most of every day, can't we? Every day, every hour...?' His voice was hushed so that no one but Barbara could hear. The other two, anyway, were engrossed in their own conversation.

Nat took hold of her hand, gazing at her intently. 'You know what I'm saying, don't you, Barbara?'

'Yes, Nat... I guess I do,' she replied as they exchanged a look of total empathy.

'Shall we go and take a look at the aquarium?' he suggested. 'It'll be nice and peaceful there, won't it?'

'I'm sure it will,' said Barbara. 'It's ages since I was down there. It's a strange place; at least I thought so when I was a little girl – all green and mysterious.'

Dorothy and Howard had gone onto the ballroom floor again, and Barbara could see them jigging about happily to the tune of the 'Woodchopper's Ball'. They seemed to be getting on very well, she pondered, but she doubted that there was the intensity of feeling that had developed between herself and Nat. Again a tiny voice at the back of her mind tried to tell her that she was playing with fire ... but it was already too late.

They wandered downstairs, hand in hand, to the dimly lit, greenish gloom of the aquarium. It resembled a cave with limestone pillars, where exotic fish from all over the world swam around in glass tanks. They strolled about, taking a brief look at the fish, but Barbara knew that what Nat wanted was a place where they could be on their own for a little while. There were just a few people, like themselves, gazing at the fish, but also enjoying the solitude of the surroundings.

They stopped near to one of the stone pillars. Nat put his arms around Barbara and drew her towards him. He leant forward and, very gently, kissed her on the lips. It was no more than that the first time, a very gentle, loving kiss. 'Barbara...' he murmured. 'You know what has happened, don't you? I've fallen in love with you. Tell me, please ... I have to know. Is it ... is it the same for you?'

She nodded. 'Yes, Nat, it is. I've only known you for a week, but I feel as though I've known you for ages. Yes, Nat ... I love you.' Her voice was the faintest whisper. 'I don't know what we're going to do. I've tried to tell myself that it's wrong, that I mustn't ... but it's no use. I feel as though we were meant to be together... Is that dreadful of me?'

'No ... no, it isn't!' he answered, quite vehemently, although he was still speaking quietly. 'I know that some might think so, that they will certainly think so. But I knew, almost the first moment I met you. I've never felt like this before, about anyone. God help me, I love you, Barbara!'

'I have a husband and a little girl,' said Barbara, although neither of them needed reminding of that fact. 'I told you so, last week. I knew I had to tell you ... and I do love Kathy, so very much.'

'And ... your husband?'

Barbara sadly shook her head. 'I'm fond of him. Albert was good to me, and I knew he'd take care of me. I wanted the security, but I know now that it was wrong of me. I should never have married him, not for that reason. I think I knew it at the time. Oh Nat ... what are we going to do?'

He smiled at her, then he tenderly kissed her again. 'For the moment, we're not going to be miserable. As I said before, we have to take each day as it comes. We'd better go back now, hadn't we, or the other two will wonder where we are.'

Dorothy and Howard were standing at the edge of the dance floor, as they had lost their seats. Barbara fancied that her friend gave her an odd look, but she, Barbara, smiled nonchalantly. 'We've been to look at the fishes,' she said brightly.

They danced again, then had a drink in the bar, and at ten-thirty they headed for home.

'How about a change of venue next week?' suggested Howard. 'I'd sure like to take a look at your Winter Gardens; that is if you girls still want to see us?'

They agreed that they did, and that they would go to the Winter Gardens, rather than the Tower. Howard hung back as Nat said goodnight to Barbara.

'Here...' she said, stopping at a shop doorway, a little distance away from the boarding house. 'My aunt and uncle might still be around. I'm sorry, Nat...'

He kissed her again, a little more ardently. 'Don't worry,' he whispered. 'I love you; just remember that. It'll all sort itself out in the end, I'm sure.'

Chapter Twenty-Six

'What you're doing is wrong,' Dorothy told her friend. 'You're playing with fire; surely you must see that? For heaven's sake, Barbara, put an end to it before it's too late.'

The two friends were walking along the promenade near to the North Pier; Barbara was pushing little Katherine, fast asleep in her pram. Dorothy had phoned her asking if they could meet for a chat. They had decided on Wednesday afternoon, which was Dorothy's half day off from the munitions factory where she worked. Barbara had already guessed that her friend might have some strong words to say to her. She knew now that she had not been mistaken about the odd looks – searching, knowing looks – that Dorothy had cast her way on Saturday night.

She had been surprised that Dorothy had agreed to go along with the Americans' suggestion that they should go to the Winter Gardens the following Saturday. But to refuse, of course, would have been to put an end to the fun that Dorothy was having with Howard – light-hearted, innocent fun, Barbara was sure. She knew that Dorothy was a far more easy-going person than herself. She seemed more able to take life as it came, in a much less serious way. Barbara did not think that her friend felt too intensely about anything, not even about her engagement to her fiancé, Raymond. All the same, she had made it clear that she would not cheat on him, and that her friendship with Howard was enjoyable, but of no consequence.

Barbara listened to her, as she knew she must. 'I understand what you are saying,' she replied, 'and only a few weeks ago I would have agreed with you. I would have thought it was dreadful that a married woman, such as I am, could even think of carrying on with someone else. But you must see, Dorothy, that we're not "carrying on". Nothing has happened between us; you must understand that. When we met, Nat and me, there was an immediate attraction, a magnetism between us; we were both aware of it. And now ... well, I'm afraid it's already too late. I love him, and he loves me.'

'But you've only known him for two weeks! You've only met him twice. You can't really be sure that you love him, not in such a short time. And what about your husband, and your little girl, bless her! Just look at her, Barbara, what a little treasure she is!'

'Do you think I haven't said the same thing to myself, time and time again? Yes, I know it's wrong, Dorothy. Not that we've done anything really wrong as yet. And I wouldn't do that anyway. You know what I mean; I would never sleep

344

with him, have an affair, whatever you want to call it, as though it didn't matter. It isn't like that; I know that Nat respects me too much for that. It isn't what either of us want ... but we do love one another.'

Dorothy glanced across at her in what looked like a pitying way. She shook her head. 'But that's what it will lead to; you must know that, Barbara. Yes, I know he seems like a very nice bloke. They both are, Nat and Howard. But we don't really know all that much about them, do we? If I were you I would put an end to it, now, before it goes any further. Look ... why don't I meet them on my own on Saturday night, and tell him that you've decided not to come? Believe me, Barbara, it'd be the best thing to do. It might hurt at first, but you're going to get in too deep if it goes on any longer.'

Barbara shook her head. 'You say "if you were me". But how can you say that? You're not me, are you? You can't possibly know how I feel, or what you would do if it had happened to you. I know you're concerned about me. You're probably annoyed with me, and I suppose you have every reason to be ... but there's nothing you can say that will make any difference.' She glanced into the pram. Katherine was just opening her eyes and Barbara leant over to touch her downy cheek.

'Yes, I love my little daughter more than I can say. It's the one good thing that has come out of my marriage to Albert. Because I know now, Dorothy, that I should never have married him. I did so for all the wrong reasons. I don't love him, not the way I should, and I know now that I never did. But there's Kathy; that's the awful part about it, and that's what hurts, so very much. It's agonising when I think how much Kathy means to me. And Albert thinks the world of her too. She doesn't really know him yet, not in the way she knows me, because he's not here very often. But I know it would hurt him if he ever had to part with her.'

She was silent for a few moments and her friend made no comment. But she could sense Dorothy's disapproval, waves of reproach drifting across to her.

'I'm so happy when I'm with Nat,' she continued. 'Yes, I know it's been only a short time, but when I'm with him I feel like a different person. I've never felt like this before about anyone; not even when I was engaged to Mike, although I was so sure that I loved him. And that's what Nat said to me, that he's never felt like this before. Oh, Dorothy, whatever are we going to do?' She looked imploringly at her friend. But Dorothy's reply was far from sympathetic.

'I've told you what to do, Barbara. It's the only way. You'll have to put an end to it, straight away. You'd get over it...'

Barbara could see that Dorothy was getting exasperated, and the last thing she wanted to do was to quarrel with her friend. Heaven knows, she might need a friend who understood before long.

'Please don't be angry,' she said, almost crying. 'I didn't ask for this to happen ... the way I feel about Nat. It's been totally unexpected, and I can't just finish it, in spite of what you say. And I wouldn't get over it, not so easily...'

'Thousands of girls have had to get over far worse things, when their husbands and fiancés have been killed, just as you had to get over losing Mike. It's wartime, Barbara. You don't know what might happen to Nat. You and Nat, Howard and me, we're what you might call ships that pass in the night.'

Barbara didn't answer, and Dorothy was beginning to realise that nothing she could say was going to make any difference. And she, too, did not want to lose her friend. 'I'm sorry,' she said. 'I don't want to quarrel with you, but I wouldn't be a very good friend if I didn't tell you how I feel. I'm concerned for you, Barbara, but maybe I can't understand what you're feeling. Maybe it hasn't happened to me. I love Raymond, but it's a pretty uncomplicated sort of relationship. Perhaps I'm better at compartmentalising my life than you are. Gosh! That's a big word, isn't it?' She laughed. 'Do you know what I mean, though? My time with Howard is separate from my feelings for Raymond. Howard and I will say goodbye at the end of the war or maybe sooner – whenever he's sent elsewhere, who knows? – and we'll have no regrets. But I can see, I suppose, that your involvement with Nat is rather different.'

Kathy was stirring now and making little cooing sounds as though she was singing to herself. Barbara stopped and sat her up against the pillow at the back of the pram. She was warmly dressed in a bright-pink jacket, bonnet and mittens. The colour suited her dark curls, peeping out from under the fur-trimmed bonnet. She smiled appealingly at both her mummy and Dorothy – she was not a shy child – reaching out her arms and saying something that sounded like 'mama', followed by 'ba-ba-ba'.

Dorothy laughed. 'Isn't she delightful? Is she trying to say Barbara?'

'I don't think so,' smiled Barbara. 'She says it all the time. It's one of the easiest sounds to say.'

The feeling of tension between them was over as Barbara turned the pram round and they headed towards home. No more was said about the situation until they stopped to say goodbye at the end of the street where Dorothy lived.

'Saturday evening, then?' said Dorothy. 'I suppose I can take it you'll be going?'

Barbara nodded. 'We agreed to meet them outside the Winter Gardens at half past seven, didn't we? Shall I see you at the bus stop, then, at about ten past seven?'

'That's OK with me,' said Dorothy. 'Er ... if you change your mind, just let me know.'

'That's not going to happen,' replied Barbara without smiling. 'Just leave it, Dorothy, OK? I won't change my mind. See you on Saturday...'

Barbara was aware of a feeling of foreboding for the next day or two. At first, little niggling doubts crept into her mind as she recalled all that her friend had said. Two weeks was such a short space of time, so how could she feel so sure? Was it just physical attraction, or the novelty of meeting someone so completely different from anyone she had known before? Did Nat really mean everything that he said? And what about the future, the time when Albert would have to be told, as he surely must? She knew, though, despite her confusion and the misgivings that Dorothy's words had given rise to, that she would be there again on Saturday night.

And, sure enough, all the negative feelings were put to one side when she met Nat again, at least for the time that they spent together. They danced and they had a drink at one of the several bars, the four of them chatting easily together. The men agreed that they were impressed with the glories of the Winter Gardens building. It was sumptuous throughout, comparing very favourably with the Tower. A flight of stairs from the Indian Lounge, which was lavishly decorated in an oriental style, led up to the equally splendid Empress Ballroom.

There were quiet walkways too, adorned with palm trees, ferns and lush foliage, where Barbara and Nat were able to be alone for a little while. They sat in a quiet alcove, looking at one another without speaking for several moments, but experiencing again the feelings and the attraction that had first drawn them together. Nat put his arms around her; he kissed her gently and tenderly, then again, more ardently.

Then he stopped. It was not the time nor the place, and both of them knew that. They did not want to make an exhibition of themselves, as very many couples were doing in wartime Blackpool. On promenade benches; on the sands or the grass in the park, if the weather was clement; on the back row of the cinema; or under the pier ... they were to be seen all over the place, girls with soldiers, sailors, airmen and GIs, and who could tell whether it was a one-night stand, a passing fancy, or something that would stand the test of time? Barbara and Nat knew that the feelings they had for one another were private and precious, and that they would have to wait.

They spoke very little of the future, not then or at further meetings. They both knew, though, that it would ultimately have to be faced; there would be a day of reckoning.

Nat told her about his life back in his hometown in Vermont, about his parents and his brother and sister. They were both older than he was and married with families. His brother, Lawrence, was thirty-five; unlike his brother he had not joined the army. Neither was he part of the family business as Nat was. Lawrence had shown no inclination for it; he was a bank manager in Montpelier, which was the capital city of Vermont. His sister, Nancy, was thirty and married to the owner of a sports emporium in Stowe, not far from the family hotel. Nat, at twenty-seven, was the baby of the family.

Barbara told Nat about her family background, how her parents had been killed when she was very young, and her upbringing with her aunt and uncle. She told him, too, about her engagement to Mike, who had not returned from Dunkirk.

She felt honour-bound to mention Albert from time to time. Nat didn't say, 'Never mind about him,' or words to that effect. Her husband was there as an undeniable fact, as was her baby daughter, and they could not be ignored.

'Albert is a good man,' she told Nat. 'I've known him ... well ... for ever, really, because he lived

350

next door. He was literally "the boy next door", although he is fifteen years older than I am. He never seemed to be all that interested in girls; I don't remember ever seeing him with one. He's more of a man's man, really, if you know what I mean. He loves his football and darts, and a pint at the pub now and again. He's been good to me, kind and thoughtful.' She did not say how Albert had spoken of his undying love for her and how he had said he would always be there for her, come what may. She tried to push memories such as those to the back of her mind.

And Albert likes his own way, she also thought to herself. He could be dogmatic and unbending, and when she forced herself to think about the future she could foresee trouble ahead.

'Let's take a day at a time,' Nat always told her when she became too introspective. 'When it's time to face up to it all, I shall be with you every step of the way.'

There was a weekend when Dorothy's fiancé was home on leave, but Howard came along with Nat – to the Tower on that particular Saturday – and he found plenty of partners to dance with. Barbara was sure he knew of the situation between herself and Nat, and he was extremely tactful and understanding. Whether he approved or not she was unable to tell.

Another time it was Barbara herself who was not there because Albert was home on leave. There were two such occasions during the time that Nat was stationed at Warton. On the first occasion she and Albert made love, though not without a sense of guilt on Barbara's part. On the next occasion, some six weeks later, Barbara was relieved when the onset of her monthly period prevented this from happening.

Occasionally she was able to meet Nat during the week. Almost every afternoon, if the weather was not too cold or rainy, she took Katherine out for a walk in her pram. It seemed that the life at the American camp was pretty free and easy because Nat was able to get time off to be with her. She met him near to the North Pier and she wheeled the pram down the slope to the lower prom. It was far more secluded than the upper promenade, where the RAF recruits who were stationed in the town were often to be seen walking along in small groups, and where the tramcars clanged and clattered by, bound for Squires Gate or Cleveleys.

They sat on a bench, Nat's arm around her, relishing their brief time together. They could hear the sound of the waves beating against the sea wall and the cry of the seagulls as they exchanged kisses of love and longing. They knew, though, that that was all they could do, that now was not the time nor the place.

Nat was enchanted with Kathy, who cooed and laughed and held out her arms to him. She had learnt to wave 'bye-bye', one of the first things learnt by all babies. She waved dutifully as they parted by North Pier where Nat boarded a tram to take him towards Squires Gate. In fact, Kathy then continued to wave to imaginary people all the way home, and was still doing it when they entered the house and saw Aunt Myrtle.

'Who is she waving to?' laughed Myrtle.

'Oh, she's been doing it ever since she woke up,' answered Barbara. 'It's a new trick she's learnt. She's waving "hello" to Aunty Myrtle, aren't you, darling?'

Barbara reflected that it was fortunate that Kathy had not yet learnt to talk. Aunt Myrtle was still unaware of the secret life her niece was leading.

Chapter Twenty-Seven

By the end of May everyone, civilians as well as the fighting forces, was aware of the tension in the air. It was common knowledge that D-Day, the start of the liberation of occupied Europe, was imminent.

'Barbara, could you meet me this week, on your own?' asked Nat. 'You know how I love to see your little daughter; but we do need to be alone for a little while. Could you possibly leave her with your aunt one afternoon?'

'Er ... yes; I'll manage it somehow,' replied Barbara, although she hated the subterfuge and the lies. She had not really told any out-and-out-lies, but she had failed to tell the whole truth. This time, though, it might be necessary to lie to her aunt.

'I could say that I have a dental appointment on Wednesday afternoon,' she suggested tentatively. 'I really do need to go before long. And the dentist will no doubt want to see me again – they always do – so I could make the actual appoint-ment for the following week. My dentist is in the centre of Blackpool, and my aunt is sure to tell me to take as long as I like, and have a look round the shops.'

'Don't look so worried, darling,' said Nat. 'I know you hate telling lies, and that's one of the reasons I love you so much. You're such a good honest person, Barbara.'

She shook her head. 'How can I be, the way I'm behaving?'

'I know … I know what you mean.' He drew her closer to him on their seat in the Floral Hall of the Winter Gardens. 'But you really are – good and honest and thoughtful. I know you don't want to hurt anyone, but we can't let anything come between us, to spoil what we have. You know that, don't you, Barbara?'

'Yes, I know that… I'll meet you on Wednesday, then, shall I? Two o'clock at the usual place?' That was near to the North Pier entrance.

Her Aunt Myrtle fell in readily with the story of her supposed dental appointment. 'I'll have Kathy for as long as you like,' she said. 'Go and have a look at the shops while you're in town; and why don't you treat yourself to tea and cakes at Robinson's café? Unless you've had a bad time at the dentist's, of course.'

'No, it'll just be a check-up the first time,' said Barbara. 'Thank you, Aunty. You're very good to me.'

'No more than you deserve,' said Aunt Myrtle, which caused Barbara a severe stab of guilt.

They met as arranged by the North Pier

entrance on the following Wednesday afternoon. Nat kissed her on the cheek, smiling broadly. 'Hi, good to see you. Glad you could make it. No problems, then?'

'No, not so far,' she replied. 'Nat ... you do love me, don't you?' Once again the enormity of what she was doing became very real to her. She knew that the time had arrived when she and Nat would bring their love for one another to its inevitable climax. 'I mean ... this is for ever, not just for now?' she whispered. 'You are very sure ... about us?'

'I've never been more sure about anything,' he answered. 'I love you, Barbara, more than I can say, and I always will.' They were talking in hushed voices, but no one was paying any heed to them. Couples such as themselves were to be seen all over the town.

'Come along...' He took hold of her hand and they hurried to the tram stop. They boarded a tram bound for Squire's Gate.

'But you've already come from there,' said Barbara.

'No matter,' said Nat smiling. 'It's a good deal quieter down there, and I didn't want you to travel so far on your own.'

She laughed. 'Why ever not? I'm a big girl now, you know. I'm not likely to get lost, not in Blackpool.'

'But I'm here to take care of you, aren't I?' He reached for her hand.

They did not speak very much throughout the journey along the stretch of Blackpool promenade. They sat hand in hand, looking out at the crowds of both civilians and servicemen thronging the promenade, and at the expanse of golden sand, and beyond it the vast stretch of sea.

It was a glorious May day. The sun shone from a cloudless sky; glinting like silver coins on the bluey-grey ocean. The sea at Blackpool was ever changing, taking its colour from the heavens – often dark grey and stormy, but today as still and as blue as Barbara had ever known it to be.

They alighted from the tram at the stop known as Starr Gate and walked towards the sandhills, as Barbara had already guessed they might do. The sandhills stretched southwards from Squires Gate to St Annes – hillocks of fine, pale, golden sand, interspersed with the clumps of star grass that helped the dunes to keep their shape. The sea never came so far inland, but could be seen in the distance beyond the stretch of coarser sand that was covered daily by the incoming tide.

This was a favourite spot for courting couples. Barbara and Nat clambered across the dunes, their feet sinking into the soft sand. It crept through the straps of Barbara's sandals and between her toes. She was not wearing stockings, an economy measure that many women were adopting, especially when the weather was warm. She pondered that every trace of sand would need to be removed before she went home.

They found a secluded hollow where the sandhills rose above them on all sides. Nat took off his jacket and laid it on the ground. They sat on it together, looking at one another speechlessly for several moments. Then he drew her into his arms and kissed her passionately, in the way they had both been yearning for and anticipating for so long.

'Barbara ... I love you,' he murmured, and it did not seem at all sordid or wrong as they made love for the very first time. She felt tears of pent-up emotion and sublime happiness misting her eyes as their love reached its fulfilment.

'I love you too, Nat,' she whispered. 'Whatever happens – and God alone knows what is going to happen – I love you, so very much.' She knew now that there was no turning back, but there was so much that was unknown, so much that they must face, together. 'Oh, Nat ... what are we going to do?'

She looked around, feeling a shade guilty; and worried lest there was anyone near enough to see or hear them. It was not the sort of thing she had ever done before. She had always thought that making love out of doors as they had just done was something rather shameful, not at all the sort of thing that a 'nice' girl would do. She adjusted her clothing feeling, now, a little embarrassed, and Nat did the same.

He clearly understood how she felt. 'I know, my darling,' he said. 'This...' He gestured with his hand towards the sandhills. 'It is not ideal. But you do know, don't you, that this was inevitable? And some day, Barbara, we will be together for always. You must try to cling on to that, just as I will, because...' He took a deep breath. 'I had to see you today, to show you how much I love you, but also because there is something I have to tell you. The first draft of men from our camp has already left for the south of England, in preparation for D-Day. And it's almost certain that I will be going with the next draft, in a couple of weeks' time. And Howard as well.'

'But I thought you were needed here. You said, didn't you, that you had an important job in charge of the catering? Oh, Nat, this is dreadful news.' Tears welled up again in her eyes, but she brushed them away. She knew that to weep and wail about this would only make things worse for Nat. She was not surprised at his next words.

'It's war, my darling, and it's far more important than cooking meals and looking after the officers. And we have to obey orders. We didn't join up just to have a cushy number and keep out of danger.'

'But how will I know where you are?' she asked. 'How will we be able to keep in touch?'

'I don't really know at the moment. But there will be an address – a sort of address – you can write to once the assault is under way. I'm sorry to have to leave you, Barbara. I'm more than sorry; I'm torn apart. I was planning to be with you, for us to be together when we tell your husband about ... you and me.'

'No, I don't really think that would have been a good idea, Nat.' She shook her head. She knew that Albert could be aggressive when he was roused and she shuddered to think of his reaction. No – it was far better that she should face him on her own, although she was already quaking at the thought. 'I will tell him,' she said. 'I'm not sure when, but I will, I promise. Will I see you again before you go?'

'Yes, on Saturday, I hope. We arranged, didn't

we, the four of us, that we should visit the Tower again?'

She nodded numbly. The sun had gone behind a cloud – a few clouds had now appeared in the formerly clear blue sky – and she shivered, although not just with the cold. 'I must go, Nat,' she said. 'Aunt Myrtle said I could take as long as I wanted, but I'd better be getting back. Don't come back with me on the tram. It would be a waste of your time, and I'm all right, honestly.' She needed a little time on her own to compose herself and to adjust to Nat's news before she joined her family again.

'OK, if you're sure, darling...'

They walked to the tram stop where they said goodbye. Their parting was far less joyful than their meeting a couple of hours ago had been.

At nine-thirty in the morning of Tuesday, 6th June, the sombre voice of John Snagge told the nation over the radio that, 'D-Day has come. Early this morning the Allies began the assault on the north-western face of Hitler's European fortress...' The news had been long awaited and the majority of Britons had felt sure that 'Operation Overlord', as the attack was called, would be successful. It was reported that before nightfall on 6th June, one hundred and fifty-six thousand men had been put ashore on the coast of Normandy. There were heavy losses, mostly among the RAF and in the American assault area known as Omaha.

Nat was not part of that first offensive but, as he had told Barbara, he was posted soon afterwards with the next draft, to somewhere in Devon. It was to be a long time before he and Barbara were in contact. She knew, though, very soon after he had departed for the south coast, that she was expecting his child.

At first she was shocked and frightened, then she realised that this was inevitable, just as their one and only act of love had been. Perhaps it was meant to be; at all events it forced the issue and compelled her to admit, first of all to her aunt, what had been going on in her life for the past few months.

She decided to talk to her aunt on her own, and she chose an evening when her uncle had gone to have a drink and a game of dominoes, as he did from time to time, with his mates at the local pub. She had put Kathy to bed, and she and her aunt sat one on each side of the fire in the family living room.

'Aunty ... I've something to tell you,' Barbara began. She did not hesitate before she said, 'I'm having another baby.'

'Oh!' her aunt gasped, then she beamed with pleasure. 'That's wonderful news. It's rather soon after Kathy, but I'm sure you're very pleased. Does Albert know?'

'No, not yet,' Barbara replied. 'Actually, Aunty Myrtle, there's something else I have to tell you. You see ... it isn't Albert's baby.'

Her aunt's expression changed from one of delight to one of horror. 'Barbara! Whatever are you saying?'

Barbara explained how she had met Nat Castillo and how their friendship had developed over the months. 'We love one another,' she said, 'in a way that I have never loved Albert. I know what you will think about me. I know what you will say – that I have behaved disgracefully and that I can't be sure that I love Nat ... but I do love him; I'm very sure, and so is he.'

Her aunt's face had blanched and she was grasping hold of the chair arms to stop herself from trembling. Barbara felt dreadful at the effect her news was having. Myrtle did not weep, or shout at Barbara. After a few moments, during which she was trying to compose herself, she said, 'That's *exactly* what I'm going to say, Barbara. You've been a silly girl. You've behaved very badly, but I suppose I can understand that you might have had your head turned by this young man. A Yank ... yes!' She shook her head despairingly. 'They're a long way from home, and who can blame them if they find girls who are willing?'

'But it isn't like that,' Barbara protested. 'I know the reputation they have, but Nat isn't like that. He's a good honest man ... and we fell in love.'

'You couldn't help yourselves, I suppose?' Myrtle smiled a little cynically, and Barbara couldn't blame her.

'Well, yes ... I mean ... no. We couldn't help – can't help – how we feel about one another.'

Her aunt sighed. 'You've been very foolish and I can't condone what you've done. Nor have we ever encouraged you to tell lies, but there is a way round this. Albert need never know, not if you let him think that the baby is his. I know it's wrong, but there's nothing else you can do under the circumstances.'

Barbara shook her head. 'I'm afraid I can't do that. The last time Albert came home on leave I was having a period, and so we didn't ... you know. Anyway, I couldn't deceive him like that. When he comes home the next time I couldn't trick him into ... doing that, then pretending the baby was his. You see, Nat and I, we want to be together, when he comes back, when it's all over.'

'And when is he due home again – Albert, I mean?'

'In just over two weeks. I shall have to tell him, Aunty Myrtle. It's not going to be easy, but I know I must.'

And what about ... the other one, Nat? Does he know about the baby?'

'No, I only found out after he'd gone. He's somewhere down south now. I don't know when I shall see him again.'

'Isn't it possible that you might be mistaken,' said Myrtle, 'about being pregnant?'

'No, not at all. I'm always so regular, you see. And anyway ... I just know.' Barbara felt instinctively at her breasts, which were already a little tender.

'I can't pretend I'm not shocked,' said Myrtle, 'especially at you, Barbara. It's the last thing I could ever have imagined you would do. But I shall stand by you. I'll help you in any way I can, and I know your uncle will too. I shall have to tell him, of course. We love you, Barbara. We've tried to make up to you for you losing your parents, and we'll do whatever we need to do now, you can be sure of that.'

'Thank you, Aunty Myrtle,' said Barbara in a subdued voice. 'You've always been so good to me, and I hate to upset you like this.'

Myrtle thought to herself at that moment, and during the following weeks, that she would not like to be in Barbara's shoes when she broke the news to Albert. And, despite her disappointment and her annoyance at what her niece had done, she reflected that Barbara's marriage was by no means the perfect one. Myrtle had come to the conclusion, over the last couple of years, that Albert was not really the right man for Barbara.

The scene with Albert, inevitably, was a bitter one, but poignant and distressing as well. Barbara had never seen Albert so angry or, on the other hand, so dejected and bewildered as he was at first. She had deliberated and agonised as to how to tell him. She decided that the bold approach, telling him straight away that she was pregnant, was not the right one to adopt with Albert. Instead she began in a regretful way, telling him that whilst he had been away she had met someone else and that they had fallen in love.

Whilst he stared at her, open-mouthed with disbelief, she went on to say that she was sorry to hurt him, but she knew now that she had been wrong to marry him, that what she felt for him was affection but not real love.

'What are you saying, Barbara?' he cried. 'That you want to leave me? You want to go off with this other fellow, whoever he is? That you want ... a divorce?' He shook his head decisively. 'Oh no,

Barbara; I shall never let you go. A divorce is out of the question.' Then, as her aunt had done, he said, 'You've had your head turned by some fancy words, I daresay. A Yank, is he?' He had guessed correctly, but it might just as well have been an RAF man. There were hundreds of them in the town, even billeted in the same house.

'Forget him, Barbara. You belong to me; I'm your husband and I love you. Maybe I'm not as glamorous or as young, eh? Is that it? But I love you far more than he ever could.'

She knew then that she had to pluck up the courage to tell him the truth. 'There's something else,' she said. 'Yes, you're right; he is an American GI ... and I'm expecting his child.'

It was then that Albert lost control of himself. He did not strike out at her physically, but she had never heard such a tirade of abuse as he flung at her, nor had she believed he could use such words.

'You're a whore, a trollop!' he yelled, as he turned white with rage. 'I said I loved you, and yes, I do – heaven help me – and I suppose I always will. But I despise you, Barbara. At this moment I almost hate you! How could you do this? I don't know what you are trying to tell me, what it is you want; but if you're expecting me ever to accept this child that you're having as mine, then let me tell you that I never will. Go to him, then, your Yank, if that's what you want. But you are not taking Katherine. She is my child and she stays with me.'

There was a lot more in the same vein before Albert left her alone that night. He went to sleep in an attic room, leaving her alone in the bedroom they shared when he was home on leave, in the Leighs' boarding house.

She tossed and turned in the bed, lying awake for hours and only falling into a fitful sleep as dawn was breaking. An hour or two later she dressed herself and Kathy and crept out of the house before anyone else was stirring, back to her home next door with her aunt and uncle.

She was left in no doubt about Albert's feelings. He would never accept the child she was carrying as his, nor did she want him to; this was Nat's child. But if she and Nat, sometime in the future, were to be together, which was what they both wanted so much, then Albert would force her to leave Katherine behind. And however could she bear to part with her precious little daughter?

Chapter Twenty-Eight

1973

'So my mother went away and left me, then?' said Kathy. 'She deserted me and married this American fellow? At least I'm assuming she married him?'

'Yes, she did marry him, eventually,' said Winifred. 'It sounds dreadful, Kathy, to say that she deserted you; it's not a word she would have wanted to use. But she really had little choice in the matter; in fact, she had no choice at all.'

Her aunt was trying to explain to Kathy about

the circumstances that had led to her father and her mother parting, all those years ago in 1944.

'There was a dreadful scene when Barbara – your mother – told your father that she was expecting someone else's child. I wasn't there, of course, but Albert told us about it the following morning, myself and my mother and father. We were horrified, as you can imagine, and Albert was so very bitter. But I'd always liked Barbara – she was such a pleasant and thoughtful girl – and I couldn't believe that she would behave like that, have an affair with another man, without it really meaning something. And I guessed she must be feeling terrible herself about everything. She was such a nice girl, she really was. Anyway, I went next door to see her, and she told me about how she had met this American soldier – GIs, they were called – and how they had fallen in love. She was already expecting his child, you see, my dear, and he'd been sent away from Blackpool, down to the south of England.'

'So ... what happened? Did she go off and join him?'

'No, how could she? He'd been posted down there in preparation for D-Day. He took part in that offensive, although he wasn't part of the first landings. Barbara didn't know when she would see him again. Anyway, she stayed with her aunt and uncle, next door, until nearly the end of the year – it was 1944. Myrtle White – she was Barbara's aunt – had a sister who lived Manchester way, and Barbara went to stay with her until after the baby was born.'

'And ... she left me here?'

'Like I said, she had no choice. It must have broken her heart to leave you; in fact, I know that it did. But your father wouldn't let her take you. And even if she had stayed here, Albert had made it very clear that he would never accept the child she was carrying as his. Yes, she left Blackpool in the December of 1944 ... and I never saw her again. You were about eighteen months old, Kathy love, and you stayed with your Grandma and Grandad Leigh, and with me, of course. Your father was in the army until peace was declared the following year, so we looked after you.

'Albert had told her that she must never contact any of our family ever again, and she must certainly not think of trying to get in touch with her daughter – I mean you, Kathy, dear. And eventually he divorced her; they'd been married long enough for a divorce to be possible, and there were grounds for it with her expecting a child by this ... Nat Castillo.'

'You never met him, then?'

'No, I never met him. I knew they got married, possibly in 1945. I didn't know all the details, of course; I just put two and two together. I presume that Nat came to find her, wherever she was in Manchester, after the war was over, or he may have been given leave before the end of the war; I'm not sure. The baby would have been born by then. They would have to be married before she went off to join him in the USA. There were strict regulations about that, from what I remember. A lot of girls became what were known as GI brides, but the men had to have married them before they set sail for America. In case the fellow changed his mind, you see, and decided he didn't want to go through with it after all.

'As a matter of fact, Barbara wrote to me, just once. She wasn't supposed to, of course, and I could never let on to Albert that I'd heard from her. He'd have gone mad! She told me that the baby was a little girl, and that she and Nat and the baby were living with his parents in a town called Stowe, in the state of Vermont. I looked it up in the atlas, and it's in New England, up near the Canadian border. Whether she is still there or not I have no idea; it's quite a long time ago.'

'Then ... she could still be alive? She probably is. She was younger than my father, wasn't she? Do you mean to say, Aunty Win, that you've known all this time that my mother might still be alive? You even knew her address, but you never told me?'

'It was the promise I'd made to your father, love. In his eyes, she was as good as dead to him, and that's what everyone else believed – what we were forced to tell them – that she'd died. I know it was dreadful, and many's the time I've wanted to break that promise, but I knew that I couldn't. It would have opened a whole can of worms, as they say. Except ... I must confess that I told Jeff, after we were married. There's nothing that I won't tell Jeff.'

'And what did he think about it?' asked Kathy.

'He thought it was one of the most dreadful things he'd ever heard, that the poor girl had been forced to leave her baby behind; and he felt so sorry for you, that you'd been told lies about your mother. But he had to try and act normally with Albert – I know he found it hard at times, especially as they weren't very much alike. I'm sorry, my dear; I can't tell you how sorry I am. Jeff and I knew that it would probably all come to light now.

'But there's one thing you must be very sure of, Kathy, and that is that your mother loved you very much. I always told you that, didn't I? I made a point of telling you that from when you were a tiny girl. It really must have torn her apart to leave you.'

'But she had another baby girl, you say?' Kathy couldn't help feeling resentful and she knew it was obvious in her tone of voice. 'She probably has lots more children by now. She'll have forgotten all about me.'

'The Barbara I knew would never forget you, my dear,' said her aunt. She smiled reminiscently. 'I wish I could make you understand what a lovely girl she was. Yes, I know she did wrong, that she behaved very badly – so did hundreds of other girls in that dreadful war – but I believe that she really must have loved this Nat.'

'And ... she didn't love my father?'

'Probably not in the way she should have done when she married him. Your father was a good deal older than she was, quite set in his ways when they got married. You must remember that, Kathy. He could be difficult. But he really did love her – he adored her – which made it so much worse when he found out what she'd done. I never thought, to be honest, that they were just right for one another. They might have found that they didn't get on so well had they ever lived

369

together. They never had the chance to have their own home because your father was in the army when they married. Barbara stayed with her aunt and uncle whilst Albert was away, and then she usually came to stay here when he was home on leave.

'And then when you were born he was over the moon! He loved you so very much. In fact, I was amazed at the way he fussed over you when you were a tiny baby. That's why he refused to part with you. The mother is usually given custody when it comes to divorce but ... well, I suppose the judge decided that she was the one at fault. So perhaps you can understand now, Kathy love, why your father behaved the way he did when you were a little girl. He was rather moody and awkward and he didn't find it easy to show you how much he cared for you. He was still grieving over Barbara.'

Kathy shook her head. 'I'm finding it hard to forgive him for the lies he told me, and her – my mother – for leaving me. It was really you who brought me up, wasn't it, Aunty Win, not my dad? He always seemed so withdrawn, so un-approachable.'

'So he was, especially at first. I really wished he would get married again and try to forget how badly he'd been hurt.'

'He nearly did, didn't he, to Sally Roberts?'

'Well, that was as near as he ever came to it. But it wasn't to be. He was upset about that as well for a while. He always had a lot to say about un-faithful women. Not that I'm saying Sally was like that; she could probably see that it wouldn't have worked out with your father. No, I'm thinking about Sadie Morris. You remember her, of course, your friend Shirley's mum? Your dad had a lot to say about that, what a flibbertigibbet she was. I think that was the word he used. She met a fellow who was staying here on holiday and went off with him. It brought it all back to your dad, you see, and his friendship with Sally was coming to an end at about the same time.'

Kathy was silent for a few moments, deep in thought about all she had heard. 'So ... my mother was brought up by her aunt, like I was?'

'Yes, her aunt and uncle. Both her parents had been killed when she was a baby. Ben and Myrtle White; they were really good to her and I know they loved her, just as her real parents would have done.'

'And what happened to them?'

'They moved away from their boarding house next door to ours just after the war ended. They gave up the business and went to live in Marton. We lost touch with them because of all that had happened. We didn't hear any more about them. It was a pity, really; my parents had always been friendly with Myrtle and Ben, but it made it all rather difficult for the friendship to continue. I doubt that they're still alive now.'

'They were my – what would they be? – my great-aunt and – uncle, then, weren't they? And you never saw them again, you say, after they left the boarding house? So they never saw me again either? Didn't they want to know how I was getting on as I was growing up? I must have lived in the same house as them when I was a baby.'

'I'm sure they would have liked to keep in touch, my dear, but as I say, it really caused quite an upheaval. No doubt they thought it was the best policy to keep their distance. Your father was so cut up about Barbara, very angry, and deeply hurt as well. And as it was their niece who was the cause of it all I suppose they didn't want to encounter Albert again. But I'm very sure they must have thought about you a lot.'

Kathy was slowly coming round to grasping the significance of all her aunt had told her. She was filled with a mass of conflicting emotions. Disbelief at first, then shock, anger, sadness, bewilderment... But one thought stood out from the rest.

'How old would my mother be now?' she asked.

'Barbara would be – let me see – she'd be fifty-three. She was fifteen years younger than your father.'

'But that's no age at all,' said Kathy. 'It's more than likely that she's still alive, isn't it?'

Winifred sighed. 'Most probably she is, Kathy love... I'm so terribly sorry. I'm wishing now that I'd told you, years ago, but you know what your father was like, and I'd made a promise, you see. I suppose I convinced myself that what you'd never had you'd never miss; and I did try so hard to make it up to you for not having your mother with you all the time you were growing up.'

'I know, Aunty Win,' said Kathy. 'I'm finding it hard to believe that you could keep it to yourself all that time, but I'm trying to understand why you did it... But it's not too late, is it? It might be possible for me to find her again?'

Winifred had feared – almost dreaded – that this

was what Kathy might say. 'Oh, I don't know, love,' she replied. 'I'm not sure that it would be a good idea. It's a long time ago. I doubt that they're still living in the same place, Barbara and Nat, and they'll probably have some children, grown up of course, though, now... She'll have made a whole new life over in the USA. It's such a long way away, and such a long time ago. Maybe it's best left alone.'

'You told me, though, didn't you, how much she loved me?' Kathy insisted. 'And that she would never forget about me? It's no use, Aunty Win; I've got to try and find her. It might not be possible ... but at least I've got to try. It's what I want to do, what I must do, can't you see?'

'Yes, I suppose I can,' said Winifred. 'No doubt I would feel the same if I were in your shoes. But wait a little while, Kathy. Wait until after the funeral at least. And then, if you're still in the same mind, we'll try and make some enquiries. It might not be so easy; it's not as though it's the same country...' And Barbara might not want to be found, Winifred thought to herself, but she could not burst her niece's bubble of hope. She had already hurt and disappointed her far too much.

The church was more than half full for Albert's funeral service. He had been a popular and respected member of the congregation and the church council, and was well known generally as a former hotel owner, and a member of the darts team at his 'local'. The vicar spoke kindly of him, praising his work for the church and community.

373

'Albert was a quiet, unassuming man,' he said. 'A little reserved until you got to know him, but his heart was in the right place, and he had a deep affection for his family.'

An appropriate cliché, thought Kathy, a trifle cynically. There was a good deal that the vicar and countless others did not know about her father; but she was trying not to let bitter thoughts spoil the reverence of the occasion. And there were many things in her father's life for which she knew she must be thankful. She knew, deep down, that he had always loved her and he had tried to do his best for her according to his beliefs.

Tim had been almost as shocked as Kathy on hearing the revelations about Albert's secret past. After he had got over his initial reaction – disbelief at first, and then amazement that Albert could have been so deceitful for so long – he came to the same conclusion as Kathy, that her mother, Barbara Castillo as she was called, would most probably be still living. And he agreed wholeheartedly with Kathy that she must try to find her.

They sat discussing it the night after the funeral. Sarah and Christopher had been in bed for ages; Kathy and Tim enjoyed their quiet time together in the evening on their own. They were still as compatible and as happy as they had been when they were first married.

'I get the impression that Aunty Win is not entirely in favour of me trying to trace my mother,' said Kathy. 'She thinks I should "let sleeping dogs lie" as they say. On the other hand she won't try to discourage me; she knows she has caused me enough distress already. I still find it hard to believe it of Aunty Win that she could have lied to me for all these years.'

'I don't suppose it's been easy for her,' said Tim. 'They all made a promise to keep up the pretence, didn't they? And you found that letter that your mother wrote, saying she would never contact your family again. It must have been dreadful for her as well, Kathy love. And I'm quite sure what your aunt says is true, that Barbara really loved you very much.'

'Yes ... that's what I'm trying to believe,' said Kathy. 'We know she had another little girl, and she may well have more children by now, grand-children as well. She'll have made a whole new life over there in America.' She was deep in thought for a few moments. 'It's quite possible that she and her husband have kept the past hidden from their children. They might not know anything about me, just as I've been kept in the dark about my parents' divorce and everything. It might come as a tremendous shock to them; I'm saying 'them' although I don't know how many children there might be, my half-sisters and -brothers...' She shook her head bemusedly.

'All the same, I've got to try, Tim, no matter what the consequences might be. You do agree with me, don't you, love?'

'I shall be with you every step of the way, my darling,' he told her.

Kathy was unsure how to go about starting the search for her mother, and it was Tim who sorted things out for her. It turned out to be much simpler than they could have believed. Winifred had the address that was on Barbara's letter, written all those years ago, but there was no telephone number. However, a long-distance call to the telephone exchange in the town of Stowe in the state of Vermont proved fruitful. Kathy and Tim were amazed to discover that a family called Castillo were still living at the same address. And now they had the telephone number.

Kathy's hands were trembling so much that she could scarcely hold the receiver when she decided, late one night in mid October, to make the all-important call to the USA. She knew that the time in America would be different, some five or six hours behind the time in Britain, so it would be early evening over there. Who would answer the phone? she wondered. Her mother, Barbara? The thought of that filled her with wonder, but also with fear. Or might it be Nat Castillo? She had tried to conjure up a picture in her mind of what he might look like, but of course, she had no idea. And what on earth should she say? She had tried to compose a few opening remarks in her head, to ease her way into the situation. She knew that she must not say straight away that she was Katherine, Barbara's long lost daughter.

It was a woman's voice that answered the phone, giving the number and saying that it was the home of the Castillo family.

Kathy took a deep breath. 'Hello... Could you tell me who it is I'm speaking to, please?'

'I'm Beverley Hanson... Who is it you wish to speak to?' The voice, with the typical accent of a north American, sounded puzzled.

'Well, I'm wondering if that is the home of ... Mr Nat Castillo?' asked Kathy hesitantly.

'Yes, it sure is. He's my father. I was Beverley Castillo before I married. I'm just visiting. Look ... who are you? Where are you speaking from?'

'From a town called Blackpool in England. My name is Katherine Fielding. I was Katherine Leigh before I was married. And I have reason to believe that your father was in Blackpool during the war...' Kathy was finding it hard to keep her voice steady '...and I believe he knew some of the members of my family. It's really important that I should speak to Mr Castillo, if you don't mind.'

There was silence for a moment, then she heard the voice again. 'My father is not too well just now, but I guess he'd sure like to speak to you when he's feeling more himself again. I've heard him say that Blackpool was the place where he met our mom.' Kathy's heart gave a jolt, but she could not pluck up the courage to ask to speak to this woman's 'mom'. 'Listen ... give me your address and your telephone number and I'll ask my dad to get back to you. Tell me again, what did you say your name is? ... Katherine Fielding, and you used to be Katherine Leigh... Yes, I promise I'll tell him. Just a minute and I'll get some paper and a pen... Yes, I've got all that. I'll tell him to contact you as soon as he's feeling better... Bye for now, Katherine.'

Kathy's legs as well as her hands were trembling as she replaced the receiver. She collapsed into the nearest armchair.

'Well?' asked Tim. 'Any joy? Who was that you were speaking to?'

'She's called Beverley,' replied Kathy in a hushed voice. 'She must be my half-sister... She says her father will get back to me. Oh, Tim... whatever have I done?'

PART FOUR

Chapter Twenty-Nine

1945

Barbara was fascinated by her new home and touched by the welcome she received from Nat's parents and the rest of his family: his brother Larry and his wife, Shirley; his sister Nancy and her husband, Frank; and their children, six in all, ranging in age from five to fifteen. The warmth of their greeting and their continuing care and concern for her helped a great deal to ease the heartache she had been feeling ever since she had been forced to part with her beloved little daughter. She knew that she would never forget Katherine; there would always be a special place in her heart and mind for her firstborn child.

She often cried about her, but always in secret. She knew that she, Barbara, was in the place where she must be, with the man she loved and who loved her, and with their own little daughter, Beverley.

It had been a traumatic time for Barbara in the December of 1944, when she had left Blackpool and had gone to stay with her Aunt Myrtle's sister, Muriel, in her Manchester home. Muriel and her husband, Jack, had been very kind and understanding. They had been made aware of the circumstances and she had met with no reproach or condemnation, only sympathy and friendliness. Muriel's commonsensical approach helped Barbara to look forward, not only to the birth of her baby, but to her future life with the man who loved her.

Beverley was born in the February of 1945. Barbara was pleased that she had given birth to another baby girl, not to be a replacement for Kathy – no child could ever be that – but to give her, Barbara, the chance to start again and to be an even better mother this time. She knew that she had failed Katherine. She did not try to convince herself that she was not responsible for what had happened. She knew that both she and Nat had been guilty of wrongdoing in the eyes of many people ... but was it wrong to fall so deeply in love? She had paid the price for it – a bitter, agonising price – but good must be allowed to come out of it. She would do her utmost to be an ideal wife and mother.

Baby Beverley did not resemble Katherine in any way, and Barbara was glad of that. Whereas Kathy was dark with Barbara's brown eyes, this baby was fair, with Nat's colouring. The little hair she had was like the fluffy down on a newborn chick and Barbara guessed she would be blonde-haired, and probably grey-eyed too, like her father, although it was hard to tell at first.

The war was drawing to a close by the time Barbara's baby was born. 'Operation Overlord' had proved to be a victory for the Allies, although not without a few setbacks and severe loss of life. Barbara had heard intermittently from Nat and thanked God that he was still safe. The German troops were in retreat; Paris had been liberated, followed by Brussels, in the late summer of 1944. In the following March the US forces had seized a bridgehead on the Rhine and British troops were now occupying the Ruhr Valley.

Probably because the conflict was in its last stages, Nat was given compassionate leave to be with Barbara and their baby daughter in the month of April. Her divorce was now absolute, and she and Nat were married quietly at the nearest register office, with Muriel and Jack, who had proved to be true friends, as the only witnesses. Unfortunately Nat had to return to Germany to await his demobilisation, leaving Barbara behind once again. She was, however, feeling much more optimistic by now, making arrangements to join him in the USA as soon as it was possible.

She sailed from Liverpool in early October. Her Aunt Myrtle and Uncle Ben, as well as her good friends, Muriel and Jack, were at the quayside to wave goodbye as the ship sailed away. Nat had been demobbed from the US army a couple of months earlier, and the letters they exchanged told of their love and their longing to see one another again. Despite her heartache over Kathy, which was still very intense, Barbara knew she must try to look forward to her new life and, first of all, to the journey.

It was, of course, the longest journey she had ever taken, and the same was true for the many GI brides who were making the voyage along with her. It was a completely new experience for all of them, and as they exchanged stories of how they had met their husbands and about where they were going to live in the USA, the time passed quite quickly. Some of the women had young babies with them. Barbara felt very proud and pleased that she had her lovely nine-month-old Beverley with her. She did not say a word to anyone, however, about the other precious little girl whom she had been forced to leave behind.

The ship docked in New York harbour. It seemed like an impossible dream to Barbara as she caught sight, for the first time, of the Statue of Liberty and the skyscrapers of New York. They were far taller than she could ever have imagined. She remembered joking with Nat about the height of Blackpool Tower. It was true, it seemed, that everything over here was so much bigger and bolder.

Her meeting with Nat, when at last they found one another amidst the milling throng of people, was a rapturous one. Their kiss was full of the delight of seeing one another again and the pent-up longing of the last few months; there was the promise, too, of the joy and contentment of a happy life together.

Baby Beverley, held by her mother, was wide awake and staring around, especially at the smiling stranger who, of course, she could not remember. She had been only two months old when her father had seen her for the first and only time. She had been nearly squashed by their embrace, but now Nat took her from her mother as they made their way to the customs hall to deal with all the rigmarole of disembarkation and entry to a new country.

Finally, they were aboard a long-distance bus, setting off on the long journey to the state of Vermont. They headed north from the state of New York to Connecticut, Massachusetts and, finally, to Vermont.

Barbara was tired and she dozed a little at first, but as they drove through the landscape of hills and valleys, streams and woodlands, she became too enraptured by the scenery to do anything but stay awake. Never had she seen such a kaleidoscope of colour, opening up on either side and in front of her, as far as the eye could see. Vibrant colours such as she had never imagined, ranging from palest yellow through the whole spectrum – gold, orange, scarlet, vermilion, russet – to the deepest brown, as the leaves of the vast variety of deciduous trees changed from their summer green to the varying hues of autumn.

'This is fantastic!' she breathed, after she had gazed at the view in awe for mile upon mile, with Nat watching her with pleasure and pride in his country, and in some amusement as well.

'You ain't seen nothing yet!' he joked. 'Just wait till we get to Vermont. All the New England states are a sight to behold in the fall, but our little state beats the lot. It's known as the Green Mountain State in the summer but it's even lovelier in the fall.'

'Look at the deep crimson,' remarked Barbara. 'I've never seen such a vivid colour.'

'Those are maple trees,' Nat told her. 'The maple leaf is the symbol of Canada, but it's one of the most common trees in New England as well. You've heard of maple syrup?' She nodded. 'Well,

385

our state is one of its chief producers. It's one of our specialities, pancakes with maple syrup. You sure have some treats to look forward to, Barbara... And not just maple syrup either,' he smiled as he leant across and kissed her.

'I'm quite overwhelmed already,' she said. 'It's just ... so beautiful.' She really was at a loss for words.

'We're fully booked with visitors at the moment,' Nat told her. 'We are very busy for most of the year, but in the fall we get a lot of what we call "leaf peepers", folks from the South or Midwest, staying maybe for only a couple of nights and then moving on to the rest of the New England states to enjoy the scenery.'

'I'm looking forward to meeting your family,' said Barbara. 'I had a lovely letter from your mother.'

'And they're sure looking forward to meeting you too,' replied Nat. 'We'll have our own quarters, you know, at the hotel, and Mom and Pop will leave us alone when we want our privacy. It won't be like living with your in-laws, I promise you. It's just that it makes sense, with me helping with the running of the hotel. And Pop has sure made me work since I came home. He may well think of retiring in a few years' time, although I could never see him giving up altogether, nor Mom.'

Barbara was reminded of her own aunt and uncle, Myrtle and Ben, still running their Blackpool boarding house, although they were talking of selling up soon. And of Albert and Winifred next door, working along with their parents in the family business. She pushed the thoughts away, though, as she always tried to do whenever they recurred. She had been instructed, and had promised, that she would have no further contact with them. She must look to the future, the future that had now become the present.

It was good to be part of a large family after being brought up as an only child, and an orphan as well, although Barbara had never had cause to doubt the love that her aunt and uncle showed towards her. Larry and Nancy, Nat's brother and sister, soon made her feel as though she was a welcome addition to the Castillo family, and their children, all six of them, were delighted with their new little cousin.

Then there were Martha and Jacob, known as Jake, whom Nat called Mom and Pop; and Uncle Elmer and Aunt Carrie who lived nearby and helped in the hotel when they were needed.

The hotel was vastly different from anything Barbara had known before. It was a wooden building, as were the majority of houses, a very large white chalet with a wide veranda where the guests could take their ease. The family, too, if and when they had time to do so, because Barbara soon realised that they were busy almost all the year round.

The little town of Stowe, and the surrounding countryside, was as beautiful as Nat had described it to be, ringed by mountains and surrounded by woods and pastureland. The highest peak in the area, Mount Mansfield, could be seen from Barbara and Nat's bedroom window. She never tired of the view: the verdant green of the spring and summertime, the glorious tints of autumn, and the pristine white of the winter snow.

Winter began early in Vermont, as it did in all the New England states. There was a decided nip in the air when Barbara arrived in mid October. By November it was considerably colder, and in the middle of that month the first snow began to fall. When they awoke in the morning it was to a very different scene. The rooftops and church spires, pavements, trees and bushes were now clothed in a mantle of silvery white, glistening in the early-morning sun, virgin white in the places where no feet had trodden.

Barbara soon learnt that the New Englanders adjusted quickly to the change in the weather. Houses were centrally heated, so there was no huddling round a coal fire, then feeling frozen as soon as you moved away, as was the case in England. The snowploughs were soon at work to clear the roads, and people took the weather in their stride, equipped with boots, fleece-lined coats and fur hats.

The snow remained all winter, fresh falls arriving throughout the succeeding months. There was none of the slushy brown mess left behind when a thaw came, as there was back home.

Nat was busy, not only with his duties at the hotel, but also as a ski instructor. He persuaded Barbara that she must learn to ski as most people did in Vermont. She promised she would do so, but not that year. Or the next as it happened...

Winter continued until the end of March, and by that time Barbara knew she was pregnant again. Their son, Carl, was born in the November of 1946, on Thanksgiving Day, to the delight of all the family members.

Another daughter, Anne-Marie, was born in the summer of 1949. Barbara and Nat decided then that their family was complete.

She did learn to ski, but not until several years later when the children were old enough to accompany their parents on a skiing holiday to the Green Mountain range.

They enjoyed many holidays, as a family, to some of the other New England states. To the city of Boston, where they walked the Freedom Trail, visited the State House of Massachusetts and climbed to the top of Beacon Hill; to the lake district and the mountains of New Hampshire; to Portland and the rocky coast of Maine; and to the beaches and quaint colonial villages of Cape Cod.

Their holiday times were precious to them, a time for relaxing together as a family and following new pursuits. They were a happy family, and although there were, inevitably, minor disagreements as the children entered their teens, there was never any serious discord.

Holidays were taken when it was convenient to Martha and Jake. Nat's father, although he had been saying for ages that he would retire, did not do so for many years, not until 1960, when he was seventy-five years of age. He and Martha then went to live in a smaller house on the outskirts of Stowe, leaving the hotel in Nat's capable hands.

Barbara had helped there too, over the years,

with various kinds of work. She became responsible for the office work and bookkeeping when Nat took control of the business. Their three children were still at school. Their parents had no wish to persuade them to take part in the family business unless they wanted to do so. Barbara and Nat had high hopes for them all, that they would go on to college and do well in their chosen professions.

What was Katherine doing now? Barbara sometimes wondered about her, although the heartache had eased considerably over the years. Her firstborn child was there in her mind, though, as a poignant memory. She thought of her especially on her birthday each year, the last day of June. Now she would be eleven, eighteen, twenty-three... She might even be married.

Nat had agreed with her that it would be better if their three children, Beverley, Carl and Anne-Marie, were never told of their half-sister back in England. Barbara had begun a whole new chapter in her life when she had come to live in Vermont. To tell the children about Kathy would only cause complications and give rise to endless questions.

There were times – although only occasionally, and she never mentioned them to Nat – when Barbara felt a deep longing to know how Kathy was faring. Had she been happy with Albert and his parents, and with his sister, Winifred? Perhaps Albert had married again, in which case Kathy would have a stepmother. She felt, though, intuitively, that Winifred would have had a lot to do with the little girl's upbringing. Barbara had always been fond of Winifred, and she felt sure she would have done her very best for the little girl entrusted to her charge.

These times of anguish, fortunately, were of short duration. Barbara continued with her new life, keeping herself busy and forever seeking new interests. On the whole she was happy and contented, and she knew that Nat loved her as much as he had always done, just as she loved him.

It was in the early spring of 1971 when Barbara discovered a lump in her right breast. She made an appointment to see a doctor – something she rarely needed to do as she was normally in very good health – and within a week she was admitted to hospital for an exploratory operation.

Nat, as always, was a great support and comfort to her and did all he could to encourage her to be optimistic about the outcome. 'Now, don't start getting all worked up about it, darling,' he said. 'It's more than likely that it'll turn out to be benign, and you'll be fine once it's been removed. You're strong and healthy, and young as well.'

She smiled. 'Not all that young, Nat.'

'You'll always be young to me,' he told her, with the same loving smile that had not diminished with the passing years. 'Still the same lovely girl I met at the Tower Ballroom.'

Barbara knew, though, that to be young – or comparatively so – was not always a good thing if what she was secretly dreading was diagnosed. The older you were, the slower the disease spread,

391

or so she had heard.

'We won't tell the children just yet,' she said. 'Let's wait until I've had the first op, then we'll know the worst ... or the best,' she added, trying to be optimistic.

The children by now were grown-up and no longer living at home. Beverley, who had trained to be a teacher, had married young and now had a two-year-old son. Carl, who was an accountant, had also married at an early age and he and his wife were expecting their first child. Anne-Marie, aged twenty-two, was still single and enjoying herself too much to marry and settle down just yet. She had taken after her father with her interest in all kinds of sports. She was a qualified swimming instructor, and in the winter, as her father had used to do, she taught skiing to the locals and the many visitors who came to the town. She was sharing an apartment with a girl she had met at college. And so Barbara and Nat had found themselves alone, apart from the few live-in staff that they had appointed when Nat's parents had retired.

Barbara seemed to recover well from the operation and they waited in some trepidation for the results in a few days' time. 'Then came the news that Barbara, secretly, had been dreading all along. The cancer – for that was what it was – had spread further than had been anticipated. A mastectomy of the right breast was deemed necessary and it was imperative that it should be done quickly.

By the autumn of 1971 it seemed that she was well on the road to recovery. She had adjusted well to her incapacity and she was hopeful that the treatment she was receiving would make sure that the dreaded disease did not recur. She had started dealing with the hotel office work again, and she and Nat were planning a trip to New York in the late spring of 1972. She had wanted to see the city for a long time, but with their commitments at the hotel and with their family, it was a visit they had never got round to taking.

She found New York to be fascinating, wonderful, awesome ... and all so unbelievably big and bold, just as she and Nat had joked about when they first met. She loved it all: Macy's and Bloomingdale's, the huge department stores; the shows on Broadway; Central Park and Fifth Avenue; Manhattan Island; the Statue of Liberty (which she had seen, briefly, on her arrival twenty-seven years ago); the blaring horns of the taxicabs; the gigantic steaks and beefburgers; and the pancakes with maple syrup and ice cream. She was no stranger to that delicacy, but here it seemed even more tempting and delicious. It was all like a dream coming true, the other face of America that she had long imagined, so different from the quiet beauty of Vermont.

She did not tell Nat that she was feeling tired, more so than she knew she should, although it was truly an exhausting holiday. She had started to feel pains in her back and abdomen, and she thought – or had she only imagined? – that there was a small lump in her left breast. She knew that it was not likely to disappear and that she must not delay to do something about it as soon as they returned home. The pains in the other parts of her body, that she hoped might be due to tiredness, did not improve either.

Nat was devastated when she told him, the day after they had flown home. She could tell how concerned he was by the look of horror on his face, which he quickly tried to hide with a show of optimism.

The operation was done quickly, a partial mastectomy, but Barbara knew, this time, that there was no point in trying to convince herself that it was not serious. All the members of her family knew too, although they tried to hide their deepest fears with brave attempts at cheerfulness.

By the autumn of 1972 she was spending more and more time resting – she was often too weary to do much else – although she was not confined to bed. She remembered how her Aunt Myrtle had used to say, when she was feeling not too well, 'I'm not going to bed! You die in bed!' Barbara's illness, of course, was much more serious, but she was determined to keep going and remain cheerful – at least from outward appearances – as long as she was able.

Thoughts of the little daughter she had left behind in England started to loom large in her mind. How old would Kathy be now? Twenty-nine years old, probably married by now with children of her own. And what of Albert? Barbara calculated that he would be sixty-seven, not a great age at all. Surely by now he would not be as bitter as he had been about what she had done? Surely he would understand if she tried, at long last, to contact her daughter?

She sat in an armchair near the window of their bedroom, one afternoon in late autumn, looking out at the view of which she never tired. The distant mountains were already capped with white after the first snowfall, and, nearer to the house, the trees that lined the road glowed with the glorious tints of the fall: russet, scarlet, orange, gold and amber. A thick carpet of leaves covered the ground, and two boys were scuffling through them, crunching the leaves underfoot and sending them scurrying away in little flurries.

She experienced a sudden feeling of joy and contentment amidst the sadness and the fear that she sometimes felt at what she knew was inevitable. Nat was wonderful, though, at helping her to keep her spirits up. She was alone, though, at the moment, and knew that there was something she must do.

She opened the drawer of her bedside cabinet and took out a notepad and pen. The urge to write to her firstborn child was so great that it could not be ignored.

'My dear Katherine,' she began. 'I have no idea how much or how little you have been told about me...' She went on to explain what had happened and how she had been compelled to leave her behind. As she wrote of how she had loved Kathy and had never forgotten her, Barbara's eyes began to mist with tears. She felt overwhelmingly sad and so very tired.

She closed the pad and put it back in the drawer underneath her private documents and photograph albums. She would finish the letter another time...

Chapter Thirty

1973

Beverley hurried away to find her father. He was not very ill, just suffering from a bad cold which threatened to turn to bronchitis if he didn't take care. He was not in bed, just resting in his favourite armchair in the bedroom, looking out at his favourite view, now at its best, resplendent with all the glowing colours of the fall. Beverley remembered how her mother had used to sit there drinking in the beauty of the scenery, almost to the very end.

He looked round as she entered the room. He was reading, one of his favourite Jane Austen novels. Her mother, Barbara, had stimulated his interest in this very English authoress, who had long been a favourite of her own. No doubt it brought back memories now of the wife he had loved so very much.

'Dad, I've just had an intriguing phone call,' she began, 'from England. From a young woman who lives in Blackpool. That's where you met Mom, isn't it?'

'It sure is,' replied her father. 'Who was it? What did she say?' His voice was a little hesitant; he sounded almost nervous.

'She's called Katherine Leigh; at least, that was what she was called before she was married.

She's called Katherine Fielding now. She said that she knew you'd been in Blackpool during the war and that you knew some members of her family. She said she would like to speak to you, Dad – to Mr Castillo, she said – but I explained that you're not too well at the moment.'

Her father's face, already pale, had blanched. 'So ... what did you tell her?' His voice sounded husky with emotion. 'Did you say I'd get in touch with her? You've got her address, I suppose?'

'Yes, and her telephone number... Who is she, Dad? Did you know her? She sounded very sure of her facts.'

Nat sighed, such a deep sigh that seemed to come from the very depths of his being. 'Yes ... I knew her. At least, I met her when she was just a tiny girl. They called her Kathy. It's a long story, Beverley. A very sad story that perhaps your mother and I should have told you. But we decided it was best not to.'

'Who is she, then, this Kathy?' Beverley asked again. She was perplexed, and concerned too, at the shock that this had clearly been to her father.

'Your mother's name was Leigh before she married me,' he replied. 'I don't think you ever knew that.' He shook his head. 'We didn't tell you, any of you, that Barbara had been married before.' He paused and took a deep breath; then, 'Kathy Leigh is your half-sister...' he said.

'What!' To say that Beverley was surprised would be a vast understatement. 'You mean ... Mom had another child, back in England? But why ... how...? I don't understand. Why didn't we know about it?'

'Because it was too painful for your mother ever

397

to talk about it.' Beverley could see that her father was very distressed and close to tears. 'Look, Beverley ... this has come as a great shock. But it's only right, now that it's happened, that you should all know about it. Let the others know, will you, honey? Tell them I'd like to see them; I mean Carl and Anne-Marie. Come here tomorrow night, all of you. I'll probably have recovered a bit by then. As I say, it's been a shock. Then I'll tell you all about what happened; I know it's what Barbara would want.' He nodded slowly, seeming to have aged a few years in those last moments.

'OK, Dad,' she said. She kissed his cheek. 'I'll phone them right away. I won't say what it's about, just that you want to talk to us all. Now, you'll be all right, will you? I must get along because Freddie will be due home from nursery school.'

'Sure, don't worry about me.' Nat smiled. 'I've been spoilt rotten these last few days, Sam and Ellie waiting on me hand and foot. They're worth their weight in gold in the kitchen, those two. We haven't many folks in at the moment, fortunately, but I hope to be up and doing in a day or two.' He nodded, seeming now a little more composed. 'I'm OK, honey, honestly I am. See you all tomorrow.'

It had certainly been a bombshell, though, Katherine phoning like that, out of the blue. Dear little Kathy... What an enchanting child she had been. The image of her mother, with the same dark curls and lovely warm brown eyes. He and Barbara had not spoken of her very much as it would have been upsetting for his beloved wife;

but he knew that the little girl had always been in her thoughts. He knew the times when she had been thinking particularly about her, so well attuned had he been to her various highs and lows.

He had wondered what to do ever since he had found Barbara's half-written letter to Katherine in her bedside drawer, soon after his wife's death. He had realised then how she must have longed to contact her firstborn child when she knew that her life was drawing to a close, although she had not told him, Nat, what she wanted to do. Had she changed her mind, he wondered, or had she become too poorly to complete the letter? He would never know. He had done nothing about it partly because there was no address and, also, it was unlikely that the Leigh family would still be at the same place after all these years. Maybe it was best, he had told himself, to leave well alone. He had no idea what Katherine, as a child, would have been told about her mother; there would be no point in contacting her now that her mother had died.

He was aware now, though, that he could not leave the matter unresolved for any longer. Katherine, too, must have had a desire to find her mother, although it was he, Nat Castillo, that she had asked to speak to. But why now, after all these years? Maybe she had only just found out... It was no use speculating. He knew he must get in touch with Katherine, either by letter or by phone. First of all, though, he had to speak to his family.

Beverley, Carl and Anne-Marie all came round

the following evening, the elder two having left their spouses and children at home. Anne-Marie was still single, but was now engaged to a fellow swimming instructor. They planned to marry the following summer.

The other two were stunned, as Beverley had been, to hear the news, but their reactions were somewhat varied.

'Gee! That's great!' said Carl, always the most outspoken of the three, forever optimistic and ready to see the best in all situations. 'A long-lost sister over in little old England! It's like a fairy story, Dad. When can we meet her?'

But Anne-Marie's response was rather different. She was always more cautious, which was probably the reason she had not married at a very early age as the other two had done. She was also a very sympathetic sort of girl.

'That poor little girl!' she said. 'Just imagine how sad it must have been for her, her mother disappearing like that and leaving her all alone. Honestly, Dad, I'm very surprised at our mom. How could she have done it?'

Nat had already tried to explain that Barbara had had no choice; her first husband had been such an intransigent sort of fellow. Also, he admitted, a little embarrassedly, that she had already been expecting a baby – Beverley. He told them how he and Barbara had been so very much in love, and that he was due to be sent overseas for the final assault on Europe. It had been a traumatic time for both of them.

'I have no idea what little Kathy was told,' he said. 'I know, though, that she would have been

400

very well looked after by her father, and particularly, I guess, by her aunt. I never met Winifred, but Barbara always spoke very highly of her.'

Beverley had had time to think about the situation. 'You must contact her, Dad, as soon as possible,' she said. 'I have a feeling, somehow, that she's just found out where her mother might be and she wants to get in touch with her. It'll be a shock to find that she's ... no longer with us.' It was a euphemism, she knew, but the word 'dead' sounded so harsh and final. 'After all, Mom was young, wasn't she? Katherine would expect her to be still living. Perhaps you should write to her first of all, Dad, and then speak to her later on the phone? But it's down to you, of course. How do you feel about it?'

'Yes, that's the best idea,' he agreed. 'I've been stunned by this, as you all have. And many, many times I've agonised about my own share of guilt in all this. I didn't like to talk too much to your mother about little Kathy; it was so painful for her. But now, maybe there's a way of putting things right. As I told you, she was such a cute, lovable little kid. If she's grown up in the same way, and I've a feeling she will have done, then I know we'd all like to meet her.'

'Kathy, there's a letter here for you from America,' Tim called out to his wife one morning in mid November. He took it into the living room where Kathy was making sure that the children – Sarah, aged eight, and Chris, aged six – had all they needed before departing for school: PE kit; recorder and music book; last night's homework;

401

and their dinner money, as it was a Monday morning.

Her face lit up with pleasure. 'Gosh, that's great!' she exclaimed. 'I'll read it when these two have gone,' she added in a quieter voice.

'I'm dying to know what it says as well,' said Tim, who had been just as excited as she had been after she had made contact with America. She had been a little worried at first, wondering what she had done. Would they really be pleased to hear from her? By now she had convinced herself that they would. That young woman, Beverley, had sounded very nice, if you could tell from a voice, and had promised that she would ask her father to get in touch.

'Listen,' Tim went on. 'I'll just drop these two off at school, then I'll come back and we'll read it together, OK? There's no rush to get to work now I'm one of the bosses!' Kathy knew, though, that he was joking and that he worked just as hard as any of the employees.

'All right; I'll wash up while I'm waiting,' she said.

Tim was back in less than fifteen minutes and they sat together on the settee as Kathy tore open the flimsy blue and red envelope. 'I'll read it out to you,' she said.

'*My dear Katherine,*' the letter began. '*My daughter, Beverley, told me that you had phoned. You won't remember me. I am Nathaniel – known as Nat – Castillo, and I met you in Blackpool when you were a tiny girl, just about one year old. I can only guess that you are trying to find out about your mother, Barbara, the dear girl whom I married in 1945.*

402

Kathy, my dear, I am not sure how much or how little you know, but I must tell you that Barbara and I had almost twenty-eight very happy years together. I am sorry to have to give you the sad news, though, that my dear wife ... died ... in the January of this year...' Kathy's voice faltered as she read the last sentence, then she burst into tears.

'Oh Tim! How dreadful! I thought I'd found her. I made myself believe I was going to meet her, and now ... this!'

He put his arm round her and she leant her head against his shoulder. 'I never knew her,' she murmured, her voice husky with tears, 'but this is so very sad. Why didn't my father tell me about her? If only he had told me ... even a year ago, then I could have gone to meet her. And now it's too late. I'm finding it very hard to forgive what he did to me, telling me all those lies. I tried to understand, and I thought maybe we could make things right, my mother and me. But she's ... she's gone!' She was not crying now, just shaking her head sadly and unbelievingly.

'I'll read the rest of it to you, shall I?' said Tim gently. Kathy nodded.

'I am truly sorry to have to impart such sad news,' Tim read. *'My dear wife had cancer, so you will understand how tragic it has been for us. But I do know that she, too, wanted to get in touch with you, Kathy. I found a half-written letter to you that I can only assume she became too poorly to finish.*

'I won't say any more now, but I would very much like to speak with you over the phone. I have your telephone number, so how would it be if I phone you on the last day of November – it's a Friday – at 8pm,

403

your time? That will be early afternoon for us over here. We can have a chat and exchange news about our families. I expect you have children, Kathy? Barbara and I had three children – two daughters and a son – and now they have learnt about you they are all longing to meet you.

'With my kindest regards, Nat Castillo.'

Kathy was more composed by the time Tim had finished reading. 'Well, I think that's a splendid letter,' he said. 'I'm really sorry about your mother, darling, but this Nat seems a real nice sort of fellow. And he remembered you, didn't he?'

'So it seems,' said Kathy. She smiled sadly. 'I know they say that what you never have you never miss. And I never knew her, did I? Barbara, my mother... But I can't help feeling there's a great emptiness ... here.' She touched the region of her heart. 'How I used to wish, when I was a little girl, that I had brothers and sisters, like my friends had. Shirley, in particular – you remember, Tim? I was so envious of her having a little sister and an older brother. And now I find I've got two sisters and a brother at the other side of the world. Ironic, isn't it?'

'Not really the other side of the world, love,' said Tim. 'Australia's the other side of the world. America isn't all that far away, comparatively speaking. And Nat says they all want to meet you. Just think about that!'

'Let's wait and see what he has to say when he phones,' said Kathy. 'My head's in a whirl, Tim. It's all happened so quickly, I can scarcely take it in.'

Nat Castillo phoned, as he had promised, at the appointed time. His voice, though so far away, came over loud and clear, and Kathy felt at once the warmth and sincerity of this man who had been married to her mother. They spoke for half an hour or so; he said not to worry about the cost – they had a lot of catching up to do. Kathy learnt of her half-sisters, Beverley and Anne-Marie, and her half-brother, Carl; and also a half-nephew and half-niece, Freddie and Patsy-Lou – they would be half-cousins to her Sarah and Chris? she pondered.

Nat told her how he and her mother had met at the Tower Ballroom and had very quickly fallen in love. 'I knew she was married,' he said, 'but I guess it made no difference to the way we felt. I just hope you can understand and forgive us, Kathy. It was heartbreaking for your mother. She had no choice, though, but to do what she did. I'm only sorry that you haven't had the chance to meet her. She was a wonderful lady...' His voice faltered as it did more than once as he spoke of her. 'I'll write again,' he promised, 'and send some snapshots.'

Another letter with the photos arrived in a few weeks' time, after Kathy had replied to the first letter. She had told Nat of her disappointment and sorrow that she was too late to meet her mother, but of how delighted she was to hear of her three step-siblings.

Kathy gasped, and so did Tim, when they looked at the photos that Nat had sent.

'Wow! She looks just like you,' he said. 'You could be twin sisters.'

The image he was referring to was that of her mother, Barbara. One was a family group – Barbara and Nat, whom they agreed appeared to be a nice, friendly sort of guy, and the three children, taken several years ago, Nat explained, before the eldest two had married. Beverley resembled her father more than her mother, and so did the son, Carl. They had the same fairish mid-brown hair and wide smiling mouths. The younger girl, Anne-Marie, looked more like her mother. She was dark-haired and petite, although a little on the plump side.

So was Barbara, Kathy noticed. She had a full face and a nicely rounded figure, dark curling hair, and the expression in her brown eyes was the very same that Kathy saw when she looked in the mirror. Barbara looked relaxed and happy; and Kathy felt, again, a momentary sadness. Why did it have to happen like this, only a year too late?

Chapter Thirty-One

Over in Vermont the Castillo family agreed that the wrong that had been done to Katherine all those years ago must be put right, or as right as they could possibly make it. Anne-Marie was to be married in early August. What a splendid idea it would be if Katherine and her husband and children were to be there as well.

The invitation arrived in the February of 1974, and Kathy and Tim wasted no time in making all the necessary arrangements. Sarah and Chris were thrilled at the prospect of flying in an aeroplane all the way to America, but no more so than their parents; it would be their first flight as well.

There was all the excitement of getting passports, visas, and buying new clothes and suitcases, before they boarded the aeroplane at Manchester airport one early afternoon in August. They touched down in Boston some seven hours later. It was evening now by their reckoning, but it was still afternoon in the USA. It was certainly going to be a long day ahead of them!

No one was sleepy, though, with the myriad sounds and sights and impressions that followed one another in quick succession. They had no difficulty in finding Nat or, rather, he found them. He hugged Kathy, making her feel at home right away, and shook hands with Tim and the children. Then they were all bundled into his Cadillac and were soon on their way along the wide straight highways leading north.

They travelled at a speed they had never experienced before, but were not scared because the roads, though busy, did not appear so, and the traffic was well controlled. Back home in England the motorways were starting to be congested at busy times, with aggravating hold-ups and traffic jams. But there was so much more space over here, Kathy mused, as they travelled mile after mile through scenery that became more beautiful – with mountains, river valleys, and great stretches of verdant trees and pasture land – as they went northwards.

The Castillo family home, where only Nat resided now, along with his live-in employees, was a comfortable, homely hotel, now partially converted to a motel. It was very different from Holmleigh, the hotel-cum-boarding house where Kathy had lived as a child. There was plenty of room for the Fielding family, especially as Nat had restricted the number of guests staying there in the weeks leading up to and following Anne-Marie's wedding.

The following day Kathy and her family had the pleasure of meeting some of the members of Nat's large family – his brother and sister, and just a few of their six sons and daughters; and there were numerous grandchildren who would all be present at the wedding. Nat's mother and father – Mom and Pop – now well into their eighties but still spry both in body and in mind. They told Kathy how much they had loved Barbara and how her death had saddened them.

'But now you're here with us, my dear,' said the old man. 'We couldn't be more delighted to see you and your family. Gee! It's almost like having Barbara back with us, isn't it, Martha?'

The dear, old, rosy-cheeked lady nodded and smiled. She hugged Kathy. 'Yes, it sure is wonderful,' she said. 'And you've brought a smile back to our Nat's face, honey!'

Then there were her half-siblings: Beverley, her husband Greg and their five-year-old son, Freddie. Beverley was the young woman whom Kathy had spoken to on the phone – they had conversed again since that first call – and she proved to be just as friendly and welcoming as her voice had suggested she would be. It was Beverley who spoke out loud what was in all their minds.

'You're more like Mom than any of us,' she said, 'and we sure are glad to meet you at last.' The two half-sisters, less than two years apart in age, hugged one another without any restraint, just a real feeling of sisterhood. They knew at once that the two of them, possibly even more so than the rest of the family, would become firm friends.

There was Carl too, with his wife Donna, and their cute little two-year-old Patsy-Lou; and Anne-Marie with her ruggedly handsome fiancé, Bruce, who would be married in a few days' time.

The wedding took place at a typical New England church, a white wooden building with a tall spire, on top of a hill and surrounded by maple trees. The church was almost full with the many wedding guests – countless numbers of relatives of both the bride and groom as well as numerous friends – and other well-wishers too, who had come along to share in the joy of the popular young couple.

The reception afterwards was held at the family hotel, an informal affair where Kathy and Tim and their children had the pleasure of meeting their many new relatives, and friends of the family too, who had heard of the daughter back in England.

Anne-Marie and Bruce had planned a honeymoon in San Francisco, far away on the west coast of the USA. They were to set off on the long journey later that evening; but before that, as Anne-Marie told Kathy, there was something that she wanted to do.

They left their children behind in the care of the many relatives, then Nat and his three children and their spouses, with Kathy and Tim, made their way, in two cars, back to the same church on the hill.

Barbara's grave was in a secluded spot at the edge of the cemetery, beneath an overhanging willow tree. There were flowers in the glowing colours of late summer – red roses, yellow and orange dahlias and early flowering chrysanths – in a large earthenware vase. They looked fresh and vibrant, and Kathy guessed that Nat renewed them frequently.

The family group stood in silence as Anne-Marie placed her wedding bouquet of white roses next to the vase of flowers. 'God bless you, Mom,' she said quietly. It was Anne-Marie's day and she wanted her beloved mother to be a part of it.

Kathy read the gold lettering on the black marble headstone.

'Barbara Jane Castillo, 1920–1973. Beloved wife of Nat and dearest mother of Beverley, Carl and Anne-Marie.' And below, in brighter letters that must have been added fairly recently, 'And mother of Katherine, in England.'

Kathy's eyes misted with tears. 'Thank you, thank you...' she whispered. 'That is ... so lovely.' Beverley, standing next to her, took hold of her hand and they smiled at one another.

Kathy's heart was too full for words. She felt very close to the mother she had never known. She knew that not meeting Barbara was something she would always regret. But now she had found two sisters and a brother ... and England and the USA were not all that far apart.

Author's Note

The question I am most frequently asked as a novelist is 'Where do you get your ideas?' It is not easy to answer.

Sometimes they just happen, but more often they arise from an incident in my own life or in that of a member of my family or a friend. In this novel it was an incident in the life of my sister-in-law, Linda, that gave me the initial idea, and I thank her for that.

The story, however, is a work of fiction, and all the characters and happenings therein exist only in my mind.

I decided to set this book in my hometown of Blackpool, as I did with my earlier books. The setting of Blackpool is, of course, real, and the boarding house where the Leigh family live resembles the one in North Shore where I was born and lived as a child.

The childhood memories are mine, as are the recollections of the day to day life of a primary school, experienced during my time as a teacher of infant and junior school children.

The publishers hope that this book has given you enjoyable reading. Large Print Books are especially designed to be as easy to see and hold as possible. If you wish a complete list of our books please ask at your local library or write directly to:

Magna Large Print Books
Magna House, Long Preston,
Skipton, North Yorkshire.
BD23 4ND

This Large Print Book for the partially sighted, who cannot read normal print, is published under the auspices of

THE ULVERSCROFT FOUNDATION

CHASING THE DREAM

Leaving the pit village of Craston, Teresa Mercer escapes with her daughter Millie to the nearby town of Ashborough. Posing as a respectable widow, Teresa secures jobs for them both and it's here that Millie begins to build a new identity for herself. Then she meets and marries Dan Nixon, the local hero: a professional footballer who sees his future not in the pit but on the pitch, playing for Newcastle United. Millie dreams of happiness and prosperity, but it's not long before Dan's drinking and womanising threaten to damage both his career and his family...

CHASING THE DREAM

CHASING THE DREAM

by

Janet MacLeod Trotter

Magna Large Print Books
Long Preston, North Yorkshire,
BD23 4ND, England.

British Library Cataloguing in Publication Data.

Trotter, Janet MacLeod
    Chasing the dream.

    A catalogue record of this book is
    available from the British Library

    ISBN   0-7505-1546-5

First published in Great Britain by Headline Book Publishing, 1998

Copyright © 1998 by Janet MacLeod Trotter

Published in Large Print 2000 by arrangement with
Headline Book Publishing

Magna Large Print is an imprint of Library Magna Books Ltd.

Printed and bound in Great Britain by
T.J. (International) Ltd., Cornwall, PL28 8RW

With love to Alan and Enid, who went to Wembley in 1951 and saw Jackie Milburn score.

CHAPTER 1
1920

Millie woke with a start, shocked out of a deep sleep by the slam of a fist on the piano below. The discordant noise set her heart hammering. Strangely, she had been dreaming of music. She had dreamt of her mother playing a duet with her older brother Graham, the warm parlour full of singing and lamplight and laughter, the table laden with food. For one confused moment, Millie thought she heard her brother's voice and jerked up.

'No!' her mother was shrieking. 'Over my dead body!'

Then the man's voice came again, a deep, indistinct rumble so like Graham's, trying to placate her. The piano keys were bashed once more and Millie sank back, realising it was only her parents arguing again. Graham was never coming back. He was dead and buried somewhere in France and the only reminders she had of him were a few treasured postcards and a silk embroidered handkerchief he had sent her. There was nothing else in the house that hinted he had once lived there, neither clothes, boots, cigarettes nor sheet music. Even his uniformed photograph had been removed from the mantelpiece, once the terrible shame of Graham Mercer had spread around the village and they had become outcasts, shunned by their neighbours.

Millie buried her head of dark curly hair under the pillow and tried to block out the shouting downstairs. Moonlight streamed in at the broken skylight above her bed and she heard the mournful call of a fox from far off. Her stomach clenched, reminding her how hungry she was. At fourteen she was constantly hungry, her body and limbs grown out of control like a stringy runner bean. But these past weeks, while the pit had been idle and the men locked out over an unofficial dispute, hunger had gnawed at her innards like a dog. Thoughts of food consumed her even in her dreams.

'They can't, I'll not let them!' Her mother's screams penetrated her muffled ears.

She'll be waking up the neighbours again, Millie thought in distress, and they already had a low enough opinion of the Mercers these days. The quarrels happened most evenings now when her father reluctantly dragged himself home from the Miners' Institute, tearing himself away from his books and periodicals. Self-taught he might be, but there were no jobs for men with a bit of learning in Craston, just the pit if they were lucky. Her parents argued about money, or lack of it. They fought about her mother's bad housekeeping, or the amount of credit run up at the drapery store. She accused him of weakness and neglect, of losing his job at the pit face through carelessness. The fall of stone that had crippled him and left him sorting coals with the old men and boys was his fault, according to Teresa Mercer. The reason Millie could not cook

12

or sew but was only interested in dancing and music was her crime, Ellis Mercer accused back.

'She'll be useful for nowt!' her father would rail. 'Our Millie will never get a place in service, let alone a husband – all because of your fancy ways, woman!'

'You'll not turn my Millie into a skivvy like you have me,' Teresa would spit back. 'I was born for better things – my grandfather was a famous musician, my ancestors were French noblemen.'

'Scotch tinkers and thieves more like!' Ellis would laugh harshly. 'Your mam followed the herring fleet, so don't go thinking you're any better than us.'

On the accusations would go. The reason there was scant food was his doing. The reason it was burnt and inedible was hers. Millie would lie upstairs and watch the clouds whip across the stars, wishing she could climb on to one and escape. All the time she wondered why they never spoke of the one thing that she wanted them to – her dead brother. The fights had never been this bad when Graham had been around, but without him they seemed to be tearing each other apart. She hated her parents for not missing him as she did. Not once in nearly three years had they mentioned his name.

But this banging on the piano made Millie anxious. Her mother had hardly touched it since Graham's death. It was the only piece of furniture left of any worth, yet it stood in the corner of the tiny parlour gathering dust, a reproachful reminder of happier days when they had gathered around it on a Saturday evening and sung songs. Those were days before the war when her father had walked without a limp and sung with off-key gusto. The cottage in Saviour Street had been full of harmonious sound then: her mother's humming, Graham's whistling, her father's hymn singing, her skipping songs with friend Ella. Now it was a house of bickering and bitter words and slamming doors. Yet there seemed to be something worse than usual happening in the dark downstairs, something else that was keeping her parents and probably their neighbours from sleep.

Millie decided to get out of bed and creep to the trap door beyond her curtained room. Shivering in her nightgown she peered down the ladder to the kitchen below. It was in darkness. But beyond she saw candlelight flicker from the parlour where her parents slept and where they now fought. The dim light threw grotesque, exaggerated shadows across the floor.

'There's nowt I can do to stop them,' Ellis insisted.

'That's typical! You've never been able to stand up to anyone,' Teresa accused.

Ellis blustered. 'We can go and live with Hannah for a bit till this all gets sorted out.'

Millie's heart sank at the mention of her aunt. She was censorious and mean with her money, and all too ready to beat Millie with a hairbrush if she broke anything or spoke out of turn. Why could her father possibly want them to go and live there? she wondered. She climbed down the ladder to get a better view.

'I'll never be beholden to that woman,' Teresa

hissed. 'She's always treated me like I've just crawled out of the midden – thinks she's above us just because she's married to that preacher. And the way she picks on Millie…'

'She's a good woman,' Ellis defended his sister. 'She sees the way you spoil that lass. It'll not do Millie any harm to have a bit of firmness for a while.'

'No, Ellis! Wild horses wouldn't drag me to live under her roof.'

'You don't have a choice. Do you want to end up on the shore in a makeshift tent like the MacAulays and the Smiths?' her father shouted. Millie's stomach turned over at his dire words, thinking of those leaking, windblown structures that were now home to the strikers' families who had been evicted from a neighbouring terrace last week. Their homes had already been occupied by strangers rumoured to have come from Cornwall.

'Don't you threaten me with that,' Teresa shouted back. 'This is all your doing.'

From the bottom of the ladder Millie could glimpse the pair through the door. The candlelight fell on her father's angry, gaunt features, creating deep shadows for eyes.

'It's not my fault the bosses tried to cut our pay by half,' he answered. 'They're the ones that locked us out. They're the ones that are bringing in scab labour.'

'Not to my house they're not!' Teresa replied with spirit.

'And how are you going to stop them?' Ellis demanded. 'They've given us two days to clear out or they'll hoy us out. Is that what you want, to be thrown out on the street in front of all the neighbours? Well, I'll not have anyone making a spectacle of the Mercers. We'll go quietly.'

For the first time Millie saw her mother's face as she stepped towards her husband. Her prominent cheeks looked sunken in the lurid light, but her dark eyes blazed with contempt and indignation.

'Is that all you care about – your precious Mercer pride? When are you ever going to stand up for your own family, Ellis? You're weak, weak as dust tea! You'd sooner see your wife and daughter evicted than make a fuss or disturb the neighbours.' She was close up to him now, jabbing a long finger into his chest. 'Why do you think they've picked on us, Ellis? Why are we the only ones being thrown out of Saviour Street when there are half a dozen others on strike down our street?'

Millie saw her father back away. 'I don't want to hear any more of your vicious tongue, woman.'

But her mother persisted. 'It's because the bosses know that there's not one family in this street will lift a finger to help the Mercers now. Not after all the shame. They'll be pleased to see us go, they'll say it's no more than we deserve. What with us raising a *coward* in our home!'

Ellis grabbed Teresa's hand with a howl of anger and shoved her back. She fell against the open piano, which squealed in protest. Turning with a sob, Teresa thumped the keys with rage, the jarring sound filling the tiny room.

'Coward, coward, *coward!*' she screamed. 'I

spawned a yellow-bellied Mercer. My son should have been a hero, but they shot him for running away. He was a coward all along – just like his father!'

'Damn you!' Ellis croaked, and lunged to silence her. He snapped down the lid of the piano and trapped her fingers. Millie heard her mother scream in pain while her father shouted, 'Shut up, shut up! I told you never to mention that lad again.'

'Graham, Graham, Graham!' Teresa taunted as she wept. It was the first time Millie had heard her mother call his name since his death, and it seemed to conjure him into the room. Millie felt winded and saw her father flinch too. Then in horror she watched as he struck her mother across the face, the name of her brother ringing around the room with the dying piano notes.

'You can't stop me talking about him any more,' Teresa howled, clutching her face. 'I want to hear his name. Graham, Graham, Graham...' She became incoherent as she gave way to choking sobs and sank to her knees.

Millie saw her father pick up the candlestick and wave it above her mother's head where she lay crumpled on the floor. Suddenly she leapt forward.

'No!' she cried.

Her mother looked up in time to see the brass holder bearing down on her. She glanced away and took the blow on her shoulder. The candle fell into her hair, and she shrieked in panic as the flame flared. Ellis stood back in horror at what he had just done. As the smell of singeing hair stung

17

Millie's nostrils, she lunged for the chamber pot under the iron-framed bed and flung the contents at her mother. Teresa gasped and spluttered with shock, but the flame fizzled out.

Both parents turned to stare at her as she dropped the chamber pot. Millie stood shaking uncontrollably in her nightgown, her tousled black hair snaking about her face, but unable to hide her appalled expression. She did not know what to think of them. They had frightened her with their talk of eviction and their hatred for each other, yet for a moment she had felt pity at the sight of their distress – her father's desolate face, her mother's agonising cry for their lost son. She was too upset to know if she hated or loved them any more.

'Millie, pet,' her father whispered, 'I'm sorry…'

'Come here, my precious!' her mother com-manded, holding out her arms.

But Millie could not move. Her father's sudden violence made her afraid of him, while her mother repelled her with the smell of scorched hair and urine.

'Where are we going to live?' she whispered in a trembling voice.

Neither of them could answer her.

She felt a small worm of bitterness twisting inside at what they had done. They had spoilt the place of her growing-up, taken away the feeling of safety and cosiness that had once been there. Ever since Graham had answered the call of the recruiting posters for the army in Flanders and been waved away at the station in Ashborough, this house had deteriorated into a worried, unhappy place. It dawned on Millie for the first time that Graham had been the one person who could hold the family together. Without his easy laugh and quick forgiveness they had fallen to pieces. She, Millie, could never be big enough to step into the role of peacemaker. In fact she seemed to make matters worse, driving her parents further apart as they argued over possession of her.

'I don't care,' she said defiantly. 'I hate this place, I hate this house. I'm glad they're hoying us out. Ella was the only one round here speaking to me and now she's gone to London. They wouldn't even let us take part in the peace tea, would they, the miserable lot? Who needs neighbours like that?'

She saw her father's eyes glisten with tears, but he could not speak. Her mother rallied at her stout words. It had rankled with her too that they had been ostracised from the end-of-war celebrations last year. Teresa had taken Millie on a rare trip into Ashborough to see a Charlie Chaplin film rather than be excluded from the street party and the fêting of Craston's surviving heroes.

'Aye, that's right, Millie,' she answered, picking herself up from the floor. 'We don't need them. We'll leave Craston. Start again somewhere else where they'll respect us for who we are.' She went over and put damp arms around her daughter.

'Go where?' Ellis asked with a despairing look. 'I'll not get another job outside Craston Colliery, not with me gammy leg.'

Teresa turned and looked at him with weary

19

contempt. 'No, most likely you won't. But that's not going to stop me. Millie and me will go to Ashborough and look for work. You can follow on if you wish.'

Ellis gawped at his wife as if he had misheard her. 'And who's going to employ the likes of you?'

Teresa bristled. 'I can get work as a house-keeper or a companion.'

Millie watched her father's haggard face crease in derision. 'A housekeeper! You can't even keep this cottage in order, you useless woman.'

Millie knew in that moment that the final thread binding her parents to each other was snapping. If her father had said something placating to show he still wanted her, Teresa might have relented, even after such a row. They had made it up before after terrible fights. But both were now at the end of their tether.

'Don't laugh at me, Ellis Mercer.' She spat out his name. 'I'll show you I can make something of myself outside this poxy village!'

She turned her back on him and spun Millie round with her, pushing her through the parlour door towards the ladder. Millie scrambled back upstairs and heard her mother follow. It was not the first time Teresa had slept with her instead of her father, but tonight, Millie knew, was different. This was no mere protest, even though her father thought otherwise.

'You'll not last more than five minutes on your own!' he shouted up the ladder after them. 'No one'll have you as their cook – not unless they want to poison someone!'

He must have stayed at the bottom of the

ladder for ten minutes or more, shouting derision and abuse at the dark hole above. Teresa removed her damp dress and ordered Millie to lie down beside her and go to sleep. 'We'll show him,' her mother whispered determinedly. 'We'll show them all!'

Millie lay awake for most of the night listening to the sigh of the sea on the nearby shore and the uneven breathing of her sleeping mother. Below she heard her father go out, and just before dawn she heard his boots returning up the cinder track to the kitchen door. He was banging about, opening and closing drawers. Perhaps he was packing up their few possessions, she thought drowsily, as sleep finally came to claim her. But just as she slipped into oblivion, she heard a strange, muted crying, like a mournful seagull. Millie had never heard her father weep before, not even when the telegram had come telling them of Graham's death, but she was sure she heard him now.

When she woke it was broad daylight and her mother had gone from beside her. Millie shot up in panic, thinking she might have been left. Struggling into her clothes she tumbled down the ladder to find the kitchen deserted and the fire quite cold. For the past week they had tried to keep it alight with driftwood and pieces of dross picked up from the shore.

Suddenly Teresa appeared from the parlour, carrying a small portmanteau that had belonged to her own mother.

'There's a lump of cheese in the pantry,' she

21

said quietly. 'Go and get it. You can have that with a cup of water, then we'll be off.'

'Off where?' Millie gulped, watching her mother take the gaudy tea caddy from the mantelpiece and wedge it in the bag on top of a few clothes.

'Ashborough, like I said,' Teresa replied shortly.

'Is Dad coming?' Millie asked. Her mother did not answer. 'Where is he?'

'Gone to beg with your Aunt Hannah, no doubt,' Teresa said bitterly. 'Now hurry up and do as I say.'

Millie felt her stomach tighten with hunger and nerves. The terrible scenes of the night before seemed like a bad dream and she was now frightened of the thought of leaving. She fetched the cheese but found it hard and indigestible, sticking in her throat when she tried to eat. Her mother seemed edgy and eager to be gone.

'Hurry and put your clothes into a pillowcase,' she ordered while wrapping her prized silver teaspoons in a cloth.

Millie's heart hammered as she ascended the ladder for the final time. She glanced around the sparse room, with its low, sloping ceiling and worn linoleum, that she had once shared with her brother. Fumbling with the chest of drawers that her mother had painted with bright flowers, she pulled out clothes at random and stuffed what she could into her pillowcase. Her eye caught the childish music box that stood on a chair by her bed. Her father had made it for her years ago and she still played it every night to get to sleep. After a moment's hesitation, she pulled out a petticoat and shoved in the music box instead.

'Be quick now!' her mother shouted up the ladder.

Millie hunted under her mattress for a precious bundle of possessions: Graham's postcards and handkerchief, a roll of purple ribbon from Ella and a miniature picture book she had been given in Sunday school. She forced them into the bulging pillowcase as she scrambled for the stairs.

Her mother had Millie's coat held out ready to put on. Teresa herself was already dressed for going out in her navy coat and best blue felt hat.

'We can't go without seeing me dad,' Millie gabbled. 'And I want to say goodbye to Ella's mam.'

Her mother considered her for a moment and then seemed to change her mind.

'This isn't goodbye,' she said briskly. 'We'll just spend the day in Ashborough looking for work and some decent lodgings. I can sell the spoons to cover the rent. Now let's get started while it's early and there're fewer busy bodies about. Don't want the neighbours gawping at us like fish, whispering about us behind our backs, do we?'

They do that anyway, Millie thought, but kept it to herself. She felt a wave of relief.

'So we're coming back later to tell Dad where we've gone?' she questioned.

'Aye,' her mother said, looking away.

Millie followed her out of the cottage into a grey, drizzly morning. Rain dripped off the red geranium in its pot on the low window ledge by the back door. Their feet squelched on the cinder pathway that was turning to black mud. Saviour Street was quiet, save for the squawk of a hen and a small group of boys playing football with a tin can. The rain was keeping people indoors, but Millie was sure they were being watched.

She hurried after her mother down the back lane and turned into Craston's main street, but instead of walking past the huddle of sparsely stocked shops, Teresa cut across the street and down towards the shore.

'We'll take the short cut along the beach to the wagonway,' she told her daughter. Millie wondered if this was to avoid bumping into Aunt Hannah or her father, who might be hanging around the corner of Main Street where the out-of-work miners squatted on their haunches and passed the tedious hours together.

Millie's heart lurched as she caught sight of the dismal tents on the beach where the homeless strikers were now attempting to shelter. There was a wisp of smoke from a spluttering fire which a thin-faced child was trying to coax into life. Her clothes and hair dripped and Millie could see her shivering from this distance. Shuddering to think that this might soon befall them, she hugged herself in her coat and clutched at her mother's hand. It was cold, but she felt an answering squeeze.

As they passed, they heard the wailing of a baby and a mother's sharp voice scolding. The sea frothed on rocks below them, a stiff breeze making the canvas shelters flap and tug at their makeshift pegs as if they yearned for escape too. Teresa pulled Millie after her, quickening their

24

step, so that she did not have time to look back at the blackened village or its towering pithead that hissed and clanked on the skyline. All she saw was a fleeting impression of dark figures crawling over the spoil heap searching for nuggets of coal. Whether they were men or children she could not tell; all she knew was that they would soon be chased off by the police. Her father had forbidden her to go there in case she got into trouble, preferring to sit and shiver by a dying fire than risk arrest. Instead he had gone each day to the Institute to read and left Teresa to worry about how to keep the fire going. But today there would be no forays to the beach to look for wood, Millie thought with relief as they hurried away from the encampment and into the fields.

When there had been a wage coming in, she had occasionally gone to Ashborough with her mother, riding on the tankey which took passengers on a Saturday. They would sit on newspaper in the open trucks so as not to dirty their best clothes. But today they took all morning to walk into the bustling mining town and were wet through by the time the familiar landmarks drew near. Millie loved the town with its solid buildings and exciting array of shops, its cinemas and concert halls, imposing church spires and pillared town hall. Its streets heaved with horse traffic and wagons, busy shoppers, paper boys and the occasional gleaming, hooting motor car.

But today she felt light-headed with hunger and fatigue, her feet aching in boots that had grown too tight for her over the summer. First her mother dragged her to a tidy house in Myrtle Avenue where she knew of a Mrs Dodswell who acted on behalf of a domestic servant agency. She was a plump woman with a florid complexion, whose front parlour looked more like a penny library, with a desk covered in paper and periodicals and shelves around the room crammed with books and ledgers.

'Plenty of work if she's prepared to go to London, Mrs Mercer,' she told them. 'I've sent many girls to place from Ashborough and they've all gone to good homes. I pride myself on the quality of the girls I send. Girls from Northumberland are sought after – very hardworking. How old did you say she was?'

'Fifteen,' Teresa lied. Millie flushed at her mother's boldness. She had already pretended that they had come from the genteel market town of Morpeth, seven miles in the other direction from Craston.

Millie was aware of the woman sizing her up with one penetrating look.

'She's a bit thin, but given training, she'd make an excellent parlour maid with her height. Of course she'd have to start off with a lesser position – a housemaid or in-between maid, perhaps.'

'We'd have to go together,' Teresa insisted. 'I'll not be parted from my Millie.'

Millie felt nauseous as they discussed her future, her head beginning to swim.

'Now that might be difficult,' Mrs Dodswell looked more severe. 'You have no training, Mrs Mercer, and your age … the agency prefers young girls who will be quick and eager to learn.

I didn't realise you were looking for a position yourself. What does Mr Mercer say?'

There was a moment's hesitation, then Teresa said stonily, 'There isn't a Mr Mercer – I'm a widow.'

Millie's heart began to hammer. She could not believe the way her mother was lying to this woman, but she knew she would be in big trouble if she said anything now.

'I'm as good as any trained housekeeper,' Teresa declared, 'and I can decorate and play the piano. I'd make an ideal companion for some elderly spinster or widow.'

Millie had been standing all this while, and now felt her legs begin to buckle, her head quite dizzy. 'Please can I have a cup of water?' Her words rang in her ears. The women looked round at her and then receded in a speckled mist as Millie blacked out and hit the floor.

When she came round she was lying on a small sofa, with her mother and Mrs Dodswell peering at her in concern. Teresa helped her sip some water.

'Look how pale she is, Mrs Dodswell,' her mother said in her trembling theatrical voice. 'I couldn't leave my little lamb to fend for herself in London. Surely you can find us something more local in Ashborough?'

Mrs Dodswell sighed with reluctance. 'Well, I do know of somewhere that is looking for a cook. It's not through the agency, mind, and I really can't vouch for the place. I've heard that people don't stay there very long, but I can't comment on why.'

'Where?' Teresa said eagerly.

'The Station Hotel,' said Mrs Dodswell with a sniff. 'It's really just a boarding house with a bar. Seen better days.'

'We don't mind,' Teresa said stoutly. 'Who runs it?'

'A widower and his daughter. A Mr Moody.'

Millie could tell by the way she spoke his name that Mrs Dodswell did not approve of the man. But her mother was undeterred.

'Will you speak up for me, Mrs Dodswell?' she pleaded.

'Very well. Perhaps you could return in a day or two and I can make enquiries for you?'

'No.' Teresa was adamant. 'We need something now. My Millie can't manage the walk back to Cr – Morpeth in her weak condition.'

Mrs Dodswell looked taken aback.

'Mam,' Millie began, 'what about–?' But her mother cut her off quickly.

'We can start right away,' Teresa insisted. 'We're not going back where we came from. Not ever!'

CHAPTER 2

Millie disliked Joseph Moody on sight. He was
large and overweight, his skin grey and glistening
around morose brown eyes. His long sideboards
were a gingery grey, yet his hair was unnaturally
black and his breath smelt of stale hops when he
came near. He stood too close when he talked,
but her mother did not seem to mind.

'The lass doesn't look that strong,' he said
dubiously.

Teresa answered swiftly, 'My Millie's a hard
worker. She just needs a bit of rest and some food
in her belly. Just give us bed and board to start
with and we'll prove we're grafters.'

Teresa smiled, and Millie could see that he was
impressed by what he saw: a good-looking, well-
dressed woman with a pleasing manner.

'Your mother's got breeding,' Moody often said
in the days that followed, which made Millie
think of horses.

He took little persuasion to take them in, and
Millie soon saw why. The boarding house that
grandly called itself a hotel was in a filthy,
dilapidated state and the previous housekeeper
had walked out after only a month. An arthritic
maid called Sarah came in daily to help, but few
travellers chose to stay there. The main custom
came from the use of the public bar. This was the
scene of many a rowdy evening brawl that made

Millie keep to her room in the attic which she shared with her mother. For several days she was too weak to get out of bed, content for Teresa to bring her offerings of bread dipped in milk and some watery broth, glad to be out of Moody's way. But even from her garret she could hear the shouting and the fist fights.

She was amazed that her mother agreed to serve in the bar without protest, as Teresa had always been strictly teetotal and disapproved of Ellis's drinking. Yet she seemed to revel in the challenge of the place. While Millie lay upstairs in the leaking bedroom, kept awake by the drip of rain into a metal pail and the snort of the horses in the stables next door, she would hear her mother playing on the bar piano. Tears would sting Millie's eyes at the sound of familiar tunes that Teresa had not played since Graham's death. She would bury her head under the damp, musty blankets and weep for home. Her only comfort was taking out her brother's dog-eared postcards and rereading the cheerful fading messages – echoes from a lost world.

Millie was soon put to work with Sarah, learning to clean and polish and wrestle with the poss tub and mangle. Gruff Sarah was a competent teacher though long past managing the chores herself, and Millie was exhausted by the back breaking work. Her resentment grew as she saw her mother coping cheerfully with the shopping, cooking and helping in the bar.

'I hate it here,' she told Teresa one night. 'Please can we go back to Craston?'

Her mother flopped down beside her, smelling

of pipe tobacco. 'There's nothing to go back for. This is your home now, Millie, you'll get used to it soon enough.'

'No I won't!' Millie contradicted. 'I miss me dad. He'll be worried about us. You said we were going back, you lied to me!' She burst into tears.

Teresa rounded on her sharply, grabbing her arms and shaking her, so that she choked on her tears. 'We've been here nearly two weeks and your father's never come looking for us once. He doesn't give tuppence ha'penny what happens to either of us! We've done him a good turn coming to Ashborough, so he doesn't have to provide for us any more. He was a bad husband and bad father. As far as folk here are concerned he's dead. And if you dare mention anything about him I'll skin the hide off you, do you hear?'

Millie was terrified by her mother's outburst and winced at the pain in her arms. Further words of protest died on her lips. She turned away and curled up into a tight ball, thinking mutinously that when her strength returned she would go back to Craston, even if it was just to assure her father she was safe. She longed to see him, for despite what her mother said, she was sure he must be fretting about her. She could not bear the thought that he did not care what had happened to her.

Later, Teresa put a hand on her shoulder in the dark and shook her gently.

'I'm doing what's best for us, pet,' she murmured. 'We'll make something of this place, make it into a proud hotel again that people'll want to visit. We can have a good life in Ashborough – better than anything Craston has to offer. The likes of you and me can't thrive in a dirty little village like that, we're meant for better things. Besides, we're not welcome there any more.'

Teresa snuggled next to her, putting a protective arm around her, and Millie wondered at how quickly her mother's mood could change. 'And Mr Moody's daughter will be back from Newcastle from time to time,' Teresa mused sleepily. 'She's sixteen – not much more than you in age – looks canny from her picture. You'll have a friend right here – and a better sort than that Ella Parks. She was as common as they come anyway.'

Millie was just drifting off into a warm sleep, comforted by her mother's arms around her, when there was a sudden banging on the stairs and loud shouts. She shot up in alarm, rousing her exhausted mother.

'What's that, Mam?' she cried out.

Teresa hardly had time to pull on her overcoat to investigate the noise before the door flew open.

'Ah! There you are!' Moody shouted, giving out a ribald laugh as he lurched into the room. Millie shrank behind her mother's protective back, disgusted by the smell of stale liquor that wafted from him. 'Why you hiding up here?' he demanded.

Teresa reached out to steady him, but he was bulky and clumsy from drink and knocked her sideways. Then he lunged at Millie cowering in the bed.

'I never see you,' he grinned at her, his face

sweaty and flushed, as he tried to stroke her curly hair. Millie froze in horror at his touch, unable to say a word. 'I like to see you. I miss me own little Ava, do you understand? You're a little picture, just like my Ava.' Millie stifled a scream and tried to turn her head away.

'Don't!' Teresa ordered, on her feet again and trying to pull Moody off her daughter. He turned suddenly belligerent.

'I'm not hurting her,' he growled. 'Just a good-night kiss for a little lass.'

'She's not your little lass,' Teresa shouted, picking up one of her boots and threatening him with it. 'So stay away from her!'

Millie scrabbled to the far side of the bed, pulling the counterpane around her for cover. Moody hesitated, his look confused. Teresa seized the advantage.

'You don't want us to leave, do you, Mr Moody? Not when we can help make something of this place.' She dropped her voice. 'I can see how you miss your Ava, but she'll be home soon. My Millie can't take her place, can she?'

All of a sudden Moody's belligerent face crumpled and he broke down sobbing. 'I'm sorry,' he wept loudly, 'I'm sorry.'

Teresa stepped towards him and heaved him to his feet. The look she gave Millie warned her not to move or say a word.

'Come on now,' she coaxed. 'You're just tired. Let's get you downstairs.'

He bawled like a baby, his face running with tears and mucus. 'I miss me wife. I miss her that much.' Swiftly Teresa levered him to the door and out on to the landing. Millie sat shaking with disgust and relief, listening to their slow progress down the stairs and her mother's gentle scolding as if dealing with a child. She heard the door to Moody's bedroom bang open and waited for her mother's footsteps to regain the narrow stairs. But she did not come. Growing bolder, Millie crept out of bed and squatted at the top of the stairs to listen. She could hear muffled grunts and words as her mother moved around the room below, helping the landlord out of his boots and on to the bed. His crying had subsided, but she could hear her mother's voice murmuring softly the whole time, though she could not make out a word of what was being said.

Millie grew impatient as the cold seeped through her old nightgown. Surely it was now safe for her mother to return and leave Moody to sleep off his drunken outburst? She heard footsteps come to the door, and leaning forward she caught sight of her mother glancing out of the gaslit room. For a brief moment they caught each other's look. Teresa's face was stern and set, but her dark eyes shone strangely. Was she trying to tell her something? Millie wondered in perplexity. Then her mother turned back and closed the door and the landing was plunged into darkness. Millie felt quite abandoned and gripped by an unknown fear. She peered into the void below, wanting to rush down the blackened staircase and seek refuge in the room of light downstairs. Whatever was happening in there, it must be preferable to this terrifying aloneness on the cold attic landing.

She remained there for ages, but her mother did not come. Inexplicable moans and creakings disturbed the night, while Millie cried quietly at her chilly outpost. Eventually she heard a strange rhythmic hum, like a distant motor vehicle, and realised that someone was snoring. Unbending her frozen limbs, Millie crept back to her now cold bed. She hardly slept that night, unable to get warm again and half listening out for her mother's return. Eventually Teresa came back, just before dawn, and Millie feigned sleep.

The terrible night had shaken her beyond belief. The fragile security she had felt with her mother tucked in beside her was now gone. Nothing was as it seemed. Something had happened in the night that had changed her world. She knew that her mother had somehow protected her, and yet she felt empty and betrayed inside. The next day she could not meet her mother's look, and nothing was ever said about what had happened. But after that there were other nights when her mother did not come to bed until the early hours of the morning, and nights when the murmur of voices from below would disturb her. Yet Moody never came near her again, hardly speaking to her unless to give some order, and she noticed how his drinking lessened under her mother's influence. Teresa seemed able to predict his moods and placate his temper like a circus tamer. Soon he was paying her a wage out of takings from the bar, and she persuaded him to retire old Sarah and give her meagre wages to Millie.

Teresa was triumphant when Moody agreed

that if they got enough custom from the hotel, he would turn the public bar into a temperance room serving tea and Bovril.

'We'll show Ashborough you can have a good time at the Station Hotel without drinking and brawling,' she declared. Millie was cheered by her mother's enthusiasm and optimism, which never stayed dampened for long. Yet there were times when Millie's own show of good humour masked the fear that plagued her within: fear of losing her mother, of destitution and home-lessness, of what went on in Moody's bedroom in the dark hours of the night.

Then, just as their new life was growing familiar and the trauma of their flight from Craston was receding, Ava Moody returned home, appearing on the station platform with a heavy suitcase and bulging packages. Millie was in the greasy, smoke-blackened kitchen, warming herself by the large range that her mother had got Moody to stoke up for wash day, when Ava burst in with a blast of autumnal air, throwing her packages on to the floor. She was round-faced, with straight brown hair tied loosely behind and unblinking hazel eyes.

'Who are you?' she demanded at once, giving Millie a hostile look. Then, 'Where's my father?' she asked, not giving the other girl time to reply.

'You must be Ava,' Teresa intervened brightly, coming out of the laundry room with a basket of grubby bed linen. 'By, you're bonnier than your picture! Your father's up at the farm visiting Mr Collins. Not be long. Why don't you have a cup of tea with us. I'm the new housekeeper, Mrs Mercer, and this is my daughter Millie. We weren't expecting you. I'd wanted to get your room nice and welcoming for you coming home.'

Ava gawped, quite disarmed by Teresa's cheerful, flattering manner. Millie watched in admiration as her mother put on her eager-to-please act and saw Ava's tight, surly expression dissolve into blushing smiles. Soon they were laughing and chatting around the kitchen table like old friends. Teresa murmured sympathetically when Ava declared that she was not cut out for service in Newcastle and had no intention of returning to slave for any banker's family in Jesmond ever again.

'It was all Aunt Effie's fault anyway,' Ava pouted. 'She sent me away but I never wanted to go. She's always interfering.'

'Well, she hasn't been near the place since we arrived,' Teresa assured her.

Millie wanted to know what life had been like in Newcastle, but the other two were more interested in discovering a mutual interest in clothes and hats, and a taste for music hall.

'My Millie loves a good sing-song and dance too,' Teresa said warmly. 'I can see you two are going to get along just grand.'

The girls eyed each other with suspicion. Millie resented the way her mother was taking to Ava so readily, and she hated the way Moody's daughter looked at her as if she were the scullery maid. But then that was what she was, Millie told herself harshly.

When Moody came back, he made a huge fuss

of his daughter, with no reprimand for having left her job in Newcastle or for returning with a purse full of clothing bills. It was immediately clear that Ava was not expected to help around the hotel if she chose not to. She leapt at Teresa's suggestion that they make social calls on the various grocers and suppliers to discuss the weekly orders.

'I think we should be attracting a higher class of customer,' Teresa suggested boldly. 'We could give the old dining room a clear-out and advertise it for luncheons and teas. Get some of the town's societies using it as a meeting place.'

Ava clapped her hands in excitement, and Millie guessed that there had never been anything so glamorous suggested before. Moody seemed quite captivated by the idea too, or maybe it was just her mother's flirtatious manner that pleased him, Millie thought with familiar dread clutching her stomach.

'We've missed a woman's touch about the place since Ava's dear mother died,' Joseph said with emotion. 'Twelve years I've struggled without her. It hasn't been easy, and no woman's come near to replacing her. Have they, Ava?'

Millie wondered fleetingly how many women had tried to replace Mrs Moody. She had noticed Joseph smelling of beer as soon as he entered the kitchen, but no one had said anything. Mrs Dodswell had hinted that his drinking was the reason why no one stayed for long, but since her mother's nocturnal visits to Moody's room, Millie knew it was more than that. She wondered what Ava would say to the clandestine arrangement.

'Father, don't upset yourself,' Ava said briskly.

'With Mrs Mercer's help we can put this place on the map.'

So it was Millie who ended up in the laundry room all day on her own, possing the sheets, wrestling with a giant wooden mangle and hanging the washing out in the yard to dry. Keeping it clean seemed an impossible job, for the coal train ran along a siding right behind the hotel and left smudges of soot on the white linen.

By tea time, Millie was quite exhausted and a sudden gusty downpour made all her efforts at drying and washing worthless. She was in the middle of draping the sheets around the kitchen when unexpectedly a group of hikers sought refuge out of the storm. Her mother, who had just returned with Ava, took command of the situation.

'Get a pot of tea made, Millie,' Teresa ordered as she bustled off to show the visitors into the parlour. 'Ava, you come and keep them talking while I lay the fire.'

Twenty minutes later, Teresa had persuaded them to book in for the night and dispatched Millie and Ava to make up three bedrooms. Alone together for the first time, Millie found herself being closely questioned.

'How did your father die?' Ava asked. 'Your mam wouldn't say. Are you an only child like me?'

Millie flushed, her throat going dry. What would her mother want her to say? she panicked.

'Am I upsetting you like your mother?' Ava asked, standing back while Millie moved around the bed, tucking in the sheets.

Millie was goaded into answering. 'She would get upset. She's not only lost me dad, but her only son as well. I had a brother called Graham.'

'Really? I wish I'd had a brother.' Ava sounded interested and Millie was at once anxious at having mentioned his name. But Ava went on, 'I've suffered as well, you know. I lost Mother when I was four years old. It was lonely growing up here just with me dad. Housekeepers came and went, of course. And there's Aunt Effie – she used to help out. She's not a real aunt – just a distant cousin – and she had her own family to look after. I've never really had anyone to call Mam. You're lucky – I like your mam.'

Millie nodded, feeling suddenly sorry for Ava and pleased that the older girl had confided in her. She felt a desire to talk of her own sense of loss, though she could not tell the truth. It was terrible being made to feel so ashamed of the brother she had loved so much. 'Aye, Mam's all right considering what she's suffered. Graham was a canny brother – I really miss him.'

'Tell me about him,' Ava encouraged, sitting on the bed Millie was trying to make.

Millie found herself gushing. 'He died at an outpost, defending it, of course. He was the last one left alive – a real hero.' It was a story she had heard about someone else's father and she did not know what had made her say it, only that she yearned for it to be true.

'Go on!' Ava gasped. So Millie gave way to a flight of fancy, describing all the courageous deeds of which she knew her brother had been capable. After all, Graham had pushed heavy

40

tubs of coal in the dark, cramped tunnels down Craston Pit, and seen his best friend crushed in a fall of stone, so he was no coward in her eyes. Her tale was interrupted by Teresa's abrupt appearance and warning look.

'Get yourself downstairs, Millie, and serve our customers,' she ordered briskly, and Millie escaped, realising too late that she had said too much.

For the rest of the evening she was kept busy waiting on the travellers and helping in the kitchen. She had to rescue the sausages from burning which her mother had forgotten all about while chatting to the guests, and she ended up baking the apples and mixing the custard too. How long was it going to be before Moody realised that her mother could not cook? Millie wondered. Somehow she was going to have to learn quickly from someone else.

After boiling up water to fill the china pigs for the guests' beds, Millie hauled her weary body upstairs and fell into her own bed. She was soon asleep and did not know at what time her mother joined her.

The following week, she was kept busy with cleaning the hotel from top to bottom while her mother reorganised the dining room. Ava was supposed to help, but always seemed to find some errand to do that took her out to the shops. Millie was impressed by her mother's work when she saw how the dingy room had been transformed with white tablecloths made out of old sheets, fresh flowers on the tables, potted palms, and new lace curtains at the windows. Teresa was triumphant when, four days later, a local leek club booked it for their show.

Word soon spread and people came to look for themselves. They were charmed by the Morpeth widow, with her smart appearance and welcoming manner, who offered to play the piano for any special events. Ashborough Cricket Club booked the venue for their annual dinner, and the newly formed operatic society showed an interest in hiring the room for rehearsals.

'I'll need a bit of help in the kitchen for the cricket dinner,' Teresa admitted to Moody. But he was so delighted by the local interest after years of being shunned that he willingly volunteered the services of his cousin Effie.

Effie Nixon was a tall woman, with fair greying hair pulled into a loose bun and a long nose dominating a pale face. She emitted a quiet energy and composure that Millie found comforting among the hectic scenes in the Station Hotel. Millie liked her immediately. It was from the calm, capable Effie that she learned to bake bread that rose, cakes that did not collapse and pastry that did not flake or crumble at a touch.

Effie's standards of cleanliness in the ancient kitchen were far more exacting than Teresa's, and she would not start to prepare anything until all the surfaces had been scrubbed, the range blacked and the floor washed down. The two older women disliked each other on sight, but Teresa could see that she needed Effie's cooperation in the kitchen. Millie also noticed that Effie quietly but firmly stood up to Ava and encouraged her to do some work.

'Come and help me peel these vegetables, Ava,' Effie coaxed. 'We can't leave everything to young Millie.'

While her mother chattered away about everything that came into her head, Effie got on with her work, dropping the occasional comment about her family of sons which seemed to annoy Teresa the more.

When Millie and Ava were sent out to buy extra groceries, Ava grumbled about Aunt Effie. 'For all she boasts about her family, I bet she likes to get away from them. Uncle Mungo's like a bear with a sore head half the time. Used to be famous round here for playing the border pipes, but now he drinks too much to be any good. And as for the Nixon lads!'

'What about them?' Millie asked, interested in Ava's gossip. At least it took her mind off Craston and how it was proving impossible to slip away for long enough to search out her father.

'Always arguing,' Ava said with a roll of her eyes. 'Grant and Walter work at the pit. They say Grant came back from France a Communist after the war – he'd fight with his own shadow, that one. Walter's canny enough – bit of a dreamer – always getting a clip from his dad for not listening. Then there's Dan, but he's away down London somewhere. Word is he's playing football – never came back after the war ended. Was always football-daft was Dan – and always getting on the wrong side of his dad and his brothers because of it. The times Aunt Effie tried to stop him getting a hiding for breaking windows and being late for school!'

'Did you spend a lot of time round at your cousins' when you were younger, then?' Millie asked, intrigued by the other Nixons, who sounded so different from the reserved Effie.

Ava said, 'Aye, I suppose I did. It was always more homely than stopping around the hotel. More lively too sometimes!' Then she sighed. 'But the war came and things changed. Me eldest cousin, Mungo, went off to sea and was killed at the Battle of Jutland. I remember the blinds being drawn at the house for months after that, and they never really wanted to see anybody very much.'

Millie's stomach twisted. She could understand that feeling so well. 'But the other boys came back all right?'

Ava nodded. 'Grant survived nearly the whole war in France. Aunt Effie called it a miracle. But he was that different when he came home, like he was angry with the world all the time.' As they turned into Dyke Road, the main shopping street, Ava added, 'Mind you, it's Dan that Aunt Effie misses the most, I reckon. He's only been home once in two years. A real war hero.' Millie winced at the thought of her own brother's cowardice and how she had pretended quite differently to Ava. How lucky Ava was to be able to talk proudly of cousins who were heroes. Ava chatted on, unaware of Millie's discomfort. 'But Dan seems to have taken a liking to London. Trying to make a go at football rather than come back and go down the pit. Can't say I blame him. He's the type of man I'm going to marry,' Ava declared. 'Someone with a bit of ambition who doesn't want to spend all his life in Ashborough – and canny-looking, too!'

Millie had never thought much about marriage before, nor of travelling any further than Ashborough. After Craston it seemed to offer so much. But here was Ava, who had lived in Newcastle and knew so much more of the world than she did, yearning for something better. And as she swung down Dyke Road in an ill-fitting dress that Ava had discarded, a restless feeling stirred within Millie too. Maybe there was a whole world of possibilities beyond the bustling shops and teeming terraces, just waiting to be grasped. Her friend Ella had disappeared to London and written once about enormous houses and parks, and visiting a Lyons coffee house. Why had she never thought of following her? Millie wondered. It had never occurred to her to leave home until she had been forced to. It was something that other people did, like her brother or Ella. Up until now, she realised, she had never had an ounce of ambition for herself.

'So why did you leave Newcastle if you don't want to stay in Ashborough all your life?' Millie asked.

Ava gestured impatiently. 'Because I don't want to skivvy for some lazy wife who thinks she's better than me, that's why! It was Aunt Effie's idea. She and that Mrs Dodswell she goes to church with. They said the hotel wasn't a suitable place for a lass to grow up. Me dad didn't want me to go. They had a real row about it – over me!' Ava announced, sounding pleased. Then she turned and gave Millie a considered look. 'Still, with your mam here now, Aunt Effie won't be interfering. Everything'll be grand, won't it?'

Millie was about to answer when she spotted a familiar figure that made her heart somersault. There, right ahead of them, was her father, limping across the road just a stone's throw from where they walked. Her instant desire was to drop her shopping, rush up to him and fling her arms about his drooping shoulders. He looked so tired and downcast, his face drawn and lifeless, his suit shabby.

If they carried on they would bump right into him. Millie's heart hammered. This was not how she wanted to meet him, with the inquisitive Ava at her side. If he spoke to her and caused a scene, then Ava would find out that her mother had lied about being a widow and discover the disgrace of their eviction and flight from Craston. She could not risk that. She felt nauseous, her heart hammering and her legs weak.

In panic, Millie grabbed Ava by the elbow and steered her towards the penny bazaar that they were passing.

'Let's have a look in here,' she urged breathlessly. 'I've never been in yet.'

Ava was dismissive. 'There's nothing in there I want. Not after the choice of shops in New-castle.'

'Please!' Millie pleaded in panic. 'Just show me what they've got. Then you can tell me all about Newcastle. I'd like that.'

To Millie's relief, Ava was persuaded, and she pushed her in quickly. While Ava picked things up and scrutinised them, Millie glanced anxiously at the window. Moments later she saw her father limping past. He stopped to glance in at the cheap goods on display and her breath froze. For a second she thought he was staring straight at her, his faded blue eyes red-rimmed and troubled. But the light must have been reflecting off the glass, because his look never quite focused on her or showed any sign of recognition. Then he turned and hobbled on down the street, leaving Millie shaking and struggling for breath, fighting the urge to run after him.

'You all right?' Ava asked her, having grown quickly bored with looking around and telling the shopkeeper that there was nothing she wanted. Millie nodded dumbly. 'Look like you've seen a ghost. Come on, let's get home. All those cricket lads will be arriving this evening. That should liven the place up!'

They emerged from the shop and hurried home. Millie did not look back in case she caught sight of her father again. For the rest of the evening she was too busy to dwell on the near encounter, as she helped with the large gathering of cricketers, serving them with soup and ham and steamed vegetables, followed by apple crumble and raisin pie. Yet she could not shake off the feelings of guilt and dread that had knotted her stomach since seeing her father in Ashborough, and she wondered if she should tell her mother.

But there was no opportunity, for after the speeches and presentation of trophies, Teresa played the piano for them, while the bearded club captain sang and provoked loud applause. Ava was flirting with some of the young men, which made Millie feel embarrassed and gauche. Everyone else was having a good time, so she forced herself to smile too and hide her unhappiness.

Moody came out of the bar to congratulate Teresa on a successful evening. Watching her mother so full of vitality and laughter just after she had witnessed her father's forlorn condition was more than Millie could bear. She escaped to the kitchen, hoping to be alone, but Effie was still there, standing at the outside door in dispute with someone. The gas lights flickered and popped, disturbed by the blast of cold air.

'I'll not gan until I've seen her,' a man was shouting belligerently.

Millie's heart thumped in recognition.

'You must be mistaken,' Effie was explaining patiently. 'There's no one here from Craston.'

'That's what I've been told. She's been seen by someone from the village. Now let me past, woman!'

'Please go away,' Effie said, a little frightened at the desperate man before her. 'Mrs Mercer here doesn't come from one of the villages; she comes from Morpeth. Besides, she's a widow. Now go before Mr Moody finds you bothering us. He'll only call the police.'

Ellis swore at Effie and tried to push past.

Millie shrank away into the shadows, trembling. She was ashamed of her father's rudeness to Effie, but more ashamed of her own instinct to hide rather than come to the rescue. What should she do? she agonised.

'No!' Effie's voice was now raised in anger. She pushed back at the aggressive caller, quite as strong as he was.

'I want to see me lass! You'll not stop me, you bitch!'

Millie forced herself to move. She must go and get her mother, for no one else could deal with him as she could. Back inside the dining room, Teresa had just finished playing and was the centre of attention among a group of men. Millie summoned all her courage and pushed between them to reach her mother.

'Please, Mam, can you come?' she urged.

Teresa looked annoyed. 'Don't speak until you're spoken to,' she scolded.

But Millie persisted. 'Please, Mam, there's someone to see you. Someone from home.' She gave her mother a pleading look and saw horror flicker across the older woman's face.

'Excuse me, gentlemen,' she smiled. 'There's work to be done.' She slipped out quickly, with Millie following. Closing the kitchen door firmly behind her, she rushed to the outer door. Effie was standing on the steps above a figure sprawled on the ground.

'I think he's a drunk,' Effie said with distaste, 'after some woman from Craston.'

From the lighted kitchen doorway, Millie could see her father's haggard face looking up at them.

'T'resa,' he mumbled, 'T'resa.' He tried to stagger to his feet.

Effie looked at Teresa, puzzled. 'Do you know this man?'

Teresa did not answer, but advanced down the steps in fury. 'You stay away from me,' she ordered, 'and don't come bothering us again, do you hear?'

Ellis pulled himself up and faced her. 'You'll come back wi' me, woman,' he growled. 'You don't belong here.' He lunged for her. 'I want to see Millie. I want to see the lass!'

'She doesn't want anything to do with you. You've failed her. We're not coming back, not ever!' Teresa shouted, and shoved him away. He was so much weaker than two months ago and it took little effort to throw him off. 'You've got nothing to offer us any more.'

Millie stood with her hands half covering her face, appalled by the scene. She had forgotten just how upsetting their arguing had been, and dark memories came flooding back. She was shaking but could not speak. To her horror, her father did not deny Teresa's accusing words; instead, he crumpled at her feet and began to weep.

'Come back wi' me, T'resa, please,' he cried. 'I can't manage on me own. I can't live on me own.' At that moment he looked beyond his wife and recognised Millie for the first time. 'Millie, pet, help me!'

A sob caught in Millie's throat as she moved down the steps towards him. She could not bear to see him brought so low, this man who had once been tall and dignified and proud of his learning.

'Dad!' she croaked, stretching out her arms to him. But her mother held her back.

'Keep away from him, he'll only do us more harm,' she ordered. 'You're disgusting!' she hissed at her husband. 'You may be fit for the gutter, but you'll not take us down with you. Now be gone, Mercer!' She shoved him away from them with her foot, as if he were a troublesome stray dog, unable even to bring herself to call him by his Christian name. She had no feelings left for this wreck of a man on the dirty yard floor. The man she had married and lain with all those years was dead to her, and the hopes she had once had of him long gone.

Millie struggled to free herself of her mother's grip, but the older woman was the more resolute. 'Stay where you are, do you hear? I'll not let you throw away your life on a waster like that. He doesn't deserve your pity.'

'But he's me dad!' Millie tried to plead through her sobs. 'We can't just leave him…'

'Get back in the house,' Teresa ordered, shoving her up the steps with surprising strength. 'If you disobey me now, I'll tan your hide!'

It was Effie who stepped forward to help Ellis to his feet again. He swayed unsteadily. 'Don't hurt the lass,' he cried. 'I'll go, I'll go. Just don't hurt her!' Then he turned without a further look or word of goodbye, wove across the yard into the blackness and was gone.

They all stared after him, surprised by the sudden capitulation, Effie speechless at the scene she had just witnessed. After a few moments, Millie slipped her mother's hold and ran down the steps and across the yard. A blustery squall hit her face with needles of rain and the smell of

51

horse manure from the adjacent stables.

'Dad? *Dad!*' she shouted after him in vain. There was no sign of him in the unlit back lane and she knew he would not turn back even if he heard her. He had shown a flicker of his old pride in the way he had gone. And even as she stood calling after him, she knew she did not want to have to choose between her parents. Her mother had made the choice for her, and even as she hated her for what she had done, Millie knew that staying at Moody's hotel was their only chance of security. Yet still she screamed his name into the dark: 'Dad, *Dad!*'

Effie appeared at her side and put an arm about her in comfort.

'Come back in, lass,' she encouraged. 'He's gone now.'

Millie crumpled against her and wept, not needing to explain anything to this kind woman. As they walked back into the kitchen, Effie and Teresa glared at each other with hostility.

'Don't look at me like that! I'm doing this for Millie,' Teresa said defensively. 'That man would have had us in the workhouse. We were evicted for him being on strike. You're a pitman's wife, you know what that means. The only difference between you and me is that your man's still in work, so don't think you're any better than me.'

Effie gave her a disdainful look, and her reply was quiet but contemptuous. 'I don't blame you for trying to protect the lass. The difference between us is that I wouldn't give my favours to Joseph the way that you have. What sort of example is that for Millie?'

Millie thought her mother would strike the other woman. She trembled as she answered. 'I'll do whatever is necessary for us to stay together!' She advanced on Effie with her finger jabbing the air in fury. 'You're a mother with plenty of sons. Well, I lost me only son in the war. He meant the world to me, that lad,' she blazed. 'But I'm not going to lose me only daughter an' all. So if you go telling Joseph about this, it'll be Millie who suffers most. Me, I don't care any more what anyone does or says to me. But I'll go to the ends of the earth before I see Millie suffer further!'

Millie had never heard her mother speak so openly about their tragedy, or so frankly about her family. She loosened herself from Effie's protective hold and rushed to fling her arms around her mother. Teresa hugged her back, the way she had done so easily when Millie was a small child, and Millie saw rare tears in her mother's eyes.

At that moment Moody came barging into the kitchen, red-faced and jovial.

'Where have you all got to? They want you to play one more time, Teresa.'

It was the first time Millie had heard him speak to her mother in such a familiar way. Then he frowned, glancing at the gaping back door. 'What's been going on?'

Millie held her breath to see what Effie would do. She sensed how much she disliked Teresa; if she wanted to get rid of her, now was her chance.

Effie closed the outer door. 'Just some tramp being a nuisance,' she answered carefully. 'Teresa helped me get rid of him. Millie's just a bit upset by it.'

Millie saw a look flit between the women, the beginnings of a wary truce.

'Well done.' Moody beamed at Teresa in admiration. 'Millie, you have a sit by the fire for a minute, then you can clear the tables. Come on then, Teresa, got to keep everyone happy.'

Teresa went at once. Left alone with Effie, Millie felt suddenly awkward. She was shaken by the terrible scene with her father and thought Effie must now feel contempt for her. She had lied as much as her mother about their circumstances. What must the woman think of them both? But Effie steered her to the chair by the range.

'Sit yourself down, you look terrible. I'll warm you up some cocoa.' Millie's resolve to be brave melted at the kind words, and she felt the tears flooding down her cheeks. Effie laid a hand of comfort on her shoulder. 'I'll not say a word about the visit from your – from that man,' she promised. 'Not for your mother's sake, but for yours, Millie. You're a good lass and I'll not see you turned out. You've been through enough already by all accounts.'

Millie smiled through her tears in gratitude. It frightened her that there was now no going back to Craston and their old life. But she knew that however precarious their security in Ashborough, she had a good friend in the quiet Effie Nixon. The thought helped ease the hurt inside her a fraction.

Effie spoke softly. 'Your mother's wrong if she thinks I don't understand what it's like to lose a son. My Mungo was lost at sea.'

Millie whispered, 'I didn't think she ever thought of Graham. She's hardly mentioned him to anyone since he died. I thought I was the only one who missed me brother.'

Effie laid a gentle hand on Millie's head. 'She probably thinks of him every day. No matter how many children you have, it's not something you get over. Not ever.'

Millie heard the bleakness in the woman's voice and wondered if she had ever said that to anyone else. For a moment she felt special, as if a secret bond had been forged between them. Taking the warm drink that Effie offered, she put her cold hands around it and thought guiltily about her father, lost in the autumn night. She wished that he had been able to hear her mother's outburst to Effie, then maybe he would have understood a little better why they had deserted him. Now he might never know, and Millie doubted she would ever see him again.

CHAPTER 3
1923

'Coal wagon's coming!' a neighbour bellowed into Effie's kitchen.

'I'll go,' Millie said, rushing at once to the back door and across the yard. She thought that Effie looked more tired than usual, labouring over the ironing. Dashing into the back lane, she began to unpeg the flapping washing before the dirty wagon delivering the coal reached them. It gave her a brief, painful reminder of Craston, where her mother and neighbours had often defied the delivery men.

'You'll just have to wait till the washing's dry,' her mother used to shout. 'Come any nearer and I'll wrap it round you and tie you up!' There would be ribald laughter from the other women, and the men would retreat, shaking fists and grumbling in defeat.

But that seemed in another lifetime, Millie thought, as she slipped around on the mud and leaves, gathering armfuls of men's shirts. She found it difficult to recall the names of some of their old neighbours, let alone their faces. It was three long years since they had sought refuge in Ashborough, and since she had last seen her father. After that night when he had come looking for them at the hotel, he had never returned. Once she had bumped into her Aunt

Hannah in an ironmonger's, but her aunt had cut her dead, barging past her as if she did not exist. In agitation, Millie had rushed after her in the street and demanded to know how her father was.

Hannah had turned on her with her frostiest look and almost spat out the words. 'How would I know? He left Craston the year *that woman* deserted him. I don't know where he went. Heartbroken he was. If he's dead it'll be her fault. We all know the bad company your mother keeps – half the village knows. Living with that publican!'

'It's not like that.' Millie had tried to defend her mother, wounded by her aunt's harsh words.

'Well, don't think of coming back, because you're not welcome,' Hannah had interrupted. 'You've a sinner for a mother and you look more like her than ever. You'll bring no more shame on my family!' With that, she had stalked off, leaving Millie speechless with anger and humiliation.

So she had never gone back to Craston. She had even lost touch with Ella, her one link with her old life. She had written to the London address where she thought Ella was working, but her lively friend had either moved on or decided not to reply, for her letters were never answered.

But Millie had made the best of her new life in Ashborough. Under her mother's influence the hotel was prospering since the rowdy public bar had been turned into a tearoom. Many respectable societies used it for their functions, and it had become a popular lodging place for travelling salesmen. They had taken on another girl, Elsie, to help with general chores, but Millie still found herself doing twice as much as Ava. She and Elsie were up at five thirty lighting fires and boiling up water to take to the guests, laying tables and cooking breakfast. Teresa would appear to chat to the residents, and Ava would emerge last, yawning and uncommunicative until after she had drunk three cups of tea. An insomniac, Moody might appear at any time or pass them on the stairs, going to bed as they were about to start the day.

Teresa had persuaded him not only to close down the bar, but also to stop drinking. He would go for weeks without drink and the atmosphere would be light-hearted and industrious. But then some black mood would take hold of him and he would disappear on a drinking binge around the town or lock himself in his room with a crate of whisky. During such bouts, Teresa would warn the girls to stay away from him, and she too ignored his presence until he emerged haggard and contrite. Millie distrusted him, still haunted by the episode in the attic when she had been a frightened and insecure fourteen-year-old. She avoided being alone with him and could not understand Teresa's friendship with such a man. While she was thankful that her mother coped with Moody and his moroseness, she could not help feeling disgust that she had left her father for this slovenly and ill-educated character.

Millie and Ava had established a volatile, sisterly relationship that suited them both at times. They were rivals, quick to argue and fall out, but also company for each other, and would occasionally enjoy going out together to the cinema or socials at Ashborough Presbyterian Church, which Effie attended. This summer Millie had been allowed to go with Ava to the carnival at the Miners' Hall, chaperoned by the Nixons, but there was little opportunity to dance. Ava had monopolised the compliant and bashful Walter Nixon, who was good at dancing, while Millie sat and watched. Burly Grant Nixon appeared to hate dancing, preferring to argue politics and football with his father, Mungo, over pints of beer until the music stopped.

Millie found Grant odd. He was ill-at-ease in company and she never saw him speak to other women. She could only get him to talk in the confines of his own home, and even then he would never look at her directly. She was forever tidying up his piles of books that cluttered up Effie's kitchen; huge tomes on history and politics, lightened by the occasional earnest novel. Millie sometimes thought he would have got on well with her father, and allowed herself to imagine them together: two stubborn, bookish men who liked nothing better than to argue and debate into the night beside a glowing fire, sharing a pipe of tobacco.

Both Millie and Ava were a little envious of Elsie, who had been to the new Egyptian Ballroom on Fern Street. She was allowed to go with her older sister, Mary, who was housemaid to a coal merchant.

'It's got a proper sprung floor,' Elsie had told them excitedly, 'and it's not just old waltzes –

there're new dances too. And they've got one of them American soda machines in the buffet!'

The more Millie heard about it the more she yearned to go. She badgered her mother to allow her to join the dance class there, but Teresa told her she would have to save up and pay for the lessons herself. Ava, on the other hand, had wangled the money out of her father during one of his brighter moods and was already learning the delights of the foxtrot and the tango, which she and Elsie demonstrated in the kitchen to howls of laughter.

'But Uncle Joseph doesn't give me enough money,' Millie had protested to her mother.

'Then you'll have to find a job that does,' Teresa had replied. 'But you'll still be expected to cook the breakfasts and the evening meals for the guests, do you hear?'

So that was why Millie spent her Mondays over at the Nixons'. Effie had agreed to pay her a little for helping out on wash days, and for running to the shops on errands. The amounts she could afford were not enough to cover the lessons, so Millie also worked at the Palace cinema on Wednesdays and Saturdays, selling sweets, fruit and peanuts. The Palace had once seen better times as a concert hall for visiting music-hall acts and travelling players, but was now known locally as the 'fleapit'. Still, Millie bore the ribald comments from the young pitmen she served, and laughed off Ava's spiteful teasing at her lowly jobs, determined that by Christmas she would have enough money to pay for dancing lessons.

Thinking about entering the mysterious world

of the Egyptian Ballroom cheered her now, with the wind biting into her reddened fingers and numbing them as she fumbled with the clothes pegs outside Effie's back door. Soon she would dance all the dances there were to learn, and maybe one day she might become a dance teacher herself and work amid the grand surroundings of the Egyptian Ballroom.

Effie, glancing out of the steamy kitchen window, saw Millie wave and smile at the coal wagon as it trundled to their back gate and let go a cascade of glistening coal. She probably knew the driver from the Palace, or maybe from the hotel. It amazed her how quickly the girl had adapted to her strange new life in Ashborough, and how little she seemed to resent the drudgery. Effie still shuddered at the memory of the fight outside the Station Hotel with Millie's father. She would never approve of Teresa's desertion of her husband, but she silently admired the woman for her determination to make a new life for herself and Millie. And she had to admit that Teresa had succeeded in curbing Cousin Joseph's excesses and brooding temper where she had failed for years.

Since discovering the secret of the Mercers' past, Effie had felt a special bond with young Millie, and she had tried to protect the girl from her mother's demands and the relentless hotel chores that were her daily lot. It was she who had persuaded Teresa to allow her to take Millie and Ava to the church whist drives and suppers, thinking how they deserved a bit of fun once in a while. Effie had half hoped that her son Walter might form an attachment to Millie, for he was kind and a bit of a dreamer and she thought they might make each other happy one day. But perhaps Ava sensed this too, for she made it her business to monopolise him. Ava, a troubled girl, alternately spoilt and neglected, Effie thought, brought nothing but discord.

Effie sighed and felt suddenly very tired. She heard Millie humming as she re-entered the kitchen, her arms full of washing. How much stronger she looked now, Effie thought. Her skinny body had filled out nicely in the past three years, and her dark hair shone in soft curls around her high forehead, framing her slim face and lively blue eyes. She doesn't realise how pretty she is these days, Effie mused. Millie still walked with quick, restless steps like a child, and blushed shyly when whistled at by the coalman.

'Sit down and I'll make you a cup of tea,' Millie insisted, plonking the half-dry washing on the one kitchen chair that was not piled with books or newspapers. 'You look done in. I can come back tomorrow and finish the ironing.'

'You don't have to,' Effie protested half-heartedly, but she sank gladly on to her worn fireside chair. 'I just seem to be short of breath these days. Must be the change in the weather.'

'Aye.' Millie nodded, glancing at her in concern. 'Mustn't let the cold get on your chest like last winter. Have you been rubbing that grease on like I told you? And you mustn't sit in a draught, you should move your chair to the other side of the fire.' She went and closed the kitchen door as she spoke.

Effie smiled, enjoying being made a fuss of by the girl.

'I should have had a daughter like you,' she wheezed. 'I get no sympathy from all my men. Wouldn't even notice if I ran stark naked down the back lane, let alone if I rub goose grease on my chest!'

'If you were waving a copy of the football pink they might,' Millie joked. The two women laughed out loud.

'Oh, Millie, you do me good,' Effie said, then her laughter turned to coughing. Millie rushed over and slapped her back, and Effie retched and spat phlegm into the fire. Dashing to the pantry, Millie returned with a cup of water from the metal jug.

'Sip it slowly,' she encouraged, and rubbed the woman's back in comfort. It alarmed Millie when Effie had these bouts of coughing. Though the older woman insisted they were not frequent and were nothing to fuss about, she looked quite drained once the coughing died down.

Millie glanced at the clock on the mantelpiece. Grant and Walter would be home from the pit soon, expecting a hot meal and hot water for a bath in front of the fire. Later, Mr Nixon would be meandering back from the club also wanting food and a few hours in bed before going on night shift.

'You go and lie down and I'll get the tea on,' Millie said. 'I'll make a thick gravy for the end of the brisket and boil up some potatoes.'

'But you'll be needed at the hotel...' Effie answered weakly.

'Not for another hour or more,' Millie lied. 'I can manage both.'

'Just for ten minutes then,' Effie acquiesced, and dragged herself upstairs.

Millie got on with the meal, worrying about the woman who had befriended her. She felt closer now to Effie than to her own mother; they shared a common outlook on life – always to make the best of what you had – and a common humour. Effie could make her laugh about the most mundane of things that happened in her street. Later, Millie went to check on her and found her asleep, her breathing noisy like the purr of a bronchial cat.

She was worn out, Millie thought. It was time her family gave her more of a hand. It was ridiculous that Effie should be left to do much of the heavy fetching of water from the pump, and the shovelling of coal into the outhouse and then humping it into the kitchen. She would have strong words with Grant and Walter to help their mother more on the days she was not there. For far too long they had taken Effie for granted, treating her more like a skivvy than a mother. Millie knew she could talk frankly to the sons and they might listen, whereas Mungo Nixon would not.

Effie's prickly husband would never take advice from a girl, especially one like Millie, who was not from one of Ashborough's respectable pit families. He was wary of his wife's friendship with Millie, and especially disapproving of Teresa, whom he thought of as common and brash. He only put up with her helping out,

Millie knew, because she made excellent stottie cake and always made sure his tobacco was in the house. Millie wondered again about Dan, the missing son. What was he like? She knew that Effie pined for her distant son, fretting that he stayed away in London for so long and never visited. It was the one tonic that might revive the ailing woman, Millie thought, to see Dan again. How selfish he was to have lost touch with his mother, so that she did not even know where he lived any more. Still, Effie had two other sons who could help her.

So when she heard the sound of Grant's heavy feet crossing the yard and Walter's tuneful whistle, she shouted a greeting through the door, which had blown open again. 'Before you take your boots off can you put the coal away in the shed, please?' Millie was stirring hard at the gravy, defying it to go lumpy, and did not take her eyes off the task. 'Your mam's gone to lie down. She's sound asleep. You could help by bringing in a bucketful for the fire once you're finished, an' all.' The footsteps stopped.

Millie, satisfied with the gravy, bent down and pulled on the heavy oven door with a rough cloth to check on the bread-and-butter pudding she had made with the stale bread from the pantry. It released a mouth-watering aroma of buttery, sweet raisins and toasting bread that made Millie realise how hungry she was. She slammed the oven door shut and stood up, face flushed, pushing away curls from her eyes.

Turning, she saw a stranger in the doorway and shrieked in shock. He was dressed in a tan coat and wide-brimmed hat, and the boots he stamped on the mat were worn but well polished. The look he gave her was quizzical.

'The Nixons still live here?' he asked.

Millie flushed. 'Aye, they do. Who are you?'

But even as she asked, she already knew. The bright-blue eyes under the thick dark brows were just like his father's; the jawline was strong but not as heavy as Grant's, the amused smile under the fair moustache reminiscent of Walter's. He had the best attributes of all the Nixons rolled into one, and as he dumped down his canvas bag and threw off his hat, Millie saw he had his mother's fair colouring and blond hair.

'I'm Dan. Dan Nixon,' he grinned, and began to unbutton his coat. 'And who are you? Don't tell me one of me brothers has beaten me to it and married the prettiest lass in Ashborough?'

The directness of his look and his teasing words turned Millie red and stammering.

'N-no. I mean, I'm not – your brothers haven't. I'm just lending a hand...'

Under his coat Dan was wearing a smart suit, the jacket of which he quickly discarded. Millie gulped as he proceeded to roll up his sleeves, revealing broad, muscly forearms.

'Well then?' he said.

'Well what?' Millie gawped.

'What do they call you?' Dan asked, advancing towards her.

Millie backed away. 'Millie,' she answered. 'Millie Mercer.'

Dan smiled. 'So are you married, Millie Mercer?'

'No,' Millie said too hastily. 'No, I'm not.' Then she blushed deeper. Not that it was any of his business, she wanted to add, but felt too inhibited. Instead she gabbled, 'I'm helping your mam out with the washing, earning a bit of money – for dancing lessons.'

'Dancing, eh?' Dan looked approving. 'I like a dance too. There's nothing better than a good game of footie on a Saturday afternoon, followed by a few beers and dancing the night away. Don't you agree?'

He was standing close to her now, and Millie had never felt her heart racing in quite the way it was at that moment. His words seemed to be suggesting so much more. She was still startled by his sudden appearance just after she had been thinking about him. It was too much of a coincidence, as if his being nearby had forced his presence into her mind. It was suddenly un-comfortably warm in the kitchen; beads of perspiration were breaking out on her brow.

'I don't play footie,' she answered.

They stared at each other a moment and then both burst out laughing. Dan reached forward, and for one heady second Millie thought he was going to grab her hand. But he seized the empty coal bucket that was standing on the hearth beside her.

'Well, you'll just have to watch then,' he grinned. 'At least I hope you'll come and support the Ashborough Comrades. I'll be playing for them on Saturday, once they know I'm back.'

'Will you? We sometimes do the teas for them.' Millie smiled back nervously. 'I live at the Station

Hotel with Mam and Mr Moody. The away teams usually change at the hotel these days.'

'Judging by the smell coming from that oven, the teas must be good,' Dan said with a wink.

'They are,' Millie said proudly. 'Your mam taught me to bake.' She suddenly remembered that they were not alone and that Effie was lying upstairs asleep. 'She talks about you a lot. You should've said you were coming.'

'I wanted to surprise her,' Dan smiled.

'You'll do that all right. She'll be that pleased to see you're back.' Millie slid him a look. 'That's if you're staying?'

'Aye, I am now,' he answered, giving her another of his cheeky looks.

Millie put her hands up to her burning face. 'What are you doing with the pail?' she asked, trying to change the subject.

'You shouted at me to fetch some coal, didn't you?' Dan gave a quizzical, lopsided smile that made one cheek dimple.

'I thought you were Grant or Walter,' Millie said in embarrassment.

'Well, I'm glad to see someone's keeping them in order,' Dan chuckled. 'I'll make myself useful, then we're going to sit down and you can tell me all there is to know about Millie Mercer before Mam wakes up or any of me interfering brothers turns up to spoil our chat.'

Millie looked beyond to the back yard and laughed. She could see the dark head of Grant bobbing above the back wall as he trudged in beside the slighter Walter.

'Too late,' she answered.

'Later then, Millie.' Dan winked, and Millie felt her heart hammering again, as if she had run all the way from home without stopping.

As he turned and strode out of the kitchen to hurl the empty bucket at his brothers in a rough greeting, Millie watched his every move and gesture with delight. She listened to the rude banter and the tussling between the men as they made up swiftly for years of absence. And she knew before they came back into the kitchen to wake up Effie with their noise that something else had happened. As swiftly as he had whizzed into her world like a dangerous firecracker, Millie knew she was falling helplessly in love with Dan Nixon.

CHAPTER 4

'And where in the world have you been all this time?' Teresa demanded when Millie rushed breathless into the hotel kitchen.

'Mrs Nixon's,' she panted, her cheeks stinging from the raw air. It was already nearly dark outside.

'You're spending far too much time over there,' her mother complained, 'and neglecting your duties here. I've had to prepare the evening meal, and we've six travellers in tonight. And that debating society want a room ready at eight o'clock, so you'll need to get laying a fire. I need Elsie to serve tables.'

'What about Ava?' Millie asked, discarding her coat and hat quickly.

'She's still out shopping somewhere,' Teresa answered sharply.

Millie was disappointed; she was bursting with her news that Dan was home and she had met him. But as she rushed off to lay a fire in an upstairs room, she felt a pang of resentment that Ava was once again out enjoying herself while she and Elsie were left to do most of the work. Her mother too had long tired of the favouritism that Joseph expected his daughter to receive, but would do nothing to upset him.

It was not until late that evening, when they were making ready for bed, that Millie had a

chance to talk to Ava. They now shared a bedroom together at the back of the hotel, above the
kitchen, which meant that it was warm. Her
mother had long ago moved to a larger room on
the main landing near to Moody's, and Millie
had given up her attic room to Elsie because Ava
refused to share with a country girl whose father
was a mere gravedigger. Yet Ava would not sleep
alone, so Millie had been made to share a bed
with her.

'So what was it you had to tell me?' Ava
demanded, clambering into bed and wriggling
around to get warm.

Millie sat on the edge of the bed, pulling a
brush through her thick tangle of curls. She
envied Ava her straight, soft brown hair and did
not understand why she insisted on Millie
helping her bind it with torn pieces of sheet at
night so that she would wake with ringlets in the
morning. Ava looked like a fierce ragdoll with
white stalks for hair as she eyed her companion
impatiently. Suddenly Millie was apprehensive
about sharing her secret and decided she would
hide her enthusiasm from Ava, not wanting to be
teased.

'Dan Nixon's home,' she said, keeping her
voice even. 'He arrived while I was there.'

Ava shot up in bed. 'Why didn't you tell me?
No wonder you took so long to come home!' she
accused. 'What does he look like now? Is he still
really handsome?'

Millie turned away so as to hide the flush she
felt creeping up from her chest. 'I suppose he is.'

'What did he say?' Ava asked. 'Did he ask after

me? Of course I'm much prettier now than when he last saw me, so he probably didn't. Oh, I wish I'd been there!'

Millie was taken aback by her eagerness. She knew Ava remembered Dan with liking, but she was surprised by this outburst.

'I thought you were sweet on Walter?' Millie reminded her.

Ava pulled a face. 'Walter's canny enough, but Dan's more glamorous. He's been living in London, he's a man of the world. And he was that popular before he went away, what with being such a good footballer. Everyone liked him. And the number of different lasses he used to court – and he only seventeen when he went away! He's probably courted half of London these past few years!'

Millie felt dashed by the news. When Dan had spoken to her she had felt special, as if he might really care for her. But he was obviously like that with all the girls; it was just his way. She was being foolish to think Dan had meant anything by his flattering words and looks, and was glad she'd decided not to speak of it.

'Well he's back now. Looking for a job at the pit. He's hoping to play for the Comrades on Saturday, so you'll see him afterwards at the tea, more than likely.'

Ava sank back with a smile of triumph. 'No, I'll go and watch him. I'll get Walter to take me.'

Millie was shocked. 'Poor Walter! You've never shown the least bit interest in football when I've suggested we go and watch.'

'Well, I'm not going to stand and freeze to

watch just anybody,' Ava replied. 'But Dan Nixon's different. I'd watch him in a snowstorm.'

Millie climbed into bed beside her, knowing she herself would not have time to go and watch. She would be too busy making the teas. Long ago, before the war, she had enjoyed going to see her brother play for Craston Colliers, and once the whole family had travelled away to see him in a semi-final of the local league against a Tyneside team. It had been the only time she had glimpsed the smoky sprawl of Newcastle and the forest of cranes along the River Tyne. Her father had lifted her up on his shoulders for a better view and told her proudly, 'That's where the world's greatest ships are built.' She had felt a shiver of excitement at the thought of the world beyond Craston, a world of busy docksides, exotic cargoes and luxury liners.

During the war she had even played a bit of football herself, for a local church team. The girl's team had been formed to help with fundraising for the war effort and she had played in several charity matches. But when news of Graham's shameful death had filtered back, she had been dropped from the team and never picked again.

Once she had tried to explain to a bewildered Elsie why support for football in a mining village was so fanatical.

'They graft hard in the darkness all week,' she had said, thinking of her brother, 'so they really enjoy the sport and the fresh air on a Saturday. It takes them out of themselves for a bit.'

'But the bairns,' Elsie had answered, 'they're

kicking stones around the streets before they can barely walk!'

Millie had laughed in agreement. 'It's in the blood then,' she had conceded. 'And there's always that dream at the back of every lad's mind that they might play for one of the big teams one day, become a hero.'

'That's lads for you,' the practical Elsie had answered. 'Always chasing dreams.'

The week seemed to drag. To Millie's annoyance Ava twice went round to the Nixons' house in Tenter Terrace hoping to see Dan, but his father had already secured him a job at the pit and so she had come back frustrated. But when Saturday came, even Moody noticed the air of excitement as the girls rushed around to get the chores done, laughing at the slightest thing.

'What's got into you lasses?' he grumbled. 'Have I forgotten someone's birthday?'

'It's the thought of all those footballers arriving,' Teresa explained, throwing up her arms in a dramatic gesture of despair. 'They'll be no use to us all day long. It's the same whenever the Comrades have a home match and the place is full of lads.'

The girls giggled and denied it. To Millie's surprise Moody just shrugged. 'Well, with you to keep an eye on them, Teresa, they'll come to no mischief.'

It struck Millie how much Joseph had come to rely on her mother for the way things were run and for the care of his own daughter. He seemed happy to do less and less, playing cards with the travellers at night or sitting in the kitchen with his feet up reading the racing news. When he had ambled out again, the chatter rose.

'I'm going to watch the match,' Ava boasted. 'Walter's taking me.'

'He's a nice lad,' Teresa said with approval. 'If you want to go back to his house for tea afterwards you can.'

Millie protested, 'What about helping out here? Me and Elsie can't manage on our own with nearly thirty teas–'

'That's all right,' Ava interrupted quickly. 'I'll come straight back.' She gave Teresa a sweet smile.

'Our Millie, you're getting too jealous by half,' Teresa complained. 'If Ava's starting her courting you shouldn't stand in her way. Your turn will come soon enough.'

Millie exchanged exasperated looks with Elsie, who understood that her resentment was only about Ava's laziness. She decided to press her own case.

'Can I go and watch the footie this afternoon, Mam?' she asked. 'I'd come straight back too.'

'No you can't,' her mother answered without even giving it consideration. 'I need you here. Besides, it's a spectacle for lads.'

Millie stared at her mother. Had she forgotten the times in Craston they had cheered on Graham and his team-mates as if their lives depended on the outcome? Did she not remember the thrill of victory and the warm feeling of togetherness felt by the whole village when a rare cup was won? But her mother had dismissed her request and was already drawing up a list of duties for the day. She had severed the ties with their old life as completely as an amputated limb, Millie realised. It was as if Craston and their home in Saviour Street had never been, and it made her feel achingly alone. At times she longed to talk about her old life and thought she might burst if she did not. But her mother had robbed her of this release, for she had forbidden her to mention any of it, even to Effie. For the past three years they had been Teresa and Millie Mercer from Morpeth, respectable widow and daughter, ignoring the whispered rumours that they were common runaways from a colliery eviction.

To counteract the rumours, Millie had invented a world of make-believe around them, of a kind father who had died tragically in a riding accident (no poor man's disease) and the loss of a comfortable house with an ornamental garden and a flush toilet. But most of all she liked to tell the story of her heroic brother who had died defending his friends. So not only had she colluded in her mother's falsehoods; she had embellished them until she almost believed them herself.

Now she turned away and swallowed her disappointment. 'Haway, Elsie, let's go and set the tables.' At least they could watch the away team arriving and savour some of the atmosphere. And later, she might catch a glimpse of Dan Nixon.

Walter was worried about his mother, who had

barely been able to raise herself from the chair to attend to Mungo when he came in from the night shift. She had dozed by the fire, unable to drag herself to bed for a few hours of rest, and Walter, on a trip to the outside closet, had found her struggling to fill the zinc tub for her husband's bath by the fire. He had persuaded her to go and lie down while he got on with breakfast.

But the noise at the Nixons' house was deafening that morning and he doubted his mother was able to sleep. Dan was arguing with Grant about his place on the Comrades team as they clattered around polishing boots and knocking into each other, trying to reach the huge wedges of bread and bacon Walter had prepared.

'You should at least be on the bench,' Grant grumbled. 'It's unheard of to turn up out of the blue and just walk on to the team – and at centre forward!'

'They need me to pull the Comrades out of the hole they're in, that's why,' Dan said cockily. 'I'm going to turn their fortunes around. They know a professional when they see one.'

'Oh, aye?' Grant spluttered over a mug of tea. 'So how come the Londoners let such a professional go?'

'Time to move on, bonny lad,' Dan said with a nonchalant wave of his huge sandwich. 'I'm going to play First Division one of these days and I'm going to play in black and white.'

'Craston, then?' Grant mocked.

Dan came at him. 'Not bloody Craston. *Newcastle!*'

Grant caught his arm and shoved him back. 'I'll

show me backside in Fenwick's tearoom the day you do.'

'Just because the Comrades haven't picked you since the Crimean War,' Dan mocked. 'You talk a good fight, but you haven't got the guts for League football. What are you? Goalie for the Bolshie debating society?' He laughed. 'Too busy arguing about the rules you've nee breath left for running!'

Grant forced Dan's arm on to the kitchen table, knocking a pile of his books to the floor and spilling a half-drunk mug of tea. 'Come on then, let's see how tough you are, you gobby little bugger!'

As they arm-wrestled, Walter tried to jump out of the way but got pinned against the heavy oak press with his newspaper. Then Mungo stormed in, eyes blinking in the light, his thinning hair tousled. He picked up one of Dan's football boots and hurled it across the room.

'How can a man sleep with you two fighting?' he yelled. 'Bugger off the pair of you!' When he reached for one of Effie's gleaming fire-irons and brandished it at them, his sons knew when to stop.

'Is Mam still sleeping?' Walter asked in concern, as the other brothers scowled at each other and began to pick up the debris.

'Of course she isn't. The dead in the cemetery couldn't sleep through that racket,' Mungo growled.

'I'll take her up a cup of tea,' Walter offered.

'Don't fuss over her,' Mungo snapped. 'She's not a bairn. If she's thirsty she can come down for it.'

Walter knew his father hated anyone being ill,

especially his wife. To him it was a sign of weakness and the patient must be bullied back to health. So Walter hesitated, waiting for Mungo to retreat to the earth closet in the outhouse with yesterday's newspaper before he went upstairs. But Dan intervened, uncowed by his father's wrath.

'I'll take it up,' he said, reaching for the teapot and beginning to pour. 'Can't have her dying of thirst up there, can we?' he challenged.

They all watched to see if this would spark off their father's famous temper, as Dan had always managed to do. But Mungo just swore at him and told him he was a nancy boy, then stormed out the back door, dropping the poker with a clang as he went.

The brothers exchanged glances. Walter said. 'He's forgotten the newspaper.'

Dan laughed. 'He'll just have to read last week's then – before he wipes his backside on it!'

Grant and Walter chuckled.

'Better get your kit together,' Grant said, retrieving the hurled boot from under the table and handing it to Dan.

Dan nodded. 'So are you coming to watch me?'

'Aye, of course I am,' Grant admitted. 'Wouldn't miss the laugh of the season.'

They shadow-boxed around the kitchen, but Dan could tell that his older brother had signalled his approval at the stand against their father. He did not know why it mattered so much to him that Grant came to watch him, but it did. Maybe because he had always been the brother he had looked up to most, rather than easy-going

Walter, or quiet Mungo who had been killed at sea. Grant had looked out for him as a boy, deflecting some of the punishment from their father on to himself and giving him rough comfort when his ears rang and his back stung from a beating. Grant was one of the few from the town who had survived the Front from 1915 to the Armistice, but he never boasted of his deeds or gloried in his heroism as Dan would have done. Grant was more likely to turn round and deliver a lecture on the iniquities of imperialism. 'Lenin's the only hero I know of,' he had once declared, which had sent his father rushing for the fire-irons.

Dan and Walter went upstairs to see Effie. Her face brightened at the sight of them, and she sipped gratefully at the tea while Dan amused her with the description of what had gone on below. But it set her coughing again.

'Do you want me to fetch Mrs Dickson to sit with you, Mam?' Walter suggested.

'No, pet,' she spluttered. 'You get away and enjoy yourself with Ava.'

Dan nudged his brother. 'Is she any bonnier these days?'

Walter gave him a shove, and Effie laughed. 'Don't you go interfering there,' she scolded mildly.

'How about that pretty lass from the hotel coming to help out more?' Dan said with a wink.

Effie sighed. 'Millie? Aye, I might need a bit more help for a week or two. But she can hardly spare the time, the way her mother works her.'

The brothers looked at her in concern. It was

80

very unlike their mother to admit she needed any help at all. She must be feeling ill.

'We'll sort something out, Mam,' Dan assured her, rising from the bed.

'Come here and let me kiss you, lad,' Effie said with an affectionate smile. Dan obliged, and his mother pecked at his forehead with dry lips. 'It's so good having you back. I've missed you. Why did you have to stay away so long?'

Dan smiled awkwardly. 'Can't think why. Not when all the best women are in Ashborough.'

She laughed weakly and gave him a gentle swipe. 'You never even told me where you were living. Did you have respectable lodgings? Did they treat you proper?'

Dan squeezed her rough, veined hand. 'Aye, they treated me canny. I'm sorry I never wrote, but you know I was never any good at that kind of thing at school.'

Effie smiled at him sadly. 'No, you weren't, were you? Anyways, I've got you back now and that's what matters.' She pushed his hand away gently. 'Be off with you. And play well. I'll be grand until you get back.'

As they went, clattering down the stairs and talking noisily about the afternoon's sport, Effie lay back exhausted and unclutched the handkerchief into which she had been coughing. It was speckled with blood. She closed her eyes, trying to squeeze back the tears that threatened to brim. She did not want to die now. She wanted to live to see her sons marry and have children of their own, to carry on hearing their banter and lively presence around the house.

Silence settled on number 28 Tenter Terrace for a few minutes, then the back door banged and footsteps crossed to the stairs.

'Are you going to get the dinner on, Effie?' Mungo shouted up the stairs. 'Or lie in bed all day like a slut?'

Effie forced herself to sit up. Her husband would never believe she was ill with consumption, even though he must know the signs, having watched his own mother die of the disease. So there was no point telling him; he would discover the truth for himself soon enough. Once she would have felt sorry for him, but not now. She could take the verbal abuse he gave her, hardly noticing the insults any more. But too many times she had had to stand by while he thrashed and assaulted her sons for their minor misdemeanours, fuelled by the drink that he consumed daily. God forgive her, she sometimes wished she could live long enough to see one of them turn the belt on him. The bitter thought gave her the strength to haul her aching body out of bed.

Ava burst in ahead of the players. 'The Comrades won! The first time since the start of the season and they won two-one. And guess who scored the winning goal?' she asked breathlessly, pulling off her gloves.

'You tell us,' Elsie said without interest, balancing plates of buttered bread on a tray.

'Dan Nixon, of course!' Ava exclaimed to Millie, who was doling out portions of pie and peas.

Millie's insides twisted at the mention of his name, and she wished she had been there to see him perform. 'That's grand,' she managed to say.

'He was wonderful,' Ava enthused, 'the best player on the field. Everyone clapped him as he came off. He's better-looking than I remember him. I can't wait to meet him properly!'

Teresa bustled in and interrupted. 'Hurry up, girls, they're beginning to arrive.'

Ava tore off her coat and flung it on a chair, patting her hair into place. 'I'll take that tray, Elsie,' she insisted. 'You stay here and wash up.'

Before Elsie could protest, Ava had seized the tray of buttered bread and was swinging through the door behind Teresa. Millie gave Elsie a sympathetic look.

'I need some help with these pies,' she said. 'Don't be bullied by Ava. You can help me.'

The young girl smiled in gratitude and followed her out. A buzz of male voices hit them as they entered the dining room, which was filling up with players. Their faces were red and gleaming from the cold scrubbing they had been given at the crude hut that passed for a clubhouse at Thomas Burt Park. Soon the tables were crowded with hungry young men, tucking into the fare and supping the beer that Moody had brought round from the Farrier's Arms.

Millie's heart lurched to see Dan Nixon holding court at the noisiest table, where Ava was hovering with a pot of tea. There was much laughter and Millie could see Ava's round face dimple and blush at something Dan was saying to her.

'Have you cut up the cake and fruit bread?' Teresa asked.

'Aye, Mam,' Millie answered, dragging her gaze away from the far corner of the room.

'Well, bring them out, and then go and help Elsie with the dishes,' her mother ordered. 'And stop standing around gawping at those lads, Millie. You're just seventeen, remember.'

Millie hurried away, disappointed that Dan had not noticed her. Her mother was right: she was too young to catch the notice of men like Dan. It was different for Ava, who at nineteen had already worked in Newcastle and been out with Walter Nixon. She seemed far more at ease chatting with the footballers than Millie ever was. Millie knew that her mother did not approve of her mixing with lads at her age and was far happier for her daughter to help in the kitchen when the Comrades or the cricket club were patronising the hotel.

Once Teresa had taken her to task for speaking to a young footballer who wanted to know if she was courting. 'Of course she isn't,' Teresa had cut in with a laugh. But afterwards she had berated her daughter. 'Don't you go flirting with lads like that. I'll not have you making the mistake I did and marrying the first man who shows any interest. I want a better life for you, Millie, that's the reason I've worked so hard to keep us here. So don't you go throwing it all away on a daft lad, do you hear?'

So Millie knew better than to argue with her mother, and disappeared to the kitchen to help Elsie. Later, when the visiting team had climbed aboard their charabanc and the locals had dispersed to social clubs or home, Millie went out to clear the tables. The sudden quietness brought a feeling of anti-climax, and she realised how much she had been looking forward to the tea. She hurried to clear up, for she had little time before starting work at the Palace. Her mother did not seem to mind her going there as long as she was earning money and 'keeping out of mischief', as she put it.

She found Ava lolling on their bed, half reading a penny romance.

'It's not fair the way you're allowed to go out and I'm not,' Ava pouted.

'It's work,' Millie reminded her. 'And you could have gone to tea at Walter's.' Ava gave a resentful *humph* in reply, so Millie quickly wrapped up in her coat and hat and hurried through the gaslit streets. Passing the end of Fern Street, she looked enviously at the dancers going into the Egyptian Ballroom in their tapping heels and best clothes. She hurried on, the more determined to get to work. Soon, she promised herself, soon it would be her going up the steps to the brightly lit dance hall.

That night she took tickets and sold sweets to the lively audience who had come to see Rudolf Valentino. In the crowded, fusty atmosphere of the old hall, Millie gave herself up to its rough glamour. She loved to watch the silent heroes and heroines with their exaggerated expressions rushing through the scenes in their fashionable clothes while Major Hall, an invalid from the recent war, banged out dramatic tunes on an old piano. Other cinemas boasted a bijou orchestra, and Elsie had told her that the new Empire had an enormous organ installed that rose from the orchestra pit at the beginning of the performance. But Millie was happy to be among the hubbub of the Palace, excited to be a part of Ashborough social life in this modest way. She liked to chat at the end of a performance with the kind major, who took an interest in her aspirations to be a dancer and had showed her how to dance a foxtrot.

'Love dancing,' he once told her as she swept up the orange peel and peanut shells. 'Was quite good at it, though I say so myself.' Then he had pointed to his missing eye. 'No one wants to dance opposite a one-eyed old thing like me though, eh?' Millie had glanced at the puckered scar where his left eye had once been and realised why he felt more comfortable sitting in the dark playing the piano. 'You could wear an eye patch,' she had suggested. 'That would look dashing.' After that the major had taken to wearing a black patch and thumped the keys with even greater enthusiasm.

Tonight the hall was heaving with bodies as late cinema-goers squashed on to the benches at the front, the main seats long since full. As the film started, Millie went to refill her tray of sweets and heard a commotion at the back of the hall.

'There's no more room,' the manager, Mr Peters, was insisting. 'Come back on Monday, we'll be showing the same film.'

'I want to see it tonight,' someone was arguing. 'Haway and let us in, man!'

'Sorry, lad, you can't.' Mr Peters was adamant, blocking the entrance.

'Do you know who I am?' he demanded, shaking off the manager's hold.

'No, but you've had your fill of beer and you're not coming in here.' Millie could hear the annoyance in Mr Peters' voice and strained to see who was causing the trouble.

'I'm a bloody war hero!' he shouted. 'And I've just scored the winner for the Comrades the day.'

'Oh aye? And I'm Rudolf Valentino,' Mr Peters said, unimpressed. 'Take him home, lads, and let him sleep it off.'

Millie gasped as she saw Dan being ejected from the cinema, with Walter and another man steering him away.

'You might think you can chuck me out now,' Dan roared, 'but one of these days I'll bloody own this fleapit! When I'm a famous footballer!'

'Haway, Dan, man,' Walter was cajoling. 'We'll gan somewhere else.'

Dan seemed about to relent, then he turned unsteadily as if he had just remembered something. At that moment he caught sight of Millie standing in the entrance, staring at the scene.

'There she is!' he announced in triumph. 'That's the lass I came to see.'

Walter told him to shut up, but Dan threw him off and lunged back through the door, grinning at Millie. She felt herself flushing with embarrassment as he fixed her with his blue-eyed gaze. His blond hair was ruffled and his tie awry, but even in his semi-inebriated state he exuded a powerful energy. Mr Peters tried to step in the way.

'Be off with you! I'll not have you causing trouble for Millie, she's a good lass.'

Without stopping to think why, Millie intervened. 'It's all right, Mr Peters, I know him. And there's room for one more – down at the front. As long as he doesn't mind squashing up a bit.'

'I don't mind a bit,' Dan grinned, not taking his eyes from her. Millie held her breath, realising she might be jeopardising her job by speaking up for Dan if the manager was in a bad mood. What had made her risk her dancing lessons on a sudden impulse? she wondered.

'You'll have to behave yourself, mind,' she warned him, suddenly unsure of what she had done. Dan just laughed.

Then Mr Peters relented. 'Gan in then,' he told Dan with a wave. 'But cause any trouble and you're out for good.'

Without a backward glance at his brother or friend, Dan stepped forward and took Millie's arm. 'Show me in then, bonny lass,' he smiled.

Millie felt a thrill at his touch and words. She did not know if he had really come seeking her, but she did not care. He was here, linking his arm through hers, and she was exultant. She ignored the smell of beer on his breath and did not dwell on Ava's gossip about all the other girls he had courted. Tonight Dan Nixon was hers, and they went into the dark hall together arm in arm. At that moment she had never felt more alive in her life.

CHAPTER 5

At the end of the film, Dan waited around for Millie to finish clearing up. He leant against a pillar with his hands deep in his pockets, whistling a tune that Major Hall had played. When the major appeared, he stopped him to chat about his army life.

'I was in the Fusiliers,' Dan told him. 'Served in France. So did me brother, Grant Nixon.'

'I know him,' Bob Hall beamed. 'He was a very brave soldier. But when were you there?'

'Nineteen eighteen,' Dan said. 'Just caught the end of it.'

'I was invalided out by then,' Bob admitted, 'but there were some fierce fights put up at the end by all accounts.'

'Aye, there were that.' Dan nodded, catching sight of Millie. 'Well, nice to meet you,' he said, 'but I have to walk this young lass home.'

'Oh, I see,' Bob said, with a surprised look at Millie. 'Well, thanks for chatting. People don't like to talk about the war these days. Find chaps like me a bit of a bore!' He laughed at himself.

'You're never boring.' Millie smiled at him. 'I'm sure Dan would like to chat about old times again.' It always gave her a pang of regret to hear old comrades reminiscing together, knowing her brother would never be one of them. But the major was such a kind man that she never resented his harping on old times.

Dan nodded as he moved swiftly to Millie's side. 'Be pleased to. Good night, Major.' He took Millie's hand possessively and pulled her after him.

Millie waved to Bob and followed, thrilled at Dan's open show of affection. He slipped her arm through his and squeezed it as the dimly lit street swallowed them up. He chattered away as if he knew her well, his breath warming the frozen air around them in billowing clouds. Millie realised after a few minutes that they were walking back to the hotel in a very roundabout way, but she did not protest. She wanted the walk to go on for ever as she listened, captivated, to his tales of London life and football. He could have recited times tables and she still would have hung on his every word, thrilled by his lively voice and animated face. In return, she recounted fanciful tales about her life in Morpeth, not wanting him to think her dull. As they passed the end of Fern Street, she gave a half-glance towards the Egyptian Ballroom. Even the lure of that forbidden world seemed to lessen in Dan's company. But he noticed her look.

'I found out from Mam that you worked Saturdays at the fleapit for dancing money. You're desperate to go in there, aren't you?'

Millie nodded. 'One day I will.'

'We'll go in now,' Dan announced, and abruptly steered her into Fern Street.

'We can't!' Millie said in panic. 'I'm not dressed for it – and the money – and Mam! I'm supposed to be home.'

'They'll let us in the buffet,' Dan said, undaunted. 'We'll just go in for a few minutes. Your mam'll not miss you. Haway, it's time you had a bit of fun.'

Millie's heart began to pound. This could not be happening to her. Two hours ago she was selling sweets in a drab picture house, and now she was about to enter the Egyptian Ballroom on the arm of handsome Dan Nixon! Any moment she would pinch herself and wake up in bed beside Ava. But she pushed away thoughts of a jealous Ava or an angry mother and allowed Dan to hurry her up the street.

At the steps Dan squeezed her arm and led her up, immediately engaging the doorman in conversation about the afternoon's game. The man appeared to know him and congratulated him on his winning goal. They were ushered in with a pat on the back. Millie smiled broadly, feeling a warm glow spreading inside at the reception they got. It happened again as they mounted the stairs to the buffet, people stopping to chat to Dan, welcoming him home, shaking his hand, talking about the match. She had never experienced such admiration, and it made her feel light-headed to be basking in the glow of Dan's popularity. She noticed too the looks that the women gave her, puzzled and intrigued to know who she was. Millie wished she was wearing something more attractive than a brown jacket and black skirt and the felt hat she had worn since she was fourteen. But Dan did not seem to mind as he ushered her into the buffet and claimed a table by the railings so that Millie could peer over at the dancers below.

She gazed around at the exotically painted walls depicting sphinxes and pharaohs, palm trees and fruit. The elaborate stucco ceiling was picked out in gold and green, and everywhere there were potted plants throwing shadows on the black and white tiled floor from bright electric lamps. Music pulsated from the well-dressed dance band below as Millie leaned over to catch a glimpse of the dancers. The ballroom was a blaze of colour and noise, every bit as exciting as she had imagined.

Dan came back with two ice-cream sodas in long glasses with spoons, and watched Millie's face light up at the sight.

'It's like a fairytale!' she grinned.

He was struck again at how unselfconsciously pretty she was, her slim face flushed and her eyes shining with excitement, black curls snaking from under her unfashionable hat. He liked the way her mouth turned up at the edges, smiling easily, and the candid look in her blue eyes under the dark lashes. There was nothing jaded or world-weary about Millie; she seemed to get pleasure out of so little and it made him feel good bringing her here. She was sweet and undemanding and listened to everything he said. He was captivated by her.

'I've never had one of these before!' she cried, eagerly dipping her spoon into the melting mountain in the glass.

'Tuck in then,' Dan grinned. She finished first, and he pushed his half-eaten one away and leaned closer. 'You never came to see me play at

Burt Park, did you?'

'Mam wouldn't let me,' Millie replied. 'There was too much to do at the hotel.'

'So you did try?' Dan asked, regarding her intently.

Millie blushed. 'Aye, I did.'

'Ava was there with our Walter. She seems to do as she pleases.'

'Her dad doesn't take much interest in what she does,' Millie explained. 'He leaves it to my mam to tell her what she can and can't do.'

'And your mam's soft on Ava and hard on you?' Dan guessed.

'She's always been protective of me,' Millie answered, not wanting to be critical.

'Protective from the likes of me, eh?' Dan grinned.

'Especially from the likes of you!' Millie laughed.

Unexpectedly Dan reached for her hand, leaning close. 'You're a canny lass, Millie. I want to see you again.'

'Me?' Millie gasped, her whole body beginning to tremble. She could not believe that the popular Dan wanted to court her.

'Aye, you,' he laughed, squeezing her hand. 'So what do you say? Will you gan out with me?'

Millie felt her face burning. 'Aye, I'd like that,' she whispered.

'Grand,' said Dan. 'Now I better get you home before your mam has me guts for garters.'

Millie gave the dance hall a reluctant backward glance as they stepped out into the chilly night once more. Dan enclosed her in his arm as they hurried along, but as they neared the hotel, Millie pulled away from him.

'She might be looking out for me,' she said nervously, her euphoria at the past hour evaporating as she thought of her mother. Suddenly Dan stopped and swung her round to face him. He leaned very close so that she could feel his warm breath on her cold cheeks. Her heart thudded.

'I'll meet you at the fleapit on Wednesday, and on Saturday I'm taking you to the Egyptian Ballroom. Properly this time – dancing and supper.'

Millie was shaking with cold and nerves. 'She'd never let me. Not just with you.'

Dan was undaunted. 'She'll not stop me seeing you. When I want something, Millie, I've got to have it.' He gave her a dangerous, glinting look that made her insides leap.

Millie returned his look. 'Then you'll have to come and ask her properly,' she answered.

Dan smiled, relishing the challenge. 'I will, bonny lass, I will.'

To Millie's amazement, Dan came seeking her at the Palace on Wednesday and treated her to fish and chips afterwards. The following evening she called on Effie with some baking and Dan escorted her home, taking a long deviation by the river. In the twilight he stole a kiss on Millie's lips and set her heart thumping like a bass drum. He laughed at her flaming cheeks and told her she was the bonniest lass he had ever kissed. Millie hurried home but hardly slept. Friday seemed to last an eternity, but then it was Saturday morning, and Dan had promised to call and see her mother before the team left for their away match to Bedlington. She was a bundle of nerves and kept dropping things.

'What is the matter with you, lass?' Teresa snapped. 'Stop staring out the window and get on with that polishing.'

All at once, Millie caught sight of Dan striding through the back gates, whistling, clutching a bunch of flowers. Her stomach lurched. 'Mam,' she began in panic, wanting to warn her. But there was a sudden shriek from Ava, who had gone to see what it was that had distracted Millie.

'There's Dan Nixon! And he's coming across our yard.' She turned excitedly. 'He must be coming to see me!'

Millie's pulse raced as she looked away. Ava did not notice her nervousness as she rushed to open the back door, but her mother gave her a sharp look. A moment later, Dan was sauntering into the large kitchen, dressed in his best suit, his fair hair combed with brilliantine, exchanging greetings with his cousin Ava.

He strode straight over to Teresa and thrust the bunch of flowers into her arms.

'It's Mrs Mercer I've come to see,' he smiled. 'Thought it was time I introduced myself properly.'

Teresa was quite taken aback. She stared at the flowers and then back at Dan. Millie hardly dared look at him; she was suddenly overawed by his appearance, although she had longed for it since their last meeting and that first kiss.

'Well, that's very good of you,' Teresa blustered, 'but I really don't see why...'

''Cos you deserve them,' Dan replied with the dimpled smile that set Millie's heart hammering faster.

Ava, hardly able to mask her disappointment, pouted. 'Well some people have all the luck. You'll stop for a cup of tea with us, won't you?' She fussed around him, but Millie could not move.

Teresa recovered. 'Of course you must. Sit yourself down, Millie, get the lad a cup. I'd like to hear all about your time in London. Your mother must be pleased to see you back.'

'I'll get the tea,' Ava said quickly, rushing for a cup and saucer.

'That's very kind of you,' Dan said, sitting astride a stool. 'But I can't stop long. I've got to meet the lads shortly.'

Millie tried to appear busy, vying with Ava to prepare a pot of tea. She suddenly realised she had not really expected Dan to turn up, and was now terrified of what he was going to ask. But he seemed quite at ease talking to her mother, regaling her with anecdotes about London life. Ava relaxed and, to Millie's embarrassment, became flirtatious.

Teresa silenced her. 'You still haven't explained why you've brought me flowers. Is there something you're wanting to ask me?'

Dan nodded. 'I came to ask your permission, Mrs Mercer.'

Millie saw Ava flush in anticipation and felt her palms go moist. She did not dare look at her mother.

'Well, ask away then, lad,' Teresa encouraged.

He stood up and went round the table to stand beside Millie, giving Teresa a challenging look. 'It's your daughter I've come to see, Mrs Mercer.' Turning to Millie, he grinned. 'I'd like to take her out to the Egyptian Ballroom tonight.'

Ava gasped, Teresa reddened.

'Millie?' she said sharply. 'Surely not! You don't even know her!'

'I know her enough to want to take her out dancing,' Dan replied, undaunted by the shocked looks. 'I met her at the pictures and I think she's canny. And I can see now where she gets her looks from, Mrs Mercer.'

Teresa's protest died on her lips, dumbfounded by his mixture of flattery and boldness. She looked at the burning cheeks of her daughter. 'Millie, you never mentioned this to me,' she accused.

Dan quickly intervened. 'I asked her not to,' he smiled. 'I wanted to do this properly and come here and ask for myself. Do things the respectable way.'

Teresa was disarmed by this. 'Well, I don't know. I suppose there's no harm in it. You seem like a good lad to me.'

Ava interrupted frostily. 'She's only seventeen! She's far too young to be going to the Egyptian Ballroom on her own,' she complained petulantly. 'You've never let me go!'

Dan turned and smiled at his cousin. 'You could come too. We'll make up a foursome with Walter. We'll have a really grand night out.'

Ava coloured, seeing it was impossible to refuse such a suggestion without losing out completely.

'That seems all right to me,' Teresa declared. 'You can both go, as long as you're safely home at a reasonable hour. And I hold you responsible for that, Dan.' She shot him a warning look.

'You can rely on me,' he smiled. Turning to Millie, he gave her a triumphant look. 'Walter and me'll come by at seven then.'

Millie's heart leapt. 'Good luck for this afternoon,' she managed to say, before Dan disappeared out the back door with a wave.

As she turned back, she caught sight of Ava's thunderous face. It was a look of pure loathing. But Teresa did not allow Ava to pick an argument. 'Back to work,' she said briskly. 'I'll not have you falling out over lads, do you hear?'

Ava pulled a petulant, mutinous face. 'Why should I take orders from you?' she said rudely. 'You're just my father's housekeeper.'

Teresa flashed her an angry look. 'Don't cross me, Ava, or you'll not go dancing tonight. Your father won't stand for any nonsense either, so don't think you can go telling tales to him. Dan has chosen to court Millie and that's his choice. You should be happy with Walter. He's a fine lad and a credit to his mother. What more do you want?'

Millie was thankful for her mother's support, but she was unnerved by the spiteful look on Ava's face. The girl did not argue further, but flounced out of the kitchen and banged the door in ill-temper. Later, making ready in their room for the dance, Millie was relieved that Ava said little, apart from a few barbed comments about keeping secrets from her. Ava wore a new dress that she had gone out and bought that afternoon, made of beige satin with black lace cuffs and collar. Millie made do with a plain purple dress that she had borrowed from Elsie. It was too short in the arms and it came to just below her knees. She kept yanking it down in case her mother thought it too short and revealing. Elsie came rushing in with a necklace of paste jewellery and a matching headband.

'Here, I've borrowed these from our Mary,' she panted. 'They'll go canny with the dress and it'll stop you wearing that awful hat.'

'Ta very much, Elsie.' Millie tried them on with delight, dashing over to the stained oval mirror that hung above the washstand. She could not believe how the cheap jewels transformed the dull dress, the headband making her look much older.

'You look like Clara Bow!' Elsie teased. 'Doesn't she, Ava?'

Ava gave them both a sullen look as she made for the door. 'Hurry up, we don't want to keep them waiting.'

As she disappeared, Elsie pulled a face behind her back. 'Old misery-guts,' she muttered. 'You look just grand.' She pinched Millie's cheeks to bring colour to her pale face and told her to bite her lips, then the girls clattered down the stairs together, laughing. Elsie had agreed to take Millie's place at the Palace that evening so she did not lose her job.

When they burst into the smoky kitchen, Dan and Walter were already there. Dan broke off his conversation with Teresa and stared. Gone was the bashful girl with the untidy curls. Millie's dark hair gleamed in snaking waves from under a silver headband like a filmstar's, accentuating her lively eyes. Her cheeks were flushed and her lips looked reddened. A simple string of silver and green jewels hung about her slim neck, bringing glamour to a plain purple dress that was too tight for her. Dan's pulse began to race at the glimpse of knee he caught as she hurried into the room and gave him a broad smile.

He stood up. 'You look beautiful, Millie,' he smiled, and stepped towards her.

Millie flushed with pleasure, glancing at her mother nervously. But Teresa was staring at her too as if she did not quite recognise her, her mouth quivering.

'Yes, you do,' she murmured, her eyes glistening in the lamplight.

'Let's be off then,' Ava snapped, breaking the intense atmosphere. 'We don't want to be late.'

Walter obediently followed her to the door, and Millie fumbled for her jacket, gabbling to her mother that they would not be late. Out in the dark, Dan grabbed her hand and linked arms possessively.

'I'm the proudest man in Ashborough tonight,' he whispered into her ear, and Millie felt the excitement leap inside her. The dark hid the daily squalor of ash lanes turned to quagmires in the rain, the billowing smoke from coal trains and the skyline of pit wheels and chimney stacks. Instead, the shops glowed with phosphorescent light like Aladdin's caves, while laughter and expectant voices rang out through the dank stillness above the soft neigh of horses from the Co-operative stables.

'So how did you get on at Bedlington?' Millie asked, trying to sound calm.

'Won three-nil,' Dan replied. 'I scored twice. And there was a scout from Gateshead watching.'

Millie glanced at his animated face. 'Did he come to watch you?'

'Well, put it this way, I reckon I'll not be staying with the Comrades long. It's just a matter of time before I'm picked for a professional team.'

Millie nudged him. 'You're very sure of yourself, Dan Nixon.'

He grinned at her. 'Aye, I am. When it comes to football, anyway.'

'And lasses, so I hear,' Millie teased.

Dan shot her a look. 'You shouldn't listen to idle gossip. There's only one lass that interests me and she's right here beside me.'

Millie laughed, delighted. 'So why didn't you stay down in London?'

Dan's face hardened. 'I was playing semi-professional, but some people had it in for me, didn't want me to get on, said I didn't have the right temperament.' He turned to her, his expression passionate. 'I play hard, Millie, and I don't mind taking a bit of punishment on the pitch. But I don't play dirty. You should see some of the kickings I've taken, but I don't complain. Maybe I have lost me temper once or twice, but I score goals. You've got to feel fire in your belly to keep doing that week after week.'

Millie looked on in awe as he continued to

speak about the game, the words tumbling out of him like coals from a tub. Up till now she had only seen the light-hearted side of Dan, his teasing and jokes and flattery. But now he spoke of football with a seriousness and intensity of which she had not thought him capable.

'It's me life, Millie. One day I'm going to play First Division. I'm not going to stop down the pit like me dad or me brothers, be worn down at forty. I'm going to play for Newcastle United – be up there with the gods like Bill Appleyard and Albert Shepherd.'

These were familiar names to Millie, who recalled Graham's enthusiasm for Newcastle before the war, when they had been League champions three times and FA Cup winners in 1910.

'Colin Veitch was me brother's favourite,' she said without thinking.

'Aye, Veitch! I didn't know you had a brother,' Dan said, regarding her.

Millie felt her stomach twist. 'I – I don't now,' she said quickly. 'He died in the war.'

'I'm sorry,' he said, squeezing her arm. And because of his sympathy and because she yearned to impress him, Millie could not stop herself repeating her fantasy about her brother's heroics and his tragic, glorious death.

All at once, they were outside the dance hall. They had been talking so much, she had not noticed. Ava turned on the steps to berate them for dawdling and they swept in past the two large potted palms in the entrance. This time they went into the main ballroom, its magnificent polished parquet floor feeling springy underfoot. The hall was already crowded and the band was playing. Even Ava had her mouth open in wonder.

The evening sped by with dancing, supper in the buffet upstairs and then more dancing. Millie, awkward at first, soon relaxed as Dan led her around the dance floor and taught her the steps. She wondered how many other girls he had held in his arms and whether they had felt as strongly for him as she did, then pushed such uncomfortable thoughts from her mind. He was attentive only to her, planning future nights together.

'There's Bonfire Night coming up, and a fancy dress here next week. We can dress up Egyptian, seeing as you're daft about all this,' he teased, waving his hand at the décor. 'We can hire costumes from that place on Dyke Road.'

'I'd love that,' Millie grinned.

All too soon the evening was over and they were tumbling out into the cold night once more. It was then that Millie was stopped in her tracks by a familiar shout from the street.

'Millie Mercer, is that you?'

The steps were crowded and Millie wondered for a moment if she had heard correctly. Dan hesitated, glancing at her quizzically. Her heart began to pound as a girl thrust her way up the steps through the departing dancers. She pushed past Ava to reach her.

'Millie, it is you!'

'Ella?' Millie cried, finding herself staring into the face of her old friend. 'Ella!' Instinctively they flung their arms around each other like long-lost sisters, gasping each other's names in joy and gabbling in disbelief.

'What are you doing here?' Millie asked.

'Visiting me auntie,' Ella explained. 'I'm back for a week from London. This is home now since me mam died.'

'Your mam?' Millie gasped. 'I didn't know.'

'Aye, two years back.' Ella grimaced. 'But how could I tell you, disappearing like that? No one would tell me where you'd gone – not even your Aunt Hannah. I heard rumours, mind, about your mam setting up with another man, but I didn't believe it.'

Millie felt panic. Ella was garrulous at seeing her; she would give her away.

'Where does your aunt live, Ella?' she asked, swiftly taking her by the arm and trying to steer her back down the steps. Perhaps no one else had heard Ella's remarks in the general hubbub. 'I'll come and see you there before you go, explain everything.'

Ella glanced over Millie's shoulder at her handsome partner and the scowling friend who was eyeing her intently. 'Yes, I'd like that.'

Millie tried to block her inquisitive stares. 'Eeh, Ella! You've picked up a posh accent,' she teased. 'You can tell you've been in London for years. I did write, at the beginning, but you mustn't have got me letters.'

'No, nothing,' Ella said. 'You could come back now to my auntie's, just for a little chat. Bring your friends.' Ella gave Dan and Walter an appreciative glance. 'Thirty-six Dene Row.'

'We can't now,' Millie said quickly. 'I promised Mam I'd be back as soon as the dance finished.'

'Are you not even going to introduce us to your friend, Millie?' Dan intervened, following them down the steps.

'Ella Parks,' Ella smiled, and held out her hand, seeing that Millie was quite tongue-tied. 'Millie and me grew up together.'

Dan shook hands. 'I didn't know Morpeth had so many pretty lasses,' he winked.

Ella's fair face blushed. 'Morpeth? No, we come from Craston!' She nudged Millie. 'Have you been trying to make us out as posher than we really are, Millie Mercer?'

Millie froze in fear. She had spent three years trying to erase the past from her mind until she had almost convinced herself it had never been. Craston belonged to the lanky, childish Millie, someone who no longer existed, who would never have been courted by the likes of Dan Nixon. But Ella continued in her usual indiscreet way, unaware of Millie's predicament, while Millie stood paralysed, not knowing how to stop her.

'How is your mam, by the way? I often used to think about you and wonder why you left. Mind you, I suppose she'd had enough. With all that business over your Graham and no one speaking and your dad locked out the pit. Do you ever see your dad these days?'

There was a stunned pause as everyone turned to stare at Millie. She was suddenly aware of Ava beside her.

Ava questioned, 'From Craston, did you say?'

'Yes.' Ella smiled obligingly, then caught the look of horror on Millie's face. 'Have I said something wrong?'

Ava rounded on Millie. 'Have you been lying to us all this time, Millie? You and your mother? Pretending to be someone you're not! Who exactly *are* you?'

Millie shrunk away from her spiteful stare, looking to Dan for help. But he was baffled too. 'Millie?' he asked. She began to shake, unable to answer them.

Ava pressed her. 'And what's this about your father? You told us he was dead. Is he, Millie? Or is that another lie? To think my father took you both in thinking your mam was a widow! What sort of woman could lie about a thing like that? It's disgusting! If he thought she was still married, he'd throw her out!'

This vitriol against her mother was too much. Millie met Ava's look as defiantly as she could. 'Yes, I am from Craston, and I'm not ashamed of it,' she said, trembling. 'I only kept quiet about it to help Mam.' She looked around at the shocked faces. They might hate her now, but they were going to hear her side of the story; she had nothing to lose by telling it. 'Me dad was on unofficial strike – they were cutting wages and we had nowt to live off. I went to bed hungry every night. Then the bosses brought in scabs. They were going to evict us.' She challenged them with her look. 'Me mam wasn't going to wait for them to hoy us out in front of all the neighbours, end up on the beach like the others. That's why she left me dad. To stop us starving!'

The steps had emptied, people hurrying away from the argument. As the doorman came over to see what was going on, Dan shifted uncomfortably. But Ella spoke up.

'But we would have helped out if we'd known, Millie,' she insisted. 'Why didn't you go to your neighbours for help? That's what they're for.'

Tears sprang to Millie's eyes as she faced her old friend. 'Because they despised us,' she hissed. 'They wouldn't have lifted a finger to help. You know very well what it was like for us after Graham died.' She turned to the others, seeing the embarrassed looks on the men's faces, the stony expression on Ava's. 'My brother was no war hero,' she croaked in humiliation. 'He was shot for desertion. A coward! It finished me dad. And now I don't even know if he's alive any more...' Tears flooded her eyes. She glanced at Dan, hurt by his silence. 'We came here with nothing, me and me mam. Just common Mercers, who no one in Craston had the time of day for. Mam was just trying to make a new life for us, that's all. Was that too much to ask? Was it!' she sobbed, pushing her way past them all.

The next moment she was running up the street into the darkness, desperate to be away from them and their accusing stares. What a fool she had been to think life was any different in Ashborough, that people would understand what her mother had done and forgive their covering up.

'Millie!' It sounded like Dan shouting after her. 'Millie, wait!' But she did not turn around or lessen her pace. The evening was ruined and her

107

secret was out. Things could never be the same between her and Dan again, and she was too ashamed to turn back now. She ran on through the smoky, frozen air until she thought her lungs would burst. The steps of the runner who had tried to catch her up slackened to walking pace. She still heard them at a cautious distance, making sure she got home safely, but reluctant to catch her up.

When Millie reached the hotel, she burst into the kitchen in a panic to reach her mother before Ava could fling her accusations. She found Teresa sitting by the fire in the hotel parlour with Moody, alone like some old married couple silently content in each other's company. Millie collapsed at her mother's feet and burst into tears.

'What in the world's the matter with you? What's happened?'

But Millie was incoherent as she tried to confess what she had said. Moody rose, stirring from his torpor by the fire.

'Has the lad harmed you?' he demanded.

Before Millie could answer, Ava ran into the room, a cold draught following her.

'Tell him,' she demanded. 'Tell my dad what you told me, you little liar!'

Millie felt her mother's arms go round her protectively. 'Hold your tongue,' Teresa scolded.

Ava advanced on her like a predator smelling blood, and Millie knew then that this was the opportunity the girl had been waiting for all these years to put them in their place.

'I'll not hold my tongue – not for you, Mrs

Mercer from *Craston!*' She spat out the name.

Moody stared in incomprehension. 'Ava?'

His daughter went to him. 'They've lied to us, Father. *She* has!' she said, stabbing a finger at Teresa. 'She's no respectable widow from Morpeth. She's married to a sacked pitman from Craston – walked out on him because they were going to be evicted! Common as muck they are, the Mercers,' Ava sneered, slipping her arm through her father's in solidarity. 'They've made fools of us, Father,' she continued, seeing Teresa's devastated expression. 'And that's not all. You won't see *her* son's name on the roll of honour at Craston war memorial. Do you want to know why?'

Teresa gave out a howl of pain. 'No!' she gasped. 'Millie, you didn't say...?'

'What?' growled Moody, quite dazed by the revelations.

'He was shot as a coward,' Ava said in triumph, 'a disgrace to his family. Millie said no one would speak to them in Craston, that's another reason they came here. To think you took them in out of the goodness of your heart, and all the time they were living a lie. To think we were taken in by all those stories of a dead father and a hero for a brother. But bad will out, I say!'

Millie watched her mother's anguished face as if she had been physically struck. But seeing the effect on Moody, she felt fear shoot through her body. He was livid.

'Teresa!' he roared. 'Is it true? Have you lied to me? Are you still someone else's wife?' He drew up his large, bulky body in a menacing posture.

Her mother stood her ground. 'I was when I first came here,' she said trembling, 'though if he's still alive, God only knows.'

'See,' cried Ava, 'I told you.'

'You've come to my bed, knowing all the time you were committing adultery?' he shuddered. 'Like a common whore!'

Even Ava gasped at the savagery of his words.

But Teresa was not cowed. 'So it was all right to bed a defenceless widow, but not another man's wife, was it?' she answered with contempt. 'You were nothing until I came here, Joseph. No one else stayed five minutes with you and your spoilt daughter. Maybe I used you, but you've done the same with me. And I'll not apologise. I'm a mother first and I'd rather have died than see Millie thrown out on the street or be locked up in the workhouse!'

Moody let out a cry of anger and shoved Teresa away from him. 'Get out of my house! You and your brat, get out!'

Teresa stumbled against the horsehair sofa, but came back at him.

'Don't be so daft! Who's going to run this place for you if we go? Who's going to see to the guests upstairs in the morning? Ava doesn't lift a finger, and neither do you. You can't do without me, Joseph, and you know it.'

Moody wavered an instant, his hand raised to strike.

'Don't listen to her, Father,' Ava pleaded. 'We can manage on our own. We've got Elsie.'

'Elsie won't stop another day if we leave,' Teresa countered, 'she's always said as much.' She could see that Moody was confused. She knew he was a weak and lazy man who would get over the blow to his pride sooner than look for another housekeeper. She appealed to him. 'We've made this into a respectable hotel, Joseph, one that decent folk like to visit. When I came here it was no more than a rough bar. Are you going to throw all that away?'

'You lied to me,' Moody accused, still red with anger.

Teresa bowed her head. 'I know I did, and I'm sorry. Not sorry for what I did, but sorry you had to find out like this.' She gave Millie a furious look.

'It wasn't my fault,' Millie whispered. 'We bumped into Ella Parks.'

'That lass!' Teresa let out an impatient sigh. 'Never anything but trouble.'

Ava stamped her foot in petulance, seeing her advantage over the Mercers slipping away. 'What about *me,* Father?' she railed, working herself up until tears came, as Millie had seen her do many times to get her own way. 'Do you care more about that woman than me?'

'Of course not,' Moody answered in agitation. He turned to his daughter, looking defeated. 'But Teresa's right, I can't do without her. You've never been interested in running the hotel like your mother was. All you care about is shopping and dancing and lads.'

Ava howled. 'You don't love me any more! You care more for Millie than me!'

Moody looked stricken. 'Of course I don't. I care about my little treasure more than anything,' he crooned, putting his arm about her shoulders. 'Please don't be upset.' She turned into his burly hug and allowed herself to be comforted. 'This has been a shock for us both,' he said wearily, 'but we'll just have to learn to live with it and get on.'

'Not me!' Ava threw Millie a hateful look. 'I refuse to carry on sharing a room with *her!* I want my own one. I don't trust her and I don't like her any more.'

'Millie can share with Elsie in the attic,' Teresa said quickly, giving her daughter a warning look, defying her to object. Moody nodded.

Millie winced at the open hostility. She pulled herself up from her half-crouched position on the floor. No one was going to stand up for her, she thought in painful realisation. Her mother might be able to overcome the humiliation of being found out at last, but she would blame her for the crisis. It was now impossible to remain friends with Ava after such a personal attack. There was no place for her here any more and no reason to stay now that Dan knew the truth about her and must surely despise her for pretending to be better than she really was.

'I'm not stopping here,' she told them bluntly. 'I'm not blaming you, Uncle Joseph. It's only right that you take your Ava's side.' She looked at her mother. 'I'm sorry, Mam, that I've brought all this on you. But I'm glad I don't have to lie any more, and if people can't accept me for who I am, then that's a problem for them, not me.' At this she gave Ava a pitying look, then walked calmly towards the door. Glancing back, she added, 'I'll go to Mrs Dodswell's on Monday and ask her to find me a job away from Ashborough.' Then she left.

They listened in silence to her footsteps mounting the stairs, growing fainter as she climbed to the attic. Teresa's heart ached to think of her daughter back in the room they had shared on their arrival. She had been so dignified in her quiet denial of them, so painfully reminiscent of her dead brother in that regretful backward glance. She wanted to rush after the unhappy girl and tell her it did not matter what she had said. But she could not go now and risk igniting Joseph or Ava's volatile tempers again. She had stood up to them, but only just. She was secretly aghast that Millie wanted to leave, but maybe it would be for the best until things calmed down with Ava. Later she would sneak up and make sure Millie was comforted. Now she had to look after herself.

She turned and smiled apologetically. 'Let me get us all some cocoa before bed,' she said briskly. 'In the morning this will all seem a fuss about nothing.'

CHAPTER 6

The next day the atmosphere was tense around the hotel. Moody kept to his room and Millie's mother seemed wary of speaking to her. After completing the morning's chores, Millie escaped from Ava's malicious looks and asides and went to the Presbyterian church. The only person she knew who would understand her situation was Effie, and she longed for her quiet advice and stoical humour. She did not often attend the cavernous black edifice on Myrtle Terrace because she was usually making the Sunday dinner, but today Elsie volunteered to do it. 'You make yourself scarce,' she ordered and shooed her out of the hotel for the morning.

So she hurried through the icy rain that was blowing inland from the sea, head bent and fingers numbed. Inside she squeezed into a pew at the back and craned around for Effie. There was no sign of her in her usual pew on the left-hand side, four rows from the front, where she liked the view of the pulpit. Millie sank back, allowing the fug from the stove to envelop her and thaw her out. Why was Effie not there? she worried. She had been tired and listless these past few weeks and her racking cough had come early this year. But she always managed to drag herself to church, however bad she felt. It was no surprise that her family were not there, for her sons had not accompanied her since they were boys. Millie had gone in the safe knowledge that she would not bump into Dan.

At the end of the service, Millie wondered if she should call round at Tenter Terrace to see if Effie was all right, but her courage failed her. She had no wish to confront Dan or Walter on the doorstep and compound the humiliation of the night before. She would be the talk of the street already, she guessed. Mungo Nixon would be confirmed in his suspicion of her as a troublesome lass with a sinful mother who had never deserved his wife's attention and care. Millie turned for home, comforting herself that tomorrow was Effie's wash day and that she would see her in the morning after visiting Mrs Dodswell. Effie would be expecting her, and if she was bound for London it might be her last chance of seeing her friend.

Dan had sat up all night with his mother, watching her frail waxen face and listening to her ragged breathing. He and Walter had gone drinking after the terrible scenes outside the ballroom, shaken by the revelations about Millie and her mother and shocked by Ava's temper. They had downed several beers in quick succession, relieved to be out of the crossfire, and made a pact not to go near the hotel until tempers had calmed.

'Who would've thought Millie was hiding such a past?' Walter had shaken his head. 'She seemed that canny and respectable – sweet-natured.'

'She still is,' Dan defended her. 'It's not her

fault what happened.'

Walter snorted. 'She lied to you, man, you should steer well clear. Imagine what Mam would say if she knew!'

Walter had added, 'By, I didn't know Ava had such a sharp tongue. Think I'll keep me distance from that one an' all. Mind that lass Ella Parks was bonny.'

'Aye,' Dan had agreed, but he felt wretched about Millie. He cared for her and wanted to tell her he did not mind about her past. He should have tried harder to catch her up and not let Walter put him off so easily. He searched his pockets for enough to buy a final drink.

'Mind you,' Walter grunted, 'I'm not surprised Millie wanted to cover up about her family. Imagine the shame of having a brother who was shot for cowardice. No, lad, you're well out of it – stick to your footie.'

So they had meandered home in the fog that was turning to a drizzly rain, and thought to find the house in darkness. But surprisingly they had discovered their father and Grant arguing heatedly with Mrs Dickson from next door.

'You should call in the doctor,' Mrs Dickson was insisting. 'I'll sit with her while you fetch him.'

'Not the doctor,' Mungo had grumbled. 'We'll see how she is in the morning.'

'I'll pay the doctor's bill,' Grant had snapped. 'I'm off to fetch him.'

'You'll go nowhere.' His father blocked his way. 'You can't call the doctor out at this time of night. Your mother wouldn't want the fuss. She just needs rest. She'll be better in the morning.'

'She might be dead in the morning!' Grant shouted.

When Mrs Dickson saw the other sons, she seized Dan by the arm. 'I'm that glad you're back. Your mam's collapsed. We think she fainted and fell down the stairs. She's poorly bad. But she's been asking for you, lad.'

Dan felt his head spin and wished he had not drunk so much. He and Walter clattered upstairs and found their mother lying in the old iron bed, propped up on pillows, eyes closed. There was a large swelling on her brow where she must have hit her head as she fell, and Dan was shocked by how gaunt and old she looked. So while the others argued downstairs about the doctor and Mrs Dickson gave up and went home, he had kept vigil by her bedside, willing her to wake up and speak to him.

As he sobered up, he was overwhelmed by remorse. Why had he stayed away so long in London, or at least not visited more often? His mother had grown old before his very eyes. But surely it was impossible that she would never wake up again and smile at him? he worried. In the depth of the night, he had held her hand and talked quietly to her about his life and his ambitions, his regrets and his fondness for her. He confessed secrets that burdened his conscience and that he could tell to no one else. Yet she did not stir or show any signs that she could hear him.

'I'm sorry I've been such a bad son – I know how much you've cared for me,' he whispered.

117

'You always tried to shield us from me dad – stuck up for me. Don't die now, Mam. Please don't die!'

As grey light finally filtered through the small window, Dan stood up, stiff and dispirited. Grant came upstairs to say he was going for Dr MacKenzie, and they tried to rouse their mother to drink a glass of water. For the first time in the long night, Effie opened her eyes. Her look was unfocused and confused, her breathing shallow.

'Dan?' she mouthed.

'Aye, I'm here, Mam,' Dan reassured, coming close.

'You're back,' she murmured with a ghost of a smile.

'Aye, I'm back.' Dan smiled too.

'Did you have a nice evening with Millie?' Effie asked.

'Canny,' Dan mumbled. His mother looked pleased. 'Here, try and sip this,' he said, awkwardly pushing the mug of water to her lips and cupping his hand around her head. The effort made her splutter and cough and she turned her face away in exhaustion.

'We won yesterday, Mam,' Dan tried to cheer her, 'and there was a scout from Gateshead Vulcans watching. We're going to have a grand season.'

But Effie had closed her eyes again and appeared to be sleeping at once. Later, when the doctor came, Dan went downstairs to douse his bleary eyes with icy water and munch on a dripping sandwich which Walter offered him. Effie's sons sat around the kitchen table, slurping tea and casting resentful glances towards their father, who was sitting by the fire reading the newspaper as if it was a normal Sunday morning.

When Dr MacKenzie appeared, his face was grim. 'She's very weak,' he told them. 'She needs to be in hospital. I'll send for an ambulance to take her in.'

Mungo flung down his newspaper. 'Hospital?' he snorted. 'She's not that poorly. She can't be!'

The doctor was short. 'She's got pneumonia. She's very ill, Mr Nixon.'

Mungo looked horrified. 'She's not going to die, is she?'

Dr MacKenzie said, more gently, 'We'll do what we can. Just say a few prayers.'

Dan saw his father sink back into his seat, his face drained in shock. Dan rushed upstairs. His mother was staring at the door as he came in, and she stretched out weak arms towards him, her breathing laboured.

'I'm dying,' she gasped, struggling for breath. Dan put his arms around her.

'No you're not!' he exclaimed. 'We're going to get you well again. They're taking you to the hospital soon.'

Effie tried to raise her head and speak, her feverish eyes full of urgency. 'M-M...'

'What is it, Mam?' Dan bent close, trying to make out her words.

'Promise me,' she whispered.

'What, Mam, promise what?' Dan asked.

'Look after her,' Effie said, her throat rattling.

'Who?' Dan asked, worried by his mother's agitation.

'Millie. Look after Millie for me.' She sank back, her face strained and her chest heaving at the exertion. 'She's been like a daughter to me.'

Dan looked at his mother in astonishment. Why should she be thinking of Millie and why ask him to take care of the girl? he wondered, with a pang of guilt for the way he had abandoned her earlier. But he nodded and said, 'Aye, of course I will,' just to keep Effie happy. It was typical of his kind-hearted mother to worry about the young girl who came to help out. Of course she would have no idea about the Mercers' shameful past, and there was no point upsetting her with it now.

Effie closed her eyes once more and drifted back into feverish sleep. She was barely conscious when the ambulance came to collect her. Dan and Grant carried her down the narrow stairs and out to the back lane. They slipped around in the black mud, nearly losing their footing, and watched the horse-drawn ambulance trundle and slither away in the rain. Dan turned to see his father, pale and fearful, standing in his braces by the back door.

'We'll visit tomorrow after our shift,' Grant reassured him.

Mungo said nothing. Shortly afterwards he went out, and did not reappear until after dark, by which time he was so drunk his sons had to help him into the house. They had just got him up to bed and he was snoring loudly when Dr MacKenzie appeared at the door with the news. Effie had never regained consciousness. She had died in her sleep at tea-time. Dan looked at his brothers, appalled. Pushing past the doctor, he rushed out into the dark before they could see him weep.

Millie sat once more in Mrs Dodswell's crowded parlour. It seemed an age since she had visited that first time with her mother, in their desperate search for work and shelter. Then, she had been timid and afraid; now she felt braver. Now, first thing on Monday morning, she was here of her own choosing, attempting to make something of her life, looking forward rather than back. She took a deep breath and explained how she was just ordinary Millie Mercer from Craston, gambling that the plump agent would care more about her commission than Millie's past. Mrs Dodswell listened with widening eyes, but at the end she patted Millie's hand and said, 'I always thought your mother was covering up for something, but she's not the first to have to do so. Besides, you shouldn't blame yourself, you were just a young lass. Your mother's brought you up well and that's all the grand folk in London need to know.'

Millie felt a flood of relief at her lack of condemnation, and she stuttered her gratitude. Mrs Dodswell agreed to write on her behalf to the agency in Baker Street, London, for whom she liaised.

'Girls from the north are very popular as domestic servants,' she assured her, with a confident nod. 'I've been sending girls to place since before the war, and the demand has never been higher. You're strong and hard-working, and you've got the height and bearing for a parlour maid. Your prospects for domestic service are excellent, Millie.'

Millie signed the form, encouraged by the woman's enthusiasm, and was about to leave when Mrs Dodswell stopped her.

'It's terrible about Effie Nixon, isn't it? So sudden.'

Millie's heart jerked. 'What about her?'

The agent's florid face flushed in confusion. 'Oh dear! I thought you must have heard, with you so keen to get away from Ashborough all of a sudden.' One look at Millie's aghast face told her otherwise. 'Oh, I'm sorry. Dear me. I just heard last night from Mrs Dickson.'

'Heard what?' Millie demanded hoarsely.

'Sit down,' Mrs Dodswell insisted, steering Millie back into a chair. 'I'm afraid Mrs Nixon died yesterday.'

Millie gasped in horror. Not Effie! she thought in disbelief. She could not bear to think of kind Effie dead. The older woman was telling her details, but Millie could not take them in. All she could think about was how she had longed to talk to Dan's mother today about what had happened on Saturday night, and explain why she was going away.

'That's terrible,' she said in distress. 'I must go round. I'm always expected on a Monday...' Then she burst into tears.

Mrs Dodswell fussed around her with a handkerchief and fetched a cup of water. 'I'm sorry you had to hear this way. I know you were fond of her – as Mrs Nixon was of you. She often said so.' Millie struggled to compose herself, but

Mrs Dodswell was dubious. 'You've had a shock, dear. Wait a few days before you visit. From what I hear, Mr Nixon wants to be left alone.'

But Millie could not wait. She insisted she was fine and rushed round to Tenter Terrace, half hoping Mrs Dodswell had got the story wrong. But as she neared number 28, she saw that the blinds were drawn and there was no sign of activity in the washhouse as normal. She slowed to a walk and fretted over whether she should call.

Deciding to be brave, she went into the yard and knocked on the closed back door. Grant loomed in the entrance as it opened a fraction. He came out.

'Er, sorry, Millie,' he mumbled, looking beyond her shoulder, embarrassed to catch her eye.

'I know, I've heard, you don't have to explain,' she said quickly, seeing his distress. 'I just came to see if I can help. With the washing and that…'

They stood in awkward silence, both feeling inadequate. Mungo's voice barked ill-temperedly from the kitchen, 'Who is it?'

'It's Millie,' Grant answered, 'offering to help out.'

'Tell her to bugger off!' he shouted back drunkenly. 'I don't want any women fussing round here, do you hear? No one!'

Grant looked at Millie, his stern brown eyes softening. 'I'm sorry. It's been a shock for us all.'

Millie nodded, swallowing hard. 'Is Dan at home?' She was sure he was nearby; she could sense it. Grant hesitated a moment, and then shook his head.

'He's very upset about his mam,' he said. 'Maybe leave it for a few days, eh?' Millie's vision blurred with tears, and she turned away, unable to speak. As she trudged back into the lane, she heard him add, 'Ta for coming, lass.'

Millie glanced back, wondering if he knew about her family shame. But Grant's impassive face gave nothing away. Yet worse than her humiliation was the knowledge that Dan did not want to see her, and she cursed herself once more for her boastful tongue. She hurried away quite desolate.

Millie never found the courage to return that week. She was subdued and kept to herself, working slavishly to stem the grief inside. Once she tried to tell her mother how much she missed Effie, but Teresa took offence. 'It's not as if she was family,' she complained jealously. So Millie kept quiet. Elsie tried to comfort her, and Millie was grateful that the country girl felt no ill-will towards them for their shameful past. But only word from Dan would ease her wretchedness. She hoped in vain that he might appear to tell her that he still cared for her and it did not matter to him that she had lied about her past.

On the day of Effie's funeral, word came through from Mrs Dodswell that the agency in London was offering Millie a job as between-maid at a house near Hyde Park. She accepted it. Millie, Teresa and the Moodys attended the funeral service at Myrtle Terrace Presbyterian Church, which was packed with mourners. While Ava fidgeted and Teresa muttered that she hated funerals, Millie watched the pale autumn sun filtering through the high plain windows and thought how Effie would have loved the burning orange of the leaves outside. Anything that brought colour into the drab streets around Tenter Terrace had always delighted her.

Only Moody went to the Nixons' house afterwards for the wake, telling the others to go home. Ava, in a sulk at not being taken to Tenter Terrace, defied Teresa and went out for a walk.

'You're in mourning, you should show more respect on the day of your cousin's funeral,' Teresa scolded.

'Don't talk to me about respect,' Ava answered scornfully, and banged out of the house. The girl was being extra difficult since the recent revelations, and Teresa had to bite back her criticism. She could risk no further upset.

Teresa waited tensely for Joseph's return, fearing his mood after a sorrowful drinking session with Mungo. 'It'll bring back his own memories of losing his wife,' she complained to Millie, 'and I'll have to bear the brunt. The funeral will set him off again, it's not healthy.'

That was typical of her mother, Millie thought, to have no truck with the past. She had not even wanted to attend Effie's funeral and had only gone for appearance's sake. Since Graham's death, funerals were to be shunned. She was right about the effect on Moody, though, who came rolling home drunk and morose and shut himself in his room for the next three days, allowing only Teresa to console him. Millie saw how Joseph leaned on her mother and realised just how much

125

he had come to depend on her. For that reason she knew her mother's position at the hotel was secure. Teresa had made herself indispensable, and not even Ava could get rid of her, despite her animosity.

With Ava's continual sniping comments and the atmosphere of gloom in the hotel, Millie began to long for her departure to London. Yet as the day approached, she became restless at the thought of leaving without ever seeing Dan again. Defying his father's strict adherence to mourning, he had played in the match that Saturday, but did not come back for tea with the rest of the team. He appeared to be avoiding the hotel, for which Ava blamed her. Millie had caught a glimpse of him in the distance, leaving Burt Park on his own with a black armband over his tan coat, an unusually solitary sight.

Time was slipping away and her mother was preoccupied with getting her fitted out for her journey to London. The agency had sent the money for a single train fare and uniform, which would have to be reimbursed out of her wages once she began work. But it was Teresa who finally exploded with exasperation.

'Go and see the lad!' she cried. 'I can't bear all this moping around.'

'But what if he won't speak to me?' Millie worried.

'Then he's not worth the bother,' Teresa answered bluntly. 'Maybe you acted a bit daft with your stories, but if he can't take you for what you are, then he's not worth losing sleep over. It's not your fault that you had a feckless father and a cowardly brother. And it's me who deserted me husband and set up with another man. I caused all the pretending and lying. I'm the one who's going to hell, not you!'

Millie rushed over and hugged her mother. 'Don't say that, Mam!' Teresa laughed bleakly and hugged her back.

'You know I don't want you to go, don't you? I'd much rather it were Ava who was leaving, but I can't force her to go. Anyhow, you'll be better off away from her, and you're lucky to have this chance of going to London. You're old enough to stand on your own two feet now.' Millie nodded bravely, but her mother held on to her. 'I'll miss you, silly Millie.' Teresa kissed her head briefly. The old childish expression and the unexpected tenderness made Millie's eyes sting with tears. For the first time in her life she was leaving her mother, and all at once she was fearful. The arguments and battles of the past did not seem so bad after all.

'I'll miss you more,' Millie promised tearfully. They hugged each other fiercely and wept.

That evening Millie went to say goodbye to Mr Peters and Major Hall at the Palace, where Elsie had taken over her part-time job.

'Don't spend all your wages on chocolates,' Mr Peters teased.

'She won't have to.' The major winked. 'There'll be too many young men queuing up to buy them for her.'

Millie blushed and told them she would be back to see them soon, though she had no idea when she would return to Ashborough. Before her courage failed her, she hurried round to Tenter Terrace. It did not matter if she made a fool of herself now, she thought, because tomorrow she would be on the train to Newcastle, and then London. She found the house in darkness, with no welcoming glow from the kitchen window. Knocking brought no one to the door. Eventually Mrs Dickson peered out of the neighbouring back door.

'There'll be no one in, pet,' she explained, picking her way carefully over the slippery yard. 'Mr Nixon's on night shift and the lads'll be out. None of them stop in any more, not since dear Effie passed away.'

Millie was seized by both relief and disappointment. 'Out where, Mrs Dickson?'

'Drinking,' she sniffed in disapproval. 'There's no one to check those lads now. They've all taken their mother's death that badly. Mind you, the biggest shock is Mr Nixon. He's taken the pledge!' the neighbour gossiped. 'Effie was on at him for years to give up drinking, but it's taken her death for him to do it. Isn't that just the way? Hasn't improved his temper, mind. Like a mad bull. You'd best keep out his way.'

'That won't be hard, I'm going to place,' Millie told her. 'I just came to say goodbye. I'm off to London the morrow.'

'Fancy that!' Mrs Dickson exclaimed. 'I'll miss you not coming around on wash day.'

Millie was touched, but she was keen to get away before being questioned further. 'Would you just tell Grant and Walter and – er – Dan that I came to say ta-ra?'

'Aye, pet, I'll do that. Take care of yourself.'

Early next morning, in the half-dark, Teresa walked her across the iron bridge to the station platform for the southbound train. Millie was glad that Joseph and Ava were still in bed, or at least avoiding her, for she wanted these last moments alone with her mother. Teresa, enveloped in steam, bustled her into a carriage, not wanting to prolong the parting. They only had time for a peck on the cheek and a stilted exchange before the whistle blew and the train jolted into life.

'Here.' Her mother suddenly thrust a scrap of paper into her hand. 'I forgot this. Ella came round last week with her address in London. I was in two minds whether to give it to you, after all the trouble she caused. But at least it'll be someone you know.'

'Ta, Mam!' Millie blew a grateful kiss.

She leaned out of the carriage to wave, unable to resist a last glance up the platform to see if anyone else had come to wish her well. But no one had. She waved furiously to hide her nerves and smiled as broadly as she could to the retreating figure in the steam and morning mist. Her mother had told her to be brave, and she would be. Millie watched the terraces of Ashborough trundle by until they abruptly petered out into low fields and straggling hedgerows. She tried to cheer herself with the thought that she was on her way to a new life. Dan Nixon had had his chance, she finally admitted.

Teresa kept glancing at the clock throughout the day, trying to imagine where her daughter was. She could not believe how deeply she felt the girl's going, how huge was the emptiness in her heart. She felt as she had done the morning the awful telegram had arrived to tell of Graham's death. She was numb and yet full of pain at the same time. Why had she let her go? she wondered. Why had she not been able to stand up to the Moodys and insist that Millie stayed? But deep down she had feared for Millie. Ava was too vindictive and Joseph too unstable. She could put up with their moods and tantrums, but there was no reason why Millie should. Her daughter would be better off starting a new life elsewhere, no matter how much Teresa would miss her.

Ava and Elsie had gone off to the pictures and Teresa was rinsing out the metal milk churn in the yard when steps approached in the dark. For a few seconds, the sound of heavy pit boots made her heart lurch and forced her mind back to her home in Craston. She straightened up in panic, only to see Dan behind her, dressed in dirty work clothes, his handsome face drawn and wolfish.

'Evening, Mrs Mercer,' he mumbled, his demeanour subdued. 'I came to see Millie.'

Teresa tensed. 'You've left it too late,' she answered. 'She went off on the train this morning.'

Dan's face fell. 'Why didn't she come and tell me sooner? I never knew she was thinking of going away.'

Teresa was instantly angry with him. It was he who had judged them harshly and caused her daughter so much pain. It was just as much this man's fault that Millie was now gone. 'She's been trying to tell you for the past two weeks! It's you that's been avoiding her. Thinking yourself better than the rest of us!' Teresa clasped her fists to her hips in fury. 'You had no business to treat Millie like that – all over her one minute and not speaking to her the next. She had feelings for you. Even this morning she was still hoping you would call round for her. But I told her she was better off without you if you couldn't care for her as she was. Those stories she told were just a young lass's fanciful dreams – there was no harm in them. You can think what you like of me, I don't give two hoots. But Millie deserves better. She's worth a hundred of your kind!'

Dan looked at her, stunned. He was unused to being spoken to so rudely by a woman. He was hurt and baffled, but under his annoyance he felt a wave of guilt. He had not wanted to be associated with Millie's public humiliation on the steps of the Egyptian Ballroom and all too easily had allowed Walter to convince him to stay away. If his mother had not died the following day, would he still have avoided Millie, not wanting to be drawn into her messy life? That was what he always did, he mocked himself, run away from trouble. Yet in the days since his mother's death, her words had kept coming back to haunt him, ordering him to take care of Millie. Keeping to himself since the funeral, he had found his thoughts straying continually to the tall, dark-haired girl. He longed to see her and knew he had judged her too harshly. Mrs Dickson had for-

131

gotten to give him Millie's message until that evening, and he had rushed straight round, still in his damp pit clothes. He felt suddenly desolate that he had missed Millie, but he was not going to be shown up by her censorious mother.

'I came as soon as I heard,' he replied defensively. 'Why did she have to rush off like that?'

'Because of narrow-minded folk like you and Ava,' Teresa said stonily. 'But Millie's made up her own mind. She's going to start a new life for herself where you lot can't hurt her.'

Dan was stung by her words. 'Well, at least me mam didn't live to see what you Mercers were really like. I'm glad of that!'

Teresa advanced towards him. 'Your mam?' she glared, eyes glinting in the gas lamp. 'She was the only one who *did* know! She covered up for us!' Dan gaped at her. 'Aye, she was a good woman, better than you Nixon men deserved. She met my drunken husband in this very yard – helped chase him away. Effie knew why I stopped here as Moody's mistress – she saw the reason sprawled out like a dog in the gutter at her very feet!'

Dan was astounded. 'Mam knew all the time and never said anything?'

Teresa nodded defiantly as they glared at each other. Suddenly the indignation went out of Dan. His shoulders sagged. How like his mother to befriend Millie without judgement. He felt even more ashamed of his own treatment of her, and now he had lost her for good.

He shook his head. 'I'm sorry. I don't know what else to say.'

Teresa's anger lessened at the sight of his forlorn face. 'Aye, well, I'm sorry too. I shouldn't have shouted at you when you've just lost your mother.'

Dan hunched his shoulders. 'No, I should have come sooner. I'm sorry I never got to say goodbye to Millie. Will you tell her?'

Teresa hesitated. She felt a stab of pity for the unhappy young man before her who so obviously grieved for his mother. Yet she was not sure about Dan Nixon. She had been charmed by him as Millie had been, but now she was wary. It would not do to rekindle false hope in her daughter. Deep down she did not trust the handsome Dan, who had turned up after years of not telling his mother where he was. She recognised a spend-thrift drinker when she saw one.

'It's best she's gone from here,' Teresa said curtly, then relented as she rolled the churn towards the back door. 'But aye, I'll tell her.'

They exchanged guarded looks.

'Ta, Mrs Mercer,' Dan said quietly, and walked away.

CHAPTER 7
1924

The job Millie enjoyed most was walking the Halletts' dog around the elegant square in front of their London home. She would take Buster the spaniel for a brisk trot after brushing the hall carpets and cleaning the day nursery and setting it for the children's breakfast. She had taken these early-morning walks right through the winter, sometimes in freezing fog or skating along icy pavements. But she relished those moments of calm, when the world was barely awake and the streets belonged only to early delivery vans and cheerful newspaper boys. She would breathe in the smell of newly lit coal fires and think of home. Walking in the early dawn, past shops that were prising open their shutters like sleepy eyes, she was reminded of Ashborough and felt comforted.

In these quiet hours she thought about her brother, who had spent his final leave in London before going back to the Front. How had he spent his last days of freedom? she wondered. Had he walked around Hyde Park as she did, regretting that he had not come home? Why had he not come home? There were so many things she would have liked to ask him and now never could. And as she tried to imagine what Graham had been doing and thinking, she peered through the dawn light at the shadowy figures as if she could conjure him up. Only recently had she admitted to herself that she was also scouring the park and streets for signs of her father. Maybe he had come to London to find work? Even before the strike, work up north was becoming harder to come by. Away from her mother, she had felt increasingly guilty at the way they had turned their backs on Ellis, and deep down she longed to see him again. Each day she imagined the emotional reunion they would have and how proud he would be to see that she was making her way in the world.

It was hard to believe that she had been working for the American Halletts for six months now. April had come and the squares blazed with spring flowers, their trees already bursting with green shoots. At first everything had seemed so bewildering in the bustling tall house, where the staff rushed about as if they had lived there all their lives. The cook complained of not being able to understand Millie's accent, the head parlour maid that she was too noisy on the stairs and the nanny that she talked too much to the boisterous children. Millie was put straight to work cleaning the servants' attic bedrooms, the nurseries, the pantry and sinks. She washed up endlessly. There were six flights of stairs between the nursery quarters and the kitchen in the basement and her arms and legs ached from the constant fetching and carrying between the two. Millie had thought that she would never last beyond Christmas. But the Halletts were pleasant people who liked to entertain and they made sure that their staff were well fed too.

Mrs Gallagher, the stout, amiable cook, kept Millie and the other maids fuelled with large meals in the servants' hall and thick slices of bread pudding with coffee in between times. Learning of Millie's interest in cooking, Mrs Gallagher gradually allowed her to help with some of the food preparation. Christmas away from home had been made bearable by the Halletts giving them a party with gifts of nuts, oranges and money, and Cook had commandeered sherry from the butler's pantry which had led to a sing-song and dance. But best of all, Millie had met up with Ella again. Her friend worked for a banker in Montagu Square and they spent their Saturday afternoons off together. Ella had long since apologised for inadvertently causing the rift between Millie and Dan. She had felt terrible for creating such a stir at the hotel too and seemed to try extra hard to make it up to Millie. 'At least it's brought you to London,' she had declared cheerfully. So she had shown Millie London, and they liked nothing better than to go to matinées and see the latest moving pictures. Once they had managed to get the same evening off and had gone to a dance and met two footmen from Eaton Square. Ella had continued to see hers throughout January, until he disappeared with a Cornish kitchen maid, but Millie had not been enthusiastic about hers.

'You can't pine over that Nixon lad for ever, Millie man,' Ella had protested. 'You make me feel terrible. You'll just have to settle for second best.'

'I don't want to settle for anyone just yet,' Millie had insisted.

Ellie had been baffled. 'London's full of canny lads. Have a bit of fun!'

Millie had laughed. 'I'm having fun with you.'

Ella had rolled her eyes in despair and declared she would find Millie a man before the spring. But spring was here, Millie thought ruefully, as she hurried back to the house with Buster, and Ella had failed to find her a match among the city's domestic servants, porters or clerks. Perhaps she would have been more keen on Ella's matchmaking if she had not received a letter before Christmas from her mother, explaining how Dan had come round to see her after she had gone. It was such a brief reference to him, among her other news about the hotel and how Ava was now helping out at the Nixons' in her place. Yet Millie's hopes had soared that Dan might still care for her, while she had fretted to think of Ava spending time at Tenter Terrace, wheedling her way into his affections.

'It's time I put Dan Nixon out of my mind,' she whispered to Buster as she cleaned up his paws in the kitchen and hurried to take the children and nanny their large breakfast tray.

Later, when she was in the pantry polishing the crystal and silverware for the evening dinner table, Ella called in on her way back from an errand. She knew Cook would be resting upstairs and the other maids bathing or changing into their afternoon uniforms in this quiet half-hour before the dining room was made ready. Millie suspected she had called round to flirt with the

Halletts' American footman, but she did not mind.

'So what are you going to do for your birthday?' Ella asked the question for the umpteenth time. 'It's next Saturday after all.'

'Eighteen's nowt special,' Millie had said, rubbing hard on an elaborate candelabra.

'All birthdays are special,' Ella insisted, tossing a fair curl out of her eyes. 'We could go to a tea dance or something.'

'Will Queen Mary let you out?' Millie teased, knowing how Ella joked about her strict and imposing lady of the house, who made her stand on the stairs in the dark, ready to turn the light on for her coming down.

'That slave-driver!' Ella grimaced. 'I don't care, I'm going out whatever. Jobs are easy to come by in this city.' She gave a cavalier wave.

Millie put down her cloth and thought. 'You know what I'd really like to do?'

'Go on, say it!' Ella urged.

'I'd like to go to the new Empire Stadium.'

'Wembley?' Ella asked, puzzled.

Millie grinned. 'Aye. I'd like to gan and see Newcastle play Aston Villa in the Cup Final.' She burst out laughing at the look of disbelief on her friend's face.

'Watch football on your birthday?' Ella gasped.

'It'd be grand,' Millie enthused. 'Half the north-east are coming down for a day out, the papers are full of it. There's that steamer, *The Bernicia*, leaving from Newcastle. Our team will be here – training at Harrow on the Hill, the papers say. Just think of it, Ella! Heroes like Stan

Seymour and Frank Hudspeth right here in London!'

Ella wrinkled her button nose, amazed at how excited her friend could become over the game. 'Well, you've got a point. I suppose there'll be lots of lads to look at.'

Millie threw the cloth at her. 'That's all you think about!'

'Oh, aye! And the thought that Dan Nixon might be one of those lads has got nothing to do with you wanting to go?' Ella teased.

Millie flushed. 'Even if he was, how would I ever find him in a crowd of thousands? I want to see the footie.'

Ella snorted. 'You were always daft that way, especially with your brother–' She broke off quickly. There was a moment of awkward silence between them.

'You are allowed to mention him, even if he is dead,' Millie answered, with a pained look. 'Graham. See, the kitchen ceiling didn't fall in, did it?'

Ella jumped up. 'Sorry,' she said, embarrassed. 'I thought talking about him might be hurtful.'

'No,' Millie said quickly, 'it's the *not* talking that hurts.' She sighed. 'He would have been twenty-seven last month. I wonder if me mam still remembers his birthday?'

Ella came round and squeezed her shoulders. 'Wembley it is then. I'll get the tickets. It'll be my treat.'

Saturday dawned overcast and drizzly, but Millie was in high spirits and determined to get through

139

her chores quickly. Mrs Gallagher gave her an extra portion of bacon for breakfast, and the other maids presented her with a bar of Lux soap and black and white ribbons to tie round her new cloche hat. There was much teasing about her proposed trip to Wembley. Sally, the kitchen maid, told her to go and get ready early as she would tidy the night nursery and the attic bedrooms for her. Millie rushed away to wash with her new soap and change into the pale-yellow spring dress that Ella had helped her choose the previous Saturday. Fixing on the new hat, which she had bought with money her mother had sent down for her birthday, she eyed herself in the mirror.

Despite the constant activity of her job, Millie's figure had filled out since Mrs Gallagher had been feeding her. Her face was fuller too, her cheeks a healthy pink and her blue eyes shining. Her dark hair, cut into a short bob, was sleek and wavy under the hat. For the first time in her life she was satisfied with the way she looked, and her new clothes made her feel good too.

As she clattered downstairs, she was met by a flustered Sally on her way up.

'Millie, come quick. Cook wants you!'

Millie's heart sank at the thought that she might be delayed in getting away. 'What is it?' she asked in annoyance.

'There's someone to see you,' Sally gasped, clutching her arm and pulling her forward. 'Well, more than one, to tell the truth.' She pushed Millie ahead of her through the kitchen door.

The room seemed to be full of people and

chatter, but when Millie took in the scene she realised that there were only half a dozen making the noise. Cook was holding court at the vast table with the two parlourmaids and Ella. But standing half turned away from the door and warming their backs at the fire were two men. Millie's heart thumped hard as they turned towards her, breaking off from the banter. Walter and Dan Nixon.

Colour rushed into her neck and cheeks like fire as Dan's handsome face grinned at her.

'Hello, Millie,' he said easily, as if their estrangement had never been. 'We thought we'd come and give you a birthday surprise.'

Millie's hands flew to her face as she stifled a cry in her throat. She wanted to laugh and weep at the same time at their miracle appearance. 'How – how did you know?' she gasped. She looked at Ella for explanation, and then back at Dan.

'Little carrier pigeon,' Dan said with a wink, and stepped towards her. 'Here, this is for you.' He thrust a wrapped and beribboned parcel at her. 'Happy birthday.'

Millie's heartbeat pounded in her ears like a bass drum to have him so close, and she thought he must be able to hear it too. She took the present with trembling hands and stood looking at Dan, unable to disengage her look. His eyes shone with warmth for her.

'Well open it then,' Ella cried, coming towards her in excitement. Millie fumbled with the fancy ribbon and tore at the tissue paper, which Ella took from her. Inside was a box. Ella helped her lift the lid, as curious as she was at the surprise. Inside lay a white silk scarf and a pair of black kid gloves. Millie touched them in awe, catching her breath at their quality.

'Beats the box of chocolates I've got you,' Ella declared, eyes wide.

'They must have cost a fortune!' Millie spluttered, looking at Dan in disbelief.

Walter piped up, 'I paid for them an' all.'

Millie smiled at the older brother standing in Dan's shadow. She was deeply touched. Walter had always been kind to her when she had worked for his mother. 'Eeh, thank you! Both of you.' She looked at them, still unable to believe her eyes. How had they suddenly appeared like this, conjured out of the rain?

'Well, you can thank us with a birthday kiss,' Dan insisted, and before anyone could argue, he stepped forward and planted a kiss on her lips. Mrs Gallagher clucked in mild shock and the maids tittered, but Millie found her face burning with pleasure. Dan took the scarf and placed it around her neck, brushing her cheek with his hand as he did so, and sending a shiver through her. Ella took her friend by the arm, seeing that she was too stunned to say anything. The quicker they got out from under Mrs Gallagher's suspicious gaze, the better.

'Come on, we don't want to be late,' she ordered, picking the gloves out of the box and thrusting them at Millie.

With cries of goodbye and promises not to be late back, they clattered out of the kitchen and up the basement stairs to the street above, laughing as they went. Dan kept close to Millie's side.

'We came down on the train early this morning. I gave Walter a sightseeing drive before we met up with Ella,' he chattered. 'Got our tickets for the match and transport to Wembley all in.'

Millie was baffled. 'How did you know where to find us? Did Mam tell you?'

'Not your mam,' Dan snorted. 'She'd not be best pleased if she knew I was here, I reckon. She wouldn't give me your address, else I would have written.' Then he grinned. 'No, it was Ella told us. Sent a telegram. Said it would be a canny birthday treat if we all met up.'

Millie stared at Ella, but her friend merely shrugged. 'Well, I wanted to make up for the mess I got you in, and I was sick of you moping around. I thought Dan was likely to be coming down for the match anyway, so what was the harm in it? I got him to ring through on old Queen Mary's telephone.' Ella giggled at her own audacity, then turned and hurried ahead with Walter, engaging him in conversation as they made for the shelter of a trolley-bus.

Millie gaped at her friend's forwardness, and then embarrassment flooded over her at the thought of what Ella must have said to persuade Dan to come to London.

She dropped her head, wishing the ground could swallow her up. 'What you must think of me…'

Dan slipped her arm through his. 'I think a lot of you,' he insisted. 'It's me who's been worrying what you must think of me. I feel that bad at the way I treated you. As if it mattered about your family. None of it was your fault and I don't blame you for wanting to cover up about your brother and that.'

Millie stiffened. Dan squeezed her arm. 'Sorry. I'll not mention it again. Let bygones be bygones, I always say. Will you forgive me, Millie?'

She lifted her head and met his intense blue gaze, her insides melting at the look he gave her.

'Of course I will,' she answered hoarsely.

Dan's face broke into a smile, his cheeks dimpling in that way that made her pulse race faster.

'Champion!' he said. 'I was that chuffed when I heard from Ella. And here we are together again just like before. By, you're looking grand, Millie. All I need is for Newcastle to win today and I'll die a happy man!'

Millie laughed as they raced for the bus, from where Ella was gesticulating.

'Don't die yet, Dan,' Millie teased him. 'Not on me birthday anyway.'

He kissed her cheek. 'By, I've missed you, Millie.'

'Really?' Millie flushed.

'Aye,' Dan insisted, 'I should never have let you run off like you did.'

They jumped aboard, laughing, and clung on as the crowded bus trundled them north through the city. Millie caught a wink from Ella and smiled back conspiratorially. She had a strong feeling that today was going to be a momentous one for them all.

CHAPTER 8

By the time they reached the newly built Empire Stadium at Wembley, Millie's excitement was soaring. She could not believe the size or enthusiasm of the crowds, bedecked in black and white scarves and hats, waving banners amid a cacophony of blaring bugles, rattles and bells. The din was so loud that she had to shout close into Dan's ear to make herself heard. She was overjoyed to hear so many familiar accents and felt a mixture of pride and homesickness to be a part of the excited throng.

'There can't be a Geordie left up north!' she cried, as they were jostled good-naturedly among the stream of supporters on the way to the ground.

Dan gripped her hand. 'Stay close,' he grinned. 'I don't want to lose you now.'

Millie smiled broadly, thrilling at his words. She could tell how excited he was by the whole occasion. The four of them had stopped at a café on the way and Dan had treated them to steak and kidney pie. Afterwards he had talked animatedly with anyone in the milling crowd who walked by, exchanging comments about the team and throwing out predictions. There was a rumour that goalkeeper Mutch was out because of injury and the older Bradley would replace him. But Dan was undaunted.

'We'll win by a goal,' he declared confidently to two men from Byker. 'McDonald or Seymour will score the winner.'

One man shook his head. 'Na. Not with our best goalie injured.'

'Bradley will do the business,' Dan said confidently.

'He's an old man,' his companion answered, spitting into the road.

'We've got experience over youth.' Dan was optimistic.

The arguments and banter continued until they got into the ground and attempted to find a good vantage point among the thousands of eager watchers. Millie stared in awe at the vastness of the amphitheatre, while Dan shouted at a man in front to put down his large black and white umbrella, despite the rain. Although not small, Millie resigned herself to not being able to see much on the pitch, so dense was the crowd. She felt Ella clutch her arm in excitement just as the teams came out and a roar went up around the ground. As the band played and royalty came to shake the hands of the players, Millie craned to get a view.

Suddenly Dan seized her by the waist and hauled her up. 'It's the Prince of Wales!' she reported to Ella, exhilarated by Dan's hold. 'What a canny dresser.'

'Give me a lift up, Walter man,' Ella ordered impatiently. With only the slightest hesitation, Dan's bashful brother did as he was told.

The game got underway and Millie was soon caught up in the drama, cheering with the rest of them and forgetting about the rain seeping through her thin coat and dripping off the ribbons of her new hat and down her neck. She revelled in the freedom that she and Ella were experiencing on their day out with these attractive men, with no one to fuss over them or criticise. Millie felt grown-up and full of anticipation at what more the day might bring. Torn between watching Dan's animated face and the game, she listened enthralled to his lively commentary, his urgings and advice to the players, his cries of disbelief as favourites Villa twice slammed in shots that hit the crossbar.

'Haway, Hudspeth, and wake up your defence!' he yelled. Around them the crowd groaned and swayed during the first few frantic minutes as the Midlands team came at Newcastle and looked likely to score. Then cheers of relief rang round as goalkeeper Bill Bradley made one thrilling save after another. From her partial view, Millie thought Aston Villa looked younger and faster, and she cringed inwardly to think how a defeat would dampen this special day out. It must not happen, she prayed, as she shouted herself hoarse in support.

But by half time, Newcastle had hung on and neither side had scored.

'By, that was a thumping tackle from Mooney,' Dan said to Walter.

'Aye, he's a hard lad,' Walter agreed. 'Canny defender.'

'And Bradley's been brilliant in goal,' Dan enthused. 'Didn't I say he would be?'

They argued about tactics. 'They're too

defensive,' said Dan. 'They want to bring their wingers back into the game, see some goals scored.'

'There speaks a forward,' Walter joked.

As they debated, Ella leaned towards Millie and whispered, 'Aren't you glad the lads came down?'

Millie nodded and nudged playfully. 'I see you and Walter are getting along canny.'

Ella beamed. 'He's a real gentleman. Not like them down here that we have to work for and call themselves gents.'

'So you prefer him to American footmen, then?' Millie teased.

'Any footmen,' Ella confided. 'I've decided, Walter Nixon's the man for me.'

Millie laughed and rolled her eyes skywards. She had heard such talk before from Ella. 'Better claim him before Ava does,' she warned.

'I've already found out he's not courting her any more,' Ella smiled. 'Not since she showed you up in public.'

Millie wanted to ask her more, but the second half was starting. She had a sudden lurch of uncertainty. What if Ava had become more friendly with Dan over the months instead? She slid a look at him, but his attention was fixed on the action, totally absorbed by the game.

The second half began and the atmosphere grew more taut, the noise more deafening as gradually Newcastle began to gain the upper hand. There were several attempts on goal that raised the hopes of all around.

'Low's got it!' Dan cried. Then, 'Ow! Just wide!' he groaned in disbelief. Millie saw every emotion flicker across his face and she knew that he was wishing himself on the pitch. She could read the desire in his face. The ambition within him was almost palpable. To be there, playing in the FA Cup Final in a black and white strip was the ultimate dream of thousands like him. But the difference, Millie knew, was that Dan believed he could get there. He exuded a belief in himself and his talents that made her feel heady just standing next to him. She knew she was hopelessly attracted to him, whatever he felt about her. It was not just his looks and sense of fun, but the vitality and ambition that stirred restlessly within him. Watching his passionate expression, Millie knew she was also in love with the idea of the man he could become – the famous footballer he wished to be. In that moment she realised that she yearned for his success as much as he did himself, and wanted to be a part of it. Nothing in her life had ever been as exciting as being in Dan Nixon's company, and she held on to his arm to convince herself he was real.

'There'll be extra time,' Walter shouted, as the match drew towards its end with still no goal conceded by either team.

As he spoke, a movement began down the line that started the crowd roaring like a great wave crashing towards the cliffs.

'What's happening?' Millie demanded, jumping up on tiptoes.

'Harris passed to Low,' Dan said breathlessly, 'now Seymour – oh, he's lost it! – no, Mc-Donald's got it! – *gan on McDonald!*' he bellowed.

Millie glimpsed the ball firing towards the goal and the Villa goalkeeper leap at full stretch to block it. She surged with the crowd and saw him just clear it with a hand. Everyone gasped. Then someone else rushed forward and banged it over the prostrate keeper into the corner of the net. An almighty cheer went up from the crowd like a clap of thunder.

In the frenzy of celebration, Dan seized Millie in a hug. 'We've *scored!* We're going to beat Villa. Pay them back for 1905!'

'Who was it?' Walter croaked in excitement, quite hoarse from shouting.

'I couldn't see,' Dan bellowed, 'might have been Harris.' But even before the cries of jubilation had time to die down, there was an echoing roar from the opposing fans. Villa were counterattacking. There was less than five minutes to go, and suddenly the Midlanders were threatening the Newcastle goal. Dan clutched his head in disbelief. 'We're going to throw it away…!'

The shouts of encouragement and warning rang around like a wall of noise as the opposition headed the ball at the net. There was an almighty agonising groan.

'Have they scored?' Millie asked, bracing herself for disappointment.

'No, it's hit the bar!' Dan screamed in relief.

Seconds later, Newcastle were surging back up the field.

'The Scotsman's got it!' Dan yelled to Millie, as Jimmy Low ran up the flank. With a long, curling pass, he sent the ball across to Stan Seymour on the left wing.

Millie clung to Dan's arm in a frenzy of anticipation as she saw the centre forward striding unchecked towards the goal. The crowd sensed the moment almost before it happened. Seymour slammed the winning goal high into the net.

The stadium erupted like a volcano, the din around them quite deafening. Caps flew into the air and bugles blared in victory. Dan turned towards Millie, his face suffused with triumph. He grabbed her to him and kissed her firmly on the mouth. Millie squealed in surprise and delight, holding on to her sodden hat. Over Dan's shoulder she could see that even Ella was jumping up and down ecstatically. She had never experienced anything like it: the crowds, the noise, the feeling of oneness, the heady scent of victory and now the taste of Dan's lips on hers. She was elated.

Even her memory of the Armistice was a pale shadow of this scene of such overwhelming joy and relief. But then for Millie the end of the war had been poisoned with sadness at knowing her brother would never return, and the shame of not being able to celebrate with the rest of the village.

She felt no such restraint now, as the jubilant crowd began to sing 'The Blaydon Races'. Millie joined in with the rest, tears of happiness on her face as the game came to an exultant finish. They stood there singing and clapping and cheering their heroes for an age, no one wanting the magical moment to end.

Eventually Dan turned to her. 'Millie, you're

crying,' he said in astonishment, brushing tears from her cheeks.

Millie laughed. 'I'm that happy. My best birthday ever.'

Dan hugged her to him, overcome with joy at the result and feeling suddenly closer to Millie than he had ever imagined possible. 'Give us another kiss!' he demanded, and planted one roundly on her lips. He felt drunk with happiness at the cup win, and a sudden desire for the girl in his arms. He had missed her these past months, his disappointment at her slipping away to London without seeing him fuelled by Teresa's refusal to tell him where Millie was working. Although there had been other girls like Ava showing interest in him, he had done little courting and spent spare moments, when he was not down the pit, playing football. For a long time his mother's death had dampened his spirits and he had kept to himself, often thinking of the promise he had made her to look after Millie. So he had been instantly intrigued by Ella's urgent telegram asking him to come down and take Millie out for her birthday. It was even more satisfying knowing he had managed to do so despite Teresa's obstructiveness. Now it seemed that Millie had been thinking of him as much as he had of her all this time. At this moment there was no girl so sweetly desirable as Millie.

Finally, after presentations and ovations, the crowds began to move and the stadium to empty, people spilling into the surrounding streets intent on celebration. Somehow Dan and Millie became separated from the other two in the crush of bodies.

'They can look after themselves,' Dan assured her, unconcerned. 'The train doesn't go for two hours, we'll do a spot of celebrating, eh?' He pulled her on to a crowded bus and set off back into central London.

Millie revelled in having Dan to herself. They went for a meal in a café that Dan knew from his time in London. Yet he was dismissive of his time spent in the capital.

'That's all in the past, Millie,' he declared. 'You've got to live for the future. Always look forward, not back, I say.'

As they strolled arm in arm along the street, Millie dared to ask, 'And what is the future, Dan?'

He grew expansive. 'I'm going to play First Division. I'm expecting to hear any day from one of the professional clubs. There've been enough scouts out watching me this season. I've taken Ashborough from the bottom of our league to second from the top. We should have won the final, but the boss wouldn't let Manners off his shift to play. Well, the sub let in five goals in the first half.'

As they neared the Halletts' house, Millie began to panic. Soon they would be saying good-bye and Dan would disappear north again on the train, with no knowing when she would see him again. She put a hand on his arm to stop him.

'But what about us?' she asked boldly. 'Are we courting again?'

Dan gazed at her, feeling flattered by the urgency in her look. His pulse quickened at the

153

thought of Millie being his lass. Steering her across the square to the seclusion of the central gardens, he sat her down on a damp bench. Not only did he want her, he had a sudden mental picture of how angry both Teresa and his own father would be if he announced he was courting her. Millie's mother seemed to have taken against him, and his father had always despised the girl from the station boarding house. Mungo had turned into a crabby old man since Effie's death, forever finding fault with his sons and threatening to throw them out of the house. It would give him a bleak pleasure to annoy his father.

'Of course we're courting,' he smiled, putting an arm around her shoulders. He leaned over and kissed her long and hard.

Millie closed her eyes, her insides melting at the feel of his mouth on hers, the warmth of his breath, the strength in his arms around her. When the kiss finished, Millie murmured, 'Take me back with you, Dan. I can't bear to think of staying on in London with you so far away.' Her heart twisted at the thought of not being able to look at his handsome face every day.

Dan fixed her with his vivid blue-eyed gaze and considered. She was as good as asking him to marry her! The thought made his head spin. He knew he ought to dismiss it at once. The last thing he needed was the complication of getting wed. Since returning to Ashborough, he had promised himself he would not become entangled with any lass for too long. Yet something deep within him yearned for Millie and what she was offering. She was different from the girls he was used to courting. She was so trusting and open and giving and loyal. With Millie at his side, Dan suddenly realised, he would have the excuse to escape Ashborough and his father's temper for good. Millie was pretty and practical and would support him in his ambition to go after his dream like no one else could. She would help him blot out his past mistakes. Looking at her adoring face, he knew she would do anything for him, go anywhere he asked. That look gave him courage, and in that instant he made up his mind. He would have Millie for his own.

He seized her hands in his, his face eager. 'Aye, Millie, I will! I want you to come back with me.'

Millie's heart jolted. 'You do?' she gasped in astonishment.

'Aye.' Dan laughed to see the pleasure his words gave her. 'And maybe in time we'll get wed.'

'Wed?' Millie let out a cry and kissed him joyously. 'Ask me properly then, before you change your mind!'

'What now?' Dan laughed, feeling drunk with the speed at which things were developing.

'Aye, now!' Millie insisted, flushing prettily.

Dan made a dramatic gesture of going down on his knees in the mud. 'Millie Mercer, will you be my wife?' he grinned.

Millie laughed in delight. 'Of course I will. I'd like nothing more in the whole wide world!'

Dan scrambled to his feet and pulled her up. He embraced her again, more boldly this time, a long, lingering kiss that left Millie strangely hungry for more.

'Oh Dan,' she cried, 'I'm so happy I could cry. I know we'll be right for each other. I've always known it.'

Glancing over her shoulder at the grand street behind her, he thought, who cared if London had rejected him? Millie wanted him, and together they would have a glorious future. Dan hugged her close to him, exultant.

CHAPTER 9

For two months Millie attempted to talk her mother round to the idea of her marrying Dan. She did not want to go ahead without Teresa's blessing, for she was the only family she had. But her return home had caused terrible rows at the Station Hotel, with Ava refusing to speak to Millie, Moody retreating to his room for days on end and Teresa putting up every conceivable argument against the match. Millie was too young, Teresa said, Dan was too unreliable, he was not earning enough to keep them, there was a shortage of housing, they could not afford a wedding that year, it was causing too much friction with Ava. Ava spoke about Millie to the others as if she was not in the room. 'She's got above herself, talking like she's posher than the rest of us! She shouldn't be marrying before me – she's nearly two years younger – it's just not fair!'

But Millie persisted, and her argument was strengthened by Ella's surprise appearance back in Ashborough a month after Millie had given her notice to the Halletts, announcing that she and Walter were engaged to be married too. Millie was thrilled, and the friends talked about a double wedding. But she was worried about Dan. He had been kicked out of Tenter Terrace by his cantankerous father – who had taken once again to drinking – and was lodging in Corn Lane with Kenny Manners, the Comrades goalkeeper.

She saw the bad influence Kenny was having on Dan, persuading him to go out drinking after work and spending the wages he should have been saving for their wedding. No offers had come from any of the professional clubs, and she could see Dan drowning his disappointment around the clubs of the town. At the same time he showered her with presents: gaudy brooches, embroidered handkerchiefs, chocolates and flowers. He took her on picnics and trips to the seaside; they went dancing to the Egyptian Ballroom, and to the plush Empire cinema.

Dismissing her fears, he would say, 'Stop worrying, your mam will come round to the idea eventually.'

'Why won't you talk to her?' Millie pleaded. 'You could win her round if you really tried.'

He swung an arm round her as they walked past the bowling green in the park. 'We could always elope,' he whispered in her ear, and grinned.

Millie was horrified by the idea. What a scandal that would be! 'No we could not,' she answered hotly. 'I want to be wed in the proper way, with me mam's blessing. Besides, we need to live at the hotel to start with – we can't afford anything else and there's a waiting list for the colliery houses...'

'Stop your fretting,' Dan interrupted, squeezing her shoulder. 'I'll have a word with your mam, make her see sense.'

'I just want us to be married,' Millie said, leaning against him. 'Isn't that what you want?' She noticed his hesitation with dismay. 'Dan?' she questioned.

Quickly he gave her his dimpled smile. 'Aye, of course I do, bonny lass.'

With renewed determination, Millie went back to work at the Palace to earn some extra money for the wedding, seeing how Dan spent his wages so freely. One evening shortly afterwards, Dan came round to the hotel bearing a large gift.

'It's a gramophone!' Teresa exclaimed.

'It's for all you ladies here,' Dan smiled, and set it down on the kitchen table.

Immediately Teresa and Ava gathered round in excitement, demanding to have a demonstration. Dan put on a record and wound it up, giving a wink to Millie over her mother's head. There was a crackling fizz, the sound of an orchestra and then a voice began to sing 'The Teddy Bears' Picnic'.

Teresa gawped at Dan and then burst out laughing.

'Well, there wasn't much choice of records,' Dan grinned.

But Teresa was entranced. 'Play it again!' she demanded. 'Show me what to do.'

The record was playing a dozen times, and Millie saw how clever Dan had been to try to win her mother round with music, her passion in life. Each time Dan called at the boarding house he would come bearing a new record of traditional songs, music-hall favourites, ragtime, or the new jazz dance tunes if he could get them. He would

159

breeze into the hot kitchen, roll back the oilcloth and get them dancing. Sometimes they would spill out into the yard, taking the gramophone with them, and the neighbours would be drawn by the music to join in. They would dance and sing and Millie would fetch jugs of home-made lemonade or ginger beer to quench their thirsts.

But despite Teresa's thawing disapproval of Dan, she still did not see him as a suitable son-in-law. The fact that he spent too much money on frivolous presents and saved nothing seemed only to confirm her opinion. So when Millie presented Dan into finally asking her mother outright for permission to marry her, Teresa said no.

'At least not until you've put enough by to support her,' her mother declared.

Millie feared that Dan would just take no for an answer and carry on as before. It worried her that he seemed resigned to their relationship as it was, happy to be courting her and free to go out with his drinking friends when it pleased him. She saw that if he did not have her beside him as his wife, supporting him and pushing him towards his ultimate goal, Dan might fritter away his chances of success. Yet she knew he possessed that ambition – she had seen it all over his face at Newcastle's victory at Wembley. Millie realised it was up to her to persuade her mother, so she redoubled her efforts to get Teresa's approval.

'Why can't you like Dan?' she pleaded for the umpteenth time since her return. They were hanging out washing across the yard, the large white sheets catching in the stiff May breeze and lifting like sails.

'It's not that I don't like him,' Teresa said briskly. 'He's very easy to like.'

'Then what have you got against him?' Millie demanded, stabbing wooden pegs on to the line.

'I'm just worried that you're too young. I'm not saying you shouldn't be courting, but there's plenty of time. No need to rush into anything. Get to know him properly first. Don't go headlong into marriage with the first man that asks you, like I did,' Teresa lectured.

Millie humphed with impatience, tired of the old arguments. 'I'm eighteen and I've worked away from home, stood on me own two feet. I know what I want, Mam. I want to be married and I want Dan to be me husband. Nothing will change the way I feel about him.'

Teresa saw the determined set of Millie's usually dainty mouth and grew annoyed. Her daughter had returned from London far more argumentative and ready to challenge her. She blamed the lax American employers and the leniency of Mrs Gallagher, whom Millie was forever praising. She felt her temper rise.

'Would it change your mind about him if you knew he had been seeing other lasses while you were in London?' Teresa blurted out. 'I thought you would have had more sense in your head than running after someone who cares more about football and drinking and having a good time than finding a steady job and a good wage!'

Millie faltered, clothes prop suspended halfway to the line of washing. Her face fell in dismay. It was the accusation about other girls which hurt the most. 'Don't speak about Dan like that.' She flushed. 'He only showed an interest in other lasses 'cos he didn't know he'd see me again – and you wouldn't give him my address,' she accused.

'He never tried very hard to get it,' Teresa blustered, taking the prop from her daughter and finishing the job. But the pained look on Millie's face made her heart twist, and she immediately regretted her hasty words. She decided not to mention that among the girls Dan had taken to the pictures these past months was Ava. There had probably been nothing in it but a bit of harmless flirtation, and Teresa was the first to admit that Ava had probably made all the running.

Teresa wanted to put her arms around Millie, thinking how young and vulnerable she still seemed under the veneer of sophistication she had acquired in London. But she feared this marriage with football-mad Dan might end in disaster, so instead she snapped, 'I don't want that lad leading you a merry dance, that's all.'

Millie shook with indignation, hurt that her mother should think Dan cared so little for her. 'He loves me, Mam,' she insisted. 'I don't care if he's courted other lasses. It's me he wants now.' She looked into her mother's distracted face and determined not to give in to her disapproval of Dan. She forced herself to speak her mind. 'I want to be married, Mam, because I want to feel secure like I used to feel when I was a bairn in Craston. When we were a proper family. I want that feeling back again!'

'What do you mean by that?' her mother bristled. 'Haven't I given you a good home here, you ungrateful lass!'

'It's not enough!' Millie cried in desperation. 'I want us to be respectable again! You can't give me that. You can never marry Uncle Joseph because you don't know if me dad's alive or dead.'

Stung by her words, Teresa sprang forward and slapped Millie hard on the face. 'Shut up!'

Millie yelped and put a hand to her cheek, but she carried on her defiance. 'I won't shut up! For years I've had to block me ears to the whisperings about us – how we're not good enough for Ashborough society, how we always had something to hide. Well, marrying Dan will make me respectable. People will look up to us. I won't have to put up with Ava lording it over me ever again.' She could see her furious mother was about to rebuke her outspokenness once more, so she finished before her courage failed her. 'Dan is going to be a great footballer. He's got ambition and I can help him. We're not going to live a life of drudgery or insecurity; we're going to make something of ourselves! I'm going to have a respectable life with a husband who cares for me, and one day we'll have our own home and family. That's what I want, Mam. And no one – not even you – is going to spoil this chance for me!'

Teresa was dumbstruck at the outburst. She felt battered and worn down by her daughter's persistence. She was shocked at how much Millie had kept bottled up inside about her feelings for their former life in Craston and the life she had made for them here.

All at once the anger drained out of her. 'I never knew you felt that way,' she whispered. Reaching forward, she saw Millie flinch away from her and felt a stab of hurt that her daughter should fear her so. She flung her arms around the young woman and hugged her close, feeling Millie relax into her hold and bury her face into her plump shoulder in relief. They cried together in the smoke-filled air, oblivious to the world around them, weeping with regret for their blighted family life and the accumulation of small, un-spoken sorrows.

'I'm sorry, Mam,' Millie sobbed. 'I didn't mean to hurt your feelings, but Dan means that much to me.'

Teresa stroked her daughter's dark hair, not caring what the passing tradesmen would make of the emotional scene in the yard. 'Don't be sorry. I can see how much you care for him. I've only ever wanted what's best for you, that's why we came here in the first place. I've tried my best for you, Millie. I never knew you were that unhappy.'

Millie sniffed. 'I wasn't so unhappy – as long as you were always there,' she admitted. 'But now I want something more, Mam.'

Millie was almost a grown woman, Teresa realised, and impatient for adulthood. If her daughter had made her mind up, she thought wearily, she would have to live with her decision. She wished she could explain why she was so wary of Dan, but it was just an instinct and not a strong enough one to stand in the way of Millie's happiness. Perhaps Millie was right and Dan would give her the life for which she yearned.

'If you two are determined to have your way, I'll not stop you,' she relented.

Millie gasped in delight and hugged her mother tighter. 'Oh, thanks, Mam!'

Teresa saw the tears spilling down her daughter's cheeks and felt guilty for not granting her wish sooner. 'I'll have a word with Joseph about a wedding party. I want things done properly, mind.'

Finally, at the end of August, just before the start of the football season, Millie and Dan were married at the Presbyterian church in Myrtle Terrace. They were married in the morning and Ella and Walter in the afternoon. As Ella's aunt could afford no more than a dress for her niece, the party for both weddings was held at the Station Hotel, at Teresa's insistence. For days beforehand, Millie, Ella and Elsie had baked pies, scones and pastries for the wedding feast, and helped Teresa decorate the dining room with paper ribbons and fresh flowers. Ava made a big fuss of feeling unwell and taking to her bed, in petulant protest at being asked to help.

'With any luck her so-called fever will last until after you're wed,' Elsie said as she polished the dining-room floor to a shine in readiness for the carpet being rolled back for dancing. 'She gets more like a bad-tempered old witch by the day.'

'She'll come round,' Millie said with optimism. 'She usually does if there's a party to sweeten her mood.'

165

As predicted, Ava revived on the eve of the wedding in time to buy a new outfit. Millie tried not to notice that the pink dress Ava had chosen to wear was of superior quality to the one she herself had bought from the Co-operative store for half the price. Her mother had wanted her to be married in a long white dress, but Millie had chosen a knee-length cream outfit with a lacy bodice and sleeves, and a straw cloche hat that she would be able to wear again.

Ava came into Millie's bedroom, the one she would soon be sharing with Dan, to flaunt her new get-up with its pink feather boa and high-heeled shoes.

'I bought it at Davidson's Emporium,' she boasted as she preened in front of the mirror.

'It's lovely,' Millie said, trying not to feel dismay at how sophisticated her rival looked. She kept reminding herself that by tomorrow she would be Mrs Daniel Nixon, and they would soon be sleeping together in this very bed on which she now sat. The thought made her excited and nervous at the same time. Naturally she wished that they were moving straight into a home of their own, but they could not afford to do so yet. Millie had not wanted them to share the same lodgings as Kenny Manners, so had persuaded Dan that they should start off married life at the hotel until they got somewhere better.

'I thought you'd like it,' Ava said, pleased. 'Dan likes pink too.' Millie shot her a look and saw a secretive little smile lift her thin lips. She was not going to give Ava the satisfaction of seeing her upset, so did not rise to the bait.

'Aye, no doubt it'll remind him of the football results in the newspaper,' Millie answered lightly, and left to have a bath.

Her mother had filled a tub of hot water in front of the kitchen range, and making sure that Moody was out of the way, insisted on washing her daughter's hair like she used to when Millie was a child. They chattered and laughed with Elsie about the day to come and were just wrapping Millie in towels when Dan burst through the kitchen door, followed by his two brothers and Kenny.

The women shrieked in consternation, Teresa flapping her hands wildly at the men while Elsie threw a coat over Millie's pink shoulders.

'You shouldn't be here the night before you're wed!' Teresa scolded.

Dan laughed and lurched towards Millie, throwing an arm around her waist. 'I've just come to see my bonny Millie,' he announced, delivering a sloppy kiss on her cheek.

'Well she's not yours until the morrow,' Teresa replied, 'so be off with the lot of you!'

'Aye, mother-in-law-to-be,' Dan teased. 'How about a quick wind-up of the gramophone?' He twirled Millie, who grabbed at the loose coat to cover herself.

'Dan,' she giggled bashfully, 'not now!'

'Haway, Dan,' the burly Grant said in embarrassment, trying to avoid looking at Millie's state of undress. 'It's time we got you back. Sorry, Mrs Mercer.'

'Aye, come on Dan,' Walter coaxed, taking his brother by the arm.

Dan gave Millie another kiss on her flushed face as they pulled him away. She could smell the beer on his breath and knew they must have been celebrating hard. Side-stepping Walter, Dan planted a kiss on an unsuspecting Teresa as he lurched by.

'Dan Nixon!' she protested.

'You'll not be able to stop me kissing you all tomorrow,' he joked, and allowed himself to be led away.

'Just make sure you're there,' Teresa snorted.

Grant gave her a nod. 'I'll make sure they're both there,' he promised, 'then we can all have a peaceful life.'

They retreated across the yard, their raucous laughter and singing echoing through the calm late-summer night. Teresa gave Millie a strange look, half amused, half sorrowful. Perhaps she was reminded of the old days when Graham had brought his friends back to the cottage in Craston and the small kitchen had rung with their joking. Millie wanted to ask her mother, but knew she could not. It was the one subject that was never raised between them, and after all this time Millie did not know how to broach it. Instead she allowed her mother to dry her hair and comb out her curls, and chatter about last-minute preparations.

When the moment finally came to walk down the aisle to meet Dan, Millie thought her knees would buckle with nerves. To her secret regret, it was Joseph Moody who took the place of her father and gave her in marriage to Dan. Teresa had made sure he was well shaven and smartly dressed for the occasion, and he seemed genuinely pleased to be there, but Millie could not help imagining her own father at her side, proudly accompanying his only daughter. Where was he on her wedding day? she agonised. Could he possibly be aware that something momentous was happening within his family?

She smothered her guilt as she entered the church. If her father had really cared what happened to her, he would have returned to find out; he would not have been so easily put off by Teresa's harsh treatment.

Once she caught sight of Dan's handsome face, smiling at her in encouragement, she knew that nothing else mattered. Her heart leapt as she stood beside him, sure that what she was doing was right. The ceremony was over in a blur, and soon they were outside being congratulated by friends and neighbours and standing while the photographer from the Comrades club took their picture.

Back at the hotel, Moody had laid on two barrels of beer, and the guests tucked into the home baking. Even Mungo's long face and grumbling disapproval did not dampen their spirits. When the carpet was rolled back and Dan and Millie led the dancing, Major Hall banged away with gusto on the piano and Teresa joined him in a duet which got everyone on their feet.

At two o'clock they all trooped back to the church for the second ceremony to see Ella and Walter married. This time the singing was lustier and the party afterwards even more livelier. Elsie brought out the last of the baking, along with jellies and puddings and cakes, while Moody tapped into the second barrel.

By the evening, even Mungo had succumbed to the celebrations and was persuaded to bring out his old set of border pipes and play. The dancing continued, and they ended up around the piano for a sing-song before Ella and Walter made their departure for her aunt's house, where they had decided to begin married life.

But Dan seemed in no hurry to end the party, and the dancing and singing and drinking continued until the beer finally ran out. Millie wished they had been able to afford to go away for a couple of days. At least there was the Bank Holiday charabanc trip to look forward to on the Monday, but there was no getting away from the hotel until then.

Teresa, sensing her daughter's mounting nervousness, began to shoo the guests out of the hotel. She saw Ava hanging around the piano, giggling at what Dan and Kenny were saying.

'Ava, come and help me clear up in the kitchen,' Teresa ordered. 'We can't leave it all to Elsie.'

Ava looked about to mutiny, but Major Hall stood up and closed the piano lid.

'Thank you for a marvellous party. It's time we left you all in peace.' He steered Kenny and Ava and the last of the guests out of the dining room with him.

All at once, Dan and Millie were alone. Dan started to hiccup and sat back down. Millie watched him, wondering if he could possibly be as nervous as she was. She had seen how much of

Moody's beer he had drunk, and how he had been in no hurry to end the party. Maybe it had been a mistake to arrange a double wedding after all. He gazed at her, unfocused, as if he was not sure where he was.

Millie held out her hands to him. 'Let's gan upstairs before we're made to do the washing-up,' she smiled.

He got to his feet, steadying himself against her with a laugh. 'I hope the landlady lets us sleep in,' he slurred as Millie steered him towards the stairs. With difficulty they negotiated the two flights up to the bedroom, where earlier his bag of possessions had been put. Then he lost co-ordination, banging into the clothes chest on the landing. Persuading him not to climb into it, Millie coaxed him into their room at last. She gulped to see his coat and spare suit hanging behind the door, and his shaving brush and razor on the washstand.

Dan flopped straight on to the bed. 'Oh, Millie, we've had a canny day, haven't we?' he hiccuped, attempting to loosen his tie.

She went over and helped ease off his well-polished shoes, while he lay back and closed his eyes. 'It's been a wonderful day,' she agreed, wondering if she should attempt to remove any more of his clothing.

She turned to the mirror and began to take off the necklace and earrings that her mother had given her as a present. She brushed out her hair, chatting all the while about the day to calm her racing pulse. Then she heard a snore from the bed, and looked round to see that Dan had fallen asleep. Millie felt dismay mixed with a little relief. She knew from Elsie that there were things that needed to be done on a wedding night and subsequent nights in a marriage. The country girl had been quite matter-of-fact about the mating of farm animals, but Millie was still vague about what might be expected in a marriage bed. Ella had been none the wiser, and when Millie had tried to raise it with her mother, Teresa had dismissed the subject. 'You'll find out soon enough. It's not the worst side of marriage by any means,' she had added bafflingly.

Millie sighed at the sight of Dan's prone, inebriated body. She went and sat on the edge of the bed, wondering if she should shake him awake. But he looked so peaceful, his face quite relaxed and boyish in sleep, that she left him. Undressing and putting on her nightgown, she pulled the covers over them both. She lay awake a long time, listening to the sounds of the others clearing up below and the distant strains from the gramophone, and wished she was with them, being useful. Later she heard the creaking of floorboards as they went to bed. Millie wondered if they were listening out for noises from the newly-weds' room too. Finally she heard Elsie tramping wearily past their bedroom up to the attic.

She put out a hand to touch Dan's face in the dark and felt him stir. He flung out an arm, which found her, and mumbled a name incoherently. Millie closed her eyes and gave in to a sudden tiredness. At least they were now married; it was still a miracle to her that she was lying next to Dan at all. She did not blame him for having a good sup of beer on his wedding day, for there would be other nights to consummate their marriage. They had the rest of their lives stretching before them together. The thought brought her warm satisfaction, and she leaned over and kissed Dan's forehead possessively.

'Good night, me husband,' she whispered, and snuggled under his heavy arm.

CHAPTER 10
1925

'Guess what I've heard?' Ava said breathlessly, dumping down her shopping on the kitchen table where Millie was rolling out pastry.

'Watch me pastry!' Millie complained, exasperated that this rare quiet moment had been spoiled.

'Millie's been keeping secrets from us,' Ava continued, deliberately leaving the groceries where they were.

'No I haven't,' Millie replied, pushing back her curls with a floury hand.

'What secrets?' Teresa asked, looking up from the menu she was planning for a debating society luncheon.

Ava pulled off her gloves and hat. 'They were talking about it in the butcher's. No doubt Millie was trying to protect Dan by not saying anything.' She picked up one of Millie's newly baked hot-cross buns and bit into it without asking.

'I've no idea what you're on about,' Millie snapped, suddenly nervous.

'You mean Dan hasn't told you?' Ava said in mock surprise.

'Told her what?' Teresa demanded, sensing another battle brewing between the women.

'They're suspending the Comrades from the League,' Ava announced, hardly able to keep a smile from her face.

Millie's heart jerked. She had known something was wrong. Dan had been preoccupied of late, spending more time round at Kenny's, telling her not to fuss him when she asked what was the matter. She had assumed he was worried about being put on short time at the pit, like many of the other men. For two weeks in February the pit had shut down completely and the men had been idle, hanging around street corners sharing cigarettes, or squatting on their haunches playing pitch and toss. It was a sight which filled her with dread, a reminder of those hungry days in Craston before their flight.

'Suspended?' Teresa cried. 'What for?'

Ava flopped into the battered horsehair chair by the fire, eager to tell all.

'They're saying the team's being investigated. Something to do with taking payments that they shouldn't have. No doubt Dan will be able to tell us,' Ava said with a malicious look at Millie. She seemed to derive all her entertainment these days from baiting her, Millie thought angrily.

She at once jumped to Dan's defence. 'You'll not go bothering him with any of your gossip!'

'Not gossip,' Ava insisted. 'It's in the evening newspaper, apparently.'

'It's rubbish,' Millie answered. 'The Comrades are amateurs, they don't get paid anything.'

'Well, the butcher says they've been fiddling their expenses – tea money and travelling. Claiming for money that they haven't spent.'

Millie put her hands on her hips. 'They're entitled to their expenses. It's little enough they get for all the effort they put in to represent the town!'

'There's even talk of some players being paid to play – make up for them losing a shift at work, that sort of thing,' Ava continued. She took another bite of bun and munched while Millie's slim face reddened.

'Well, that's rubbish! But most of the lads can't afford to play if they don't get expenses,' Millie said, flustered. 'I don't blame them if they decide to walk miles to a match and save the bus fare – they're still entitled to it! I don't see the harm in that.'

'Keep your hat on, Millie,' Teresa warned, seeing how Ava had so quickly needled her daughter. 'You don't have to convince us. Ava, move those parcels now. Grant Nixon will be calling shortly about the debating society lunch.'

Ava got up slowly, finishing her bun. 'Umm, that was tasty. That's what you do best, Millie, cooking.' She strolled over to the table and, picking up the parcels, headed towards the larder. Millie wanted to hit her for trying to put her down all the time. She was beginning to feel like the drudge that Ava thought she was, still doing the main share of the chores despite her married status. And if Moody's daughter was not ridiculing her or flirting with Dan, then she was making impertinent remarks about how slow they were in starting a family. Millie longed for a baby, and to escape the restrictions of the hotel, but both dreams were receding along with Dan's dwindling pay. This new shock about the Comrades would make things worse, for football was the one thing that might release them from a future of poverty.

Millie went back to thumping pastry with the heavy rolling pin, determined to ignore Ava, but the other girl turned and added softly, 'You never did tell us where Dan got the money for your birthday clothes, did you? What with him being laid off so much recently, it's a wonder he had any wages put by for that fur-trimmed coat. Even in the sale it must have cost at least a guinea. I wonder if he's ever been offered money for a match? He is the Comrades' best player, after all.'

Millie's patience snapped. In an instant she was across the kitchen and seizing Ava by the arm. 'How dare you!' she yelled. Ava screamed in pain and dropped the parcels. Sausages, bacon bones, dripping and offal fell from their paper wrappers on to the oilcloth as the girls pushed and tussled. Ava pulled Millie's hair and bit her hand, while Millie pummelled her stomach. Teresa shouted at them to stop, but they fought on, giving vent to their years of antagonism.

Millie forced Ava to the ground. 'You're jealous!' she accused. 'You can't stand to see me happy with Dan!'

'I couldn't care less about your precious Dan,' Ava shouted, shoving Millie away. 'He came after me ages ago, but I told him where to go.'

'You're lying!'

'He'd kiss anything in a skirt!'

Millie howled in rage, 'I hate you!'

'Look at the pair of you,' Teresa bawled. 'Stop this at once!'

As they rolled on the ground, spitting bitter

177

accusations at each other, someone knocked on the back door and entered. Teresa cried out, 'Help me separate them before they kill each other!'

Millie felt strong, rough hands pull her off Ava, and looking up, she saw the brawny figure of Grant Nixon looming over her. His look was one of astonished revelation. Millie threw off his hold, humiliated that Effie's eldest son should have seen her like this. What would the gentle Effie herself have thought of her? she thought in sudden self-disgust.

'Thank you, Grant,' Ava gasped, leaning dramatically against him as he helped her to her feet. 'She just came at me like a wild animal.' Then she burst into tears. Grant, quite at a loss as to how to react, gave her an awkward pat on her shoulder and produced a white handkerchief.

Teresa took charge of the situation. 'You were just as much to blame. Millie, get yourself upstairs until that husband of yours comes back from wherever he's drinking.' She turned to Grant. 'I'm very sorry you had to witness that. Would you like to come through to the dining room while we discuss the luncheon arrangements?'

Grant hesitated, looking between the women. Millie was shaking, unable to move, and she had a sudden urge to justify her actions to him. She had always been rather in awe of the stern older brother with his bookishness and politics, but she knew he was a fair man. His disdainful look was worse humiliation than her mother's scolding.

'Ava was bad-mouthing our Dan. Surely you

178

don't believe the rumours about the Comrades?' she appealed to her brother-in-law. 'Ava says everyone's talking about how they've taken money when they shouldn't. But I know they're not bad lads.'

Grant stared at her with dark, hooded eyes, his heavy jaw set, and she thought he would criticise her too. 'You're right, they're not bad. No one complained when they won their games most Saturdays this season. What do they expect these lads to live on? If they won't pay them a decent wage at the pit, the lads must do what they can. It's the middle-class amateurs who complain the loudest, but they're not the ones who are tightening their belts. The rules are made up by officials who've never had to worry where the next penny's coming from. It's the system that's to blame, not the players.'

They were all stunned by his speech. It was the most Millie had ever heard him say. Teresa broke the silence. 'Well, we can see why you're in the debating society, Grant Nixon!'

He smiled sheepishly and followed her out of the room, but not before Millie had given him a grateful look. Without another word to Ava, she ran upstairs to wash and change and went out to the Palace, thankful to escape the hotel for an evening's work. Dan came in for an hour's nap before going on night shift, but there was no chance for them to talk alone. Millie left a supper of ham and pease pudding for him and woke him just before she left. As she took tickets, she determined that she and Dan must find a place of their own as quickly as possible. It was as if they were not properly married, the way they lived under her mother's rule and she carried on working there as before. Maybe Dan would not stay out so much if he had a real home to which to come back.

She tried to talk to him about it in the morning when he returned from the pit and after she had helped him bath. Finally they were alone together in their cramped bedroom. Millie had attempted to make it homely with a vase of flowers on the washstand and embroidered pictures on the wall that she had bought from a bazaar. But she could not hide the fact that it was a dismal boarding-house bedroom with a view over the Co-operative stables and a pungent smell of horse muck that grew worse with the summer weather.

'Tell me what's happening with the Comrades,' Millie insisted, as Dan flopped down on the bed to sleep.

'It's nowt for you to worry about,' he insisted, pulling her down beside him. 'It's all a fuss over nothing. All that I'm bothered about is winning the Northumbria Cup this time.'

Millie allowed herself to snuggle up to him; the chores downstairs could wait for once. 'I'll stick up for you, whatever they say.'

Dan kissed her. 'That's my lass.' Then he slumped back on the pillow and Millie feared he would be asleep before they had time to talk any further.

'Dan,' she said, shaking him. 'I've been putting a bit by now from me wages at the Palace. Not a lot, but enough for a deposit on a bigger room than this.' Dan grunted his surprise. Millie wondered if she was wise in telling him about her savings; he was so generous he would be out tomorrow spending it on gifts for her if she told him where it was hidden. But she decided to continue.

'Major Hall says there're rooms to rent in Ivy Road, just along from him. We could go and have a look,' Millie suggested.

Dan snorted. 'When we move from here, pet, it'll be for something grander than Ivy Road.'

'Oh aye! And when's that going to be?' Millie demanded in exasperation, sitting up.

Dan pulled her down beside him again. 'Soon,' he promised.

'I want to get away from here,' Millie protested, resisting his placating kiss. 'I can't stand any more of that Ava!'

Dan just laughed. 'I wished I'd been there to see you going three rounds with her in the kitchen. Hammer and tongs, your mam said!'

'Don't!' Millie said, flushing with remorse. 'It was all over you, anyway.'

Dan tickled her. 'How about we gan to the seaside in a couple of weeks – after the final? There's a charabanc going from the club. We'll have a canny day out, eh?'

Millie sighed. 'And how are we going to afford it?'

Dan grinned. 'You've just said you had a bit put by. We should enjoy ourselves while we can, not be worrying about the morra.' And he kissed her before she could protest.

Millie gave up, realising that it was partly his

happy-go-lucky nature that made her love him so much. Dan was never plagued with the anxieties over the future that kept her awake at night. With his optimism and her practical nature they would succeed, she determined. Millie believed that if she could just get him into a place of their own, or even away from Ashborough altogether, she could change his profligate ways. With that thought, she kissed him back.

When the Comrades won the Cup for the first time since before the Great War, Dan and the rest of Ashborough were ecstatic. The team played their final game in front of an enthusiastic crowd of six thousand. Millie went along to support Dan, thrilled to see him play before so many spectators and seeing him respond to their cheering by scoring twice. The season over, they went on the charabanc trip, spending some of Millie's hard-earned wages, and early summer came with a measure of freedom from the hotel. They borrowed bicycles and went cycling with Ella and Walter to Morpeth. But in the weeks that followed, the victory became tarnished when the players were suspended while the allegations over illegal payments were investigated.

Dan shrugged these off. 'If they declare us professionals, so what? That's what I intend to be anyway.' He went off on the club's annual trip quite cheerful, for a day of sport and drinking, leaving Millie morosely wondering if the day would ever come when his talents would be spotted. Her mother was beginning to make pointed remarks about how little Dan was bringing into the household, and that he should be concentrating on getting a better pit job. 'Life's all about putting food on the table, not wasting time hankering after what you can't have.'

Millie was always quick to defend her husband and argued back, 'That's rich coming from you, Mam! You've always cared more about singing and playing the piano and chatting to folks than bothering what's cooking for tea!'

Teresa glared. 'I've worked my fingers to the bone keeping you all these years – and now I'm keeping that lazy husband of yours!'

They argued constantly through the summer, while Dan kept out of the way, refusing to be drawn into their battles. Ava, in the mean time, had astonished them all by courting surly Grant Nixon. Millie was amazed to see him quite boyish in her company, seemingly endlessly patient with her possessive, bossy demands.

'He'll never stick it,' Ella said to Millie, 'not once he gets to know what she's really like.'

Ella and Walter had managed to secure a small colliery house back in Tenter Terrace, a few doors away from Mungo and Grant. Millie enjoyed her visits there, admiring the way they had decorated it with flowery curtains and some of Effie's old brass ornaments for which Mungo had no use. Millie wished that she lived in such a private haven, despite the constant fight against coal grime and dust from the unpaved lanes around that quarter of the town. Millie would escape to Ella's to help her work on a hooky mat, sitting either side of the frame by the kitchen range, or outside in the yard in the sunshine, as they were one day in June.

'Grant needs his head examined,' Millie laughed. 'And there was his mam always worried he was too serious about books to get himself a wife to look after him.'

'I think that's why he's courting now,' Ella mused. 'Mungo's in poor health these days, and Walter says I'm not to spend me spare time round there running after him. It's little thanks I get when I do. Mungo's got a temper like a bear and Grant's too busy with his debating and his politics to notice I'm there.'

'Well, they should just get themselves a housekeeper,' Millie answered.

'Cheaper to marry,' Ella snorted. 'But I can't see Ava wanting to settle to a life of skivvying for them.' Ella sighed and put down her hook. 'Oh, it's too hot for this.'

Millie, noticing her friend's unusual lethargy, got up to make them a pot of tea. When she came back, Ella said, 'I've got something to tell you.' Millie saw her blush and look away.

'What is it?' Millie asked, her stomach suddenly clenching.

Ella smiled coyly. 'I'm going to have a baby.'

Millie gasped and then flung her arms around her friend. 'That's grand! I'm that pleased for you.' Yet at the same time she felt envy twist her insides. They had married on the same day ten months ago, and had done everything together since. Now Ella was pregnant and she was not. She would have given *anything* for them both to be going through their first pregnancy at the same time, comparing experiences and revelling in the anticipation together. But this was something that she could not share with her oldest friend, and she tried to hide her disappointment.

Ella seemed to read her mind. 'Likely you'll be next.' She smiled awkwardly. 'Then we can help each other poss the nappies!'

Millie agreed, but on the way home she held back tears of panic that she and Dan might never have a baby. Even with him working night shift, they still found time for snatched lovemaking. They had done it dozens of times since getting married, yet nothing had happened. Why had the old wives of Craston always muttered darkly about the dangers of being left alone with a man, and how this could ruin a young girl, as if getting pregnant was like a contagious disease? Millie thought tearfully that she did not know what the secret was. Perhaps she ought to ask Ella, for she was the only person in the world to whom she could speak about such things. But when she arrived back home, such thoughts were banished instantly by an unexpected caller.

'Is this where Daniel Nixon lives?' asked a stout man in a smart suit and trilby hat.

'Aye,' answered Teresa suspiciously as if the visitor might be some dubious tick-man.

'Is he at home?' the man persisted.

'Yes,' Millie said quickly, 'he's sleeping before his shift. Can I help you? I'm Mrs Daniel Nixon,' she said proudly.

The man smiled and took off his hat. 'Mr Coburn.' He extended his hand. 'I'm from Gateshead Vulcans. The football club.'

Millie gaped at him and then seized his hand and shook it quickly. 'Please come in. I'll go and get him straight away.'

She raced upstairs and shook Dan awake, gabbling the news to him. She had never seen him react so fast off the pitch, pulling on trousers and jacket over his pyjamas and rushing down the stairs. Millie insisted that they went into the dining room for privacy, and brought them in tea and biscuits. When the club official went, Dan could hardly contain his excitement.

'They want me to play in a trial next week! There's a touring side from France visiting and I'm getting a game for the Vulcans reserves.' His face was lit with happiness as he swung Millie off her feet and twirled her round. Millie screeched with pleasure. 'This is it, bonny lass, I know it!'

Millie caught sight of her mother's sceptical look, but ignored it. 'You show them how good you can be,' Millie told him, kissing him boldly in front of Teresa.

The following Saturday, Millie took the train to Newcastle with Dan to watch him play. 'You'll bring me luck,' he told her, insisting that she come. That morning she got up early to cook him a mammoth breakfast of four eggs, six rashers of bacon and toast, to keep him going after a full shift at the pit. Fuelled with food and nervous energy, Dan showed little sign of fatigue.

Millie was bursting with excitement at the sight of Newcastle's impressive buildings emerging out of the steam as they drew into Central Station: the delicate crown tower of the cathedral, the ornate redbrick buildings of commerce, the squat castle fortress and the span of a railway bridge across the teeming River Tyne. She had never been so close to it all before, and she clutched Dan's arm in excitement as they crossed the high-level bridge to Gateshead on the south side of the river. The place was bustling with shops and tramcars and horses pulling trolleys laden with goods. The smoky air held a whiff of the sea, blown upriver like the gulls, while below, the quayside rang with the unloading of cargo and the hoot of tug boats.

Millie was amazed at the size of the Vulcans' ground, further upriver from the town centre, near some coal staithes. Thousands of people had turned out to see the friendly game between the Third Division side and their French visitors. She willed Dan to do well and he rose to the occasion, rushing around the pitch like a man possessed, tackling keenly and stealing the ball again and again. Millie sensed he was going to score as soon as she saw him receive the ball on the edge of the penalty area, his back to the goal. She held her breath as she craned to see him. With supreme confidence, he pivoted on the spot, jinked between the two defending backs and whacked the ball past the advancing goal-keeper and into the net.

Millie leapt in the air, with thousands of other fans, nearly choking with pride. She knew she was witnessing something momentous, some-thing that would change their lives for good, and she relished it. She hung around afterwards, waiting for Dan to emerge from his meeting with the managing board. Mr Coburn came out beaming and shook her hand. 'I'm pleased to say, Dan has accepted our offer to join the club. Part-time to start with, and see how he comes on.'

Dan took Millie out to celebrate with drinks in a prestigious hotel near the station, and a fish-and-chip supper. 'Three pounds a week extra, Millie,' he crowed, booting his empty fish paper in the air and catching it. Millie hid her initial disappointment that he was not to be full-time, for her mind had raced ahead with plans of moving to Tyneside.

'I suppose you'll just have to keep on at the pit in the mean time,' she said, slipping her arm through his.

'Aye,' Dan agreed. 'But it'll not be for long. I'll be full-time before the year's out, I reckon.'

'And we can put some money by, save for our house when we move here,' Millie said enthusiastically.

'Little Miss Thrifty,' Dan teased, and kissed her cheek.

They got a train home, returning triumphant. The news soon spread, and all week people called at the hotel to congratulate Dan and talk football. He was toasted around the town wherever he went, refusing to allow friends to dip their hands into meagre pockets. Millie knew he was buying most of the rounds because she noticed with concern that his pit wages were gone in three nights' drinking. Yet Dan was so happy, she could not deny him this period of celebration, even if it meant him spending too much time with the likes of Kenny Manners.

With the end of summer, Dan began his regular

trips to Gateshead and beyond to play for the Vulcans most Saturdays, sometimes having to stay away all weekend. She hated these separations, yet it was better than worrying about him down the pit pushing coal tubs, bent double in wet seams. Her anxiety over his pit job increased. What if he got injured? she fretted to Ella. He might ruin his chances and never play football again.

'I wish he would give up his job at the pit,' she said, noticing how much Ella had thickened out at the waist this past month.

'Count yourself lucky he's got work. He's got more than any of the other lads around here,' Ella replied sharply. 'You've two wages coming in. Walter's back on short time. I don't know how we're going to manage once the bairn's here.'

Millie bristled. 'Aye, but Dan's that generous he spends as fast as he gets it – more often than not on your Walter!'

'Well, I'd rather he didn't,' Ella complained, heaving herself out of the chair where she had been sewing cot sheets out of an old tablecloth. 'Walter's too easily led.'

Her friend seemed so irritable these days, Millie thought in annoyance. If this was what being pregnant did to you, then perhaps she was not missing out after all, she decided. Ella had lost her sparkle and sense of fun, as well as any interest in going dancing on a Saturday night. To Millie's irritation, all she did was make endless things for her baby and grumble about lack of money.

Then, shortly before Christmas, events came to

a head. Dan was due to play for the Vulcans away in the Midlands. To do so he had to miss the Friday-night shift down the pit and travel with the team. But the pit manager refused to let him, and he came storming home in a terrible temper that Millie had never before witnessed.

'He says I'll be out on me ear if I don't turn in for work Friday,' he fumed.

Millie exchanged anxious looks with her mother. 'They can't stop you! It means that much to us...' She swallowed angry tears.

To her surprise Teresa came to Dan's defence. 'If the game's that important to you and Millie, you've got to go.' She was adamant. 'Tell them to go to the devil. This is your big chance to give my Millie a better life, so take it!'

Millie fought down her usual caution. 'Aye, Mam's right, the match is far more important, even if it means losing that job. I'd be glad if you weren't ganin' down the pit any more.'

But as Friday neared, events overtook them. Grant organised an unofficial strike among the face workers, threatening that they would all walk out if Dan was not allowed to travel away with the Vulcans. The bosses backed down, quite taken aback by the strength of feeling over the matter. Dan went, and Millie waited nervously for the result to filter through, rushing out for the evening newspaper.

'They won!' she cried, running into the kitchen to find Grant waiting for Ava. 'It doesn't say who scored, but they won!'

In her excitement, she swung an arm around her brother-in-law's neck as he sat waiting, and kissed him on the cheek. She laughed as she saw Grant flush with embarrassment. 'And it was thanks to you that he got to go.'

Grant began to mumble a denial when Ava entered, throwing Millie a suspicious look.

'Come on, Grant,' she ordered, 'or we'll be late for the concert.' He followed quickly, without a backward glance at Millie.

Millie could hardly wait for Dan's return late that night. She met him off the train in the frosty dark and he grabbed her in an emotional hug.

'We've done it, Millie!' he cried. 'They want me full-time at the club, so the bosses at the pit can stick their job – it's no more hauling coals for Dan Nixon, centre forward!'

Millie screamed with delight. 'I'm so happy!' she cried.

Dan laughed. 'You can start packing your bags, we're off to Tyneside.' But Millie suddenly burst into tears, and Dan held her in concern. 'I thought that's what you wanted?'

'I do!' Millie was laughing and crying at the same time. 'I just can't believe it's happening.'

'Well it is,' Dan reassured her with a grin. 'And I know something else – I can't do it without my Millie beside me.'

'You'll always have me,' Millie promised him, smiling through her tears of pride.

'I've missed you, bonny lass. Give us a kiss,' Dan whispered. And they kissed long and hard on the frozen platform, warmed by their passion for each other and the thrill of their new life beckoning.

CHAPTER 11
1926

Millie was up early preparing the picnic for the charabanc outing to the seaside. They were to meet outside the Waterloo public house at the end of the street by nine o'clock. She bustled around her small, neat kitchen with its gas stove and green-painted cupboards and gleaming linoleum floor, making salmon-paste sandwiches with the fresh loaf she had just bought from Tilley's the baker's. It was still a delight to descend from their upstairs flat in Paradise Parade and walk along the wide street to the shops as they put out their awnings for the day, beckoned by the yeasty smell of baking bread, the spicy whiff of hanging cured meat and the delicious aroma of coffee beans from the grocer's.

Millie loved the shops of this residential area, with their windows piled high with fresh fruit and pyramids of tinned peas, the mouth-watering pastries in Tilley's, the choice of gloves at the haberdasher's and perfumes in Laurie's hair-dresser's, where she had her hair bobbed. Her friend, Dinah Fairish, who worked for Mr and Mrs Laurie, was coming on the trip too, with her husband Bob, a drinking friend of Dan's. Dinah was small, plump and lively. She reminded Millie of how Ella had been in the days when they had worked in London and had gone to dances and the pictures and shared their wages and jokes about lads. Millie never heard from Ella these days, despite having written and asked her to come and stay and bring her bairn. She had only seen Ella's daughter Marjory once, when she had returned at Easter time for a snatched visit while Dan was playing away in the south. Marjory was already four months old, and yet the dress and matinée coat that Millie had bought her swamped the tiny, sallow-faced baby.

'She's bonny,' Millie had said, thinking quite the opposite and noticing for the first time how sooty Ella's kitchen was. Her friend did not appear to have decorated her cottage that spring, and she looked careworn and far older than twenty. She showed no interest in Millie's new life on Tyneside, so preoccupied was she with the impending threat of a lockout at the pit.

'They're threatening to lay them all off if they don't sign new agreements to cut their wages and increase their hours,' she had fretted. 'There's going to be a strike, Millie, you're lucky to be out of it.' And Ella had given her such a look of resentment that Millie had not stayed long.

'You will come and visit us, won't you?' Millie had insisted. 'It'd do you good to get away from here for a few days. I'll show you the sights, introduce you to our new friends at the Waterloo. I can tell you'd get on with Dinah like a house on fire.'

Ella had nodded. 'Aye, I will.' But Millie had known from the dull look in her eyes that she would no more think of travelling the twenty miles to see her than fly to the stars. She offered to pay her train fare, but Ella had bristled and said that would not be necessary, and Millie had left, pulling her warm coat with the fox-fur collar around her self-consciously and wishing she had not been so well dressed. But Dan insisted on buying her new clothes every month, and they revelled in going round the large Newcastle stores together, choosing outfits and buying each other gifts. It was something she would have loved to do with Ella, treating her to new clothes and spoiling baby Marjory with treats, but she knew her friend was too proud.

Millie cut off the crusts and quartered the sandwiches into triangles, wrapping them in greaseproof paper and placing them in their new wicker picnic basket. She filled the thermos flask with tea and secured it with leather straps in the basket. She added slices of cherry cake, bananas and a packet of fig rolls, then turned her attention to cooking bacon and eggs and black pudding for breakfast. By the time Dan emerged from bed, his fair hair standing up in spikes and his eyes bleary, it was almost ready. She shooed him away when he tried to cuddle her.

'We haven't time for that,' she smiled. 'We have to be at the Waterloo in half an hour.'

Dan grunted and staggered off to douse himself in cold water. Millie was proud they had their own bath, even if it was wedged into the corner of the kitchen. It made a useful extra surface when it was covered over with a washboard, and she had hot water coming out of the taps. She did her washing in it too, so there was none of the back-breaking chore of fetching water from standpumps, laying a fire under a washpot or dashing out in the pouring rain to an outside washhouse as she had once done for Effie. Not for the first time, Millie said a silent prayer of thanks that Dan was no longer a pitman.

Millie eyed her husband as he leapt into a tub of cold water, splashing and roaring as the shock woke him up. He was lean and fit, despite the amount of beer he drank, his legs and arms well muscled. Soon the season would be starting, and Millie felt a sudden surge of relief. Dan was always happiest when he was playing and working at the club. He was their top goal-scorer of the previous season and took the credit for lifting the Vulcans into the Second Division. He was already becoming recognised around Tyneside, enjoying the attention and looking with hope towards the prestigious St James's Park of Newcastle United. All his drinking mates told him it was only a matter of time.

It had been fun, Millie reflected, having Dan around during the summer months, but he spent too much and drank too heavily when there was no work. Luckily he still got paid while he was not playing, but only at half his normal wages, and they had precious little left to live on. Their flat was carpeted, crammed with new furniture from the co-operative cabinet-makers at Pelaw, and filled with crockery from Malings pottery, for which Millie was developing a passion. Their wardrobe was bursting with stylish dresses, fifty-shilling double-breasted suits from Montague Burton and new Aertex undergarments instead of old-fashioned long johns.

As Dan whistled a Count Basie tune, Millie went to open the kitchen window, feeling suddenly nauseous from the smell of frying. She had felt this way on and off for several days now and hoped she was not going to be ill on the trip. The sea air at Whitley Bay was what she needed, she told herself firmly. Hearing the postman's footsteps below, she served Dan's breakfast on to a flowery plate and went downstairs. There was a letter in her mother's handwriting, formal and elaborately looped, and she could imagine Teresa sitting at the desk in the kitchen laboriously copying her darting thoughts on to paper with the slowness of an old scribe.

Millie's nausea rose. She would not read it now. It was probably another letter complaining that she had not been to see her mother for months, rebuking her for spending too much money and telling her it was high time they started a family. Millie could put up with Teresa's bluntness, but what she dreaded was any reference to the lockout at the pit. She knew she was being cowardly, but the reason she made excuses not to go back to Ashborough was the fear of seeing the men out of work hanging around the street corners, reminding her of Craston. She did not like to contemplate how Ella and Walter were surviving with no wages coming in. Her mother had told her that the hotel was running an unofficial soup kitchen, filling up empty milk jugs and tins with broth. Millie had sent money to her mother to salve her conscience, and hated herself for the relief that she felt that she and Dan had escaped when they had.

She never showed these letters to Dan, in case he saw the criticisms about them being slow to have children, and he never asked for news of home. He did not dwell on the past, and Millie knew that when his friends and family were out of sight, they were out of Dan's mind. He took up and left off friendships as easily as changing clothes, living for the moment. Millie was different. She often caught herself thinking about Ella and Walter, her friends at the Palace and Elsie at the hotel, and wondering what they were doing. But most of all she missed her mother and the intensity of their relationship. It was rooted in a time before memory; demanding, exasperating and argumentative, but loving. They frequently disagreed, but they always knew what the other was feeling, as if bound by an invisible umbilical cord that had never been cut. It did not matter that they were miles apart and had not seen each other for months; Millie thought of her mother every day and knew that Teresa did the same. She had tried to get her mother to visit Tyneside, but first she had used the hotel as an excuse not to come, refusing to leave Ava in charge, and now it was the strike.

Well, a reproachful letter from her mother was not going to spoil this special day, Millie decided, stuffing it into her pinny and going to get ready. She would read it after the trip, when Dan was asleep, or maybe tomorrow. Whatever bleak news it carried from Ashborough could wait.

At the top of the street, Millie caught sight of Dinah waving excitedly at her, peering from under a new purple hat that swamped her round face. Millie had helped her choose it on their recent trip into town. She waved back and called cheerily, 'Have you packed your bucket and spade?'

'Aye, and you should see me new bathing suit!' her friend shouted back.

'Can't wait,' Dan joked.

Millie laughed and quickened her pace beside her husband. The crowd of onlookers gathering around the charabanc to gawp at the day trippers in their finery, turned to watch them approach. They made a handsome couple, Millie tall and elegant in a yellow summer dress and matching ribbons in her hat, while Dan looked debonair in a light-coloured suit, spats and well-polished shoes, sporting a boater, gloves and cane.

One of the barefoot children who was hanging around shouted out, 'It's Charlie Chaplin!'

His older brother gave him a reproving shove. 'Shurrup! That's Dan Nixon of the Vulcans.'

But Dan grinned, and putting down the picnic basket gave a twirl of his cane and mimicked the film star's waddling walk, to the delight of the children. The proprietor of the pub came out to wish them well for the trip, and they piled into the open bus with much merriment and promises to return and drink at the Waterloo before sundown.

The warm morning turned into a hot, sultry late-August day, with little breeze stirring the sunbaked streets of Tyneside, where children played in the dust and the smell of fresh horse manure mingled with the smoky haze from chimneys. They passed acres of housing stretching in solid redbrick ranks down to the Tyne, with the skeletal necks of the dockside cranes rearing up like giant birds. Millie, already feeling the sweat prickling her back and her heart beating erratically, craved the fresh sea air that would bring relief.

Then, as the motor vehicle laboured up the hill and turned towards the coast, Millie caught sight of a distant pit wheel and its nearby slag heap. As they skirted past the village she could see clearly that the wheel was still and that no smoke rose from the chimneys of the pit cottages. Bile rose in her throat as she was struck by this rude reminder of her past. It was as if she had suddenly come across a long-forgotten photograph of her childhood, one she had kept buried at the bottom of a drawer and hoped to forget. She knew that within that village there would be children whose stomachs twisted with hunger as they watched their mothers boiling up nettles for soup, while their fathers risked arrest picking over the pit heap for dross.

Millie wanted to look away but could not, like those drawn to the scene of an accident by fascinated horror. No one else seemed to even notice, or if they did, they saw nothing but a grim little pit village like any other. All she could do was stare, and wonder at the hidden suffering. The miners had been on strike for four months now, longer than any dispute she had ever lived through, and she shuddered to think what life was like for them. Suddenly she caught sight of Dan's unconcerned, laughing face and felt an inexplicable anger. Leaning over the side of the charabanc, she pressed a handkerchief against her mouth to stop herself retching.

'What's wrong?' Dinah demanded behind her. 'You've not been drinking stout for breakfast, have you?'

Dan turned to her in concern and immediately put a comforting arm about her. 'Millie?' He raised his voice to the driver. 'Hoy, stop the bus! The missus is going to be sick.'

Millie shook her head, feeling despair. 'No, please don't,' she whispered, and retched over the side. They were past the village when the driver pulled on to the verge.

Dan climbed out of the charabanc and helped her down. Millie was sick into the ditch, though there was little to show for it as her breakfast had been a cup of tea and a plain biscuit.

'You're not much of a traveller, are you?' Dan teased, wiping her mouth with his own hand-kerchief. 'We're only a couple of miles from home!'

Millie gave him a weak smile. She could not begin to explain to him how a vision of the past had frightened her into being sick. It was a part of her life that she kept locked away from every-one, even Dan, too full of ghosts and fears and painful, hungry memories.

'I'll be fine once we get to the seaside,' she assured him.

And once they reached the promenade, Millie did begin to feel better. They hired deck chairs, and bathing huts for those who wanted to swim, and spread out picnics on rugs. Dinah and Millie changed into their new bathing suits and caps and ran down to the water's edge, where Dan and Bob were standing with their trousers rolled up to the knee, swigging out of beer bottles.

Dan whistled at the women, who splashed them as they ran past and fell into the shallow water. Neither of them could swim, but that was not going to stop them having fun. Yet all through the day, Millie could not quite shake off the feeling of dread that the sight of the pit village had evoked. She touched little of the picnic and could not wait for the fish-and-chip tea at the café to be over so that they could return home.

She hoped that she and Dan could go straight back to the flat when the charabanc drew up outside the Waterloo, but he was keen to carry on drinking in the pub with their friends. He was the centre of attention there, being asked questions about the coming season and the Vulcans' surprise promotion to the Second Division. Millie, seeing that he was in his element, resigned herself to staying.

But Dinah took her to one side. 'You don't look at all well,' she told her. 'Are you sickening for something?'

Millie shrugged off her concern, but her friend insisted on taking her home.

'I'll sit with you till Dan comes home if you like,' Dinah offered.

'You don't have to do that,' Millie assured her. 'I'll just put myself to bed. I'll be right as rain in the morning, after a bit of sleep.'

Most other nights she would have welcomed Dinah's company and her chatter, but that night she did not want to talk about clothes or furniture or the gossip from the hairdresser's. She wanted to lie down and be alone. She wanted to read her mother's letter.

Much later, when Dan came fumbling in at the door and tried to find the electric light switch, he found Millie curled up on a chair, wrapped in a blanket.

He stopped whistling. 'What you doing there?' he slurred, swaying in front of her.

She pulled out a piece of paper from under the blanket, and Dan noticed that her face was puffy from crying.

'It's a letter from Mam,' Millie said in a small voice. 'It came this morning.'

'What's the old dragon got to say?' Dan asked, collapsing in a chair beside her.

'Grant and Ava got married a fortnight ago,' Millie said with a tremble.

Dan gaped at her. 'Me own brother got wed and didn't tell us?' he laughed.

'Dan! It's not something to laugh about!' Millie said with a sniff. She felt desolate, imagining them all there together without them. They had not even had the courtesy to let them know, so that they could at least have sent a present! Millie fumed, 'Mam's making excuses for them, of course. Says they couldn't afford a party so they didn't invite us. But it'll be because of me. Ava wouldn't have wanted me there. Now you've missed your own brother's wedding because of me.'

Dan reached across to give her a clumsy hug. 'Don't you go saying you're sorry. It's none of your doing. It doesn't bother me! I'd've been surprised if that miserable bugger Grant *had* invited me. And if they didn't have a party, I'm glad we missed it. Imagine, tea and Bovril in your Mam's temperance bar!'

But this just made Millie the more indignant. 'But it's family! Walter was there – he was best man!'

'Good for him,' Dan hiccuped, unconcerned. 'If you're that bothered, we can go and visit them soon. Take them a present. You can choose some nice crockery or som'at.'

Millie suddenly burst into tears. Dan pulled her into a comforting hug. 'Haway, you're never upset over Ava? You can't stand her anyway. What's really the matter?'

Millie sobbed. 'I want to see Mam!' She had not known until that moment quite why she was so upset. Dan was right; it was not really about missing the wedding. Neither of them was close to Ava or Grant. She felt childish crying over her mother, yet that was how she felt. She was tearful and moody for no particular reason and did not know what to do about it.

Dan pulled her on to his knee and kissed her short, curly bob of hair. 'We'll go and see her then. I just thought you didn't like going back to Ashborough. You tried that hard to get away.' He pointed at the letter in her lap. 'What else does it say?'

Millie hesitated, knowing he would not like what she heard, then decided it was time he knew what was going on too. She read: '"Ava and Grant are living with Mungo, so they don't have to furnish a house, which is lucky. There's no sign of the men being put back on at the pit. What little they have to start their married life is what Joseph has given them for a wedding present. Mind you, there is no business at the hotel. A few travellers, that is all. All the dinners have been cancelled this summer. The temperance bar is closed. People have no money. Grant says the Comrades might have to disband because they cannot pay their subs…"'

'The Comrades?' Dan said, sitting up. 'But they've just been readmitted to the League! They can't close them down. I don't believe things are that bad!'

Finally something had been said to make Dan take notice of what was happening at home. Millie thought it was typical that only football could make him do that.

'Things *are* that bad,' she insisted, 'Mam's letters have been full of it. People don't have enough to live on, let alone find the money to go to the football.'

Dan's face was appalled. 'Why didn't you tell me all this before?' he accused.

'You've never been interested,' Millie defended herself. 'When have you ever asked for news of home? You've never once been in touch with your family. It's me who writes to them and visits!'

Dan turfed her off his knee, suddenly aggressive 'Don't go on at me! You haven't been back since Easter! Hardly the dutiful daughter, are you?'

Millie glared. 'Well, I want to go back now! I want to see me mam. Maybe if you'd shown more interest in your own family we might not have been left out of the wedding!'

'Bugger the wedding!' Dan shouted, getting to his feet. 'I'm more bothered about the Comrades. I'll pay their subs if they can't afford to!'

'With what?' Millie demanded in exasperation. 'We spend it as soon as we get it.'

'I'll raise a loan,' Dan said, undaunted. 'I'll be worth plenty once they pay me transfer to Newcastle or a First Division club. I'm going to save the Comrades.'

Millie looked at him in disbelief. His own family were on the breadline, but all that concerned him was that they might lose their precious football team.

'Even if you bail them out,' she argued, 'they'll not be getting the gate money they need to keep going. People aren't going to choose football when they haven't got enough to eat! Anyway, the Comrades are probably still paying off the fines from the season before–' She broke off quickly. She had not meant to refer to Dan's suspension from the amateur league for taking payments. She knew he was deeply ashamed of his part in getting the team banned, and it was something about which they never talked. He had escaped to Gateshead just in time, while other team mates had been suspended from local football all year.

But it was too late. She could see by his injured expression that he was stung by the reminder. He lurched at her, taking hold of her arms and gripping her painfully. 'They won't go to the wall because of anything I've done,' he hissed at her.

'I'll make sure the Comrades survive. I owe them that much.'

When she protested that he was hurting her, he shoved her away from him and shouted, 'Shows what little you know about football. Ashborough lads will always find the money to watch good footie, even if they're starving. It's what keeps them going!'

She felt like asking him, 'What about their starving families?' but kept silent. The look he gave her, and the way he had roughly handled her, had left her in a state of shock. They had never had such an argument before, and his rare temper had never been turned on her. She did not want to experience it again, so she bit back a reply and watched him stagger off into the bedroom. She heard him relieving himself into the china chamberpot they kept under the bed. She felt drained and very tired. Her cheeks were still hot from the sun and her silk stockings were gritty with sand, yet the carefree trip to the seaside seemed an age ago. With a huge effort she dragged herself to bed and lay beside Dan, who slept with his back turned towards her. Millie shed silent tears on to the new embroidered pillowcase, comforted only by the thought that he would probably have forgotten their row by the morning, and that soon she would be seeing her mother again.

CHAPTER 12

It was a month into the season, and after several promptings from Millie, before Dan finally borrowed Bob Fairish's Austin and drove Millie up to Ashborough with a car full of gifts and food. Millie was wary about arriving in such style, but Dan was as eager as a schoolboy with a new toy. He had every intention of giving rides to all his friends and relations. They had wrapped a present of Maling pottery for Ava and Grant, a large hand-painted plate of flowers with a motif of Newcastle in the centre.

The day was autumnal, with leaves gusting about the car and banks of grey fog rolling in off the sea. Their arrival in Ashborough was heralded by noisy tooting on the car horn at everyone Dan recognised. Yet the town was disturbingly quiet, with the streets empty of traffic and no sounds of industry from the pithead. Some shops were boarded up, while others advertised sales. Occasional groups of men sheltered near pub doors, and small numbers of women trickled in and out of shops. Millie noticed that the windows of a pawn shop were laden with goods. There was a lethargy about the place, the bystanders hunched with blank expressions, the children strangely quiet and pinched with hunger.

The knot in Millie's stomach tightened as they neared the hotel and saw a thin woman scurry

207

out of the kitchen entrance with a steaming jug, followed by a gaggle of dirty, unkempt children who disappeared down a muddy back lane. Dan parked the car at the front entrance, which they had never used, and sounded the car horn ostentatiously. He jumped out, grinning at Millie, and helped her out, as if he had noticed none of the grim sights on the way in. She swallowed her dismay and smiled half-heartedly.

'Wait till your mother sees the car,' he beamed. 'I'll have her on it's ours!'

Before Millie could protest, her mother was at the door and running towards them.

'Mam!' Millie cried as her mother flung her arms around her and they hugged in delight.

'Not before time an' all!' Teresa scolded. 'I'm surprised I recognise you!' She looked directly at Dan. 'You didn't have to wait till you had your own car before you visited.'

'Do you like it?' Dan teased.

'It's not ours,' Millie confessed, not wanting to see her mother made a fool. 'We borrowed it from our friends, the Fairishes.'

'You'd like a spin though?' Dan said, throwing Millie a look of annoyance.

'Of course I would!' Teresa replied. 'Just let me get my coat.' She was back in seconds. 'Run us round to Ava's. I take it you've come to see the newly-weds?'

Millie realised that her mother was as keen to show off in front of Ava and the other neighbours as Dan was, so she was not going to spoil their fun. Dan put Teresa in front beside him, and Millie climbed in the back.

'Very smart,' her mother nodded, impressed. 'Smells like the Store's furniture department.' Dan began to boast about their life in Newcastle, but as they bumped away down the road, Teresa interrupted. 'It's really bad round here with the strike. Folk have nothing left. We've been doling out soup now for two months to the neighbours. Everyone's living on tick where they can get it. Walter and Ella have no savings left – they've had to sell all Effie's brasses. And the bairn not a year old yet; it's a terrible business! Don't expect to get much of a reception at Ava's. If you're lucky, Grant'll be out picketing or making speeches, so at least you won't have to listen to him ranting on.' She craned her neck round to look at Millie, while gripping on to the dashboard. 'I don't blame you for staying away, pet, but I'm that pleased to see you. You're looking too thin, mind. I know it's the fashion and you look like a real lady in that hat, but are you eating enough? You can afford it, thank the Lord! Dan, is she eating proper meals?'

'Eats like a queen, Mrs Mercer,' Dan assured her. 'I give my Millie anything she wants.'

Millie felt her eyes sting with tears at her mother's fussing. She had expected to be scolded, but this acceptance that she would stay away now that they were well off cut her like a knife. She felt engulfed in guilt.

'I'm eating fine, Mam,' she gulped, the familiar bile rising in her throat. 'And I'm sorry I've stayed away so long. I didn't mean to.' She leaned forward and put a hand on her mother's shoulder, which Teresa quickly covered with her own. Her mother looked stouter, or maybe she was just wearing more clothes, yet her cheekbones were more prominent in her face. She was still beautiful and looked younger than the other Ashborough women her age; only her hands belied her forty-six years. They were old hands, large-knuckled, with veins standing out on them like ropes. It shocked Millie that these were the same slim hands that had once played the piano so gracefully, before the drudgery of the boarding house had taken its toll.

They knocked at Ava's closed, peeling door, Millie remembering how everyone had walked in without knocking when Effie had lived there. She glanced at Dan, trying to gauge what he felt as he stood on the doorstep of his old home, but he was too busy bantering with the children who had swarmed around the gleaming car and were eager to speak to him. She saw how they looked upon him as a heroic god whom they wished to emulate, and she imagined how Dan had once been the same. He hoisted up a small, skinny barefoot boy who was tugging at his suit trousers.

'You look like a Dickson,' Dan smiled. 'Matty, is it?' The boy nodded with pleasure. 'Can you play as well as your dad?'

The boy wriggled out of his hold and ran across the yard, dribbling a pebble with his filthy feet. Dan clapped his hands and followed him. 'But that won't do,' he said. 'You need a real ball.' He went straight to the car and produced a leather ball that he had brought for Walter. He dropped it at his feet, scooped it up with his shoe, kicked it in the air and headed it to Matty Dickson.

The boy caught it, nearly knocked over by the force, and gawped. 'It's a caser!' he cried, stroking the leather ball with reverent fingers.

'Aye, and it's yours to keep,' Dan grinned. 'As long as you share it with your marras.'

There was uproar among the children as they all tried to touch the ball, pulling Dan along with them to play.

'Ava's not in,' Teresa said, turning to watch Dan too with a mixture of impatience and admiration. 'Maybe she's round at Ella's.'

'Ella's?' Millie asked in surprise.

'Yes, they've been in each other's pockets since you left,' Teresa said, giving Millie a wry look. 'Ava likes to have someone to lord it over, remember?'

They drove round to Ella and Walter's home in the next street, with children hanging off the car running-boards and whooping excitedly. The noise brought Walter to the door in his shirt-sleeves. His unshaven face brightened at the sight of them, and he hugged Millie and tussled with Dan, shouting to his wife to come and see. A small girl with an unruly mop of fair hair tottered on to the top step and clutched at Walter's leg, staring wide-eyed at the visitors.

'Is that Marjory?' Millie gasped, holding out her hands. The girl flapped a delicate hand at her and nearly fell. Millie rushed forward and caught her, lifting her gently into her arms.

'You're a little pet,' she smiled. 'Have you got a love for Auntie Millie?' She pressed her cheek to the child's soot-smudged one, delighting in the smell of baby skin and coaldust.

211

'Haway in and see wor lass,' Walter told her. Millie followed, still clutching the child, but Marjory struggled out of her arms when she caught sight of her mother again. Millie handed her over, kissing Ella as she did so and trying to hide her shock at how thin and pasty-faced she looked.

'Well, get the kettle on then,' Walter said cheerily.

'We don't have any tea to spare,' Ella said in a small voice.

'We've brought you some tea – Ringtons,' Millie answered hastily, turning to Dan, who stepped forward with an armful of parcels.

'Aye, something for everyone!' he cried. Suddenly a figure stood up in the gloom and came forward. It was Ava.

'So you've come back to show us all up?' she accused in a brittle voice.

Dan ignored the remark, thrusting the wedding present into her arms and planting a kiss on her lips.

'Well, Mrs Nixon, you're one of the family now,' he teased. 'Married life treating you canny, by the looks of it.'

'Not really,' she pouted, only half mollified. 'Not when me husband's out of work. I'm the one putting bread on the table just now, still working at the hotel. I can see that you're doing all right for yourselves though.'

Millie stepped forward and tried to greet her, but Ava held herself away, crossing her arms in a defensive gesture. She had abandoned the present on the table without opening it. Millie swallowed and turned to Ella.

'So how are things?' she asked.

Ella shrugged and looked at Walter. 'The same. There's talk of some lads returning, but...'

'Not round here they won't,' Walter said stoutly. 'They'll not bring scabs into Ashborough.'

Ava made a derogatory noise. 'Stop sounding like Grant. I'm sick to death of the whole business.'

Dan intervened quickly, clapping Walter on the back in a hearty gesture. 'By, it's good to see you, marra! Still playing for the church team?' Walter grinned and nodded. 'The bairns tell me there were riots at Burt Park at the start of the season,' Dan laughed. 'The Comrades that good without me that folk are breaking in to see them, eh?'

Walter laughed weakly too, but Ava answered waspishly, 'Tell him then! Tell Mister High-and-Mighty with his posh clothes and car!'

'Shurrup, Ava,' Walter mumbled.

'Tell me what?' Dan smiled at her quizzically. But Millie's mouth went dry at Ava's venomous look, realising with a shock how much Ava resented Dan. When had her admiration for him turned sour? Millie wondered.

Ava's voice rose dangerously. 'They broke in at the gates because hundreds of them wouldn't pay – *couldn't* pay – and the club were trying to lock them out. Haven't you seen the posters round town cancelling Saturday's match because they don't want a repeat of the rioting?' She looked at Dan with narrowed, contemptuous eyes. 'You tried your best to ruin the Comrades last year;

213

now the strike's finally finished them off. Not so funny now, is it?'

There was a moment of stunned silence. Dan's face looked harrowed, Walter's angry and embarrassed. Then Teresa stepped forward, taking Ava to task. 'That's enough from your sharp tongue…!' The room erupted in quarrelling.

Suddenly there was a movement at the door and Millie turned to see Grant, blocking the dull daylight with his broad frame. Teresa's scolding died on her lips as the others stood back to let him in. Millie noticed how his presence at once commanded respect, the bickering silenced. Here was the eldest brother, veteran of the Great War, union man and supporter of the Bolshevik revolution. Millie watched him in awe.

'Lockout,' he said clearly. 'It's a lockout, Ava, not a strike. The bosses threw us out of work, remember?'

Millie thought Ava was about to argue, but she thought better of it, dismissing her husband with a petulant gesture. Grant ignored this and turned to Dan, shaking him by the hand.

'I'm pleased to see you, lad,' he smiled. 'You're looking well. Does the car outside mean you're the manager now?'

'Not yet,' Dan laughed, visibly relaxing at his brother's civil greeting. 'We've brought a few presents, mind. Just wanted to wish you and Ava well.'

Grant glanced at his wife. 'That's kind of them, isn't it, Ava?'

His conciliatory attitude was too much for Ava. She had expected Grant to back her up; instead he had made her look petty and foolish in front of the others. 'I thought your precious principles would have stopped you taking charity from the likes of them,' she sneered. 'It's all very well for Millie and Dan to waltz in with their fancy presents – they can go back to a warm house and plenty food. What do we have to go back to? An empty grate and your father complaining about what I cook him.'

'That's enough, Ava,' Grant warned, his dark eyes watchful.

'No, it's not enough!' she screamed. 'It's not nearly enough. They've got everything and we've got nothing. This isn't what married life's supposed to be like!'

Grant's square face reddened. 'It's the life you chose,' he said quietly.

Ava glared at him. 'More fool me!' She pushed past him.

'Ava,' he said, trying to stop, 'please don't...'

But she brushed off his hand and stormed out of the cottage, banging the door behind her. Millie watched Grant swallow his embarrassment and shrug.

'It's hard on her,' he said in excuse. 'It's hard on all of us.' The familiar edge of defiance crept back into his voice, but Millie felt a wave of pity for the way this proud man had been reduced to humble words. She even felt sorry for Ava, despite her hurtfulness, for she recognised the fear that gripped them all – fear of the present, fear of tomorrow. It could so easily be her and Dan in the same situation.

She stepped forward and touched Grant's arm.

'You don't have to explain, we can see how it is. All we ask is that you let us help you.'

He gave her a strange look, half surprised, half contemptuous.

'Aye, that's right,' Dan agreed. 'We'll not see you starve. We've things we can sell.'

Grant held up a hand to stop him. 'You can't feed a whole town, lad, not even on your pay.'

'No, but I can look after me own family,' Dan insisted.

'Give to Ella and Walter if you must,' Grant answered. 'They have the bairn to worry over.' He glanced at Marjory. 'Ava and I can manage.'

Dan gave him an impatient shove. 'Don't be so bloody proud, man!'

Grant was sharp in reply. 'Pride's important to a man even when he's out of work.'

'Food's more important,' Dan scoffed, 'and your wife thinks so an' all.'

'You can leave Ava out of this,' Grant said, suddenly angry. He glared at Dan and Millie. 'What have you come back for? Can't you see how turning up in your fancy clothes and car just upsets everyone? Look at the pair of you – just like bosses! You can't change things by bringing a few presents. It might dull the hunger for another week, but it doesn't give us our jobs back.'

'Well, that's gratitude for you!' Dan exclaimed, flushing. 'I wouldn't have bothered, but Millie got this idea in her head that we should come back and help. But you don't deserve it. I pity poor Ava, stuck with a man who thinks more about winning a bloody strike than he thinks of her!'

'Dan, don't,' Millie pleaded, but he ignored her.

'At least I'm doing something useful,' he went on belligerently, 'something people really care about in the north-east. I'm playing footie – the game of the gods, of real working men – and I'm playing well, and people will remember that long after any strike!'

Grant clenched his fists. 'Then get yourself back to Tyneside and play football!' he barked. 'But don't think you can come here and expect us to fall over you in gratitude. You've turned your back on your own kind – the people who put you where you are now. But we've got a hard fight on our hands – we're part of a much bigger struggle. You've gone soft,' he accused. 'We don't need you.'

'What struggle?' Dan said with scorn. 'This isn't Russia; you're not going to get revolution here. People just want to make their way in the world like me and Millie, they don't want all the good things in life done away with.'

Millie could see that Grant was livid. He came at Dan, shouting, 'You should be ashamed of yourself! The General Strike was all about working men standing up for themselves, demanding decent pay and living conditions. We were promised those things after Flanders, for fighting the bosses' war. You were there, don't you remember?' he bawled. 'So what did *you* do in the General Strike, Dan?'

Dan squared up to him and Millie held her breath. 'I drove a bus so that we could get to a midweek away game! There, I'm a capitalist and proud of it!'

'You bastard!' Grant fumed, and pulling back his fist he swung it into Dan's stomach. Dan doubled up, winded. Marjory laughed, thinking it a game, until her mother grabbed her. Dan recovered and came back at Grant with fists flying. Walter tried to intervene and was hit in the face. Ella screamed and Marjory wailed. Millie and Teresa shouted at the men to stop, but to no avail. They brawled on the floor, knocking over chairs and sending the wedding plate flying. It smashed on the ground, still in its wrapping.

Millie seized Marjory from a petrified Ella and whisked her outside, followed by her mother. They calmed the terrified infant with hugs and soft words, while the fight inside raged on.

'We should never have come, should we, Mam?' Millie asked in distress. 'You warned me how bad it was, but this is even worse.'

Teresa tried to comfort her. 'It'll probably do some good to let off steam. Grant's at the end of his tether with talk of the strike breaking down in defeat. And Ava gives him a terrible time. He was a strange choice for her, but she just wanted to be wed. It's a bad start for them.'

'We have to stop them, Mam,' Millie fretted. 'If Dan's injured, he'll ruin his chances and be out of work.' She hugged Marjory close. 'Please stop them!'

Teresa touched Millie's cheek with her hand. 'That's not all that's worrying you, is it?' she said, scrutinising her closely.

'What do you mean?' Millie asked, feeling sick with an unnamed dread.

'You're carrying a baby, aren't you?'

Millie gaped at her mother's wild suggestion. 'No! I – I mean, I don't know,' she stuttered. 'I don't think ... why would you possibly think that?'

'I just sense it – you look pregnant to me.'

Tears welled up in Millie's eyes. It would explain why she was feeling so odd these days, sick and tearful and as if her body was changing without her consent. She could not remember how long it was since her last bleed. She leant towards her mother, weak at the revelation, and burst into tears.

Teresa put her arms around her daughter and the tiny Marjory imprisoned in her hold. 'See, that proves it,' she smiled. 'You're going to have a baby at last.'

CHAPTER 13
1927

Dan insisted that their firstborn should be attended to by a doctor, like the middle classes did, and had arranged for Millie to be seen by one in the city. Millie was nervous of the red-faced man, who was off-hand until he was assured they could afford him and then took pleasure in showing his array of metal instruments that he could use on her to ease the birth.

'I'd be far happier just calling in Mrs Hodges, the midwife,' Millie said afterwards, 'and she'd only cost a few shillings rather than two pounds for that doctor and his instruments of torture!'

But Dan would not hear of it. 'I want the best that money can buy for my son,' he declared, 'and for you.' He had taken to kissing Millie on the head in a protective manner since the pregnancy had been confirmed, and their love making had ceased on his insistence, 'In case we harm him.'

Millie had given up asking what he would do if the baby turned out to be a girl. Dan just did not expect it. He came from a family of boys and could not imagine that his own child might be otherwise. The impending birth seemed to have given a fresh impetus to his football and he was playing brilliantly for the Vulcans. Supporters constantly told him that if Hughie Gallagher had not been brought from Airdrie to Newcastle United as their star centre forward, then Dan would definitely have a place on the First Division team. But Gallagher was their star player and captain, and seemed set to break club records with his goal-scoring. There was excited talk that Newcastle might become League champions for the first time since 1909, and a huge crowd of over 67,000 had crammed into St James's Park the previous Saturday to see them beat local rivals Sunderland one-nil, with Gallagher scoring the crucial goal.

Dan's admiration for Gallagher was transparent and Millie knew that he sometimes joined the Scotsman's group of footballing friends who congregated at the William IV pub on Bottle Bank in Gateshead, to drink and play billiards. Now that Millie was so heavily pregnant, she no longer went with Dan on nights out, but he would roll home in a taxi, full of beer and laughter and stories about Gallagher's generosity and good company.

But Millie sensed his admiration was mixed with envy that it was the tough young Scot who had been wooed by Newcastle for undisclosed thousands of pounds and wore their coveted number nine shirt, instead of him. So she was pleased that the thought of their first child was giving her husband such pleasure and anticipation. It had sweetened the bitterness of that terrible trip to Ashborough when Dan had ended up with a broken nose from his brawl with Grant. They had left with acrimonious words being shouted on both sides, and Dan had sworn never to visit his family again.

'They can all gan to hell, Millie!' he had ranted all the way home. 'We're better off without them.' She knew deep down he did not mean it, but his pride had been hurt. He had wanted to help them, but they had thrown his generosity back in his face. They had not been back since, not even at Christmas, though she kept in contact with her mother by letter. From Teresa's short notes, Millie gleaned that there was still little business at the hotel, even with the strike at an end, and although Walter was working again, there was no mention of Grant or Ava. She longed to see her mother again and was exultant that Teresa had agreed to leave Moody in charge for a week when the baby arrived and come and stay with them in their Tyneside home.

So as the March days lengthened and daffodils bobbed brightly behind the railings in the nearby park, Millie's impatience grew to bursting point. She felt well and rested, but her baby now weighed heavily and stirred within her restlessly.

'I've never seen a home this ready for a bairn,' commented Dinah on one of her visits after work, as she gazed around the box room that they had decorated for the baby. They had painted it blue and yellow, with a stencil of toy soldiers and drums. The cot was in place with new sheets and blankets washed and pressed, Dan had painted an old chest of drawers blue, and there were blue and white gingham curtains at the narrow window. Dan had already bought several toys – a train, a duck on wheels, Dinky cars and wooden bricks – which lay piled in a box on the floor waiting to be used.

Millie caught Dinah's look. 'I know. I told him the baby won't be able to play with these for ages, but he wouldn't listen!'

Dinah laughed and touched Millie's large bump gently. 'I just hope you're a boy in there, or God help you!'

'It'll play football whatever it is,' Millie replied, hugging her baby with a tender smile.

It was while Millie was out buying bread at Tilley's that she was gripped by a sudden acute pang. She had felt twinges before, a tightening in her belly that had sent Dan rushing out into the street to start up the engine of their new black Ford. But they had eased off and Millie had ended up laughing and feeling silly.

This time she gasped and clutched her bump. 'I think it's coming!' The shopgirl came running round the counter and steered her into the back of the shop, where she plonked her on a chair.

'Shall I go for Mr Nixon?' she queried, glancing at Mrs Tilley for permission.

Millie winced as the pain came back again, and looked at them with anxious blue eyes. 'He's already gone. He's playing away,' she answered in panic. 'The baby can't come till he's back!'

The women exchanged wary glances. 'Who else can we call?' Mrs Tilley asked kindly. 'Dinah Fairish?'

'Aye,' Millie said breathlessly, 'Dinah will help me.'

Dinah came rushing round from the hairdresser's, squealed in delight and then rushed out again to fetch Bob before Millie could stop her. They drove back round in their car and made a fuss of helping her into it.

'I can walk,' Millie protested, gasping at another contraction.

'Don't be daft,' Bob chided. 'We'll get you home and then I'll go for that doctor Dan's been on about. What's his name?'

'I'm not telling,' Millie said stubbornly. 'I'm not having him near me with them forceps things!' She doubled up, convulsed in a new wave of pain. 'Help me,' she wailed.

She hung on to her friend's arm so tightly that Dinah yelped. 'All right, we'll take you home!'

By the time they had driven the few hundred yards down Paradise Parade, parked and helped Millie upstairs to the flat, she was in agony.

'You gan for Mrs Hodges in Cedar Crescent,' Dinah ordered her husband, while she hauled Millie into the bedroom and helped her to undress. She rushed around the flat looking for newspaper to lay on the bed as she had done for her mother when younger siblings had been born.

'You can't use the sports pages,' Millie cried faintly, clutching the bedframe.

'Shut up and get into your nightgown,' Dinah answered, stripping the bed of covers and laying out the newspapers. 'It's the racing results or a new mattress.'

Millie flinched, frightened by Dinah's words, her mind filling with appalling thoughts of blood and mess. The doctor had never actually told her what would happen at the birth, and she had been far too in awe of him to ask.

'What do I do?' she pleaded.

'Mam used to walk around the room singing the hundredth psalm,' Dinah suggested.

'Walk?' Millie gasped. 'I can hardly stand.'

'Then lie down,' Dinah ordered, and helped heave her on to the bed. 'I'll put the kettle on and make us some tea. Mam always drank gallons of tea.'

Millie watched her through her bouts of sharp pain as Dinah brought in freshly brewed tea and poured her a cup. Then her friend disappeared into the adjoining sitting room.

'What are you doing?' Millie asked anxiously, wondering why she was taking so long.

'Winding up the gramophone,' Dinah called through. There was a crackle, followed by a jaunty burst of jazz.

'This isn't a tea dance!' Millie shouted in disbelief.

'It'll take your mind off it,' Dinah assured her, dancing back through the door with a grin and humming along to Count Basie.

By the time Mrs Hodges had been found, Dinah had been through the entire record collection and was starting again, while Millie was already gripped in the final stages of labour.

'Turn that thing off,' the craggy-faced midwife commanded in disapproval. 'What will the neighbours think?'

Chastened, Dinah was put to dousing Millie's sweating face with a wet cloth, though she continued to hum defiantly. Millie would have wanted to laugh if she had not been in such pain. Outside, the sky was a dull metallic grey, and she

225

tried to concentrate on the sounds beyond. A delivery cart trundled up the street, a horse neighed, voices called, two dogs snapped as they passed each other, someone whistled. She had no idea what time it was, though she felt as if she had been lying in a red fog of pain for hours. A hooter sounded far off, somewhere down by the river, and then a strange sensation gripped her body and she shrieked aloud.

'Quiet now,' Mrs Hodges soothed. 'The baby's about to come.'

Dinah grabbed her hand and squeezed it so hard, Millie cried out. 'This is it, Millie!' Dinah squealed.

'You keep quiet an' all,' the midwife ordered sternly, 'or I'll send you into the next room.'

'I know what to do as much as you do,' Dinah pouted. 'You don't want me to go, do you, Millie?'

Millie fixed her wide-eyed look on Dinah. 'No, don't go anywhere,' she pleaded.

Then she was consumed by a searing pain, a force that seized her lower body as if it would rip her apart. The pain flooded her, pushing its way down like a tidal wave that would not be stopped. Mrs Hodges commanded when to push and when to stop, and Dinah broke into frantic song.

The small bedroom rang to the sounds of Millie's panting and exertions, Dinah's hysterical singing and the midwife's chorus of instructions. Suddenly she felt the solidness of her baby push its way between her legs in an agonising rush that nearly made her pass out. Then there was relief, like the backwash from a ferocious wave. She sank on to the pillow, numb and shaking from the ordeal. It was over.

'Is it a boy?' she gasped.

There was a cry from Dinah: 'What's that?'

'The cord's wrapped around the bairn's neck,' Mrs Hodges hissed. 'Quickly, pass me that bag.'

'Is he all right?' Millie wailed. 'Oh, God, my baby! My baby!'

There was a frantic bustling around the bed where the baby lay motionless, an unrecognisable bloodied bundle. Millie howled in distress. Dinah was not singing now. The room was strangely quiet after the noise of moments before, while Mrs Hodges struggled with the umbilical cord and the lifeless baby. She should have called the doctor, Millie tortured herself. Dan would never forgive her for this!

Suddenly Millie was gripped once more by birth pains. She could not believe it was happening to her again. She grew almost hysterical. Dinah rushed to her aid.

'It's all right,' she assured her. 'It's just the left-overs.'

As Millie's body rejected the afterbirth, a tiny cry rose from the bottom of the bed. She tensed, too fearful to ask. Mrs Hodges looked up with relief and wrapped the baby in a towel, handing it over to Millie.

'Is he *alive?*' she screamed.

Mrs Hodges smiled for the first time, and Millie saw tears in the old woman's eyes. '*She's* alive, hinny.'

Millie grasped at the towel and peered at the whimpering infant. 'A lass,' she spluttered, half crying, half laughing. 'What will Dan say?'

Dinah came and scrutinised the baby too. 'It doesn't matter what he says,' she replied. 'He's got a bonny baby daughter.' She looked over at the midwife. 'And thanks to Mrs Hodges, she's alive.'

Millie looked up, still trembling from exhaustion and elation, and smiled at the older woman.

'I can't thank you enough,' she said, then broke down sobbing, clutching her daughter to her as if she would never let her go.

'What you going to call her?' Dinah asked, hugging them both and wiping Millie's tears with a handkerchief.

Millie shook her head. 'I don't know. Dan was so sure it would be a boy we never decided on a girl's name.' She watched the stern old widow clear up the mess of afterbirth into newspaper and carry it through to the kitchen, looking for the range.

'She doesn't have a fire,' Dinah called after her.

Mrs Hodges returned with a grunt. 'I'll get rid of it later,' she offered. 'Now, let me show you how to set the baby on.'

Millie looked at her, baffled. 'On what?' she asked weakly.

'For a feed, lass,' she said, as if dealing with a dense child.

To Millie's embarrassment, the woman tugged at her nightgown and exposed her breast. She guided the baby towards it and Millie's new daughter snuffled blindly at her like an inquisitive animal. All at once her little mouth latched on to the breast and gave a sharp tug that was almost a nip. Millie gasped at the unexpected pain.

'Just take it easy, hinny,' the old woman said gently. 'Here, hold her like this.'

Millie saw Dinah look away awkwardly. 'I think I'll be more help making another pot of tea,' she said, and hurried out of the room.

As the baby began to suck, Millie found her fear lessening and the sensation not unpleasant. Mrs Hodges sat beside her, watching quietly and occasionally throwing out pieces of advice like someone feeding titbits to pigeons. 'Your milk will come in proper in a few days ... don't tense yourself ... that's it. Now this is how you take her off without it hurting. That's it, hinny – now try the other side.'

Dinah came back with tea, and Millie carried on feeding, feeling proud and content in her new role as mother. Dan had got her to buy bottles and brushes in their spending frenzy on the new baby, but now that Millie had felt her daughter's trusting tug on her breast, she knew she wanted to feed her herself.

After a while, Mrs Hodges suggested that she stop. 'You don't want to overdo it at the beginning – make you sore. I'll give the bairn a wash and you can get some sleep.' She looked at Dinah with suspicion. 'Are you going to stop with her, or is someone else coming to help out?'

Dinah looked tired. 'I'll stay.'

Millie looked at her gratefully. 'Don't you have to get home for Bob?'

Dinah snorted. 'He can get his tea at the café

for once. I'll stop until Dan gets back. Bob knows where I am.'

Millie closed her eyes and felt the pull of sleep immediately. 'Thanks,' she murmured, unable to open her eyes even to watch her daughter lifted from her arms by the midwife. She heard them talking about her, insisting that she too should bathe and change into clean clothes, but she was asleep before the end of the conversation.

When she woke again, it was to the sound of a door banging below. Millie looked around, wondering where she was. The curtains were drawn and a lamp glowed from the room beyond. It took her a few seconds to realise that it was night-time and she was in her own bed. The familiar throbs and aches of her body as she stirred instantly brought back the memory of the birth. Someone had covered her over with bedclothes and wiped down her face and the blood from her hands while she slept. As she pulled herself up to look for her daughter, she heard the door to the flat open and Dinah's voice greet someone with the news.

'The bairn's come?' she heard Dan gasp with disbelief.

Dinah laughed. 'Aye, she had her right here.'

'A lass?' Dan questioned. Millie tensed herself for the disappointment in his voice, but none came. 'By, she's bonny, isn't she?' he exclaimed.

'A little picture,' Dinah agreed.

Suddenly it dawned on Millie that Dinah must be holding the baby, showing her daughter off to Dan. She felt a stab of resentment, excluded from the warm scene beyond the open door, where they laughed and cooed over her baby girl.

'Do you want a hold?' Dinah asked.

'Aye, if you show me how,' Dan laughed.

'Careful now … that's the way.' There was a small, querulous wail, then a giggle from Dinah. 'She's letting her da know who's boss.' Dan's laughter came again.

Millie waited to hear him ask about her, but they carried on chatting and she could tell that he was moving around the room as he cradled the baby, for she soon quietened. Finally it was Dinah who mentioned her.

'Millie's been asleep for hours,' she said. 'She refused to call the doctor. I got old Mrs Hodges in instead. She wouldn't take any payment.'

'I'll make sure she gets paid,' Dan insisted. 'Daft Millie. I wanted her to have the best. Ta for staying, Dinah.'

'I was glad to,' she said warmly. 'I'd do anything for the pair of you.'

Millie could not listen to any more. She pulled herself up, wincing at the pain between her legs and down her back, and called, 'Can anyone join in the party?'

There was a moment's pause, then Dan pushed the adjoining door wide with his foot.

'Millie!' he cried, steadying himself on the doorframe before launching into the bedroom. She smelt a waft of stale beer as he wove towards the bed and plonked himself down, still clutching their daughter. This produced a wail, and Millie quickly reached to rescue the baby from his precarious hold.

'Isn't she bonny?' Dan hiccuped. 'You should have called the doctor, mind. What if something had gone wrong?'

Millie glanced at Dinah. 'Mrs Hodges was grand. The cord was tied around the baby's neck when she was born–'

'Her neck?' Dan cried in shock. 'Millie! You should never have taken such a risk with our bairn.'

Dinah intervened. 'Mrs Hodges knew just what to do, Dan,' she reassured him. 'She saved the bairn's life.'

'That doctor couldn't have been any quicker, even with all his instruments,' Millie added. 'I was much happier having a woman with me – and Dinah.'

'Aye.' Dan smiled at their friend. 'Ta for looking after my stubborn wife.'

'Oh, I just sang a few songs,' Dinah laughed.

The baby's whimpering grew more insistent, and Millie decided to feed her again.

'What you doing?' Dan asked in alarm.

'What does it look like?' Millie laughed. 'Mrs Hodges told me how to do it.'

Dan stood up. 'Sounds like a saint, this Mrs Hodges. Let's celebrate and drink to the woman. There's some beer in the larder. I'll go and get Bob.'

He returned an hour later, having found Bob in the Waterloo just before closing time. By this time Millie was trying to sleep, the baby having dropped off at her breast. But both were woken by the shouts of the men, and soon Dinah was winding up the gramophone. After two hours of celebration, all the beer was drunk and the needle was wearing out on the gramophone. As the Fairishes called loud goodbyes to a drowsy Millie, Dinah said, 'You still haven't given the bairn a name.'

Dan asked as he swayed in the doorway, 'What's that woman called?'

'Which woman?' Dinah giggled.

'The midwife,' Dan said. 'Mrs Hedgerow or som'at.'

'Hodges,' Bob laughed. 'Edith Hodges.'

'That's it then,' Dan declared. 'She saved me bairn, so we'll call her Edith. What d'you say, Millie?'

Millie grunted agreement, too tired to protest that a family name might be more suitable. Right at that moment she would have called the baby anything to get some peace and rest. As she drifted into an exhausted sleep, she comforted herself with the thought that once her mother arrived, the parties and drinking would have to stop.

CHAPTER 14

Teresa came and stayed for nearly a month, revelling in her new granddaughter and in her first proper visit to Newcastle. Once Millie was back on her feet, they went out every day, proudly pushing Edith in her new pram up to the shops and round the park in the late-spring sunshine. Teresa loved it all: the wide, bustling streets, the myriad of shops, the ice-cream parlour on Cedar Crescent and the bands that played in the park. She made instant friends with Dinah and was persuaded to have her hair done at Laurie's. Several times Millie and Dinah took Teresa into the centre of Newcastle to look round the shops and have tea at Fenwick's or Tilley's. On other occasions, Mrs Hodges minded the baby while Millie took her mother to the music hall and to a concert of touring American gospel singers.

Bit by bit, Millie learned just how grim life had been in Ashborough over the past year; of the debt that saddled the hotel because of Teresa's generosity to starving neighbours, and how little Marjory had nearly died of whooping cough that winter.

'She's better now, but they had a terrible shock. Ella won't let her out of her sight. Walter's quieter than ever, he's a good family man. Ella's expecting again.'

Millie listened aghast to the tales of hardship, silently vowing that she would write to Ella. It pained her to be estranged from her oldest friend. She heard how Teresa had been forced to lay off Elsie, who had gone to work on a farm. But her greatest shock came with news of Grant and Ava.

'He's been blacklisted from the pit,' Teresa confided one time when they were out and Dan could not complain of them speaking about his family. 'I blame him for joining the Communist Party. Anyway, there's no work for him around Ashborough. They've only got a roof over their heads because old Mungo is still working. We'd've taken them in at the hotel, of course, but Grant's too proud to live off the likes of me and Joseph.'

'Is Ava very unhappy?' Millie asked, feeling sorry for her old rival.

'Aye,' Teresa sighed, rocking the pram with her hand as they sat on a park bench. They watched a boy run past rolling a hoop. 'She's got this bee in her bonnet about emigrating to America; thinks Grant could work in the mines out there.'

'America?' Millie gasped.

'She got hold of one of Grant's periodicals and read about it – Virginia or somewhere. Anyway, she's set on this idea. She gives him a terrible time, never a minute's peace. I think they'll go. That's why I'm making the most of this visit – it'll be the last if Ava leaves. I'll have no one to help me in the hotel.'

'I could always come home for a bit and help out if you want,' Millie offered at once. 'You only

235

have to ask.'

Her mother gave her an odd look. 'That's the first time I've ever heard you call the hotel home,' she answered. Millie flushed, and Teresa put a hand quickly over hers. 'It's kind of you to offer, but your home is here now. You've got everything you ever wanted, haven't you?'

Millie looked into the pram at Edith's sweet, soft, sleeping face and thought of their cosy flat full of sunshine and gramophone music and the way Dan would rush in cheerfully impatient to see them after a match. He was full of optimism these days, full of energy and fun. Even having Teresa around for a month, critical of his visits to the pub, his habit of leaving his crumpled clothes lying around and his occasional rash gamble on the horses, did not dampen his zest for the future.

'Yes, I've got everything,' Millie agreed. 'I've never been so happy.'

Teresa's eyes shone as she looked at her daughter, plumper now but still pretty. 'I'm glad for my silly Millie,' she smiled, feeling a rush of relief that she had made the right decision in leaving Craston all those years ago, and the two women hugged each other tight.

The summer passed happily, with Dan and Millie taking their daughter on trips to the seaside and into the country in their shiny black Ford. She was too young to even sit up and admire her surroundings, but they laid her on a rug, shaded from the sun, while they picnicked and splashed in the river and collected bunches of flowers to place in Edith's tiny bedroom. Sometimes Dinah and Bob would come with them and they would end up calling at some wayside pub on the way home, where the men would bring their pints to the door while the women sat in the car and Millie fed the baby.

The men were ecstatic over Newcastle winning the League that season and chatted about football for hours. Dan began to talk restlessly about making a move from the Vulcans. 'I've been with them two seasons now; it's only a matter of time before I'm transferred to a bigger club,' he declared to Millie. They were taking an evening stroll around the park in the late summer. Her heart sank at his words.

'But we're so happy here,' she protested. 'I love our flat – and the neighbours – and you're doing that well at Gateshead. Can't you just stop where you are?'

He gave her an impatient look. 'I can't stop there forever, Millie. I'm nearly twenty-seven. I've got to get on while I can.' He saw her disappointment and swung an arm around her shoulders. 'Don't look so sad. A transfer doesn't mean we have to move, does it?' he grinned.

She knew he was thinking that if Newcastle United or Sunderland approached him, they could stay on Tyneside. But the season started again and no offers came. Dan hid his disappointment and went back to playing for the Vulcans, and Millie felt secret relief that life could go on as it was.

Through that autumn, she heard intermittently from her mother. Ava had finally persuaded

Grant to leave for America, and they were making preparations to go before the winter set in. Teresa confided that while Grant would be working his passage, Joseph was helping pay for Ava by selling his dead wife's wedding ring and some of the furniture. He had been plagued by gout in one foot and was increasingly confined to his bed, worse at the thought of his daughter leaving. She had news that Elsie had married a shepherd, and that the Palace had closed, unable to compete with the newer, grander cinemas. Major Hall was looking for work.

Then, a month before Christmas, Grant turned up unannounced one afternoon as Millie was decorating the sitting room with tinsel. She was playing 'The Teddy Bears' Picnic' on the gramophone and Edith was sitting on the floor chewing paper decorations and gurgling to the music.

Millie flushed and stammered with awkwardness when she went to answer the door. 'I didn't expect... Where's...? Dan's not here.' She clasped Edith to her hip.

He stood in a worn suit and scarf, his broad face pinched with cold under an ill-fitting hat of Mungo's. 'I'll not stop long then,' he promised.

'Sorry, come in,' Millie said hastily, opening the door wide and leading him upstairs. She saw him glance around the cosy sitting room with its electric fire and comfortable chairs, its tidy surfaces and smell of polish. The record had come to an end and was hissing repetitively. Millie went over and lifted the needle. 'You'll have a cup of tea?'

He nodded. She went into the tiny galley

kitchen, still clasping Edith, who was making blowing noises to Grant. Millie was unnerved by his coming and wished Dan would hurry home from the club. She turned back.

'It's not bad news, is it?' she asked tensely.

Grant was still standing where she had left him, clutching his hat and loosening the scarf around his neck against the sudden heat. He shook his head. 'Nothing like that. I just wanted to come and make me peace with Dan before we leave. You've heard...?'

'About America?' she asked. 'Aye, Mam told me.'

He seemed to lose his nerve. 'Listen, I'll not stop. You can give Dan a message.'

Millie felt guilty for making him feel so ill at ease. 'No, stay, please, you must,' she insisted. 'You can't come all this way and not tell him yourself. Sit yourself down.' Impulsively she held out her daughter to him. 'Here, this is Edith, you've never met your niece, have you?'

'N-no,' he answered, unsure. But the infant held out her hands to the stranger, intrigued by the large hat, and he took her tentatively in out-stretched arms.

'She won't bite,' Millie laughed. 'Least not until nearer teatime.'

Grant gave a shy smile and held the child carefully, lowering himself into a chair and placing her on his knee. She smiled and made noises at him and tried to grab his hat. Grant let her inspect it, and when Millie came back through, Edith was trying to eat it while Grant spoke to her softly about how it belonged to her

Grandfather Nixon.

'Here, she can sit on the floor while you drink your tea,' Millie said, placing a cup on a square table by his chair. But Edith protested when she was plonked on the rug, and she grasped Grant's legs, attempting to pull herself up. He chuckled and hauled her up again. Millie had never heard him laugh out loud before.

'I'm sorry you're having to leave Ashborough,' she said suddenly. 'I can't imagine you living anywhere else.'

He gave her an appraising look. 'I have been out of the place before, you know,' he teased gently.

'Yes, of course you have,' Millie said quickly, recalling how he had spent most of the war away from home. 'You've seen more than most. But America seems so far away – so final somehow.'

They looked at each other in discomfort. She would have liked to ask him about the war, what it had been like and whether he had ever heard of her brother as they had both been fusiliers, but she did not have the courage. Effie had always told her not to mention the war in front of him, and so she let the moment pass.

'It's what Ava wants,' Grant said quietly.

'What about you?' Millie asked, wondering how she dared.

Grant shrugged. 'It's a new start for us. Things haven't been easy.' He cleared his throat. 'Anyway, you've got a nice place here – and Edith's a little charmer,' he smiled, changing the subject. He ruffled the child's honey-coloured curls and she gurgled in conversation. Millie had never seen her take so quickly to any man, except Dan.

She smiled back. 'Aye, she is. And how're Ella and Walter and little Marjory?'

Grant's face fell. 'They're getting by.'

'I hear they're having another bairn,' Millie said, sipping her tea.

Grant gave her a sorrowful look. 'Ella's bairn was born too early. It only lived a few hours.'

Millie put down her cup with a clash. 'That's terrible!' she gasped. 'When did that happen?'

'Maybes a fortnight ago,' Grant said, allowing Edith to grasp his hand.

'Mam's not written for a month,' Millie murmured. She gulped. 'Was it a girl or a boy?'

Grant shifted uncomfortably, unused to speaking about such things. 'I don't know. No one ever said – least not to me.'

Millie's eyes stung with tears. What agony for Ella to lose her baby like that, she thought. A baby dying after all the pain and effort of childbirth, slipping away without a name or a memory. 'Poor Ella and Walter!' Millie's voice trembled, and instinctively she reached for Edith.

'Here, I'll take her while you have your cup of tea – it's getting cold.' She almost grabbed the girl from him and cuddled her firmly in her arms.

After that they talked of Dan's football, and she told him about their life on Tyneside and he spoke of the debating society and how her mother had helped so many people out during the lockout. He told her about the ship that would take them to America, where the economy was booming, and talked of American politics.

241

'I'll be working my passage, of course,' he said with a proud jut of his chin. Only afterwards, when she was recounting the visit to Dan, did she realise that Grant had not mentioned Ava again.

Eventually, when Dan did not come, Grant took his leave. 'I have to catch the train.'

'You could stay the night,' Millie suggested.

'No,' Grant said quickly, 'I'll be expected home.'

'Aye, of course. I'm sorry you've missed Dan, I don't know why he's this late back. Maybe buying something in town.' Millie made excuses. 'He'll be that sorry to have missed you.'

They exchanged looks. 'Aye, well, you'll tell him I came. No hard feelings on my part,' Grant said in his usual gruff way. He fixed on his hat and patted Edith once more on the head. 'Ta-ra, pet,' he smiled at her. 'Ta-ra, Millie. I'll see myself out.'

They regarded each other, then awkwardly shook hands. 'Ta for coming,' she said, suddenly regretting that she had never made the effort to know Dan's older brother better. 'And good luck.' He nodded and left. She looked out of the window, holding Edith, and watched him walk past the streetlamp. Something made him look up, catch sight of them both and wave. Millie saw he was smiling. Then he was gone into the dark and she was left feeling strangely sad.

That night, when Dan finally returned with Christmas toys for Edith, Millie was tearful as she told him the news about Ella's lost baby. But Dan seemed annoyed rather than pleased by Grant's attempt to see him and make amends.

Perhaps he felt guilty, Millie thought, because he had not been there to see his brother or because he had not thought of the gesture first.

'You never told me he was serious about emigrating!' Dan exclaimed. 'I would have tried to see him.'

'You knew as much about it as I did,' Millie defended.

'And fancy turning up here without any warning,' Dan said indignantly. 'He knew I'd be at the club working. I think he came at that time knowing he'd only catch you in.'

'Don't be daft,' Millie said, losing patience. 'He's been out of work that long, he probably didn't think about the time of day.'

'Well, that's not my fault. Anyway, why you sticking up for Grant all of a sudden? You never used to like him,' Dan accused.

'Don't let's argue over him,' Millie sighed, giving in. 'I've bought some chestnuts for a treat. Why don't we have Bob and Dinah round for the evening?'

Dan brightened at this suggestion and calmed down. He was soon playing with Edith, trying out the presents that he could not wait to give her for Christmas. Their friends came round, bringing a bottle of sherry, and soon the argument over Grant was forgotten and the visit was never mentioned again.

Christmas came and went with happy activity: a service in the local parish church, Christmas dinner at the flat with their friends and the widowed Mrs Hodges, and a trip to see Dan play in a Boxing Day match.

At New Year they went round to the Fairishes while Mrs Hodges minded Edith. They celebrated at the Waterloo and then called in on neighbours, before ending up back at their friends'. Dinah said tipsily, 'Dan, you be our first caller of the New Year. Out you go! I'll show you where the coal is kept.' They disappeared into the back yard, and when Millie thought they'd been gone too long, she went looking for them. When she called there was a scuffling in the doorway of the darkened coal shed and Dinah appeared, stifling a giggle.

'What's going on in there?' Millie said tartly to Dan, as he appeared looking dishevelled.

'Couldn't find the coal,' he laughed.

But after that the party went flat and Millie persuaded Dan to leave. 'You've got the match tomorrow, remember?'

Later she tried to question him about the incident in the shed. 'Were you kissing Dinah?'

Dan lay on the bed. 'We were having a laugh, that's all. It's New Year, Millie man. Come here and give me a kiss.'

Millie shrugged off her feeling of disquiet. Everyone had had too much to drink, that was all. Dan loved her and was devoted to Edith, so she had nothing to worry about. The next time she met Dinah, her friend showed no embarrassment and the incident was never mentioned again. Millie decided to forget about it, thinking she must have imagined the sight of them embracing in the dark. Yet after that, she and Dinah were never quite as close nor as keen to spend so much time together as they had done over the past two years. When she observed Dan and Dinah in each other's company there was never an improper gesture or word, though now and again she caught a look that passed between them and wondered if it meant anything more than it should.

Nineteen twenty-eight rushed by with Dan enjoying his football and Millie delighting in every advance that Edith made. She found herself writing long letters to her mother about the child. '...*She won't stop in her pram if she can help it, she wants to be running round the park. She chats to anyone who passes, mostly nonsense, but she makes noises as if she's having a great long chinwag! Dan has bought her a little ball and she kicks it to him and he dives to save it as if she's made a great strike at goal. Who would have thought I'd have a daughter who could play football before she can walk properly! She's the apple of her daddy's eye, of course. He's never regretted that she wasn't the boy he thought we were getting. She can tell when he's coming home before he reaches the outside door. She toddles towards the window and demands to be held up and nine times out of ten, he's there in the street, walking up to the flat. It's a feeling I used to get when Dan was nearby and I think Edith's got it too. I wish you could see her. Maybe when the season's over, Dan will drive us up for a visit. You'll never believe how much she's grown. I show her your picture on the mantelpiece – the one from the wedding – and she says Nana every time...*'

She never mentioned to her mother her concern that they were spending too much money. It had been fun at first, buying whatever they wanted. But now that they had Edith to care for, Millie wanted security more than ever and would have been happy to forgo some of the treats Dan brought home for them. She began to worry over his extravagance and how having Edith around had done nothing to curb his appetite for drinking his way around town after matches. For some reason Dan also felt a need to keep up with the Fairishes, who were happy spenders; hence the need to have their own car. Bob had made money on the horses and he and Dinah were in the process of buying the hairdressing business from old Mrs Laurie. Bob was a risk-taker, but a shrewd one. 'There's a future in hair,' he kept declaring, and when Millie thought of how the fashion in hairstyles was forever changing these days, she wondered if he might be right. But when Bob had suggested that Dan put some money into his new venture, Millie had not encouraged it. 'We don't have that sort of money,' she pointed out. Privately she pondered whether her reluctance was more to do with keeping Dan and Dinah apart. They saw enough of each other socially without them becoming business partners, Millie thought, and then felt churlish at her suspicions.

When the season ended, Dan came home and announced that the Vulcans were going on a foreign tour during June. 'We'll be playing in Italy and Hungry!' he enthused. 'And I'll be getting a full wage – so that should please you.'

'How long will you be gone?' Millie asked, pleased for him but dismayed at being left alone. She had been so looking forward to the summer break when they could spend time together and take Edith out on trips.

'We'll be gone about three or four weeks, not long,' Dan assured her, kissing her. 'It'll fly over.'

'I'll miss you,' Millie told him, snuggling into his hold.

'Not as much as I'll miss the pair of you,' Dan replied. 'But you'll have Dinah to keep you company.' Millie slid him a look. Had he really not noticed that her friendship with Dinah had cooled since New Year? Dinah always said she was too busy at work these days to come round as much, and Millie used Edith as an excuse not to go into town as often as they used to. She suddenly thought how lonely she would be, left in Newcastle without Dan.

Later Millie said what was on her mind. 'I think I'll go back to Mam's while you're away, instead of stopping here on me own. She hasn't seen the bairn all year. And I can be useful lending a hand in the hotel.'

'I'll not have you skivvying there like the old days.' Dan was dubious.

Millie laughed. 'You know I'm not the kind who can sit around doing nothing all day long.'

'Well, if that's what you'd rather do, I'll drive the pair of you up to Ashborough before I go,' Dan insisted.

The evening before they left, they took Edith for a walk round the park and watched the bowlers playing on the green in the mellow sunshine. Dan treated them to ice-creams at the parlour on Cedar Crescent and carried his daughter home on his shoulders, singing football chants, while she giggled to be up so high.

Later, as they lay in bed, the window open against the stuffy, airless night, Dan and Millie made love with a tender urgency. 'We've never been apart this long since I went away to London as a lass,' Millie mused sadly.

'I know,' Dan whispered, caressing her hair, 'but it's worse for me. You'll have Edith with you – I'll be stuck with a bunch of footballers.'

'You'll love it,' Millie answered with a wry smile. 'Just don't pay too much attention to the foreign women.'

Dan rolled over and tickled her. 'You've nothing to be jealous about,' he assured her. 'You're the only lass for me, Millie.'

'Good,' she laughed, and kissed him.

'I mean it,' Dan said, suddenly serious. 'I'd be nothing without you and the bairn. The footie wouldn't be enough.'

Millie answered his tender smile, realising how deep her love for him still went. 'Kiss me again then,' she whispered, 'while we've still got each other.'

Millie closed her eyes as Dan's lips pressed down on hers, urgent and possessive, showing he needed her as strongly as she yearned for him. She lay for a long time afterwards, warm in his hold, listening to the night sounds of tugs on the river, a distant train and someone singing their way home up the street. Edith lay sleeping peacefully in the next room and Millie felt a deep contentment, wishing life could go on like this for ever.

Edith cried loudly when Dan drove away in the car, disappearing down the street with horn hooting. Although the road was no longer cobbled but laid with a proper surface, dust rose up in clouds from his speedy departure. Millie, standing waving goodbye, knew he was just showing off rather than being in any real haste to get away. Yet he had declined her suggestion of visiting Walter and Ella before he left. 'You're much better at knowing what to say,' he had answered. 'I just seem to spark off the fights.'

'You'll come for us when you're back?' Millie had asked.

Dan had promised her he would and kissed her roundly in front of Teresa, then made a fuss over leaving Edith.

So Edith was now in tears and her grand-mother was ready to spoil her with cuddles and sweets. But the small child clung to her mother, not yet sure of this loud woman with the untidy hair, who smelt of carbolic soap and lavender water. She was more intrigued by Joseph, who snoozed in the sunshine with a newspaper over his face and his bad leg propped on a footstool that Teresa carried around for him.

'That's Grandpa Joseph,' Teresa told her grand-daughter. 'He likes to sleep a lot.' She glanced at Millie and lowered her voice. 'Either that or he's sitting at the dining-room window watching the trains come in, hoping Ava will be on one of them. Can't accept she's gone for good. Mind, it's been bliss round here without her constant complaining.'

'Have you heard from them recently?' Millie

asked, following her mother into the kitchen carrying Edith. The room seemed smaller than she had remembered, and gloomy after the brightness outside.

Teresa nodded. 'They've settled somewhere called Pennsylvania, but Ava was vague about Grant's work. I'm not even sure he's down a pit. Still, she goes on about how great the place is – living off ice-cream sodas by the sounds of it.'

'Well, I'm glad they're happy,' Millie said, removing Edith's matinée coat and thinking how sooty all their clothes were going to get. The kitchen was filthy. There appeared to be no travellers staying and the hotel wore a forlorn, down-at-heel look that reminded Millie of when they had first arrived there. With Moody to nurse and no Elsie or Ava to help out, her mother seemed sapped of the energy or enthusiasm to make the place attractive. Millie resolved to have a good scrub-round in the morning. Her mother was far more interested in winning the approval of her granddaughter.

'Give the little pet to me,' Teresa insisted, sweeping Edith on to her knee and ignoring her protests. As soon as biscuits and milk were produced, the girl acquiesced. At bedtime that night, Teresa played nursery rhymes on the piano and sang through her old repertoire of music-hall songs, which delighted the child. Before long Edith was like her grandmother's shadow, tottering along behind her, calling 'Na-na!' and pulling her hand until she got what she wanted.

Teresa delighted in showing her off around Ashborough, taking her into shops and calling round on friends like Mrs Dodswell. Millie was sure Edith would burst with the amount of cake she was fed on these visits, though judging by the mess of crumbs, more ended up on the floor than in her mouth.

For a week, Millie worked at smartening up the hotel, scrubbing down the walls, washing the windows and polishing the furniture. She did enormous washes of table and bed linen that had sat in damp cupboards since before the strike, and baked scones and current loaves to entice shoppers in for a refreshing cup of tea. By the end of the week, with a board outside to advertise their teas, the dining room was once more in use and Millie found herself enjoying the work.

But the frantic activity was not just to fill the emptiness of not having Dan around, as her mother suspected. 'You can't go putting off seeing Ella much longer,' Teresa said, in gentle reproof. 'She knows you're back. Her aunt was in here having tea yesterday.'

Millie felt like replying that she had been too busy and that Ella could just as easily have called to see her. But she knew that was not fair and that she would have to make the effort to salvage the friendship. She dreaded the encounter. What would she say to her estranged friend? Would she be received in her house at all after the terrible fight between Dan and his brothers nearly two years before? Finally she took Edith round shortly before tea-time, so that she would have an excuse not to stay for long.

It was Walter who answered her knocking, looking bleary-eyed from sleep.

'I'm sorry, I've woken you,' Millie apologised. 'I'll call another time.'

He blinked at her a few seconds before recognition dawned. 'By, you're looking well, Millie,' he smiled. 'I was just taking a nap before night shift. Ella and the bairn are up at Drake's farm – picking strawberries. Why don't you gan up and meet them?'

Millie was encouraged by his welcome and the fuss he made over Edith, leaning into the battered pram Teresa had borrowed for her and tickling her chin.

'You're a Nixon,' he chuckled. 'You could be sisters with our Marjory.' As she left, Walter asked, 'Dan not with you then?'

Millie shook her head. 'On tour abroad,' she explained.

Walter gave a twisted smile, the nearest she had ever seen to envy on his fair face. 'By, the lad's done well for himself, I'll say that.'

Millie found Ella and Marjory in one of the lower fields at Drake's, where the farm bordered the edge of the town. Ella was wearing an old-fashioned bonnet to keep off the sun, while Marjory's mouth and fingers were stained with red juice. The small girl came running up to scrutinise the object in the pram.

'Hello, I'm your Auntie Millie and this is your cousin Edith,' Millie explained with a nervous smile.

Marjory grew quite excited, not knowing what a cousin was but aware that the gesticulating baby somehow belonged to her. 'Dith! Dith!' she lisped. 'Look, Mammy, at the baby!' The two women regarded each other in awkward silence while their daughters prodded one another with inquisitive fingers and Marjory asked questions that received incomprehensible babbling from Edith.

Millie thought Ella's face had hardened; there were lines around her mouth and eyes that had not been there before. It appeared Ella had nothing to say to her. Millie saw her stare at Edith with a strange look. Was it resentful, or just pained? Millie wondered.

All of a sudden Millie was swept by a wave of sympathy for the anguished woman. Taking a step towards her, she held out her arms. 'I'm sorry about your baby, Ella. I really am sorry!'

Ella's stern look crumpled like a child's and she fell forward into Millie's outstretched arms. They hugged while Ella broke down sobbing and clung to her friend.

'Oh, Millie, it was terrible! *Terrible!*' Millie held her while she shook with bitter crying. 'And n-now,' Ella spoke with difficulty, 'n-no one wants to mention him,' she wept.

Millie stroked her hair, knowing that somehow she had to comfort her friend, yet feeling quite inadequate to do so. She asked tentatively, 'It was a boy, then?'

'Aye,' Ella sobbed. 'A little l-lad.'

'Did you – see him?' Millie asked gently.

Ella nodded, her face red and swollen, but for a moment the question seemed to calm her. 'He looked that like his dad – a miniature Walter. And he was still breathing. I felt his breath warm on me fingers. But they took him away and I never got to see him again...!'

Ella broke down once more, and Millie held her tight as she cried uncontrollable tears, stored up and forbidden until this moment. No other words were necessary, just comforting arms. Ella had confided her innermost feelings and Millie knew she had never lost her friendship. It might have been damaged by jealousy, neglect or too much money, but it was still there.

Marjory gazed at her mother and the stranger in apprehension. She hesitated a while and then, growing distressed, pulled on Millie's linen dress, saying, 'Don't make Mammy cry.'

Millie felt tears flood her own throat at the girl's words. Bending down, she swung Marjory into her arms too, kissing her sticky cheek. 'I'm sorry. I won't make Mammy cry again, promise.' She looked at Ella. 'I've kept away too long. I should've been more help. Do you forgive me?'

Ella sniffed, gulping back her tears. 'Aye, of course I do.' She wiped her wet face on her sleeve. 'I feel bad myself about the last time you came – letting Ava say all those spiteful things in me own home, and you me oldest friend.'

'Maybes we both said things we shouldn't have.' Millie flushed with shame. 'You must have hated the way we came visiting like Lord and Lady Muck – and in that car. When I think of what it must've been like for you during the strike...!'

'We got by,' Ella said stiffly, lifting Marjory from Millie's arms. For a moment Millie feared she had wounded her friend's feelings again by mentioning that terrible year. But Ella gave her a bashful look and added, 'I've missed you, Millie. Ashborough's been that dull without you and Dan here.'

Millie felt a great surge of relief to be forgiven. She vowed she would never be so selfish again. 'Well, I'm here for the summer,' she promised, 'so we're going to make the most of it.' And for the first time in too long, the friends smiled at each other.

CHAPTER 15

Millie found herself enjoying being back in Ashborough far more than she had expected. Her enthusiasm for bringing life back to the hotel seemed to infect her mother, and she noticed how Teresa began to care about her appearance once more. Her step was brighter and she showed interest in the customers who came for tea or Millie's homemade lemonade and shortbread biscuits. Millie began to realise just how much the strike and its impoverished aftermath had taken a toll on her mother's health and spirits. While she had been enjoying life in Newcastle as never before, Teresa had been barely scraping a living at the hotel, worn down by helping out her neighbours and Dan's family and nursing Moody.

But now her hands, which had stiffened up over the winter and made it painful to play the piano, were loosened by the warm weather and she delighted in playing for customers, but especially for Edith. The pair were inseparable. While Millie worked and enjoyed the purpose and activity to her days, her mother would spoil Edith with treats and visits, games and music. Millie thought about the months in Newcastle she had whiled away doing nothing very much except spend money, and wondered how she had managed to fill her days.

At the hotel, she got up early and breakfasted with Edith before her mother and Joseph awoke, then lit the fire and planned the modest menus and shopping for the day. After a morning of chores and dealing with deliveries, she would take Edith to the park, returning in time to serve teas. A trickle of travellers began to turn up at the hotel enquiring about bed and board, and for the first time in two years her mother placed an advertisement in the local newspaper encouraging societies to hold their annual dinners and functions there once more.

On sunny days, Teresa would shoo them out of doors and Millie would push Edith round in the pram to Ella's house. If the weather stayed fair, they would take the girls for a stroll along the river, packing a picnic of egg sandwiches, buttered teacake and a flask of sweet milky tea. They would trail their bare feet in the water and throw sticks into the current with Marjory, while Edith crawled around trying to eat the soil. They talked and talked, catching up on the years they had been apart, reminiscing about London, speculating about Ava and Grant in America and talking of the future.

'I wonder where you'll go next?' Ella mused, as they lay in the dappled shade of a willow tree sucking strands of grass. 'It must be exciting not knowing. I suppose me and Walter will stay in the same house in the same street until they put us in our boxes.'

Millie laughed. 'It used to excite me, the thought of going to different places. But I think I'm happiest when I'm settled and know the folk that live around me. I like living in Newcastle. I don't want to leave. But I know I'll have to if Dan's to get on.'

In fact the thought of the upheaval of moving and starting somewhere new filled Millie with dread. She knew it was likely once Dan returned from tour that he would be looking for a transfer, if only to pay off some of the debts they were accumulating. But she hated the idea of moving any further away from Ashborough and her mother. She pushed it from her mind. For now she was going to enjoy the sunshine and the countryside and the freedom to do as she pleased with Ella and their daughters. She knew that Ella felt the same. Since losing the baby, her friend had been nervous about going out and meeting people, shying away from company. But with Millie she could be herself because her friend was patient when bouts of grief gripped her. To Walter's obvious relief, Ella was learning how to laugh again in Millie's company.

During that month they went to the annual pitmen's picnic, when all the mining villages from around Northumberland unfurled their banners and marched together behind their brass bands. Millie watched Edith's animated face as she carried her through the crowds to the field where they gathered for the picnic, speeches and games. She was reminded of her own earliest memories, riding high on her father's shoulders or piggy-back on Graham, almost sick with excitement at the enormous gathering. Living on the coast at Craston, they would have to rise at dawn to walk into Ashborough in their finest clothes and catch the special train laid on from the colliery gates, or one of the horse-drawn carriages.

Millie's vision blurred at the sudden recollection and she scanned the crowds for any sign of her long-lost father. She spotted the Craston banner with its revolutionary figure declaring 'Emancipation of Labour' and the pile of brass instruments being minded by picnicking families. One or two faces were familiar, and she edged closer, wondering if she dared ask after her father. It was nearly eight years since she had lived in the village, and she doubted whether anyone would recognise her with her bobbed hair and plumper features. But before she could pluck up the courage, Ella was dragging her off in the other direction.

'I don't want to be spotted by some nosy old neighbour,' Ella hissed. 'They'd only ask questions and I don't want to talk about … you know.' So the moment passed and Millie banished her curiosity, half disappointed, half relieved not to speak to anyone from her old village.

A week later was the Ashborough Carnival, and the women spent many happy hours preparing for the fun. Millie insisted that this year the hotel should have a float in the parade through the town, and she set about organising it with Ella's help. They decided to dress up as American jazz musicians and inveigled the help of Major Hall, who agreed to play the piano and borrowed black jackets and bow ties for the women. Millie persuaded the Co-operative store to lend them a horse and dray by promising to advertise them on their banner, and then decorated it with red, white and blue bunting. With the help of Walter and some of his friends, they hauled the hotel piano on to the float and lassoed its feet with rope. Kenny Manners, who owned a trumpet, took little persuasion to play, while Millie and Ella and Elsie's sister Mary – who now worked at the Co-op – got hold of football whistles, tambourines and two banjos from the pawn shop. Major Hall taught Millie and Walter how to play three chords.

Millie secretly hoped that Dan might be back in time for the Carnival, for it was the end of June and she expected him to appear any day. But the Saturday came and he did not arrive. Instead Millie threw herself into last-minute preparations for the tea dance that she had organised for the afternoon.

The morning was bright and blustery and she thought their banner and bunting would be blown away before the parade had started. Kenny and Walter turned up looking smart in dinner jackets, while Major Hall wore a striped blazer and boater, grinning beneath his eye patch. They laughed at the women dressed up in baggy trousers and waistcoats, their hair oiled with brilliantine, their bow ties at raffish angles. Teresa and the small girls were dressed in pale-blue frocks with matching headbands. Teresa and Marjory wore false pearls and feathers in their headdresses, while Edith kept pulling off her headband in annoyance.

They were the noisiest float in the whole

parade, riding up Dyke Road and turning down Fern Street, Teresa and Bob Hall thumping the piano in a jazz duet, Millie and Walter on banjos, Kenny on trumpet and the others a discordant mix of whistles, tambourines and shrieks from the children. As they went, Ella and Mary threw out handwritten bills inviting people to come to the afternoon tea dance at the hotel. The crowds clapped and cheered and laughed, while children ran alongside shouting out requests.

They ended up at Thomas Burt Park, ranged around the football pitch, besides stalls selling pies and peas or seafood, and hand-carts offering drinks or ice-creams. There were several bands playing, including the colliery band, a veterans' military band and a couple of church bands. Millie and her mother got carried away by the music and the children dancing in front of the bands, and egged on by the crowd they played again, banging and screeching their way through an improvised rendering of 'When the Saints Go Marching In'.

By early afternoon it had started to cloud over, and before they had lurched their way back to the Co-operative stables, the rain began, huge, steady drops out of the thunderous air that soon turned to a downpour. They tumbled into the hotel laughing and shaking off the rain from their costumes and hair, wrapping the children in towels and plonking them by the hearth. Teresa was worried the weather would keep people away from their tea dance, but the town was full of families from outlying villages looking for something to do out of the rain.

Millie persuaded Kenny and the others to stay. 'Major Hall, you could lead the dancing, get people on their feet,' she suggested, 'while Mam and Kenny play.'

An hour later, Millie and Ella could hardly keep up with the demand for teas and refreshments, while Teresa played the piano and Kenny gave sudden bursts on the trumpet. The Major went around the room, offering to partner different dancers. He seemed to have the knack of searching out the maiden aunt or widow who longed to dance but needed coaxing on to the floor. Millie noticed that they were soon won over by his natural courtesy and shy charm, and the dance was a huge success.

As the numbers eventually dwindled and they began to clear up, Millie went outside to shake the tablecloths. The rain had eased off and the sky was clearing once more. Three women passed her on their way out of the hotel, and the oldest one gave her a sideways look. Millie had been half aware of being watched by this particular woman during the tea dance and thought there was something familiar about her weathered features. But under her purple pudding-shaped hat, she could have been any of several women she had seen around Ashborough.

The woman walked on, hesitated, then turned round and came back.

'You don't remember me, do you?' she asked. Her companions stood apart, waiting, looking ill at ease.

Millie smiled. 'I'm sorry, I don't quite...'

'Your mam doesn't either,' the woman grunted,

'or pretends she doesn't. Which is strange, since I lived five doors up from you for long enough.'

Millie stared harder at the ageing woman, confused. Then suddenly a memory sparked. She was talking about Craston. This was a neighbour from Saviour Street, the first she had come face to face with since their undignified flit. Millie's heart thumped nervously to be so abruptly confronted with the past they had disowned.

'Mrs Gilfillan?' she whispered. The woman nodded, triumphant.

'Aye, I thought you'd remember, for all your mam doesn't want to know her old neighbours.'

Millie almost leapt to her mother's defence, wanting to tell this woman that it was folk like her who had ostracised her mother and made life unbearable in Craston. But she bit back her retort, realising that it would only do harm to her mother's business if she was rude. It was all too long in the past to stir up old enmities.

'It's nice of you to come. Have you enjoyed your tea, Mrs Gilfillan?' Millie forced herself to ask with a smile.

She nodded. 'Aye, I have. It's the first time I've been in and I must say I'm surprised at how respectable it is. Not what I'd heard. I wouldn't have gone in, but me daughters wanted to.' She nodded at the others. Millie did not recognise the Gilfillan girls; they had been younger than her by three or four years. 'Course, your mam was always one for the piano.' Mrs Gilfillan gave a sniff of disapproval. 'We were all that shocked when she left like she did. The shame for Mr Mercer!' she tutted. 'Don't suppose you ever see your father these days?'

Millie felt winded. She groped for something to say to this woman who had so casually insulted her mother, and asked such an impertinent question. But something in Mrs Gilfillan's voice alerted her. If she was asking if she ever saw her father, did this mean that she knew he was still alive? Millie dared to wonder.

She stepped forward and put a hand on the older woman's arm. She smelt of damp tweed and cinders, and the smell brought back the memory of Saviour Street more powerfully than any words. 'Do – do you know where he is, Mrs Gilfillan?' she gasped.

The woman stepped away, alarmed at the pained look on Millie's face.

'Well, no, I don't,' she blustered. 'He hasn't been in Craston for many years.'

Millie persisted, her heart hammering. 'But you've never heard that he's died?' She forced out the question, her throat drying with nervousness.

Mrs Gilfillan grew uncomfortable. 'I really wouldn't know about that. But I'm sure if your Aunt Hannah had heard anything she would have told me.' She looked around in panic. 'Now I really must catch up with me daughters.' Millie saw the woman was about to walk away, yet this might be her one chance of learning some clue as to her father's whereabouts.

'Please, Mrs Gilfillan,' she stopped her, 'can you just tell me where you think he went? Anything!' she pleaded.

The woman shook her head. 'He just disappeared one day – walked out of Craston like your mam did. We'd heard he'd tried to see you in Ashborough, but hadn't been able to persuade that woman to come back. So I suppose he had nothing to stop around for. Your aunt's never got over the shame of it all.'

Millie's look was one of bitter disappointment. She thought the old neighbour would say nothing more, but Mrs Gilfillan added in a kinder voice, 'Mind, I did hear from your aunt that she'd met someone who thought they'd seen him a couple of years back.'

'Where?' Millie whispered.

'In Newcastle. Thought he'd got work on the new Tyne Bridge. That's all I know and it might not be reliable. Now I must be off.' Mrs Gilfillan turned and hurried away, leaving Millie staring after her, feeling faint.

Was it possible that her father could have been living in Newcastle all the time that she had? Millie wondered. Had she unknowingly passed him in the street? Dan had sometimes taken her to watch the building of the new bridge and its bold arch of girders growing across the Tyne. From a distance she had gazed at the men crawling up scaffolding and working cranes and wondered how they had the nerve for such heights. Could she possibly have observed her own father at work? She tortured herself with the thought.

Ella appeared at her side. 'What's wrong?' she asked, catching a glimpse of the departing women. 'Who was that?'

Millie stood trembling and shook her head. 'No one important,' she gulped, too shocked to speak of the encounter, even to Ella. Her friend gathered up the tablecloths where Millie had let them fall. 'These'll need a good wash now. Haway, Millie, your mam's saying we should gan to the carnival dance the night. We haven't been to the Egyptian Ballroom in years. What do you say?'

Millie gave a guilty glance towards the hotel, hoping her mother had not been watching. Teresa would only be angry and upset if she knew she had been talking to Mrs Gilfillan and trying to find news of her father. It seemed somehow disloyal. Ellis Mercer had made only one drunken, half-hearted attempt to see her in all these years, while her mother had worked tirelessly and sacrificed her reputation for her. She knew Teresa would go to the ends of the earth for her and Edith, whereas her father had been weak and buckled under the weight of responsibilities. He had not loved her enough, else he would have tried harder to win them back, Millie reasoned harshly. So why make herself so upset thinking she might have been living near him for the past two years? Her memories of him had faded; if she met him they would probably have nothing to say to each other.

She forced herself to be composed. Looking at Ella, she realised her friend was suggesting going to a dance for the first time since her baby had died. It was a brave step. She took Ella's arm.

'That would be grand, I'd love to go to the dance,' she agreed. Taking a deep breath, she hurried Ella back into the hotel. 'Let's get out of these lads' clothes,' she said. 'You can wear one of me dresses if you like.'

Ella grinned at the familiar phrase. In London they had constantly swapped clothes, unable to afford new outfits. 'Just like old times,' she laughed, as they went in together.

It was the middle of July before Dan finally came for her. Millie had grown worried at not hearing from him and had sent a telegram to the club. They had replied the next day, saying the touring side had returned ten days previously. Millie was all for rushing back to Tyneside with Edith, but her mother persuaded her to send another telegram.

'What if he's not at the flat?' Teresa argued. 'You'd have gone back early for nothing.'

'Well, where else could he be?' Millie demanded, knowing her mother wanted to delay her departure with Edith as long as possible.

'Maybe he's taking a few days' holiday, just having a quiet time,' Teresa answered. 'He'll turn up when he's ready.'

One afternoon, when Millie was returning from Ella's pushing a sleeping Edith, she saw the black Ford parked outside the hotel. She raced towards the open back door, shouting for Dan. He came running out, grinning, his face tanned and his hair glinting in the sun, and opened his arms wide. Millie ran into them, laughing as he picked her up, swung her round and kissed her hard on the lips.

'By, I've missed you!' He kissed her again.

'Where have you been?' Millie cried.

267

'Sorting out me transfer,' Dan grinned. 'We're off to pastures new, Millie. The Black Country! Kilburn Wanderers. Still Second Division, but they're on the up.'

Millie felt a lurch of disappointment. This was the news she had not wanted to hear. 'How far away is that?' she asked, as Dan let her go and went eagerly to see Edith.

'Still as bonny as ever,' he crowed, gazing at their daughter.

'Don't wake her,' Millie said hastily, but he was already plucking her out of the shaded pram.

'Let me have a look at you!' he cried. 'By, she's heavy. What's your mam been feeding her?' Edith woke up, startled, and began to cry. But Dan just laughed and bounced his daughter around in his arms. 'You'll love it where we're going,' Dan said to the small girl. 'There's a big viaduct just opposite the house we're getting – you can see all the trains going by. And there's a canal with boats on.'

'A house?' Millie asked with more interest. 'They're giving us a house?'

'Aye,' Dan smiled, 'they really want me.' He kissed Edith happily and her crying subsided.

Millie slipped her arm through his, determining to put a brave face on the move. At least the three of them would be facing the unknown together.

CHAPTER 16

Dan and Millie moved that August, hastily packing up their flat in Paradise Parade and saying goodbye to their friends. Bob and Dinah seemed strangely distant, as if they had already lost interest in Dan now that he was moving away and was no longer a local celebrity on the street. Bob had pressed a sovereign into Edith's plump hand and wished them well, and Dinah had kissed them all and told Millie, 'You take care of your lass – and keep a good eye on Dan.' She had laughed as she said it, and winked, but it had made Millie uncomfortable and she had almost been relieved when they had gone.

'What did she mean by that?' she had asked. Dan had swung an arm around her carelessly and said, 'Just Dinah being Dinah. I hope we make as good friends as the Fairishes in our next place.' But Millie was doubtful just how close they had been. She could not shake off the notion that their friends had been attracted to Dan because of his local popularity and his generosity. Bob and Dinah had never been so eager to delve into their own pockets for others. They were now running a prosperous little business while she and Dan were leaving for the Midlands with their furniture only half paid for, the car sold and nothing in the bank.

She found it harder to say goodbye to Mrs

Hodges, the woman who had brought Edith safely into the world. 'You go and enjoy your life, hinny, with that beautiful bairn,' the widow said, unusually tearful at kissing Edith goodbye. Promising to keep in touch, Millie left the midwife a studio photograph of her, Dan and Edith taken the previous Christmas and set in a tortoiseshell frame.

The train journey south and west was long and tiring, and Millie was not cheered by what greeted them. The terraced house the club had provided was damp and dingy, any daylight blocked out by the towering viaduct that arched overhead. The windows and walls vibrated when trains rattled by and the wallpaper in the front room was lifting with mildew. Millie's spirits sank even further when she surveyed the antiquated kitchen with its old black range and open fire. It would be back to humping coal, blackleading the grate and keeping the fire stoked for boiling water and cooking.

'Just until we get turned around and find somewhere else,' Dan said, catching her look. 'You'll make it cosy, I bet.'

But the winter came and there was never any mention of moving house. Millie managed as best she could with the temperamental range and the lack of space to dry Edith's nappies. They were too near the railway line to hang the washing out; it was blackened with soot marks in minutes. Night after night, Millie would be startled out of sleep by the thunder of a train above that sounded as though it was coming in through the window. Neighbours and shop-keepers were friendly, and occasionally Millie would meet the wives of other players, but she found it hard starting again knowing no one.

Their sitting room was too damp to use and so they did not invite people round to the house. Sitting in the fug of her cramped kitchen for hours on end, trying to prevent Edith from tottering into the fire or pulling everything off the table, Millie thought nostalgically of the freedom of the previous summer at home: the riverside picnics, the bustle of the tea room, chats in the kitchen with a constant stream of callers, the music and dancing. For in her heart, Ashborough was still home, and she longed for her mother's company. She missed Ella and Walter and little Marjory, she missed the banter and laughter of Bob Hall and Kenny Manners. She even missed the solid, dependable presence of Joseph Moody, snoozing under his newspaper, for at least he was around, whereas Dan frequently was not.

Christmas that year was dull, despite Millie's attempts at decorating their leaking house and making mince pies with Edith, and there was no visiting of neighbours at New Year. Dan was often absent, the cramped house unable to contain his restlessness. Millie was aware of him drinking more frequently, and he came home one night with cuts about his face, having been involved in a fight. Millie's fussing only worsened his temper.

'It was over nothing,' he insisted. 'Just some so-called supporter having a go at me. It's not my fault the team's doing badly, I'm not being fed the passes to score goals.'

'Shouldn't you have gone to the police?' Millie asked, trying to bathe his swollen eye.

Dan shook her off. 'I can handle myself. I'm not the type to go crying to teacher.'

Only Millie could tell how unhappy he was becoming, for he kept up his cheerful bravado to the outside world. She guessed that for the first time in his life he was anxious about the way he was playing, worried that his talent might be on the wane. He would grumble about the meagre pay footballers received.

'It's the poor man's sport, Millie,' he would complain. 'Only the managers do well out of it. Look at other sports – golf, boxing, tennis – they all get better paid than we do. Do you know what baseball players get in America? Ten thousand pounds a year! Even cricketers are getting ten or fifteen pounds a match – more than double my wages.'

Millie too began to fret that the move had been a bad one for them, for not only their dreams but their very livelihood depended on Dan's footballing success. Up until now, she had never questioned that he would succeed. He tried to keep from her how badly the season was going at the club, but she read the results for herself in the local newspaper, and the creeping criticism of her husband. He was becoming known for his aggression and fouling on the pitch, his sudden bursts of temper and name-calling. Frequently he would return home after matches with his shins lacerated and bleeding from the boots of opposing players. But he suffered these attacks in silence.

'Why don't you do something about the way you're being picked on?' Millie asked in outrage. 'The papers never mention anything about that!'

'They go for me 'cos they know I'm a hard tackler, Millie man,' Dan said, wincing as she dabbed on iodine. 'They know that if they stop me, they stop the scoring. In football you've got to take the knocks.'

Only gradually did Millie learn, from gossip in the press, that Dan had been transferred from Gateshead for his poor performance in the latter part of the season and on the continental tour. But what hurt her most were the rumours that he had spent too much time around the pubs on Tyneside and that he was labelled a ladies' man. So-called friends were quoted as saying that Dan was boastful and extravagant and squandered his talent on drinking and socialising. Millie was outraged and challenged him with the report.

'It's lies!' Dan was indignant. 'I grafted harder than any of them! But I've always been one to work hard and play hard – and what's wrong with that?'

'Play hard with who?' Millie demanded, pacing the tiny area in front of the hearth, feeling un-usually hemmed in. 'What do they mean by "ladies' man"?'

'Millie!' Dan said in exasperation. 'That's just the press. They like to make som'at out of nowt. They're digging for dirt so they've someone to blame for the club doing badly. For some reason they've chosen me – maybes 'cos I let me mouth go too much.'

Millie was not convinced. 'But these stories

have come from your so-called friends. Why should they be lying?'

Dan grew agitated. 'I was a name on Tyneside. I had my fair share of hangers-on – people after free drinks, free meals. Some lasses just like to be part of it too – they're no different from the men. There was nothing in any of it!'

Millie glared at him. 'Like there was nothing between you and Dinah, you mean?'

Dan looked at her angrily. 'How can you say that, Millie? Dinah was a good friend to us – especially to you and the bairn!'

'To you, you mean!' Millie could not help accusing. Her unhappiness and frustration were compounded by these rumours that stung her pride and made her unable to face people in the street. She was humiliated and could no longer contain her anger. 'How do I know there weren't other occasions when you and Dinah cuddled in the coalshed? Times when you were out and I was looking after Edith. What about after the trip to Italy? You were back for two weeks before you came and fetched me and the bairn!'

'Shurrup!' Dan sprang up, stepping on one of Edith's dolls. Their daughter looked up at them in alarm. 'Da-da, dolly!' But Dan was too riled to notice.

'I was down here, getting fixed up. Finding a home for us!' he shouted.

'Some home!' Millie cried, eyes blazing. 'It's a slum! You should never have left the Vulcans.'

Dan pushed her roughly away from him. 'Well, they didn't want me any more, did they? This move was the best thing on offer. Is it too much to expect a bit of support from me wife?' he yelled.

All at once, Edith stood up and began to wail, covering her eyes with her hands. Both parents stopped and stared at her. Quickly Millie rushed to comfort her, but Dan reached her first and swung her into his arms.

'Don't cry, pet,' he said, suddenly gentle. 'Dada's sorry for shouting.'

'Mammy's sorry too,' Millie was quick to add, caressing her soft curls.

Dan hugged the small girl tight until her sobbing subsided. Millie, heart still hammering from the argument, bent and picked up the damaged doll.

'I'll mend it,' Dan promised quickly, wiping Edith's wet crimson cheeks with his hand. He exchanged looks with Millie. 'I'm sorry,' he said hoarsely. 'All I want is to do the best for you and the lass.'

Millie's eyes stung with tears at his conciliatory words. 'I'm sorry too,' she whispered. 'I shouldn't have said those things...' She felt a pang of remorse for having accused him so disloyally, when he was already under attack from the outside world.

He stretched out an arm and pulled her into his embrace with their daughter. 'I tell you what,' he smiled, 'when the season's over, I'll take you both back to Ashborough for the summer – spend it with your mam.'

Millie felt her spirits lighten at once. 'And you'll stay with us too?' she queried, knowing how he had avoided the place since his fight with Grant.

Dan hesitated only for a moment. 'If you want me to,' he grinned. 'No doubt that mother of yours will find plenty of jobs for me to do – keep me out of bother.'

Millie smiled, wiping a tear of relief from the corner of her eye. 'That would be grand!' she agreed, kissing him.

Edith's face broke into a smile of gleaming, neat teeth. 'Kiss, kiss!' she insisted. They both laughed and kissed her, and Millie felt Dan's hold tighten around them both.

The summer could not come soon enough for Millie, as she made impatient arrangements to leave their dismal house and travel north. Finally, in May, they packed three suitcases and clambered on the train, Millie silently praying that they would never have to return. Edith, now over two years old, was excited by the bustle on the station and the movement of the train. Her lively company was the one thing that had got Millie through the drab winter. Perhaps because of Millie's incessant conversation with her daughter as they spent long days alone, Edith was already talking. She spoke in a clear, high-pitched, penetrating voice that caught everyone's attention, showing her delight in all that she saw with her sharp blue eyes. Heading north, Millie and Dan sat proudly beside her in the carriage while she reported on every cow, tree and house that they passed.

At the end of a very long day, they reached the station at Ashborough, with Edith asleep in Dan's arms. Teresa was there to meet them and cried openly at seeing them again. She took them back to a cold supper of ham and egg pie, potato salad, tinned pears and cream, then helped Millie put a drowsy Edith to bed, the little girl still trying to talk about the train journey.

'She's twice as bonny,' Teresa cooed, binding her granddaughter into the bed so she wouldn't fall out. 'I've missed her that much. It's been too quiet around here without you both. I never managed to keep the tea dances going after you left; I've had my hands full looking after Joseph,' she confided. 'He keeps to his bed these days, doesn't even watch at the window any more. If only Ava would write a letter once in a while, he might show more interest.' Teresa shook her head. 'She was always a little madam!'

The next day, Ella came round with Marjory and the friends spent the afternoon in happy conversation while the small girls stirred cake mixture with Teresa and dipped their fingers in cocoa powder. Dan, at a loose end, went for a walk. Two hours later, when Millie went looking for him, she found him with Walter on the rough ground behind the Presbyterian church, surrounded by boys eagerly kicking a football to him. She was thankful to see him reconciled with his brother and watched him for a while, unobserved. Millie could not remember when she had last seen him look so relaxed. He was happy demonstrating his skills to the keen young crowd, giving them encouragement and words of advice. When he caught sight of her, he relinquished the ball and ran over, grinning.

'You should help out at one of the boys' clubs

over the summer,' Millie suggested, linking her arm through his.

He smiled ruefully. 'I need to find something that'll bring in a bit of money.'

'Maybe you could do both,' Millie smiled, optimistically.

Dan eventually found delivery work for Davidson's Emporium, which now stretched for a whole block on the west side of Dyke Road. As well as driving a delivery van and chatting to the weekly customers, he did jobs around the hotel for Teresa, painting the window frames and whitewashing the yellowed kitchen walls. At times he escaped to play football with Walter and Kenny after their shifts, or with the dozens of young boys who hung around the lanes banging makeshift balls against brick outhouses, play-acting at being professionals.

Millie threw her energies into helping with the hotel, once more calling on Major Hall to help with tea dances. To her dismay she saw that her mother's arthritis had worsened and that she could no longer play the piano for any length of time. So Bob Hall provided the music and Millie and Ella served the teas, while Teresa looked after the small girls. The cousins soon became used to each other and Marjory took delight in telling Edith what to do, being bossily protective towards her while Edith followed eagerly in her wake.

Some evenings, Teresa would bed the two girls down together, while their parents went out dancing or to one of the picture houses. That summer talking films were the rage. Millie loved

278

their visits to the Empire, the huge picture palace, which had got rid of its cinema organ and put in extra seating to accommodate the hordes wanting to hear their matinée idols speak. In the plush velvet seats, surrounded by gold-painted columns, she listened enthralled to Greta Garbo and Douglas Fairbanks and heard her first musical, *Broadway Melody*. Dan took her to see Mickey Mouse talking in *Steamboat Willie,* and the adults shouted at the children to be quiet and stop hissing and booing as they had been used to doing during silent films.

'I can't wait until Edith's old enough to take to the pictures,' Millie declared.

'We'll take her Saturday, to the matinée.' Dan was enthusiastic. 'She's bright as a button, she'll sit through a film.'

So they did, sitting near the front either side of her. Edith clutched their hands tightly and hid her eyes to begin with, but was soon gazing in wonder at the large screen. She laughed at the slapstick antics of Mickey Mouse and cried out to him to be careful. She talked about the film during it, after it and for the rest of the day until bedtime.

'Nana come and see Mickey,' she told her grandmother as Teresa got her ready for bed. So the next week Teresa went too, and marvelled at the talking films as much as Edith had.

Only Bob Hall bemoaned the changes. 'Think of the thousands of musicians who've been put out of work by the talkies,' he grumbled. 'It's hard enough finding work these days as it is.'

'Well, there's work at the hotel as long as you

want it,' Millie assured him, not liking to dwell on the scarcity of jobs. Dan still had to negotiate a contract for the coming season, and she fervently hoped that some northern club would want him. At times she wished their life could just continue as it was in Ashborough, where they had a sizeable roof over their heads, Dan was happy doing deliveries and coaching football and she had her family and friends around her. But she knew that for Dan it would never be enough; he needed the thrill of playing professional football, of proving himself against some of the best in the country. So she lived life to the full all summer and did not think about what the autumn would bring.

At the end of July, Dan went south again to agree his contract for the coming season and to begin training. Millie hated him going and Edith made a terrible fuss seeing him off on the train.

'I'll be back in a fortnight,' he promised with a kiss, while Millie tried to pull a screaming Edith away from her father.

For a couple of days Millie felt bereft without him, but her daughter's high spirits soon made her cheerful again. She did not like to admit her relief at not having to return with him. They had agreed that she should stay for the rest of the summer in Ashborough and only bring Edith down once the season had started. No date had been set, and Millie avoided bringing the subject up. She wanted to stay at home as long as possible, partly out of selfish reasons, but also because she was growing concerned about her mother.

It had struck her more forcibly this year that Teresa was ageing. She was plagued with arthritis in her hands and had recently complained of back pain. She was slower at everything, her old briskness gone, and she lay in bed longer each morning, delaying the effort of getting up. Millie worried that she would soon not be able to carry on running the hotel on her own. Moody was almost a recluse, and without her and Ella's help over the summer, Millie was doubtful Teresa could have managed. She would have to persuade her mother to pay for some help this winter, unless she could stay on herself for longer... Millie pushed the enticing thought from her mind. It would be disloyal to Dan not to return sometime in the autumn, she told herself firmly. In the mean time she would do as much as possible to help.

When Dan appeared in August, expecting Millie to be packed, ready to return with him, he lost his temper.

'Mam needs me here,' Millie insisted. 'She's not well.'

'She's taking advantage of you, as usual,' Dan replied impatiently. 'She should take on a lass to do the heavy work, not you. You give in to her too easily, Millie, you always have done.'

'No I don't,' Millie replied, indignant. 'I'm happy to help out. It's my choice. She's in pain with her hands and back. She needs me.'

Dan gave her a furious look. 'I need you, Millie! You're me wife and your place is with me. I want you back in Kilburn.'

She stared at him in dismay. She did not want

to go, but she could hardly argue otherwise. What would people think of her if she remained with her mother instead of going back with her husband? She had chosen Dan and his footballing career rather than stay in Ashborough, so she could not complain now.

Millie bit on her trembling lip. 'I'll come back,' she agreed, 'but just give me a bit longer with Ma. Let me sort things out here for her first.'

Dan relaxed. 'Aye, for a week or two then.' He gave her an awkward smile. 'I don't like ganin' back to the house without you and Edith. It's not home without the pair of you.'

Millie smiled back, but inwardly shuddered at the thought of the depressing place.

'Then you promise me something,' she urged. 'That we look for somewhere else to live when we come back.'

Dan put his arms around her and gave his dimpled grin. 'Promise. Anything to keep you happy.'

So Dan left to start the new season and Millie made arrangements to follow. But first she went to Mrs Dodswell and asked if she could recommend a maid to help at the hotel. Mrs Dodswell sent round a dark-haired girl called Sarah from Corn Lane, one of five sisters. Millie offered her food and lodgings and twelve shillings a week, and set her to work laying fires, making beds, washing and cleaning. The two extra weeks turned into a month, while Millie taught Sarah how to bake large batches of scones and breads, as well as how to wait on tables. The young girl seemed obliging, but Millie noticed how she was easily distracted by Edith's chatter and demands for attention.

Millie decided it was time to leave. To her concern, her mother grew visibly upset when she returned from buying her train ticket.

'I don't want you to go!' Teresa cried, bursting into tears. 'I can't manage without you.'

Millie tried to calm her. 'Yes you can. Sarah's here to help out now, and she'll be living in.'

But her mother grew hysterical. 'You don't understand,' she wailed. 'I need you!'

Millie was alarmed by this unusual display of emotion. Her mother had grown increasingly quiet and withdrawn over the past month and had spent several days in bed complaining of tiredness, but never this hysteria. Millie coaxed her to bed.

'I'm calling the doctor,' she insisted, ignoring her mother's protests. 'I don't care what it costs, you're not well.' She was haunted by Dan's angry recollection at his father's delay in calling out the doctor for Effie until it was too late.

A new young doctor from the practice on Ivy Road came later that day. Millie looked at him anxiously, thinking he seemed no older than Dan, but he smiled reassuringly. 'I know your mother; I've treated Mr Moody before.' Millie flushed, wondering what he must think of their irregular arrangement, but showed him up to Teresa's bedroom.

She waited downstairs with Edith while her mother was examined, watching the clock anxiously and thinking that the doctor was taking a long time. Her fear grew as to what might be the matter; she could not bear the thought of losing her mother. Teresa had always been there, whether scolding or supporting, and she could not imagine a world without her.

Dr Percy appeared at the kitchen door, looking hesitant.

'Come in and have a cup of tea, Doctor,' Millie insisted, trying to read the look on his expressionless face.

'Thank you,' he accepted. Momentarily he was distracted by Edith running over to him, waving a paper figure that Millie had cut out of newspaper for her.

'Look! Look! It's my dada,' she cried.

Millie could not bear the waiting any longer. The tea spilled over into the saucer as she held it out to Dr Percy. 'What's wrong with Mam?' she asked nervously. 'Is it serious...?'

The young doctor gulped, his face flushing. 'Well ... I don't quite know how to tell you. It's rather awkward.' He looked away from her and down at Edith's eager face. 'Your mother, she's – she's going to have a baby.'

CHAPTER 17

When Millie had recovered from the initial shock of her mother's news, she was furious.

'How could you!' she railed at Teresa, who cowered pale-faced in bed. 'And I thought you were dying! It's disgusting – and with that man! I thought he was an invalid?'

Teresa buried her face in her gnarled hands and wept. 'Don't think badly of me!'

Millie was too appalled to comfort her. She could not imagine that someone of forty-nine would still be doing such things. She had never liked to think of her mother 'doing it' at all, even when she knew that she often spent the night in Moody's bed. It was something on which she had never dwelt. But now Teresa had disgraced them all by what she had done. She was bearing Moody's illegitimate child and soon the whole world would find out about it. She felt faint to think what Dan would say, let alone the rest of Ashborough.

'I can't stay here any longer,' Millie shouted. 'You'll have to face this one on your own. It's too shameful!'

'Millie, don't!' her mother wailed. 'I'm sorry. I never expected it. Please don't hate me...' She turned into her pillow and wept uncontrollably.

Millie watched in horror. She had never seen her mother break down like this before and it frightened her, so she fled. They did not speak again until the day she left. By then Teresa had emerged from her room, haggard but composed, to fuss around the kitchen, making sure they had food for the journey. Sarah watched warily, witness to both the shouting and then the silence between the women, and wondered what it could have been about.

For the first time in several days, Teresa stepped outside the hotel to walk them over the iron footbridge to the station platform. She moved stiffly, clutching Edith's small hand as the child chattered excitedly about going on the train.

As they stood waiting, Teresa gathered Edith up in her arms for a moment, before the pain in her weak hands forced her to put the girl down. 'I'll miss you, pet,' she said, kissing her pink cheek. Millie's eyes stung with tears at the sight and she felt engulfed in remorse that she had been so hard on her mother. How was Teresa possibly going to manage on her own? she fretted. Her very life might be endangered by having to give birth at such an advanced age. Millie realised too late that she should have blamed the feckless Moody for the trouble instead of letting it come between her and her mother.

As the train pulled in, she asked anxiously, 'Mam, will you be all right?'

Her mother's face took on her stubborn look. 'Of course I will. I've always managed, haven't I?'

Millie nodded, feeling wretched, but unable to bring herself to say sorry for her harsh words. She was in a turmoil of conflicting emotions: fear, anger, guilt, shame. If only her mother had not complicated their lives so! It was best if they had a time apart, while they both grew used to the idea of the baby and what should be done. Perhaps she should bring the child up as her own, Millie contemplated fleetingly, as Edith's brother or sister.

Then her mother was pushing her on to the train and waving them away. As Edith pressed her nose to the window and shouted goodbye to her grandmother, Millie's eyes blurred with tears. She watched Teresa standing alone on the chilly platform, proud and upright in her bearing, blowing a kiss to her granddaughter. Millie waved at last, wishing she had said a proper goodbye. They had left so many things unsaid and unresolved and she had no idea when she would see her mother again. Shutting the window against the steam and setting Edith on to a seat, Millie resolved that she would write to her mother and make amends.

Millie had meant to keep the shameful news of her mother's pregnancy from Dan until much later, but found herself blurting it out soon after their arrival back in Kilburn. The house seemed even more cramped and damp than she had remembered it, having stood empty and unused for several months. Dan had only used it as somewhere to sleep, but he had made an attempt to rake out the range and get a fire going for their return. He had changed the sheets on the bed too, and put pink carnations on the table for her and a new doll in a sailor's outfit for Edith.

'By, I've missed you both!' he cried. 'Now we

can be a family again.'

It was the mention of families that had provoked Millie's confession. Dan's reaction had been incredulous and then amused.

'Well, that's the last time the old baggage can criticise me about anything!' he crowed. 'To think of the times she's called me irresponsible!' He chuckled. 'Who would have thought old Moody would've still had it in him.'

Millie was astonished. 'Aren't you going to take it more seriously? It'll ruin her!'

'I doubt it,' Dan grunted. 'She hasn't paid two hoots to people's gossip in the past.'

'But what will folk think?' Millie fretted. 'I couldn't bring myself to tell Ella before I left. I keep wondering if we should adopt the bairn when it comes.'

Dan took her in his arms. 'Have you talked about it to your mam?' he asked.

Millie shook her head. 'I've hardly said a word to her since I found out – except to shout. We had a terrible row.' She closed her eyes and shuddered at the memory.

Dan was philosophical. 'Well, that's not going to change anything, is it? What's done is done. I wouldn't mind bringing up another bairn, if that's what you and your mam decide.' He looked adoringly at Edith, who was engrossed in conversation with her new doll. 'The more the better, as far as I'm concerned.' He gave Millie his impish grin.

That night they made love eagerly, making up for the time apart, and fell asleep wrapped in each other's arms. The next day Millie visited her neighbours, eager to show off how Edith had grown over the summer and to talk to anyone about home. To her disappointment, the friendly family from two doors away had gone, and she reluctantly allowed Edith to spend the afternoon playing with the Dyson girls across the lane. Millie thought them unkempt and sickly children, but Edith was happy. The following day, no one appeared to play, and Millie found it hard to entertain her daughter, confined indoors by the rain. Once again she badgered Dan about moving.

Within two days he came home excitedly to say he had heard of a flat further away from the football ground and the railway line. 'It's near a park with swings and there's a swimming baths nearby. It'll be grand for Edith to learn to swim.'

Millie laughed in relief. 'She's a bit young for that!' Then she asked anxiously, 'Can we afford the rent?'

Dan shrugged off her concern. 'We'll find the money if you like it.'

They arranged to go and view the flat the following week. Millie could not wait. She dressed Edith up in her best frock, coat and hat, chiding her for whingeing and pulling the ribbon under her chin.

'Keep still and let me tie it,' Millie scolded, impatiently. She wanted them to look their best for the landlord. Edith worked herself into a tantrum and began to scream and push her away.

For the first time she could recall, Millie slapped her legs, hard. Edith wailed louder and Dan arrived home to find Millie in a state. 'She won't do as she's told. She's becoming as wilful as her nana!'

Dan picked up the kicking Edith and carried her out. To Millie's annoyance the girl quickly quietened down and buried her head into her father's shoulder in exhaustion. By the time they reached the flat she was asleep, and Dan had to carry her around in his arms. The flat was on the top floor of a large terraced house that had been divided up into smaller dwellings. It was dark, with only skylights for windows, but there were two spacious bedrooms, a living room and a small kitchen with a gas oven. There was a shared bathroom on the floor below, which was preferable to trailing to an outside toilet in bad weather. It did not offer the comfortable cosiness of their Tyneside flat, but Millie knew she could make it homely, and the street itself was far quieter and more pleasant than their house under the viaduct.

'Let's take it,' she urged Dan. 'We'll be happier here.'

Millie spent the week making preparations to move, hunting round drapery stalls in the market for cheap bright cotton to make into covers for the skylights and matching antimacassars for the chairs. She planned where their few bits of furniture would go, and her pieces of Maling pottery of which she was so proud. The planning and day-dreaming took her mind off her mother's problems, which plagued her daily. Several times she sat down to write to Teresa, but got no further than addressing the envelope. Edith seemed to sense that there was change in the air, or that her mother was preoccupied, for she became difficult. Usually sunny-natured, the child began to cry a lot, refuse her food and generally try Millie's patience.

Millie, who hated to spend a minute more in the house than was necessary, could hardly cajole Edith to go out. The small girl threw herself on the floor and refused to put on her coat, preferring to lie on the rug by the hearth. The weather was autumnal and becoming colder, so Millie did not force her, deciding instead to sit and make curtains.

It was Dan who, at the end of the week, commented on Edith's behaviour. She curled up in his lap while Millie sighed with annoyance that she had refused her scrambled egg yet again.

'She's getting that fussy with her food,' Millie complained.

Dan scrutinised his daughter. 'Maybe she's not well. It's not like her to sit still for so long.'

Millie thought impatiently that Dan was just making excuses for the girl. Then Edith looked up at her with large blue eyes that seemed full of pain and Millie's heart jolted; she had not noticed the feverish shine in them before. She had been too busy all week, preoccupied with thoughts of the new flat and with her mother's predicament, to see the change in Edith as anything more than contrariness.

She went over to the child at once and put a hand on her forehead. It felt hot, but then she had spent the day next to the fire. Millie tried to tilt her chin, but Edith pushed her hand away, pulling a face of pain. Millie exchanged worried looks with Dan. As the girl twisted away, Millie saw that her neck was swollen.

She spoke softly, urgently. 'Let Mammy look in your mouth, pet.'

Edith shook her head and gave a whimper, flopping back into Dan's chest. He pulled her gently away. 'Open your mouth for Dada.'

Edith turned large frightened eyes on her father and attempted to open her mouth. She did not seem able to move her jaw. He peered but could not see anything. Millie said, 'Turn her towards the light.' She went down on her knees in front of the girl. 'Show Mammy too.'

Edith's face crumpled and Millie had to force her lips apart, wincing at the pain she must be inflicting on the reluctant child. At first she saw nothing; she was just aware of a strange smell, a whiff of something unpleasant. Then the light caught something white at the back of the tiny throat. Millie's pulse began to race. 'There's a big thing of pus in her throat,' she gasped. 'No wonder she couldn't eat anything.'

Dan saw her alarm. 'What does that mean?'

'I don't know,' Millie whispered, suddenly seized with fear of the unknown, 'but it must be sore.'

'I'll gan and get the doctor,' Dan said at once, and sprang to his feet, bundling Edith into Millie's arms.

Millie panicked. 'It's probably just a sore throat. Don't you think we should wait for the morning and take her round the surgery...?'

'No!' Dan was adamant. 'I couldn't sit through the night waiting. Not like...' Millie stared at him in horror, knowing he was thinking of his mother's final night and how they had delayed calling the doctor.

'No, of course not,' she said, trembling and clutching the whimpering Edith tightly to her. 'Go quickly then.'

Dan was out of the door without stopping to put on a coat, and racing round to the club doctor, who lived six streets away where the terraces broke up into large, redbrick semi-detached houses with gardens. He hammered on the door, the drizzle of rain sticking to his hair and face like ghostly gossamer. A maid answered. Dr Knight was out to dinner on the far side of Kilburn. Dan's distress was so obvious that the girl suggested another doctor, one who ran the surgery near the station.

Shouting his thanks, Dan ran as fast as he could through the increasing rain to the modest house and surgery where Dr Michael lived and banged on the black door until it opened. The young doctor left his half-eaten supper and came with the anxious father at once.

Dr Michael found Millie cuddling the listless child and soothing her with soft words of comfort. Edith's breathing was growing more rapid and she shrank away from the stranger with his leather bag. After a few minutes of coaxing, Edith lost the will to struggle, and with Millie still holding her, the doctor managed to investigate her mouth and throat.

He stroked the girl's head and stood up, his face betraying his concern.

'What's wrong?' Millie asked fearfully, seeing

that Dan was speechless.

'We'll have to get her straight to hospital – the fever hospital,' the doctor said, his look pitying.

'The fever hospital?' Millie repeated hoarsely.

Dr Michael nodded. 'It's diphtheria. If we can get her treated straight away, there might be a chance...'

Millie felt punched in the stomach. Diphtheria. One of those terrible names that stalked childhood, sending fear into parents, throwing the shadow of death over their babies.

'Wh-what?' Millie stuttered, trying to grasp the implications. 'But how has she possibly got it?'

'Maybe someone she's played with,' Dr Michael said gently.

Millie thought with alarm about the Dyson girls, whom she had not seen for several days, and gave out an agonised wail.

But Dan leapt forward and seized Edith, gathering her to him. 'Where's the hospital?' he demanded.

'To the north of the town,' Dr Michael answered, turning from Millie's stunned in-comprehension. 'I'll ring for an ambulance.'

Dan stepped towards him. 'Don't you have a car?'

'Yes,' Dr Michael admitted, 'it's outside my house.'

'Take us then, please!' Dan urged. 'It'll be quicker.'

Millie put a hand to her mouth, trying to swallow her panic. She gulped and grasped the doctor's arm. 'Please save her,' she whispered. 'Please save me bairn!'

294

He did not answer, but nodded to Dan and followed him out. Millie grabbed a blanket from the chair to wrap around Edith and rushed after them, leaving the lights on and the door unlocked. They ran down the street and turned towards the station to where the doctor lived. Squeezing into the back of the car, both parents cuddled Edith, trying to comfort the frightened girl. No one spoke as they sped across town and out into the countryside. The old mansion now used as a hospital loomed out of the dark, lights glinting from high windows.

It all happened so quickly, Edith being transferred to a trolley and whisked away, while Millie and Dan were left feeling helpless in the echoing hallway.

'Can't we go with her?' Millie pleaded. 'She needs me!'

A matron insisted that this was out of the question and tried to shoo them out of the building. Dr Michael said, 'Let me take you home. There's nothing more you can do tonight.'

Millie could not bear the thought of leaving Edith alone. 'I must stay!' she cried. Dan took her hand and squeezed it hard. He faced the doctor. 'Can't we just see her settled before we go?' he asked.

Dr Michael hesitated, then nodded and went away to see what he could do. Returning a little later, he said they could look in briefly on Edith. 'She's very sick, though – you mustn't upset yourselves, or her.'

Millie almost ran down the corridor and up the stairs to the high-ceilinged room where their daughter had been taken. Her heart pounded in her ears and she felt sick as she clutched Dan's hand. They were made to put on masks and overalls and told by the matron to be brief.

Millie's eyes smarted to see her beloved Edith lying in the spartan room on the narrow iron-framed bed, her small head in the centre of a starched white pillow, her fair curls damp on her face. Millie could hear her ragged, rapid breathing; her eyelids were pale and closed, her neck looking swollen to her chin in the short hours since teatime. How could this have happened so quickly? Millie agonised. Why had she been so caught up in her own concerns as not to notice what was happening to her precious child? When Millie thought of the times that week she had scolded Edith for crying or wilfully refusing her food, her heart was seared with guilt. She wanted to gather the weak girl into her arms and hold her tight until she was better, kissing away her fear and pain. Edith was everything to her, and without her daughter life would not be worth living. Millie glanced at Dan's harrowed look and knew he felt the same. Their lively, loving little girl had become their reason for being.

They crept forward and knelt down by the bed, Millie stroking Edith's forehead while Dan held her limp hand. Edith's eyes opened and looked scared for a moment, until Millie pulled the mask from her face and the girl recognised her parents. She tried to speak but could not, and Millie saw the puzzled look on her face. Her throat was so swollen that she could not even cry any more.

There was just this strange silence and the large eyes pleading for them to help her.

'The doctors are going to make you better,' Millie whispered, forcing herself to smile. 'You mustn't worry.'

She glanced at Dan, seeing the muscles working in his cheeks as he tried to compose himself to speak. He croaked, 'We'll be in to see you tomorrow. I'll bring the sailor doll for you.'

Edith looked at him, and for a moment her eyes seemed to brighten, lit by a small spark of interest. She tried to nod, but the movement caused her pain and tears welled in her eyes. Millie picked up Edith's other hand and pressed it to her lips.

'Mammy loves you very much,' she whispered.

The matron came in and told them they must leave. Millie thought she would break down there and then, but she forced herself to be brave in front of Edith. She smiled and, leaning forward, kissed the girl tenderly on her swollen face. 'Be brave, my little lamb,' she added, gulping back tears. She saw Edith struggling to say something, her lips working to form the word 'Mammy', but she could not make a sound. Her breath was laden with the peculiar smell Millie had noticed before and her hand tried weakly to hang on to her mother's. Millie was rooted to the spot; she did not see how she could ever leave. She watched numbly as Dan kissed Edith too, and then the matron was hurrying them out.

Millie stifled a sob as Dan reached for her and pulled her away.

'We'll come tomorrow,' he assured her. She

craned for a last glimpse of Edith at the door, but the matron marched them swiftly down the stairs. Neither of them could speak as they stumbled out after Dr Michael, who was waiting to drive them the five miles back home. The journey passed in silence. At their door he asked if there was anything they wanted, but they just stared at him mutely, too shocked to answer.

'I'll ring the hospital tomorrow and pass on any news,' he promised, and left.

That night they did not go to bed, but sat up through the night, keeping the fire going, saying little. Their thoughts were focused on Edith lying in a strange hospital. Millie had never been forced to be without her before and the separation felt like an amputation. She sat clutching the sailor doll where it had been discarded by the fire, and looked around at the evidence of Edith's existence: the box of toys under the table, the photographs on the mantelpiece, her favourite eggcup on the dresser next to a pile of her un-ironed dresses. The room was full of reassuring signs of Edith's presence, so palpable that she had to stop herself from rushing up to the bedroom to check if she was really just lying asleep and that she had dreamt the whole awful nightmare. As day dawned, Dan made a pot of tea, splashed his haggard face with water and pulled on his coat.

'Where are you going?' Millie demanded.

'To the club,' he answered. 'Tell them I'm not ganin' to play this afternoon.'

'Why don't you wait?' Millie pleaded, not wanting to be left alone with the thoughts that plagued her.

'I'll not be long,' he promised, and was gone with a draught of icy air from the door.

For hours Millie sat numb and dispirited, listening to the clock ticking and the trains rumbling overhead, until she could no longer bear the emptiness, the lack of Edith's chatter that normally filled the room. She forced herself to do jobs; menial tasks to occupy her shaking hands and paralysed mind. She cleared the table of the previous evening's tea – she despised scrambled egg – and washed the dishes. She set to scrubbing the kitchen table, the hearth, the doorstep until her hands were red raw. She swept the whole house and banged the mats on the yard wall, she ironed Edith's dresses, finding a strange comfort in the task, and polished the brass fender. After hours of chores she sat down feeling faint and sick and realised she had eaten and drunk nothing since the previous afternoon.

She helped herself to some of Dan's cold tea made that morning, but it tasted bitter. Millie's stomach churned with anxiety as to why Dan had not returned and why no word had come from the hospital. How could he stay away at the club while she worried herself sick? she thought angrily. Finally, exhausted, but unable to bear another moment in the house alone, she brushed her hair in the mirror and pulled on a hat and coat. She would go down to Dr Michael's surgery and wait until there was any news. Maybe he would drive her over to the hospital, she thought with optimism. If not she would take a taxi, for she could not stand another minute away from her daughter's bedside.

Millie was just stepping into the yard as the daylight was fading when she saw the doctor's car pull up outside. Her heart began to bang in fear. Did he have news or was he coming to fetch her? His face was pinched in the cold evening air as he came round the car towards her, but she could not read his expression clearly in the shadows.

'Where is Mr Nixon?' he asked.

'At the club,' Millie replied, her throat painfully dry. 'Have you heard something?'

Dr Michael steered her back across the yard. She allowed herself to be taken inside, grasping at the silence optimistically, for as long as he said nothing then she could still hope. In the house he looked at her warily.

'I rang the hospital an hour ago.' He took a deep breath. 'I'm terribly sorry, Mrs Nixon, but Edith died this afternoon. The membrane – she couldn't breathe – it was too far gone,' he tried to explain. 'But it must've been quick, just like going to sleep.'

All strength drained out of Millie at the words. She had an awful image of Edith struggling for breath, alone in that stark hospital room. Had she tried to call for her? Millie wondered. Did she die afraid, wetting the bed? She must have been in agony! She felt dizzy with disbelief. All the time she had been ironing her dresses, Edith had been dying. Turning on the young doctor she shouted, 'No! Not dead! She can't be dead!'

'I'm very sorry,' he repeated nervously. 'Please sit down. I'll wait with you until your husband returns if you like.'

But she shook him off. 'You should have let me

300

stay with her!' she accused. She glared at him even as the faintness flooded over her. 'I should have been with her!' she screamed. 'Me bairn. *Oh, Edith!* I want to see me bairn!'

She was aware of the doctor reaching forward to catch her, and then, collapsing on the floor, blacked out into blessed oblivion.

CHAPTER 18

Millie would not be comforted. She spent the next days in a twilight world between hysteria and numbness, neither eating nor sleeping. Sometimes in her exhaustion she would almost forget what it was that upset her so. Then the memory of leaving Edith alone in the hospital room would come back so vividly that she was consumed by acute pain and all she could do was scream with grief.

She was aware of Dan being there, though when he had come back on that terrible day she did not know. All she could remember was that he had not been there to hear the news when she did and suspected he had stayed away at the club rather than face the worst. Millie knew he must be grieving too, but to her surprise and hurt he was not showing it. He would not talk to her about Edith. He was withdrawn but calm, trying to make her eat and take the doctor's sedatives as if she were ill.

Sometimes he lost patience and would disappear, leaving her alone in the bleak house, curled up in a chair with one of Edith's dolls. He would come home after dark, reeking of drink, and fall up the stairs to bed.

The hospital wanted to know what funeral arrangements to make, but Millie could not talk about that. Once her baby was in the ground then she would have to admit she was gone forever. Dan did not know what to do with her. Eventually, in frustration, he sent a telegram to Teresa begging her to come down and reason with Millie.

Her mother appeared two days later, Dan meeting her at the station and guiding her to the house. Millie flew into her mother's outstretched arms, crying uncontrollably.

'I would have come as soon as I heard,' Teresa said, cradling her daughter's head, 'but I didn't know if you'd want me...'

'Of course, I do,' Millie sobbed. 'You're the one person who can understand – you loved Edith that much.' She wept anew.

Dan watched in discomfort, then made for the door. 'I'll leave you two alone then. I'll be at the club if you want me,' he said stiffly, and left.

Teresa, alarmed by how haggard her daughter looked, sat Millie down and insisted on making her a drink. Searching the gloomy kitchen, she could find no tea but boiled up a pan of milk with cocoa and sugar. She made Millie sip it while she raised the blind a fraction to let in some daylight so that she could move around the room tidying away dirty cups, discarded clothes and half-sewn pieces of material. Her heart lurched to see Edith's hat and coat lying over the back of a chair; it was the outfit she had been wearing when she had waved her away from Ashborough on the train. She wanted to pick it up and crush it to her, breathe in the girl's smell, but she resisted. It would not do for her to go to pieces in front of the traumatised Millie.

The drink appeared to calm Millie, and her mother managed to coax her upstairs to bed. She tucked her in like a child with Edith's doll, noticing the smell of damp in the poky attic and averting her eyes from her granddaughter's cot. Millie had talked about getting the girl a bed in the spring. She sat on the end of the bed until Millie fell asleep, a deep, exhausted sleep that lasted until tea-time. Teresa felt tired and uncomfortable; she had been able to feel the baby moving for the past week. She was depressed by the house and bewildered by Edith's death, still too shocked to take it in. She wanted to get this visit over with as quickly as possible and take Millie away from this terrible place.

When Dan returned, Teresa made him carry water from the scullery, boil it up on the fire and fill the tin bath they kept hanging on a nail in the yard. She sent him out to buy fish and chips while she bathed Millie in front of the fire and washed her lank hair. Millie sat mutely allowing her mother to take control, finding comfort in the mechanical actions of washing and drying and putting on clean clothes. Her mind seemed dislocated from the nightmare of the past few days, as if sleep had sealed it off, cocooning it from the raw pain of Edith's sudden death. If only it could always be like this, she thought numbly, if only she could carry on forever in this strange, detached state, she might be able to exist. But when Dan came back with their tea, he could stand the silence no longer.

'Have you decided about the funeral then?' he

asked, eating his fish and chips straight from the newspaper while Teresa fussed around with plates and cutlery. Millie began to shake.

'No we haven't,' Teresa said shortly, giving him a warning look.

'Well, it's time you did,' he answered angrily. 'The bairn needs a proper burial. I don't like to think of her lying in the hospital.'

'Neither do I!' Millie cried.

'Then let me make the arrangements,' Dan insisted.

'I don't want her buried here among strangers,' Millie blurted out. The other two stared at her.

'What *do* you want?' her mother asked. 'Dan's right, you can't put things off any longer.'

Millie looked back defiantly. 'I want to take her home to Ashborough. I want her buried there, where she was happy.' She glanced at Dan. 'Where we were all happy,' she added quietly.

Dan's face looked gaunt and miserable. She knew he just wanted it all to be over, to go back to playing football where he could immerse himself in the game and wall up his grief. He wanted a quick, private ceremony with no fuss and no relations.

'What's the sense in that?' he cried. 'It's too far away. If she's buried here then at least you can go and visit the grave – put flowers on it and that.'

'No, not here!' Millie was adamant. 'I can't stay here, Dan, not without the bairn. I want to go home.'

He looked at her appalled, and then to Teresa for support. But his mother-in-law held his look. 'I think it might be for the best if Millie comes back with me for a while, seeing the state she's in.'

Dan's anger erupted. 'Best for who? Not for me. I can't gan back to Ashborough – me work is here. Millie should stay with me.'

'Don't be so selfish,' Teresa replied, her look disdainful. 'She's not well.'

'I'm not the selfish one, you are!' He glared. 'You just want her back to help you around the hotel while you have Moody's bastard!'

Teresa flushed puce and Millie gasped. 'Don't speak to Mam like that!'

'I'll speak to her how I want in me own house,' Dan shouted, thumping the table.

Millie pushed away her untouched food. 'I'm going home, Dan,' she said in a flat voice, 'and I'm taking Edith. I couldn't bear to stay here without her, can't you see that? Not even for you.'

Dan winced at her words. He pushed back his chair and stood up. 'Go then!' he raged. 'I can't stand your twisty face around here any more. You think you're the only one who minds about the bairn, but you're not. And do you know what I keep thinking?' His blue eyes blazed angrily. 'I keep thinking that you should have noticed she was ill – you were with her every day.'

Teresa saw Millie's mouth drop open as if she had been punched. 'How dare you?' she scolded. But Dan would not be stopped.

'Why didn't you notice, Millie?' he demanded. 'Were you too bothered about moving house? If you'd just tried to make a better job of this one, you might have had more time for the lass!'

Millie gave a cry of pain, covering her face with her hands. Teresa rounded on Dan. 'And has it ever occurred to you that Edith died because you made her live in this hovel? She would never have caught diphtheria if you hadn't insisted that Millie come back when she did. If she'd stayed on in Ashborough a bit longer, Edith would be alive today!'

Millie watched Dan reel backwards at the verbal assault, his face haunted. 'You'll not blame me for this,' he cried.

'Why not?' Teresa flared back. 'You're blaming Millie!'

Dan gave them both a look of hatred and then rushed for the door. He grabbed his coat from the peg and stormed out of the room, banging the door behind him. For a moment the house seemed to reverberate with the noise before it died away, leaving only the poisonous argument ringing in Millie's head. He had spoken the thoughts that plagued her own mind. She should have done something sooner; she had noticed that Edith was acting differently. How could she not have seen that the girl was ill? She tortured herself. Why had she not taken her to the doctor to be checked? She let out a howl of distress, her mind no longer numb to pain. Her grief was compounded by lacerating guilt. If only Dan knew that she blamed herself far more than he ever could.

'If only I could relive that week again,' she wept. 'I'd do anything for it to be a fortnight ago, for Edith to be alive – then I'd do everything differently! *Everything!*'

She crumpled into her mother's arms and gave in to her grief.

Teresa took Millie north on the train and arrangements were made to have Edith's body transported to Ashborough, Millie pawning all of the jewellery Dan had ever given her to cover the cost. She sent a telegram to Dan to confirm the date of the funeral, fearing that he would not come, but he was given leave to attend and arrived late the evening before. Dumping his bag he went straight out again, drinking with Kenny Manners until closing time and ending up sleeping on the kitchen floor.

On the morning of the funeral he looked old and grey-faced, his lack of colour accentuated by the black suit he wore. Millie's features had shed their healthy plumpness and she too wore the same harrowed look. When she looked at Dan as they set out for the service in the Myrtle Terrace church where they had been married, she wanted to say something to comfort him but could not. She was too deeply hurt by his accusations to try and relieve his obvious suffering. She tried to recall their wedding day and the love she had felt for him, but could not. It all seemed a lifetime ago.

Somehow Millie got through the ordeal, given courage by the friends around them and the balm of words and hymns. She did not remember much of it afterwards, except Dan's ghostly whiteness and eyes red-rimmed from crying or drink. There was a small solemn gathering back at the hotel for tea and cake, but Teresa put an exhausted Millie to bed, allowing her a liberal dose of whisky in a hot drink to help her sleep.

When she woke later on that October evening, the room was in darkness. She stumbled for the door and met her mother climbing the stairs breathlessly. It struck Millie for the first time that Teresa's pregnancy was beginning to show. Things sounded quiet below.

'Where is everyone?' Millie asked. 'Have I been asleep long?'

'Yes,' Teresa panted. 'It's past eight o'clock. They've all gone home.'

'Where's Dan?' Millie asked, shivering in her underclothes.

Teresa's look hardened. 'He's gone too. Took the afternoon train back to Newcastle, said he'd get a connection tonight or tomorrow.'

Millie felt unexpected disappointment grip her. 'Did he say anything … a message?' she asked quietly.

Teresa shook her head. 'He couldn't get away quick enough; it's clear he wants to forget the whole thing. But that's men for you. Don't expect them to be any help when you need them.'

Millie bowed her head, feeling panic engulf her at being left alone. She fought the urge to cry; she had cried herself dry in the past month. Steeling herself, she lifted her chin and faced her mother, quelling the fear inside her. This was what she had chosen, she reminded herself, to return to Ashborough and grieve, leaving Dan to cope in the only way he could – playing his football. Whether their marriage would ever recover from the wreckage of Edith's death, it was too soon for her to say.

'I'll get dressed,' Millie said, 'then come and help you clear up.'

Her mother nodded in approval and retreated downstairs without another word.

CHAPTER 19
LATE 1929

Millie did not see Dan again that year. He stayed away in the Black Country and all Millie knew was that he had moved into digs with some of the other players. She imagined that he carried on his playing and drinking, for he did not return north or answer her letters, though he did send her a trickle of money. She followed the club results in the newspaper and saw that they were mediocre. Christmas passed painfully, with Millie plunging herself into work at the hotel, refusing to relax and trying not to recall the happy Christmases of their days on Tyneside. She saw few people apart from the lodgers, who came and went and did not ask questions. There were no tea dances since Major Hall had left the area with a travelling concert group, and the place was quiet, which suited Millie's fragile spirit.

Occasionally Ella and Walter managed to entice her round for tea, but she kept the visits short, unable to bear Marjory's puzzled questioning. By February, her trips to Edith's grave were still almost daily, as spring flowers appeared in the muddy ditches and they prepared for the arrival of Teresa's baby. Millie defended her mother against the gossip that blew around Ashborough like the March wind.

When Teresa's pregnant state became increasingly difficult to conceal, Sarah the maid was let go and Millie was left running the hotel. Teresa retired to bed with swollen ankles and breathlessness, while Joseph remained a bed-ridden recluse in his room, ordering up newspapers and existing on pots of tea and toast. Millie questioned his sanity, doubting that he understood that Teresa was close to giving birth to his child. When she mentioned it on one occasion, he asked who Teresa was, and he absently called her Ava on several occasions. This prompted Millie to urge her mother, 'You must get Joseph to make a will leaving the hotel to you. You have to think of the babe and its future as well as your own.' So Teresa did just that shortly before the birth of her child.

On the day her mother went into labour, Millie received a letter from Dan saying he could not send her any money that month as he was short. She threw the brief note on to the fire in disgust and went to fetch Mrs Dickson, Effie's old neighbour, who had agreed to come and help with Teresa's confinement and whom Millie knew would be discreet.

The labour was long and painful and went on through the night. At one point, as she watched her mother's sweating, twisting face glistening in the gaslight, Millie feared the exertion might kill her. Teresa cried out in agony and wept for relief, while Mrs Dickson sat knitting at the bottom of the bed, exhorting her to be calm. Occasionally she would come and lay a hand on Teresa's womb and instruct Millie to wipe her brow.

'This is taking too long,' Millie fretted in the

small dark hours of the night. 'Shouldn't I go for Dr Percy? He could do something to help the baby come.'

But Mrs Dickson shook her head. 'You don't want the expense of all that,' she declared. 'The babe will come when it's ready.'

Finally the labour proper started shortly before dawn, by which time Teresa had hardly enough energy left to push. Millie gripped her hand and encouraged her, while Mrs Dickson finished off the sock she was knitting and scrubbed her hands ready to receive the baby. When it came slithering on to the bed, Millie burst into tears at the reminder of Edith's birth.

Yet when Mrs Dickson announced, 'It's a little lad,' she felt a wave of relief. Somehow she could stand her mother giving birth to a boy, whereas a girl would have been unbearable. As she stared at the crinkled creature, Millie wondered suddenly if a boy would be a consolation to her mother, helping fill the void left long ago by Graham. Or did her mother never think of her firstborn son? Millie looked at the exhausted woman for signs of her delight, but Teresa had taken one look then collapsed back on the bolster, gasping with fatigue.

'What are you going to call him, Mam?' Millie asked gently.

Teresa groaned, without opening her eyes. 'I don't know,' she whispered. 'I was sure it would be a lass – to comfort me after Edith...' Millie's heart squeezed in pain at the regret in her voice. 'I wanted a lass to give us something to smile about again,' Teresa said, slow tears oozing from under her lids.

Mrs Dickson could not get Teresa to look at the baby again, so Millie bundled up the nameless boy and took him downstairs, leaving her mother to sleep.

'She's all done in,' the neighbour said later as she drank tea in the kitchen with Millie. 'You'll have to keep an eye on her. Giving birth at her age – it's enough to finish a woman off.'

Millie shuddered at her tactlessness. 'Of course I'll look after her,' she replied stoutly, then glanced over at the baby, feeling less sure. 'But what shall I do with the bairn in the mean time? Mam's not strong enough to feed him.'

'If you ask me,' Mrs Dickson said between slurps, 'you'd be best giving him up for adoption. What sort of life is he going to have here?'

Millie peered at the sleeping baby in the drawer where she had laid him in place of a cot. He looked long and skinny, like a rabbit, and quite defenceless. She had no great feelings towards him, but she felt this small scrap of humanity did not deserve the indifference that he provoked.

'No, he's me half-brother,' she said stubbornly. 'No one's going to adopt him. We'll just have to manage as best we can. I'll not have him disowned.' Tentatively she reached into the drawer and lifted the baby out, holding him against her. He snuffled and felt warm in her arms. Suddenly Millie experienced an unexpected rush of affection, the sort of emotion that she thought had died for ever with Edith. Tears sprang into her eyes, and she bent down, kissed his cap of soft black hair and whispered, 'Welcome, little man.'

While Millie's new half-brother thrived, Teresa did not recover her health. The exertions of the birth had left her almost crippled. Millie turned the travellers' sitting room on the ground floor into a bedroom, getting Walter and Kenny to shift the bed, washstand and cumbersome wardrobe downstairs, so that she could answer Teresa's calls without having to run up and downstairs all day long. Her mother was a far more demanding patient than the solitary Moody, who showed not the slightest bit of interest in his new son or comprehension about what was going on outside his hermit's existence.

But Teresa shouted constant instructions about the hotel, or the feeding of her son, through the open door. She was not interested in dealing with the baby herself, except to cuddle him when the mood took her. Her one real pleasure appeared to be listening to records on Millie's gramophone – the one possession of any value she still had left. Like Moody, Teresa showed no interest in venturing out into the world beyond the hotel, and Millie's coaxing was only half-hearted, for local gossip about them was still rife. She steeled herself against the pitying looks and the half-finished conversations that dried up the minute she walked into a shop, guessing that they were discussing her own bereavement and estrangement from Dan as much as the scandal over her mother.

Millie, however, found a new strength and purpose in looking after the baby, whom her mother had finally named Robert after no one in particular. She determined that she would defy the gossips and not buckle under her grief. Her days were long and tiring, filled with running after others and seeing to their needs, preventing her from dwelling on the emptiness inside. It was the only way she could cope with Edith's loss, and she fell into bed at the end of the day too tired to think or remember her dreams in the morning. She wrote to Dan and told him about Robert, hoping that it might bring him home for a visit, but she heard nothing. Neither did she receive any more money from him. She had to be frugal in her housekeeping and accepted second-hand clothes for the baby.

There was increasing hardship in the town as the pits went back on short time and a rash of small businesses folded. Some people were blaming the slump on the Americans and the stock-market crash in New York the previous year. But Millie did not like to think of the Americans suffering too, because it made her worry about Ava and Grant. She wondered how they were faring and if she would ever see them again. Travelling salesmen came, but not so frequently, yet Millie refused to fret. Strangely, since Edith's death, such things as money and security did not preoccupy her as much as they had done in the past. She did not look beyond the end of the week when budgeting. Death had snatched away her most precious possession while she was not looking. There could be nothing more terrifying than that, Millie admitted, nothing that could possibly hurt as much again.

When the days lengthened into early summer,

she would snatch the odd hour away from the hotel and wheel Robert round to Ella's home. They would sit and drink tea and work on a hooky mat together while Marjory played out in the yard with a Dickson grandchild and Robert slept in the sunshine.

'How's your mam?' Ella asked one day in early May.

Millie shrugged. 'She's like an old woman, lying in bed all day long. I sometimes wonder if she'll ever get up again.'

'You're making life too easy for her,' Ella chided. 'She'll not *want* to get up.'

Millie sighed. 'I would never have believed it a few months ago, but she's lost all her energy and interest in the outside world. She's still one for dramatics – says she's a melancholic since Edith died,' Millie said, finding it easier to mention her daughter now she had Robert to care for. 'Not that it's affected her appetite. She eats more than the rest of us put together. Soon she'll not be able to get out of bed even if she wanted to – she's grown that stout!'

'Just as well you put her on the ground floor then,' Ella joked. 'At least she won't come through your ceiling!'

'Aye,' Millie laughed. 'I think she's just decided the leisurely life of a lady suits her after all those years grafting in the hotel for Moody.'

'By, you should put signs out saying you're running a home for invalids, Millie,' Ella teased.

Millie enjoyed these times at Ella's, for she was the one friend with whom she could discuss anything, even Dan.

'How's the vanishing man?' Ella would ask her, and Millie would be able to laugh about her situation and not feel so alone. 'Don't worry, he'll turn up when he's ready to face you.' Ella was certain. 'Nixon men can't survive on their own. Even old Mungo has a housekeeper these days.'

In the end it was Mungo's sudden death from a heart attack in midsummer that brought Dan home. Millie sent a telegram to the club relaying the news, and another one to Grant in America, though she had no idea if he and Ava were still at the same address. Three days later Dan sauntered through the kitchen door, whistling, as if he had just left that morning. Millie was holding Robert, feeding him a bottle of milk. Dan stopped, taken aback by the sight, and the two stared at each other, speechless. Millie was aghast at the sight of his thin, drawn face with dark shadows beneath his eyes, his once stocky frame no longer filling his suit. He looked ten years older and she noticed how his hands shook as he reached for a battered packet of cigarettes and lit up quickly.

'This your mam's bairn?' he asked, inhaling deeply, keeping his distance.

'Aye,' Millie answered, hating the trembling in her voice. 'This is Robert.' She bent her head over the contentedly sucking baby, heart hammering. So often she had wanted to see Dan walk in through that door, ready with a thousand questions to ask him, but now he was here she was dumbstruck, overcome with nerves.

Dan drew nearer, still cautious. 'He looks a grand lad.'

318

Millie chided, 'Don't blow smoke in his face.'

Dan stepped back and threw his cigarette into the fire. 'How've you been?' he asked.

Millie looked up at him, overwhelmed by fierce emotions of anger, remorse, pity and indignation. 'Why didn't you answer me letters?' she cried. 'Just a word now and again to tell me you were all right! I've worried about you. And then when the money stopped, I didn't know what to think.'

Dan gave a bitter little laugh. 'So it was the money you missed?'

'No!' Millie was indignant. 'It's been a struggle, but I've got by on what I've earned keeping this place open.'

Dan's look was stubborn. 'I didn't want you to struggle! I hoped once your mam's bairn was born you would have come back to me. You're still me wife, Millie.'

'How could I have left?' Millie demanded. 'Me mam's bedridden now as well as Moody – I told you that! Someone had to look after the baby and run the hotel. I couldn't have left them on their own!' Robert spluttered as she jostled him in agitation, breaking into a coughing fit.

Dan moved swiftly to help. 'Here, give the bairn to me before you choke him.' He held out his arms. 'I'll give him his bottle.'

Millie handed him over warily, watching Dan carefully as he cradled the red-faced baby and spoke gently to him. She passed over the bottle, astonished at how quickly Robert calmed down and settled in Dan's confident hold.

'Tip it so he doesn't fill with air,' she instructed.

Dan glanced at her with a sad smile. 'I know,'

he replied, 'I remember.'

Suddenly Millie's eyes flooded with tears. She could picture him feeding Edith her evening bottle so vividly that she could almost imagine that he held her now. She wiped the tears away with her hand. 'Oh, Dan!' she whispered. 'Why did we quarrel so badly? We should have been helping each other instead of blaming!'

He came and sat beside her, lowering himself and the baby carefully on to the chair.

'I'm sorry, Millie,' he apologised, his eyes shining with tears. 'I said some terrible things to you that I never meant.'

'Me too,' Millie admitted, putting a hand out to touch him for the first time. 'I was hurting so much, I think I was mad with the pain. And I felt that guilty. Guilty about Edith dying...'

'No,' Dan stopped her, 'don't ever say that again. I'll never forgive myself for blaming you. I only said such a thing because I couldn't accept our Edith was dead. I still can't. But it was never your fault, it just happened.'

Millie felt a great release at his words, and she leaned into his shoulder and wept. They sat in silence together as Robert guzzled happily. When the bottle was finished, Dan winded him. 'That's a good lad,' he grinned. Millie took the baby and changed his nappy, then laid him in his pram. As she turned, Dan came and put his arms around her.

'I've missed you, lass,' he whispered, hugging her. She could feel how much thinner he was as she answered his embrace.

'Oh, Dan, I'm glad you're back!' she said,

kissing him. It felt so good to have comforting arms around her once more, and she realised how much she had missed him. The past months had been the loneliest of her life. 'It's been so terrible without Edith or you,' she said sorrowfully.

'Aye, for me an' all,' admitted Dan. 'But we've still got each other. Nothing's going to come between us again.'

As Millie smiled at him and they kissed again in renewed yearning, a voice shouted down the passageway, 'Who's that? Millie, have you got company?'

Millie pulled away with a regretful smile. 'Mam,' she sighed.

Teresa's commanding voice came again. 'If you're making tea, I'll have a cup, pet.'

Dan gave a quizzical look. Millie whispered, 'She never leaves her room now. But she does receive visitors.' She gave Dan a wry smile. 'This'll make her sit up – seeing the prodigal return.'

'Aye, I bet,' Dan grimaced. 'Well, you get the tea brewing and I'll get the sandbags.'

Millie laughed. 'You'll need them, the things she's said about you this past year.'

Dan glanced over at the gurgling Robert. 'That's the pot calling the kettle black, isn't it?'

Millie wagged a warning finger at him. 'Don't you go upsetting her, do you hear?'

'As long as she doesn't go taking advantage of you,' Dan countered.

Millie felt a stab of apprehension that marred the joy she felt at seeing him again. She wondered how long it would be before her mother and husband were rowing once more and the dull equilibrium of her existence was shattered. She had no idea how things were going to work out for them, but then she had decided she shouldn't worry about the future. Warming the teapot, she reminded herself once more not to look beyond the day.

CHAPTER 20

After Mungo's funeral, Dan stayed on for the rest of the summer, declaring to Millie, 'It's the best thing me dad ever did for me – dying. Brought us back together again.' His reappearance seemed to galvanise Teresa and she made attempts to leave her bed and sit in the kitchen, where she could keep a better eye on Dan's comings and goings.

'He's drinking too much,' she told Millie in disapproval. 'You should try and stop him.'

Millie silently agreed that he spent more time than she would have liked with his old drinking friends, and she noticed how small amounts of money that she had hidden around the house to pay bills were disappearing. At first she was just relieved to have him back again, and enjoyed their walks along the river, picnics in the park with baby Robert and watching Dan organising games of football with children in the street.

But Dan made no attempt to find casual work and Millie found it increasingly difficult to make their meagre takings at the hotel last the week. She could not understand why he could not make do with what the club must be paying him over the summer. But try as she might, she could not get him to talk about money.

'I can't give you any more,' she told him. 'You'll just have to stay in.' He looked about to protest and then stopped. 'At least you'll be earning a full wage again shortly.' Millie tried to be optimistic. 'When will you have to go back to Kilburn?' She looked at him warily, wondering if he was going to try and insist that she return with him. But his look slid away from hers as he lit up a fresh cigarette from the one he was already smoking.

Millie felt a flicker of apprehension. 'Dan?'

Dan coughed and looked edgy, pacing the kitchen where Millie was ironing.

'The thing is, Millie,' he began hesitantly, 'the thing is ... I don't know if I'm going back.'

'What do you mean?' Millie demanded, banging the iron on to its stand.

'Well, I'm sure I will be,' he answered. 'It's just...' He gave her a helpless look. 'I was suspended twice last season,' he said in a low voice. 'That's why I couldn't send you any money – they stopped me wages for two months, and I got into a bit of debt. But nothing I can't pay off once I'm earning again.'

'Are people after you for money?' Millie asked, her mouth going dry. Dan did not answer. Millie stared at him in dismay. 'What were you suspended for?'

Dan drew hard on his cigarette. 'I lost me head on the pitch a couple of times – had a go at the referee.'

'Dan!' Millie cried.

'Well, they were having a go at me – dirty tackling, calling me names, trying to get me to lose me temper,' Dan defended himself. 'I used to be able to handle it.' He gulped. 'But – well – since the bairn died...' He gave Millie a bleak look, flicking his cigarette into the fire. 'I started taking nips of brandy before going on. Thought it would give me courage, but it just made me lose me temper more.' Millie watched his face crumple like a small child's. 'God, Millie! I wasn't right in the head,' he sobbed. 'I thought I'd lost you as well as the bairn.'

Millie came swiftly round the table and put her arms around him. 'Oh, Dan!' He wept in her arms and she was shocked to see him cry. She had never seen him like this before and it was the first time he had shown such emotion over Edith's death. Even in private he had not allowed himself to weep and she had been left with this image of his stony, impassive face at the funeral. For too long she had thought it was only she who was drowning in grief, quite alone.

'I should have known how badly you'd take losing our Edith,' Millie comforted, hugging him tight. 'But drinking like you do isn't going to bring her back,' she added gently.

'Aye, I know,' Dan sniffed, wiping his face on his sleeve, embarrassed by his show of emotion. 'I'm going to stop the drinking, Millie, I promise.' He blew his nose. 'And I'm going to sort things out with the club, get me career back on course.'

'Good.' Millie smiled with relief, hoping that he meant it.

The autumn came, but rather than being welcomed back by his club, Dan found himself being transferred swiftly to a Third Division side in east Yorkshire. Millie could tell he was dashed by the demotion, but she was secretly relieved that he was now near enough to travel back to Ashborough more often.

'At least you can come back during the week when you're not playing,' she tried to cheer him. 'It's just a couple of hours on the train.'

She resisted any of his attempts to get her to go with him, saying that there was no point in moving for just a few months in case he was transferred somewhere else at the end of the season. It was the only thing they argued over, but Millie was adamant she would not leave her mother alone to cope with Moody and Robert. She could not bring herself to tell Dan that she could not bear the thought of leaving Ashborough again because that was where Edith was at rest. She felt near to her dead child and spent the anniversary of Edith's death putting fresh flowers on her grave and sitting in the October sunshine writing her a letter. She hid this in her coat pocket, telling no one of its existence, ashamed of her sentimentality yet finding comfort in the action. She told her daughter how much she was missed by her parents, how many hopes they had had for her and that she would never leave her again.

But she could talk to Dan about none of this. How could she say that she would rather stay close to the grave of her daughter than follow him to some unknown town, trying to fill long, empty days of inactivity? Once she dared to suggest, 'Why don't you give up the football and come back here? Help run the hotel? We could make a real go of it together.'

Dan had looked at her, incredulous. 'Give up

football!' he exclaimed. 'For this dump? Not on your life! Don't ever ask me that again!'

When he returned to spend a few days with her just before Christmas, he put pressure on her to join him once more. 'You've never even been to see where I live – or the club, or anything,' he said, pausing on the ladder where he was hanging up battered decorations in the dining room. 'The other lads think it's odd you not being around; they have a good laugh at my expense. It's as if you've stopped believing in me, Millie,' he accused, 'stopped thinking I'm any good as a footballer.'

Millie glanced up from setting a table for the drapery salesman who was staying for the night. She could hear Robert shouting from his pen in the kitchen where she often put him when she had jobs to do. He was crawling so fast now it was not safe to turn her back for two seconds. Gone were the days when he would lie contentedly in her lap and sleep. Now was the time to tell Dan, before the predictable argument spoilt their few days together yet again.

'I'm not stopping you playing,' she said, rearranging the place setting, 'but I can't travel. I–'

'Don't be daft,' Dan interrupted. 'Listen to me, I've been thinking. You could bring Robert with you. We could pretend he was ours like you once suggested. He thinks he's yours anyway, calling you Mama all the time. So does everyone else. We could get Ella and Walter to keep an eye on your mam and Moody – pay someone to live in like before.'

'Pay with what?' Millie laughed shortly. She pushed dark curls out of her eyes, her hair having grown long since her return to Ashborough. 'No, I'm not going to go travelling about now,' she went on quickly. 'Not in my condition.' She looked at him squarely.

Dan stared back, puzzled. 'What do you mean, in your condition?'

She could not help a nervous smile. 'I'm expecting again,' she told him, feeling a thrill inside, despite her apprehension. At first she had ignored the signs of pregnancy, not wanting it to be true. It felt disloyal to Edith. As if she could ever be replaced! But after a couple of months of no periods, swelling breasts and the constant taste of bile in her mouth, she could deny it no longer. How they were going to afford another child or manage the hotel she did not like to think.

Dan scrambled down the ladder and rushed towards her, flinging his arms wide.

'Is it true? Are you sure?' he gasped in excitement. Millie nodded and laughed. He kissed her enthusiastically. 'That's champion!' Then he steered her to a chair. 'You shouldn't be working so hard. Your mam'll have to help out more.'

Millie gently disengaged herself. 'I'm perfectly all right,' she insisted. 'There's no need to fuss.'

'There's every reason to fuss,' Dan replied. 'We're going to be parents again, Millie. It's the best feeling in the world!'

Dan managed to return home about once a month through the spring, and Millie looked forward impatiently to the end of the season, when he could come back to Ashborough and be present for their baby's birth in June. She was apprehensive about the new baby, constantly concerned for its safety and anxious when she did not feel it kicking. Yet she felt guilty at allowing herself the pleasure of thinking about being a mother again or planning for a baby that was not Edith. Bearing another child made her think more acutely than before of her dead daughter, bringing back vivid memories of the happy days on Tyneside when she was carrying Edith. It made her miss her daughter more rather than less, but she tried to mask her grief and did not speak of it even to Dan. He seemed so thrilled by the thought of a second child, and it had given him new motivation. She noticed that his drinking had lessened and he appeared settled and happy at his new club, despite playing in the Third Division.

His old optimism returned. 'We'll finish near the top this season,' he predicted, 'and next year we'll get promotion to the Second Division, you just see.'

Dan never mentioned playing for Newcastle United or one of the First Division clubs, but Millie knew he still harboured dreams of making it to the top. She no longer believed that he would. Looking back, she thought he had frittered away his talent at Gateshead, enjoying life too much to apply himself to the hard graft of top football. Perhaps he had never had the talent of a Hughie Gallagher after all. Millie was no longer concerned. All that mattered was that he had a job and was content with it, while she had a roof over her head and was managing to scrape a living for them all at the hotel. Their baby would not be indulged the way that Edith had been, but at least she could offer some security and prospects, which in the growing depression around them was an achievement.

When Dan returned in May, he managed to pick up a couple of weeks' casual work on Drake's farm, labouring out in the fields. He enjoyed the physical exertion of working outdoors and came home with arms aching and face ruddy, his fair hair bleached by the summer sun. Millie ignored the barbed comments around the town that he was taking work from others worse off. With the baby on the way, they needed what little extra they could get. She became increasingly tired, running after an active Robert whom chair-bound Teresa could not cope with, as well as cooking and laying tables, making beds and cleaning for the household.

'When the bairn comes, I'll have to get some help,' she told Dan as she hauled herself into bed one hot May evening, quite exhausted.

'Maybe that lass Sarah might come back,' he yawned.

'Her mam doesn't approve of us,' Millie sighed, trying to shift into a comfortable position and failing. She threw off the covers.

Dan put a hand over her bump. 'I'll have a word with her mam if you like. Folk can't be too choosy these days. I bet she could do with one less mouth to feed.'

Their preparations were overshadowed by a

sudden event. One morning Millie hauled herself upstairs with a breakfast tray for Moody as usual, followed by an unsteady but eager Robert, who liked to come and peer at the man in bed. But that day Millie found him lying stone cold, his eyes staring at the damp, flaking ceiling. Millie spilt the tea over the counterpane in her shock and found herself gasping for breath as if she had been punched. Robert tried to climb on to the bed and howled when Millie grabbed him and pulled him away.

'Leave Grandda,' she gasped, bundling him towards the door. Shaking, she hurried from the room and called for Dan, but he had already left for the farm. Teresa, hearing Robert's protests and Millie's cry, demanded, 'What is it?'

Millie rushed breathlessly into the kitchen where her mother was sitting. 'It's Joseph,' she hissed. She did not have to say anything more, for her ashen face betrayed what she had found.

'Dead?' Teresa whispered, her hands moving in agitation. Millie nodded, bracing herself for hysteria from her mother. Robert was already screaming the house down, having inherited Teresa's temperament. But Teresa merely closed her eyes and gave a shuddering sigh.

Millie stared at her while Robert bawled and clawed at her skirt. 'Mam, are you all right?' she asked in concern, but her mother did not speak. To Millie's astonishment, a slow smile spread across Teresa's haggard face.

'The old lecher's gone,' she said with quiet relief. 'I'm free of him.'

Millie gawped at her mother's muted elation,

quite baffled. She thought Teresa had come to love Moody, or if not exactly love, then grown fond of the strange man. Surely Robert was proof of that? Millie thought, bending to console the screaming infant clamouring for her attention. She tried to lift the stocky boy, but felt a pain shoot through her at the effort, and gasped in agony. She felt odd, her pulse racing uncomfortably.

Teresa opened her eyes at Millie's cry of alarm. Millie clutched her swollen womb, feeling ill. 'Oh, Mam,' she groaned, 'I think the baby's coming.'

When Dr Percy came to certify Moody's death, he found himself helping out at the birth of Millie's baby. Teresa had crawled to the kitchen door and bellowed for attention as Millie doubled up on the kitchen floor. A delivery boy from the Co-operative store had been passing and ran for help. Dr Percy just had time to get Millie on to Teresa's downstairs bed before she went into labour proper. Half an hour later, faint with the shock of discovering Moody and the speed of the delivery, Millie was presented with her newborn.

'It's a boy,' Dr Percy told her. 'Mr Nixon will be pleased.'

'Aye, he will,' Millie whispered, unable to look at the young doctor. She was mortified that a man had witnessed all the mess and intimacy; she would never be able to look Dr Percy in the eye again. Millie's head swam. She had been certain she would have a girl to plague her with memories of Edith and a life of constant comparisons. But here was an unexpected boy. She gazed at the tiny, red-faced creature that Dr Percy had placed in her arms. He looked sleepy, as if he too had been taken unawares by his sudden arrival into the world. Millie experienced a surge of delight, coupled with relief.

'I never dared hope...' she began. 'Is he all right?'

'Perfectly all right,' Dr Percy assured her.

Millie felt herself choking with emotion. 'Thank you,' she gulped, giving way to tears of relief.

By the time Dan returned home at tea-time, Moody's body had been laid out and measured by the undertaker and Millie was already sitting up in a kitchen chair feeding their son. She had never seen her husband so lost for words. But he recovered swiftly, kissing her with delight and swinging the baby into his arms.

'I want to call him Albert,' he announced.

'I thought he was to be called Daniel, if he was a boy?' Teresa questioned. 'Millie said she wanted him called after you, and she's done all the hard work.'

Millie sensed a quarrel brewing. 'Daniel could be his middle name,' she said quickly, too weary for argument. 'And I like the name Albert – sounds regal.'

'Grand!' Dan grinned happily. 'Albert it is.'

Teresa snorted. 'Think you're royalty, do you? Naming him after Prince Albert!'

Dan looked at her, puzzled. 'No,' he insisted. 'After Albert Shepherd – centre forward before the war. Scored ninety-two goals in five seasons.'

Millie caught her mother's scandalised look and burst out laughing. Dan smiled down at the tiny-featured infant. 'My Albert will play like him one day, won't you, son?'

Millie smiled at them both as Robert whined at her side, resenting the lack of attention. She glanced down at the fractious child and had an acute pang of regret that it wasn't Edith there, sharing the moment. She smothered the ill-feeling towards Robert and put an arm around him.

'That's your new brother, Albert,' she told him as she hauled him on to her knee, glancing at her mother to see if she would protest. Millie thought it best to avoid the future embarrassment of Albert having to call Robert his uncle. But Teresa said nothing. It appeared she did not care enough about her young son to make a fuss, or maybe she really did think it the best arrangement for Millie to pretend to be the boy's mother.

'Does Robert want to give the baby a kiss?' Millie encouraged.

But when Dan lifted Albert down for the small boy to inspect, Robert shoved a finger in the baby's face and scratched him. Dan snatched him quickly out of reach while Millie smacked the boy's hand.

'Naughty Robert!' she scolded. 'You mustn't harm the baby!'

As Robert burst into tears, Millie was filled with foreboding. He would just have to get used to having a baby brother around, she thought fiercely, and she was going to have to do everything in her power to protect her new son. She felt overwhelmed with possessiveness for her newborn. She was never going to lose this child, never!

CHAPTER 21

Messages were sent to America to try and discover where Ava and Grant were living and tell Ava of her father's death. No reply came back, and Teresa went ahead swiftly with arranging Joseph's funeral. Within five days of his death, Joseph Benjamin Moody was cremated after a modest ceremony attended only by Teresa, the Nixons, his old friend Collins from Drake's farm and two retired draymen from the Co-op who were former drinking companions. He had no close family to mourn his going. Millie stayed at home with the baby boys and prepared a few sandwiches.

Dan insisted that they buy in several jugs of beer for Moody's wake. 'We were second-cousins-once-removed, as Mam always used to say, so we should give him a proper send-off.'

Teresa agreed to lift her temperance rule for the occasion. 'But after this there'll be no drink brought into this house.'

The atmosphere that afternoon was that of a party rather than a wake. Moody's morose spirit had gone from the hotel and, in the days that followed, Teresa wasted no time in having his room cleared, directing Millie and Sarah – whom Dan had persuaded to return – to throw out his old clothes. An out-of-work miner who had a small business cobbling and selling second-hand footwear came round for Moody's boots and shoes, that had hardly been worn in years. Millie was astonished at the number of old newspapers they found laid under the carpet, the mattress and piled high in the wardrobe. They discovered dusty empty whisky bottles in an old chest, along with further newspapers dating back to the Great War.

The women took down the threadbare curtains, which reeked of stale cigarette smoke, and burnt them in the back yard, then unnailed the window and threw it open to the fresh air. Teresa gathered his few trinkets, including a photograph of Ava before she was married, a snuff box and a print of Queen Victoria, and put them in a box for Ava if she ever returned. After the room was given a thorough scrubbing-down, Dan set to work painting the walls a primrose yellow.

'We'll turn it into a nursery for the two lads,' Teresa ordered. 'It's the biggest bedroom and they should have somewhere to play so they're not in the way of the lodgers.'

Millie watched for Dan's reaction, thinking he might object to Albert being given a permanent room in the hotel. It was an admission that Millie would not be following him back to Yorkshire when the season started. But Dan seemed pleased with the idea of his son being given the best room in the house and fussed over in the manner he deserved.

Albert was christened a fortnight later, but Teresa declared that only tea and ginger beer would be served with the celebratory tea. Dan and Walter disappeared swiftly to the Farrier's Arms in defiance, Dan muttering that he would not wet his baby's head with anything less than Federation Ale. Millie was annoyed with both her husband and her mother for being so stubborn over the occasion, but endeavoured to enjoy the day, inviting Mrs Dodswell, Mrs Dickson, Ella and Elsie, who to Millie's delight travelled the twenty miles from the farm where she now lived. She came with her sister Mary and brought her twin daughters, Nelly and Doris.

Yet Millie's joy at seeing her old friend was marred by the unexpected pain she felt at the sight of the small girls. They were five years old, just a few months older than Edith would have been had she lived. Although they looked nothing like her daughter, with their dark-red hair and freckled noses, she felt a pang to hear their chattering talk and watch their restless play with Marjory. They were boisterous, strong-limbed country girls, too loud for Teresa's approval, and Millie's heart ached anew to think how much Edith would have relished their company. She would have been singing songs too, and learning to hopscotch in the yard, Millie thought mournfully.

She found herself suddenly tearful and made excuses to leave the gathering to feed Albert, telling Ella to stop the clinging Robert from following her. She shut herself in her bedroom and wept as quietly as she could, while Albert struggled to suckle at her shaking breast. She wondered despairingly if she would ever be able to control her grief for Edith, ever feel it lessen its savage grip on her emotions. It was nearly two years since she had died, and yet Millie still missed her desperately, her feelings as raw as ever.

By the time Millie emerged, having lain down and slept for two hours, the guests had gone and only Ella remained, helping Teresa clear up. Her mother could now stand and walk short distances with the aid of two sticks, so she could issue orders but did little of the actual work. As soon as Robert spotted Millie he hurtled across the kitchen and threw himself at her legs, whining in protest at her neglect of him.

'You were missed. They've all gone,' Teresa said in disapproval. 'I had to make excuses for you.'

Ella said in quick support, 'But it's good you had a bit of sleep, you were looking tired. Elsie understood. She's promised to visit later in the summer.'

Millie smiled at her friend, distractedly handing her the baby while she tried to pacify Robert. She picked him up, but he continued to cry and she lost patience. Plonking him into Teresa's lap, she said irritably, 'Here, you do something with him for a change. He wears me out and I've got me own bairn to think about now!'

She hurried from the room, escaping from Robert's howling and Teresa's irritated scolding. Ella found her on the steps of the hotel, face buried in her hands.

'I don't know what comes over me,' Millie said in despair. 'I don't mean to take it out on the bairn like that, but I can't help it.' She looked at her friend, shamefaced, and whispered, 'I can't bear him for not being Edith. Is that very terrible of me?'

Ella put out a comforting hand. 'I know what you mean. I couldn't bear other people's bairns for a long time after we lost ours. It'll just take time.'

'Aye,' Millie sighed. 'It's just Robert's so wearing. He used to be such a contented baby... It might help if me mam showed a bit more interest in him.'

Ella reminded her, 'Aye, but you were the one who wanted to keep him, remember? You didn't want him adopted, did you?'

Millie felt herself flush with guilt. 'No I didn't. Poor Robert!'

She dragged herself up from the steps, resolving to try harder with the small boy in future.

The end of the summer came and Dan went back to Yorkshire, cheerful about his prospects for the season and no longer nagging Millie to return with him. They both knew that they could not afford to rent rooms down there as well as keep the hotel going, and Dan appeared to accept that Albert would thrive better in Ashborough. So he went into shared digs with two other footballers and promised to return as frequently as possible. Millie suspected that he was relieved to get away from Teresa's censoriousness and back to a life of football. She missed him at first, but soon her life was too busy with the baby and Robert, the hotel and her mother, who relapsed into long days in bed once Dan left. Her life was too full to fret over what Dan might be doing in the days and evenings when he was not playing.

But her heart lurched one day when a telegram was delivered to the hotel, thinking something awful must have happened to him. Only after she had torn it open did she realise it was addressed to her mother.

She stared in amazement at the stark message, then ran in to see Teresa, shouting, 'You'll never believe this! It's from Ava. They're in Liverpool – on their way home. They said to get a room ready for them!'

Teresa snorted. 'Well, that sounds like Ava! Let me see.' She took the telegram with a shaking hand. 'So she's on her way back,' she said, breathing hard. 'I suppose the news about Joseph finally caught up with her.'

Millie exchanged looks with her mother. 'Why do you think she's coming back now, if she knows her father's dead?' she asked nervously. 'She never came back when he was alive.'

Teresa's face looked sombre. 'I don't know. But we could have a battle on our hands when she finds out Joseph left the hotel to me.'

Millie prepared one of the rooms normally kept for travellers, laid a fire and put out clean hand towels. She invited Ella and Walter over for tea to greet them, and her friend came early to help prepare a meal, having collected Marjory from school. There were two other visitors staying that night who needed to be fed, and the Co-operative women's society were holding a meeting in the dining room at eight o'clock and would be needing refreshments.

'What time's their train get in?' Ella asked as

she peeled potatoes to go with the special roll of brisket that Millie had extravagantly bought.

'Half past four,' Millie said, nervously glancing at the clock. There was an hour to go. Teresa sat at the back door keeping an eye on the children playing in the yard. It was an unusually warm late-September afternoon, with just a hint of sharpness in the air, warning of changing weather. Marjory was helping Robert push a heavy child's wheelbarrow full of wooden alphabet bricks that Millie had bought cheaply at a bazaar for the boy's birthday the previous spring. The wheelbarrow had been built by Grant for Marjory before he had left for America. Ella had asked for a pram for the girl's two dolls, but that had appeared too much of a challenge for Grant's rough carpentry skills.

Millie, listening to the rumble and crash of the barrow as it hurtled around the yard, grew increasingly anxious at the impending arrival. How would Ava take her father's death? Did she now have children of her own, and would she resent the presence of these new boys occupying Moody's old room? Perhaps they had been too hasty in clearing out the old man's possessions, she fretted. The only trace left of his having lived there was a formal portrait of him in Edwardian coat and bowler hat that hung in the hallway. Even then he had been portly, but there was still an air of vigorous prosperity about him that made Teresa think it suitable to display in the hotel.

Ella sensed her disquiet. 'You've no need to worry. We're all older now – and Ava's had four years out in the world. She's bound to have changed her ways.'

'Once spoilt always spoilt,' Teresa snorted. 'Except now there's no Joseph to give in to her all the time. But no doubt we'll still have to listen to hours of how grand America is compared to Ashborough.'

'Well, I can put up with the boasting,' Millie replied, 'if Ava can accept the way things are here.'

The women exchanged glances, each thinking of Robert and wondering how scandalised Ava would be were she to discover she had an illegitimate half-brother. Only Ella, Walter and Mrs Dickson had been told the true parentage of the boy, and all three, along with Dr Percy, had long ago sworn to keep it secret. The story they circulated after Robert's arrival was that he was an orphan who had been adopted by Millie and Dan. Their neighbours appeared to accept the situation, keeping to themselves any suspicions that Teresa had been pregnant. Millie suspected their tolerance was in return for Teresa's efforts to save them from starvation during the strike. Ava was unlikely to find out about Robert, but not for the first time Millie was plagued with uncertainty that she had done the right thing in keeping the boy in the family.

Millie trooped on to the platform with Ella and Marjory to meet the train, her heart hammering with nervousness. A handful of passengers disembarked and Millie stared through the steam but could not see Grant and Ava.

'They're not on it,' she gasped, feeling a flood of relief.

But Ella nudged her. 'Look, up the far end, with all those boxes. That must be Ava!'

The friends hurried up the platform to help. The thickset man in a gabardine coat and black hat hauling luggage off the train turned out to be Grant. He looked thinner, his face more lined, but the brown eyes were still vital under their bushy eyebrows. They hesitated, then Grant put out a hand, which Millie shook, embarrassed by the formality. Ella, feeling less in awe, gave him a kiss on the cheek and gestured at the pile of boxes.

'We'd have hired porters if we'd known you had all this,' she joked.

'Ava likes her clothes,' Grant began to explain, but he was cut short by a shout from inside the train.

'This one's too heavy for me. Come back and help!'

Millie recognised Ava's peevish voice, though it held a distinct American twang that made her want to laugh. Moments later, Ava stepped off the train, almost unrecognisable. Her brown hair was tightly permed under a jaunty red hat that sloped down at one side. Her eyebrows were plucked to a thin line, and she was wearing red lipstick that matched her hat. She was wrapped in a tan-coloured coat with a fur collar, but Millie noticed it was well worn. Nevertheless, the effect was like that of a film star arriving at Ashborough station; there was an air of glamour about Ava that made Millie feel dowdy, even though she had changed out of her work clothes and made an effort to be smart. She still could not fit into most of her skirts since Albert's birth, and was wearing a loose dress that she had bought in Newcastle five years before.

Millie stepped forward to greet Ava. 'You look grand!' she cried in admiration. Ava looked at her in satisfaction, presenting a cool cheek to be kissed.

'You look just like that cartoon character, Betty Boop,' Ella teased, holding Marjory up for Ava to kiss. 'Isn't Auntie Ava like something out the films? Go on, give her a kiss!' But Marjory was suddenly shy and craned away from Ava's red lips and cloying smell of cheap perfume.

'She'll come round,' Millie said quickly. 'Here, let me help you carry some of these,' she said, bending to lift two boxes.

'Well, you've put on weight, Millie!' Ava cried in her new sing-song voice. 'You used to be so slim.'

Millie flushed. 'That's what having bairns does for you,' she answered with a self-conscious smile.

Ava gave her a sharp look. 'That's one thing I've avoided, then.'

Grant glanced up and Millie saw a redness creep into his prominent jaw.

'You haven't got...?' Millie asked awkwardly. Grant shook his head.

'It doesn't bother us,' Ava said stiffly, picking up a battered hat box and a canvas bag.

As Grant turned, he said quietly, 'We were sorry to hear about your Edith, a terrible thing.'

Tears stung Millie's eyes at the unexpected mention of her daughter's name. 'I remember her as such a bonny bairn,' Grant added kindly.

Millie gulped, remembering how he had visited their flat on Tyneside and how easily Edith had taken to his gentle, gruff manner. 'Aye,' she murmured, 'thanks.'

Ava cut in, 'But your letter said you'd got another one, so at least you should be thankful for that.'

Millie felt bruised by her lack of sympathy, but tried not to show it, not wanting to cause embarrassment for the others. 'I am,' she answered, turning away.

Ella spoke up. 'It doesn't stop her missing Edith, mind. It's not just something you forget.'

They all walked along the platform in silence while Marjory skipped ahead. Millie took a deep breath. 'So you got our letters? We thought you must have moved when we heard nothing.'

'We've moved around,' Ava said shortly. 'I didn't hear about my father until a month ago.'

'I'm sorry about that,' Millie said. 'We'll tell you everything you want to know. He died in his sleep, quite peaceful. I went up with his breakfast–'

'I don't want to hear any more!' Ava snapped. 'Talking about him won't bring him back. You should have written to tell me he was so ill. I could have come sooner and taken care of him properly.'

Millie was stung. 'He never wanted for anything, Ava. Mam and me looked after him well. He's been bed-bound for years. You knew that. He used to write to you but you never once replied.' She stopped as Grant gave her a warning look.

'His letters must have gone astray.' Ava was defensive. 'And we've moved that much. You should have tried harder to contact us. I'm very upset to think I'll never see him again!' And she burst into instant tears.

Millie plonked down the boxes and rushed to put her arms round her. 'I'm sorry, Ava, really I am. Of course it's upsetting.' But Ava shrugged her off and pulled out a handkerchief, dabbing her eyes and nose quickly.

They reached the hotel in a tense silence to find Teresa standing by the range, leaning on her sticks. She was wearing a black dress that made her look matronly and emphasised the sallowness of her face. Millie saw at once that her mother was going to play the grieving widow for all she was worth. Ava looked visibly shocked to see how Teresa had aged. They greeted each other stiffly, with formal words, and Millie was thankful to occupy herself with preparing the evening tea.

Ava flopped into a chair, looking warily askance at Albert, lying kicking on a rug inside the playpen, where Millie had put him out of Robert's reach. But Grant went over and made a fuss of him. 'By, I bet Dan's proud of him. Got his colouring, just like–' He broke off suddenly, throwing Millie an apologetic look. She knew what he had been going to say, and he was right; Albert looked painfully like his sister had done at the same age, which was both a comfort and a trial. But she was grateful to Grant for noticing.

'Aye, he has,' she smiled.

'Where is Dan?' Ava asked, giving Millie a hard look. 'Your letters never mentioned him. I suppose that means he's not done as well as you hoped.'

Millie reddened. 'He's playing for a Yorkshire side – they're doing well enough. He's in lodgings, comes home as often as he can.'

Ava carefully unpinned her felt hat and shook out her tight brown curls. Millie could not help noticing how much the hairstyle suited her, giving shape to her thin face, while eyeliner made her small eyes seem bigger. 'That must be difficult for you,' Ava commented, raising her pencil-thin eyebrows. 'I can't imagine letting a man like Dan live away from home.' She gave an irritating little smirk, implying so much more.

Teresa answered before Millie lost her temper. 'Needs must. He's got to go where the work is. He knows that Millie's needed here to keep the hotel going, and it's a better place for Albert to grow up. They've lost one child with living in bad housing; they're not going to risk that again.'

That seemed to silence Ava, and she was persuaded by Grant to go to their room to unpack. Later, when Walter had arrived and given his cheerful greetings, they all sat round the kitchen table eating Millie's tea, while Millie dashed in and out serving the two lodgers and trying at the same time to listen in to snatches of conversation in the kitchen. Ava talked a lot about America and going to the movies, as she called them. But she was evasive about what they had actually done for four years, or where they had lived. Grant muttered about working in a factory and then a garage.

'I did a bit of carpentry on the side,' he told Walter. 'Would have liked to do more, but the work dried up. Things were getting really bad, we had to give up–'

'I wasn't keen on him doing work that no one was paying him for,' Ava interrupted sharply, 'so we moved to a better part of town. He got this very good job at a top department store.'

Grant looked uncomfortable. 'Just a night-watchman.' Ava's glare was so fierce that he gave no more details.

'So is that why you decided to come home?' Walter questioned. Grant nodded. 'Well, things are tough here too. Have you thought what you might do?'

There were anxious glances around the table, and Millie wondered how they were going to support two more mouths if Grant and Ava stayed on here.

Then Ava spoke. 'Of course we've thought. We didn't come back because life was too hard in America, we came back because of the hotel. Now that my father's gone, we want to sell it.'

There was an intake of breath around the table. Millie put down her knife and fork with a clatter.

'Why do you want to do that?' Ella was the first to speak. 'It's Mrs Mercer's livelihood – and Millie's and the bairns'...'

Grant said quickly, 'We hadn't decided–'

'Oh yes I had,' Ava contradicted her husband. 'It was my father's and I can do what I want with it.'

'No you can't,' Teresa said in a triumphant voice. Everyone looked at her. 'Joseph put in writing that I was to have the hotel. He made a will.'

Millie felt her pulse quicken, thankful that she had made her mother act when she did.

Ava was furious. 'My father would never have disinherited me like that!' she cried. 'I don't believe you.'

Teresa gave her a fierce look. 'It's true, and I'll not let you or anyone else throw me or my family out! Not after all the work we've put into this place.'

Ava stood up. 'What about me? I need to live too! I can't rely on *him* to provide for me.' She gave Grant a contemptuous look. 'It's mine by right and I will have it!' She stamped her foot like a child.

Millie was appalled by her outburst and the way Grant just sat there submitting to her waspish tongue. The man who had once lectured them passionately on the rights of the working classes would never have sat mute with bowed head like this. His pride had been punched out of him, Millie thought. Whatever else had happened in America, he had lost all self-respect. Everyone was looking at him, and he gave his wife a bleak look.

'We came back to sort things out, not throw people out,' he said, his anger suppressed. He regarded Teresa. 'We thought you'd be wanting rid of the place now that Joseph's gone...'

'No.' Teresa was adamant. 'It's the only security we've got. I can manage here with Millie's help and the wages Dan sends home. It's not the best of situations – and it's not what Millie's been used to – but we get by.' She turned her defiance on Ava. 'This hotel would have closed down years ago if it hadn't been for me – you wouldn't have had anything to come back to at all!'

'I don't believe that for a minute!' Ava shouted, losing her affected accent. 'You've used me dad all these years, scrounging off him like leeches. Well, not any more. I want you all out!'

'Ava!' Grant protested half-heartedly.

'Haway!' Walter added in disbelief.

Ella cried, 'You can't mean it!'

Millie stood up, realising that neither her mother nor Ava was going to give ground. She was thankful that they had bundled all the children into bed before the meal so that none of them had to witness the savage bickering. Now she intervened. 'Ava, the hotel's not worth anything at the moment,' she said, keeping her voice low but firm. 'We're in a slump. No one would buy it, and even if they did we wouldn't get fair money for it. The best thing we can do is hang on here and make what living we can from it. You could do that too – live here, I mean. Couldn't she, Mam?' She gave Teresa a pleading look.

Teresa struggled a moment and then said, 'Aye, of course.'

Ava, face puce with indignation at being out-manoeuvred, answered, 'Well, that's a cheek! You giving me permission to live in me own home! By, you're a bit high and mighty for a pitman's daughter from Craston,' she sneered, 'and an

351

evicted one at that. This is my house – I grew up here. My father saved you from the workhouse and destitution, remember?'

Teresa tried to rise, shaking with fury. 'And that's where you would have ended up, you spoilt bitch, if I hadn't come here and saved your father from drinking himself into bankruptcy and death! I ruined myself for you and Joseph – ruined my health and my reputation.'

'Reputation?' Ava scoffed.

'Aye!' Teresa cried, unusually flushed. 'Submitting myself to that weak, selfish man all those years – for Millie's sake and for yours. It kept his attention off both of you! I deserve this house, and it's mine–!' She broke off, panting.

'Mam, don't upset yourself,' Millie warned, seeing her agitation.

Ava was furious. 'Don't you dare speak about my father like that! You were nothing but his whore,' she hissed.

'That's enough!' Grant protested.

But Teresa struggled to rise again, livid at the accusation. 'How dare...!' Then she gasped in pain and sat straight down again.

'Mam?' Millie cried, rushing round the table. She just caught her mother as she toppled sideways off her chair, making a horrible gurgling sound as she fought for breath. 'Mam!' Millie gasped. 'Help her!'

At once Grant and Walter were out of their seats. 'I'll go for Dr Percy,' Walter offered swiftly, and escaped out of the back door. Grant helped Millie lay Teresa on the floor, and Millie fumbled with the buttons at the back of her mother's dress to loosen the collar, while Ella rushed for a glass of water. Teresa's eyes stared at them in fear as she struggled to breathe.

'Don't try to speak, Mam,' Millie urged gently.

Suddenly Teresa went limp, as if she had fallen instantly asleep. Millie felt for a pulse but could not find one.

'I think she's stopped breathing!' she screamed.

Grant pushed her aside and bent over the collapsed woman, listening for her breath. He placed his mouth over hers and tried to resuscitate her. Millie watched in horror as Teresa lay quite still and unresponsive. Grant straddled her and pressed down hard on her chest with three short blows of his hands, then repeated the breathing, blowing more air into her mouth.

Millie was aware of Ava hovering over them, frightened. 'I didn't mean...' she whispered, nearly in tears. 'It wasn't my fault.' No one answered her as they fought to save Teresa's life.

'Please, Mam,' Millie sobbed. 'Please don't die!'

Grant looked grim. 'I don't know what else to do, Millie,' he confessed.

'Try again!' she demanded.

Grant leaned forward, placing his hands over Teresa's ribs once more. Suddenly there was an exhalation of air from her mouth and she began a ragged, shallow breathing. Grant and Millie exchanged astonished looks.

'She's breathing,' Millie gasped. 'You've saved her!' Instinctively she threw her arms round Grant's neck and hugged him, shaking with relief and joy. 'Thank you,' she wept, 'thank you!'

Briefly she felt Grant's burly arms go round her in a comforting gesture, and then he pulled away. Teresa's eyes opened, looking confused.

'It's all right, Mam,' Millie reassured her, stroking her forehead, 'the doctor's on his way.'

Ella bent down with the glass of water and they helped Teresa to sip. Glancing up, Millie caught the look on Ava's face and felt a chill go through her. The fear of moments before had given way to loathing. Ava stood alone, separated from them by the bitterness and resentment that plagued her. Millie felt a mixture of pity and anger at Moody's daughter for throwing their lives into turmoil once more. At that moment she doubted whether they could ever live together in harmony.

CHAPTER 22

It was Dan who finally resolved the situation. To Millie's surprise he came rushing home in concern when he heard of Teresa's heart attack and near-death. Teresa was kept under observation by the doctor and administered to by Millie, who tried to calm her mother about the cost of medical bills. Ava hung about the hotel or walked aimlessly around the shops, while Grant went out each day in a fruitless search for work, often walking miles to follow a rumour of a day's factory work or labouring. But Ava perked up at Dan's arrival, and Millie watched with a mixture of admiration and unease at the way he won her round.

'You mustn't blame yourself for the heart attack,' Dan reassured her. 'It could have happened any time. Teresa's not been well for a couple of years now. But you're a canny lass, Ava, you could put her mind at rest by dropping this thing about the will. No more talk of selling the hotel, eh?'

Ava looked nonplussed, confused by Dan's words. They seemed to both flatter her and somehow imply she had an obligation to Teresa because of her ill-health. She had not seen the heart attack as her fault anyway.

'We can hardly stay under the same roof after what's happened,' she pouted. 'And I've got no-

355

where else to go. Why can't you look after your own family and find somewhere for them to live down in Yorkshire?'

Dan laughed, then spoke confidingly. 'Because the old woman would drive me crackers, that's why.'

Ava smirked and glanced at Millie, who was across the kitchen kneading dough and pretending not to listen.

'But you've seen how poorly she is,' Dan continued in a low voice, offering Ava a cigarette. 'She's in no state to move next door, let alone down to Yorkshire.' He lit Ava's cigarette for her. 'Mrs Mercer's bed-bound, she's not going to be in your way if you stay. It'll just be you and Millie, you'll be like sisters again.' Dan raised his voice. 'Isn't that right, Millie?'

Millie looked up, biting back the retort that they had never been like sisters. Only in the early days had they ever got on, in the days before Dan had come into her life. Instead she nodded.

Ava looked over, blowing smoke in her direction. 'Well, as long as she keeps those boys under control,' she said to Dan. 'Your Robert is so noisy, and the baby cries half the night.'

Millie expected Dan to defend them, but he merely laughed. 'She will. Millie's good with the bairns.'

Millie could no longer contain her annoyance at the way they spoke of her as if she was not there. 'As long as Ava's prepared to do her bit around the hotel,' she warned.

Ava carried on smoking as if she had not heard, and Dan stood up, winking at them both. 'That's grand,' he said brightly. 'I knew you'd come to an understanding.' Then he sauntered out, leaving the women staring after him, Millie furious that he had pandered to Ava's vanity. The hotel belonged to Teresa now and there was nothing Ava could do about it. Grant could not support her, so Ava had no option but to co-exist with them.

So after that there was no more talk of anyone moving out or the hotel being sold, and the women came to an uneasy truce. As Millie could have predicted, she was left with the responsibility of the day-to-day running of the boarding house, as well as caring for her mother and the boys and trying to eke out their modest budget, while Ava did the shopping and attempted to bring custom into the hotel. She had a new self-assurance that went with her change of hairstyle, looks and speech. Millie had to admire the way she managed to persuade a choral group and a dance teacher to use the hotel on a weekly basis.

But Ava was basically lazy and avoided doing any of the menial work, so Millie was thankful to have young Sarah's help. The girl no longer lived in, but came three mornings a week to clean, lay fires, change beds and poss the washing. Grant, when he was not tramping the countryside for work, could be cajoled into helping around the hotel, and Millie came to rely on him for odd joinery jobs such as mending chairs and replacing rotting window frames. Yet Millie sensed that he felt such work beneath him, a man who had once been a skilled face worker in the pit. He had grown moodier and more irritable than Millie remembered him, and she found his surliness as trying as Ava's constant nagging and criticism. Despite his help, he took no real interest in the hotel. The only time she saw his face light up was when he was making something for the small boys or listening to their chatter.

Millie was baffled and irritated by his indifference, thinking that he should be more grateful for the roof over his head and the meals that appeared on the table when he returned from his wanderings each day. It was more than many had, she thought impatiently. But even if Grant had not been blacklisted from the pits, there were no jobs on offer. Walter was back on short time, and there were families whose breadwinners were heading for the cities in an attempt to find work. Others were subjected to the new means test, with relieving officers prying into their affairs and ordering them to sell possessions before notifying the employment exchange of what relief, if any, they should receive.

The queues outside the labour exchanges grew, and business in the town slumped. To Ava's humiliation, Grant attempted to sign on the dole, but was declared ineligible because of his wife's involvement in the hotel. Millie watched with mounting concern as he struggled to fill the idle hours, drifting around the streets of Ashborough in increasingly half-hearted attempts to find odd jobs. He had pawned all the books he had ever owned and no longer seemed to find enjoyment in reading. Robert followed him around like a thin shadow, but he appeared not to notice. It suddenly dawned on Millie that he was beginning to give up like her father had. It appalled her to think that he might buckle under the weight of unemployment and depression in the same way. Ava appeared to despise him just as Teresa had Ellis. They squabbled constantly, and the hotel became a place of slamming doors and frosty silences, reminding Millie painfully of her last days in Craston.

Yet she did not like to interfere; she had enough to cope with as it was. She made an attempt to open up the temperance tea room once more, selling Bovril and hot soup through the winter, tea and scones during the summer. Gradually it became a popular meeting place again and brought in a steady trickle of income. But Ava complained at the number of unemployed men who hung around the converted bar, sitting for hours in the warmth reading old newspapers and making one cup of tea last an afternoon.

'It's putting respectable folks off, having these idle men filling up the place,' she told Millie, 'and they make the tea room smell.' Millie was glad that Grant was not around to hear her; he was one of the few jobless men who did not stay around the hotel if he could help it.

'They're not doing any harm,' Millie insisted, darning under the electric lamp in the kitchen. 'And no one's complaining. They're not going to criticise their neighbours when they might be next to lose their jobs.' She quietly resisted Ava's demands that she put up a sign discouraging people from bringing in their own sandwiches, and kept quiet about the number of times she had let someone off without paying for a second cup of tea, or slipped a hungry child an extra biscuit. Her mother would have done the same, Millie thought, if she had been in charge.

But Teresa had taken to life in bed once again and showed no inclination to get up. Whenever Millie suggested she try and walk further than the commode or mind the children in the kitchen, she refused, complaining about pains in her chest or aching in her limbs. She was content to let Millie run things while she listened to the wireless set that Dan had bought her and knitted ill-fitting garments for the boys or Marjory out of unravelled jumpers and socks. Occasionally, on warm summer days, she would emerge to sit in the sunshine, peeling vegetables and sparring with Ava. But mostly she left Millie to cope alone.

There were times when Ava's carpings about the jobless in the tea room became too much and Millie would argue back about Ava's squandering of their precious income. She was furious when she discovered a hidden pile of film magazines and sixpenny romances in Ava's room.

'Where did you get the money for these?' Millie demanded.

'You've no right to go snooping around in my bedroom!' Ava was equally outraged.

'No one else cleans it, do they?' Millie pointed out, throwing the offending magazines down at Ava's feet. 'We can't afford these! I'm working me fingers to the bone trying to make ends meet, and what do you do? Spend a week's house-keeping on nonsense like this!'

'It's not nonsense,' Ava pouted, bending to retrieve her scattered belongings. 'Life wouldn't be worth living if I didn't have the odd magazine to look at.'

'Why can't you go to the library like everyone else?' Millie snapped.

Ava pulled a disdainful face. 'I hate the library – it's full of people who haven't washed for a week. And the books are all grubby and used. I need my own. But you've no imagination, you wouldn't begin to understand what a woman like me needs. I've travelled the world, I've seen things. You're just a small-minded common pitman's daughter and always will be, just like all the other village girls around here. I don't know what Dan ever saw in you.'

Millie answered hotly, 'He saw what he wanted – a lass who truly loved him.'

Ava gave her a withering look. 'There've been plenty of *them*,' she said waspishly.

Millie was outraged at the slur. 'Maybe there were, but he chose me. And I've given him happiness, and bairns that he adores.' She glared at Ava. 'And it would be nice to treat the boys to some meat now and again instead of you wasting money on rubbish for yourself!'

But any mention of the children made Ava behave worse. She constantly complained about Albert's messy eating and smelly nappies, or the way Robert bounded around after her, grabbing her second-hand American dresses with sticky hands. The more she shouted at the small boy, the more he sought out her company and gave her unwanted attention. Grant would intervene

361

and try to distract the boy, but this just seemed to irritate Ava the more. He had endless patience for the boys, yet was short-tempered with her.

When Dan came home at the end of the season, the atmosphere improved. He dismissed Millie's grumbling about Ava's rows with herself and Grant, and her awkwardness over the running of the hotel.

'She seems happy enough to me,' he shrugged.

Millie eyed him suspiciously. 'Aye, well, it seems to have something to do with you being back. I don't like the way you flirt with her,' she blurted out.

Dan just laughed. 'Come here, silly Millie,' he said, mimicking her mother, and pulled her on to his knee. 'Are you telling me you're jealous of Ava?'

Millie flushed. 'Should I be?' she asked, remembering Ava's insinuations about other women and feeling drab in her faded cotton dress and pinny. It seemed an age ago when she had strutted around Newcastle in fine new clothes with a figure like the women in Ava's magazines. Now she was skin and bone, the bloom having gone from her face and the sheen from her dark curls. For the first time in her life her hair was dry and brittle, and she thought nostalgically back to the days when she had been able to afford to go to Laurie's salon in Newcastle. But she had grown used to smaller portions of food in order to provide the boys with milk and eggs, going without so that they could stay healthy.

Dan squeezed her, seeming not to notice her

362

thinness. 'Course not,' he grinned, and kissed her. 'You're the only one for me. And to prove it, I'll take you dancing on Saturday night. A night out at the Egyptian, eh, like old times?'

Millie was reassured and ignored Ava's resentful comments that she should not be spending money on dancing. She aired one of her old dresses to rid it of the smell of mothballs, and put on some lipstick. Dan paid for Walter and Ella to join them, and they had one of the best nights out Millie could remember in years.

That summer, despite the hardship, the town seemed buoyed up by Newcastle's victory over Arsenal at Wembley. 'The first time the FA Cup's come back to Tyneside since 1924!' Dan kept telling Millie. 'Do you remember the grand time we had then?' It lifted Millie's spirits to see him so cheerful and to hear people talking happily about football rather than the lack of work. The back lanes were full of children playing the game until late in the evening, re-enacting the Wembley win. Wherever she went, there was a constant thud of balls against brick walls, shouts, and the occasional smash of glass followed by angry scoldings and the sound of children running away.

They celebrated Albert's first birthday with a party outside, stringing bunting across the yard and carrying out the kitchen table and chairs. Millie and Ella made potted meat sandwiches and a cake and invited in children from the surrounding terraces, while Albert sat in his high chair and banged his spoon in delight at the noisy tea party. Afterwards Dan organised games of

Blind Man's Buff and the Farmer's in his Den, and gave out twists of barley sugar.

It was a happy summer, despite the worries over money, and Millie felt optimistic for the future. Dan was talking of a possible transfer to Teesside and a Second Division team, and she day-dreamed about him returning to Tyneside. He would never play for Newcastle now, she thought privately, but he might get a job in training or management one day. So often she had seen him coaching boys in the back streets, inspiring them with his passion and skills, that she was sure he could have a role in the game for years to come. But she kept her thoughts to herself, knowing Dan still hankered after glory as a player.

For the first time in three years Millie felt real happiness again as she and Dan managed to escape the confines of the hotel for brief picnics or walks by the river, taking the boys with them. Albert was such a happy baby, with an engaging smile for everyone and an infectious chuckle. Dan doted on the boy, taking him everywhere with him and showing him off. Robert, who had been openly jealous and often lashed out at Albert, was beginning to find him more interesting. He would rock the pram too vigorously, but Albert would laugh out loud, thinking it a great game, and Robert would laugh back, feeling important. Gradually Millie noticed Robert's aggression towards the baby wane. If he bothered with Albert at all it was to be protective and shout loudly at people who came near that the baby was his.

The only thing that saddened Millie was Dan's refusal to visit Edith's grave with her. He complained that she went there too often, while she was hurt by his ability to cut himself off from the past. She still grieved for her daughter deeply and there was an emptiness in her heart that she knew would never be filled by anyone else.

'All I'm asking is for you to come with me, put a few flowers on,' Millie urged.

'No, I can't,' was Dan's stiff reply. 'It's not healthy for you either. It doesn't do to dwell, Millie. Maybe it's time you moved down to Yorkshire with the bairns, got away from Ashborough,' he said, fixing her with a hard look.

But Millie shook her head, swallowing her disappointment. 'You know I can't do that while Mam is so ill.'

Dan snorted. 'That woman'll outlive us all.' So Millie never mentioned going to Edith's grave again; indeed, they never talked of Edith at all. And Dan dropped the subject of moving. The summer ended all too quickly, and soon he was away again, returning only for snatched days or when he was playing in the north-east, and they slipped back into their separate lives as before. As the months sped by, Dan's visits grew less frequent and Millie had to contend with Ava's snide remarks about what must be keeping him away.

'Football, of course,' Millie protested. 'Dan's always put his job first, it's just something I accept.'

'I wouldn't,' Ava replied. 'A man as good-looking as Dan – I'd want to be near him all the time to make sure he wasn't up to something.'

'He isn't up to anything,' Millie said sharply, thumping the rolling pin on to the pastry and sending up a cloud of flour.

'How do you know?' Ava persisted. 'You've never even been to see where he lives. You've no idea what sort of life he leads. Not like me, with a husband who's under my feet all day long with nothing better to do than make stick-men for your boys. Mr Misery!' When Millie would not be provoked, Ava added, 'It's just that I've heard stories – from lads like Kenny Manners. But if you're not worried...'

Millie stubbornly refused to talk about Dan with Ava, but it did not stop the doubts from creeping into her mind. She remembered how partial Dan had been on Tyneside to a night out drinking and fending off attention from admiring women. She knew he probably drank too much for his own good, but it did not appear to be the problem it had been in Kilburn. He had never been suspended again or got into trouble with his club, so there was no need to worry. But what did he do when he was not playing? Millie was increasingly plagued by the thought. So the next time he returned to Ashborough, she suggested that she took a trip and came down to stay with him.

'But how will they manage without you here?' Dan asked.

'They'll just have to,' Millie answered. 'It'll only be for a few days. Ella said she'd take Albert, and Grant will help with Robert.'

She noticed his reluctance, but then maybe he was surprised at the suggestion after she had spent so long making excuses not to go.

'Maybe it's time I did think about joining you,' she continued. 'We could look for a house when I'm down.'

'But your Mam,' Dan reminded her, looking askance, 'you've always said you couldn't leave her.'

'And you said she'd outlive us all!' Millie reminded him. 'Why are you against the idea now when it was yours in the first place? Have you something to hide down in Yorkshire?'

'Of course not,' Dan said quickly. 'It would be grand to have you visit.'

'Good,' said Millie, satisfied. 'And if we move down, Mam could always come with us. It might do Ava and Grant good to have the responsibility of running the hotel for a while.'

Eventually, just before Easter, Millie got her way and travelled down on the train, leaving baby Albert with Ella and a reluctant Ava in charge of Robert and the hotel. It was the first time she had been parted from the boys and she missed them at once. Dan met her at the station, but Millie was dismayed at the sight of the poky room that was his home. Yet the landlady, Mrs Dawson, was friendly, and the atmosphere congenial in the cosy parlour that the lodgers shared. They sat around after tea, playing cards and drinking bottled beer like in a men's club.

Dan showed Millie around the industrial town and she went to see him play, taking her mind off fretting how Albert and Robert were doing without her. But it soon became clear that they could not afford the rents in the more well-to-do part of town and Millie would not contemplate bringing up the boys in the dismal rooms to which Dan's modest wage would stretch. They might just afford a couple of rooms in one of the more respectable streets, but nowhere that would provide space for her mother as well. Millie was reminded of the damp house under the viaduct in Kilburn and realised that she could not go back to such an existence again.

She enjoyed her few days and parted from Dan at the station with a pang of regret.

'I'll miss you,' he told her with a kiss, 'and I miss the bairns. But I'll be back soon for the summer.'

Millie journeyed home realising that she must be content with the arrangement they had. It was not ideal spending so much time apart, but she could see that Dan was happy enough and she had grown accustomed to getting on with her busy life in Ashborough and looking forward to their summers together. Others might think them strange, but at least they were not squabbling all the time like Ava and Grant, or like her own parents had. Even Ella and Walter had arguments, usually over lack of money. So at least when she and Dan were together they were happy, and that was proof to Millie that Dan was faithful to her. There was no reason for him not to be and she had found no evidence to the contrary. She returned to Ashborough resolving not to listen to any more of Ava's spiteful gossip, and once she was home she had no more time to dwell on it. Having rushed first to Ella's to be reunited with Albert, joy at seeing him again was overtaken by dismay at finding the hotel in chaos.

The tea room was closed. Grant was burning fried bread in the kitchen, muttering that Sarah had stomped out because Ava had treated her 'like muck'. There was a group of singers practising in the dining room complaining that it was too cold and no one had come to lay a fire. Ava was nowhere to be found and Teresa was banging her stick against the wall demanding that someone come and see to her.

'No one's fed me for two days!' Teresa wailed. 'Not properly. And no one's emptied the potty. That madam Ava's upset everyone. Don't ever leave me with her again, Millie, not ever!'

Millie calmed her mother down and helped her to the commode, nearly retching at the stench that came from it.

'I'll give you a bath, Mam,' Millie promised, seeing how distressed Teresa was at her unkempt state. 'And make you something to eat. Where is that Ava anyway? And where's Robert?'

'I don't know, she wouldn't tell me,' Teresa said querulously, 'but it'll be up to no good. She's got the bairn with her – been spoiling him rotten since you went, probably to get at you.'

Forcing herself to dump a clinging Albert into his pen, Millie got Grant to fill a tub of water in Teresa's bedroom, and changed the sheets on the bed while her mother was in the bath. After she had brought Teresa a boiled egg and toast on a tray, she stormed back into the kitchen and confronted a morose Grant, who was sitting in his vest, smoking and staring into the smouldering fire.

'Where's Ava?' Millie demanded, hands on hips. 'And where's my Robert?'

Grant did not answer, merely giving the ghost of a shrug. Millie advanced on him, prodding him on the arm. 'Don't ignore me! I asked you where your wife was. Or are you so sunk in self-pity that you haven't noticed she's not here?' He looked at her slowly. His silence maddened her. 'Does nobody care what happens round here? Look at the state me mam's been left in – I've seen animals tret better! And why's the tea room closed? We'll have them singers walking out and not coming back an' all if no one sees to them. What's ganin' on? You at least used to care about the bairn. Speak to me, you useless man!' Millie cried.

'She's gone out,' Grant said quietly.

'Where?' Millie demanded.

'Taken Robert to the films,' Grant answered. 'Wednesday matinée.'

Millie exploded. 'That's just typical! She's left this place looking like a pig sty, we've got customers to look after, and where is she? At the flicks spending the housekeeping! Am I the only one capable of running this place? Doesn't anyone else care whether we've got a roof over our heads?' She glared at him, not knowing why she was taking her anger out on Grant, just that he was there. The dull look in his eyes told her that he had given up caring. 'Look at you, sitting in your vest like a navvy! You're a disgrace. What sort of man are you to let yourself go like you have? Have you no pride? Your mam would have been ashamed to see you like this, all your learning and fine words gone to nothing!'

For a moment she saw him frown, but it was gone as quickly as it had come, leaving his face empty of emotion. In her fury and frustration, Millie drew back her hand, shouting, 'You can't even provide for your own wife – I have to do that!' and slapped him hard on the face.

Grant reeled slightly with shock and Millie gasped at what she had done. They stared at each other for a moment, then Millie stuttered, 'I – I didn't mean to...'

Grant stood up, his eyes haunted. She expected him to be offended, angry, but his subdued manner was much more frightening. 'I'm sorry, Millie, we've all let you down,' he said, his voice weary and full of regret. 'I'm no use to you. I'm no use to anyone.'

With that he walked to the door, unhooked his jacket and left the house without another word. Millie stood shaking, the smell of burnt food making her queasy and Albert's plaintive cries from the pen growing more insistent. She instantly regretted her brutal words to Grant, ashamed at the way she had taken out her anger at Ava on him. She wanted to run after him, but knew she could not leave the hotel unattended. She waited until the singing group had left, then, bundling Albert into his coat and pram, hurried out to look for him.

Millie searched the town, the park and the back lanes, her fear increasing as she did not find him. She went round to Ella's, but he had not gone there, and no one she asked had seen him. She doubted whether he had gone to the Institute reading room, as he had not been there in months. If he was to do something impulsive or foolish, Millie agonised, she would never, ever forgive herself for the cruel words she had flung at him.

On the point of giving up, she turned into the cemetery, not expecting to find him, but thinking she ought just to look. Skirting round the trees, she caught sight of a figure crouched against the far wall, capless and hunched into his jacket. With a jolt she realised it was Grant, and he was squatting next to Edith's grave, near the Nixon family plot. She hesitated, then continued to push Albert in his pram towards the solitary figure.

Millie spoke straight away. 'I know you want to be on your own, but I came to say sorry for the terrible things I said. And I was worried about you...' She glanced down, flushing.

Grant rose slowly to his feet and looked at her with fierce eyes. She had done the wrong thing, Millie realised in panic; he was even more angry that she had hunted him down, compounded his humiliation.

'You,' Grant said in a hoarse voice. 'You!'

Millie backed away. 'I'm sorry, I shouldn't have come.'

But he stepped forward, leaning across the pram, and held her. 'Don't go!' She saw him struggling to compose himself. 'It's been so hard for you,' he whispered. 'You've been through that much, ever since you were a lass. And there you are trying to make ends meet and keep everyone going and what do you get? Not a word of thanks from anyone, just Ava's tongue and Mrs Mercer complaining and me worse than useless.'

'Don't say that,' Millie protested, colouring with embarrassment. But he shook his head. Millie noticed how he was staring at Edith's gravestone, at the loving words and stark dates marking her short life, adorned with a protective angel.

'I think about your little lass sometimes,' Grant rasped, 'and remember how she sat on me knee. And I think how if I can miss her when I only ever saw her the once, what must it be like for you, Millie, as her mam?' Millie felt a sob catch in her throat at his words. His eyes were swimming with tears, but she could not look away. 'Yet you keep on going, carrying all that suffering inside and never complaining. It makes me feel humble, Millie, it makes me realise how worthless I am...'

Suddenly his voice broke and his hand dropped to his side. He bent his head and Millie heard him try to bury a sob deep in his throat. She stood, shocked, as he broke down weeping. Never in all her life would she ever have imagined seeing tough Grant Nixon weep. Swiftly she stepped around the pram and put a tentative arm round him. She felt him stiffen and try to control his sobbing, but she did not drop her arm.

'Not worthless,' she said gently, feeling tears trickle down her own cheeks. He was the only person apart from Ella who had ever spoken to her so frankly about Edith, and yet he was the last person she would have expected to do so. This unapproachable, disillusioned, unhappy

373

man, bruised by countless rejections, had touched her in a way no one else had. She and Dan could never talk about Edith; it was too painful a subject and there would always hang between them the memory of their bitter accusations of each other at the time of her death. But Grant felt no such difficulty. Beneath his exterior of blunt defensiveness lay a kind, tender nature she had not appreciated. It struck her suddenly how Edith must have sensed it, and in that moment she felt a strong bond of closeness forming to Dan's eldest brother.

'Thank you,' she smiled through her tears, 'thank you for saying that. You don't know how much you've comforted me.'

Grant looked at her in surprise, his eyes red. 'Me comfort you?' he whispered, puzzled.

'I know it's been hard for you, not finding work, having to be kept by others,' Millie said gently, 'but you mustn't let it break you. I saw what it did to me dad – he lost everything. I'd hate to see the same happen to you.' She squeezed his hand. 'You could help around the hotel more – it's work of a kind. Or you could protest more, like you used to – go on marches like other Communists. Anything but sit around getting melancholic.' Grant shot her a look and saw the teasing smile on her thin face. He nodded, with the ghost of a smile. 'Come back with me,' Millie encouraged. 'I need your help. We'll face Ava together, eh?'

'Oh, Ava,' Grant said with a deep sigh. 'I've been nowt but a disappointment to her.' He pulled away, taking deep breaths to calm himself.

'I doubt there's a man in the world can make

that one happy,' Millie sympathised. Grant gave her a strange look and then bowed his head in resignation and followed Millie out of the cemetery without another word.

Later, while Grant was raking out the neglected fire and Millie was making pease pudding, Ava and Robert returned. The boy threw himself enthusiastically at Millie and she hugged him back, surprised at how much she had missed him. He was so full of excitement about the cartoons he had just seen that she did not have the heart to scold Ava for spending money.

'He was Popeye! And he was big and strong. Popeye the sailor man!' Robert rushed around the table, knocking into Albert's high chair and nearly toppling it to the floor while Albert giggled.

'Careful!' Millie warned.

'No!' Robert defied her and rushed to Ava, pulling on her spotted dress. 'Auntie Ava, you're my best auntie. You be my mammy!'

Ava flicked Millie a look of triumph. 'Ah, isn't he sweet?' she said, giving him an indulgent pat on the head. 'It seems to me that no one gives him enough attention. That's what I've been trying to do these past few days. I thought you'd be grateful, Millie.'

Millie was stung by the remark. 'Some of us are too busy working,' she pointed out. But she said no more. She was not going to allow Ava to provoke a slanging match in front of the boys. From Grant's silence she knew he was in agreement. 'Come on, Robert, it's time for your tea. Tell me more about the film,' Millie said, trying to sound calm.

Ava looked suspiciously from Millie to Grant, noticing how her husband had given himself a shave and was wearing a clean shirt, having not cared about what he wore for months.

'How was Dan?' she persisted in a needling voice. She'd lit up a cigarette, knowing how this would annoy Grant, who did not approve of her smoking.

'Grand,' Millie answered evenly.

'So are you going to live down there after all?' she asked.

Millie held her look. 'No, we're not.'

Ava gave a smile of derision. 'No, I didn't think you would be. Some women would put up more of a fight for a man like Dan. But then if you're happy living this way, who am I to say...'

Millie felt her indignation rise, but before she could answer back, Grant rose to his feet, clutching the fire poker.

'Aye, Ava, who are you to say anything to Millie?' he growled. 'You've said quite enough already. So hold your tongue!'

Ava gaped at her husband. He had seldom defended Millie like that before, or rebuked his wife so roundly in front of someone else. She threw them both a hateful look, ground out her cigarette on the kitchen floor and marched to the door.

'I'm going out,' she announced, with a look that defied Grant to stop her. He watched her go, and Millie pretended not to see his look of humiliation. Robert ran after her, crying out to be taken, but she slammed the door before he got to her and left him howling on the other side.

Millie rushed to rescue him, but the boy struggled and kicked and bit her hand, screaming, 'Gerroff me! I hate you! I want Auntie Ava!'

Millie let go in surprise, gasping with shock at the unexpected attack. As she sucked her sore hand, she wondered in distress how much more heartache and disruption Moody's spiteful daughter was going to inflict on her family, and how much more of it she could take.

CHAPTER 23

That summer, Dan delayed his return, writing to say he had found employment in a bicycle factory. Millie was disappointed, but mollified by the wages he continued to send. He appeared briefly for Albert's second birthday, but it was a tense few days. Dan grew irritated by the amount of time his son spent sitting beside Grant looking through picture books, and argued with Millie that she was being too soft with him.

'He'll never learn to play footie if you don't let him out with the other bairns,' he chided. 'At his age I was scoring goals down the back lanes as often as older lads.'

'He's only two! Give the lad time,' Millie protested. 'And if you were around more often he might learn faster.' Dan took offence at this remark and shortly afterwards returned to Yorkshire. Millie resigned herself to the hard work of making the hotel pay and running the household. Her mother was making attempts to walk again, which Millie encouraged, even though it meant greater friction with Ava once Teresa was giving orders from her chair in the kitchen.

But Grant had become a quiet help and ally amidst all the warring. He now helped lay fires and stoked the boiler without being asked, and under Millie's guidance was learning to cook, despite Ava's ridiculing. He would go over to Walter's during summer evenings and help him work the narrow strip of ground in front of his house that passed for a garden, often taking Robert with him to dig his own small corner. Grant was endlessly patient with the boys, reading them stories and carving figures out of wood. Now that Dan was gone, only he seemed able to cope with the boisterous and demanding Robert. It saddened Millie that Teresa, his real mother, showed little interest in the boy at all, while Ava ignored or spoilt him on a whim.

Just before Christmas, Dan came home unexpectedly and in jovial mood once more. The boys enjoyed the sudden playful attention, but his attempts to get Albert out kicking a football ended in an attack of wheezing.

'Don't do that again!' Millie scolded in fright. 'The bairn's chest's not strong enough.'

Dan stormed out and did not come back until after the pubs had closed, reeking of beer and maudlin in his drunkenness, waking Millie to tell her he was sorry. They had a special dinner on Christmas Eve, the day he had to leave, which Grant helped Millie cook, taking Dan's teasing in good humour. Against Teresa's wishes, Dan fetched a jug of beer from the Farrier's Arms, and Walter and Ella joined them.

'Haven't you heard, Mrs Mercer? Prohibition's just ended!' Dan teased his mother-in-law.

Afterwards Millie brought out the long-neglected banjos, which she and Walter strummed, while Grant fetched his father's old set of border pipes. He gave a passable attempt at

379

a tune, working the bag and bellows in haphazard harmony and reducing the boys and Marjory to fits of giggles. All too quickly it was time for Dan's train, and the children clung on to him, begging him to stay. Albert burst into tears when he realised that they were not going on the train with his father, and Millie was left holding the screaming boy while Dan waved at them and blew her a kiss. She watched his handsome face recede into the distance and wondered when she would see him again.

Suddenly she felt weighed down by her responsibilities, by the people who depended on her, by the daily grind of the hotel. For a moment she was swamped by the desire to leave it all behind, wishing herself on that train with Dan, remembering how they had gone together to Tyneside all those years ago with hopes and expectations so high. She envied him his freedom and his appetite to still chase dreams. It struck her that Dan was just the same as he had been when she had first met him, still as full of hopes and desires, still as single-minded and pleasure-seeking. It was she who had changed, she realised. Sometime in the past nine years of their marriage she had grown up, or grown old, or maybe just grown to accept that life was more about survival than dreams. Either way, it dawned on her in painful realisation that she and Dan were growing away from each other as relentlessly as the disappearing train. Her eyes flooded with tears as she clutched the sobbing Albert, not knowing how she could bridge the chasm between them.

The following year, 1934, was a grim one. Dan's team only just survived relegation and he was unceremoniously transferred to a Third Division club in East Anglia. He came home for the summer, but spent much of his time back on Tyneside. He had contacted the Fairishes after many years of absence, and Bob, now the prosperous owner of two hairdresser's, had secured him a job at the Waterloo. Millie imagined him holding court behind the bar with tales of his travels, embellishing his footballing career and drinking more than he should of the profits to forget his humiliating demotion.

He would appear for snatched days, which he spent taking Albert and Robert to the park or along the river with a makeshift fishing net. Outwardly he was cheerful, but Millie noticed in unguarded moments that his face was drawn and his look sallow from too many hours in the bar. She sensed his fear of the future, his creeping sense of failure and having to admit that he would never now become a footballing legend like his boyhood heroes. She day-dreamed of him finding a job at Davidson's Emporium, or even back at the pit when work picked up again. No longer did she waste her hopes on an unattainable life beyond Ashborough like Dan did. She now realised that she would be quite happy for him to have an ordinary job like Walter, so long as they could all be together as a family, living in the security of the hotel. If only he would come home, she could help him adapt to a new life in Ashborough. But when she tried to suggest this, Dan was indignant. 'I know what you're thinking,' he accused her just before departing for the south. 'You think I'm past it. But I'm only thirty-four. Players can go on for years in their thirties. Look at Hampson playing for Newcastle until he was forty-four!'

They argued over his drinking and parted in discord, so that Millie was unable to tell him why she was so anxious. Teresa found her in the kitchen late one night.

'Why can't you sleep?' her mother asked.

'I've never been a deep sleeper,' Millie answered, mixing them both an Ovaltine, 'not since having the bairns.' She glanced at her mother.

'You worry too much,' Teresa answered, taking the cup she offered. 'You always have done.'

'Aye, well, there's something else to worry about now,' Millie said, sipping at the hot drink. 'I'm expecting again.'

Her mother shot her a look of surprise. 'Does Dan know?'

'Not yet,' Millie sighed. 'I wasn't sure when he went away.' Her voice trembled. 'I don't know if he'll be pleased or not.'

Teresa put a hand briefly over Millie's. 'He will. That lad of yours may be many things, but he's bairn-daft, that's for sure. Maybe it'll help mend things between the pair of you.'

Millie could no longer put on a brave face; she crumpled into tears at her mother's words. Teresa put down their cups and pulled Millie into her hold, as she had not done for years. 'How will we manage with another mouth to feed?' Millie sobbed. 'How can I keep this place going if I'm nursing another baby?'

Teresa hushed her. 'We'll manage. I know I've been nothing but a burden to you since Robert was born, but I'll try harder. I don't know what I'd've done without you, Millie, all these years.' They hugged tightly, comforted by their support of each other.

'We've helped each other, Mam,' Millie answered softly. 'That's what families are for.'

The following day she wrote to Dan about being pregnant, and was heartened by a tender letter in return. But the pregnancy was long and tiring. Sapped of energy to cope with the boys, Millie vowed this baby would be the last.

In early April of 1935, Millie went into labour in the middle of the night and Teresa sent Grant racing for Mrs Dickson. An hour later, Millie gave birth to another boy. Secretly she had wished for a daughter, but she cuddled the long-limbed baby in relief that he had come swiftly and safely. The next morning Teresa sent a telegram to Dan and he appeared just in time for the christening with flowers, a small teddy bear and bags of sweets for Albert and Robert.

The placid baby was named John Graham, but was soon known simply as Jack. Dan stayed around for the Silver Jubilee celebrations of King George and Queen Mary in May and helped string out bunting across the back lane and around the hotel entrance. There were flags all over Ashborough, and Dan took the older boys with him to march through the streets behind the colliery band and mingle with the large crowds. Afterwards there was a big tea laid on at the hotel and the women were rushed off their feet trying to meet the demand. Teresa stood propped at the kitchen sink with the aid of a stick and washed up endless tea plates, cups and saucers, while Millie, Ava, Ella and Sarah served teas and cleared tables.

At the end Millie collapsed into a chair, unable to move. Dan was all for going to the dance at the Egyptian Ballroom, but Millie was too exhausted.

'I'll go with you,' Ava volunteered at once. 'I can't remember the last time I went dancing. Grant's got two left feet.'

Millie was past protesting that Ava got out far more than she did. She would be glad of the peace, for Ava had been resentful all through her pregnancy, taking up keep-fit and showing off her trim body in front of Millie, chanting, 'Use your vigour to keep your figure!' Just now, Millie relished a quiet evening without Ava and her exercising more than going dancing with Dan.

Only afterwards, when Grant returned from clearing up at the Comrades club, where they had held races for the children, did Millie realise that no one had even thought to ask if he wanted to go dancing. Instead he read stories to the boys and Marjory, while Millie went away to feed Jack. She fell asleep on the large double bed in the nursery that had once been Moody's room and woke much later to find the children sleeping all around her. Too tired to contemplate dragging herself back to her own bed, she spent the rest of the night there, feeding Jack each time he woke.

Her mother was of the opinion that she should bottle-feed her baby and be done with the tying role of breast feeding. 'It's not seemly having you feeding him all over the hotel,' she had complained. But Millie enjoyed the closeness and the comforting suckling with her baby and would not give it up, no matter how tiring.

There was also another side to her desire to keep Jack with her. She had quite lost her appetite for sex. She feigned sleep when Dan rolled in after a drinking session with Kenny, or escaped down to the nursery to feed Jack and did not return. She felt overwhelmed with tiredness just thinking about having to make love. It surprised and dismayed her that she should feel this way, for she did not want to upset Dan. But after a couple of attempts at lovemaking, he gave up and left her alone. Millie wondered if this was what happened to all couples after eleven years of marriage, but she could not bring herself to ask either her mother or Ella. So she kept her feelings of guilt to herself.

Dan left soon after for Tyneside and another spell as barman at the Waterloo, only appearing at the beginning of August for the Bank Holiday to whisk them on a trip to the seaside. He came with the Fairishes and three other couples in a hired charabanc. They piled in with children and picnics, sending word round to Walter and Ella. Ava and Grant came too, and Dan even persuaded Teresa, carrying her like a child into a front seat and wrapping a rug around her knees.

The weather was glorious and the children

scampered about on the beach with buckets and spades bought by Bob and Dinah, while the adults hired deck chairs and sat in the sweltering sun with too many clothes on.

'Remember the times we used to go in the sea?' Dinah reminded Millie. 'Weren't we brave?'

Millie laughed. 'I'd never get into a bathing costume now – not since having Jack!' He was a plump baby, a demanding feeder, and she felt the need to fuel herself with stodgy food in order to keep up with his voracious appetite. Her trim waist had not returned after the birth and she felt dumpy and uncomfortable in the heat. Worse still, she had lost some bodily control, and to her great embarrassment a sudden sneeze was liable to make her wet herself. In contrast, the talkative Dinah had changed little in ten years. She was still attractive, fun-loving, childless and well dressed. Then Dinah said something that spoilt Millie's enjoyment.

'Did I ever tell you about that tramp who turned up looking for you after you'd left Newcastle?'

'For me?' Millie asked in surprise. 'No, you didn't. What tramp?'

Dinah waved a hand carelessly. 'I meant to write, but it wasn't really important. He was that common and scruffy – walked with a bit of a limp, I remember.'

Millie flushed, suddenly uneasy. 'What did he want?'

Dinah shrugged. 'Obviously just after your money – must have heard about you and Dan. Wouldn't tell me his name or anything about him. I told him to make himself scarce, but Mrs Hodges took him in for a cup of tea. Never saw him around again.'

Millie's heart began to pound. She wanted to ask more, but Dinah was already gossiping about something else and she was left feeling perplexed and ill at ease.

But what really upset her as the day progressed was the way Dinah looked and behaved with Dan. Millie observed her former friend's flirtatiousness. At the start she had her suspicions; by the end of the day she was certain.

That night after the charabanc had departed, leaving Dan behind, and they were alone in their bedroom, she challenged him. 'You're having an affair with Dinah Fairish, aren't you?'

She thought he was going to bluster, deny it, and suddenly Millie realised that that was what she wanted. But he faced her stubbornly and said, 'Aye, I am.'

Millie gave him a look of despair. She was hurt, but she felt more defeated than angry. To think that she had feared Dinah's rivalry for his affections all those years ago, when they had been neighbours, and now it had finally happened.

'How long?' she asked hoarsely.

'Just this summer,' Dan confessed.

'Just!' Millie spat the word back at him, not knowing if she believed him. He reached towards her, but she recoiled from his touch as if it would burn her.

'Millie, I'm sorry. It doesn't mean anything. I'd never leave you or the bairns,' Dan insisted. 'Dinah doesn't expect me to. It was just a daft thing that happened.'

She looked at him fiercely, swallowing the tears in her throat, wondering at his ability to wreck their marriage with those few words. 'How stupid can you be?' she accused him. 'You've spoilt everything for a selfish woman like Dinah Fairish! Of course she doesn't expect you to leave me – she wouldn't want that. Dinah would never give up Bob and all his money for you, would she, Dan? A third-rate footballer who drinks away what little money he makes!'

Dan was stung by her scorn, whipping across the room to seize her by the arm. He shook her hard. 'Don't ever call me that!' he blazed. 'Not ever again!'

She fought him off, pushing him away from her and escaping to the door. 'I'll sleep downstairs with the boys,' she hissed.

'Good, go on! That'll make a change!' he lashed out sarcastically. 'Who would blame me for looking for it elsewhere?'

Millie picked up her hairbrush and hurled it across the room at him, maddened at the accusation.

'Don't you go blaming your adultery on me!' she shouted. 'It's your own selfishness that's done it! To think I've just given you another son, and what do you do to show your thanks? Go off with the wife of an old friend! How do I know you haven't been carrying on with her for years?'

'Because I haven't!' Dan shouted back.

'Well, there've been tongues wagging round here about you for long enough,' Millie accused. 'Have there been others, Dan, like Ava says?'

'Ava! You shouldn't listen to her gossip, woman! She's been trying to come between us ever since we were first courting.'

Millie wanted to believe him, but she no longer trusted what he said. She had dismissed Ava's insinuations about other women for so long, not wanting to believe them, that now she was confronted with evidence of her husband's unfaithfulness she felt physically ill. She tried to control her shaking voice. 'You can go tomorrow. I don't want you back until you finish with that woman, do you hear?'

Millie walked out and slammed the door. She was aware that the whole household had probably heard their row, but she was past caring. She hurried to the nursery and climbed into bed beside the sleeping boys, their cheeks still hot from the sunshine, the sheets gritty with speckles of sand. She lay numbly, feeling a strange mixture of fury and regret. Later she shed tears as quietly as she could, unable to imagine the future without him, yet determined that she would not accept him if he carried on his affair.

Just before dawn she heard him descend the stairs and let himself out of the house. She got up, still dressed in yesterday's clothes, and hurried down to the kitchen. She caught a glimpse of Dan disappearing across the yard and out into the lane, and thought she heard him whistling a Cole Porter tune that he had been humming all summer.

Millie felt sick and empty. She sank into a chair and cried, thinking how she might never see her husband again. Perhaps this was the excuse he was looking for to leave her, she thought miserably. Had she brought the whole situation on herself? She was startled by a door opening behind her, appalled to think of being found in this state. Grant walked in and closed the door quietly behind him. They looked at each other in silence and Millie saw that he'd guessed, too.

'He's gone then?' Grant asked gently. Millie nodded, wiping her face with a handkerchief.

'I'm frightened,' she whispered. 'I told him to go – but I'm frightened he's never coming back...!'

Grant crossed the room and laid a hand on her shoulder. 'He'll come back, Millie, if that's what *you* want,' he said kindly. 'He's got that much to come back for.'

Millie glanced at him in surprise, feeling his hand heavy and comforting. She covered it fleetingly with her own. 'Thank you,' she murmured, filled with sudden strength from his touch and presence. Then she stood up and Grant withdrew his hand. Together, without another word, they got on with stoking the fire and making the breakfast.

The following months seemed interminable to Millie. She did not hear from Dan and found it hard to answer Albert's constant questioning about when he would next see his father. She went through periods of anger, then remorse, her guilt at separating Dan from his sons increasing as the winter wore on. Albert would take down his father's team photograph from his Yorkshire

390

days and point him out, speaking to the picture as if Dan could hear him. He was developing a stammer, and it twisted Millie's heart to hear the unhappy boy, but her mother told her not to weaken.

'It's Dan's fault he's not seeing the bairns,' Teresa insisted. 'He knows where they are and what he has to do.'

By now the rumours about their estrangement and Dan's affair were common knowledge around the town. Millie was certain Ava had been the one to spread the story so rapidly, although she denied it. Millie determined to hold her head up when she went out, and kept herself busy around the hotel and with the children. Business had picked up since the Jubilee party and the tea room was once again a popular meeting place. They installed a soda fountain and the children of the more prosperous business owners were encouraged to hold birthday tea parties in the dining room, newly decorated by Grant.

On Jack's birthday Millie hoped in vain that Dan might appear. Albert grew impatient for his fifth birthday, convinced that his father would turn up for that.

'He always comes for my b-birthday, doesn't he, Mam?' he asked.

'Don't expect it this year,' Millie warned. Even Dan's erratic payments had stopped after Christmas, and Millie had no idea where he was.

But Albert's faith in his father was unshakeable. Over the winter, with long hours studying Dan's team photograph, he developed an interest in football, and would escape into the back lane following Robert whenever the door was left open. Millie would run after him, calling him back, to no avail.

'Cars go down that lane now,' she fretted.

'Hardly ever,' Grant pointed out, fetching the boy back.

'He's not strong enough to play with the other lads,' Millie objected. 'They're too rough with him.'

'He's a strong little lad now, Millie, as big as Robert,' Grant smiled. 'Haven't you noticed?'

Millie realised that it was true; her baby Albert had grown into a robust small boy who was now ready for school. She could no longer mollycoddle him as Ava accused, for he would have to hold his own in the school yard this term. Eventually Grant persuaded her to allow him to take Albert out in the back lane as long as he stayed and kept an eye on the boy. Sometimes Grant would take him and Robert along to the Comrades to watch a match or kick about in the corner of the ground while he helped coach one of the youth teams.

On the day of Albert's birthday, after the boys had returned from school, Millie laid on a special tea and invited in the neighbouring children for games. The family had clubbed together to buy him a second-hand Meccano set, a pack of Happy Families and some comics. Grant had spent hours making him a bagatelle board. But despite Albert's obvious delight at his presents and the fuss they were making of him, Millie could tell the boy was fretting for his father. He kept glancing towards the open door as the children tucked into jam sandwiches, cake and jelly. She felt a wave of guilt, mixed with anger at Dan, that turned into annoyance towards the boy for not appreciating what she had done for him.

'Stop looking for him, he's not coming!' she said, prodding Albert to eat his tea. 'Just be grateful for all the things you've been given. And we're going to have party games just like you wanted.'

He gave her a look as if to say it would not be the same without his dad. She was exasperated at him, amazed that he kept such a clear memory of Dan, having not seen him for nearly a year. What had Dan done to deserve such admiration when she was the one who did everything for their son? Millie thought, aggrieved. Grant saw her tenseness and suggested they get on with the games.

Just as the children scattered from the table to play in the yard, she heard a familiar whistle that made her heart miss a beat. In seconds Albert was off his chair and racing for the door, jumping from the top step into the open arms of his father.

'Dad!' he shrieked.

'Ha, ha! Bonny lad!' Dan laughed, swinging him around in a hug. 'Am I in time for the party?'

'Y-yes!' Albert cried, and buried his face in his father's neck, ecstatic.

The other children swarmed around while the adults stood and stared, feeling awkward. Dan glanced over the boy's shoulder and caught Millie's tense look. She saw tears in his tired eyes.

'I told M-mam you'd not m-miss me birthday!'

Albert said in triumph, craning to look at his mother. Millie's heart twisted at the sheer joy lighting his fair face. 'Didn't I say so?'

Millie gulped, 'Aye, you did,' unable to bring herself to say anything more coherent.

Robert pulled at Dan's leg in excitement. 'Are you stopping for long this time?'

Dan grinned at the boy and ruffled his hair, bending to haul him into his arms too. 'Depends if your mam'll have me,' he answered.

The boys chorused together, 'She will! Won't you, Mam?'

Millie and Dan stared at each other. She thought how jaded he looked despite his attempts to be jovial, his face drawn and grey, his eyes deeply shadowed. He had aged years in the months of his disappearance and she wondered what could have happened to him.

Dan looked at her pleadingly. 'I want to come home, Millie,' he said, his voice cracking, seemingly oblivious of the others in the room. His appeal was only to her. 'I've finished with football and all that life,' he said in a sad, broken voice. 'Will you have me back? Please, Millie?'

Teresa made an impatient noise, but Millie stopped her before she could rebuke her son-in-law.

'This is your home, Dan,' she said, her voice unsteady. 'Of course you can come back.'

She stepped forward, seeing his face break into a smile of relief, the old dimpled smile that had set her heart racing so often in the past. He lowered the boys to the floor and put out his arms to Millie in recognition. They hugged tightly, thankful that the barren time apart was ended, not caring in that moment what anyone else thought of them, only that they were together again.

CHAPTER 24
1936

It was not easy having Dan around the hotel permanently, chiefly because of Teresa's resentment towards him and Ava's flirtatious manner. At first he just slept a lot, content to potter about the house entertaining the boys when he was awake rather than seek the company of his old drinking mates. Millie was pleased that he was making an attempt to stop drinking, for she saw that as a major cause of past friction between them and of his health breaking down. She tried to get him to eat more, but he preferred to smoke cigarettes from the moment he woke up to last thing at night. Bit by bit she pieced together what had happened to her husband after she had sent him away the previous August.

Dan had returned to Tyneside, but Bob Fairish had also grown suspicious and Dinah had sent him packing at once to protect her own marriage. Back in East Anglia, he admitted to going off the rails, drinking too much, fighting round the pubs and being undisciplined on the pitch. By Christmas he had been suspended and dropped from the team twice; by early in the New Year he had been sacked and no other team would take him.

'Why didn't you come home then?' Millie asked, feeling both ashamed of him and pitying.

'All I knew was that you'd disappeared. Didn't you know how worried I'd be?'

Dan looked at her guiltily. 'I was too ashamed to show me face,' he whispered. 'I'd thrown away everything we ever hoped for and I thought I'd thrown away the chance of getting back with you and the boys.' His eyes glinted with emotion. 'After the way you stood up to me – over Dinah – I thought you'd never want to see me again. I've tret you that badly, Millie, I can never forgive myself...'

Millie put her hands up to his gaunt cheeks protectively. 'Maybes not,' she said gently, 'but I can.' She kissed him tenderly, wanting to dissolve all the hurt between them and the cruel words of the past.

Gradually Millie saw Dan reviving, his health and confidence returning, nurtured by her care and the love he received from the boys. Just before Christmas, he was taken on as a part-time delivery man at Davidson's, where the manager was an avid Newcastle supporter who was happy to listen to Dan's colourful stories of the game. Grant soon persuaded him to help coach the Comrades, and by the spring he was playing again on a regular basis for the amateur club.

His old optimism returned. 'We're doing our bit for the government's campaign for fitness!' he joked as he taught Albert how to dribble the ball past an opponent. 'That's the way, tap it left. By, you're coming on grand!'

Albert revelled in his father's praise and in the popularity he acquired at school by having Dan Nixon as his father. Millie tried not to intervene when he fought with Robert for Dan's attention or when the older boy pushed him around jealously. She had to restrain herself from taking Robert aside and telling him he was not Dan's child and that Albert should not be denied his father's attention. But she knew she must not, and it grieved her to see that Robert was a natural ball player whereas Albert improved only through sheer hard work and gutsy determination to please his father.

At least, she consoled herself, all the boys were receiving plenty of attention. Dan and Grant would take them down to Burt Park to see the Comrades play or to kick a ball around the newly laid playing field in the municipal park. Ava treated them to the cinema every week, while Millie and Dan took them swimming in the new public baths opened on Fern Street. By the summer, two-year-old Jack, a quiet but determined boy, was attempting to join in too. Once on his feet he lost his baby plumpness and was soon racing about after the others.

In May there was excitement over the coronation of the new King George, after the shock of King Edward's abdication over an American divorcee. Ava had become an expert on the matter, reading anything she could get hold of in newspapers and magazines about the royal love affair, revelling in the scandal and the illicit romance.

'I think it's lovely he gave up all his privileges and the Empire for Mrs Simpson,' she declared, in tears when she heard the abdication speech on the wireless. 'Fancy doing that! All for the woman he loves...'

Millie noticed wryly how Ava became just as fixated with the lives of the new king and queen and their young daughters, Elizabeth and Margaret Rose. As soon as the newsreels of the grand coronation were shown in Ashborough, Ava was queuing to view them, dragging Robert along with promises of lots of soldiers on parade. Robert came back disappointed, but Ava eulogised about the royal pageant of carriages, ermine cloaks and diamond crowns. A month later she was poring over reports of the Windsor's quiet marriage in France and reading out descriptions of what they wore.

'They're in Austria on honeymoon,' she announced to anyone who would listen. Albert obliged.

'W-what's a honeymoon?' he asked, intrigued by the word.

'It's a holiday you go on after you get wed,' Ava explained. 'It's very romantic.'

'Where did you go, Auntie Ava?' Albert asked.

Ava's lips pursed crossly. 'We didn't have a honeymoon,' she answered tersely, flinging a resentful look at Grant, who was shelling peas newly picked from Walter's garden. 'Uncle Grant couldn't afford to take me anywhere – never has done.'

'B-but you went to America,' Albert pointed out. 'Mam says that's very far away – thousands and thousands and thousands of miles away.'

'That was no honeymoon,' Ava replied sniffily.

Millie saw Grant flush. She knew he was as irritated with Ava's obsession over royalty as she

399

was with his lack of interest in it. But he did not retaliate.

'Where did you go, Mam?' Albert persisted. 'D-did you go in a honeymoon?'

Millie laughed. 'No, we stayed here too.'

'So do only royal people have them?' Albert puzzled.

'Or rich,' Grant grunted.

'Oh.' Albert frowned in concentration. 'I d-don't think I'll bother getting wed,' he decided, 'not if you don't get a holiday.'

Millie and Grant laughed, but Ava made an impatient noise and stalked out with her pile of magazines. Sometimes Ava's retreat into her magazine world concerned Millie, for she would fill the children's heads full of gossip and yearnings for things they could not have, bringing them home comics and annuals too. Any new title that came into the shops she snapped up, spending half the housekeeping on a new weekly called *Woman* or the more expensive *Picture Post*.

But by then there were other events to worry over. Teresa's wireless and travellers to the hotel had brought news of the scare of war abroad. The Germans had marched into Austria and claimed it as their own; their own Prime Minister, Chamberlain, had returned from Munich that summer claiming to have secured peace with the Führer. While Ava pored over photographs of British life caught candidly by *Picture Post*, Grant grumbled with concern over politics abroad and the advance of the fascists on the Continent.

The boys found it exciting that they had to practise gas-mask drill at school, and they careered around the house pretending to be aeroplanes. By the spring the government was making preparations for war, drawing up an evacuation programme for women and children and the distribution of air-raid shelters. Millie discussed with Ella the possibility of evacuees coming to the town.

'We'd certainly have room for city bairns,' Millie declared. 'How we'd feed them all is another matter.'

'I hate all this talk of war,' Ella said fearfully. 'I'm glad we're out of London, they keep talking about bombs being dropped...'

'Things won't change that much round here,' Walter assured her. 'They've told us to carry on working as usual.'

But Grant was less sanguine as he scoured the newspapers daily. 'Look! They're introducing conscription for lads of twenty. It's pandering to the generals and warmongers like Churchill. It's the thin end of the wedge.'

Ava did not hide her irritation at her husband's preoccupation with the threat of war. 'Why don't you stop talking about it?' she snapped. 'You're frightening everyone with your doom and gloom.'

'It's more important than your silly films,' Grant retaliated. 'This is reality, Ava. We could be at war again with Germany after only twenty years. It seems like yesterday to some of us!'

'Well, I'm going to enjoy life while I can,' Ava huffed, and took herself off to see the handsome Laurence Olivier in *Wuthering Heights*.

Dan kept out of these arguments about the

401

war, preferring to take the boys off to play football after he had finished his deliveries. He did not boast about having served in the army during the Great War as Millie would have expected, and would not talk about it to Albert and Robert when they demanded heroic stories.

'Your Uncle Grant was the hero,' he would answer. 'You go and ask him what it was like.'

Millie found such conversations uncomfortable as they reminded her of her dead brother and the family's humiliation over his execution. She grew alarmed when Dan talked of joining up himself. The hot summer was advancing and the rumours and scares of imminent war were mounting.

'You're not serious, are you?' Millie asked. 'It's the younger men they'll be wanting.'

Dan gave her a reproachful look. 'I'm not forty yet. I'm as fit as any man ten years younger.'

'Aye, I know you are,' Millie agreed quickly, conscious of how sensitive he was about his age or athleticism. He had tried hard to curb his drinking over the past three years and only occasionally had he lapsed and gone 'on a bender', as Teresa accused. When this happened, Millie would be summoned by a neighbour or publican to go and retrieve him, and she and Grant would hurry to bring him home while Dan sang drunkenly or cursed them for interfering.

One time after they had frog-marched him to bed, trying to keep him quiet passing Teresa's room, Dan collapsed on the bed quite maudlin.

'I'm sorry, Millie, I'm sorry!' he slurred. 'I've been a disappointment to you.'

Millie sighed and pulled off his well-cobbled

402

shoes, remembering when he had bought them in Newcastle over a decade before. 'Quiet,' she hushed him. 'I knew who I was marrying.' She thought back and wondered if that was true. She had been so much in love with Dan in those early years, quite besotted, that she had been blind to any shortcomings. She had chosen to ignore his fecklessness with money, his fondness for drink, and had believed that once married to her, Dan would be faithful.

'No you didn't,' he protested, trying to sit up. He focused on her blearily from under his ruffled receding fair hair. He looked old, Millie thought in shock. This was how he would look in ten years' time. Yet he was still handsome, still recognisably the man she had determined to have all those years ago. And without him she would not have had her precious children, she reminded herself. No matter what they had been through, she would still have done it all over again for them. No other man had ever attracted her like Dan or had such a hold on her heart. Besides, these recent years had been ones of contentment, even happiness with Dan at home. They had been a family again for the first time since their early married days, and she had watched the boys thrive under their father's attention.

Albert, in particular, had blossomed, and was now a lively, affectionate eight-year-old with an enthusiasm for life that reminded her of how Dan had once been. Since his father had come home, the boy's stammer had almost disappeared. Jack was more of a loner; quiet, determined and independent even at four and a half, insisting on doing everything for himself, from tying his boot laces to carrying his own garden implements as he followed Grant around. Only nine-year-old Robert was more of a handful than ever, easily distracted from school work and bored with inaction. He had boundless, destructive energy that only Dan seemed able to cope with, channelling it into running or football.

Above all Dan had given them the security and respectability of the Nixon name, which had helped her to be accepted into Ashborough society in a way that she never would have been as Millie Mercer, outcast from Craston and daughter of Joseph Moody's mistress. And Dan had given her love, and a bit of glamour, and experience of the world beyond a pit town.

'Go to sleep,' she told him as she undressed for bed.

But Dan was agitated. 'I'm not who you think I am, Millie,' he continued, shaking his head, looking doleful. 'It's been on me mind that much recently...'

Millie gave him a wary look, not wanting to hear any more revelations about past affairs. 'I don't want any confessions,' she told him brusquely. 'What's in the past can stay there.'

But he carried on as if he had not heard, his glazed blue eyes haunted. 'I was no war hero,' he mumbled. 'I never got to the Front.'

Millie stared at him. 'But I thought you were wounded out of action?' she answered. 'You always said...'

'I know what I said.' He gave a mirthless laugh.

'But I never got beyond the field hospital – went down with chicken pox, got it bad. I was sent straight back to England and kept in isolation. Never fired a shot. Then the war was over and I hung around London, couldn't face going home and telling them what a useless soldier I'd been – not with two older brothers such heroes!'

Millie wanted to laugh at the sorry tale in her relief that it was nothing worse, but she saw how humiliated he felt and quickly reassured him.

'You can't blame yourself for catching chicken pox,' she said, putting her arms about him. 'You went prepared to fight, and that's what counts.'

But Dan would not be consoled. 'No it's not,' he moaned, brushing her off. 'Even your brother did better than that. He fought out there for two years before he cracked up, didn't he? He probably had that shellshock – they know about these things now. Should never have shot him at all, poor bastard. But me,' he said harshly, 'I did nothing, just pretended I did. Me and me big mouth – always boasting about things. And I felt that guilty at the way I never stood up for you when it all came out about your brother being shot. I of all people should have spoken up for you, Millie!'

Millie saw the self-disgust in his face and tried to comfort him. 'That was all years ago. I was hurt at the time, but you made it up to me by coming to London to find me. Besides, no one can blame a young man for doing a bit of boasting. It doesn't matter to me.'

Dan gave her a strange look. Was it anger or guilt or relief? Millie wondered.

'Why do you keep forgiving me, Millie?' he demanded.

'Because I love you,' she answered simply.

Dan groaned and buried his face in her hair. 'Do you really mean that?' he asked hoarsely. 'Can you forgive me for the way I've let you down?'

'Aye,' Millie said quietly, 'I think I could forgive you anything.'

She felt Dan clutch her tighter as if he would never let her go. 'Oh, Millie man, I don't deserve you!' he cried.

She soothed him with soft words and caresses, holding on to him until he fell asleep in her arms. Yet Millie remained awake a long time afterwards, pondering his words and wondering for how long his guilt had been gnawing away inside him. No wonder he was full of talk of joining up for this war, she thought anxiously. Although she considered it of no importance that he had never fought in the Great War, it troubled her that Dan had kept his past a secret. She lay fretting about war and what it would do to their lives, filled with foreboding for the future.

CHAPTER 25
1939

Dan never referred to his late-night confession again and Millie wondered if he remembered having told her. His spirits picked up quickly when he was given a new contract with the Comrades for the coming season and play started towards the end of August. Millie was cheered to see him recover much of his old optimism and joy for life, and he spent all of his spare time training and coaching the younger men, his talk of enlisting forgotten.

There was a bravado about the town that late summer. The pit was working full-time once more and there was an air of prosperity about the shops that Millie had not experienced for years. Yet they were all issued with ration books and preparations had been made to take evacuated children. Millie had volunteered three of their rooms, despite Ava's protests that they had enough 'brats' under the roof.

Grant, who had become withdrawn during the summer, came home one late-August day, beaming. 'They've set me back on! It's only part-time, but I'm working down the pit again.' Millie went and gave him a hug of congratulation, seeing from the joy on his face how important this was to him. He was winning back some self-esteem at last. Everyone expected Ava to be pleased that he was at last working again, but she seemed more put out by his lowly position in the joinery shop than when he was out of work.

'It's hardly much to get excited about,' she said dismissively, 'a part-time job making pit props!'

'So what are you going to do for the war effort?' Millie demanded, seeing how dashed Grant was by her scorn.

'It might never come to that,' Ava pouted.

'You can't live in that dream world of yours forever,' Grant said quietly, his shoulders hunching in that familiar defensive gesture. Millie watched him retreat outside with Jack to dig in the yard, which he had turned into a vegetable garden in preparation for the extra mouths they might have to feed come an evacuation. At least Jack provided him with uncritical companionship, Millie consoled herself, and bit back her anger at Ava.

The first Saturday in September, Dan's team won three-nil at home, with Dan scoring the winning goal. The teams came back to the hotel for tea like in days gone by, an arrangement Millie had suggested and one that her boys were thrilled about. They milled around the players, listening to their banter and eager to be noticed, forgetting their mother's instructions that they were supposed to be handing round sandwiches.

That night, Teresa told Millie and Dan to go out for the evening while she looked after the boys. They chose to go dancing at the Egyptian Ballroom like old times. Grant was persuaded to accompany Ava; Walter and Ella came too. For a short while Millie imagined that the threat of war was exaggerated and that their lives might continue as they were, unaffected by the world beyond. But there was an expectation about the place, hushed conversations, a sense of desperation in people's determination to enjoy themselves. And there were men in uniform, young recruits about to leave for the south and strangers whom Millie did not recognise.

'They'll be from the camp over Drake's farm,' Ava speculated. 'Go and find out, Grant.' But her husband refused, and it was Dan who engaged one soldier in conversation and brought him over to their table. The tall, sandy-haired quartermaster was called Bain and came from the Borders.

'You'll have to patronise our hotel,' Dan told him, with a wink at Millie. 'Best baking in Ashborough. And Grant here plays the border pipes. You tell your mates.'

But the next day, as Millie was standing over the stove cooking the Sunday dinner, feeling hot and listless after the late night, the announcement they had all been dreading came over the wireless. Prime Minister Chamberlain had declared that the country was now at war with Germany. That evening they gathered around the wireless to hear King George broadcast to the nation. Millie felt a great weight bearing down on her spirits at the gravity of his sombre words: '*We can only do the right as we see the right, and reverently commit our cause to God.*' To her dismay, Dan went out and got drunk.

The following week their lives were thrown into upheaval with the arrival at Ashborough station

409

of dozens of evacuated schoolchildren from Tyneside. Millie opened up the hotel dining room as one of the reception centres, and they were busy all day long providing drinks and cups of tea to the chattering, wide-eyed children and a handful of mothers. Billeted on them were Nancy Baker, a shipyard worker's wife, her two boys and six-month-old baby, as well as two girls, Patience and Charity Armstrong, whose father was in the navy and whose mother was ill with pleurisy and unable to travel.

'Auntie Rachael wouldn't have us,' the solemn Patience announced. 'She thinks a bomb's going to drop through her ceiling if she has us in her house.'

Jack looked up suspiciously at the kitchen ceiling after this pronouncement. 'Will the Jerry know where to find you?' he asked, quite troubled by the thought.

'Aye,' Robert teased, yanking Charity's long, dark pigtails viciously, 'the Luftwaffe'll have their sights trained on this pair! Ack, ack, ack!'

Patience burst into tears, but small Charity swung round and slapped Robert on the mouth, causing his lip to bleed. Ava yelped at the girl and smacked her back for her insolence, but Millie quickly intervened.

'Stop it all of you,' she ordered. 'There's to be no fighting in this house. Robert, you deserved that for picking on the lass. You'll go and sweep out the dining room as punishment.'

He scowled back, but grabbed the brush and stormed out, leaving the newcomers gawping. Nancy Baker smiled at Millie and rolled up her sleeves. 'Here, let me help you with that washing-up,' she said, adding, 'Looks like you're well in charge here.'

At that Ava stalked out of the room, flinging a look of disdain at them all. 'This is *my* home, remember. It belonged to my father. Millie will never be anything more than a glorified house-keeper!'

Millie ignored her, no longer bothered by Ava's insults. She dried her hands. 'Patience, you come and help me roll out this pastry,' she told the sniffing girl, putting an arm about her thin shoulders. The girl obliged, and Millie looked around to involve Charity, but the younger girl had already escaped outside to play catch with the boys. At six years old, Charity had something of Edith's spirit, Millie thought with a pang, though she looked nothing like her. By now Edith would have been twelve and a half and on the verge of leaving childhood behind. Millie had no idea what her daughter would have looked like, but it never stopped her trying to imagine – not for one single day. She forced herself to turn back to the fearful Patience and gave her a smile of encouragement.

'You'll soon settle in,' she told the girl, 'and when your mam's better, she can come and stop here too.'

For the first time, she saw Patience's anxious face light up with a sweet smile.

In all the flurry of activity surrounding the new arrivals, the sorting out of ration books, attend-ing to crying children in the night and worrying

411

over Teresa, who had taken to bed with a heavy cold that she blamed on the evacuees, Millie did not at first notice Dan's morose behaviour. But it soon became obvious that something was wrong. The football had come to an abrupt end, the season being abandoned with the outbreak of war and contracts cancelled. Apart from early-morning deliveries for Davidson's, Dan drifted around the hotel like a lost soul, or sat around and smoked with no interest in doing anything.

Millie grew quickly impatient. 'You could at least make yourself useful around the place – there's that much to do.'

'Not for me there isn't!' Dan snapped back.

'What is the matter with you?' Millie cried. 'Is this all because the League's disbanded?' She sighed. 'There'll be charity matches – raising money for the war effort. It's not the end of the world.'

'It's the end of me career, woman!' he shouted.

Millie gawped at him. 'But that's been over for the past three years or more! You haven't played...' He gave her such a bleak look that she stopped. Suddenly realisation dawned. Dan had never thought of his footballing days as over. All this time, while Millie had thought her husband had come to terms with a routine family life at the hotel, he had secretly being pursuing his dreams hankering after a return to professional football.

'The Comrades were just till I got me total fitness back,' Dan said defensively, 'but they were better than nothing.' He spread his hands in a hopeless gesture. 'Now it's all finished. No one knows how long the war'll last, but chances are I'll be too old to play professional again when it's over.' His expression was desolate. 'It was me life, Millie,' he admitted. 'I need the other lads, the crowds, that surge inside that makes you want to run till your lungs burst. Banging that ball in the back of the net – there's nothing sweeter!' He looked panic-stricken. 'What do I do now, Millie?'

She stared at him, disappointment welling up inside her. 'You grow up, Dan,' she told him sharply, 'like the rest of us. Do something useful to see us through this war.'

Her anger with him soon subsided, but Dan stayed out of the way, drinking where he could, until Millie regretted her harsh words and felt guilty for his unhappiness. Teresa, who had been frightened by her bronchial attack into thinking she was dying, recovered and galvanised herself out of bed. She seemed to have found a new zest for living while everything around turned precarious and uncertain. She took to exhorting Nancy Baker and the children to tidy their rooms, encouraging Ava and Millie to run a canteen for passing forces personnel, and ordering her grandsons to collect scrap for the war effort. But she appeared to get most enjoyment from goading Dan into doing something worthwhile.

'There'll be no more money for drinking,' she lectured him, 'so don't go thinking you can get round Millie when me back's turned. Stop feeling sorry for yourself and make yourself useful. You boasted all summer about joining up, but now that we're at war I don't hear any brave words!'

Millie tried to defend him, but this just angered Dan the more. 'I don't need you to fight me corner!' he shouted, and banged out of the house. He stayed out that night, Millie did not know where, but when he returned it was to announce that he had been to the recruiting office in the town hall.

'An orderly with the medical corps,' he told them, flinging Teresa a look of satisfaction. 'I could be in France by next month.'

Albert and Robert threw themselves at him in their excitement. 'Will you see the fighting, Dad?' Albert asked, his look adoring.

'Very likely,' he answered, swinging the boy over his shoulder, 'I'll be shovelling up bits of the enemy!'

The boys whooped in glee, but Millie covered her face with her hands in horror. This was all her fault, she realised, and her mother's for ridiculing Dan's feelings of worthlessness. Now he was going away, leaving his sons fatherless and her bereft, not to play for some distant club but into the dangers of war.

A week later they saw him off at the station. Millie watched him buoyed up by the attention, enjoying being seen once more as a hero around the town, the famous footballer turning his efforts to serving his country. She kept secret her knowledge that he was proving his bravery to himself as much as to everyone else. Even Teresa came out to wish him well, surprised and pleased with her son-in-law for once. Millie, used to partings, steeled herself for his final embrace and the tears on the faces of her sons. But no matter how many times it had happened, she was filled with a sick emptiness at his going.

The following month she got word that Dan was working in a military hospital outside London. Then, just as they were growing used to blackouts, daily huddles around the wireless for news and growing rationing, he came home for Christmas, saying he was being posted abroad.

'It'll likely be the Middle East,' he told them as their extended household gathered in the dining room for a special dinner of pork, which Millie had managed to purchase, and large helpings of Grant's vegetables. Nancy Baker had grown homesick for Tyneside and returned with her children to be with her husband for the holidays, but Patience and Charity remained while their mother recuperated with Auntie Rachael and seemed in no hurry to join them. Millie could not imagine Dan being so far away from them and tried to hide her anxiety from him and the boys.

'I'll bring you back a camel,' he teased Albert before he left.

'Never mind about camels,' Millie said tearfully, 'just you come back safe.' This time she could not stop herself weeping at their station parting. With him going so far away, it somehow seemed terribly final. She was filled with an unnamed dread that clawed at her insides. Dan saw her distress and tried to comfort her.

'Take care of yourself and the lads,' he said, kissing her tenderly. 'We'll all be together again soon.'

Millie tried to smile. 'Aye, of course.' But as she watched the train pull away and Dan's waving arm disappear from view, she was filled with foreboding that she would never see him again. She clutched Jack tightly to her and tried to comfort a howling Albert with words of reassurance that she did not believe.

It was several weeks before she received any news of Dan's whereabouts and months before any letters came through, describing life in a hospital in Egypt. *'We've got a couple of men on the ward waiting to be hanged, but they've got dysentery and we've got to get them better first,'* he told her with grim humour in one of his short, un-sentimental letters. *'Playing a bit of football, tell the bairns. There's nothing like the Egyptian Ballroom out here,'* he joked, *'or if there is I've not found it. Send me a picture of you and the lads. My love to you always, Dan.'*

Millie treasured his brief notes and tried to imagine what his life must be like. But she had little time to dwell on how much she missed him, for the news at home grew more alarming, with the German invasion pushing relentlessly into France, cutting off the British Expeditionary Force from the ports. In May, just as the shock reports were coming through of the British retreat and evacuation at Dunkirk, news arrived of the death of Patience and Charity's mother. A short note, edged in black, came from Aunt Rachael bearing the news and asking if the girls could remain in Ashborough for the time being. Millie sent back a telegram asking if she wished her nieces to attend the funeral, but by the time she received a reply, the girls' mother had been buried a week.

'I'm sure your father will come to visit,' Millie tried to comfort the distraught pair. Seven-year-old Charity cried every night for a month for her dead mother, then stopped abruptly on Albert's ninth birthday. But Patience, who was Robert's age, grieved more deeply, waking with nightmares, fearing the dark and sticking close by Millie as if she could not bear to let her out of her sight. Upset for the girls, Millie did not allow herself to dwell on how appalling it would be to have to break the news of Dan's death to their boys, should the worst happen.

At the end of the summer, the girls' father finally appeared on leave, a small, handsome sub-lieutenant whom Ava, having been to see *Gone with the Wind* six times, declared looked like Clark Gable. Millie was furious with the blatant way she flirted with Gordon Armstrong and disapproved of the time he spent chatting to her rather than to his bereaved daughters. She saw plainly that this man had little interest in his children, mixing up their names and smacking Charity on her legs when she refused to sit still and be quiet. The younger girl stuck her tongue out at her father and ran from the room, hiding until after he had gone, in a place Albert used as a den at the back of the station. Only Albert could coax her out that evening, long after her father had departed. It occurred to Millie that she might have to look after these girls for longer than she had anticipated. Nancy had returned with her children too, so Millie was grateful when

Ella suggested that Marjory, having recently left school, came to help out at the hotel.

That August, air battles raged over Britain and the spectre of invasion seemed to grow ever more real. Even Grant, a critic of war but disillusioned by Russia's pact with the Nazis, volunteered for the Home Guard like other veterans of the Great War, and went on night-time manoeuvres. Millie wondered if he knew about the two postcards that had come for Ava from Gordon Armstrong, or noticed the number of times the quarter-master, Bain, came in from the nearby camp to have tea in the hotel.

Millie's private fears mounted as news came of Italian advances on Egypt from Libya, and she fretted over Dan so far away. She gathered the children around the wireless to listen to Princess Elizabeth give her first public broadcast, speaking to the evacuee children. But she did her best to comfort them and shield them from the news when all around it was so bleak. She organised them into ducking for apples instead of having fireworks on bonfire night, and used up precious rations of sugar to make a cake for Charity's eighth birthday, filling the tea room with children to give her a memorable party behind the blackout curtains.

That Christmas Millie and Teresa made puddings using carrots instead of dried fruit, and ceremoniously divided the last bananas that they were likely to see while Britain remained blockaded and for which Ava had queued at the grocer's for two hours. They managed to procure a turkey for their dinner, and ate it cheered by the news that the British had begun a counter-offensive against the Italians in the Western desert.

In the New Year, Millie's heart lightened at the news of the capture of Tobruk by British and Australian troops, her mind briefly distracted from rising food prices and the problem of how she was going to keep the hotel running. But the relief was short-lived, for Marjory came rushing round with a message.

'Mam says there's been someone asking round Tenter Terrace for Dan. She thought you ought to know.'

'Why?' Millie asked in surprise. 'Who is it?'

Marjory blushed. 'A lass, Mam said. She told her to come round here, but sent me to warn you first.'

'What lass?' Millie asked suspiciously, her heart lurching.

Marjory shrugged awkwardly. 'Not from round here, spoke quite posh.'

'What did she look like?' Millie questioned, her heart beating uncomfortably.

'Bonny looking – blonde. She was in uniform,' Marjory said, giving her a cautious look.

'What did she want?' Millie asked, feeling herself redden and glad that Ava was out.

'She was looking for Uncle Dan – asked Mam a lot of questions about the family,' Marjory told her, quickly tying on her apron and setting to work so that Millie would not question her further.

Millie's pulse raced and she felt sick as she waited for the stranger to appear at the hotel.

What if she was some younger woman that Dan had taken up with? she agonised. Surely he would not have been unfaithful to her again after the heartache his affair with Dinah had caused? She forced herself to carry on with her jobs and said nothing to her mother or Ava about Marjory's message, thinking they would find out soon enough. But the morning dragged on and no one called. The afternoon wore on and she busied herself with preparing tea for the household, while Marjory and Ava served in the tea room and Teresa sat mending the evacuees' clothes. The children rushed in from school, darkness fell, but the mystery blonde did not come. The following day Millie went round to Ella's and questioned her about the woman.

'But who was she?' Millie worried.

'I don't know,' Ella said with a helpless shrug. 'She never gave her name and I was too taken aback to ask. She was smartly dressed, in army uniform – stationed outside Newcastle somewhere. Asked a lot about you and the bairns. Said she'd never met you, but Dan was a friend of her family's.'

Millie let out a shuddering sigh and confided her fears in Ella. 'What if Dan's been unfaithful to me again? What if this lass has come to show me up?'

'You've no reason to think that, have you?' Ella asked.

Millie flushed. 'He always swore that Dinah was the only one – daft little fling, he called it. Said it never meant anything, just that he was lonely without me.' She gave Ella a defiant look.

'I believed him when he said there'd never be anyone else – that's why I took him back. For the sake of the bairns. But now I can't stop thinking of the old rumours about him and other women.'

'That was just Ava's spiteful gossiping!' her friend retorted.

'But you said this lass was in the army,' Millie continued to fret. 'Dan must've met her since he joined up.'

Ella pushed a weak cup of tea towards her. 'You don't know that. I think you're worrying over nothing. This lass might be the sister of a friend of his in the army or an old team-mate. I'm sorry, it's my fault for not asking. Anyway, she can't be that interested if she didn't bother to turn up.'

Millie allowed Ella to calm her fears, and when the woman did not appear she was soon immersed once more in the daily struggle of making ends meet, caring for the children and keeping the peace among the squabbling evacuees and her own boys. Spring came and she forgot about Ella's caller. April brought news of a German counterattack in North Africa and the worry of the British being driven back from Libya once more. Her last letter from Dan had been cheerful and affectionate, but it had been written before the reversal in fortunes.

She was clearing a tea table, thinking about Dan and how Albert kept asking anxiously for reassurance that his father was safe, when she noticed a woman hovering in the hallway. Something about the way she held herself, the flick of her blonde hair away from her face, made Millie stop and stare. The stranger looked back at her, then took a tentative step forward, and Millie knew in that moment that this was the woman Ella had met. There was something familiar about her pretty face, the lift of her chin maybe, or the dark lashes against her pale skin, yet Millie could not place her. Perhaps she had seen her when she had visited Dan in Yorkshire, yet the woman did not seem very old, given the wavy starlet hairstyle and the red lipstick.

Millie's heart grew heavy at the sight of her and she felt suddenly old to be confronted with such a young rival. At that moment, before either of them could speak, Albert and the Baker lads raced in, chased by Charity and Jack. They flew around the dining room, knocking into tables and screeching at the tops of their voices. Millie shouted crossly, 'I've told you to keep out of here! Out, the lot of you!'

As they scattered out of the open doorway, Teresa hobbled in on her stick, drawn by the commotion, and apologised to the young woman for nearly being knocked over.

'It's these townie evacuees, they've got no manners,' she explained.

'I'm a townie myself,' the woman answered in a stiff, well-spoken voice.

'Is it tea you'd like?' Teresa asked, ushering her towards the empty tea room and Millie.

'No thank you,' she replied. 'I'm looking for Millie Nixon.'

Millie faced her, saying as calmly as possible, 'That's me. Can I help you?'

The woman did not answer at first, just stared

at her in curiosity, making Millie feel even more uncomfortable.

'You're not what I expected,' she said at last, her blue eyes critical. 'You're taller, but not as pretty. But then I suppose you must have been as a young woman.'

Millie flushed and asked indignantly, 'And who are you?'

'I'm Helen Nixon,' the woman replied, lifting her chin stubbornly. 'I'm stationed up here. Been plucking up courage to come and visit. It took a bit of asking around to find you, but I knew to come to Ashborough. I funked it the last time. Mother didn't want me to track any of you down, but I've always been curious.'

Millie's heart pounded. 'Nixon, you say? Are you related to us?'

Helen gave her a hostile little smile. 'I am to your husband.'

'Dan?' Millie asked, quite baffled.

Teresa elbowed forward. 'Stop playing games with our Millie,' she scolded, 'and tell us what you're up to! If you're some little trollop of his, I'll send you packing.'

The young woman turned on her, shaking with nervous anger. 'I'm not the trollop, *that* woman is!' she declared, stabbing a finger at Millie. 'I'm Dan Nixon's daughter!'

Millie was flabbergasted. 'What?' she demanded. 'What do you mean, *daughter?*' She was incensed by the claim. Dan's daughter was their beloved Edith, the only child who had the right to call herself that!

But Helen advanced on her, just as angry,

423

glaring at Millie as if she were the devil.

'I came to find my father,' she hissed, 'to ask him why he deserted me and my mother all those years ago – the real Mrs Nixon!'

Millie's breath stopped in her throat, her head dizzy with incomprehension. 'How dare you!' she gasped.

Helen's attack faltered for an instant and confusion flickered across her young face. 'He's never told you, has he? You really don't know anything about us. I always wondered how you could live with yourself for taking another woman's husband like you did, marrying him as if you had any right to!'

Millie felt her legs begin to buckle; she slammed the tray she was still clutching down on to the table. 'I've taken no one else's husband!' she exclaimed. 'Dan and I were married good and proper in church, nearly seventeen years ago!'

Helen gave her a look, half pitying, half scornful. 'Well, he married my mother over twenty years ago, because she was carrying me – his child! Grandfather might have forced him to, but he did it. Cleared off before I was born, but he was still married to Mother at the time. She wouldn't divorce him at first, because of the scandal it would've caused to the family. When he married you, he should've gone to prison for bigamy, but Mother would never do anything to harm him. She only divorced him after he wrote and told her he had another daughter. That was typical of Mother, to bother about my father's bastard child.'

Millie was speechless. She collapsed into a chair. 'I don't believe you,' she whispered. 'How dare you call my Edith that! Why are you saying such things?'

'Because it's true.' Helen was adamant. 'I wanted to see what my father is like and I was curious to see his other family too. I find it hard to believe he would turn his back on my mother and me, and the life he could have had with us in London, for this!' She gave a dismissive wave of her hand.

Teresa cut her short with a jab from her walking stick. 'Stop that! I'll not have you say any more against my Millie, and I'll tell you now, you'll not find a better lass or a more loving wife and mother than she is. I don't care who your mother is and I don't see why we should believe any of your fanciful story! If you've nothing better to do than cause trouble, you can clear off somewhere else!'

'Wait, Mam!' Millie stopped her. 'Let the lass have her say.' She fixed a steady gaze on Helen and demanded, 'Where's your proof that Dan's your father and that he was married to someone else?' She could hardly believe she was asking such questions, let alone with such a steady voice. Inside she felt so fragile that another harsh word or gesture might shatter her into tiny pieces.

Helen walked over to the table and pulled out some papers from a neat handbag.

'Here's their marriage certificate, September 1920. And this is my birth certificate – look, it's got Daniel Nixon as the father, February 1921.

They didn't divorce until 1928.' Millie handled the documents with shaking hands, as if they scorched her fingers, but Dan's name was on them both, along with a scrawl that could have been his careless signature. 'Grandfather gave him his first break in football, signed him up for his club. That's how he met Mother. She thought Dad was so dashing, with his army uniform and his good looks. She was very young and easily impressed.' Helen laughed mirthlessly. 'I was a mistake, of course. Nobody wanted me at first. But I don't think Dad liked being told what to do by Grandfather. He ran away from his responsibilities,' she said critically, 'changed clubs. Grandfather never forgave him for letting everyone down, had him branded as a troublemaker around the local clubs. I suppose that's why he came north again.'

'Did he know about you?' Millie gulped. 'Did he know he had a daughter?'

Helen gave her a look of surprise. 'Of course he did! He used to send me presents and money when I was little, and I could never understand why he wasn't living with us. I still remember my mother crying for days when she got a letter from him asking for a divorce. All because of you!' she said, her look resentful. 'I didn't know the reason until much later, but my grandfather told him that she never would. Grandfather wanted to ruin his career when my father married you, but Mother wouldn't let him go to the newspapers. In the end both of them thought Dad wasn't worth it, that's why she finally agreed to divorce him and why she wouldn't see him when he tried

426

to come back a few years ago. But I always longed to meet him. After all, he is my father!' she said defiantly.

Millie's insides turned cold. 'What do you mean, when he tried to come back?' she gasped.

Helen's blue eyes, so like Dan's, glinted with triumph. 'A few years back he got in touch with Mother again. Said he was living in Kilburn. He wanted to see me, started sending presents again. But Mother wouldn't let me keep them, threw them out. They were little girl's toys anyway,' Helen said dismissively, 'and I was nine by then.'

Millie sat there, stunned, gazing blindly at the proof in front of her. She thought she had been able to bear all the betrayal and disappointments of her marriage to Dan and survive them, clinging on to the belief that for all his mistakes he still loved her deeply and above all others. Yet at their wedding he had been married to someone called Clementine Mary. Her marriage had been a sham and her beloved Edith had been born out of wedlock, disgraced by Dan's bigamy, while this hateful young woman who stood before her now could claim to be Dan's true daughter! Not only that, but Dan had tried to seek out his first daughter maybe just months after Edith's death, Millie thought in acute distress, while she was lost in the darkness of her grief. How could he have done that to her?

She felt a scream welling up inside her, a cry of pain and rage that had to escape out of her, else she would be torn apart by its force.

'No! *No!*' she yelled, gasping and panting for breath as she rose and grabbed the table,

427

overturning it. The papers went flying and dirty cups smashed on the polished floor. *'No!'* she screamed again. 'The lying bastard! He's weak and selfish! I hate him, hate him, *hate him!'*

She picked up her chair and hurled it across the room, and then seized another. Helen backed away, alarmed by the madness that had suddenly gripped this dark-haired woman she had dismissed as dull and inferior. The second chair broke the window with a deafening crash. From nowhere the children appeared, to gawp at the jagged glass and a raging Millie.

As she set about smashing the dining-room furniture, Millie was vaguely aware of her mother shouting at her to stop. She saw Ava and Marjory appear in the doorway, their mouths open in horror, followed by a grim-faced Grant.

'You were right about Dan!' she screamed at Teresa. 'A good-for-nothing womaniser! I can't believe I was taken in for so long! I've wasted my whole life on him!'

Grant dived across the room and seized her. She fought him off, scratching his face, beating him with her fists and kicking him, hardly aware of who he was. All she could feel was the rage that consumed her. She gave vent to her pent-up fury at all the years of slights and setbacks, broken promises and hurtful words. But worst of all was the thought of Dan's betrayal of her and the children that enveloped her like a suffocating mist. It was too much to bear. She felt the fight draining out of her, faintness overcoming her pain. Someone was struggling with her but she did not want to struggle any more. As she collapsed, she heard Albert's voice clearly, full of concern and panic.

'What's wrong, Mam?' he cried. 'Tell me what's wrong? H-has something happened to me dad?'

Millie gave way to uncontrollable sobbing as she crumpled on to the floor.

CHAPTER 26
1941

Millie remembered almost nothing of the following weeks. The end of the Blitz came, and a postcard from Gordon Armstrong, whose ship was involved in the evacuation of Crete. The news was full of the German invasion of Russia and Japanese attacks in Malaya, but Millie was aware of none of it. For a time she was in a state of total collapse, unable to drag herself out of bed or cope with the most mundane of chores, let alone see to the needs of the children. At times she would wake up and look around her bedroom and wonder where she was or who she was. Then the pain of memory would flood through her and she was engulfed in the shame that Dan had brought on her, and she wished she did not have to wake up at all.

Shocked by her daughter's breakdown after all her years of coping with life's tragedies and setbacks, Teresa galvanised herself into running the hotel once again. Crippled though she was, she hobbled around giving out orders, working out menus, disciplining the children and damping down the rumours about Millie's bigamous marriage with strong denials. It was she who arranged for Millie to stay at Ella and Walter's house for a month of rest and quiet, while Marjory lived in at the hotel and looked after the

children. Teresa could see how Albert's querulous demands about his father and Robert's
boisterous aggression were distressing Millie. She
needed to be away from the hotel and its daily
demands else she would never have a chance to
regain her strength, Teresa believed. To vent her
anger she wrote to Dan about Helen's visit and
how the news of his bigamy had destroyed
Millie's health. He would not be welcome back in
Ashborough, she told him. When letters began to
arrive for Millie she kept them unopened until
Millie felt strong enough to read them.

Meanwhile Ella nursed Millie, bringing her
food upstairs if she wished to stay in bed and
keeping prying neighbours from the kitchen
when she ventured downstairs. Millie was
plagued by dark thoughts, unable to imagine
herself coping with life again. Even the smallest
of tasks, like rising and getting dressed, seemed
as daunting as climbing the Alps. She tortured
herself with thoughts of Dan's marriage to
another woman and the daughter he had known
about all these years and kept secret from her.
How was it possible to live with someone and not
know such devastating secrets about them? she
agonised. It made her think she had never known
the real Dan at all.

Worst of all, the truth of Dan's past made her
question everything about herself, leaving her
feeling vulnerable and anxious, just as she had
when Edith had died. It was like another
bereavement; she had lost her husband as surely
as if she had received a telegram from the army
reporting his death. Except it was not final; this

431

bereavement was like a shadow cast across the rest of her life as if he had gone missing in action. The Dan she thought she had known would never return to her, yet the bigamous Dan might. Should she allow him back after what he had done to her? she questioned. Part of her never wanted to see him again, yet there were the boys to consider. They adored Dan, especially Albert. Did she have the right to deny all contact with their father? Then there was Helen. Millie wanted to hate the young woman for devastating her world and for being the grown-up daughter that Edith should have been. She could almost picture Edith as looking like the wavy-haired, blue eyed Helen. Yet Dan's daughter had sent her flowers and cards, shocked that Millie had known nothing of her existence, and at the havoc she had caused by her appearance and revelations. Teresa had forbidden her to go near Millie, yet Millie could not help being curious about Helen, secretly wanting to find out more about her in the hope that such knowledge might explain Dan to her better.

But the only visitors she was allowed were the children, twice a week after school, and she braced herself for these brief, noisy appearances, yearning for their company yet knowing that she could not stand more than ten minutes at a time. She felt guilty at neglecting them, but Ella kept the visits short and assured her that Marjory was enjoying looking after them.

As the summer wore on, Millie gradually became aware of her surroundings and began to take more of an interest in them. She and Ella would sit and work on a patchwork quilt that they were making out of an old serge suit of Mungo's and scraps of material from Marjory's childhood dresses. If they talked at all it was to reminisce about their days in London, a subject that held no pain for either of them. Occasionally the talk would stray back to their childhood in Craston in the days before the Great War, and Ella would remind her of people and incidents that she had long forgotten.

Sometimes Grant would call round after a shift at the pit, with a volume of poetry or a D.H Lawrence novel for her to read. Millie felt weak at the thought of struggling through the books, but not wanting to hurt his feelings, she would ask him to read her bits while she sewed or simply closed her eyes and listened. Whereas Walter had fulminated about his brother's disgraceful betrayal and said he would have nothing to do with him again, Grant made no judgement in front of Millie, for which she was grateful. In the quiet of Ella's kitchen, Millie found she could talk to Ella and Grant about thoughts long buried that she had never been able to voice to her mother. Her mind, so disturbed by the revelations over Dan, had unearthed her early past too, and she found herself wanting to talk about Graham, and her father, and the war that had torn her family apart.

One time she asked Grant to talk to her about Flanders. He was reticent at first, and then told her some of the anecdotes about his fellow fusiliers. 'The best thing was getting a parcel or letter from home,' he admitted. 'That kept us all

433

going. We'd share out what came – even the love letters,' he blushed.

'And who was sending you love letters?' Ella teased.

'No one,' Grant answered with an embarrassed smile. 'I was one of those who got to read other marras' postcards!'

Millie mused. 'I remember the only thing our Graham wanted was Woodbines. They had a nickname for him; I'd forgotten it until recently.'

'What was that?' Ella asked.

'Furnace,' Millie chuckled weakly.

Grant gave her a strange look. 'Furnace?' he questioned. 'I've heard that before...' Millie watched his brow unfurrow as a memory came back to him. He held her look with his dark, brooding eyes.

'Tell me,' Millie whispered, her heart beginning to pound.

'It was in a field hospital. I was visiting a marra of mine – wounded on the Somme. There was this lad visiting the same ward – we got chatting and discovered we both came from the north-east. I remember now, I'm sure it was Craston he talked about.' Millie felt a shiver go down her back as she saw Grant struggling to recall the details.

'Can you remember what he said?' she urged.

Grant shook his head. 'Not after all this time.'

Millie looked down at her lap in despair. It was tantalising to think he might have met and talked with her brother so soon before his death. It was a result of his running away in action later that summer of the Somme that Graham had been shot. There was a huge dark hole in her family's memory and understanding of what had happened to Graham that made it impossible to imagine what those last days must have been like for him, and impossible for her to come to terms with his shameful death. How she yearned for anecdotes about him in the way other people talked about their sons and brothers with such pride.

Grant touched her shoulder lightly. 'But I do remember having a cigarette with him outside. The matron chased him out for trying to light a Woodbine for his friend. I went out with him and he shared it with me. I remember he laughed a lot and he told me his nickname was Furnace.'

Millie looked up, wondering if Grant had been one of the last people to speak to her brother. 'And I remember this,' Grant said quietly. 'When I went back in to say goodbye to me marra, he was talking with the other wounded lad about Furnace. He said that underneath all the smoke and the banter, Furnace was one of the bravest in their company. He'd volunteer for night raids at the drop of a hat. Hadn't been home on leave for two years.' Millie's eyes swelled with tears. 'If he was your brother,' Grant added gently, 'then you've no reason to feel any shame for him. His own mates were a better judge than the men who court-martialled him.'

Millie felt tears of loss and regret for her brother trickle down her cheeks. 'It sounds like Graham,' she murmured. 'I've never believed he was a coward.'

Grant reached over and squeezed her hand. 'I

fought alongside lads like your brother and I saw the same sort of comradeship and courage that I was used to down the pit. A few lads did reach the end of their tether or went mad with the noise of the shelling, but only after they'd put up with months in the trenches. The only cowards in that war were the ones stuck far behind the front lines, giving out the orders,' he said bitterly.

Ella went and fetched a cup of water while Millie clung on to Grant's hand and cried quietly. She felt strangely close to him, as if in some way she had reached her brother through him. Grant had known Graham, however briefly, in that part of his short life that was a blank to her, and it gave her comfort. After a while they talked again, Millie telling Grant about her brother, with Ella joining in her reminiscences about Craston.

'I've been thinking a lot about me dad an' all,' Millie confessed to her friends. 'All this business with this lass, Helen.'

'Don't go worrying yourself over her,' Ella said stoutly. 'She'll not come near you again if I can help it.'

Millie shook her head. 'No, but she's got me thinking. All these years she's been without her father, wondering what he's like or what he's doing or whether she'll ever see him again. And when she got the chance she took it. She came looking for him, not caring what her mam or grandfather thought – or any of us, for that matter.' Millie flushed, but continued in a small voice, 'She had the guts to go after him, go after what she wanted, no matter what others thought

436

of her. It makes me feel guilty that I never tried harder to find me own father – discover what happened to him. I've thought about him all these years, but never done anything about it. I've always thought it was 'cos I didn't want to upset Mam, but I think it's really because I've never been brave enough to go searching.'

'He never made the effort either,' Ella pointed out.

Millie felt uneasy. 'He might have done,' she confessed. 'Dinah told me that time we all went to the seaside, you know, before...' Millie broke off, reddening at the memory of that awful night when Dan's affair with Dinah was discovered.

'What did she tell you?' Grant asked quietly.

'She said that she'd always meant to tell me but hadn't,' Millie continued, 'that this man had turned up asking for me at Paradise Parade. It was after we'd moved away to Kilburn. She sent him away, thinking he was just a tramp after money – probably heard about me and Dan and the way we spent so freely. She said Mrs Hodges took him in and gave him a cup of tea, but she never saw him around again.'

'Why do you think it was your father?' Grant asked.

'Because Dinah said he walked with a limp,' Millie replied, trembling, 'and me dad walked with a limp after a fall of stone at the pit.'

'It could've been anybody!' Ella exclaimed.

'I know,' Millie admitted, 'but it doesn't stop me thinking, wondering...'

Grant said, 'Mrs Hodges might be able to tell you more, if you really want to find out.'

Millie gave him a desperate look. 'I do,' she whispered. 'All this business with Dan and Helen – it makes me wonder if I've been right about anything. I've always thought badly of me dad for letting me mam down and not providing for us, but maybe I judged him too harshly. I just saw it all from a child's point of view. I've blamed him all these years for Mam having to slave for Moody, but it was really because of me that she had to.'

'Don't you go blaming yourself for what your mam did,' Ella insisted. 'As you said, you were just a bairn. What either of your parents did wasn't your fault.'

'You're right,' Millie sighed, feeling her guilt easing a fraction. 'But I really would like to know what happened to me dad.'

'Then when you're feeling stronger, I'll take you to see Mrs Hodges,' Grant promised. 'At the very least you can find out if this man was your father or not. And if it was, then at least it shows he cared something for you, tried to find you,' he said kindly.

Millie gave him a grateful smile, surprised as much by his sympathy as by her ease in talking to him about such personal fears. 'Thank you,' she answered, already feeling stronger for having unburdened herself to her friends. Maybe soon she would have the strength to write to Dan and tell him what she thought of him. She knew from her mother that he had been told about Helen's visit and warned to stay away, but she had been unable to bring herself to read his letters, not wanting to hear any more of his excuses.

It was the autumn before Millie felt strong enough to face the journey to Tyneside in search of information about her father. By then she was back at the hotel, working as hard as ever but still troubled with sleeplessness over Dan and how her life had unravelled so quickly after Helen's revelations. He should have told her the truth at the beginning, Millie raged in the dark hours of the night, alone in the bed she had once shared with him. How could he have been so selfish? But as the weeks wore on, she began to question whether she had been partly to blame. Was it not she who had yearned to be respectably married above all else? she accused herself. Had she not pushed him into marriage against her mother's better judgement? Thinking back, Millie had to admit that Dan had shown a certain reluctance in the face of her eagerness. She had assumed it was just his bachelor cautiousness at settling down. But had it been guilt or a fear of not wanting to own up to the mistake he had made as a young soldier newly released from the army? Helen had said Dan had written asking for a divorce, but had been refused.

But he still should have told her! Millie railed as she tossed in her bed. Many times during these tortured moments she wondered if she would have waited for him to divorce had she known about his first doomed marriage, or would she have got over him and married someone else? He never gave her the choice! she concluded bitterly.

Teresa was horrified by Millie's desire to waste precious time and money on a fruitless search for

Ellis. 'He'll be long dead,' she snapped, 'and it's disloyal to me! Your place is here, looking after your boys. Besides, it's not safe, there's still a chance of bombing over the Tyne.'

But Millie could not settle for thinking about her father. 'I want to know the truth,' she insisted. Her chance came when a message arrived from Gordon Armstrong that his ship was docked on the Tyne and he wished to see his daughters. Ava and Millie argued over who would take them, and Grant said that whoever did, he was going to accompany them. In the end they all went on a crowded train and the girls were briefly reunited with their father at Aunt Rachael's house near the docks. Millie took a trolley bus and travelled the mile uptown to Paradise Parade, Ava insisting that Grant accompany her.

Millie had not been back since they had lived there, and the street looked drab, the doors flaking with paint and the railings removed for the war effort. She found herself shaking as she walked past her old flat and saw that the same ivory blind hung in the sitting-room window. She slipped an arm through Grant's for comfort and he did not pull away. Without a word they hurried on, avoiding the shops at the top and the Fairishes' hairdressing business, skirting down a side lane into Cedar Crescent. She knocked nervously at Mrs Hodges' door, half expecting some stranger to answer. But to her delight, the old midwife herself opened it. Mrs Hodges peered short-sightedly for a moment and then threw wide her arms.

'Why, hinny! Haway in!' the old woman cried, flushing with pleasure. Millie fell into her plump, welcoming arms and burst into tears, overwhelmed by sudden memories of living in the cosy flat in the neighbouring street with Edith and Dan in those happy days.

After a pot of tea, with a sprinkle of precious rationed sugar and a slice of indigestible cake made from powdered egg, Millie broached the reason for her return and her quest to find any trace of her father. Mrs Hodges paused in thought for a minute.

'My memory's not what it used to be, but yes, there was a man came looking for you after you left,' she nodded. 'He was very down on his luck, shabby clothes, and he had the look of someone with consumption. Can't imagine he'd still be alive, hinny, I'm sorry to say.'

'Did he give his name or tell you anything about himself?' Millie persisted.

The old neighbour shook her head. 'Eeh, hinny, I didn't remember.'

Grant suggested, 'Did he say where he was living, perhaps?'

Her eyes suddenly lit with the spark of a memory. 'Aye, he did say his address. Now what was it...? It was somewhere near the Quayside – he'd been labouring on the new bridge.'

'The Tyne Bridge?' Millie asked.

'Aye, that was it.' Mrs Hodges pulled herself to her feet and disappeared out of the parlour for a minute. Millie and Grant exchanged hopeful looks. When she came back she was leafing through an old notebook. 'I've kept diaries and

441

notes for years about the births I've attended,' she muttered. 'Ah! This might be it. October the fifteenth 1928. A Mr Mercer called.' Millie gasped at the name. 'He was staying at Mrs Hardy's, All Saints' Buildings on the Quayside,' Mrs Hodges continued. 'I don't know if it still exists, but he must've wanted me to tell you in case you ever came back.' The old woman looked at Millie with shining eyes. 'I always hoped you would.'

Millie stood up and hugged her. 'I never was brave enough,' she confessed. 'There were too many memories of our Edith...'

'I know, hinny,' Mrs Hodges sympathised, holding her tightly. 'I missed the bairn too. I was that upset when I heard.' She patted Millie's back. 'See, I still keep that photograph you gave me of you all together.'

Millie pulled away, blinking back the tears that blurred her vision. There on the mantelpiece was the studio picture of her and Dan with Edith between them, sitting still just long enough for the photographer to capture her quizzical look and enchanting smile. She had always loved that photograph as being the epitome of their happily married days. How different things might have been had Edith lived, Millie thought painfully. Then, looking closer at Dan's lopsided smile, she was struck by the thought that even if their daughter had lived, the seeds of destruction of their marriage had already been sown. He had always been someone else's husband, someone else's father, she thought bitterly. At that moment an anger filled her, boiling up inside as dangerous as hot oil. She resolved that when she returned to Ashborough she would write to Dan and tell him just what she thought of his betrayal! She would not take him back even if that was what he wanted, she determined, and no amount of pleading would change her mind.

They took their leave of Mrs Hodges and promised to keep in touch.

'I hope you find out something about your father,' she told Millie with a parting kiss. 'You take care of yourself and that family of yours. Tell Mr Nixon I was asking after him.'

Millie nodded, turning away quickly, not wanting to talk about Dan.

As they made their way back down Paradise Parade to catch a tram, Millie said forlornly, 'We haven't time to go looking round the Quayside now; we might miss the train back to Ashborough.'

'We have if we're quick,' Grant replied. 'You'll only fret if you don't go looking now – wonder what you might have found.'

Millie smiled at his strong, compassionate face. 'You've been that good to me,' she said quietly, slipping her arm through his. 'I sometimes wonder...'

'What?' Grant asked her, his dark eyes scanning her face.

'Oh, nothing,' Millie said, flushing. She could not say what was in her mind, that maybe they had both married the wrong people. There appeared to be no love between Grant and Ava, but they had stuck together through bad times and maybe they were resigned to the life they led.

443

'Haway,' Grant encouraged, 'let's run for that tram into town.'

In Newcastle, they walked down the steep streets from the tram stand to the bustling alleys of the Quayside. After asking around, they found All Saints' Buildings tucked beneath the graceful eighteenth-century church which gave it its name. It was an old tenement block of lodging rooms which had never been grand but was now reduced to little more than a dossing house. Millie looked in dismay at the badly lit, ill-smelling stairwell as they searched in the gloom for Mrs Hardy's rooms.

The door was answered by an elderly man with a waft of burnt toast. There was a wireless on in the background. When Millie asked for Mrs Hardy, the man grunted that she was not in, but that he was her husband.

'Don't know when she'll be back,' he said. 'If it's a room you're wanting, we're full to bursting.'

'No, I'm trying to find someone – one of her lodgers,' Millie persisted. 'Perhaps you know him, Mr Ellis Mercer?'

The man sucked in lips over toothless gums as he thought. 'Mercer?' He shook his head. 'There's no one here of that name.'

Grant, seeing the look of disappointment on Millie's face, asked, 'Maybe not now, but this man lived here over ten years ago. He's a pitman from Craston.'

'Up the coast?' the old man asked.

'Aye,' Millie said, her hopes sparking once more. 'He's a tall man, but walks with a limp.'

'There was a man from up that way a long time

back,' the man answered. 'Can't recall his name, mind. Aye, he was one of the men working on the bridge back in the twenties. We had a few of them staying here. Could have called him Mercer – he certainly had a gammy leg.'

'What happened to him?' Millie asked breathlessly. 'How long did he stay here? Do you know where he went?'

'I can't rightly remember,' Mr Hardy said. 'I was working on the keelboats at the time, wasn't around much. It's the missus you'll have to ask.'

Millie could barely hide her frustration. 'But we have to go back to Ashborough tonight and I don't know when I'll be able to come back. Did she not keep any records? Can't you remember anything else?'

Mr Hardy glowered at her. 'As I said, you'll have to ask Mrs Hardy. The lodgers are her concern.' He began to shut the door.

Grant wedged his foot in the door frame. 'Just a minute. Mrs Nixon is trying to find out what happened to her father. She hasn't seen him for twenty years. Can she leave her address, and if Mrs Hardy remembers anything about Ellis Mercer she can write and tell her?'

The old man grunted in agreement and Grant pulled out a stub of pencil and wrote Millie's name and the hotel address on the back of his tram ticket. He pushed it through the gap and Mr Hardy grabbed it, then closed the door on them. Grant steered Millie down the stairs and out into the October gloom.

'He'll not give me name to his wife,' Millie said angrily.

445

'You never know. Anyway, you can write to her yourself now you've got something to go on.'

Millie turned and gave him a bleak look. 'I hope it wasn't me dad. I hate to think of him living in such a place – with people who didn't care about him and can't even remember his name any more!'

Grant held her by the shoulders. 'You wanted to know, Millie, didn't you? You should've been prepared for this. What sort of life do you think an out-of-work pitman with a damaged leg is going to find?' he demanded.

She shook him off and began to walk quickly back up the hill towards Central Station, where they had agreed to meet Ava and the girls. She did not speak to him about the visit again, but as they travelled home with the chattering children, Millie had to admit that Grant was right. She had been hoping for some fairytale ending, where she discovered her father and plucked him from a desolate life of old age and poverty. He would be eternally grateful, of course, and be reconciled with her mother at last. But that was just foolishness, she told herself harshly. All she had discovered was that her father may have lived in a dingy lodging house while he carried out some menial task for the bridge-builders, separated from family and the relative prosperity of his past. That night, filled with disappointment and bitterness about their fruitless search, Millie vented her fury in a letter to Dan.

'I will never forgive you for betraying me and the bairns or for the shame you have brought on this family. You'll not set foot inside this house again. I

don't wish you any harm out in Egypt, but you might as well go crawling back to your first wife when you come home. Your Helen wants to see you at least. I can't tell you how hurt I am that you tried to go back to them after our Edith died. You've wronged us all too much this time, Dan. I could never take you back.'

Millie posted it the next day while still in a fury, and made her mother burn his unopened letters. A month later a further letter came from Dan but she steeled herself to throw this on the fire too before reading it. Albert saw her doing this and asked in amazement, 'W-wasn't that from me dad?' When Millie did not answer, he asked, 'W-what did he say? Is he coming back on leave soon?'

Millie faced him and answered, 'He's not coming back here when the war's over. He's got another family.'

Albert looked as shocked as if she had slapped him, and Millie felt anger surge at the absent Dan for having brought about such misery for them all. Robert looked up from his homework anxiously. 'Do you mean that lass Helen?'

'Aye,' Millie said, her throat tight. She could feel herself begin to shake.

'B-but she can't take our dad off us!' Albert cried. 'That's not fair!'

Ava interfered. 'She can and she has done. He was her father first.'

'Ava!' Grant warned, stormy-faced.

'Well, it's true!' Ava lashed out. 'There's been too much covering up and pretending going on for my liking.' She gave Millie a hostile look.

'They don't need to know any more,' Millie

447

said in a panic, regretting her outburst at once. 'Not at their age.'

'They've a right to know.' Ava warmed to the argument, scenting trouble. 'They've a right to know what sort of man their father is – one who marries a lass when he's already married to someone else!'

'Shut up!' Teresa said, rising to her feet and dropping her knitting.

'No, I won't shut up!' she replied. 'It's been nothing but lies and deceit for years. Millie's been a fool to have stuck with Dan so long. He's been unfaithful to her, the whole town knows that! I'm not surprised what's happened, just that it's taken her so long to see him for the waster he is.'

Before anyone could say a word in reproach, Albert had sprung across the room towards Ava and started punching her. 'I hate you!' he screamed. Grant leapt to pull the boy off as Ava screamed in pain. Jack and Charity watched wide-eyed and alarmed from their crouched positions by the hearth, while Patience ducked behind Millie in fright. But Robert, now stocky at eleven, waded in, kicking Albert.

'Leave off her!' he shouted.

Grant heaved them apart and pinned Robert with his arms, while Millie went to grab a sobbing Albert. Robert tried to wrestle free from Grant's hold. 'You should stick up for Auntie Ava. She's only telling the truth about me dad. I hate him for what he's done. He's never around here anyway!'

Albert wailed at him, 'D-don't you say anything against Dad or I'll kill ya!'

Robert just laughed at him harshly and shoved Grant away. Ava, recovering, went to hug the boy.

'You needn't worry about any shame,' she consoled her favourite. 'At least Dan's got nothing to do with you.'

Millie looked at her, appalled. 'Ava, don't say another word!' She turned to Patience quickly. 'Take the bairns upstairs to play, pet. Go on!' She bustled them all out of the room, but Robert refused to move.

He looked between them, his surly face unsure. 'What do you mean, he's got nothing to do with me?'

Ava gave Millie a challenging look. 'Why shouldn't the boy know? He's old enough now. He's always known he was different from the others, the way you've favoured Albert and Jack.'

'You don't know what you're saying,' Millie warned. 'I'll never forgive you if you hurt him now.'

Robert demanded. 'What should I know?'

'That Dan and Millie aren't your real parents,' Ava said, undaunted by the furious looks around her. 'They adopted you – brought you up from the Midlands. That's why I've always tried to give you a bit of extra love, because I never felt you got enough from them!'

'God forgive you!' Millie hissed. But the ferocious look that Robert gave her made her heart stop. She put her arms out to him. His face was ashen.

'Is it true?' he demanded, clenching his fists and holding himself away from her. 'You're not me mam?'

They stared at each other for a long moment, Millie's heart breaking at the shattered look on his young face. She shook her head. 'I'm sorry. I didn't think you ever needed to know,' she whispered. 'But I've loved you like me own – always will do.'

His stunned expression turned to pain, and fierce tears shone in his eyes as he accused her. 'Then I don't belong here! I never have done, have I? It's not just me dad who was a liar, it's you an' all!'

Millie felt punched by the words, but at that moment she heard her mother's voice come clearly from behind her.

'Oh, but you do belong here, more than any of us,' Teresa said, her voice trembling but sharp. 'Ava's wrong about where you come from.' She hobbled towards him. 'And you've no right to speak ill of Millie – she took care of you when your own mother wouldn't. She'd just lost her own daughter, but she gave you all the love she had in her sore heart.'

Robert shook as he demanded, 'Tell me who me mam was!'

Millie held her breath while all around her there was tense silence.

'I am,' Teresa confessed, 'and your birth left me crippled.' Robert looked at her, speechless. 'You might as well know the rest of it – the harm's already been done. Your father was Joseph Moody. So Ava and Millie are your half-sisters.'

There was a horrified gasp from Ava. Robert turned to her, bewildered, but she just covered her face in her hands as if she could not bear to look at him. The boy gave out a cry of fury, like an animal in pain. He glared around at them. 'You're all a bunch of liars! I don't know who to believe any more. I hate the lot of you!'

Grant put out a hand to grab him, but he bolted for the kitchen door, flung it open and dashed out into the dark.

'Go after him!' Millie urged.

Grant turned to his wife and said grimly as he went, 'Look at the damage you've done now with your vicious tongue!'

Ava screamed and pointed at Teresa. 'I didn't have the little bastard; she did – my father's whore!'

Millie, seeing Teresa buckle into a seat at the savage words, sprang over and shook Ava hard. 'Don't you ever call her that again.'

'I'll call her what I like,' Ava wailed, half hysterical, pushing Millie away. 'She ruined my life and my father's. I wish I'd never set eyes on the pair of you!'

Grant strode back across the room. 'Millie's worth ten of you, you wicked woman.'

She spat in his face. 'That's right, stick up for her! You deserve each other, you're both failures. Well, I've had enough of you all. I'd leave here tomorrow if I had somewhere to go!'

Grant said through gritted teeth, 'And I wouldn't stop you!' Then he marched from the house without a backward glance.

CHAPTER 27

The uneasy harmony that had held the household together was shattered by the terrible rows of that winter night. Millie tried constantly to comfort Robert and explain about the past, but he spurned her attempts. He became increasingly wild and uncontrollable and resentful of them all, suspicious of any kindness Millie tried to show him. She felt deeply ashamed of the way he had discovered the truth of his parentage, and she turned to Grant for help. He was the only adult that Robert would trust, and while he disobeyed everyone else he would find solace in gardening with the man he still saw as his uncle. Meanwhile Millie worried about Albert too. His stammer grew worse as he withdrew into his own world and never mentioned his father, until Millie despaired at knowing what the boy thought about at all.

Ava went out with soldiers in open defiance of Grant, until he could stand it no more and moved out of the hotel, lodging with Walter and Ella. He would still come around occasionally to help with small joinery jobs or to take the boys out to play football at the Comrades' ground, but he did not stay long. Millie missed his company.

The war dragged on and the hardships became greater, but somehow Millie managed. By 1943 the British were victorious in North Africa and

452

she wondered whether Dan would be sent home, but no word had ever come from him after the unread letter she had thrown on the fire. She often wondered during her nights of insomnia what he had written to her and whether she had been rash to burn it. But whatever it had been, it could not have changed anything and she was determined never to be hurt by him again. She decided that a life without men was simpler.

All her time was taken up with keeping the hotel going and bringing up the children as best she could. She wanted nothing more now than to get them all safely through the war. Nancy Baker had taken her boys back to Tyneside once the threat of invasion had passed, but the Armstrong sisters were still with them. Postcards came from their father, but mostly they were addressed to Ava, and Millie secretly feared the girls might not be reclaimed should Gordon Armstrong ever return safely from sea.

The following year, when the talk was all of the expected second front and a British invasion of France, Robert turned fourteen and left the school he had been truanting from for the past two years. He talked so much of running away to lie about his age and join the navy that Millie feared he would.

'Talk to him,' she pleaded with Grant. 'I think Ava's put him up to this nonsense.'

To her relief, Grant secured Robert a job working as an apprentice in the joinery shop at the pit, and as the year wore on, Millie saw a gradual change come over the boy. He was no less surly or rude to her or Teresa, but his aggression towards Albert and Jack lessened. Perhaps because he felt like a working man in comparison with them, or because he realised that they shared the same pain over losing Dan as he did, Millie could only speculate. Still, it heartened her to see the boys getting along better.

On the other hand, they teased the timid Patience mercilessly, while Jack and Charity fought like cats and Millie was forever intervening to restore peace. Marjory still came to help out, but she had begun courting one of the 'Bevin boys' who had been drafted in to work at the pit, and Ella fretted that he would marry her and take her away to his native Somerset, so that she would never see her daughter again. To the relief of them all, the romance broke up, and the following year Marjory surprised them by enrolling as a trainee nurse and disappearing off to Newcastle.

Excitement grew that spring as the end of the war seemed possible, the Allies pushing into Germany in March while the Russians advanced through Poland. Then a package came for Millie that took her mind completely off thoughts of victory. It was wrapped in creased brown paper and tied with string, which she unknotted and saved. Taking it out into the blustery yard, she looked up at the pale April sky through the flapping washing and sat down on the low stool Grant had made for Jack when he was two. She was strangely apprehensive.

Inside was a note scrawled in pencil and a bundle of what appeared to be yellowing and musty newspaper clippings.

'Dear Mrs Nixon, Sorry I haven't wrote sooner. I looked these out for you an age ago, but then Mr Hardy was taken poorly. He died at Christmas. These bits belonged to our lodger Mr Mercer and I kept them in case any family could be found. He was a nice man and I wanted to do something for him. He died in 1930. He was cremated. Are you the woman in the picture? I know he tried to find you once. Sorry I cannot remember very much, but I hope he was your father and that these bring some comfort. Yours faithfully,
Mrs J Hardy.'

Millie gulped as she leafed through the faded papers. They were mostly cuttings about Dan's performances at Gateshead Vulcans, some with team photographs. But there were others: a newspaper picture of her and Dan at a civic reception, another of them on a team charabanc trip, and a birth announcement about Edith. Millie's heart twisted to think that her father had known about his granddaughter. How he must have longed to see her! she agonised. She delved further to find two dog-eared postcards sent from Graham in France, and wrapped in a screw of tissue paper was a tie pin that she remembered her mother giving her father one birthday. So pathetically little to mark anyone's life, Millie thought in distress, yet she was overwhelmed at what these small tokens told her. Her father had never completely turned his back on her as Teresa had always said. He had followed her life from a distance, only plucking up the courage to contact her when it was too late and they had gone from Newcastle. If only she had been there when he had called! Millie cried inwardly. She would have given anything to have seen him one last time, to have talked together and forgiven each other for past hurts, to have seen him hold his granddaughter.

Picking up the precious evidence of her father's love for them, she rushed to find her mother, tears streaming down her face.

'Whatever's the matter?' Teresa demanded. But when Millie showed her the contents of the parcel, Teresa was lost for words. For a long time she fumbled with the collected treasures in her lap, shaking her head in disbelief, then she reached for Millie, hugging her quickly so she could not see the tears that flooded her eyes.

'Oh, poor man!' she whispered. 'Would that things could have turned out differently!' And they cried together for the life they had lost and could never recapture. When Teresa gained control of her emotions once more, they talked quietly about their early life in Craston with Ellis and Graham, touching on things they had never spoken openly about before. Millie was able to tell her Grant's story about Graham, and they hugged each other again, brought closer than ever by the sharing of their long-smothered feelings.

'That gives me great comfort to think our Graham was highly thought of,' Teresa admitted. 'All those times they called him a coward,' she shuddered, 'said it was my fault, that I must have passed on my weakness to him, it was in the blood.'

'I never believed them,' Millie comforted. 'That's not the way I ever saw him as a lass.' Teresa gave her a grateful smile, but Millie could tell something still burdened her. 'What is it, Mam?'

Teresa confessed, 'It's cruel, but I've never been able to accept Robert because he wasn't Graham, because he didn't look like him. I foolishly hoped that he would, poor lad. I've so much to feel bad about – what with the way I've neglected him, and the hardships you've been through. Maybe I should have stuck with your father...?'

'Don't, Mam,' Millie stopped her. 'There's no point wishing things that can't be changed. You did what you thought was best for me at the time and I couldn't ask for more than that. As for Robert, you've still got time to make things up with him.'

'Aye, you're right.' Teresa smiled wanly. 'Thank you, pet.'

Learning the truth about what had happened to her father brought Millie a new peace of mind that she had not enjoyed for years, and she noticed how her mother seemed less fraught and made a real effort to be kind to Robert. Teresa forced her stiff and arthritic body out of bed early each morning to make her son's breakfast before he went off to work, and only Millie guessed at the pain she put herself through to do so. Robert made little comment, but Millie could tell that it pleased him to be fussed over, for Ava no longer paid him any attention. While Robert's relationship with his mother grew and deepened, Ava seemed to resent his presence as the manifestation of her father's weakness for Teresa.

Instead Ava had transferred her attention to the pliant Patience, passing on her old *Picture Posts* and taking her to the pictures as she had once done for Robert. Patience was obliging, whereas Charity was noisy and spoke her mind, and Ava had no time for her. Patience was quiet and industrious and wanted to stay on at school, while Charity fought with the boys and lived in a pair of dungarees that Millie had made her out of old curtains.

But even Ava's squabbling and petty favouritism could not dampen the feelings of euphoria when news came over the radio one Tuesday in early May of the German surrender to the Allies. People rushed out into the streets to share the news and hug their neighbours, while the children rushed around helping to build a bonfire, and that night fireworks went off and the pubs stayed open in celebration.

That weekend Millie had them all decorating the dining room and laid on a victory tea, begging and borrowing rations to put on a spread for their friends and neighbours. She felt a great sense of relief that things could now begin to get better, the threat of death and war lifted and the thought of their daily hardships diminishing. When Churchill resigned and an election was swiftly called, Grant was enthusiastic about the chance of a socialist government.

'They'll never reject Mr Churchill,' Teresa ridiculed the idea, 'not after what he's done for the country. The Tories are bound to win.'

'It'll depend on all those being demobbed,' Grant replied, 'and what sort of world they want to come back to. If it's anything like the last war, they'll be expecting a lot. Only socialists have the vision for a better post-war world.'

Teresa rolled her eyes at Millie. 'And when are you going to stand for Parliament, Grant Nixon?'

He grunted. 'They'd not have a Bolshie like me.'

Millie looked up from her mending. 'You don't know till you try. I think you'd make a good politician, your heart's in the right place.'

Grant gave her an embarrassed look as he left with Jack to help in Walter's garden, and said nothing.

Millie sighed at her mother, putting down the trousers she was unhemming for Albert, thinking how tall her son had grown in the past year. He had just had his fourteenth birthday and left school, despite her wanting him to stay on like Patience. But he had a job at the pit with Robert and was eager to start work.

'They grow up too quickly, don't they?' she commented. 'I can remember so clearly being Albert's age. I was fourteen when we came here, remember?'

'Yes,' her mother agreed, 'but at least it's a different world for them now. There'll be more opportunity now the war's over. At least Robert and Albert have escaped the fighting, we should be thankful for that.'

'Aye, you're right,' Millie mused, 'and there's Patience staying on at school and wanting to be a teacher or work in a government office. It's grand to think of it. I hope her father will let her carry on her schooling once he's home.'

Teresa regarded her closely. 'And what will you do if Dan turns up here once he's demobbed?'

Millie felt her pulse thud in agitation. 'I'll not have him back, Mam, not after all this time. I feel stronger without him and I don't want to go through all that pain over him again. He can visit the boys, but he'll not live here again. I'm not his wife and he has no claim on me,' she said brusquely.

But secretly Millie could not help imagining what it would be like to see Dan again. He had hurt her deeply, but a small part of her hankered after seeing him, wanting the past to be erased. She could not admit this to anyone, least of all her mother, but she sometimes dreamed of their days in Newcastle and knew that losing Dan was something she might never get over. But busy as they were rebuilding the hotel business and adapting to having the two boys working shifts, she did not realise quite how much Albert had been affected.

As summer turned to autumn, he grew un-characteristically argumentative and aggressive towards his family. At first Millie thought it was the strain of starting work at the pit, which left all the new boys physically exhausted. But one night he came home drunk. Millie laid into him, shocked by the smell of beer on his breath and his bad language towards her.

'You said you'd been to the pictures!' she cried. 'You're a disgrace. You remind me of your father!'

The words were out before she could stop them, but Albert looked as if he had been stung. He lurched over to the sink and threw up. Millie went to help him, washing his face and pulling off his clothes, thankful that her mother had gone to bed.

Albert looked at her with haunted eyes, his face a ghastly white. 'I'm not like him,' he slurred. 'Don't say I'm like him!'

Millie made him sit down. 'This is not like you – drinking and swearing. What's really the matter?' she asked him.

Albert leaned forward, buried his face in his hands and began to weep. 'I h-hate him,' he sobbed. 'Hate him for what he's d-done to you – to all of us.'

'You mean your father?' Millie asked quietly.

'Aye,' Albert sniffed. 'I thought he'd come b-back and see us. I've always thought he'd turn up when the war ended just to see how we were. But he doesn't care about us – he's never even written to me.'

Millie put her arms around her son, her heart breaking at his desolation. She should have known how badly Albert would have taken to not having Dan around, for of all the boys he had adored his father the most. He had striven the hardest to please him at everything, especially football, yet often his father had seemed not to notice. Dan had always said that Robert would be the one to play professionally one day, and Millie had seen how this had only made Albert the more determined to improve. At least with Dan gone the pressure on her son to strive for the unattainable was removed. She was secretly relieved that Albert's obsession with football had waned, for it was not a life she would wish on him.

'Wherever your father is, he still cares about you,' Millie assured him. 'It's just between him and me that things have changed. I could never take him back – he's not mine to have. He belongs with another woman. But if you want to see him I won't stop you.'

Albert wiped his face and gave her a fierce look. 'I d-don't want to see him. I don't care if I never see him again!'

Millie was taken aback by his vehemence, but said no more. Instead she got him to bed and let him sleep on in the morning instead of accompanying her to church with the other children. Neither of them referred to the incident again, but Millie took Grant aside and asked him to keep an eye on the boy.

'You could get him involved in your politics or debating,' she suggested, 'anything to take his mind off his father.'

Grant said he would be pleased to help, and Millie thought how much more cheerful he had become since war ended. He had been cock-a-hoop about the Labour landslide in the summer election and he appeared to be working on a reconciliation with Ava. Many of her dancing partners had now left the town, returning to civilian life, and she allowed her husband to accompany her instead.

Then, just before Christmas, Gordon Armstrong appeared out of the blue, demobbed from the navy. He came armed with presents of cigarettes, a bottle of whisky, tinned fruit, and dolls for the girls.

'We don't play with dolls any more,' Charity told him frankly.

'Don't be so ungrateful,' Ava scolded, preening in the spotted silk scarf he had bought her.

Patience watched anxiously. 'Are we coming home with you now?'

'Course you are,' he declared. 'I've got a good job lined up at the yards and I've rented a place near Aunt Rachael's house. She thought you'd be a help in her sweet shop.'

Patience looked horrified. 'After school, you mean?'

Gordon laughed. 'You won't have to bother with boring school any longer; you'll be out earning your keep, young lady.'

Millie, seeing that Patience was on the verge of tears, ushered the girls out of the hotel and told them to get some fresh air. She turned on Gordon. 'That lass has a good brain and she wants to make something of herself. You should let her stay on at school. If you're worried about the cost, she can stop here until she gets her certificate.'

Gordon blustered and protested, but to Millie's surprise Ava backed up her offer. 'Millie's right, the girl's always got her head in a book. Millie knows how to look after her.'

At Millie's insistence Gordon stayed on for Christmas, and she did her best to put on a tasty spread for everyone and small treats for the children. On Boxing Day she found Ava packing in her bedroom.

'What are you doing?' Millie gasped.

'What does it look like?' Ava replied, unconcerned.

'Where are you going?' Millie demanded, with a sinking feeling of already knowing.

Ava faced her with a triumphant smile. 'I'm leaving with Gordon. I've been waiting for this moment for so long, I can't believe it's finally come.'

'Don't be daft!' Millie flustered. 'You hardly know the man.'

'Well enough to know I love him,' Ava snapped. 'He makes me laugh and he spends money on me. I've thrown away too many years on that useless husband of mine, expecting him to make me life better. But he just makes it a misery and I've had enough of him and this place and all of you! I'm going to take this chance while I've got it.' She turned and clicked shut her suitcase, reaching for her coat and the scarf Gordon had given her for Christmas.

'And the girls?' Millie demanded angrily. 'Are you going to be a mother to them?'

Ava laughed. 'Not if I can help it. You do that so much better than me, remember? I'm thankful I never had any of me own to worry about.'

Millie blocked her way. 'Does Grant know anything about this?'

'No, but he'll sharp find out,' Ava replied. 'You can break the good news to him for me.' She pushed her way past a dumbfounded Millie and headed down the stairs.

Within minutes she and Gordon were out of

the house and heading across the bridge for the southbound train. Patience and Charity stood staring out of the window after them, their father's words – that he would come back and collect them when he had made the house homely – ringing in their ears. Millie went and put her arms around the girls, seeing in their eyes their disbelief. Patience cried into her shoulder, but Charity declared, 'I'm glad she's gone, she was as bossy as Aunt Rachael. I'd much rather live here with you, Auntie Millie, you're nearly like a real mam.'

Millie's heart ached for the girl as she kissed her dark head. 'This is your home as long as you want it to be,' she promised, and knew that she must keep to it. These children had been let down too many times before, she thought. As she comforted them, she wondered nervously how she was going to explain Ava's cowardly escape to Grant. He was a proud man, whose pride was about to be badly wounded once more.

CHAPTER 28

Life during those years immediately after the war was not as easy as Millie had hoped. The hotel was peaceful after Ava ran off with Gordon Armstrong, but rationing continued and making a living never ceased to be a struggle, despite the rash of wedding teas that peace brought. A lot of the time Millie felt achingly tired, as if her body was finally slowing down after years of restricted diet, gruelling work and scant sleep. She saw in the drawn, ageing faces of other women how the war had taken its toll of them all, not just the combatants. But they had been unprepared for the post-war hardships, when rationing grew worse, and the severe winter of 1947 brought food and fuel shortages. Coal stocks piled up at the pits, unable to be moved, and countless families were reduced to using candles and going to bed hungry and cold.

Occasionally a letter would arrive from London from Helen bringing the unsettling news that Dan was living nearby and working in a hospital. Part of Millie craved news of him, yet these snippets merely left her resentful that Helen now had his attention. Ella, who was the only one she showed the letters to, would tell her she was better off without Dan. 'Put him from your mind and get on,' Ella advised, and so Millie tried.

Patience and Charity remained in Millie's care,

their father always putting off the day when they could rejoin him, until Millie was sure the girls would refuse to go even if he finally asked them. Patience finished school when she turned sixteen and went to work as a clerk in an accountant's office, where she thrived. Charity, who had always outstripped Jack in races, excelled in sport at school and ran for the county, while Jack was content with a book or helping his Uncle Grant with gardening. Sometimes they would go fishing together, comfortable in each other's quiet company.

Grant had taken Ava's final rejection of him badly. A year after her move to Tyneside, she wrote to him demanding a divorce. When he refused, she turned up furious in Ashborough, berating him for his pig-headedness and assuring him she would never return.

Millie asked afterwards, 'Why don't you agree to a divorce? It's just causing you both extra misery.'

Grant told her bitterly, 'She's made me suffer, so why should I let her have what she wants?'

'That's just being petty!' Millie reproved. 'You should put your past behind you like I have.'

Grant fixed her with a hard look. 'You might pretend to yourself that you're over Dan, but I'm not fooled,' he said.

Millie flushed. 'What do you mean by that? I never mention him.'

'Maybe not,' Grant answered, 'but Ella's told me how you get letters from that lass Helen telling you how he is.'

Millie glared at him with indignation. 'She

467

shouldn't have told you! Anyway, Helen's only written a couple of times and I didn't ask for news of him. I don't care what he does with his life.'

Grant shook his head. 'Then why do you let his memory hang like a shadow over this place?' he accused. 'It's as if he haunts it still. Whenever anyone comes through the door you turn with that look on your face, as if you're willing it to be Dan.'

'No I don't!' Millie cried in fury.

'And that's not all,' Grant went on forcefully. 'It affects the way you treat the lads – especially Albert.'

'In what way?' Millie demanded angrily.

'By the way you discourage his football, show no interest in his playing,' Grant accused. 'You asked me to help the lad when he was down and I encouraged him to keep on at his football because he's a canny player. But you don't like to see that, do you, Millie? Because when you look at him out on that pitch you see Dan. He looks more like his dad every day.' Grant's accusing look bore into her. 'You've every right to feel bitter at Dan, but because of that, you don't want Albert to succeed at the game when he's got a good chance of doing so!'

'Stop it!' Millie cried. 'That's not true! I just don't want a son of mine to waste his life trying to copy what Dan did. Look how it ruined our family! Dan was eaten up with his ambition to play alongside "the gods", as he called them. Well, it didn't happen. And I threw away me life trying to make it happen, more fool me! I'll not have our Albert making the same mistake! You should be encouraging him in his work, not on fanciful notions about football!'

'Let the lad decide for himself,' Grant said with a glare, 'and you stop interfering in other folk's lives for once!' He stormed out before Millie could have the last word and they did not speak again for weeks. Eventually, with Ella's intervention, they came to a civil truce, but each remained angry about the brutal criticism of the other.

As time went by, Millie had to admit that she had never really given up hope that Dan would at least visit them. The letters from Helen stopped abruptly after a couple of years and Millie wondered if she had emigrated to Australia with the engineering fiancé she had written about. The notes had been brief and stilted, but she had learned that Helen's mother, Clementine, wanted nothing to do with Dan, but that Helen herself kept in occasional contact and had seen him for Sunday teas. Helen indicated that he drank too much and that she had tried to make him stop, to no avail. Millie could well imagine.

But when the letters stopped, the scant information on Dan ceased. Gradually Millie came to terms with the probability that she would neither see nor hear of Dan again. Perhaps he had emigrated with Helen and her husband; perhaps Clementine had given in and finally been reconciled with him. Or maybe the drink had killed him. Millie kept her tortured thoughts to herself and tried to hide her bitterness that he had given them up so easily. Still, the abrupt ending of news made it easier for her to bury the past.

Millie took Grant's words to heart and curbed her criticism of Albert's footballing passion. Yet she no longer found the enjoyment she once had in the game and did not share the town's revival in enthusiasm for the sport. Grant would pester her for clothing coupons to kit out the swelling Comrades teams, and Albert would be out in all weathers kicking a ball around with huge packs of boys or training at the club. But she closed her ears to their constant chatter about the local league and the hysteria in the spring of 1948 when Newcastle were promoted to the First Division after thirteen years in the doldrums.

It was Robert who caused more concern when, one summer, during the town's carnival, he disappeared with the travelling fair for two weeks. When he returned to a furious and concerned Teresa and Millie, he announced that he did not want his job at the pit back and was going to join the navy. Millie persuaded Teresa that he should be allowed to do so if that was what he wished, recognising her mother's tempestuous spirit in his defiance.

'With this National Service coming in,' Robert pointed out, 'I'll be called up anyway. And I'd rather go to sea than be stuck in some army canteen.'

'You know I don't want you to go, don't you?' Teresa told him tearfully. They exchanged looks.

'I know,' Robert said awkwardly.

Millie hugged him. 'We'll miss you. Just remember to come home as often as you can.'

470

'Aye, I will,' Robert promised, and rewarded them with one of his rare bashful smiles.

With the crisis over Robert, Millie was taken by surprise by Albert's promotion to the Comrades' first team at the start of the 1949 season. He rushed home bursting with excitement at the honour, but Millie caught his wary look when he asked, 'Will you come and see me, M-mam? We're playing away near Newcastle on Saturday.'

She felt suddenly irritated. 'When do I ever get a Saturday off to do anything?' she demanded. 'And even if I did, I wouldn't spend it watching football. I've seen enough games to last me a lifetime!' It was blurted out and she regretted the harshness at once. Why was she always so impatient and bad-tempered with him? she wondered in bafflement. But the damage was done and Albert rushed away.

Millie looked at her mother in despair. 'I just want him to be settled,' she defended herself. 'Grant's filled his head full of daft ambitions as if he was the lad's father!'

Teresa shrugged. 'Well, he's been closer to him these past years than his real father,' she said pointedly.

Such a thought left Millie feeling guilty. 'Well, he's not his father and I'll not have him taking my Albert from me!' she snapped. 'He's happiest here in Ashborough where he belongs.'

So Millie did not go and watch Albert play, and football was never talked about in front of her. She was too busy in the hotel to notice how little time Albert spent at home and how any spare moment he had away from the pit was spent at

471

the club. She found only irritation in shop-keepers' comments about how well he was doing in his position as left back for the Comrades.

'Aye, well, he's also been promoted to working on the cutters at the pit,' she would reply tartly, 'and there's not many his age do that!'

With the new year came the start of a new decade, and the family brought in 1950 with a small party at the hotel. Marjory was back briefly from nursing in Newcastle, and Ella, Walter and Grant all came over. Teresa was thrilled that Robert had managed to get home for a few days, and the young ones planned to first-foot their neighbours after midnight. Walter was persuaded to play his old banjo and Grant gave a few tunes on the pipes, while Robert banged out some popular songs badly on the piano.

'I'm pleased to see one of us has inherited the family gift for music,' Teresa crowed proudly, putting a possessive arm around her son's shoulders. 'Your great-grandfather was a famous musician, you know, and your ancestors were French noblemen.'

Robert laughed with embarrassment but Millie could tell he was pleased. He had grown up suddenly, much more sure of himself since being away, and Millie was gladdened to see how much he loved the navy. It made her so happy to see them all gathered together safely, the young ones enjoying themselves with their whole lives before them. She had never seen her mother so relaxed and content since those distant days in Craston when they had sung around the piano and been unsuspecting of the traumas to come. She could

472

tell from the fondness between Teresa and her son that Robert was finally filling the empty place left in her heart by the long-dead Graham, and that Robert was coming to accept her too as his mother.

Millie was basking in the congenial atmosphere when Marjory turned to Albert and said, 'Congratulations, by the way. Mam says you've been picked for a trial with Newcastle!'

The noise of chatter in the dining room fell away as everyone stared at Millie. Albert shot his mother an anxious look.

'Have I said something wrong?' Marjory said, puzzled. 'It's true, isn't it?'

'Aye, it is,' Albert flushed. 'It's just w-we haven't told Mam yet.'

Millie went puce. 'You? Newcastle?' she gasped.

'Aye, a t-trial for the reserves,' Albert stammered. 'W-we were going t-to tell you soon...'

'We?' Millie questioned.

'Aye.' Grant spoke up. 'The lad was afraid to tell you, so we thought we'd wait till after the party. But the cat's out the bag now. He's got a trial in two weeks.'

Millie just stared at them in dismay, humiliated by the way she had been kept out of the secret. 'You all knew and nobody told me?' she accused sharply, and rushed from the room, suddenly overcome with emotion. She knew she was spoiling the party, but she could not help the churning apprehension she felt. Grant went after her and found her shivering and weeping under a starry sky on the steps of the hotel.

'Why are you so full of anger all the time, Millie?' he demanded. 'Can't you just be pleased for the lad? It's what he wants after all.'

Millie sobbed. 'I can't help it! I worry for him being disappointed.'

'That's not it, is it?' Grant persisted. 'You're angry at the lad for reminding you of Dan!'

Millie raged, 'Well, maybe I am! But why's he doing all this to please a father that doesn't care about him any more? I don't want him throwing his life away on dreams like Dan did!'

Grant seized her hands. 'Millie, he's eighteen, he's not your little lad any more. Albert wants to play football because he's *good* at it. What does it matter if a little bit of him wants to prove to his father that he can succeed? Most of all he wants *you* to be proud of him, Millie, his mother. He thinks the world of you! And you should be proud of him. He's been playing in front of crowds of nine thousand already, but never in front of you. Now he's got a chance of the big time – something Dan would've given his eye teeth for. But Dan squandered his talent – Albert's grafted like a Trojan for his. Why can't you let him have his own dreams? Is it just because yours didn't come to anything?'

Millie gasped and pulled away from him.' You're a fine one to lecture me about failures in life,' she hissed.

Grant flinched and stepped back, his dark eyes angry. 'Even if I tried you wouldn't listen to me,' he answered coldly. 'But for what it's worth, I think you're doing your son down. Underneath you're still that bothered about Dan that you can't believe Albert could do better. You think he'll make the same mistakes and that's why you're punishing him. But he's not Dan, he's Albert. They're quite different men, Millie. When will you ever accept that?'

He turned from her and walked back inside, leaving her shaking with indignation. Millie buried her face in her hands and wept in distress in the icy dark.

The atmosphere was strained around the hotel that following week, with Albert keeping out of Millie's way and Millie unable to bring herself to congratulate her son. The thought of how pleased Dan would have been had they still been in contact just made her the more angry and bitter. It was she who had brought up their boys, without any help from him, and she cursed Albert's inherited passion. She would not listen to her mother's attempts to reason with her, and she especially ignored Grant after his brutal accusations that her opposition was merely bitterness over Dan.

It was eleven o'clock on the following Monday, while Millie was midway through hanging out the washing under a glowering, wintry sky, when the pit buzzer blew. The siren's insistence made her heart jump. It was far too early for the end of the shift, and it sounded alarm.

She dropped the washing basket and flew into the lane where others had already appeared to look anxiously up the road. Charity, who was off school with bronchitis, was peering out of the bedroom window above, her pale face creased in worry. Millie realised with a lurch that the girl was thinking the same thing: Albert was one of those underground. For a fleeting second she was caught by the surprise notion that Charity might be sweet on the boy who had spent the last ten years teasing and aggravating her. Then the panic she felt overwhelmed her again.

'Tell Mam I'm going up the pit to see what's happened!' she yelled at Charity's pasty face. Seizing Jack's bicycle from where it leaned against the yard wall, Millie clambered on and wobbled precariously up the slippery lane. She fell off twice before she reached the main street that led into the middle of town. Dodging a bus, two vans and three dogs, she crossed this and cycled down the long terraced row that led eventually to the pit gates. By the time she got there, there was a large crowd of onlookers already gathered. They stood around numbly, asking questions that no one could answer while others ran around, shouting that they wanted to help. A car drove up carrying three men.

'They're rescue workers,' someone commented. 'That's Billy Hill from West Avenue.'

Then a dark-blue pit ambulance clanged through the gates. Suddenly Millie spotted Ella among the crowd. They went to each other at once.

'Walter's down there too,' Ella cried. 'Oh, Millie, I'm that scared!'

It was another twenty minutes before word seeped out that a shot-firer's explosion had caused a fall of stone in the new flat and up to ten pitmen were trapped.

'That's where Albert is!' Millie gasped, clutching on to her friend.

'Walter could be anywhere mending things,' Ella agonised too. 'There's been no sign of him.'

Millie fought to hide her terror with brave words. 'That doesn't mean anything – it could take over an hour for some of them to travel to the shaft.'

They stood around shivering for an hour as men began to emerge from the pit, and cries of relief went up from those who spotted a husband or son. Grant appeared, sweat running in rivulets through the grime on his face as he shouldered a young man to safety. Ella dashed forward.

'Have you seen Walter?' she demanded, clinging on to him. 'Tell me what's happening!'

Grant spat out the tobacco, now tasteless, that he had been chewing. 'I saw him about an hour ago – mending one of the cutters,' he said, breathing hard. 'I thought he would've been up by now.' He looked at Ella in concern. A woman shrieked and rushed up to Grant, claiming the youth he was supporting.

'Thank you, thank you!' she kept repeating as she led the stunned young pitman away.

As he turned back, Grant's look met Millie's. She could not move for the fear which gripped her, or speak the words that were frozen in her throat. Somewhere beneath them her son was trapped. She knew it with all the intuition of years worrying about her children, knowing their wants and feeling their needs. Yet she had let Albert go off that morning with hardly a word exchanged, still punishing him for being the last

477

to know about his trial for Newcastle. She tried to mouth Albert's name, but the effort just brought blinding tears to her eyes. For a moment she saw her anguish reflected in Grant's face, then without further hesitation he said, 'I'll go back and see what I can do.'

Another long hour passed as they hung around waiting in the cold. Neighbours came out with flasks of tea for the anxious onlookers and shared cigarettes. Charity appeared, muffled in a hat and scarf, carrying a coat for Millie. Millie took it gratefully. 'You should be in bed, lass!' she scolded half-heartedly. 'But ta for the coat.'

'Granny Mercer's going to send some soup over,' Charity said wheezily. 'Is there any word of Albert or Uncle Walter?'

Millie shook her head and put an arm about the slim, pale girl. 'You take the bike and get yourself off home. There's nothing to be done except stand around. I'll come as soon as there's any news.' She was determined young Charity should not witness any distressing scenes. 'Go on, off you go!'

The girl pulled a face but did as she was told. Shortly afterwards there was a flurry of activity around the pit entrance, shouting and running and men bearing stretchers.

'Who is it?' Ella demanded, standing on tiptoes next to the taller Millie.

Millie craned over the crowd. 'I can't see, but they're putting someone in the ambulance.'

A moment later the ambulance bell sounded and the vehicle came trundling out of the gates. The crowds stood back to let it through and a

478

buzz went up about who might be inside.

'I think I see Grant,' Millie said, her heart pounding.

In another moment Grant appeared on the other side of the pit yard, beckoning to Millie. She exchanged a frightened look with Ella and then rushed towards him. He met her breathlessly. 'They're taking two lads to the hospital – one of them's Albert.'

He steadied her as she fell against him. 'He's alive?' she gasped.

'Aye,' he replied, 'but he's unconscious – a head injury, they say.'

Millie's initial relief was immediately shattered. 'Will he be all right? I should be with him!' she sobbed. 'What shall I do?'

'I'll take you to the hospital,' he said in a low voice, 'but I need you to help me first – with Ella.' The way Grant looked into her eyes made Millie's heart lurch.

'What's happened? Is it Walter?' she whispered in fear.

Grant nodded grimly, his face harrowed. He could hardly speak. 'They've laid him out in the medical centre,' he gulped. 'He got caught in the fall of rock, broke his neck–' He stopped, unable to go on.

Millie gripped his arm in support. 'Oh, dear God!' she hissed. 'I'm so sorry, Grant. Poor Walter!'

She turned back towards her friend, knowing she would have to be stronger than she had ever been in her life. Her mind in turmoil, thinking of Albert lying injured, being jolted down the road. She longed to be with him, yet she knew that Ella needed her too. Dear, kind Walter dead! It was unthinkable! As they walked towards her, she saw the fear on Ella's appalled face.

'Walter?' she trembled. 'It's my Walter, isn't it?'

Millie rushed forward as Ella buckled at the knees and gave out a wail of anguish. She caught her friend in her arms.

'Oh, Ella!' she cried. 'I'm so sorry!'

CHAPTER 29

Millie did not go to bed for two days. With Grant's help, she eventually got the hysterical Ella back to the hotel. She was mad with shock and grief, her screams and wails echoing down the lanes. Dr Percy came and gave her a sedative and they put her to bed, where she finally slept. By this time Millie was quite exhausted, but nothing would stop her from going to the hospital to find out what had happened to Albert.

'Someone will have to tell Marjory,' Teresa said, pale and trembling from the shock of it all. They all agreed, but no one wanted to contemplate the task.

'Ella needs her with her as soon as possible,' Millie agreed. 'I'll telephone the hospital and leave a message for her to ring us here.' She shuddered. 'Oh, that poor lass!'

'Let me do that,' Patience offered. She had come rushing home from her office during the lunch hour to see if she could help. 'You've had enough strain on you already.'

'Thank you, pet,' Millie said gratefully. She pulled on her coat and hat and said she would go by bus to the hospital, but Grant, having just seen the doctor away, stopped her.

'I said I'd take you,' he insisted. 'I've asked Dr Percy to give us a lift. He said he'll be back for us in twenty minutes.'

Millie was thankful to have someone to go with, and she tried to pacify the tearful Charity. 'I can't take you with me this time,' she said distractedly.

Patience swiftly took over. 'I need your help here,' she coaxed her sister, 'for when Jack gets back from school – and in case Auntie Ella wakes up.'

When Dr Percy returned, he told Millie he had rung the hospital. 'He's still unconscious, Mrs Nixon. I don't see there's any point going just now–'

'There's every point!' Millie answered desperately. 'I'm his mam and he needs me whether he's conscious or not.'

'Please, Dr Percy,' Grant added quietly. 'Can't you see how worried she is?'

'Of course,' the doctor agreed at once, and they followed him out to his car.

Half an hour later, Millie was standing beside Albert's bedside in the high-ceilinged ward, with its arched windows and rows of uniform beds. Beside her son an old man cried out deliriously for someone called Bella. Millie looked down tearfully at Albert's pale face under the swaths of bandages around his head and left eye. She silently took his hand in hers and noticed it was still grimy from the pit.

'You haven't even cleaned him up!' she said angrily to the nurse who had brought them in.

'We wanted to move him as little as possible before the doctor sees him,' she answered defensively. 'We don't know how bad his injuries are until he regains consciousness.'

Millie covered her mouth to stifle a horrified sob.

'Maybe we should go,' Grant suggested, twisting his cap awkwardly in his hands.

But Millie shook her head and knelt down at Albert's side. Squeezing his hand, she whispered, 'Mam's here now, pet. You're all right. We're all going to get through this together.'

'He can't hear you, Mrs Nixon,' the nurse declared. 'You'd be better coming back later, like your husband said.'

'He's not me husband,' Millie snapped. 'And how do you know he can't hear me?'

'Millie, she doesn't mean any harm...' Grant tried to calm her.

But she would not be pacified. 'I want to be here with him even if he can't hear. At least I can hold his hand and be near him. He's me son and he means the world to me!' she choked.

'I'm sorry,' the nurse said, embarrassed.

Just then, Millie felt a faint twitch in the hand she held, and she gasped. They all stared at Albert's prone figure. His eyelids flickered and then opened. Millie clutched his hand and leaned towards him, her mouth trembling.

'Mam?' he whispered, his eyes unfocused.

'Aye, Albert, I'm here, pet,' she answered, emotion welling within her. 'Right beside you.'

A faint smile of relief crossed his colourless face. 'G-good, I thought I heard you.' Millie's throat flooded with tears as she glanced up at Grant. 'W-where am I?' Albert asked groggily. 'I thought...?'

'There was an accident at the pit,' Millie told

483

him softly, stroking his cheek. 'You've had a blow to your head. But you're in hospital now and they're going to take good care of you.'

'Hospital?' he murmured in confusion.

'Just for a bit,' Millie promised. 'We'll have you home soon. I'm going to take such good care of you, bonny lad, you'll be up and about in no time.' Then she forced herself to add, 'I want to see you playing football again.'

Albert's gaze rested on her a moment and they both smiled. Then his eyes closed again. She felt Grant's hand squeeze her shoulder.

The nurse spoke up. 'You should let him get some rest now.'

Millie nodded and stood up, kissing Albert on the cheek. 'Take care of him for me, won't you?' she said trembling, fighting to control her emotions so she could speak. 'I lost one bairn a long time ago – I couldn't bear to lose another. It would kill me,' she croaked.

The nurse put out a hand and touched her arm. 'Of course I will,' she assured her. 'That's what I'm here for, Mrs Nixon.' Millie saw the compassion in the young woman's face and was comforted.

That night Millie sat up with Ella, talking about Walter, seeing that her friend was too over-wrought to sleep. The next day, while Grant made the funeral plans, Marjory arrived from Newcastle to console her mother.

'You can both stay here for as long as you want,' Millie insisted. But Marjory declined.

'Thanks, but Mam would like to be at home,

Auntie Millie. She feels closer to me dad there,' she explained quietly.

Millie gave her a quick hug. 'If you need help in any way, or just a bit of company, mind you say so.'

Every day that week, Millie made the trip to the hospital. To her utter relief, Albert's head injury had caused no paralysis, but they had to operate on his left eye. It would be several weeks before they knew if his sight had been saved, so Millie hid her anxiety from her son and said he must be brave and she would help him recover. She was grateful to see how the staff cared for him, especially the nurse she had met on the first day, and she marvelled at how she no longer had to worry about paying doctors' bills now that it was all part of the new NHS. Yet she agonised over whether to tell Albert about his Uncle Walter. In the end, Grant came with her on the eve of the funeral and they broke the news to him.

Grant told him as gently as possible, 'He and the shotfirer, Cook, were killed. It would have been instant.'

Albert's unbandaged eye began to blink back tears and for a few moments he could not speak. Millie just held his hand in sympathy.

'Marjory's home with her mam for a bit,' she said. 'She's being very brave and a grand help.'

But Albert's mind seemed far away. 'He was m-mending the cutter,' he mumbled. 'I'd just got off. Me and Billy were having some bait. I remember Uncle W-Walter by the machine, then...' He closed his eyes and groaned.

'Don't talk about it, son,' Millie pleaded. 'It's over now.'

'There's nothing anyone could've done,' Grant added softly. 'Walter was doing his job and it was just bad luck.'

Millie was silently thankful that her son had been taking his break further down the tunnel when the explosion happened. The blow he had taken from falling stone was bad enough.

After they left Albert, Grant said, 'I think you should try and find out where Dan is.'

Millie was startled by the suggestion. 'He ought to know about Walter – he was his brother, after all, and they used to be close.' He gave her a bleak look, adding, 'And wouldn't it be fair for him to know about Albert?'

Millie bristled. 'Albert wouldn't want to hear from him even if we found out where he was – he's too loyal to me. And Dan's never tried to contact Walter in years!'

Grant said nothing. They walked for the bus in silence, but before they reached Ashborough Millie relented. 'Perhaps Dan should know about Walter. But how could I possibly find him?'

'Why not send a telegram to that address you had for Helen? Or place an announcement in a London paper? Someone might see it who knows him,' Grant suggested.

Millie gave him an anxious look. 'I've sometimes wondered over the past three years ... wondered if Dan is still alive.'

'All you can do is try,' Grant answered, his face drained. Millie realised suddenly how much he must be suffering too. He had lost a dear brother and continued to worry over Albert as if he was his own. Yet he had been a tower of strength for her to lean on this past week and she doubted she could have got through it without him.

'Aye,' Millie sighed, placing her hand briefly over his. 'Ta for all you're doing to help.' She saw him flush and withdrew her hand quickly. They did not speak again, but Millie felt strengthened by his presence.

They were consoled by a brief visit from Robert, who was given two days' leave to attend his uncle's funeral. His appearance helped revive Albert's spirits and spur on his recovery. But Millie's telegram to Helen and notice of Walter's death in the London *Evening Standard* drew no response. She concluded that Helen must have long gone and doubted she would ever discover what had happened to Dan. Maybe he had created a new life for himself with a new wife and family ignorant of his past. Perhaps it had caused a rift with Helen, and that was why news of Dan had dried up. The idea of Dan turning up again in her life was so painful that Millie felt more relief than disappointment when the weeks went by and not a word came back. She finally forced herself to admit that she would never see him again. He was lost to her now and she must dismiss him at last from her mind and her feelings.

With Albert coming home after a month in hospital, this was easier to do. She made a big fuss of his homecoming, preparing his favourite meal of liver stew followed by treacle pudding and custard. Ella had come to live with them once Marjory had gone back to Newcastle, and it was an emotional night, but Millie sensed that Ella felt comforted having Albert back, someone who had seen Walter just before he died and knew how she grieved. Grant, who had taken on Walter's colliery house, came round for the meal and talked of little but the coming election, fretting that the new Welfare State and the nationalised coal industry might be in jeopardy if the Tories got back in. That night, Millie was filled with thankful joy that her eldest son was back under the roof with them.

Within a month Labour had scraped back into government, and a few weeks later Albert was pronounced fit enough to go back to work. Millie was thankful that there was no lasting damage to his left eye, and his fair hair was already growing back over his head wound. But she was gripped by anxiety at the thought of him going back down the pit, and Ella too became tearful at such talk. Her friend busied herself during the day, helping with the hotel, but when Millie got up during the night to sit in the kitchen sewing or reading, she often heard Ella weeping. Sometimes she would go in with a cup of tea and sit with her on the bed; at other times she left her alone.

Albert gave her concern too. So cheerful on his arrival home, he had become withdrawn and edgy.

'Are you worried about going down the pit again?' Millie asked him one night. 'Because I'd much rather you looked around for something

488

else – even at less pay.'

Albert shook his head. 'I'm not scared, Mam,' he insisted impatiently.

'Then what's troubling you?' Millie pressed.

'Y-you wouldn't understand,' he muttered.

Millie felt her heart squeeze. 'I can try. Please tell me.'

He gave her a look of despair. 'I m-missed the trial,' he said miserably. 'It's all I ever w-wanted. Now I might never have the chance again.'

Millie put an arm around his shoulders. 'Oh, pet,' she sighed. 'Uncle Grant wrote and explained about the accident. You've got to give yourself time, get your fitness back.'

Albert shook his head. 'I don't know if I'm good enough any more.'

Millie took him firmly by the shoulders and made him look at her. '*I* know you're good enough. You've shown great courage over these past weeks and I've been that proud of you. It's up to you to show them that you're still as good as before. You're young and you've mended fast; you just need to get your confidence back. Uncle Grant thinks the scouts will be back to watch you, so you just go and show them!'

Albert smiled foolishly at his mother. 'I c-can't believe I'm hearing this from you!' he said bashfully. 'You sound like you w-want me to play.'

'I do,' Millie told him, with a tender smile, 'because I know that's what you want more than anything. And I'd much rather you were playing football than going back down that pit. I'm sorry I didn't support you before, pet, but I'm going to now.'

489

The revival of Albert's spirits after their talk that night helped Millie through the anxiety of seeing him off to the pit each day, yet she never completely relaxed until she heard him coming stamping through the back door at the end of his shift. With Grant's help, he trained harder than ever, consumed by his determination to gain a second chance with Newcastle. It was just before the end of the season that a postcard came from St James's Park inviting Albert to play in another trial. He went sprinting round to Grant's house to share the news.

On the day of the trial, Millie cooked him a massive breakfast, using up her ration of eggs and bacon to do so. Grant and Jack went with him and Millie spent a tense day waiting for their return, unable to settle to her work.

'I was wrong being so against him playing,' she confessed to Ella as they changed the bed sheets in a lodger's room. 'I was still that bitter at Dan, I couldn't see how much it meant to Albert. I thought I was protecting the lad, but all I was doing was standing in his way.'

Ella stopped and looked at her. 'And you're not so bitter now?' she asked.

Millie plumped a pillow as she thought. 'No, I don't think I am. More sad than angry. Sad that Dan couldn't tell me the truth all those years ago – and for the heartaches we've had along the way. But I've got the boys to comfort me; Dan – if he's still alive – is left with no family to grow old with.'

They stood for a moment in silence, then Ella said quietly, 'Remember how happy we were when we both started courting the Nixon lads?

Going to Wembley...! Who would've thought we'd have lost them like we have?'

Millie saw the tears slip down Ella's cheeks and went to her at once, putting comforting arms around her friend.

'It's as well you cannot see into the future, else you'd end up too frightened to do anything. And they were good times at the beginning, weren't they?' Millie encouraged. 'You wouldn't have swapped your happy years with Walter even if you'd known how it would end, would you?'

'No,' Ella sniffed, 'not for anything.'

Soon afterwards Millie was called to the telephone in the station office next door to find Grant on the line. 'The lad's done it, Millie,' he shouted into the receiver excitedly. 'He's got a game for the reserves next week!'

Millie shrieked with pleasure and rushed around telling everyone she could think of, so that by the time Albert returned, all the neighbours were out to congratulate him.

'You would think I'd played in the Cup Final or som'at,' he said, embarrassed but delighted at the fuss being made.

'And I'm going to see you play,' Millie announced. 'Ella will run things here for the day.'

Albert and Grant gawped at her. 'By!' Grant chuckled. 'This must be the biggest conversion since St Paul's!'

Millie swiped at him playfully. 'Don't be so cheeky! I'm not going to miss one of the proudest days of my life.'

Albert played twice for the Newcastle reserves

491

before the end of the season, and Millie went to watch him both times, joining the enthusiastic crowds and making a day out of it with Jack, Grant and Charity, who proved the most vocal supporter of them all. The summer came, and with it the offer of a full-time contract with the club. Albert and his family were ecstatic. Millie made him go straight to the pit management and hand in his notice.

'I'll sleep easier in me bed to think you won't have to go down there again,' she told him.

That summer was one of optimism after the tragedy in January and the hardships of the past years. Millie would often pack up a picnic and chase the young ones out, telling them to go to the seaside or along the river with their friends. Charity finished school and to Millie's delight secured a place at teacher-training college, having set her heart on becoming a PE instructor. Millie noticed how she increasingly spent time in Albert's company and was secretly pleased. Millie revelled in the activity around the hotel all that summer as her children and their friends congregated in her new café. Ella had helped her decorate the dingy, down-at-heel dining room which had not seen a fresh coat of paint since the early years of the war. They had run up new curtains of bright-red gingham check and invested in a freezer chest to sell ice-cream. A telephone was installed in the hall at Teresa's insistence, so that Robert could ring home from far-away places and for which he helped pay.

'Maybe with petrol being de-rationed we'll get more people stopping on days out to the coast,'

Millie said brightly to Ella. 'I'll get Grant to make a sign to put outside saying we're selling ice-cream.'

'Nothing ever gets you down for long, does it, Millie?' Ella smiled.

'Well, that's som'at we always had in common,' Millie grinned. She knew how much her friend grieved for the quiet, genial Walter, but she also noticed how frequently Grant called at the hotel for a friendly word and to see if there was anything he could do for Ella. When Marjory came home for weekends, Millie would send the three of them off on the bus to the coast or out to the pictures to a new Cary Grant film. She often caught herself wondering if the friendship between Grant and Ella might grow into something more.

Teresa, who had spent much of the winter confined to bed with arthritis, revived with the warmer weather and a brief spell of leave that brought Robert home from sea. Millie was gladdened to see her mother doting so fondly on her son, her enjoyment only marred by Robert's announcing that his ship was to sail for the Far East to help the Americans in Korea.

'Don't fret over him, Mam,' Millie said gently. 'Look how happy he is these days. To him it's all just a great adventure; don't spoil his leave with worrying.'

Teresa gave her a wry look. 'And that from the lass who used to be the world's worst worrier!'

'Aye, well, not any more,' Millie assured her. 'The future can't frighten you if you just live for each day.'

Come the autumn, Charity was seen off at the station for her new college and Albert travelled in each week to play for Newcastle reserves. Millie could hardly believe she had a son who had done so well and was so fêted around the town. But he was far more modest than Dan and did not lord it around Ashborough as his father would have done. Neither did he drink too much, and he was bashful with girls. Only when Charity came home did he go out to dances or the cinema. The rest of the time he kept himself fit with long runs around the countryside, or spent time working in Grant's garden.

In early October he was picked to play for the first time away against Aston Villa, and Millie could not help recalling that great day at Wembley when she had watched Newcastle beat the Midlands club. How ironic that Albert should play his first-team début against them, and how proud Dan would have been of him, she thought with a pang. To Albert's disappointment they lost, three-nil, but he was full of the experience of playing in front of a crowd of over forty thousand and alongside men like big Frank Brennan and 'Bobby Dazzler' Mitchell. Just before Christmas, he was given another game on the first team in place of the injured McMichael, home against Stoke City. All the family, apart from the frail Teresa, went to watch, and Millie marvelled to see her own son playing on the famous Gallowgate pitch. To everyone's delight, Newcastle won three-one and afterwards they went for a celebratory tea in the city, goggling at the displays in the shops and the Christmas decorations. Millie and Ella gazed and gasped over displays of fashionable coats and winter dresses and felt dowdy in their old utility outfits. But it did not spoil their enjoyment of the day, and Jack must have listened to their envious talk because he and Albert presented both women with colourful silk headscarves for Christmas.

'You can't afford this, you're still at school!' Millie gasped.

'No, but our Albert can,' grunted Jack, pleased at his mother's surprised delight. She smiled in affection at her dark-haired son. He was a self-contained thinker, content to read or do crosswords when he was not posing questions about the world. With Grant he would argue politics and economics and football, but always with a slight detachment, never losing his temper as his uncle did, to Millie's amusement and Grant's annoyance. Occasionally she would chase Jack outside for fresh air and exercise, but usually he would slope back in and be found squatting on his haunches hiding behind a newspaper or reading a library book.

That Christmas was quieter than for years. They all mourned Walter and tried their best to comfort Ella through the difficult time. Robert was at sea and Patience and Charity had been pressurised to spend Christmas with their father and Ava, who was still badgering Grant for a divorce. Millie noticed with concern that Albert seemed unusually withdrawn and preoccupied, but he brushed off her questions and she put down his subdued mood to dwelling on the awful pit accident. The young women returned on Boxing Day, earlier than expected, complaining they had been left to make the Christmas dinner while their father and Ava went out drinking.

'And it's like living in a fog,' Charity said disdainfully, 'both of them puffing away on cigarettes all day long. I told them it would give them lung cancer, and they said they'd never heard anything so daft, but it's true. There's been a study in America.'

Patience, amused by her sister's censoriousness, added, 'Ava just said she smoked Craven A to keep her throat healthy. You can imagine what Charity said to that!'

'So not a very happy visit then?' Millie guessed.

Charity slid a look at Albert, whose mood had suddenly brightened at her return. 'I'm just thankful to be home again.'

Nineteen fifty-one came, and with it the painful anniversary of Walter's death. Millie went with Ella to put flowers on his grave and spent the day with her friend. 'I ought to think about the future more,' Ella murmured, contemplating her husband's headstone sadly.

'Not today,' Millie answered gently. 'And you mustn't think of moving out of the hotel. Not unless you want to,' she added, a little less sure. She suddenly wondered whether Ella had plans that she had kept secret and was trying to tell her. Maybe she had hopes of marriage to Grant; they seemed to have become closer this past year, Millie thought.

Ella shook her head. 'You've been that good to me, Millie, I couldn't have coped this last year without you. But I can't just stay at the hotel forever.'

Millie slipped her arm through Ella's. 'You stay as long as you need to. It's grand having you there and you've been such a help to me too.'

Ella wiped her tears with a large man's handkerchief, one of Walter's. 'By, you're the best friend anyone could ask for,' she whispered and they hugged each other in sympathy.

As winter turned to spring, Millie noticed Ella's spirits revive, while her own pride in Albert soared. He played three more games for the first team at left back, including the fourth-round match against Bolton Wanderers in the FA Cup. Millie went along to see him, overawed by the vast crowd of over sixty-seven thousand. She was squashed in beside Jack, Charity and Grant, her arms pinned to her side, at the mercy of the swaying, heaving mass. The only time she saw the ball was when it soared into the air, and at one point she was swivelled round and carried off her feet. She only knew what was going on by what was reported around her, but the tension was contagious. At half-time the Wanderers were leading two-one, but the fanatical support of the massive crowd seemed to lift the team and Millie screamed herself hoarse when the heroic Jackie Milburn scored twice to bring the home side to victory.

'Well, he comes from round our way,' Millie said proudly afterwards to a thrilled and exhausted Albert, while she shook with relief that they had all survived the bruising crush on the terraces.

'I'll never forget the noise of the crowd,' he told his mother with shining eyes. 'It gave us such a lift – like a roll of drums!'

Excitement mounted as Newcastle won the next two rounds. Then there was a tense semi-final against Wolves that resulted in a replay. When Newcastle won it, the town was at fever pitch at the prospect of a Wembley Cup Final against Blackpool. To Albert's frustration, he was kept out of the first team by the more experienced Bobby Corbett.

'You're just young,' Grant encouraged, 'and there'll be plenty more chances. It just shows how much talent there is to choose from at Newcastle at the moment.'

Millie, seeing how disappointed her son was, declared that they should go to Wembley anyway, as there was always a chance of Albert replacing an injured player nearer the time. But he remained so strangely down in mood and edgy that Millie wondered if there was something else worrying him. He avoided her questioning so she persisted in making plans for the family to travel down to London for the event at the end of April. It was just then that Albert was injured in a reserves match. He was carried off the pitch and Millie got a call that he would be put on a train if someone could meet him at the other end. The muscles in his knee were torn and he would have to rest up for several weeks, she was told.

As Albert lay nursing his bandaged knee in agony, sunk in despondency at the thought that he no longer had a chance of going to Wembley, one of the trainers, Bob, came in to console him.

'Listen, lad, you're young and keen,' he said. 'This seems like the end of the world now, but there'll be other moments of glory. Newcastle's standing at the dawn of a new golden era – I can feel it. With players like Milburn and Cowell and Crowe and young lads like you coming on, it'll be like the old days again, when Stan Seymour and Hughie Gallagher were playing, you'll see.'

Albert fiercely blinked away the tears that threatened to spill down his sweaty face. At that moment he could not share the older man's enthusiasm. He thought about how disappointed his family would be, how they had all planned to travel to London. He had so wanted to make them proud of him; his mother, Uncle Grant who had encouraged him since boyhood, Charity whom he loved but could not bring himself to tell.

'Here's a funny thing,' the trainer said, helping to gather up Albert's kit. 'There was that man hanging around outside asking for you again.'

'What man?' Albert said, feeling himself tense despite his grogginess from the pain.

'That old tramp that hangs around, half drunk he was. Got a bit aggressive when he was told to push off.' Bob laughed. 'He still insists he's related! So it shows you're already famous when complete strangers claim you as their own – even if they are down-and-outs. He was probably just after a bob or two for his next drink.'

He turned to go, but Albert felt thumped in the stomach. 'What did he look like?' he asked, beginning to shake. This was the third time this had happened. Just before Christmas someone had spotted the tramp, and again more recently after the semi-final. Each time he had asked for Albert.

Bob shrugged. 'Couldn't really see under all that beard. And he was wearing a dirty old fedora – the type that used to be fashionable between the wars.' He caught the young man's shocked look. 'Haway, don't worry about it. We weren't going to let him in.'

By the time Albert had made the uncomfortable journey home, he was too exhausted to think about the mystery man. He was probably just some drunk like Bob had said, he decided, and there had been no sign of him outside the ground when he had left. Why should he keep worrying over these strange incidents? he chided himself. As before, he decided to keep quiet. It was not worth upsetting his mother with the tale, and he allowed himself to be put to bed to sleep off his pain and disappointment. By the next day he had dismissed the matter as unimportant, for all he could think of was the Cup Final that he was now missing. Then Charity came home for the weekend to see how he was and he forgot about everything else.

On the day of the Cup Final, Teresa and Millie were thrilled by the sudden appearance of Robert, whose ship had docked on the Tyne for several days. Robert helped Millie and Ella decorate the café in black and white bunting and Grant came round with some bottles of beer for the afternoon. They all gathered around the wireless to hear commentary on the match and were soon caught up with the excitement of it all.

Marjory was seen hurrying across Gallowgate, already late for meeting a group of friends at the Haymarket, where they were planning to see the new Vivien Leigh film, *A Street Car Named Desire*. It was mid-afternoon and for once birds could be heard twittering above the hum of light traffic. The town was half deserted, with thousands having travelled to Wembley and many more at home listening to the match on the wireless. As she crossed the road, she was aware of a figure stumbling down from the direction of St James's Park football ground. It was not unusual to see drunks congregate in this part of town to share bottles of gin or methylated spirits. But something about this man caught her nurse's eye. He was pitching forward slowly, a choking sound rattling in his throat. He was having a heart attack, she was sure of it. Instinctively she rushed to help him, narrowly missed by a bus that honked at her furiously.

The man collapsed at Marjory's feet, a crumpled heap of old tweed coat and worn-out boots tied up with string. Her nostrils flaring at the stale smell that permeated him, she turned him over and quickly loosened his scarf. To her surprise he was wearing a threadbare tie and a collar with studs. She wrested at them frantically to try and relieve the pressure on his throat. His eyes stared at her in fear out of a jaundiced face.

'Don't be frightened,' she soothed. 'I'm a nurse. I'll get you help.' She tore off her coat and put it under his head, then ran into the nearest shop, shouting for them to ring for an ambulance. She got back to find the man had stopped breathing. She felt for his pulse but there was none. Kneeling down on the pavement, she gave him artificial respiration and, locking her hands together, thumped on his heart to get it beating again. He regained consciousness with a sigh just as the ambulance arrived. Shaking with relief, she picked up her coat and the old man's hat as he was lifted into the vehicle. Something in his terrified eyes made her decide to accompany him. She could not sit through a film now without worrying what had happened to him. Her friends would assume she had been delayed at work and would go in without her, she decided.

The man drifted in and out of consciousness, muttering incoherently, and Marjory was thankful it was only a short distance to the hospital. They soon had him stretchered inside and on to a ward. She gave what details she could about the incident and then decided she could do no more. She would check up on him on Sunday night when she was back on duty – if he was still alive, she thought grimly. Hurrying back to Haymarket to catch the second half of the film, Marjory heard a roar from an open shop door. Someone rushed out roaring, 'We've won the cup!' and startled her with a hug. She thought of cousin Albert and the family and grinned.

'What was the score?'

'Two-nil. Milburn got them both!' the man said gleefully.

'That's grand!' she cried, shaking off her gloom

over the destitute man who had almost died at her feet. 'That's made my day.'

They celebrated well into the evening at the Station Hotel, Millie giving away free ice-cream and lemonade to the children who swarmed around wanting to see Albert. He might not have played in the final, but to Ashborough he was their very own hero and Millie basked in the warmth and generosity shown to her son. Patience was being courted by a clerk at her office, who came to collect her for a dance at the old Egyptian Ballroom which had been renamed the Mayfair after being renovated the previous year.

'You get yourself along too,' Millie told Albert, 'and take Charity. This is your night and you should enjoy it.'

'Mam!' Albert laughed. 'How can I dance with a gammy leg?'

'I'll support you round the dance floor,' Charity replied. 'Probably no one'll notice the difference – the way you dance!' Albert pulled a face, but needed no further persuasion. Robert went with them, Millie thinking how handsome he looked in his naval uniform.

Millie helped her mother to bed and then sat up with Ella, reminiscing about the marathon dancing of the twenties and how keen they had been as girls to learn the latest dances.

'That's all I thought about at one time,' Millie chuckled, 'working at the old Palace to earn money for dancing. To think I once longed to become a dance teacher!'

'Do you remember that couple who tried to break the record by dancing for a day and a half at the Egyptian?' Ella recalled.

'Aye,' said Millie, 'and when her heel came off, the lass just kicked off her shoes and carried on in bare feet!'

'I wonder what happened to Major Hall?' Ella mused.

Millie shrugged. 'The last we heard was a postcard from Brighton where he was playing in a band – but that was before the war. He was such a good man. I always hoped he and Mam might marry one day... But she always saw her security in keeping Moody sweet. I think the Major saw it was a lost cause.'

Grant left them to their reminiscing and Millie sat up late, waiting for the dancers to return, making them hot drinks and demanding to hear what the Mayfair was like and what tunes had been played.

'One of these days, Auntie Millie,' Charity insisted with a yawn, 'Albert and I are going to drag you along to a dance with us, then you can see for yourself!'

Millie laughed, pleased at the closeness between her son and this vivacious girl she had come to love as her own. She would like nothing better than to have her as a daughter-in-law, but she kept the thought to herself. If she had learned one thing in life, it was not to expect too much of the future, but be content with the here and now.

Marjory had just finished attending to an elderly

woman who had been trying to climb out of bed, convinced she was trapped in the workhouse. She had calmed her and tucked her back in and the ward was quiet but for the woman's soft whimpering. Soon she would be handing over to the day staff and the place would be a bustle of activity once more. At the end of her shift, she decided to look in on the men's ward and ask about the vagrant.

'He's very poorly,' the sister confided. 'Cirrhosis of the liver and a heart condition, as well as being malnourished. He's comfortable, though, and talking a bit – showing off some medals which are all he seems to possess. Asking to speak to the lass who rescued him.'

'I better see him then,' she smiled.

As she turned to go, the nurse added, 'You're not related, are you?'

'To the old man?' Marjory asked in surprise.

'It's just he's got the same surname as you,' she explained. 'We checked with the Salvation Army hostel and they confirmed they'd had a man staying there of that name – a regular of theirs. Daniel Nixon.'

It took a few seconds for the name to register, and then Marjory's mouth gaped open.

'Something wrong?' Sister asked.

Marjory shook her head. 'No! It's just coincidence, but I had an Uncle Dan. He left the area years ago.'

Still, as she hurried to find the patient, her heart began to hammer at the possibility. She found him lying in the corner bed. He had been shaved and his gaunt face looked younger, but thin and tinged with yellow. His hair was sparse, his closed eyes hooded and the fingers that lay on the white sheet were orange with years of clasping cigarettes. She felt a moment of relief that she did not recognise this pathetic figure as her handsome uncle; the name had just been a coincidence. Then he opened his eyes and as she glimpsed their faded blueness she was not so sure.

'I came to see how you were,' she said. 'I brought you in on Saturday.'

'Hello, pet,' he wheezed. 'I'm glad you came.' He stopped while his chest pumped like bellows and then continued. 'I wanted to thank you.' When he smiled, his mouth turned up crookedly, dimpling his sallow cheek, and Marjory's heart thumped in recognition.

She came towards him cautiously. 'They said you're staying at the Salvation Army hostel – have you no family in the area you could go to?'

She noticed his hands trembling as he answered. 'Not now, pet,' he answered breathlessly. He fixed her with troubled, rheumy eyes. 'Will you do something for us?' he gasped, waving a shaking hand at the chair beside him. 'I want these sent on to someone.' She bent down and picked up a clutch of medals on faded pieces of ribbon. They were amateur cup medals, including ones from the Northumbria League dated 1924 and 1925, and she had seen them before, long ago. 'Millie Nixon,' he wheezed, 'for her lads, Robert, Albert and Jack.'

Marjory felt her heart jolt. She looked down at him, covering his shaking hand.

'Oh, Uncle Dan!' she cried. 'Don't you know me? I'm your niece, Marjory.'

Puzzled by her words, his eyes clouded then unexpectedly brimmed with tears. 'Walter's lass?' he said, trembling. She nodded. His chest heaved as he tried to clutch her hand in return. 'By, but you're as bonny as your mam.' Then he burst into tears.

Millie answered the telephone wondering who could be ringing them this early on a Monday morning. She was the only one up, stoking the increasingly temperamental range that she longed to replace with a modern cooker. Later in the day, they planned to take the train into Newcastle and see the victorious team make their progress through the city, welcoming them home. At least Albert would not be denied the celebrations. She went through to the hall.

'Marjory?' she answered in surprise. 'Is it your mam you're wanting? Is anything wrong?'

Albert limped out of his room, yawning, woken by the telephone echoing through the hall. He stopped in mid stretch at the sight of his mother's stricken face. 'Aye,' she whispered, 'of course I'll come.' She said a faint goodbye and hung up the receiver.

'What's wrong, Mam?' Albert asked, hobbling towards her as quickly as he could. She put her arms out to him, quite overcome. 'Who was it?'

'Marjory,' she croaked. 'From the hospital.' Her voice was almost inaudible. 'Your father's there – he-he wants to see us,' she gulped.

'Me *dad?*' Albert asked, astounded.

'She rescued him off the street,' Millie said, trembling. 'He's a vagrant.'

'N-no!' her son replied in agitation. 'I don't w-want to see him. H-how can you w-want to after what he did? He doesn't deserve it!'

'Please, Albert,' Millie pleaded. She saw his shock, but knew that for the sake of her sons she must convince him as well as overcome her own reluctance to face Dan. 'What your father did to me was wrong. But I punished him for it – told him to stay away. And because of me you've never been able to know him properly. It's as much my fault as his.'

'No it's not. I d-don't want to know him!' Albert said angrily. 'He was a drunkard and a waster. He never tried to come back and I'll never forgive him for that!'

Millie seized his arms before he could turn from her. 'But he's back now. You must see him for your own peace of mind. I'd have given anything to have spoken to my father before he died. I don't want you to suffer in the same way, always wondering for years afterwards, regretting the things you never said.'

'W-what do you mean?' Albert asked, confused.

Millie said urgently, 'I mean that this is your only chance. Your father is dying.'

CHAPTER 30

Marjory had warned Millie of Dan's state, but she was still shocked by what she found. They clustered around his bed – Millie, Robert, Albert, Jack and Grant – the curtain drawn for privacy. He looked so frail, and painfully thin, lying there, hardly recognisable as the man she had loved with such a passion. In her mind, all these years, she had continued to think of Dan as the handsome, impulsive man she had last seen. No doubt she had aged in his eyes too, but he smiled at the sight of her and she caught a glimpse of the old Dan.

'Hello, Millie,' he rasped. 'Still as bonny as ever.'

She blushed at the flattery. 'No I'm not,' she answered. 'But I can see you haven't lost your cheek!' He chuckled and it broke the awkwardness.

'Sit on the bed, lads,' he encouraged. 'By, look at our Robert in uniform!'

Robert smiled bashfully. 'Aye, it's a canny life. I've been right round the world.'

'That's grand,' Dan smiled. 'And I recognise *you* from the papers, bonny lad.' He focused on Albert. 'I'm that proud of you too. You did what I never managed.' He broke off, coughing, and fought to regain his breath.

'H-have you tried to see me?' Albert asked. 'At the club?'

509

'Aye,' Dan admitted. 'They wouldn't believe me ... when I said I was related. Wasn't looking me best, mind. I just wanted a bit of a chat, tell you how proud I was.'

Albert felt his heart pounding. He had come here feeling angry, wanting to confront the father who had betrayed his mother and abandoned them. He had nursed his fury for years, imagining the day when he could accuse Dan of deserting them and hurting him back. But he could not hate this frail, ageing man with the familiar smile and the gleam in his blue eyes that reminded him of the father he had hero-worshipped. He had already done better than Dan ever had at football, and was a man himself now, but he still felt like a child standing in front of him, wanting his father's approval. Deep down he felt relief that Dan knew about his achievement.

'You'll be pleased about the Cup result then? Did you listen to the match?' Albert asked.

Dan shook his head. 'I went up to Gallowgate and stood there imagining. Remembering the time I went to Wembley with your mam. What a day that was, eh, Millie...?' He broke off, his eyes glinting with emotion, and cleared his throat. 'I knew we'd win. I was off to get a drink when Marjory rescued me.'

Albert found himself talking to his father enthusiastically about the match, describing Milburn's goals. Millie saw Dan's eyes light with interest as he listened to his son and asked him questions about his team-mates. Her heart ached to think how close they could have been.

Tiring, Dan told Grant to hand his medals over to the boys. 'Divide them between you. Though Marjory tells me you're more interested in books, young Jack?'

Jack nodded, not knowing what to say to this stranger whom he hardly remembered. So he stood there mute while Grant talked to his brother quietly about Walter, and Dan lay catching his breath.

Then Grant turned to the boys. 'Let your mam have a minute on her own with your dad,' he suggested, sensing that Millie was finding it hard to say anything. He nodded at Dan, and the boys trooped after him muttering their goodbyes.

'Grand lads, all three of them,' Dan wheezed. 'You've done us proud, Millie.'

She sat beside him. 'How long have you been back, Dan? We tried to find you when Walter died – thought you were in London.'

He looked away. 'I've been back in Newcastle about three years,' he whispered. 'Lodged near where we used to live for a while.'

Millie's insides churned. 'Did you go back to Dinah?'

Dan looked at her in surprise. 'No. That was over long ago. I lodged with Mrs Hodges for a few months, but she got sick of me drinking and put me out. Said she didn't know how you had put up with me for so long. I've been on the streets on and off since then, I think. Don't remember too much.'

'You should have come home,' she chided him. 'I never wanted you to end up like this.'

He fumbled for her hand. 'I was too ashamed.

511

I let you down that badly, I couldn't forgive myself. I knew you'd be managing and the last thing you needed was me turning up like a bad penny.'

Millie gulped. 'So you never went back to Clementine? Helen wrote to me for a while, did you know?'

Dan shook his head. 'There was nothing to go back to – I never thought of her as me wife. And Helen emigrated. But we'd fallen out before that. She couldn't stand me drinking. And I just wanted to forget...'

'What did you fall out about?' she asked quietly.

Dan whispered, 'You, of course, and the lads – and our Edith.' Millie felt tears prick her eyes. 'Helen tried to help me, but she saw it was useless. She and her mam could never replace you and the bairns. You always meant the world to me, Millie. Nothing could ever change that.'

Millie felt the tears begin to trickle down her cheeks. 'Then why did you try to get back with them after Edith died?' she whispered. 'That hurt me so much.'

Dan's breathing was laboured as he struggled to explain. 'Because I was that gutted when the bairn died! I wanted to replace her – smother the hurt inside – so I went looking for Helen. It was a mistake, I soon saw that.' He looked at her with regret. 'That's what I tried to say in me letter. I knew by then that Edith could never be replaced. And I knew that I wanted you and the boys more than anything else – but if you wouldn't take me back I swore I'd never bother you again. I

512

couldn't have gone back to Ashborough if you wouldn't have me, Millie.'

Millie clutched his hands in her. 'I never read your letter – I threw it straight on the fire!' she cried. 'I always thought that some day you'd walk back through the door whistling as if none of it had ever happened. I thought you'd at least come back to see the boys. I was angry at you for so long…!'

'I'm sorry, Millie,' Dan panted, his eyes full of tears. 'I've been a daft fool all me life! I wish I'd met you sooner; you were the best thing for me.'

Millie gave him a sad smile. 'Aye, I was!' she teased. 'But there's no good fretting over what might have been.' She squeezed his hands. 'I've found you again and at least I can take you home now, look after you while I can. When you're well enough to travel, you'll come home to Ashborough, do you hear?'

Dan looked at her wonderingly. 'You'd really do that for me?'

'Aye,' Millie insisted, 'despite the fuss Mam's bound to make!'

'Thank you,' he said, his lips trembling.

They sat in silence for a few minutes, each trying to take in the enormity of what had happened. When both had regained composure, Dan was able to talk a little about the war. He had been ill with dysentery after the recapture of Tobruk and his health had never totally recovered. He had ended the war in Italy, but to his shame had sold his war medals years ago in exchange for whisky. Only his amateur football medals had survived.

513

'I'm that proud of our Albert,' he smiled. 'Prouder than if I'd done it myself.'

Millie told him quietly of the years he had missed, of Robert's painful discovery of his parentage. 'Robert took it very badly for a long time, poor lad. But he's happier now and Mam's grown to love him at last.'

Dan's eyes shone. 'He was always a grand lad – I always thought of him as one of ours.'

Millie gave a trembling smile. 'Aye, you did, and he thought the world of you.'

The nurse announced the end of visiting time. They clung on to each other another moment.

'I'll come later in the week and visit,' Millie promised. She leaned forward and kissed him on his pale lips, feeling a great weight lifting from her heart. The bitterness she had stored up against him all these years was dissolving.

'I love you,' he whispered hoarsely, taking in every detail of her face. 'I've always loved you more than me own life, Millie.'

She turned from him, blinking away hot tears. Just then there was a noise outside, a dull droning. Dan's misty gaze lifted to the window. The noise grew louder and more distinct; the hubbub and cheering of crowds.

'It's the team back,' Millie murmured. 'There were thousands gathering on the streets to see them when we came in.' She saw Dan smile.

'Aye, I can imagine,' he said, craning towards the window. Millie saw his face contort as he struggled to speak. 'Haway the lads!' he croaked, then tears began to spill freely down his jaundiced face.

'Aye,' Millie smiled, the words catching in her throat, 'haway the lads.'

They travelled back to Ashborough largely in silence, yet each feeling closer to the others for having shared the trip to see Dan. Millie was drained. As the train squealed to a halt and Jack leaned out to open the carriage door, they heard the sound of brass striking up and the thud of a bass drum. In the evening light, Jack peered up the platform.

'It's the colliery band,' he said, puzzled. 'What are they doing here at this time?' He jumped out ready to help Albert. 'And look at all the people!'

Grant smiled as they disembarked. 'They've come to give a bit welcome to one of the Newcastle team – even if he didn't play in the final.'

Albert stared at Grant and then at the advancing band. 'Did you have anything to do with this?'

Grant shook his head. 'No, you did, bonny lad.'

Millie gave Grant a grateful smile as she linked her arm through her son's. It was a proud moment after an emotionally shattering day and she was thankful to be home. Yet part of her thoughts still remained with Dan in the stark hospital ward, and his tender parting words. How he would have revelled in such a homecoming!

She never saw Dan again. Marjory rang two days later to say he had died peacefully in his sleep during the night. So instead of making arrangements to have him brought to Ashborough to be nursed during his final days, Millie found herself arranging his funeral. A week later, Dan was buried in the local cemetery after a service at the Presbyterian church in Myrtle Terrace, which was packed to overflowing. Millie was touched by the number of people who came to offer condolences after the years of rumour and scandal surrounding her doomed marriage to Dan.

On a warm summer's day, with the smell of newly mown hay heavy on the air, Dan's remains were laid in a freshly dug grave opposite Walter's and next to Edith's small headstone with the carved angel. Millie was comforted to think of them reunited at last, no longer alone. The hotel was thrown open to large numbers for tea afterwards, yet Millie felt strangely detached. There had been too many years without Dan for her to really feel his loss now, and she realised she had done her grieving a long time ago. What gave her most solace was the memory of their final meeting in the hospital and the way they had been able to forgive each other past hurts.

As the days passed after the funeral, Millie came to understand that she had never really felt free of Dan until that moment of reconciliation. She had spent the years of absence in an emotional twilight, neither bound to him nor totally free of him. She recalled Grant's angry accusation that she allowed Dan's shadow to hang over the place and haunt their lives. He had been right. Yet now she felt free of that burden. Dan was at peace and she could let go of her grieving.

Robert rejoined his ship, Millie feeling that the reunion with Dan and his funeral had brought the whole family much closer together.

When Marjory appeared one weekend, Millie took her for an evening walk along the river and thanked her for being the one who had found Dan and given them the chance to set things to rights. Marjory gave her sunny smile and linked arms with her aunt.

'I'm glad,' she answered, 'I'm really glad I could. It was a good thing I was always more interested in films than football, else I wouldn't have come across him at all!' she joked.

'So what are you doing while you're home?' Millie asked.

'Oh, just helping Mam and Uncle Grant sort out a few things from the house,' the younger woman answered. 'Things of Dad's she hasn't been able to face until now.'

'Oh,' Millie said in surprise, wondering why Ella had not asked her for help and finding the thought unsettling. Were they keeping something from her? she wondered, but could not bring herself to ask.

The next day on the Saturday afternoon, when Teresa was resting and the younger ones had gone to the park to listen to a visiting band, Grant appeared.

'Would you like to go for a cycle?' he asked, as Millie was filling a pot of tea. She looked at him in astonishment. She had hardly cycled further than the local shops in years. It was something the boys and Charity liked to do with Grant.

'I've got the tea room to mind,' she told him. 'Why don't you ask Marjory while she's home?'

'It's you I'm asking, Millie,' he replied firmly.

517

'Patience and Sarah said they'll keep an eye on things for the afternoon. I want to take you somewhere.'

She shot him a look and saw how determined he appeared. 'Where?'

'Craston,' he said quietly.

Millie's heart lurched. *'Craston?* Whatever for? I've never been back since...!' She was flustered. 'Ella's the one you want to ask if you're thinking of Craston. She doesn't mind the place.'

But Grant stood before her stubbornly. 'Haway, Millie. It's time you went back.'

Still feeling it was unwise, Millie reluctantly fetched her shoes and jacket and pinned on her hat, looking in on her mother and giving out instructions to Patience.

'Just go, Auntie Millie,' the young woman urged. 'We can manage.'

Despite some initial stiffness, Millie found herself relaxing and enjoying the freshness of the air as they neared the sea. Gulls wheeled lazily overhead and the sun sparkled off the water, but she felt a flutter of anxiety as the hunched shape of Craston appeared, straggling along the shore like a beachcomber. What if she ran into someone from her past? she worried, then reminded herself that she looked nothing like the fourteen-year-old who had run away so long ago. No one would notice, and if they did, no one would care after all this time.

The pithead still dominated the skyline, but its clankings and sighings were muted by noise of a different kind: cries from children making sandcastles on the beach, chattering people strolling in their best clothes along a new promenade. Drawing closer, Millie saw that the old ironmonger's had been turned into a café with large windows revealing tables and chairs of chrome and plastic. It was crowded with people having afternoon tea and ice-cream.

'It's all so smart!' she cried in astonishment. 'And look at the new promenade!'

Grant laughed. 'Millie, it was built in the thirties.'

'Well, it's new to me,' she insisted, leaning her bike against the wall and gazing out to sea. 'I hardly recognise anything. The last time I walked along here there were tents on that beach – families evicted from their cottages.' She shuddered at the memory. 'Why have I been so frightened to come back?'

'I wanted you to see how it had changed,' Grant said. 'I've been back often with Ella and Marjory.' Millie felt her insides twist at his words and wondered why she minded him mentioning such trips. 'Maybe you could bring the lads some time? Show them where you came from.'

'Maybe,' Millie murmured, feeling troubled.

They began to cycle again, and Millie had the feeling he was leading her somewhere for a purpose. A minute later they were at the bottom end of the village, dismounting in the old churchyard where her grandfather Mercer was buried and where her father should have lain. Suddenly Millie realised why they were there. Leaving the bikes, she followed Grant to the tall monument with the cross on the top. It was Craston's war memorial, now carved with the names of the dead of two world wars. She watched Grant bend down, pick a handful of bluebells from under a tree and hand them to her.

'Here, put these on,' he urged. 'For Furnace. It's his memorial as much as any of these men.'

She hesitated only a moment and then stepped forward with her modest tribute. She had always winced at the sight of such monuments, feeling a mixture of envy and shame. But at that moment, even though her brother's name was not there, she felt that his spirit was, and she placed the flowers at its base with pride.

'Thank you,' she said, turning to Grant with tears in her eyes. 'I never thought of doing such a thing. You're the only one who's ever made it possible for me to be proud of our Graham. You're such a kind man.'

'One day, Millie,' he said, fixing her with his penetrating look, 'we'll have his name added to this stone.'

She gulped at his words and turned away, quite overcome. Walking on a little bit, she found a bench and sat down. Grant stood over her and she felt suddenly nervous at his closeness.

'Millie,' he hesitated, 'Millie, I've got something to tell you.'

'What is it?' she asked, feeling apprehensive.

'I've decided to let Ava have her divorce,' he said with difficulty. 'It's time to move on.'

Millie nodded. Then realisation dawned. This had something to do with Marjory coming home this weekend and Ella clearing out Walter's things from Grant's house. They were preparing for the future, she thought, preparing to get married at last. Was this why Ella had stayed away today, she wondered, so Grant could take her out and break the news to her? Her heart hammered. She felt suddenly excluded. But why should the idea upset her so much? she thought in confusion. Ella deserved such happiness and Grant was an attractive, warm-hearted man. He deserved a second chance too, after the bitter years with Ava.

'Are you going to remarry?' she asked awkwardly, feeling herself flush. Grant shot her a look of alarm. 'Sorry,' she said quickly, 'it's none of my business what you and Ella do.'

'Me and *Ella?*' Grant said, nonplussed.

Millie's embarrassment deepened. 'I thought … oh dear, I'm making this worse!' She stood up to walk on, but Grant stopped her with firm hands on her shoulders.

'Ella's decided to move to Newcastle to live with Marjory. She wants to make a home for her daughter, now that Walter's gone. She wanted me to tell you because she didn't know how to start – you two being so close.'

'Oh, dear Ella,' Millie cried. 'I can see how she must want to be nearer Marjory – but leaving Ashborough? I can't imagine it! I always thought you and Ella…'

Grant shook his head and looked at her urgently with his dark eyes. 'Hasn't it been obvious all these years, Millie?' he demanded.

'What?' she asked, her pulse racing.

'That it's you I love!' He forced out the words, his eyes shining.

521

'Me?' she asked incredulously, 'I thought you didn't care that much for me!'

'I've cared for a long time,' he answered, 'but I've always tried to hide it because I never thought I had a chance. As long as Dan was alive I knew it was hopeless, no matter what you said about him.'

Millie stared at him. 'Yes,' she whispered, 'you were probably right. Even if we were never properly married I felt we always belonged to each other.'

Grant looked crestfallen. 'I shouldn't have said anything,' he answered in a low, almost inaudible voice, 'only Ella kept on at me. She saw how I felt about you – said we'd both wasted too many years...'

Millie placed a hand on his cheek. 'Grant, what are you trying to say?' she asked gently.

He took her hands in his. 'I wondered whether – maybe in time – perhaps you could come to feel the same way...?' He looked at her anxiously with his dark-brown eyes, fearing rejection, oblivious to his own attractiveness after years of being told by Ava that he was worthless.

Leaning towards him, she stopped his worrying with a light kiss. 'I do feel the same,' she answered with a tender smile. 'Ella's right. For such a long time I've thought we both married the wrong people.'

He looked at her in astonishment. 'Really? But Dan...?'

'Oh, aye, I loved Dan with a passion,' she admitted, 'but it was a young lass's passion with a young lass's impossible dreams. I stopped chasing them long ago.' She looked into his strong face and knew that she was being given a second chance of happiness. Grant was offering a mature love that had grown out of friendship and compassion and a sharing of each other's burdens, and her heart sang with joy that he had found the courage to speak out. 'With you it's been different.' She smiled. 'I used to be scared of you as a girl! And I haven't always wanted your advice, but the number of times I've been in despair and you've been there to support me... The boys and me couldn't have got through these past years without you, I know that much. I just couldn't bear the thought of not having you around.'

Grant said nothing, his eyes shining with passion. He pulled her into his arms under the shade of the large sycamore and kissed her. It had been so long ago since she had felt a man's arms around her like that, or the tenderness of a man's lips, that Millie wanted to cry with happiness.

When they broke off, she whispered, 'I do love you, Grant. I love you so very much!'

Grant gave a laugh of delight. 'Marry me then,' he challenged, 'and make me truly happy!'

Millie laughed back. 'Aye, I will!' she said without hesitation. And they kissed again, with deep tenderness, exultant at the thought of their future together.

The publishers hope that this book has given you enjoyable reading. Large Print Books are especially designed to be as easy to see and hold as possible. If you wish a complete list of our books please ask at your local library or write directly to:

Magna Large Print Books
Magna House, Long Preston,
Skipton, North Yorkshire.
BD23 4ND

This Large Print Book for the partially sighted, who cannot read normal print, is published under the auspices of

THE ULVERSCROFT FOUNDATION

1	21	41	61	81	101	121	141	161	181
2	22	42	62	82	102	122	142	162	182
3	23	43	63	83	103	123	143	163	183
4	24	44	64	84	104	124	144	164	184
5	25	45	65	85	105	125	145	165	185
6	26	46	66	86	106	126	146	166	186
7	27	47	67	87	107	127	147	167	187
8	28	48	68	88	108	128	148	168	188
9	29	49	69	89	109	129	149	169	189
10	30	50	70	90	110	130	150	170	190
11	31	51	71	91	111	131	151	171	191
12	32	52	72	92	112	132	152	172	192
13	33	53	73	93	113	133	153	173	193
14	34	(54)	74	94	114	134	154	174	194
15	35	55	75	95	115	135	155	175	195
16	36	56	76	96	116	136	156	176	196
17	37	57	77	97	117	137	157	177	197
18	38	58	78	98	118	138	158	178	198
19	39	59	79	99	119	139	159	179	199
20	40	60	80	100	120	140	160	180	200

201	216	231	246	261	276	291	306	321	336
202	217	232	247	262	277	292	307	322	337
203	218	233	248	263	278	293	308	323	338
204	219	234	249	264	279	294	309	324	339
205	220	235	250	265	280	295	310	325	340
206	221	236	251	266	281	296	311	326	341
207	222	237	252	267	282	297	312	327	342
208	223	238	253	268	283	298	313	328	343
209	224	239	254	269	284	299	314	329	344
210	225	240	255	270	285	300	315	330	345
211	226	241	256	271	286	301	316	331	346
212	227	242	257	272	287	302	317	332	347
213	228	243	258	273	288	303	318	333	348
214	229	244	259	274	289	304	319	334	349
215	230	245	260	275	290	305	320	335	350